I0600926

Summer Romance
on
Main Street

Summer Romance

on

Main Street

The Authors of Main Street

Participating Authors in this Collection:

Carol DeVaney
Jill James
Jude Knight
Kristy Tate
Lizzi Tremayne
Leigh Morgan
E. Ayers

Summer Romance on Main Street
An anthology by The Authors of Main Street
First Paperback Edition
copyright © 2018
All rights reserved.
ISBN-13: 978-1-62522-125-4
July 2018

PUBLISHER INFORMATION
Indie Artist Press
P. O. Box 131
Brackettville, TX 78832
www.indieartistpress.com

This literary work is independently published by the authors collectively known as The Authors of Main Street in association with Indie Artist Press. Each author retains copyright of her individual contribution to this anthology. If you receive this book in print format with or without a cover, or electronically by any means other than purchase through established channels or participation in a bona-fide ebook sharing subscription or program, the authors did not receive compensation. Piracy of electronic or literary works is a crime.

All rights reserved. This book or any portion thereof may not be reproduced or used in any manner whatsoever without the express written permission of the author or publisher except for the use of brief quotations in critical articles or reviews.

This is a work of fiction. Names, places, businesses, characters, and incidents are either the product of the authors' imaginations or are used in a fictitious manner. Any resemblance to actual persons living or dead, actual events or locales is purely coincidental.

Contents

Forget Me Not

Carol DeVaney

For Michael, Beverly, Emaleigh and Owen.
You are unforgettable.

One

*I*f Sarah Hall had the tiniest inkling that a simple mid-morning trip to the post office would spin her life into utter chaos, she'd have hopped back in bed and pulled the covers over her head.

The line inside the post office zigzagged from the first postal worker's counter all the way back to the main entrance. A fleeting glimpse at various customers revealed not many were in a much better mood than she was. Their arms were laden with letters and packages, and as had she, they'd probably anticipated a lengthy wait, though from the look on their faces some had begun to lose their patience. Not a happy group this morning, and she was close to getting there herself.

Sarah studied the woman in front of her who showed signs of an elevated blood pressure as she wrestled an armload of mail, but that wasn't her only dilemma. Her young son, who appeared to be about five, pitched whatever advertisements or other papers he could put his hands on in the air and over the floor. She reached out and caught a handful of the woman's letters before they tumbled onto the young boy's pile of paper, which he had promptly turned into a sliding racetrack.

After a ten-minute wait and with a groan, Sarah counted to fifteen. She was still sixteenth in line from attaining a get-a-way and on to the shop.

She'd promised her sister, Lisa, a Shrimp Po Boy from the Crab's Head today. Now lunch didn't look as though it would happen on time, and Nate had agreed to open Crab's Head early to prepare their lunch. A call to Nate that she'd be late was in order. It was hard enough working closely with Lisa without creating more issues, especially with a late lunch, since Lisa was a stickler and ate on schedule daily, which was directly related to her diabetes.

Working with Lisa shouldn't, and wouldn't, have been an issue if her mom hadn't passed on Creative Gifts to the them. Oh, they got along well enough most days, but the past had a way of rearing its head.

Five years ago on a rainy night in 2013, Sarah had picked up her nephew, Gavin, Lisa's fifteen-year-old son, from ball practice. On the way home, she'd had an accident that had almost taken his life. That incident would forever remain the worst anguish Sarah had ever experienced and shaped a powerful wedge between herself and Lisa.

Thank God, Gavin had survived and had now fully recovered from his injuries, though it had taken a year and half for him to mend. In addition, Gavin had forgiven Sarah and never let his mother forget that, or that the accident had been unavoidable.

If not for Gavin's forgiveness and explaining repeatedly to his mother that Sarah wasn't to blame, Sarah would have without doubt lost her sister and Gavin. Family was all that mattered; they had to stick together and work out their differences.

Still, occasionally, she'd caught Lisa's expression of suspicion and intentional glare before she'd lowered those hazel eyes of hers. Lisa and Gavin were all she had left of family, and she shuddered at the thought of losing touch with them. Sarah had always disregarded Lisa's skepticisms, since every time she brought it up, Lisa restrained any uncertainty she may harbor, yet her expressions gave her inner thoughts away.

She understood Lisa's moods, since she'd experienced some of the same reservations before she was finally able to forgive herself. Gavin had turned twenty this year, in college and doing great. Yet the nightmares of that night troubled her still. Total forgiveness was a daily effort.

Sarah glanced at the slow-moving line and rolled her eyes. She and Lisa had orders to box and wrap for Mayor Conley's daughter's baby shower this afternoon. Every minute was crucial today.

She slipped off one of her shoes and pressed the ball of her foot against her opposite leg to ease the ache from standing too long in the heels she should have changed before walking to the post office, then to work… when she finally got out of there.

Her arms loaded with mail and packages, Sarah glanced at her watch, and then struggled to reach inside her purse for her phone to call Nate. "Why does everyone choose to mail their letters at the same time?" she mumbled.

"The same reason we're here," a voice from behind confirmed.

Sarah's breath caught while the color drained from her face. *I know that voice. Oh, do I know that voice.*

When she wrapped her hand around the phone, the purse strap slid down her shoulder, along with her purse, which tumbled with a thump against the man's hands. The next thing she knew the box he'd held flipped over, tossed the letters. and scattered them across the floor.

Wide-eyed, she peered up into his big dark chocolate eyes… and melted. As she always had when Sarah laid eyes on the man, she'd—of course—become an out-and-out klutz. She did her best not to stare, but this time instinct had her checking out his hand, more specifically his ring finger, which was now tangled in her purse straps. The man wasn't wearing a wedding ring, and with another brief peek, the tan line she half expected to see wasn't there.

Will I ever lose the ache in my heart at my rejection of this man, years ago? Okay. That is a no-brainer. I already know the answer to that one. The biggest mistake I ever made was when I'd cut off all contact with him because I'd felt unworthy of his love. He'd tried to discourage my decision, but I was determined to ruin both our lives. And… I did. Huge mistake. But it isn't supposed to be like this, is it? I've gotten Ted out of my system. Or have I?

Her own gaze traveled down the length of the man and for the first time in her life, Sarah stuttered. "Ted. Ted W-West. W-what brings y-you b-back to Savannah?"

As her fingers tightened around the purse straps, she caught a quick, deep breath. Why someone hadn't snagged him already was beyond her. Ted had matured over the past five years and was more handsome than ever.

When she'd last seen him, he'd jogged alongside her for a few minutes on the running track in E-Way Square Park. He'd made an effort at conversation, but Sarah wasn't in the mood for chitchat. So much for making amends.

Now, Ted made no secret of sizing her up either.

His eyes found hers and held for a moment. "Visiting a friend."

A friend. Okay, then. That was that. He wasn't going to explain.

Sarah flipped her shoulder length dark auburn hair behind one ear and bent down. She hoped to refrain from stuttering again. "I-I'm so s-sorry. H-here. L-let me h-help you." So much for not stuttering.

Ted chuckled and flashed a warm smile. "No problem," he said, then set the empty box on the counter while he sidestepped around the young boy and his makeshift racetrack to gather his mail. "I have it under control, Sarah."

Aren't I the klutz? And where did that stutter come from? Again.

"Okay, thanks." She moved aside to give him room to gather his mail, then repressed a grimace and blurted out, "So you do remember me?"

He gaped at her as though she had two heads.

Of course, he'd remember her. They'd been as fused as chocolate and warm milk.

"Remember you? Of course… my goodness, Sarah. How do you think I could ever forget you? It's good to see you again. We have a history. The most exciting time I ever had was with you on the Ferris Wheel. Remember?" he asked. His eyes smoldered, yet appeared to question her sanity.

She couldn't blame him. She waited while he stuffed the box with his letters, and assumed her brain had taken flight, then gained her composure. "Yes, I remember. It's good to see you, too," she commented, her eyes fixed firmly on his handsome face, butterflies airborne in her stomach.

Ted was as charming as ever, and even now, his appeal had

the ability to captivate her. Not to mention his very presence launched her into teenage mode… stuttering, and temporarily asking awkward questions.

Ted pointed ahead of her. "You can move up. There are only nine more in front of you now." His smile widened. "There's no escaping now… unless you'd like to take a chance at waiting again later."

"No way. I'm here now." She shifted the packages in her arms, slow to move forward behind the little boy who was at this point lying on the floor, on his back, spinning in circles. As she moved forward, her foot slipped on scattered papers that were part of the little boy's makeshift racetrack, and she all but fell on her face. Ted grabbed her by the arms before she hit the floor, and then he picked up a package that had fallen from her grip.

Even if was for protection… he would have to touch me. Every muscle in her body tightened while her rattled brain flooded with many of the times they'd shared. Good and bad.

Sarah resisted the urge to run out the front door and never look back. "Thanks." *Great. Just great. I've made a fool of myself again.*

"It seems I'm forever coming to your rescue." He grinned. "Not that I minded. Ever. Remember when you almost fell backwards off the diving board?"

"Yes. I do. I also remember almost losing my bathing suit when you pulled me back." *I wonder how many shades of red my face is?* "You were always there for me."

Ted gave the impression of too many thoughts running through his head. Sarah didn't need to wonder what some of his thoughts could be. Then his expression changed to normal and a warm smile spread while a twinkle lit up his eyes.

"Being there for you was all I ever wanted."

"Ted…"

He raised a palm-out hand. "Put your mind at ease. I'm not going to dredge up the past. It's enough to see you and that you're doing well."

"Yes. We-we had some beautiful memories. Let's not spoil them." A sad smile crossed her lips. If only… if only fate hadn't dropped down that night… that night long ago. *Too many years, almost five to be exact, have passed for you to know how I'm doing though.*

"I agree." Ted stared off into the distance, then fastened a concentrated gaze on her. "The past is the past. Let's leave it there."

Beginning to feel ill at ease with discussing their past-history, Sarah moved closer to the long counter, set her armload of mail down, then changed the subject. "So, Ted. You didn't tell me how long you'll be in town, after your visit."

He responded, with a challenge. "Interested in getting together?"

Sarah peered at him through squinted eyes, and swallowed back a sour taste, still wondering if he was married. "I don't believe I insinuated any such thing, Ted."

"Sorry." He paused while his face softened. "At six tomorrow I have a birthday party dinner to attend. The rest of the week is filled with real estate agent meetings."

"Really?" Sarah gulped. "Here? Here in town?"

His gaze flicked over her face. "Where else?"

Sarah all but choked. Why must he choose Savannah, of all places? "That means you're relocating to… to, back to Savannah, Georgia?"

"The notion has been in the back of my mind for a long time. Now that college is over and done with, I chose to move back to my roots and open my own engineering firm. The offer I received from a reputable firm in Atlanta made my decision difficult, but my heart remains in Savannah. It's home."

"I'm sure you've made the right decision. Good luck locating a suitable building. If I can help, let me know." *Why? Why did I ask him that?*

"The real estate agent has got this. She's aware of the area I'm interested in and the office space the firm will require." He reached over and pushed Sarah's packages closer to making her second in line to the actual postal worker. "Actually you could point me in the direction of a shop that offers unusual gifts for a four-year-old little girl's birthday."

Her mind whispered one thing, yet her heart expressed another. She should have left well enough alone, but she couldn't resist the urge to see him again.

"Why don't you visit Creative Gifts when you finish up here? Here's my card. If I don't have what you want, I'll find it for you." She grinned. "You haven't forgotten how to get to River Street, have you?"

"Certainly not. I can smell candies, nuts and desserts now that the fantastic shops offer." Ted slid the card in his shirt pocket. "Thanks. I'll see you as soon as I finish up here."

"Anytime. Oh, give me about thirty minutes. I need to make a quick stop first."

Ted pointed toward the next postal worker's counter. "You're up next. Need some help?" he asked.

"No, thank you. I've got this. Maybe I'll see you later."

Two

At six the next morning, Sarah turned left on Main Street and maneuvered down the sidewalk toward her shop, Creative Gifts. A gentle rain had begun to fall, but the darkened sky promised more. In a matter of minutes before she arrived at the shop, the light drizzle had developed into a heavy shower, which set in as the clouds opened up. Sarah walked briskly toward the shop, the rain needling her face, Ted and his purchase of yesterday on her mind. By the time she'd practically run the last three blocks, her hair and everything she wore was soaked.

While exercise was more or less nonexistent, her preference was to walk to work, but today turned out to be the one nasty morning she should have skipped. She hadn't brought an umbrella with her, neither had she checked the weather last night or this morning. Not real smart. Where were the cabs when you needed one? With the shop a few steps away, she breathed a sigh of relief.

Sarah locked the door behind her, flipped on the coffee pot, then set soft music to drift throughout the shop while she functioned through the early hours. With any luck, and working non-stop, time would pass quickly and keep her lively thoughts from wandering in Ted's direction. Too, staying busy would put a damper on her feelings that involved Ted, best forgotten. Orders were boxed, labeled and stacked, ready for pick-up at nine and throughout the morning. Lisa had also arrived early, around seven, so they could get a jumpstart on the day.

Purchases for Mayor Conley's daughter's baby shower, this afternoon at five, were separated, wrapped and set aside ready for pick-up or delivery. With the rain showing no sign of slowing down, Sarah hoped the shower wouldn't be cancelled. There'd been too many preparations, and for the mother-to-be, a delay would be disastrous since she was less than two weeks away from her due date. Sarah wondered why the shower hadn't taken place last month. Babies were unpredictable and sometimes delivered early. They had a mind of their own.

By eight, even before the store opened, she'd barely managed a half cup of coffee when customers began knocking on the door. Every minute counted in this storm, so Sarah granted them access as they pushed inside from the wind and rain. Sarah helped some last minute shoppers choose their purchases without delay, while others quickly paid for their deliveries to the baby shower. Obviously, the ladies were unprepared for the early morning showers, too, and were anxious to get back home or wherever their day would take them.

By ten that morning, since most of the ladies had decided to visit the shop early, customer count had dwindled to a trickle. Each time Ted hadn't appeared at the door, Sarah's disappointment was unquestionable. Much to her demise, though she tried her best, not thinking of him had not succeeded.

Ted was the one she wanted to see today. He was also the one she shouldn't want to see today, or ever again, for that matter.

Disappointment at letting him get to her played heavy on her emotions. He'd only been back in town two days, as far as she knew. In her mind, the years he'd been gone simply slipped away.

The care he'd taken yesterday at choosing an ornate toy chest, a lamp to match and the special teddy bear, revealed the child meant a great deal to him. At first she'd assumed the gifts were for a friend's child. Now she wasn't so sure. Perhaps it was his daughter. Did he have a daughter? Perhaps not. Perhaps she'd been too quick to pass judgment. Then, she told herself, the man was none of her business, that even if he didn't wear a wedding band, he was probably already taken. The good ones always were… and she had no doubt that Ted would be one of the good ones. He always had been.

Besides, she'd been the one to dissolve their relationship years ago. Now wasn't the time to linger on the past and its regrets, and she'd certainly had plenty of time to relive the regrets she'd imposed on herself.

"He'll be in. Stop pacing," Lisa said, and grinned.

Sarah had finished wrapping the gifts except the Teddy Bear. She grabbed a huge box from under the counter to measure and wrap the bear in, then delivered a sideways glance toward Lisa. "Who?"

"Sarah, really. Who knows you better than yourself?" Lisa dangled the shears above the flower arrangement she was working on for the afternoon's baby shower. "You're only kidding yourself. Ted West—of course. Admit it. You haven't been yourself all morning. I've watched your expression change from expectation to disappointment every time the doorbell chimed and he didn't walk into the shop."

Lisa was right. She had made an effort to be there every minute hoping he would stop in early to pick up his wrapped gifts. "You know he's probably married with umpteen kids anyway," she offered.

"Maybe. He doesn't appear the married sort though, especially—and yes I noticed—since he wears no wedding band." Lisa stretched and rubbed her lower back. "I'm headed to the bank then I'll grab a salad. Why don't you finish up here and meet me?"

"Umm. No thanks. You know we can't close for lunch. Think I'll skip lunch today, or maybe I'll grab a health bar and a soda."

"Not as healthy as you may think. But then, love does strange things to the mind and body." Lisa laughed, then grabbed her coat. "No appetite, huh?"

"Love? Get a grip, Lisa." Sarah cocked an eyebrow at her nosey sister while her face flushed. "You understand what a pushover I am for big dark chocolate eyes—that's all. Go on. Get out of here," she said, then rolled her eyes. "Okay. For health's sake, and if you don't mind, bring me back a salad. Dressing on the side."

Love for Ted, as Lisa put it, was no longer part of her existence, but if she were honest with herself, she'd admit that wasn't true. Maybe they never had been truly in love, or maybe it was never meant to be. She knew better though.

Yet she'd thought of nothing but Ted since yesterday. The

old inclination to throw her arms around Ted and never let him go again rose inside her. But... no... it wasn't love, not by any stretch of the imagination. Ted and Sarah's connection was over. Besides, who knew if he was still available?

She couldn't stand the fact that she was being so wishy-washy, but there they were... feelings she obviously wasn't able to break away from.

Too much time had passed. Once, in another lifetime, being with Ted had filled her with so much love she thought her heart would explode. But that was before the accident... the accident, and the guilt that left her feeling she was no longer allowed happiness. That was when her world had fallen apart. That was when she'd pushed Ted away.

Out of her life for good... or so she'd thought.

Halfway outside, Lisa stuck her head back inside the door. "Sarah, admit it. You know you must still hold an attraction, if not more, for Ted," she said, then laughed and pulled off a comical face. "Yes, this is your big sister being bossy. I'm allowed. I know we have issues, but we're still family and... and... I love you. Think about it, okay?"

She couldn't believe what Lisa had said. A knot formed in her throat so heavy she could barely breathe. Lisa hadn't told Sarah she loved her since before the accident.

"I love you too, Lisa." Sarah shooed Lisa toward the door. "Go to lunch. Please... and stop putting ridiculous thoughts inside my head."

At 2:15 the bell on the door chimed. Sarah raised her head in interest as a gorgeous woman rushed through. Hair the shade of dark honey fell into place with a couple of shakes of her head and a quick run through of her fingers. How some women managed a polished appearance in the worst of times was something Sarah had rarely cared about the past five years.

Until now.

Now that Ted was back in town... but the matter of his marital status was first on the agenda. So that was it then. Interest in Ted most definitely could lead to a compromising situation.

Was she prepared for a day of reckoning?

"Good afternoon." A soft, pleasant voice greeted her. "Is Sarah around?"

Sarah smiled at the woman and extended a hand. "I'm Sarah. How may I help you?" The chicly-dressed woman stood in front of her. The out of the ordinary, buttercup yellow, crisp cotton blouse and linen slacks wasn't exactly the style her regular customer's chose. Regulars, or even tourists, were normally dressed in casual attire. Sarah caught the look the woman slid over her when she gave her the once over. She wondered why, since they'd never met.

"Hi. I'm Karen. Ted West said you have some gifts ready for him." She glanced around the shop and smiled. "Oh, he wondered if you'd be kind enough to wrap them for us."

"Yes. Of course." Her heart sank as she swallowed back the lump in her throat. She hadn't missed the 'us' part, or that when she started to hand Karen the credit card, the last name on the card was West. Sarah held the card for Karen to take. "The gifts are already paid for and wrapped except the Teddy Bear."

"Hold the card. I may find something else," Karen said.

"Wrapping the Teddy Bear will take a few short minutes. Would you like a cup of coffee, tea, or hot chocolate while you wait?"

Karen busied herself by thumbing through a discount rack of little girl's clothing. "Hmm… yes. Hot chocolate would be fabulous."

Sarah pointed toward a counter at the front of the store. "Please, help yourself."

Karen spent more than a few minutes at the clothing rack, then passed Sarah six dresses, a pair of lavender shorts and a frilly top to match. "Could I impose on you to choose lace topped anklets to match the dresses? Oh and would you also wrap these items?"

"Certainly. Someone's going to be a happy little girl."

"Yes. Even though she's young, and like any other female, Emma loves new clothes," Karen said, and flashed her a genuine smile.

Sarah snagged a paper towel and dabbed at the coffee droplets on the counter she'd spilled in her haste to gather the extra gifts, then removed her cup to the side-table and tucked it far underneath. It wouldn't do to stain the little girl's clothing, especially since no replacements were available.

Disheartened that Ted hadn't picked up the gifts himself, Sarah endured the slow moving afternoon by taking inventory of additional items to order. Once the day was over, she flipped the closed sign around. She was about to lock the door, when she was taken aback at a figure that suddenly loomed in the doorway. Ted's big dark chocolate eyes peered through the door, the rain coming fast and hard again around him. Her heart pounded with such force, she was sure he'd heard it.

"Glad I caught you, Sarah." Ted shook off the rain from his Trench coat and stamped his feet. "I forgot a couple of items. I noticed yesterday you have CD's for children. Would you mind picking out four or five with teaching material? You deal with them often and your selection will be more appropriate than mine."

His intoxicating, masculine scent filled the air. So did his dog's odor. She cared a lot for dogs, but thought there was nothing worse than the smell of a wet dog. She rubbed at her nose, and gave the dog a once over. Ted had caught her holding her nose.

"Sorry about Prissy. She's a lab and too rambunctious if not exercised often. A little wet outside for her, but the sweater and socks keep her warm and somewhat dry."

"She's fine. I have a sensitive nose, that's all. However it seemed, I do love dogs. Love her name, too." Sarah moved a safer distance from the wet dog, who insisted on shaking off the rain across her clean floor. "I understand. She's a chocolate, right?"

"Yes, and you needn't worry; she's harmless. A sweet and lovable big baby."

Ted rubbed Prissy down with the towel Sarah had thrown him to dry her off with as he watched with interest while she thumbed the music section for CD's. "You might add a yellow blankie to the list."

Without thinking, she questioned Ted. "You don't remember that you purchased two yesterday?"

"Perhaps I did. I don't recall at the moment." Ted grinned, revealing a slight dimple in his right cheek. "Emma's only four, and it's still a security thing… and well, she's really attached. A little old for a blankie I suppose, but she's having a tough time giving it up," he offered. "Throw in three more. We seem to lose them every so often."

Sarah laughed. "She won't have a chance to give it up if you keep buying more of them."

Ted hung his head, then smiled up at her. "I don't want not having a blankie available to stress her out. As I said, the blankie is her security. Her friend, she says."

"Oh. I'm sorry." Embarrassed at being so personal, she managed, "Don't feel as though you need to explain."

"I don't mind. Wait, I have Emma's picture in here somewhere. She's the light of our lives. I love talking about her."

Our lives. There was the reference to someone else in his life again.

Sarah concentrated on the light brown curls—streaked with blonde—and startling blue eyes. "I can see why you're fascinated. She's absolutely a beautiful child."

"Thanks. We call her our Angel-girl."

That name tugged at Sarah's heart. "I can see why. She looks like the perfect little angel."

Ted smiled warmly. He changed the subject by explaining his short-term new position as an Engineer two blocks away. "By the way, thank you for taking care of the gifts this afternoon. Maybe I can return the favor in some way. Perhaps, ah, you'll have dinner with me one night when you're free?"

Sarah stiffened at the implication and Ted's strong fingers lingering on hers longer than necessary as she handed back his credit card. She tried laughing it off, but because she hadn't encouraged him, she was resentful that he'd consider such an improper get-together and ask her to dinner.

"You're welcome. Please don't feel obligated. It's part of the store's service." Sarah's heart squeezed, but until she was sure of his marital status, she couldn't chance giving him the wrong impression. She wasn't a home-wrecker.

"Fine." Puzzled, Ted stepped back, then ran a hand through smoky-black hair. "I simply wanted to show my appreciation for all you've done for me, Sarah."

At the last minute, he added a music box like the one on display. It had an illuminated carousel that played Carousel Waltz. At odds with anything to talk about, he commented, "Guess I'll see you at the party tomorrow."

Dismay registered when it dawned on her that in Lisa's haste to catch her flight, they'd failed to go over the birthday party's schedule.

Ted smiled at her discomfort. "You forgot," he said.

"Yes and no. Lisa was scheduled for this party, but she had a last minute trip out of town." Sarah retrieved the schedule from Lisa's desk, flipping to Sunday. "There's no need for concern. Actually, I do my best work under pressure.

"Prissy was such a good girl while we talked, and she's really a beautiful breed." Sarah bent and rubbed a hand down Prissy's head and back. "The party will go over without a hitch. Not to worry."

Ted slid his credit card inside his wallet, then gazed up at her. "Somehow I knew that."

Three

At noon the next day, dressed in form fitting jeans, Ted paid an unexpected visit to Creative Gifts. Sarah despaired at being so drawn to the man she was duty-bound to forget again. Uncomfortable that he'd caught her staring at his muscular legs, she stooped to pick up a box and regain her composure.

"What can I help you with today, Ted? Did you forget something again?"

"No. I believe we bought everything Emma wished for. And then some. Since you weren't scheduled to organize the party, I thought I'd drop by to lend a hand," he announced, amusement playing at the corners of his full lips.

Did the man have no shame? If he was married, he surely didn't give that impression. Sarah was livid. "Thank you, Ted. I appreciate the thought and generous offer, but I'm afraid your effort is wasted. I'm good." *Why don't I simply ask if he's married? Coward. Now would be the perfect time.*

Ted eyed the boxes then turned back toward Sarah. "That's quite a load to handle alone. A bit of help wouldn't hurt. Would you care for lunch first?" Ted didn't wait for an answer. "Could we… are you hungry? I'm starved. Let's do a quick lunch, then we can get this stuff loaded."

"We?"

"Sure. After, I'll even coax Dad into helping with decorations."

Sarah wondered about Karen since he hadn't mentioned her. Was she the woman who had stolen Ted's heart? What part did she play in this special day? In Emma's birthday? In both their lives? The situation was getting more complex by the day.

With Lisa out of town, she could use the extra help and time was limited. Yet, what if he was married? What then? She wondered if he could betray so easily when he appeared so noble. "It's a generous gesture, Ted. But—no thank you. I don't believe lunch is a good idea."

Ted shrugged and accepted her answer, then began stacking boxes next to the door. Annoyed, she asked, "Isn't there someone waiting for you at home?"

The impression of confusion fell across Ted's face. "If you mean my Dad, then no. Since retirement, we rarely see him. We've a big house and it's lonely at home with Mom no longer with us, so he travels often. He'll be here this evening for Emma's party though. Karen and Emma visit often, but they have their own lives... for now anyway."

A peculiar statement... Karen and Emma visit often?

She wondered again if she should just come out and ask if he were indeed married, separated or divorced, but time was short, leaving precious little time for a drawn out conversation. Besides, she was fearful of his answer.

An hour and half later, despite her insistence that she hadn't needed help, the task was well under control and almost completed.

Her stomach growled. It was still early and it wouldn't do to go hungry to a three-hour children's party.

She willed her thoughts to regard Ted's suggestion as nothing more than lunch. That's all. An innocent lunch. She shouldn't feel guilty having a simple lunch with Ted.

Sarah grabbed her purse from her desk and an umbrella from the stand by the door. "If you're still open for lunch, there's a sandwich shop a few blocks down E. River. We can grab something quick and still have plenty of time to arrive and set up before the party."

"Excellent," Ted said, and patted his stomach. "Thankful you changed your mind. I'm starving."

"As I recall, you always did have a huge appetite," she responded, then turned the key in the door's lock. "You are looking a bit green around the gills."

"No one has told me that in years," he replied with an awkward grin. "The last time I heard those words was when I drove Grandpa's tractor into the lake."

She laughed. "Sorry, but that's the funniest story."

"I'm sorry, too. He grounded me for a month."

Sarah snapped her fingers. "I remember when that happened. You were fourteen."

Ted groaned. "Yes. Fourteen and a novice driver."

On the way back from lunch, Ted reached for the umbrella when the rain picked up again. Sarah turned toward him, nodded, and released her hold on the handle. As she did, the umbrella dipped and she noticed an electric blue convertible that idled at the traffic light on the corner. Mayor Conley was the only person she knew who drove such a flashy car. She did a double take on the woman next to Mayor Conley, seated sideways, her fingers tangled through his thinning, gray hair.

She didn't recognize the woman, but no way was that blonde the mayor's wife. If she hadn't been falling all over him, Sarah wouldn't have given it a second thought. But now... what was she supposed to think? What was she supposed to do? Put a bug in his wife's ear? Keep quiet? Hard decision, especially since she wasn't even a friend of the mayor's wife. Yesterday, during the baby shower that Sarah had organized at the mayor's house, he'd been all lovey-dovey with his unassuming wife, and gave the impression of being the ideal husband. Yet today, here he was with another woman. The scene that played out in front of Sarah wasn't innocent by anyone's perception.

"What?" Ted followed her gaze to the car. "What, or who, are you staring at?"

Sarah held up a hand and pointed discreetly with the other hand toward the car. "The passenger in the mayor's car—the one who isn't his wife."

"No kidding?" Ted said. "I wouldn't have recognized him."

"Oh, it's him all right." Sarah drew in a deep breath, then let it out in a long whoosh. "OMG. This isn't any of my business… but that car and those two will be burned inside my head forever. I can't ever… not imagine that image."

"Try, Sarah. You're right, you know. Neither of us should concern ourselves with the man's private life."

"He's the mayor. For the town's sake, and his own, he should honor that position and not dash around in public with someone who isn't his wife."

"I agree, but it's his business. His private business. It isn't up to us to pass judgment." Ted moved closer and held the umbrella over her head. "You're getting wet."

Ted's words burned inside her head, too. Sarah knew he was right, it wasn't Christian to pass judgment, but her feet were frozen in place, and she wasn't able to take her eyes off the mayor and his lady friend. "I hope he doesn't see us. That would be an embarrassing moment for all of us."

Ted took her by the arm. "Then let's go. No reason to stick around until he notices you, or the both of us."

The light changed then and the electric blue car took off, as a darting Bumble Bee would to escape a bird.

"So what do you think? Think he recognized us?"

"On second thought, he may have seen and recognized you, but not me. I haven't been around here in years, except for periodic visits."

"To visit your dad?"

Ted glanced sideways at Sarah. "Well… yes. Dad and my brother, Robert. Sadly, Robert passed away three months ago from kidney failure."

"I'm so sorry, Ted. I didn't know."

"Thanks." Ted wedged the last box inside, closed the door, then leaned against Sarah's Explorer. "How do you spend your weekends?"

"My weekends? I only have Sunday, except when a lady who works part time for us covers the shop when we need to get away. Normally I go to my grandfather's at St. Simons every other weekend. Working out my horse, Winston, usually takes most of my time there though."

Ted's face lit up. "We have something in common. Dad still has Grandpa's small place outside St. Simons. What is it, around eighty miles from Savannah? I love riding and plan to go up a couple times a month. Maybe we'll run into each other sometime."

"Maybe. There isn't much time left for get-togethers though. My Grandpa would take us fishing, we'd have picnics, swim in the lake. Lord! Remember the snakes in that lake? Scares me to death when I think of how fearless we were."

"Do I ever. Swinging from the hill on the vines, then we'd drop into the lake." He laughed. "Guess we scared the snakes away, because we never were bitten."

"We share a lot of memories."

"Good memories, Sarah."

They'd already spent too much time at lunch, and the afternoon was growing short. "The party won't set itself up. It's time for me to get going. You didn't mention Karen or Emma visiting the cottage, Ted."

"Karen isn't crazy about horses. Emma loves to go and ride the pony Dad bought for her." Ted cast a disappointed gaze at her. "Sorry our time together is so short. Would you like to follow me to the house?"

"Sure. That would be great, I won't need to use the GPS. Lead the way."

At 2:45, Ted finished tying balloons around the room while Sarah added last minute touches to the table. Karen swept through the room, barely acknowledging Ted was there, and nodded her approval. Perhaps marital problems were the reason for Ted's sad eyes. No matter. Their life was none of her concern. She had to remember that.

"Fantastic job, Sarah. You're welcome to join us," Karen said.

Sarah welcomed the chance to relax for a while. "The library looks inviting. I think I'll use the extra time and curl up with a good book, if you don't mind."

"Not at all. Please make yourself at home." Karen turned before leaving. "I'll send in refreshments. Which do you prefer, coffee, tea, or punch?"

"Thanks. Hot tea would be great. Sugar, no cream, please. I guess I'll see you in a couple hours. If there's a problem come and get me. Have fun."

Time passed quickly, but she grew tired and had also grown sleepy. She replaced the book she'd chosen on the bookshelf. The last few minutes before the party was to end she roamed the cozy room to stay awake. Intrigued with a photograph of a man, maybe a couple of years older than Ted, she acknowledged that Robert and Ted's uncanny likeness was astounding. She scrutinized the framed wedding photo.

Karen was Robert's wife. Everything she'd thought and created in her mind, was nothing but pure speculation. She'd been foolish making her mind up about Ted and Karen, but also relieved.

Ted knocked lightly on the door, then slipped inside the library and stood beside her.

"That's Robert and Karen's wedding photo. My brother — and Karen's husband. You must remember him. People often said we could pass for twins. We used to have great fun with friends pretending to be one another." Ted's smile sobered. "As I said earlier, he… he passed away of kidney failure three months ago."

"Again, Ted, I'm so sorry. Of course I remember Robert. I'd forgotten how much the two of you look alike." She glanced back at the photo. "According to this photo, the older you became, the more you two resembled each other."

"Robert was larger-than-life. A terrific brother and he doted on Emma. I'm staying with Karen and Emma a short while. To help Karen get back on her feet. To help her through the grief."

All at once, Ted's previous behavior fell into place. "Then Emma's your niece? But all those gifts… and Karen."

From the look on his face, and if she read him right, Sarah could tell Ted understood the reason for her coolness toward him at times.

"You haven't changed a bit. Your imagination clearly worked overtime," Ted teased. "It didn't occur to me to explain. I never dreamed you'd assume Karen and I were married."

Sarah pushed back a strand of hair from her forehead and set the wedding photo back on the desk. "It certainly appeared that way."

She noted the tension that rose in his shoulders, then the ache that settled in his dark chocolate eyes.

"I apologize." Ted drew in a deep breath, but never took his eyes off Sarah. "Since I'm being honest, there is one very important detail I think I should share with you."

"What's that?"

"Four years ago, my life changed. Though the decision was a difficult one to make, in the end the final choice I came to was the only solution left. Family was important. Finishing college was important. Without an education, taking care of my family would've been much more of a challenge." He hesitated before continuing. "The challenge I wasn't ready to accept... considering my circumstances."

"What circumstances? What decision?" she asked.

He stared long and hard, making her uncomfortable.

"I should have explained earlier. Robert and Karen were loving, but temporary parents for Emma during my absence."

"Temporary?"

He studied her face again before answering. "Emma is my little girl. My daughter."

Four

*S*arah's breath hung in her throat for a split second. She placed a hand over her hammering heart and willed herself to continue breathing. Had she heard him correctly? Yes... yes she had.

Ted heaved a sigh. "I'm no longer married. The marriage lasted long enough for her to have the baby and restore her health. She wanted out. No husband, no child. That's why Robert and Karen were taking care of Emma. I'm in the process of moving in with Dad, and once Karen is comfortable living alone after Robert's death, Emma will move in for good with me. Dad's gone most of the time and his home is close to Karen. Best of all, in Emma's school district."

Sarah's eyes squinted beneath her wrinkled forehead. "I'm confused. She, your wife, is still around, but didn't want her little girl? I can't imagine not wanting your baby after holding her. That's a natural instinct between mother and child." Sarah bit the corner of her lip. She was entirely too nosey. "I'm sorry, Ted."

Ted pointed toward the sofa. "Can we sit while I explain?"

Sarah had an uneasy awareness that she was getting in too deep concerning Ted's issues with his wife and child. She did want to know, but knowing may not allow her to back off sooner than she should. Like now, before things became complicated.

"You needn't explain anything more to me, Ted. Your wife was a private part of your life. Again, I'm sorry. I shouldn't be so curious."

"Yes. Yes, it's private, but we're friends." He glanced at her. "At least, I hope we're still friends."

Sarah nodded, then waited for Ted to sit beside her. But he didn't. Ted paced the space between the sofa and the fireplace. Finally he leaned against the fireplace and shoved his hands inside his pants pockets while his intent stare bore into hers.

"When you refused to have anything else to do with me, I resigned myself to the fact and realized that was the way you wanted things to be. I was angry, and confused, but had no choice except to step out of your life."

A thousand reasons and regrets of how and why she'd pushed Ted away flooded Sarah's thoughts. The look on his face when she'd told him it was over between them would forever haunt her. She'd painstakingly shattered their relationship and future plans. She hadn't even told him why or justified her decision.

"Look. I'm not proud of the way I ended things with you. No excuse in the world can make up for what I did. I was young. I was hurting. I blamed myself for the accident that all but cost Gavin his life. I didn't handle the accident well and forgiveness was the one thing I didn't allow myself. I turned my back on family, friends... and you. I didn't handle that well either."

She stared out the window at a few of the children who ran into their mother's arms; others who dragged their feet while frowns crossed their faces.

"Guilt and grief are painful issues to live through."

"I agree. I can only hope Emma's mother feels a glimmer of remorse for walking out on her baby. The baby she'd never wanted. Didn't want. I'm somewhat responsible for not trying to talk her into staying. I didn't agree with her leaving her baby but... I am thankful Emma's here with us, well taken care of, safe and happy."

Digging in deeper, Sarah probed further. "How did the two of you meet?"

"We should have never married." Ted simply shook his head. "There was no love between us, we'd only met that one night."

"Then why? Why did the two of you decide to marry?"

"There was no decision." Ted threw up his hands and whooshed out a lengthy breath. "I'd taken off a few days during a break at college. It was one of those nights I'd had too much to drink. The next morning I awoke in a motel room with a wife by my side.

I barely remember meeting her and certainly have no memory of the wedding. So... the wedding wasn't planned. Las Vegas makes it entirely too easy to get married."

"I can only imagine how being married to someone you barely know went over."

His hands gripped the edge of the fireplace as he pushed off and plopped down beside her. "That's the least of it. She went back to her mother's home and I headed back to college. We hadn't filed for a divorce yet because of money. Two months later she called with the news that she was pregnant."

"Oh, Ted. I'm so sorry."

"I would say me too... and I was when she first told me. Emma is the best thing that's ever happened to me." He smiled. "Life sometimes throws you for a loop. I did the right thing and moved her into a small apartment close to the college, then moved in myself to take care of her, should anything go wrong."

Sarah didn't want to step on his toes, but the question kept roaming around her head. "You don't have to answer, but I'm wondering if you had any problem believing the baby was yours?"

He stared into the unlit fireplace. "She knew I'd have doubts. She insisted on a DNA test, which my dad paid for. Emma is indeed my child."

"What a nightmare."

"You're telling me. The best thing that came out of the marriage was Emma. I don't regret the marriage, if only for her."

"She's beautiful. I'd like to get to know her."

Surprise flashed over Ted's face. "I'd like that too. For you two to get together sometime would be fantastic. You'd be a good friend for Emma."

"You shouldn't be so amazed at the offer." Sarah laughed. "I'm not so bad."

"No, you aren't so bad." Ted beamed at Sarah. "I never said you were."

"Thanks. That means a lot coming from you... especially after the way I left things between us years ago." She held the fixed gaze that linked them and whispered, "I'm sorry, Ted. I'm sorry I handled things so badly."

"I forgive you," he whispered back.

"I'm so happy to hear you say that. You're a special person." Sarah drew in a deep breath and looked Ted in the eyes. "Thank you for forgiving me."

Ted reached over and put a hand on the back of her neck. "Our problems are in the past. Let's leave them there." He dropped his hand and gave her a loving gaze. "You're the special one, Sarah. Special to me. Always." He reached to take her hand, but promptly withdrew the gesture. "I never got over you. We had a heartbreaking, long stretch connecting with each other again."

Sarah let out a long sigh. "Yes. It seemed a lifetime. Now that you're here, I hope our time apart has ended. Can we become friends again?"

"We're still friends, remember? Time has a way of absolving issues."

"True. You have my number. As for getting to know Emma, call me and we'll set a time that works for both of us. Maybe a weekend at one of the St. Simons cottages? I think Emma would be more comfortable at your dad's place."

Ted pushed a photo of Emma back from the edge of the mantel. "Sounds great. Emma hasn't been riding in a while. I'm sure she'll enjoy a weekend away. I know the time will be good for the both of us. Plus, it will give Karen some much needed time for herself."

Ted had left the door to the library open and Karen knocked quickly, then walked inside.

"Did I hear my name mentioned?"

Ted turned and faced Karen. "Has everyone gone?"

Karen eyed Sarah before answering. "Yes. We've almost finished cleaning up and Emma is down for a short nap."

Sarah wondered if the late nap would keep Emma from sleeping at night, but decided it wasn't her place to interfere.

"Good. I'm sure she needs a nap after the party," Ted replied. "I don't think she was still much today."

Oh well. Since her dad agrees, I should mind my own business.

"We were discussing maybe meeting at Dad's place at St. Simons one weekend. I thought Emma would enjoy some special time riding her pony." Ted glanced at Karen. "Plus, you would have time to spend doing things you'd like or need to do."

Karen's face reflected a momentary miff. "Emma doesn't keep me from doing anything. I love Emma and love having her around. You know that, Ted."

"Of course I do. I meant nothing by the comment." Ted walked over to Karen and hugged her around the shoulders.

"I should go," Sarah said. "It was wonderful seeing you again, Karen."

"Yes. Please allow me to thank you for such a lovely party," Karen replied.

"You're welcome. I'm pleased I could join in and make this a happy day."

"Karen, as always, thank you for making this day so special for Emma." Ted kissed her on the forehead and turned back to Sarah. "I'll round up Dad and help you load everything back in your car."

"If you don't mind, Ted, I have a question before you leave," Karen said.

Sarah picked up her phone from the chair arm and slid it into a pocket. "Please don't feel obligated, but your help is appreciated. I'll go get started while you and Karen finish up here."

When Sarah had almost pulled the door to, she heard Karen whispering. She didn't sound happy...at all. Right before she closed the door, and when she heard her name, she realized they were discussing her.

Five

Sarah loaded the last of the decorations, slid the box inside the trunk, then placed an arm across her forehead to block the bright sun. "Have I done something to offend Karen?"

"No. She's simply being protective of Emma." He closed the trunk lid, dusted off his hands and gave her a brief, if not somewhat frustrated, stare. "And that protection often flows onto me. She's concerned I'll marry some wild woman and take Emma away."

"But, what you do is your decision. Emma is your daughter."

"Yes, it's my decision and yes, she is my daughter. Karen has taken care of her since birth, so she feels as though she's her mother. And... well, she has been and still is, a mother to her, blood related or not. Emma doesn't know anyone except Karen as a mother figure. She doesn't call her mom or mother, but simply calls her Karen. Karen is okay with that, too."

"I understand all the reasoning, believe me. But is it healthy that Karen is so attached she couldn't bear to think of you having a life with Emma... without her?"

"How could she not be? I refuse to hurt Karen's feelings. She's fine. She knows Emma is going to move in with Dad and me, once we get settled in. Emma's just turned four and is excited to start Pre-K this year. Karen will help by picking her up and keeping her a few hours a day when Dad isn't available. It isn't as though I'm separating the two of them. Splitting them up would be cruel."

"I agree. Hurting Karen would be cruel."

He leaned against the car and studied Sarah. "The situation presents a fine line to tread. It was my responsibility that Karen was placed in the position she's in, but there was never any question that she wouldn't pitch in and care for Emma. That's the type person she is. She and Robert took on the responsibility without hesitation while I finished school. It's normal they shared a strong love for her. I've never doubted either of them."

"I'm sure Emma will always love Karen and Robert, too. Do you think she remembers Robert?"

Ted grinned. "She's a funny little girl. When she walks by his photo, she points and says, Robert, then kisses the photo. So, yes she does remember. I'm happy about that. We won't let her forget him either."

"It sounds as though Karen is a good woman. You are blessed she has a big heart."

He shook his head. "Robert chose well."

Sarah checked her watch. "It's getting late. I'm sure you have things to do."

"Nothing pressing. If it's okay, I'll follow you back to the shop and help put these decorations away. It's the least I can do."

"Sounds good to me… are you sure?"

"Certainly. If we get separated, I'll see you there."

The drive only took about fifteen minutes, as Karen lived just outside the city limits of Savannah. By the time they'd unpacked and added boxes to the shelves, the sun was beginning to hide behind a glorious orange and pink sunset.

"I appreciate your help. Believe me, you saved me a lot of work and time today." She covered her mouth and yawned. "It's been a long day, Ted. I think I'll grab some take-out and head home."

"My dinner invitation is still open. Tonight… if you're free… and if you can stay awake."

If she were free? He had no idea how wonderful being free and dinner with him sounded.

Sarah bit down on her lip. "Are you asking me on a date, Ted?"

He snapped his head around and found her, clearly taken aback. "If you're open to spending some time with me."

"Well, is it a date or not?"

"How shall I answer that question? If I say yes, you'll think I'm being pushy. If I say no, you'll wonder why."

Sarah frowned. "Are you hungry, Ted?"

"Have you ever seen me not hungry?" He laughed.

"Not that I recall, and I doubt you've changed in five years."

"Okay then. Let's eat, please," Ted appealed to her.

"You sure do talk a lot for a hungry guy."

Ted took the shop keys from her and locked the door. "Would you like anything other than Italian?"

"As long as it's food, I could care less. But Lasagna sounds too good to pass up. Just feed me," she said

Ted seated her inside his SUV, gave her a wink, then turned over the motor. "I know this great little Italian restaurant on the other side of town. They make a mean Lasagna."

"You remember I like Italian. But then there wasn't too much I didn't, or still do like."

"Of course I do. There's little I don't remember about you, Sarah. For me, you're like one of those beautiful Forget Me Not flowers."

Six

I can't believe I let you talk me into walking on the beach," Sarah commented. She looked down at Ted's bare feet and rolled up jeans. The sight took her back a few years.

He glanced up at the stars and drew in a deep breath of the ocean air. "The beach is the perfect ending to a fabulous evening with you. Besides, I've wanted to drive to Tybee Island sooner, but being with you makes it even more special."

Sarah gazed out over the incredible moonlit water, and focused on the gentle laps that caressed the sand. She didn't admit coming to the beach made her sad. The last time she'd visited, she'd left in tears. Memories of the two of them playing on the beach, Ted searching seashells for her, had sent her flying back home.

"It's been too long since I've driven to Tybee ," she said. But then not long enough.

Ted handed her shoes back after shaking off the sand and seated her in the car, but before they pulled out of the parking space, he excused himself. He walked back to the trunk and came back with a beautifully, and familiar, wrapped package.

He held it out and smiled. "This is for you."

Sarah tore off the paper and stared down at the contents. Not that she didn't already know what it was. Inside was the music box he'd bought at her shop. She'd wrapped her own gift. "You shouldn't have, Ted. But thank you."

"Sure."

"Didn't you purchase this for Emma?"

"Not really. She already has three. I don't believe Karen would appreciate having to find a spot for another." Ted laughed and crumpled the wrapping paper, then threw it in the back.

"Still, Emma would have loved another, especially from her dad. Is that the only reason you'd like me to have the music box, because she already has three?"

"Of course not. Please accept the music box in appreciation for all you've done." Ted hesitated. "Anyway, I'd like for you to have it. Actually, you're the reason I bought it."

Sarah thought back to the day he'd absently asked her to add a music box to his list of items. "But you bought it while shopping for your daughter. Remember?"

"Certainly. Except with you in mind."

Sarah leaned her head sideways and sent Ted a curious squint. "Without knowing you'd have the opportunity to give it to me?"

"A guy can hope can't he? Besides appreciation isn't the only motivation."

Disappointed at his answer, she gritted her teeth and wondered what his purpose was. "Then what else did you have in mind, Ted?"

"What would you think if I said I forgive you? That I hoped one day we'd get the chance to connect once more and work things out? You've never been far from my thoughts, Sarah."

Her mouth suddenly went dry, while a twinge of guilt rushed through her. *How can you forgive me so easily?*

"Ted—"

He didn't let it go and continued. "Wouldn't it be incredible if, after all this time, we've actually found each other again?"

"It's only been three days since we ran into each other at the post office. Don't you think it's a bit soon to expect to pick up where we left off?"

"No. We know one another. Nothing can change that. Nothing. We were together long enough to look back, realize what went wrong, rectify the problem, and deal with the issues."

Her mind was in a whirl. She hadn't expected Ted to approach her with a serious discussion so soon. "Getting to know each other again might not be as easy as you think or expect. We've both changed, grown further apart—maybe."

"As I said, I haven't forgotten you, Sarah, and you were always on my mind." He scrutinized her and the way she had twisted around to face him head-on. "I may be taking too much for granted, but I'm of the opinion you may feel the same. I hope that's enough for us to build a renewed relationship. Forget changing. We have too much history. Sometimes change is a good thing."

Now wasn't the time to let Ted know how she really felt. Of course she still cared for him, maybe even still loved him, but she definitely wasn't going there this quickly after he'd relocated to Savannah. They'd both changed and only time would tell how much. Maybe they wouldn't even like each other now.

"I'm willing to think about it, Ted, but let's consider this as a new beginning and take it one day at a time. There's a lot for us to discover about each other now. Five years can make a huge difference in how we really perceive one another."

"Five years, fifty years. I'll always feel the same."

I'll find out soon enough how you feel, Ted. And myself. Only time will tell. Some things are best left in the past. But... can I do that? Or should I take advantage of a second chance?

Ted cranked the car and pulled slowly from the parking space with an air of anticipation that gathered as his eyes met hers.

Seven

Ted stood back and noted that Karen gathered two extra sets of clothing for Emma to take on her trip to the cottage. She didn't look happy despite Emma's excitement about the weekend and going to ride her pony, Baby. Emma had been a bundle of delight all morning.

"I've packed snacks, sunscreen, and bug spray. There's also a small First-Aid kit with antibiotic, alcohol and Band-Aids, among other items, in case they're needed."

"Thanks. Karen. Hopefully we won't need First-Aid, but thanks. You never know. We'll stop by the store and stock up on staples and whatever else we need, so it really isn't necessary to go to so much trouble."

"I don't find doing things for Emma trouble." Karen folded her arms across her chest and pursed her lips. "Do you think it's a good idea for Emma and Sarah to spend time together this weekend?"

Ted's eyebrows shot up, as surprise exposed his expression. "Why not?"

"For one thing, she doesn't know her that well. She may be uncomfortable, not to mention anxious. She's never spent the night away except with your dad. Even then, most of the time, you were there. I'm simply concerned for Emma and the influence Sarah may have on her."

"Karen, there isn't any reason for your concern. The three of us have spent time at Sarah's shop, dinner, picnicking, the movies and Putt-Putt Golf. The two of them get along fine. Besides, this weekend will give them a chance to further bond."

Karen nodded and met Ted's scrutiny. "That's what I'm

concerned about."

"What? The two of them bonding? Please. Being together will be a wonderful experience for them. They're already comfortable with each other. This trip will be good for Emma. I promise."

"I'm not so sure. What if Sarah decides to break off your relationship. What then? How will Emma deal with an abrupt disappearance?" Karen took a deep breath. "She did it once before. She may repeat the incident."

"First, we aren't in a relationship. Not yet anyway. We're taking things slow and easy. No pressure on either of us. You mustn't worry about our future. We don't even know how it will turn out… but we've agreed to give it our best."

Karen managed to smile, albeit a forced smile. "That's what I mean. You two may not be together long. Why bring Emma into the triangle?"

"Believe me, both Sarah and myself have Emma's well-being in mind." Ted realized Karen was voicing her anxieties, but alarmed that her uneasiness ran a bit deeper than he'd first thought or even imagined. "Emma is young, but a smart little girl. You and I both know she deals with problems much better than either of us ever thought she was capable. You've taught her well."

"Thank you, Ted, but I…"

"Daddy?"

Ted turned around to find Emma fully dressed and ready to go, her backpack in place. "Hi, sweetheart." He reached down, picked her up hugged her tight, then perched her atop his shoulders. "You're getting to be such a big girl."

"Yes, I am. I'm four now," she said, then giggled. "Can we go now, Daddy? I'm ready to ride my pony."

Eight

arah slipped Emma's dolls inside her backpack, then picked up the sleeping little girl from the car seat. Sarah hoped she'd sleep through them getting settled in, but the moment she moved her and tried to remove the blankie, Emma woke up.

Emma yanked at her blankie with one hand and shaded her eyes with the other. "Are we here yet?"

"Yes, little one, we finally made it to the beach." Once Sarah set Emma down, she ran up onto the porch and climbed in one of the rockers, rocking as fast as she could.

"Come rock with me, Sarah," she called out. "It's so much fun."

"I will in a few minutes, sweetie." Sarah giggled. "Be careful and don't turn over. You're going awfully fast. Why don't you play the slow-rocker game?"

"But that's no fun, Miss Sarah," she said, and pouted.

"I want you to be safe, sweetheart. That's all. Okay?"

"Okay," Emma managed to say, through a frown that covered her pretty face.

Sarah took a moment to gaze out over the ocean and pulled in a breath of crisp, salty air. The sheer beauty of the ocean and the sunset crawling across the sky was breathtaking. She glanced around at the well-kept cottage and its immaculate grounds, then hugged her arms over her chest. "I love this place," she said, then grinned from ear to ear. "Ted, I can't believe our cottages were this close all these years and we weren't even aware of the other having a place here."

Ted grinned and held the door open for Sarah. "There's a good reason for that. Dad only bought this place while I was in college. I've only visited a few times during summers, when I could get away." He let out a silent sigh. "Which wasn't often. I've grown to love it here, and find it comforting to have a place to lessen the stress that comes with being a part-time parent. Emma and I connect on her level here, with time at the beach and especially since Dad gave her the pony."

"Ted, you couldn't have known about our cottage, because Grandfather refused to come here after my grandmother passed away. He missed her terribly and said the place was too sad without her. She passed away before I started grade school. You and I never had cause to discuss the place. Mom and dad never talked about the beach or took advantage of the cottage out of respect for my grandfather."

"That's a shame," Ted replied.

Sarah peeked out the door to check on Emma and make sure she hadn't slipped off somewhere. "Yes. We would've enjoyed the Summers more had we spent time here. But with the shop to run, Mom didn't have much time to spare. She brought us here a few times after dad passed away. And, after she passed away, Lisa and I usually tried to visit at least monthly. Separately of course, since we don't normally leave the shop without one or the other in charge. After I bought Winston, Gavin, Lisa's son, came up more often. He's made a few friends here, so the beach has been good for him."

Ted shook his head and laughed. "I understand. That's why, not once, did we have reason to sneak off and enjoy the beach up here. At any rate, we're here now. Speaking of now, groceries are getting warm in the car, and that won't do. I'll be right back."

Sarah finished wiping down the refrigerator and had barely dried the counter before Ted came back in, Emma holding the door for him, and stacked several bags on top. "I'll put these away while you make a run through the cottage," she said.

"Is there anything in particular you think I should look for besides checking power, gas and water? Maybe a ghost or two?" He chuckled. "You know how rumor has it that Savannah is a town occupied with ghosts."

She gave him a thumbs up. "Of which you should've checked before we bought bags and bags of food. I seriously doubt there are any ghosts around here. I'm not spooked that easily."

"Now, now. I'm kidding about the ghosts, but you never can tell what's lurking in the shadows. I called Jasper and had him check out everything the week before we left. Why do you think the grass is cut, or the fridge is cold? The list goes on and on with things you haven't noticed yet."

"Smart man." Sarah laughed. "I should have known you'd be on top of everything."

"Chalk one up for me." Ted picked up the bag of canned goods and stacked them on the counter, then wiped off the shelves before adding them. "Oh, by the way. You needn't worry about the beds. Jasper's wife Anna, aired the mattresses and added clean linen, including towels for the bathrooms."

"Thanks. Knowing we won't need to start washing linen makes things a lot easier while we're getting settled. By the way. Jasper and Anna also take care of my place and board Winston."

"I put your bag in the bedroom facing the ocean view," Ted commented, then snapped his fingers. "Emma will share the room with you, unless you'd like me to move her twin-bed in my room."

"I have no issue with sharing the room with Emma. We'll have fun." Sarah sent him a quick, uneasy glance. "I hope she's okay with those arrangements. She's young and you never know how she'll react, since kids are unpredictable."

"She's quite taken with you in case you haven't noticed. If she isn't content away from me during the night, it'll be easy enough to move the bed. No need for concern." Ted picked up his bag and headed to the smaller bedroom. "We'll ask her how she feels about it at dinner."

Emma hugged her blankie and frowned. "Daddy. Your marshmallow is getting black."

Ted had observed as Sarah and Emma bonded further and

had forgotten the marshmallow, which was now in flames. "Thanks, sweetheart. Good thing I like mine a little overdone."

Emma scrunched her nose and continued eating her lightly toasted marshmallow. "Eww, Daddy," she managed to express, through the sticky sugar, and while she snuggled the blankie under her arm.

"Ted," Sarah whispered. "Emma's blankie is like a second skin. If it isn't in her hand, it's in her mouth. A friend had an idea to get her daughter to give up her blankie, and the concept worked. If you're open to weening her from the habit we could give it a try."

Ted didn't say anything for a moment. "She's still young, Sarah. She'll probably give it up on her own, given enough time."

"She'll be starting Pre-K soon. The other kids may make fun of her, and I know you don't want her to deal with that kind of pressure."

"Okay. I'm willing to listen while you run the idea past me. I'm not promising anything though. Not yet anyway."

"Great. What she did was, once every two or three months, she trimmed all of her daughter's blankies. She thought she was outgrowing it and when it became too small, she gave it up."

Ted had serious doubts that Emma wouldn't guess their trickery. "What? Are you kidding? She's too smart to fall for that, Sarah."

"Not if we do it properly. She'll never know the difference. If she does figure it out, you can keep extras on hand." When Sarah had unpacked Emma's bag, she'd seen the extra blankie among her clothing. She couldn't imagine Emma dragging a blankie to school. Plus the school would most likely require she leave it at home.

Ted's expression was dead-pan while he sat in deep thought. "I'll consider the idea. But taking it away could create an issue for her. I won't add anymore anxiety in her life. Besides, as I've said earlier, she's really attached to her blankie. She considers it her friend."

Ted wondered how Karen would react to Sarah's suggestion. He had a feeling it wouldn't sit well with her, since she had been the one to make most of the decisions concerning Emma so far.

Of course, Karen had called Ted on really important issues, but as usual he'd left the decisions in Karen's capable hands.

He realized now that he should have become more involved and hoped it wasn't too late to rectify the mistake he'd made at leaving Karen in charge of Emma's nurturing.

He rolled his shoulders to release the tension that had developed. He was Emma's father and it was time he took back charge of his daughter's future and her progress.

Nine

The next morning, Ted knocked on the bedroom door. "Wake up sleepy heads. Breakfast is ready. It's half past eight. The day awaits you lovely ladies."

Still groggy, Sarah opened one eye and pushed back a strand of dark auburn hair then kicked the sheet from her still half-asleep body. "Fine. Just fine. What time did you wake up, early-bird?"

"I've been up for a couple of hours and have already gotten in a run on the beach. Did Emma sleep well in the small bed beside you?" Ted asked.

Sarah sat on the edge of the bed and looked over at Emma, her light brown hair sprawled over a pillow. "She's still asleep. As far as I know, she hasn't had a problem all night."

"I'm glad she had a good night. Is it safe to come in?"

"Yes."

Ted handed Sarah a steaming cup of coffee, then whispered. "Tell Emma I made chocolate pancakes with strawberries on the side. That should get her attention."

"I'm sure it will. Now, get out of here so we can shower."

Attention. What if Emma had needed me during the night? She'd slept so hard last night, harder than she normally did. Children needed someone who could sleep with one eye open. The thought that she hadn't shook her to the core.

An hour later, her tummy full of pancakes, Emma stood beside Sarah with a huge smile, ready to spend time with her pony.

As she held out her tiny hands, a carrot in both, and as Baby took the carrot from her, Emma giggled "She's tickling my fingers. Sarah, come help me feed Baby. She loves apples too. Do you want to feed her?"

"If you'd like me to. What a great idea to let me help feed your pony. Thank you, sweetheart." Sarah took a carrot broke it in two, and watched Baby nibble on the treat.

"You're welcome. See? She likes you," Emma said, then giggled again.

"I think she does. Probably because you're here with me though." Sarah rubbed Baby's head and gave her the other half. "That's all there is, Baby. We'll bring apples next time."

Emma stood beside Sarah and gazed up at her, obviously a little anxious. "Miss Sarah?"

"Yes, sweetie?"

Her eyes grew larger as she continued to stare at Sarah. "I like you too."

"Oh, sweetheart. Thank you." Sarah reached down and hugged her, and she hugged back. Sarah's heart swelled, while she fought back happy tears. "I love you, little one."

Emma grinned and slipped her small hand inside Sarah's. Hand in hand, they led Baby around the other end of the stables to join her daddy.

Ted secured the small helmet on Emma, then settled her atop the Shetland pony. He led Baby at a slow pace around the circle, as he kept a close eye on Emma. She waved to Sarah, who stood at the sidelines waving back. Once, Emma even threw a kiss at Sarah.

"Daddy, I'm thirsty. Can we ride Jack now?"

"Are you sure? Baby might feel left out."

"No she won't. She's getting tired."

Ted sent a fleeting glance at Sarah, while he led Baby over to the stall. "She wants to ride Jack because he's bigger and she can sit with me," he whispered. "Plus she always says Baby is getting tired when she's the one who is actually tired."

Sarah winked at Ted and laughed quietly. "Admit it. She's a little con."

Ted threw back his head and roared with laughter. "Of course she is. She's her dad's girl. That's okay though. I wouldn't want her to be disappointed at not being able to ride Jack."

After they'd taken the horses and pony back to Jasper's stables, they drove back to the cottage. Ted glanced at Emma fast asleep in the car seat, the blankie safely tucked in her mouth.

"Wonder what's up with Emma? Her mood is lighter and she appears happier than I've seen her in a long while."

"I really can't say. You know her better than I do. She told me she likes me while we fed Baby a treat. After I hugged her, she gave me a hug and took my hand." Sarah laughed. "It looks as though I'm making some awesome points with her."

"Wonderful. Absolutely wonderful. I was concerned that Emma wouldn't take to you as well as she has. I'm thrilled to know the two of you get along so well. That news makes me a happy man. You can't imagine how relieved that the relationship between you two has improved day by day." He placed his hand over hers and squeezed. "Please know I'm thankful."

"No need to thank me. Emma is lovely and easy to be around... and love."

Ted locked eyes with her. "You mean that don't you?"

"Of course I do. There's no reason to lie or try to make you think I care if it's not true."

"I can always trust you to be honest. I appreciate that too." Memories flooded through Ted's head. "Do you remember the night my car ran out of gas coming home from the lake?"

"For sure I do." Sarah chuckled. "My mom threatened you within an inch of your life if you ever brought me home after midnight again."

"Yes and she made a believer of me too. I never made that mistake again. If I had to beg or borrow, I made sure I had enough gas money. Your mom's wrath put the fear of God in me."

"Mom certainly had a way about her. Sweet, and I loved her more than anything, but she had strict rules and expected Lisa and me to abide by them. When she had her mind made up, we were allowed no questions and definitely no argument. *Nada.*"

"I remember that in particular about your mom. She was a tiny woman, and feisty when it came to her girls. I loved the woman though, she was always good to me. I know you miss her."

"I do. Every day. Some days more than others." Sarah looked over at Ted's profile and spoke softly. "I'm sure you miss Robert terribly."

"Of course. His passing is still raw. There are days I forget and pick up the phone to call him. Then it hits me. I won't ever talk to Robert ever again."

"I'm so sorry, Ted." While Ted's hand still lay across hers, she squeezed and looked at him. "Oh, but the memories... those memories will last a lifetime."

Emma woke then. "Daddy, can I have an ice cream?"

"Sounds good to me right about now. How about you, Sarah?"

"Nothing would be better. I'm game. What do you say we stop at a place that has tables outside?"

"Yeah, 'cause I'm messy." Emma's lower lip dropped. "That's what Aunt Karen said."

Ted and Sarah cast a surprised glance at each other.

Sarah reached across the table and patted Emma's arm. "Being messy isn't so bad, sweetheart. I can't eat ice cream without being messy either. Please don't worry your pretty little head. I believe that's what napkins are for. Okay?"

Emma was still a bit saddened, but Sarah could tell she was considering what she'd told her. Karen should know better. There were other ways of getting your point across rather than upsetting a child. Messy wasn't the end of the world.

"Okay, Miss Sarah." Emma perked up, then stuffed her blankie in her mouth as they pulled into the Tasty Ice Cream Parlor.

Sarah leaned back in the bench and waited for her ice cream to begin to melt, then run down her hand. She proceeded to yank napkins from the holder on the table. "I sure made a mess with my ice cream."

Emma's eyes widened when she saw Sarah's hand. "Oh," she said.

Ted jumped up to help Sarah and immediately turned over

his cup of water. He started to laugh and caught Emma's stricken face. "It's okay, Emma. We'll get it cleaned up."

"You're messy too, Daddy," she commented, and giggled.

"No one is perfect, sweetheart. Life goes on, no matter the mess we make," Sarah replied. She made contact with Ted. "Whether it's a food mess or our lives."

"That's so true. What would you like…"

"Hold on, Ted."

Sarah pulled a napkin from the holder on the table and wiped a dribble of ice cream from Emma's chin. "Well, that treat was good, huh?"

"Yes. Thank you, Sarah. May I have another?"

"Sarah laughed. "One is enough before dinner. Okay?"

Her mouth shaped a pout, which showed clearly, she wasn't happy with Sarah's response. "Okay," she finally replied.

"Sarah, if you're bushed, we can order in Chinese, pizza, Mexican, or pick-up whatever you'd like tonight. We have some steaks. I'm a pretty good cook… on a grill, that is."

Sarah whispered in Emma's ear. "What do you think about a steak tonight, sweetheart? Are they something you like?"

Emma's mood improved immediately. "Yes. Daddy cooks them really good."

Sarah turned back to Ted. "There you have it. Emma and I feel like a delicious steak. She laughed. "One that you prepare for us. Are you up to the challenge?"

"Are you kidding? Be prepared for an excellent dinner, because you're about to witness perfection in action. Guaranteed."

Ten

Ted's cell phone beeped as Sarah settled Emma down for a short nap before dinner. They'd planned earlier for a game of Putt-Putt on the outskirts of Savannah later and she wanted her to feel good during the game.

There was no way to eavesdrop politely, but since Sarah was within earshot, she couldn't help but overhear Ted's side of the conversation. If she were a betting woman, guessing who was on the phone would render her a ton of points.

"Yes, she's fine. Yes, she slept good last night. No, she hasn't cried to come home. Sarah and Emma are getting along great." Ted said into the phone, pointed, then mouthed, *Karen.* "I'm not really sure. We'd planned on coming home tomorrow, but may stay until Monday. It all depends on how tomorrow goes. Yes, I'll call to confirm. Thanks, Karen. We'll see you soon."

Ted slid his phone across the counter, then bent down and grabbed a bag of charcoal from inside a cabinet. "I marinated the steaks earlier. Would you mind bringing them out in about ten minutes?"

"Sure."

Sarah put in a call to Lisa. "Sorry this is such short notice. In the past few minutes, Ted has let me know he is contemplating staying here until Monday. Are you okay with the timing? Since I don't have my calendar with me, is there anything upcoming or urgent that I need to be there to help with or take care of?"

"No. All is well here. I'm glad you and Ted are together again. Don't be such a worrywart. If I need help, Gavin is available since school is out. Enjoy every moment away from work and I'll see you whenever; that is, when you get here."

"Thanks. Lisa. I'll let you know only if I'll be back before Monday."

Sarah clicked off the phone, checked on Emma, then went outside. "Potatoes are in the oven and Asparagus is ready to grill when the steaks are done." She took off the plastic wrap, set down the platter of asparagus, then laid a hand on his arm.

Ted stared at her with a half-smile.

"Are you okay? You're awfully quiet."

"I hope I'm wrong, but I think Karen has a growing dislike toward you. I'm not sure how to handle the issue, but I know you'll agree we must deal with her problem soon." He flipped the steaks and closed the lid momentarily. "Karen's behavior couldn't come at a worse time."

Sarah nodded in agreement. "It's clearly becoming a difficult situation. I don't know if she's always tense, but I've noticed she is certainly tense when I'm around."

"It's a touchy matter. Karen has taken care of Emma all her life. I'm sure she has her well-being at heart." Ted placed the steaks on a clean platter, closed the grill and walked inside while Sarah held open the door. "I'm afraid her emotions are getting the better of her."

Sarah recalled the way Karen had regarded her when they'd first met at the shop. She'd brushed aside the look Karen had given her. Jealousy had never been one of Sarah's traits, but it looked as though Karen was about to become full blown with the warning signs she had revealed thus far. She didn't want to take Karen's place. Couldn't take her place. Ever. There would be plenty of love to go around, if only Karen could see it that way.

"Go wake your daughter so she'll have time to wake up and not have to eat while she's half asleep. I'll put herbed butter on the steaks and set the table. Hey. Let's eat outside. Emma will probably enjoy watching the ocean instead of four walls. I know I will."

"Sounds perfect to me. I'll be back as soon as Emma becomes fully awake." Ted closed the distance between them, gently placed a finger under her chin, then kissed her on the cheek, a bit too close to her lips.

When Sarah caught her breath so quickly and lifted a hand to her cheek, the gesture prompted Ted to back away. "Oh, Ted. Please, don't. We're taking it slow and easy, remember?"

"Yes, I remember. I must admit though, I acted on impulse. I won't apologize. That was simply a casual kiss, more of a response, since I care so much for you."

"It's okay. I'm simply not sure how we should handle this situation either. It seems as though we're moving at high-speed... much faster than we had intended."

The moment passed, but in her heart, she accepted that Ted still cared... more than a little.

Eleven

When Ted had kissed her, even on the cheek, there'd been no denying the fireworks were still alive and well... and coursing through her veins. All it took was a touch. Why she was surprised made no sense. At all. She'd felt the same way when he'd stood behind her at the post office a few weeks ago.

Sarah had begged off going to the beach with Ted and Emma. As much as she'd rather have gone to build a sand castle with them, they needed some alone time. Time to make up for four long years between home and school commutes. He'd admitted to Sarah the guilt that ate at him. But he had convinced himself being away at school, and having his brother and Karen raise his daughter for four years, was something necessary. He and Emma had to survive to ensure their future wouldn't be a hardship on him or his daughter. He'd said being a dad was a huge responsibility, and he wanted to do it right.

Sarah admired him for sticking it out to graduation, though he'd rather have been with Emma. She didn't blame him. Emma was a precious gift. The years away from her everyday activities were something he'd never experience but he'd made every effort to be with her when he could.

The cookies she and Emma baked earlier had cooled, and Emma was excited they would decorate them after playtime at the beach. Karen had taken good care of Emma, but she'd said she'd never made or decorated cookies with Karen. Sarah thought that a bit strange since she recalled having fun in the kitchen with her mom. All little girls liked to help and learn from their moms, no matter what it was.

Sarah squeezed two slices of lemon in a glass of water, dropped in ice cubes, then went to the porch to watch Ted and Emma teasing each other in the water. Today was their last day to enjoy each other. They'd be leaving for home in the morning. Saddened, and as though she could slow time, she pushed off the rocker into a gentle movement.

An enormous wave crashed over Ted and Emma while their backs were turned to the incoming surf. Emma began to cough and spit out ocean water. Ted reached down, picked her up, and patted her on the back several times.

Sarah ran inside, grabbed an extra towel, then ran across the road to the beach. By the time she arrived at their sides, Emma was doing fine. She laughed and begged to go back into the water.

"Please, Daddy. Just a little longer," she asked, then pouted through quivering lips. "Please?"

"You're cold, sweetheart," Sarah said. She wrapped the towel around Emma and hugged her close for warmth, then whispered to Ted. "Do you think she's scared?"

"Ha. Does it look like she is? I don't think so. She isn't scared of much," Ted commented. "I guess she's that much like me."

"I've noticed that about her. You are definitely her daddy."

"That I am," he said, and beamed. His eyes full of emotion, he looked at Emma a long while with tremendous love, then nodded. "And she's my girl."

"I've seen that you're a super guy and a wonderful father. You don't mind getting your hands dirty either. I like that about you. All good qualities." Sarah spun around and faced Emma. "The cookies are cooled now. What do you say we head back to the cottage and decorate?"

Emma jumped up and down. "Yes. Let's decorate." She thought for a second. "Can we eat the cookies after we finish?"

"Yes, and this is your lucky day. There will be enough for you to take home, too."

Emma ran over and hugged Sarah. "Thank you, Miss Sarah."

Sarah hugged her back and pushed a strand of wet hair from her face. 'You can call me Sarah. It isn't necessary that you say

Miss Sarah. Okay?"

"Okay," she said, and twisted out of Sarah's hug to bounce across the sand.

Ted laughed. "Just like a kid. Nothing is as important as the next moment."

Back at the cottage, Ted marinated shrimp, prepared broccoli and put water on to boil for angel hair pasta. Pasta was a favorite of Emma's.

He took pleasure in his observation of Sarah and Emma together. The two of them had bonded quicker and considerably closer than he imagined they could or had. Sarah would make the perfect wife for him and mother for Emma. Now all he had to do was convince her of the desire in his heart.

Surely she must know how much she meant to him. Though he hadn't told her he still loved her yet, he'd declared his feelings, certain that she understood his love for her. Only time would tell if they would become the happy family they all needed. So far his fixation at making her his bride had taken a positive direction. She hadn't thrown him out on his ear. Still, the practical side of him realized some things were out of his reach. Sarah wasn't entirely out of his reach though, and he'd do everything within his power to make sure of that one thing.

Sarah sat beside Emma in a chair where she swung her legs and called out to Ted. "Hurry, Daddy. Don't you want to decorate some cookies with me?"

"Save me some. I'm on my way." He stood over the table filled with cookies and whistled. "You ladies sure know how to paint cookies. Great job."

Emma beamed up at him and took a bite from her plate of goodies. "They're good too. Here, Daddy. Take a bite. I made this one 'specially for you."

Ted bit down on the colorful, icing laden cookie and groaned. "This cookie is the best one I've ever eaten. Bar none. You ladies are professional bakers." He grinned over Emma's head and winked at Sarah. "It's true. Absolutely delicious."

"Thank you, Daddy," she said, then giggled.

Ted kissed her on top of her head then hugged her. "Will you always be my best cookie maker?"

Emma gazed up at her daddy. "Only if Sarah can help me. Miss Karen said making cookies is too much trouble."

Ted's heart dropped while his stomach churned. Karen shouldn't be telling Emma that spending time with her was too much trouble. "That's it. How would you like to move in with grandpa and me when we get home?"

Twelve

Tuesday afternoon, Sarah stood in her shop facing Karen, her mouth hanging open.

"You know all of this change with Emma is your fault, don't you?" Karen propped her hands on her hips and all but snarled. "I've taken care of that little girl all her life. Now you come into the picture and, boom. Everything shifted in a matter of a few short weeks. How dare you interfere?"

Karen's questions and comments surprised her, which she'd not expected, nor was she prepared for. "Frankly, I'm unsure of exactly what you're talking about." Sarah almost felt sorry for her. Almost. "Karen, you're mistaken. You have twisted the entire relationship we have formed with each other."

"I've twisted nothing. It's you. You've broken this family and all it stands for. I think you should step aside and leave us be."

Annoyed wasn't the word to express her frame of mind. "I'm sorry you feel that way, Karen. Nothing is broken, as you put it, that can't be fixed with understanding. But that understanding must come from you, since you're the one with issues. Ted, Emma and I have a strong friendship, one I don't regret."

"It's more than friendship, and you know it. Ted has removed Emma from my home. The home where she spent the past four years living under my care. Tell me what that's all about."

For the life of her, Sarah couldn't wrap her thoughts around the fact that Karen stood here, in her shop, and vented her frustrations on her.

Sarah chose to give Karen the benefit of doubt. She spoke in a gentle manner, hoping to alleviate some of her fears. Still it was up to Ted to make decisions concerning his daughter. Not her, or Karen.

"Excuse me, but I believe you were aware that Ted was going to be moving Emma in with him and his dad. I hardly see where you think any of this is my doing. I'm sorry you feel it's my fault when clearly it isn't."

"The move wasn't supposed to happen until next month. They aren't even finished with renovations, for heaven's sake. She will have no room of her own until then. I hope you're satisfied."

Sarah controlled her irritation that Karen would even suggest she'd had an underhanded motivation and struggled to ignore Karen's outburst. "They'll make out just fine the way things are. Now... if that's all, I have work to do."

Karen aimed her nose in the air, turned to leave, then whirled back around. "There is one more thing." She pointed her finger at Sarah and exhaled loudly. "You once broke Ted's heart. I see that happening all over again."

Ted pushed open the storeroom's door. "Karen, I think I've heard about enough."

Sarah glanced up. "What are you doing here, Ted?"

"Lisa knows I'm here. I called and spoke with her. She must have forgotten to tell you. Remember the boxes you said I could store here? I used the key you gave me and came in the back door."

"Oh, I forgot. Sorry," she said.

One glance at Karen, told Sarah all she needed to know. She looked embarrassed to have been discovered in her confrontation with Sarah. Still, she knew Karen wasn't about to let it go.

"How much of our conversation did you hear, Ted?"

"Everything. I heard it all." He glanced at Karen. "I can't say I'm real happy about it either."

"My apologies. I'm sorry you heard our discussion. Our difference of opinion," Sarah commented.

"No need to apologize. Didn't sound as though you were at fault," he directed at Sarah, then faced Karen head-on. "Karen, first, I'm sorry you're upset. You must know you have my undying appreciation and love for the sacrifice you and Robert made to care for Emma. Dad would have cared for her, and was willing, but you and Robert were parent figures and provided her a loving, stable home. I'll never forget, and will always love you for Emma's nurturing. But, I'm home now. She's my daughter, and I'm more than ready to take on the responsibility. I hope we can rise above whatever problems the past few weeks have caused. None of our arrangements were meant to hurt you, or make you feel left out."

"Ted. Sarah has no right. This problem is between—" Karen attempted to inject.

"Sarah has every right. We're working on a relationship… and our efforts are ours… ours alone." Ted held up both hands and directed a stone-faced gaze at her. "Karen. None of what you accused Sarah of is her responsibility. The decision to move Emma today was entirely my idea. I simply believed the time was right for the move." He moved farther into the shop and stood beside Sarah. "I hope you can understand why I believe an apology is in order."

Sarah saw the shock on Karen's face as she glared at Ted.

A tear ran down Karen's cheek. "I'll do no such thing. Everything I've said is the truth. I hope you don't live to regret the choice you've made." With that, Karen twirled and bounded out the front door.

Thirteen

Sarah's heart went out to Karen. Obviously, she was more than a little distraught. As Karen knew it, her world had ended when Ted had made a necessary decision concerning his daughter, Emma. The child she'd reared, almost from birth, was removed from her home. She'd made mistakes, but who of us don't? Still, Sarah believed Karen could have been a little kinder.

"Ted, I can't do this. I'll bow out if nothing but trouble is going to come from our being together again. The last thing I want to do is divide your family."

"You can't… or won't? Please, Sarah. Reconsider. If I know your heart, even the least bit, allowing Karen to destroy what either of us want isn't acceptable. I know what I want. What do you want? That's what's important—not what Karen wants."

"Of course I will, reconsider that is. It isn't that I'm allowing Karen to dictate my decisions, but I care enough for you and Emma to not separate either of you from family. I want what's best for everyone, including Karen, believe it or not."

Sarah thought back to the first time she'd met Karen, which was at her shop. Karen had been polite, but had given her the once over when she'd picked up Ted's gifts and purchased a few of her own. She'd wondered what, if anything, Ted had discussed with Karen pertaining to her before their meeting. If they had, then whatever conversation they'd had could have spurned her interest, or dislike. Too, she'd been rather cool at Emma's birthday party Sarah had coordinated.

"And you? What's best for you, Sarah? Be honest with yourself. You didn't answer the most important question," Ted asked, his gaze intent, then he reached out and pushed a strand of dark auburn hair behind her ear.

"We're still working on that, aren't we?" she said, then smiled. "One level at a time. But I am pleased with the headway we've made."

"Yes, we are getting along better than I expected. This may sound crazy, but I think it's only a matter of time until we both agree we were meant to be together. Forever."

Sarah recalled Ted saying almost the same words many times when they were younger. She grinned. "You've always said we were meant for each other. We'll see how your family feels about our being together. Of course in the end, it's who we both choose."

"I'm sorry Karen was so nasty to you. Normally she's a good-natured person. I have no idea what's gotten into her these days." He ran a hand through his smoky black hair and shook his head. "At some point, I have to confront her concerning some of Emma's treatment. I'm definitely not looking forward to further provoking her. I could have brought it up today, but she was already upset enough. But Emma's upset and so am I. You too. I will get to the bottom of the disturbing actions she's turned to."

"Agreed. You did the right thing by holding back until she's had a chance to cool off a bit, because you'd not get any answers that would make much sense. She was Robert's wife and I know you're taking that into consideration. Still, it's Emma who's protection is relevant now."

"Of course. I feel the same."

Sarah glanced at Ted, a question in her eyes and a twist in her stomach. She drew in a lungful of air. "Don't take this the wrong way, Ted. I sure pray there isn't anything more damaging within their relationship. There could be, though I certainly hope not. For Emma's sake... and hers."

"I intend to speak with Emma. She's pretty honest. But she's young and impressionable, so I'll need to be careful of how I go about asking questions, and what I think she'll be open to answer. This is a delicate situation for Emma, for me and for Karen. I know she's a stickler when it comes to keeping her home in tip-top shape. Always has been. That could be part of the problem. Still…"

"That's right. When children are involved most mother's throw caution to the wind. Kitchen's, or wherever, can be cleaned and a messy project isn't the end of the world to deal with. You'll do the right thing. I have no doubt you'll get to the bottom of the matter."

"I won't hesitate one second to do what I must – if problems escalate or the answers aren't to my liking." He closed his eyes and shook his head. "I cannot wrap my head around what Emma said to us. Can you?"

"No. I can't. Even not being that close to either of them, it's hard to fathom. What Emma told us and how Karen reacted to her is an awful set of circumstances to put all of you through."

Ted drew Sarah close, wrapped an arm about her shoulder and hugged her. She didn't resist the gesture, instead placed a warm hand over his.

"Ahh, Sarah. Emma and Karen's involvement is foremost, of course. One I sure don't relish dealing with, but I will."

"I have every confidence that you'll do the right thing."

"No question about it." Ted stepped back, his hands resting on both her shoulders. "As for us, we simply need to do what feels right for the both of us. For the present, we'll settle any concerns that arise a day at a time. That sound okay to you?"

"Yes." Sarah ducked under his arms as the doorbell chimed, letting her know she had a customer. "Our future depends on day-by-day challenges if required," she whispered. "Now please get out of here. I have work to do."

Fourteen

$\mathcal{S}$arah hadn't shared with Ted she was going to St. Simons, only that she'd be unavailable for the weekend. What she had needed was time alone, time to sort her feelings. Any other stage in her life wouldn't be as complicated, but this was one of those instances where the merry-go-round refused to stop. She had a lot to consider and couldn't concentrate with anyone around. Too much had been thrown at her the past few weeks.

First was Ted. Ted her love, though she hadn't admitted it to him as yet. As difficult as the effort to forget him had been, and she'd struggled daily, she'd never forgotten how much he had, and still did, mean to her. How she'd missed him over the past five years, and those five years had crawled by as drawn-out as a lifetime.

Second was Emma. Even as surprised as she was to have found that Ted was a father, fatherhood looked good on him. He was loving and attentive with Emma, who looked so much like her dad. Those dark chocolate eyes of hers could melt the coldest of hearts. Her dimpled, sweetheart shaped face, surrounded by long, curly, light brown hair, was a lovely vision. Sarah had immediately fallen in love with Emma and she, in turn, had caused Sarah to understand the feeling was mutual.

At half past six in the morning, Sarah pulled onto the graveled drive in front of the family cottage. Had it not been for Lisa, Gavin, Jasper, Anna, and herself, the place would've fallen apart. Somehow they'd all managed to keep the cottage in fairly good shape, and for their help, she was grateful.

She paused in the car several minutes, overcome at the sight of weed tangled Forget-Me-Nots in full bloom under the old Oak tree, planted a few years ago, for the one who was far away from her. Ted.

Though she'd tried hard enough, she'd never forgotten him. Neither had the dreams stopped, nor her love for him. How could it? Even as young as they'd both been, they'd recognized true love for what it was. He was the love of her life, and always would be.

Five years ago, she'd accepted the reality that they'd forever be apart, but a chance meeting at the post office altered everything she had believed would never change. Now that Ted was back in her life, there were different issues, other than missing him, to reckon with. All things considered, a second chance at a new beginning was going to require effort on both their parts.

The glider, which had seen better days, beckoned to her — well that and the lavender Forget-Me-Nots surrounding it. She swiped away a light dusting of sand, then flipped back the opening from the cup of steaming coffee she'd stopped for a few miles back. Screeching gulls flew overhead while she gazed at the sunrise that splattered the sky with a brilliant combination of pink, purple, and golden hues and reflected off the water.

Sarah dropped down on the glider, wrapped both arms across her chest, and hugged herself while she gazed out over the sparkling water. The sun had already warmed a gentle breeze that played with strands of her hair. There was something hypnotic about being at the beach. The soft splashes of waves colliding with sand somehow comforted her, knowing she'd be digging her toes in the warmth of sand before long. Her entire mindset changed in an instant, for the better. But it didn't last long.

Where had the rumbling emotion come from this morning? She wiped away a single tear as she thought about her mom and dad. They were both gone now and she grieved for them terribly, but their memory lived on and they were in a better place. Still, there were sad moments she could barely get through. Sure, she had Lisa and Gavin, but they had lives of their own. Thank goodness, now that she and Lisa had a better understanding toward one another, their time spent working at the shop was a lot less stressful.

With forgotten lunch and dinner purchases still in her trunk, she pulled herself out of the glider and picked up the bags, then headed into the house to deal with memories of her mom.

As Sarah pulled open the squeaky screen door, memories hovered heavy on her mind. The lingering scent of lemon furniture polish hung in the air as Sarah walked through the door. Her mom had preferred lavender, and Sarah liked it too, but lemon reminded her of her grandmother.

Even though she'd called Anna at the last minute, there were results that she'd left her mark at the cottage. A basket of fresh fruit rested on the island, with a note alongside scribbled in Anna's handwriting. *'Welcome Home, I love you.'*

"You're a jewel, Anna," Sarah said, then smiled at Anna's thoughtfulness.

Though her mom had only been to the cottage a few times before her health had gone downhill, like Anna, she'd left evidence that confirmed love of the cottage. Photos of the family were in every room, especially ones of Sarah's dad, with his children at a number of stages.

Sarah's mom had dabbled in watercolors over the years and exhibited several paintings at home. But the one Sarah loved most was the one hanging above the fireplace at the cottage. She'd painted Lisa, Gavin and Sarah sitting in the glider under the old oak tree, the Forget-Me-Nots in full bloom bordering the bottom portion of the painting.

On their last visit together at the cottage, Sarah's mom brought up the flowers. 'The Forget-Me-Nots you planted will always play a part in your future,' she'd said.

Speechless, Sarah had no idea what her mom meant by that statement, except that she was sure it had something to do with Ted. She had indeed planted the flowers for him; rather, for his memory. Now, her mom's words came back to haunt her. Ted was back, and so were the memories.

She and Ted were back together, so to speak, but their future remained to be established. She knew what she wanted, but was it for the best?

Sarah walked the mile, give or take, to Jasper and Anna's. She'd rather have jogged on the beach, but Winston needed attention, and she looked forward to a ride before she left for home in the morning. Besides, Anna always expected a visit when she came to the cottage.

Anna wiped her hands on her apron, pushed back a strand of graying hair, then shouldered the screen door wide and grinned. "Come on in, sweet girl. I've been expecting you." Anna winked. "I have some Blueberry Muffins fresh out of the oven."

"My favorite." Sarah hugged Anna and kissed her on her soft, plump cheek. "I smelled them when I walked up on the porch. You're a doll. I'm starving. What can I help you with?"

"Nothing. You sit there and let me wait on you while I still can," she said, then laughed. "Don't worry, sweet girl. Nothing but a touch of Arthritis today, that's all. I'm not going anywhere anytime soon. I have too much left on this earth to do."

"We'll have many years together, Anna. I don't know what I'd do without you." Sarah eyed Anna's small kitchen while she bustled around this morning. She'd eaten many of a meal sitting at Anna's island. Not to mention the hugs and kisses she and Anna had shared. Sarah sent a sideways glance at her. "Are you taking your meds?"

Anna cocked an eyebrow. "Of course. Can't get by without them." She slid a mug of coffee on the other side of the island, cream and softened butter for the muffin. "Well sit down then and tell me what you've been up to the last two weeks. I've missed you."

"I've missed you too," Sarah said, and took a bite from the muffin. "Umm… delicious as always… and thanks for the fruit basket. You know me well."

"That I do, sweet girl."

Anna was her rock. She'd been there for her when her mom had passed away, so it was only natural she'd discuss issues concerning Ted and his family. "You know Ted and his little girl Emma. You cleaned his house two weeks ago, and Jasper takes care of his horse, Jack, and Emma's pony, Baby."

Anna slathered butter on a second muffin then glanced over her glasses. "I do. Ted has been around here for a while. He is a nice young man and a good dad to that pretty little girl of his."

"Emma is the sweetest. Smart too. Full of questions," she said, then laughed. She decided against heaping her problems on Anna this morning. "Is Jasper around this morning? I'd like to get him to cut our grass if he has time."

"He'll be back from George's in a few minutes." Anna refilled Sara's mug and flipped off the coffee pot. "George's riding mower wouldn't crank again this morning. He needs to replace that old thingamajig. He's had that mower for over thirty years and keeps having the poor thing repaired…and he has a fortune tied up in it. Jasper says it's been on its last leg for years, and he may not be able to repair it this go-around." She laughed again. "I'm rather glad, because Jasper spends more time repairing George's equipment than he does on ours. That's the reason your grass isn't mowed. He'll get to it today though."

"Ha. George will miss his old mower. He probably gave it a name."

"As a matter of fact he did. Old Betsy. Can you believe he named that mower Old Betsy?" Anna giggled as she set their dishes in the sink, then went to the window and pulled back the edge of a curtain. "I think I hear Jasper now. Give him time for coffee before he's off and running again."

"Of course. George most likely ran him through the mill to save Old Betsy. Oh, tell Jasper no hurry on the grass, after I leave will be fine. I don't want it to get too snaky though."

The thought struck Sarah that she and Ted could possibly be hanging onto their old love and life the same way George held to Old Betsy. Hoping against hope the past few years were not beyond repair.

Did they actually have the courage to develop a love strong enough to build a lasting future?

Sarah wanted a love and marriage that would last a lifetime, as her mom and dad had.

Fifteen

ell good morning, Sarah. Did you have a good time? Get some rest while you were gone?"

"Absolutely. I really needed the time alone."

"Time away on your own is the best way to clear your head, but I'm glad you're home. I've missed you." Ted cleared his throat. "Much more than I expected... though I don't know why."

Sarah laughed at the low chuckle in his voice. "Okay, you missed me — why wouldn't you? No surprise there. You should've known that would happen."

"Ha. Pretty sure of yourself, aren't you?"

"Well... yes. Yes I am." She imagined the look on his face and all but laughed out loud. "Absence makes the heart grow stronger. Isn't that the old saying?"

"It is. I must say it worked. Did you leave just to see how I'd react or be affected by your not being here to lean on?"

"Come on. I hardly think you need someone to lean on, Ted. The beach revives me. The beach and Anna. I'm here for you though. You know that." Ted was one of the strongest individuals she'd come across in a long time. But then, even as a teenager, he'd always been the strong type, especially when it came to her.

"I do. And you must know I'm here for you, too. Any time, any place, and for any reason. Count on it."

Ted's familiar words floated over the phone line. "Thank you, Ted. You haven't changed a bit, and you're still a big-hearted man. It's comforting to know I have you back in my life to count on."

Sarah reflected back to the younger man who had promised to take care of her. Always. She'd ended that devotion with a few curt words five years ago. But now the years and hurtful words she'd spoken had somehow slipped away in one afternoon. She was undecided how they'd seemed to pick up where they'd left off five years ago, and how it had happened so quickly, but for that she was surprised and thankful. She knew it had been Ted's big heart and his love for her that had been the force to bring them back together. She doubted, if getting back together had been left to her, they'd ever have made it. But she never doubted that God's hand was foremost in their reunion.

Ted had forgiven her and the terrible thing she'd done to him. And he had not brought it up until she had.

Reservations at their outcome were still there, but she lived each day with a positive outlook. Well mostly. Karen posed a set of concerns, but Ted didn't seem too wary of her. Sarah knew how spiteful some women could get when backed into a corner, and in her mind, Karen would be one of those women. Still, Sarah thought she deserved benefit of doubt and hoped against hope that Emma had taken what Karen had said the wrong way. Then again, Emma's speculation may have been right on, and both she and Ted had to believe in her.

She'd been in such deep thought, she jumped when Ted's voice echoed over the line.

"Say. Emma has a ballet lesson tomorrow at five. Want to go with us? We can have dinner afterwards if you'd like."

"Sounds good to me. Why don't you invite your dad to meet us for dinner? I'd like to get to know him better." She'd answered before she thought to check her calendar or with Lisa. She thumbed through her calendar just in case her memory had failed today. "Wait. I'll call you back. I have a meeting scheduled with one of my suppliers' tomorrow night. I'll see if Lisa is available to attend in my place."

"I hope so. Emma has been asking for you. Nonstop. What do you say to a surprise visit? If you can't make it tomorrow, let's make it real soon, otherwise Emma will make being with you again a priority, as if it isn't already. You know she doesn't forget a thing and brings up whatever is on her mind over and over. Say you'll save me," he said, then laughed.

Sarah giggled. "Like you need saving. I certainly know how her mind works by now. I'll do my best." She adored Ted's little girl. "Give her a hug and kiss for me and tell her I'll see her before long."

"That I will."

"While I have you on the line, have you any news from Karen?"

"No. She's been quiet. Not a peep out of her. Dad said he passed by the house saw her working in the flower garden. He blew the horn and she waved at him. So… she may or may not be upset with him."

A shudder ran up her spine. She hoped Karen wouldn't take revenge on Emma. Surely she wouldn't. Her mind was simply working overtime. "Quiet can be good, but it could also be unpleasant considering the mood she was in last week," Sarah replied.

"I've given that some thought. It isn't like Karen not to keep in touch, then of course she is upset with me."

Sarah's thoughts wandered back to that day in the shop, when Karen had lowered the boom on her. "Probably more so with me, since she believes I'm to blame for your moving Emma out of her home."

"Moving Emma was my decision based on the information she gave us," Ted commented. "Emma and her safety must come first. I had no other choice."

"Yes. But Karen doesn't know the reason."

"She will after I confront her… and I will."

Sixteen

Karen signed the last of the papers, leaned back and felt pretty good about the deal. "So the building is all mine now. Legally mine right?"

The real estate agent jogged the contract together, then stacked it on his desk. "It's a done deal."

"I appreciate you handling the sale so promptly," Karen replied.

"You were right on time. Mr. Kane has wanted to sell it for a while now, but hadn't actively sought a buyer because of his children. They'd drug their feet making up their minds whether they wanted him to keep it or not. Both his son and daughter live out of state and didn't want the headache of entrusting someone else with the property should anything happen to their dad. When I sent Mr. Kane your offer, he didn't hesitate. He jumped at the deal."

"The children will have no recourse, is that correct?"

"Of course not. Mr. Kane owned the property lock-stock-and-barrel," he said, then leaned back and popped his suspenders. "It's a done deal."

"Miss Sarah Hall will be out on her ear within the month," Karen commented and laughed quietly to herself.

"Why would you want to evict a long-time tenant? Sarah's mom had the shop for over twenty-five years. Her daughters have been there on their own for three years. I know for a fact Mr. Kane has had no issues with them."

"It's a personal matter," she said. "One I don't wish to discuss."

"You'll have problems evicting them. There is a clause, in the contract, that gives the tenants, Sarah and Lisa, rights. It also states, should Mr. Kane ever sell the property, the clause remains in effect for as long as they continue to be the lessee."

"I don't see how that can be legal." Karen sat upright and fisted her hands. "But I own the building now. I can do whatever I want with the tenants."

"I'm afraid not in this instance. Sarah and Lisa have the rights to give you three a month notice, if and when, they plan to vacate the property. Otherwise their month-to-month lease is binding."

The real estate agent pulled back on the contract and shuffled through the pages.

"Why didn't we discuss such an important issue before I signed?"

"We did. Here is the proof," he said, then presented the clause page for her evaluation.

Karen jerked the contract from him and read over the clause. "I still don't remember reading this." Karen drew her lips into a tight straight line and narrowed her eyes. "Are you sure we went over it? And... if we didn't, does that void the contract?"

The agent threw out his chest and straightened his shoulders. "Of course we went over those details. I wouldn't omit something so significant to the sale. So, no. The contract isn't void."

Karen had rushed through the reading the day before she'd signed. She did remember that. Too much on her mind, she'd completely forgotten the agent had specifically made a point to draw attention to that particular clause to her. She'd shoved it aside thinking somehow she could maneuver around its legality, but now she was stuck with the property and couldn't do a thing to oust Sarah from her lucrative business.

Unless...

As much as Karen wanted to tear up the contract, she realized she no longer had a leg to stand on. The plan forming in her head was to make Sarah and Lisa's remaining time at the shop so miserable, they'd request to be relieved of their contract on their own.

"Okay. Okay. It took me a while, but I admit I do remember

going over that section now. I can't believe it totally slipped my mind." The detail had slipped her mind momentarily, but the legal ramifications hadn't necessarily registered at the time. "It goes without saying. I'll have to live with the clause in the contract."

The agent shook his head and breathed a sigh of relief. In one swift movement, he placed the contract in a yellow envelope, then handed it to her. "I'll send a letter of change in ownership to the tenants right away. Thank you, Mrs. West. Please don't hesitate to call if I can be of further service to you."

Karen glanced at the agent's fake Southern smile and wondered how he still worked in real estate. "Thank you, but I think we're done here."

Seventeen

Lisa shoved her purse inside the cabinet and locked it back. "Excuse me?"

"You heard me right." Sarah held the letter from the real estate agent toward Lisa. "It isn't as though we hadn't known at some point Mr. Kane would sell the property. He's getting up in age, and probably wanted to rid himself of the responsibility. I assumed his children would take over, but that didn't happen. But sell to Karen West? How did she ever choose to become a landlord, much less the very building we've occupied for over thirty years?"

From the look on Lisa's face, her mind was trying to digest the other letter Sarah had plunked down on the counter. "I smell a rat," Lisa blurted.

The other letter was from Karen. She'd had the gall to ask them to consider vacating the premises so she may begin renovations, including new electrical wiring. Next week.

"I don't get it either. If she thinks we're going to give up and cower to her demands, she may as well get ready for the battle of her life." Sarah slammed the cash drawer shut. "I will not let her destroy what our mom built from nothing except long hard hours away from her family."

"Listen, Sarah," Lisa said. "There's nothing wrong with this building. Mr. Kane kept it in tip-top shape. Always. I say we bring in an inspector to check out the electrical. If she replaced the wiring, that would mean our entire displays on the walls would need to come down. That's major, and we'd be out of business for weeks."

"All this is my fault. If I hadn't reconnected with Ted, Karen wouldn't be in our lives. Now that she is, I can see the situation will become worse by the day."

Lisa laid a hand on Sarah's arm. "You mustn't blame yourself. The way I see it is… this is nothing but Karen getting revenge for Ted removing Emma from her house."

"Yes and another one of the reasons is because I spent a lot of time with Emma, and she was afraid she was losing her. She lost Emma of her own deeds, but doesn't recognize that, or simply won't admit it. I'm sorry she's still grieving Robert's death, and I'm sure grief plays a huge part of her decision. She's grasping at straws."

"I agree. She's probably lonely and now running scared of losing Emma entirely. She isn't thinking clearly. What she's doing now is pushing Ted and Emma farther away." Lisa folded the letters, inserted them back inside their envelopes, then clicked on the coffee pot. "We need hot, strong coffee."

Sarah sighed and began to unload a box of china dolls. "We can't afford it, but we'll need to hire a lawyer if we want to beat her at her own game."

"Oh, no. That's not happening," Ted said. "She'll need to prove the renovations are necessary safety modifications. She can't simply come in on a whim and set your daily business operations back. Even on a remote chance that should happen, I believe she'd be responsible for your day-to-day losses. I seriously doubt she's thought of that consequence. If I were you, a sales spreadsheet for the past year would be in order. Just in case."

"We have that information up to date. All I'd need to do is print it out, but do you really think sales information is going to be necessary? Do you think she'd go that far?"

"As I said, be prepared. That's all." Dark auburn hair slid through Ted's fingers as he pushed back a tendril from her forehead and caught her gaze.

Sarah stared into his chocolate eyes, unable to make sense of why her heart lurched at the touch, when everything else was going against her. She tore her stare away and changed the subject. "By the way, Lisa will fill in for me at the meeting tonight. Is the ballet lesson still on?"

Ted smiled and gave her a knowing look. "It is. I'll pick you up around four if that's okay."

Right now, anything is okay. "Text me when you get within a block, that way you won't need to park. That time of day can be awful maneuvering around traffic."

Ted had rolled down the passenger window, which allowed Sarah to hear Emma's squeal before she even got to the car.

Emma barely waited until Sarah sat down before she unbuckled her seat belt and threw herself over the seat to hug Sarah. "Oh, Miss Sarah. I didn't know you were going with us. Are you going to dance, too?"

Sarah laughed. "No, sweetie. This is your dance class. It isn't for adults. I'm excited to see how much you've progressed since I saw you last. I think dad's ready to go, do you need any help with your seat belt buckle?"

"No, ma'am. I'm a big girl. Daddy taught me how."

"Yes you are." Sarah turned and grinned at Ted. "Good girl." She reached back, clasped Emma's hand, then buckled her own seat belt.

"Daddy says I'm doing very well. He says I'm his special little ballerina." Emma frowned. "Do you think so, too?"

Sarah smiled, gave Ted a sideways glance and a wink. "Of course I do. I thought you were the best dancer on the floor when I watched you twirl around a few weeks ago."

"Thank you." Emma grinned, then pooched her lips.

"Remember you don't need to call me Miss Sarah. Just Sarah is fine. Okay?"

"Okay," Emma said. "Sarah, when can we bake cookies again?"

Sarah glanced at Ted for confirmation that it was okay, but he'd evidently misunderstood.

Ted looked in the rearview mirror at Emma. "Hon, Sarah may be busy this weekend. She has the shop to take care of, remember?"

"But Daddy!" Emma's voice quivered. "It's been forever since we colored cookies."

"Ted, it's fine. I'll get Lisa to fill in for me this weekend. She and Gavin were away last weekend also. Or maybe our weekend lady may want the extra work. I'll work it out."

"If you're sure. Emma will be happy and I'll get to spend more time with you."

He patted her arm and took his eyes off the road for one second. When he did, an electric blue convertible missed hitting them by a hair causing him to slam on the brakes. The car slowed down enough for Ted to pass it.

Sarah gulped and turned to make sure Emma was okay. "Are you okay, sweetie?"

"Yes. That scared me."

"I know it did, sweetie. It's over now though. We're all okay."

Sarah lowered her voice so Emma wouldn't hear her. "Ted, do you know who that was?"

"I'm afraid I do. Mayor Conley and his blonde friend. I've heard he's a big drinker. If so, he doesn't need to be behind the wheel."

"You're right. He could cause a horrible accident or worse, kill someone. Something needs to be done. Monday morning I'm going to see him and let him know he almost hit a car with a child inside. That's some dangerous driving."

Eighteen

Emma's practice went well, and she fell asleep almost as soon as they got back inside the car, her blankie stuck inside her mouth.

"She's too tired to try to go out to dinner, Ted. Why don't we pick up Chinese, which will make her happy, and go to your place or mine?"

Ted put an arm around her shoulders and nodded. "It might be best to go to my place. That way I can get her ready for bed when she finishes dinner."

"Your place is fine. She needs to rest before we drive back to St. Simons tomorrow anyway. I'll call in a take-out order from the restaurant around the corner from you. Tell me what you and she would like."

Sarah had barely finished their order when Ted pulled into the restaurant's parking lot. "I'm leaving the car running so it won't get too hot. Keep the doors locked."

"Yes, sir! Bossy aren't you?" Sarah said, then saluted Ted.

"Not at all. Keeping my two girls safe," Ted replied, then closed the car door.

My two girls, he'd said. How wonderful those three words sounded. I could get used to hearing that.

Twenty minutes went by, then thirty. Sarah wondered what in the world was taking so long for a pick-up order. She couldn't leave Emma out there alone and certainly didn't want to wake her. Ted had left his phone on the console, so she wasn't able to call him.

In a few minutes, Karen walked out of the restaurant right

before Ted came out. She glanced over at Sarah and gave her a strange look.

When Sarah saw Ted as he walked briskly to the car, she hit the door's unlock button. Emma woke as he handed Sarah the bag of food.

"I saw Karen as she left the restaurant. She gave me a peculiar look before getting into her car. What's that all about? Did the two of you speak?"

"You will not believe. We'll talk later," he whispered, then put the car in drive and pulled out into traffic. "My apologies at leaving you alone for such a long time. Karen was ready to talk and I couldn't pass up the chance to meet with her face to face, even if it was in the restaurant."

"It's okay. I did get concerned though."

Emma yawned, then stretched still holding onto her blankie. "I'm hungry, Daddy. Where are we going?"

"Instead of going out, we decided to pick up some Chinese. How does that sound to you?"

"Yay." She clapped her hands. "Can I watch a movie on the way home?"

Ted glanced at Emma. "Yes, but you won't be able to finish it. We're about fifteen minutes from the house. Okay?"

"Yes, Daddy."

They finished dinner and Sarah was about to put Emma down for the night. She could barely wait to hear the discussion Ted and Karen had. It must have been something, the way Ted reacted.

"Sarah," Emma's tearful voice called out. "You forgot my blankie. I want my blankie, Sarah. Sarah!"

"I'm coming, sweetie. Don't get upset." *That does it. I'm definitely talking to Emma tomorrow about that blankie. I hope I can say the right things and get her to at least think about giving it up.*

Ted was clearing off the table when Sarah called out to him from Emma's room. "Ted, do you want to read Emma a story or is it okay if I do?"

"I want you to read to me, Sarah."

"Go ahead, Sarah. I don't mind. Make my girl happy," he

said, then chuckled.

Sarah couldn't believe she wanted her to read instead of her dad. That had to say something wonderful about their relationship.

"Do you have a special book you want to hear tonight? Any book you want me to read, just name it."

"Yes. It's over there." She pointed to her nightstand.

"What is the book's title?" she asked, and drew attention to the nightstand. "You have a stack of books there."

"Raz, the Bear Who Had No Nose," she said. *"I love Raz."*

"Got it." Sarah tried to remember the book, but no way had she ever heard of it. Neither had she heard of the author. The book must be interesting, because the pages were well worn.

Sarah pulled a blanket up around Emma, then settled down beside her and began to read.

"Raz, was a very unhappy little bear. Raz was different. You see, Raz had no nose. And a bears with no nose knows no nose."

Emma giggled. "Everyone has a nose."

Sarah smiled back at her. "Well, sweetie. Evidently Raz doesn't. Not right now anyway."

"He doesn't. Just wait, you'll find out. And you'll like it, Sarah," Emma said. Halfway through the book, Emma nodded off into a gentle sleep.

She bent down and kissed Emma on the forehead, adjusted her blanket, then put the book back on the nightstand. When she turned to leave the room, Ted was there, leaned against the doorway.

"You kind of like my little girl, don't you?" he whispered.

Sarah recognized the pride on his face and in his voice as she edged by him while he held open the door. "My goodness, Ted. Who wouldn't fall in love with her? She's such a blessing."

"Yes. I think so, too. I don't have any idea what I'd do without her." He hugged her tight and bent to kiss her, but thought better of the gesture. "I don't know what I'd do without you now that we've found each other again."

"I'm beginning to feel the same, Ted. We have a lot to be thankful for." She hugged him back and laid her head on his chest. "For our lost years, I have lived with a lot of regret... and it hasn't been easy, but there isn't anything I can do about the past. What's done is done." When she raised her head, there were tears forming. "Thank you for forgiving me."

"Aww, Sarah. We're making such an enjoyable progress. Let the past remain in the past. I've told you many times, I'd never forget you, and I haven't."

"I hadn't forgotten you either, but learned to live with my mistake." Yes, she'd lived with a heavy heart so long, she'd forgotten how good it was to be carefree. Ted had wanted to kiss her, and she'd wanted him to, but they had plenty of time for love to play out. Time to discover the other again. They'd both grown, but hadn't yet outgrown their young love. She was as sure of that one thing, as sure as she knew her own name.

Ted closed his eyes and beamed. "Aside from all that, I wouldn't have Emma if we had stayed together."

"That's true. Emma is more than a consideration. Our separation was worth the pain and heartache we endured. It's all in God's plan."

"Yes and she's worth it all," Ted agreed.

One desire had been on Sarah's heart for a while, especially since she and Ted had reconnected. She longed to have a baby. A little baby brother for Emma. What was she thinking? Ted had not mentioned marriage, and neither of them had inclinations thus far that she was aware of, except the dreams inside her head, but it was too soon. She should keep a low profile on the baby issue... *if* that were possible. Now that she'd admitted a baby was the one hope she wouldn't be able to shake any time soon, she had found a place in the back of her mind to bury it for the time being. Until it became safe to nudge it out again.

Sarah shook her head and brought her thoughts back to normal. "You were going to share what you and Karen discussed. Is this a good time?"

Ted slid a steaming mug of tea in front of her, then grabbed his, threw the tea bag in the trash can, and sat down across the island from her. "Yes, sweetheart. Now is a good time."

Oh... He called me sweetheart. I'm not even sure he realized what he said. He's comfortable easing into that old familiarity we once shared. She dunked the tea bag, removed it, stirred sugar, then squeezed lemon in her cup, tolerant while she waited for him to launch into Karen's explanations.

"First things first. When I shared with Karen all of the things Emma told us she'd said to her, she actually seemed shocked that Emma had been distressed, because she hadn't noticed a change in her behavior. She didn't deny saying any of them, that she believed she'd said everything with and out of love for Emma."

"I'm happy to hear she took what you said to heart. This is a family issue that needs to end, preferably on a positive note."

"Karen's not a bad person, never has been. That's why I was so troubled when she spoke to Emma with such disrespect, then acted and spoke to you the way she did."

"As long as she didn't abuse her, the police can be kept out of the situation," Sarah commented.

"I considered calling the police, though. What she said to Emma borders on mental abuse, but hoped we could settle the issue without taking extreme measures." Ted crossed his arms and reflected for a moment. "Karen has had an awful time with Robert's death. Her grief almost wiped her out. If she hadn't had Emma to care for, I don't know what would've happened to her. We never considered in a million years that Karen would abuse her. She was always a happy and outgoing child."

"Many children hide their abuse," Sarah reminded him.

"Of course they do, but if you look close enough, there's always something that stands out. Emma's doctors haven't brought any such information to our attention either. Even Karen agreed and insisted we have Emma periodically speak with a child psychologist because of her mom leaving her. By the way, I've already spoken to her psychologist and he gave me a clean bill of health on Emma's development. He repeated that he'd not seen any indication of abuse, but to bring her back in for a number of visits and he would concentrate on that aspect of her treatment."

"Excellent. That's wonderful news," Sarah commented.

Ted ran a hand through his smoky-black hair and lowered his chin. "When Robert passed away, I thought Karen would die with him. I'd never seen such a love between two people other than my mom and dad.

"She's apologized profusely to me and asked to meet with you and Emma so she may apologize in person. She also admitted purchasing the building you're in, was a terrible mistake. She wants to make amends, somehow."

"An apology is absolutely in order. I'm willing to listen anytime she wants to meet. I'm happy to hear we may not have to close for business. Speaking of Emma, I'm going to check on her." She set her mug in the sink and wondered if Karen was being truthful. Still, she'd give her the benefit of doubt. "I'll be right back."

When Sarah returned, he asked, "So, is she still asleep?"

"Like a baby. Kicked the covers off though," she said, and grinned. "You know she's beautiful and looks a lot like you."

Ted threw back his head and laughed. "So...do you think I'm beautiful, too?"

"No, silly." She slanted her eyes at him. "But you are handsome, as always."

"My mom always said I was handsome, but you know, I think she was prejudiced."

"Certainly she was. I wish I'd gotten to know your mom better. She was a lovely woman. If I remember correctly, an awesome cook, too."

"Yes she was. To all you stated." Ted smiled, and hugged her tight. "Mom would be delighted to know we're back together. She liked you... a lot, said you were good for me. Dad's also thrilled. He always said one day we'd get back together."

"Are we? Are we back together, Ted?" she asked, hope in her heart.

Ted held her by the shoulders and gazed into her eyes. "Sweetheart. What do I need to do to prove we are meant for each other?"

Nineteen

Are you sure we can bake cookies?" Emma asked, while she made her baby dolls comfortable in the portable doll bed her dad had made for her.

"We have everything in the kitchen or in the grocery bag your dad is bringing in we bought at The Piggly Wiggly. You mustn't concern yourself, sweetheart. I didn't forget you and the cookies." Sarah unzipped Emma's overnight bag, placed it on a blanket chest, then stared down at the yellow blankie. "Change your clothes so they won't get color on them from the icing. Okay?"

"Okay. Can we take my Papa home some cookies?"

"Wonderful idea. Won't he be surprised?"

"Yes, he will. He loves my cookies." Emma pulled out a movie and eyed it for a minute. "Is it okay if I watch a movie before we make cookies?"

"Of course. That'll give me time to get dinner started." Sarah settled her down with a movie and her blankie. "I'll check on you in a little while. Enjoy the movie."

"It's my favorite. I've seen it a lot," she said, giggled, then patted her baby dolls on the back.

Ted put a can of oil back into the shed, joined Sarah on the swing, then looked around at the yard. "Charming place you have here. I've seen it from a distance, but have never driven this far down your street."

"Thanks. I'm happy to have you and Emma visit. The place

was getting a little too lonely. I'm actually not too far from your cottage. Jasper and Anna are around a mile from here if I cut through the other yards and streets." She pulled the icy pitcher closer and poured him a glass of iced tea.

"Thanks. There's nothing like a cool drink on a sultry day. I got the screen door as well as the swing oiled." He gave the swing a push and listened. "Nice and quiet now. I'll replace the loose board on the porch the next time we come up. Wish I had the lumber and paint today. Anything else you'd like done while I'm here? Or is there something else we need to buy for a repair?"

"Since you asked, you might replace the lock on the shed. It seems to wobble quite a bit, and the wind blows the door ajar once in a while. I wouldn't want an animal to get inside."

He laughed and laid his arm across her shoulders, then set the swing in motion. "Good as done. I noticed the door didn't want to close all the way, so I leaned a concrete block to keep it snug. I also noticed a bag of grass seed. I'll spread it for you in the fall, if you'd like."

"Sure, that would be great." She turned to face him and grinned. "Not that I offered my cottage this weekend for your handiwork, but you're a good man to have around."

"So you're using me," he said, with a pretend shocked look on his face, then laughed. "But you have no idea how happy I am to hear you say that."

She brought the glass to her lips, took a sip and swallowed back the tea. "I mean every word. I love having you and Emma near. It feels like home again."

Ted leaned forward and twisted around to face her. "Do you remember yesterday when I said I'd never seen such a love between two people other than my mom and dad?"

"Of course I remember. Those were some endearing words for your mom and dad."

He glanced at Sarah and winked. "Except the love I have for you."

"Oh, wow, Ted. You're moving a bit fast for me." *But is he? Isn't this what I wanted... a commitment?*

"The truth is never spoken too soon. It's a simple fact, Sarah.

I love you. I always have, I always will. Believe me when I say I tried to stop loving you, but my effort was a battle I couldn't win. I've dated some, but not much. It wasn't fair to the ladies I dated, because I always compared them to you. None of them stood the test. I couldn't get you out of my mind or my heart. You were always there…there in the shadows…waiting. It was then I knew we'd be together again. I bided my time."

"Ted. I thought we decided we weren't going to rush into a relationship." *Ted committed, why can't I? What's wrong with me?*

"Sorry. I don't mean to push you. It's been almost three months now. I want you to know exactly how I feel. Leave nothing to your imagination. Nothing to question. Ever."

"Give me time to digest all you've said. And it's a lot, believe me. I need time."

What time she had would mainly be spent reflecting on why she couldn't, or wouldn't, admit she loved him too. She did love Ted, and she'd never forgotten him either. Why wouldn't she tell him when he had been so open with his feelings? It certainly wasn't because he had a child. She loved Emma with all her heart… and Emma loved her. Without a doubt.

Ted slid back in the swing and gazed at her. "Take all the time you need, Sarah."

She leaned over and kissed him on the cheek and placed a hand on his chest. "Thank you, Ted. Thank you for understanding."

He placed his hand over hers, and brought it to his lips, then kissed her palm. "I understand you more than you probably know. I never forgot you or anything about you."

They both looked up as the crunch of tires turned onto the driveway.

Sarah waved when she recognized Anna exiting the car. "Hi, Anna, Jasper. To what do we owe this unexpected, but lovely visit?"

Anna came over and hugged both Sarah and Ted. "We decided to take a walk on the beach and wondered if the two of you and Emma would like to join us."

"A walk sounds wonderful." She glanced at Ted. "Are you up to a walk?"

"Absolutely. I'd like to stretch my legs."

"I'll run in the house and get Emma," Sarah commented.

When she opened the screen door, she heard the sounds of the movie that still played. "Emma, you can finish the movie later, okay? We're going for a walk. Grab your hat and sandals."

Emma raced to get her sandals and back to Sarah. "I'm ready." She turned back toward the bedroom. "Wait, I want my blankie."

Now is as good a time as ever to persuade her to leave the blankie. "Looks like blankie is still sleeping, sweetie. What do you say we let it sleep and not get it wet at the beach?"

Emma pooched out her lips. "I won't get it wet."

"The waves come quickly, sweetie. Remember? We won't be gone that long. Hey, we might be able to find some seashells. Won't that be fun?"

"Really?" she asked, as her eyes lit up.

"Yes. I've seen some pretty good sized ones here."

Emma studied for a minute. "Okay. Maybe blankie needs a nap." She reached over grabbed her blankie and hugged it against her chest. "I'll be back soon," she whispered.

Oh. This child has it bad for that blankie. Her dad said it was her friend, now she really, really believed those words. Getting her to give up blankie was going to be an enormous challenge. Sarah rubbed Emma down with sun block and out the door they went to join the group under the old oak tree.

"Anna, I'd love for you and Jasper to stay for dinner, if you'd like. I have a huge pot of Clam Chowder simmering on the stove."

"Oh. Chowder sounds delicious. Are you sure?" Anna asked, then grinned. "Jasper would love someone else's cooking for a change."

"Certainly. It's more than enough. I'm forever making too much food."

Twenty

"Emma," Ted called over his shoulder. "Come up and say hello to Jasper. He sure is finding some beautiful seashells."

When Emma looked up at Sarah, she nodded. "Coming Daddy," she yelled. With pail in hand and a skip in her step, she ran up to her dad and slipped her tiny fingers around his long slender, yet masculine ones.

"Just look at those beautiful curls bouncing in the sunlight," Anna said. "I hope Ted realizes how blessed he is."

"Yes, he does. She is the light of his life. They're crazy about one another." Anna's voice held such sincere yearning, that Sarah's heart embraced the pain of the sweet woman beside her. Anna and Jasper hadn't had children. She'd never mentioned why, and Sarah had respected her enough not to meddle. In the time she'd known Anna and Jasper, she'd convinced herself they would've made excellent parents.

Sarah and Anna walked along the water's edge, side by side in silence, and observed the three of them ahead as the men enjoyed gathering, or pointing out shells for Emma's pail.

Anna pulled her hat further down her forehead to shade the sun, then turned her head toward Sarah. "I don't mean to be nosey... but do you see children in your future?" she asked.

"Surprising you should ask me about children today. Actually, children and family have been in my thoughts a lot lately." Sarah pulled her gaze from Anna's and dug her toes into the warm sand, while the water splashed over her feet. "We all want children, don't we?"

"Yes," she said, then sighed. "It's heartbreaking we can't all be that blessed."

Sarah felt the blood drain down her face. When would she learn to consider others before she spoke? "Oh, Anna, please forgive me. I wasn't thinking." More than anything, she wished she could take back the words she'd uttered... but that wasn't happening.

"Never you mind, Sarah. I've come to grips with not having children. Though I do have moments of regret that we couldn't fill the house with the pitter-patter of little feet." She sighed, then pointed to Jasper. "He's always wanted a son... and a daughter. You can see he is completely comfortable with Emma, as she is with him. He calls her our little beach princess."

Sarah laughed. "She's definitely a little princess, in every way. Now if I can get her to give up the blankie."

"You will. It takes time for the little ones to give up their steady security. Time and patience is all you need." Anna laughed. "Lots of love on the trying days, too, and... there will be difficult times."

"Well, we have plenty of time to work on giving up old habits. I hope. Ted may not appreciate my interfering with the process. He wasn't real open when I brought up my idea that would help her give up the blankie. We'll see how things go from here on out. If there is a *from here on out*."

Wisps of gray played around Anna's sun-weathered face from a wind gust that tipped her hat to the side. "You need to know your mom and I had several conversations that if you and Ted could get back together, she'd be a happy mom."

"Really?" Sarah asked. "I had no idea she thought of Ted and me together again."

"Yes. She said many times that you were too hard on yourself. That you would die an old maid if you didn't get your head on straight. She said you were afraid to get your heart broken and that concerned her. She was saddened when she thought of you never having a life with the one you loved. All she ever wanted for her girls was for them to be happy."

Sarah recalled her mom had said the Forget-Me-Nots under her old tree would always play a part in her life. She wiped a tear from her cheek and smiled. "How is it that a mom can understand their children so well?"

Anna stopped Sarah and turned her around. "Your mom knew you well. She was aware that Ted was the love of your life, and would always be the one for you. Her hope was, one day you'd realize he was the person you shouldn't let go."

"I miss mom. I miss her so much," Sarah said.

Anna gathered Sarah in her arms and hugged her tight. "I know you do, honey. I know you do. If it's any consolation, I'm here for you. Anytime. Your mom is always with you. Inside your heart. Never forget that."

"I do realize that and I love you, Anna. You've been here when I had no one else to lean on. Thank you for being here."

"No need to thank me. I love you," Anna replied." Now, what do you say we herd those three up and head back to the cottage?"

Anna and Sarah picked up their speed and caught up with the three seashell finders. "Maybe we should head back. I believe we've walked almost two miles already."

"No kidding? I didn't realize we'd walked that far." Ted leaned back and whispered in Sarah's ear. "Surprise. Emma hasn't complained once that she's too tired."

Sarah laughed. "Don't ask her if she's tired, because then she will become exhausted and you'll have to carry her the rest of the way."

Sarah ran up behind Emma, picked her up, and swung her around and around. "Who's ready for some Clam Chowder?"

Emma squealed. "Me. Me. I'm starving."

"Let's go home then," Sarah answered. "You can help set the table. Have you ever helped?"

"No. Are we still going to bake cookies?" Emma asked.

"Yes. Maybe Anna would like to stay and help us."

Anna looked to Jasper for an answer. "There are horses to tend. We'll do whatever you think is necessary."

"Fine by me," Jasper said. "Whatever you'd like to do, hon. The horses can wait a few extra hours today."

After dinner, the guys rinsed and loaded the dishwasher. "You two are such gentlemen. Thanks," Sarah said.

"Happy to help. I've never had a more delicious bowl of Clam Chowder," Jasper commented and rubbed his tummy. "Thanks for the invite. I know Anna was happy not to cook today."

"What do you say I go with you to check on the horses, Jasper? That is if you want. It will give us something to do while the ladies spend some time together," Ted said.

"Sounds like a plan," Jasper said and pointed to his twenty-year-old faded, blue truck. "Come on and hop in. I'll drive us over."

Twenty-One

*I*t was one of those unexpected drops in temperature and rain that blew in over the area right before Jasper and Ted made it back to the cottage. A rare evening that left the beach cooled down enough for a fire in the fireplace.

Sarah heard the guys drive up then stamp their feet on the porch, so they wouldn't bring wet sand into the house.

"Something smells good in here," Ted called out. "Is it a cake? A cobbler? What?"

"Daddy." Emma placed her hands on her hips and pouted. "Did you forget we were going to make cookies?"

Ted touched his forehead with the palm of his hand and pretended he'd forgotten. "How could I forget? That's all you've talked about ever since we arrived, little one." He picked her up and hugged her, then kissed the top of her head. "Does that mean Jasper and I can't have any of your delicious treat? Did you ladies eat all of them?"

"No, Daddy. We still have your cookies on a plate." She pointed to the island. "Yours and Mr. Jasper. See?"

Ted put a hand over his heart and smiled at Emma. "Thank you, sweetheart, for remembering us." He stood her back on the kitchen floor and sniffed the air. "Do I smell coffee?"

"You do," Sarah said. "Both of you grab a mug, and then, if you don't mind, get a fire started. Cookies, roasted marshmallows, and melted chocolate to dip them in for everyone."

Ted gasped. "Yes, and a sugar high all 'round."

Sarah and Anna both laughed. "It isn't as though we do something this excessive every day," Sarah said, grabbed a bag of marshmallows and tossed them to Ted.

Jasper sent his booming laugh throughout the room. "I was telling Ted how lucky he was that he'd found the perfect wife and the perfect mother for Emma."

Sarah bristled, set her coffee mug down, eyed Jasper, then observed Ted's reaction. When she saw his composure hadn't changed, she was confused, then turned back to Jasper. "And what did Ted reply to your opinion?"

"Why, hon? He knows you're the best thing that's ever happened to him and Emma. He agreed with me, of course. Why wouldn't he? The man has a good head on his shoulders."

Sarah opened her mouth to speak, but chose instead to keep to herself, the confrontation she wanted to bombard him with. But now wasn't the time. She'd been through too much over the years and had developed a tough defense when it came to shouldering someone's hurtful or misconstrued words. Too, she may be making too much of Jasper's comment—still, she wasn't certain.

What did unkind words mean? Nothing. She'd learned a long ago to overlook immaturity, and she'd accepted that she was better off for the choice.

But she did wonder how sensitive she'd be if Ted had used Emma to get to her… that was the one thing she couldn't bear. She would wait until an appropriate time to discuss the situation with Ted. Aside from that, Anna and Jasper were still there and so was Emma. She refused to create a scene in front of everyone.

They'd be home soon and away from curious ears, mainly Emma's, and she wouldn't argue in front of her. It would harmful to the child to overhear the conversation they were certain to entertain.

She'd manage to get through the rest of the evening and tomorrow somehow without the loss of her dignity.

Twenty-Two

Emma had begged for Fettuccine Alfredo on the way home. Ted noted Sarah was quiet all day and appeared anxious and ready to get home. "Let's see how Sarah feels, okay?"

"Okay. I still want Fettuccine."

Ted laid a hand over Sarah's, but she brushed it aside. He glanced at her and asked. "Are you feeling okay, sweetheart?"

Sarah replied with an abrupt, "I'm fine."

Uh-Oh. I'm not so sure about that. "All right, then. You haven't been quite yourself. I wondered if you were coming down with a virus or something." Ted knew Sarah. He knew her well She wasn't all right. He hadn't a clue exactly what was wrong, but there was an undeniable chill in the air between them.

"No. Nothing. No virus. No fever."

"Would you feel up to having an Italian dinner with us?" Ted's favorite was Angelo's Italian, a small, yet excellent restaurant close by his place. Angelo, who owned the place, as did his father before him, was a friend of his dad.

"Say yes, Sarah," Emma said, as she bounced in her seat. "Please."

Sarah sighed, smiled back at her, and nodded. "No problem. You'll have Fettuccine Alfredo tonight and I'll join you. Sure sounds good."

The waiter greeted them warmly as he seated the three at a cozy candle-lit table with a window view of a walkway and a delightful pond out back. Emma crossed her hands on the table, looked up and asked. "Hi, Luigi. May I have crayons and a coloring book?"

Luigi, the waiter, leaned down and whispered to Emma. "I saw you the moment you entered the restaurant." With those words he produced what Emma had requested from behind his back as one would a bouquet of flowers. "What do you know? Service with a smile, little lady."

"Thank you, Luigi." She giggled and twisted around to face Sarah. "Do you know Luigi's name means famous fighter?" She rested a finger on her chin and pondered for a second. "No that's wrong. His name means famous warrior. I forget the right words sometimes."

"Interesting history. Thanks for telling me," Sarah said, and laughed. "Do you know what your name means in English?"

Emma's eyes opened wide. "No. What does it mean?"

"Well, I was told it meant, Whole. Complete," Sarah commented.

Emma pooched out her lips. "I guess that's okay. Not as exciting as Luigi's name though."

Sarah reached over and tickled Emma. "It means you're all girl, silly. A complete beauty. I consider that a great meaning for you and your name."

Emma mulled over what Sarah had expressed, as though she were wondering if indeed the explanation of her name was a good thing, shrugged, then went back to her plate of Fettuccine Alfredo.

"Emma, I get how much you love Fettuccine Alfredo, I really do." Sarah laughed. "I have no earthly idea where you put all that food. I'm happy you have a good appetite."

When her plate was still half-full, Emma leaned back, rubbed her tummy." I'm full," she said, then pushed her plate aside and grabbed the coloring book to finish her page.

Once the waiter cleared the table and added Emma's leftovers to a *tow-ko-box*, as she called it, Ted ordered Strawberry Ice for the three of them.

Ted winked at Sarah. "It seems she isn't too full to indulge in a light dessert."

A smile flickered across Sarah's face. "Surprise, surprise. I haven't seen a child yet who doesn't have room for dessert. Any dessert. It's a good thing you didn't give her a choice, or you'd have chocolate to deal with."

"Eat up, young lady. From the look on your face, you're more tired than you imagine. We'll be ready leave in a few minutes."

"I am tired." Emma said, then yawned and grinned. "The beach was fun, Daddy. When can we go again?"

Ted pulled into Sarah's driveway and switched off his SUV. He opened the door for Sarah, then went around back to get her bag. He slid her bag inside the door, came back, sat down on the steps and patted the space beside him.

"Could we talk while Emma sleeps?" he asked.

"After the weekend we've had, I'm really tired and all I want to do is go to bed," she said.

A million thoughts ran through Sarah's head as she studied him. He was as handsome as ever and a gentleman. At least she'd believed him to be a gentleman until she'd listened to Jasper repeat his and Ted's conversation. From the day she'd thrown caution to the wind and began seeing him again, she'd envisioned years of happiness for the three of them. Now she wondered why she'd imagined things would work out between them. Her biggest regret right now was Emma. She was sure to be hurt if she and Ted ended their relationship. The decision would be a difficult one, and not one she thought she'd ever make.

"Please, a short talk to ease my mind. Okay?"

"Very well." Sarah sighed and sat down beside Ted. "This is most likely not the best time to have this discussion, but since you brought it up, we may as well get it over with."

"I detected a change in you yesterday afternoon. Those beautiful eyes lost their sparkle almost immediately. I'd hoped we could discuss the issue, if there is one. And… I believe there is. Whatever is going on, I'd like to get it out in the open and clear up any second thoughts you may be considering. If… you are having second thoughts."

She stared into his eyes and almost gave up on her indecision, but backing down wouldn't solve a thing. "Indeed I am having second thoughts."

Ted jerked to attention, never taking his eyes off hers. "Okay. Tell me what's wrong," he replied. "I want to know if I've annoyed you in some way… and evidently I have, so I can make it right. Whatever it takes."

Annoyed? I'm more than annoyed. "We must have been insane to think we could pick up where we left off years ago… to begin again. We've both changed and our lives have moved in different directions. I'm not so sure we want the same things anymore."

Ted ran a hand through his hair, a nervous gesture he'd always made. "I thought we were getting along rather well."

Sarah reminded herself how much she loved the way a lock of his smoky-black hair fell over his forehead, but pushed back the image. It wasn't smart to dream of things that would possibly never be. She was upset, and thinking good thoughts of Ted wouldn't get her the answers she needed.

Sarah again locked her gaze with Ted's. "I guess you were doing fine," she commented, and tried to keep her voice from shaking.

"What do you mean?"

"Finding a mom for your daughter."

Shocked, Ted stood above her and exhaled. "What? How in the world did you reach such an outrageous conclusion?"

"Jasper said as much yesterday and you agreed."

"Of course I agreed, because it's true. You'll make a wonderful mom especially for Emma. It's plain as the nose on your face that you and she love each other. This conversation is absolutely judgmental."

"Judgmental? You think I'm the one who is judgmental, now? I'm not the one who tried to use you." She jerked her purse off the steps and headed across the porch, but Ted grasped her hand and pulled her back.

"Use you? That's a horrible thing to accuse me of. Sarah, because I love you, I would never stoop that low."

Sarah twisted her hand from his hold and remained standing beside the door. "Then make me believe you didn't discuss needing a mom for Emma with Jasper."

"We certainly did discuss you. Not in the way you took it though. Jasper knows how I feel about you. I'm not giving up on my dreams, Sarah."

"What might those dreams be, Ted?"

"I've waited too many years for us to be together again. I—we—cannot give up on us now. We've come too far the past few months. I'd love for you to become my wife. That's my dream."

Being his wife had been her dream, too, but she wasn't admitting it. "Some dreams aren't meant to be, Ted."

"I need you, Sarah. I need you back in my life, in my arms. For you to believe all I've anticipated is for you to become Emma's mom is asinine. It's also an insult."

"I hope you're right, Ted. Because what's going down between us now is a lot of pressure. Look, Ted. You're a really great guy... but I think we need some time to sort out what we really want. More so, what we're really about as a couple."

Ted looked as though she'd slapped him. "Time apart may not give us, or you, the answer. It may tear us apart forever. If we can't work things out, then maybe we weren't meant to be together. But I'll respect your wishes. You have time, time to think things over. What we mean to each other." He got up to leave, then turned on one heel to face her. "What about Emma? What do I tell her?"

Sarah's throat tightened and she bit back the tears that threatened. She simply couldn't stop being with her all at once. She wouldn't understand. "Tell her I love her and will see her soon. If... that's agreeable with you."

Twenty-Three

Two weeks later, without notice, Karen made a visit to Creative gifts. When she came through the door, she wore an unexpected yet repentant smile. Sarah froze, wondering if she were about to lower the boom on her livelihood. She knew how scheming Karen had been with the purchase of the building she rented, and needless to say, she was ready for anything Karen would bring today. Good or bad, and in her mind bad was the word to plunk down the finishing touch on her day.

"I came to offer an apology to you, Sarah...to you as well as Lisa. I'm sorry for the grief I've caused. I had no right to extend my own grief onto you and your sister. Please forgive me."

Instead of the dispute she thought would happen, Karen had, of all things, apologized. "Of course, Karen. Thank you for the apology. Yes, I forgive you. I realize you've been under a great deal of pressure." Sarah extended her hand and Karen took her hand warmly into hers.

"This may be too much to ask, but I hope we can be friends," Karen said.

Sarah smiled. "I'd like that."

"By the way, there won't be any remodeling to the building, unless it's absolutely necessary." Karen glanced around at the store and nodded in appreciation. "You have a great business here. I've said what I came to say, so I'll leave now, but I'd like to thank you for seeing me. Let's do lunch one day," Karen commented. She looked at her and grinned. "Maybe we can take Emma along with us."

"I'm sure Emma would like that. Perhaps we can get together

soon. Possibly take her to the park for a picnic or perhaps a movie, or simply lunch."

"Anytime. Here's my card, but if you should misplace it, Ted has my number." Karen waved and left Sarah and Lisa both staring at each other in astonishment.

"Miracles will never cease." Lisa had stood back behind the counter while Sarah had dealt with Karen. "I can't believe she apologized. Strange. I wonder what happened to change her state of mind and attitude?"

"Your guess is as good as mine. She's definitely completed a three-hundred-sixty degree turn around. I imagine Ted and Emma could have had something to do with her way of thinking. I'm sure I don't know."

"You may be right," Lisa replied. "All I know is, I'm thrilled she isn't going to put us through the nightmare of a remodel."

"Me too, Lisa. Maybe she prayed for her own forgiveness from Ted and us. Whatever it was, I'm grateful. Tearing apart this store wasn't something either one of us would enjoy doing. Plus, she could have dragged remodeling out for months and our bank account would have suffered. Tremendously."

Twenty-Four

Three weeks later, a FedEx package addressed to Sarah arrived. She checked the return address and saw it came from a lawyer's office in town. Thinking it was a duplicate copy of their new lease, she laid it aside until she'd restocked the gift card racks. Restocking was one job she wasn't particularly fond of, but the card section was necessary to the shop's sales. The card section eliminated an extra shopping stop for her customers, since everyone chose a card to accompany their gift, a simple card for a friend or loved one.

While she struggled with breaking boxes down to take to the dumpster, the phone rang. Of course it did. Where was Gavin when she needed him? Sarah's heart warmed when she thought of him. He was such a fantastic young man and had never given his mom a minute of trouble, except when he was younger and would get into a fight on the baseball field. Gavin was pitcher and the bully he usually fought with was first baseman. Gavin had never started a fight, but he never ran from one either. Thank goodness the fights, all but one, were verbal, but Lisa still reprimanded him when necessary, which was seldom.

Sarah sidestepped over the cardboard, hoping not to slide, and grabbed the phone. "Creative Gifts, Sarah speaking."

"Hi, Sarah. Ted. Glad you answered. How are things with you?"

"I'm good. Tell me how you and Emma are doing." Her heart skipped a beat at the sound of his voice. *Will I forever be tempted by the young man of my teenage years?*

"We're good, too. Emma misses you. I miss you. I know I said I wouldn't push or bother you, but I thought you may be interested in my conversation with Mayor Conley."

"Mayor Conley?"

"Yes. Remember when he almost hit us?"

"Yes. I do. I'd forgotten you were going to speak with him." Sarah said. She kicked the stray cardboard away while making her way to her desk.

"I spoke with him early this morning. He did not take kindly to me bringing up the near mishap a few weeks ago. Anyway, he did remember when he almost sideswiped us, though his agitation at my reminding him was clearly apparent. Being the cocky mayor he is, and having to present himself as the well-mannered Southern Mayor Conley, he apologized." Ted laughed. "I saw how bitter the apology nibbled on his behavior. Anyway, he excused himself rather hastily and left it at that."

Sarah, muttered. "Think of how he would have reacted if you'd mentioned the blonde we saw him with earlier."

"Nothing would have pleased me more, but his personal life is his own, unless it hinders his official duties," he said.

"I suppose you're right. I feel sorry for his wife though, " Sarah said. "Speaking of apologies, Karen came by a couple of weeks ago to apologize. Also, she isn't going to remodel the store and said she hopes we can be friends."

"Really? An apology was big of her. So. What did you say?"

"I told her I'd like that. I saw no reason to hold a grudge against her, especially since you and she had come to an agreement. It was kind of her to drop by and offer an apology. We discussed tentative plans to take Emma on an outing… but only if you're okay with one or both of us being with her."

"Thank you, Sarah. I'd like very much for you to take Emma anywhere you'd like. If Karen would like to go along, I have no problem. I know you wouldn't let anything happen to Emma. Oh! She's still in ballet, so check with me before making plans, okay?"

"Certainly. I appreciate that, Ted. Thanks for your trust."

"Of course. I've always trusted you. And—I'll never forget you. Remember that, Sarah."

Sarah laughed. "There isn't any way I could forget. You won't allow me that courtesy."

"How good it is to hear you laugh again, Sarah. Look, I don't mean to push, but if and when you're ready to talk about us, let me know."

Us? A million thoughts ran through her mind. It was now or never—she had to know. "It's time we talk, Ted. Time to discover if we have enough between us to go forward. We need to find a solution to our problem so we can get on with living without a cloud over our heads."

"Thank you, my dear Sarah. You've made me a happy man. You can't imagine how I longed to hear you say those words."

"Why don't we run over to Tybee Island Sunday? Emma can go with us if you think she'll be alright while we talk."

"Why wouldn't she be alright? I can ask Dad to go and watch her while we talk. Is that acceptable with you?"

"Yes. It will be wonderful seeing her again. There is a delightful seafood restaurant we can go to for dinner. Does Emma like Crab Legs?"

"Does the sun come up every morning? If it's food, she likes it. Well. Most everything."

"I've seen her eat. She has a huge appetite for one so small," Sarah said. "Sorry, but I have a customer. Gotta run."

"Great. We'll pick you up after church. About one?"

"That time works for me. See you then."

Sarah finally got around to opening the FedEx delivery. She squealed so loud Lisa came running out of the stockroom. "What's wrong?"

"Nothing is wrong. Take a look at this contract."

Lisa pulled her glasses from the top of her head and began to read. "This has to be a terrible mistake."

"No mistake. My name is right there in black and white. The building is mine." She glanced at Lisa. "Of course that means it's both of ours. Nothing has changed, Lisa. I wouldn't do that to you. We'll get you added to the contract. I have no idea who did this for us, but it looks as though Christmas came early this year."

Lisa hugged her as a tear ran down her cheek. "I love you Sarah. You're my favorite sister."

Sarah chuckled. "I'm your only sister, you nut. I love you too."

"Let's get busy and make some money. We're going to need it to pay the taxes on this old building."

Tybee's beach was as beautiful as Sarah remembered. Serene and inviting. The breeze tossed Ted's hair into an untidy state, but he'd never looked more handsome. She'd hate to see what her hair looked like since she'd forgotten her sunhat.

Ted explained the conversation he and Jasper had. "And... so what you heard Jasper say about me wanting a mom for Emma, wasn't exactly our entire conversation. He's a kind man, and didn't think when he blurted out those words. I promise finding a mom for my daughter is the last thing on my mind. All I want is for us to spend time together and see what's in store for us."

Ted had never lied to her, and she didn't believe he was lying now. "I'm sorry I didn't give you the benefit of the doubt, Ted. I hope you can forgive me for being so skeptical. It's just that—."

Ted clasped a hand around the back of her neck, gazed into her eyes, then pushed a strand of dark auburn hair behind an ear. "You're forgiven, sweetheart. I love you. There isn't anything I couldn't forgive you for."

Sarah reached over and kissed Ted. When she did, he pulled her into his arms and kissed her back. "I love you, too," Sarah said. "We were meant to be together. Always."

Ted hugged her as they strolled arm in arm down the beach toward Emma and her grandfather.

"By the way, Ted. You wouldn't know anything about my owning our building now, would you?"

"That was supposed to be a surprise. You weren't to receive the contract until next week. It's a gift from me and Dad. I'm hoping it's a gift for my future bride, and now the future mom of my daughter."

"You took a lot for granted, Ted."

Ted grinned at her, walked her to Emma's side at the edge of the water. "I'd never take you for granted. I simply prayed you'd find it in your heart to give us another chance."

Sarah placed her hand in Emma's and kicked at the waves. "We both deserve another chance. We're good together…and we'll make awesome parents."

With a twinkle in his eye and a shocked look on his face, Ted stood back from her. "Now who's taking things for granted?"

"Not me. Remember you promised to never forget me?" she said, then giggled. "I'm making sure I'm always on your mind."

About the Author

Carol's roots are sown in the South. Her writings are Southern, small town based and include romantic comedies, contemporary romance, and romantic suspense.

She believes in falling in love, family values, and happy endings. When time allows, she dabbles in art, and always has popcorn, pickles, and hot chocolate on hand.

While a dose of humor sprinkles throughout her stories, they may or not be based on real life characters. Some are convinced they are, but only she knows for certain, and she won't gossip.

Carol currently resides in Georgia with her husband and family.

A multi-published eBook author since 2011, Carol's won numerous awards and has previously published poetry, short stories, and novels.

Find Carol Online

http://www.caroldevaney.weebly.com
http://www.caroldevaney.blogspot.com
http://www.facebook.com/carol.devaney
http://twitter.com./caroldevaney

More Titles from Carol DeVaney

Coming November 2019
A SMOKY MOUNTAIN CHRISTMAS WEDDING (Bk 2)
Coming November 2020
A SMOKY MOUNTAIN CHRISTMAS BABY (Bk 3)

Retreat Interrupted

Jill James

One

No matter how many times Cassie Stone closed her eyes, when she opened them, the sign was still there.

Welcome to Lake Willowbee. Home of the Stone Book Festival.

Except, in her mind, it said home of the Stone Book Failure.

Crawling home with your tail between your legs was bad enough. To be doing it after ten years of top-of-the-book-charts success was so much worse. Cassie squared her shoulders and exhaled a shaky sigh.

Her cell phone rang. A glance at caller ID showed Anna, her former agent and supposed friend. She clicked the ignore button and tossed the phone to the other car seat. A glance in the rearview mirror showed bloodshot eyes reddened from constant swiping of tears.

Forging ahead was the only option as her father liked to say. A reminder of her dad's recent passing only caused more tears to fall. How many tears had to fall for the body to dry up and blow away? Because, she was pretty sure her limit had been reached.

Turning the car back on and driving into town was harder than she thought. Her hands gripped the wheel as she glanced over her shoulder and got back on the road. Mirages rose from the summer-heated asphalt. Summer lingered long into autumn in the Sierra Nevada foothills. September, if not October, would be just as hot.

A slight right off the freeway and she glided down Main Street into the town of Lake Willowbee. There was the hardware store on the left. The bakery with free cookie Tuesday still sat on the corner of Main and Pine. At the only stop signal on Main

Street she glanced into the window of the antiques store. The same old cracked Tiffany lamp knockoff sat gathering dust in the display.

She huffed a breath to blow her bangs out of her eyes. A dozen years and it was as if she had never left. A few familiar faces walked along the street, but no waves came her way. Why should they? Cassie Stone hadn't been home for longer than a weekend since she left the day after high school graduation.

Her shoulders slumped. Millions of dollars will do that to you. Make you believe there is tons more where they came from. Make you believe everyone is your friend. She blew her bangs out of her face. *Sure, they are. Until the money dries up, and the fun is over.*

She averted her gaze as she passed the Stone bookstore. Her heart cracked with the memories of seeing her dad in the doorway, waving hello to everyone driving or walking by. Pressing harder on the gas petal, she sped up and drove to the edge of downtown. A long, winding road brought her to the lake the town took its name from.

Emerald pine trees covered the golden-brown land as far as she could see, straight to the water's edge. The browns and greens of lakeside homes peeked out from the forest. Spotting the familiar stacked-stone mailbox, Cassie turned into the driveway and stopped in front of the house.

Through a veil of tears, she stared at the closed door and empty porch. No flung open door greeted her. No parents rushing to hug her and show their excitement at her arrival.

Not now.

Not ever again.

She turned off the car and sat there. In moments, the heat overcame the air-conditioned interior of the vehicle. Perspiration ran down her neck and soaked her bra. Still, she sat there.

"Okay, are you going to bake or get out of the car?"

The personal admonishment drove her to push the door open and get out. Her legs ached from the drive from the airport. A few steps toward the front door and pins and needles shot through her and pain throbbed in her back and hips.

Lifting the verdant jade plant, she palmed the housekey and unlocked the door. An unfamiliar musty scent greeted her. Dust motes floated in the torrid heat. The house was lifeless and empty.

Mrs. Johnson had called and told her of her father's death and her mother's mental forgetfulness, but in the bottom of her heart she still held on to the hope her mom's condition was temporary. Brought on by dad's death. She expected her mother to be here, at home, in the kitchen waiting for her.

A sob broke free and wrenched her heart. How was she supposed to fix this? She couldn't even fix her own life.

Cassie girl. Time to pull it together.

She started. Her head whipped around, searching for her father. That had been his voice. His words.

Wrapping her arms about herself, Cassie stiffened her spine and squared her shoulders. His voice might only be in her head and her heart, but that didn't make it any less real.

Allowing herself a few moments to settle in, she went back to the car and got her suitcases. Bringing them to her room was like a trip down Memory Lane. In all these years, her parents hadn't changed a thing. From her rose petal-printed bedspread to the old-fashioned typewriter on her desk.

Her fingers lightly trailed over the keys. She'd used the antique device to write everything from teenage angsty poetry to her first novel. The novel which got her the big contract deal and took her away from Lake Willowbee.

She stared out the window to the sun-drenched lake. Calmness always filled her looking out her bedroom window. The words had flowed as she daydreamed a sleepy summer day away. Biting her lip, her fingers swept over the typewriter again. She could do this. How hard could it be to help her mother and get back to writing? A nagging voice in her head reminded her she hadn't written a word in two years.

Spinning in a circle, she knew she was putting off the inevitable. Her mother was not Amelia Johnson's responsibility. The elderly woman had been kind enough to care for Molly until Cassie could get home. She was here now, and it was time to pull it together, as the voice in her head and her heart had said.

Two

olly. Get down out of that tree right now. I don't have time for this. I have to get to work."

"Meow."

Meow? What the heck was going on? Police chief Ben Bridges stared up into the branches of the oak tree. Against the green leaves and black bark, he spotted the bright pink bathrobe wrapped around Molly Stone.

"Meow."

The plaintive cry came again.

His gaze swept from the woman's tear-filled eyes to the belt of her bathrobe caught and wrapped around a thick branch.

A sigh deflated his chest as he reached to grasp a handhold. Hefting himself into the centuries-old tree, he eyed Molly.

The woman settled on her precarious perch, waiting for him to reach her. For the hundredth time since Leo Stone's death last week, Ben wondered how he could have kept his wife's condition a secret in a town where people knew you sneezed two seconds before it happened.

He sighed, his fingers working on the twisted belt knotted around the branch. Molly stared at him with all the curiosity of the cat she seemed to think she was this morning.

Blowing out a breath in frustration, Ben snapped open a carrier on his gun belt and retrieved his Leatherman. A flick of the wrist opened it and a simple tug sliced through the soft, terrycloth material. The woman fell into his arms and wrapped herself around him.

One branch at a time, Ben moved down the tree, his work

boots slipping on the bark. His breath caught as a small slide almost sent them both crashing to the ground.

"This would be easier if you helped, Molly," he whispered, out of breath as they reached the grass-covered yard. The drought-tortured blades crinkled beneath his boots and Molly's bare feet as he settled her to the ground.

As if the painful prickles woke her scrambled mind, Molly stared up at him in confusion. Her eyes widened as she stared around the yard. Eyes as deep brown as her daughter's.

"Ben Bridges, what am I doing outside?"

As if she remembered her state of undress, she whipped bright-pink terrycloth around her body and tightened the frayed remains of the belt around her waist.

He placed his hands on her shoulders and stared into her frightened eyes. He gentled his voice as much as possible.

"We discussed this, Molly. You're having some forgetful moments. Where is Amelia? She was supposed to be watching you this morning until Cassie gets here."

The woman's brow furrowed.

"Who is Cassie?"

His heart skipped a beat. Molly was getting worse by the day. They couldn't do anything until Cassie returned to town. How long did it take to fly from New York City to California? With her money, the woman should be able to hire a private jet. Decisions needed to be made, but they weren't his to make.

"Cassie is your daughter."

He wrapped an arm around Molly and steered her to Amelia's front porch. The screen door stood wide open, the elderly figure standing at the threshold, wringing her hands.

"I'm so sorry, Chief Bridges. I overslept this morning. We were up half the night with her trying to get out the door. My grandson finally put a chair under the doorknob about dawn. I thought I could get a couple of hours of sleep."

"Cassie is my daughter," Molly informed the woman as she slipped out from under his arm and skipped across the porch into the house.

Amelia patted his arm and turned to go in as well. "Don't worry, Ben. We've got this covered until Cassie gets here. Eddie is on summer break. He can help me today."

"How is little Eddie doing?"

She laughed. "Not so little anymore. After this summer, he'll be heading to Sac State."

The screen shut as Ben stood there staring, his thoughts tumbling a million miles a minute. Would Cassie be able to take care of her mother? The teenage Cassie had been responsible and serious, her nose always buried in a book. He didn't know the adult Cassie at all. She'd dusted her hands of Lake Willowbee right after high school and never looked back.

He'd caught glimpses of her in the rare visits she'd make, but truth be told, he hadn't seen her for any length of time in a dozen years. Not since the multi-million-dollar publishing deal for a series of cozy mysteries had the whole town talking and sent Cassie clear across the country to the opposite coast.

Back in his patrol car, the radio crackled with talk between his three deputies. Not that Lake Willowbee needed him and three deputies, but the town charter said he could have three and his nephew needed a job. Thank goodness, William was good at his duties, because nephew or not, he would have fired him if he'd screwed it up.

He smiled at the radio chatter. Life in a small town. A case of vandalism at the high school was some kids with chalk, drawing on a wall. A fender-bender on Oak Drive on the far side of town. That would be old man McDaniels.

The man had seemed old when Ben had been in high school. The man's kids kept taking his car keys and the old man kept finding them. He never made it past the driveway before he hit the old clunker they'd put there. One of these days, the McDaniels kids would wise up and sell the old man's car. He laughed. The old man would probably just take the riding mower into town instead.

As he cruised down Main Street, he passed Stone's Bookstore. He was thrilled to see the door wide open and customers coming and going. Leo had hired some of the brightest and the best of the teenagers in town for his store. The kids competed to get one of the best jobs in town. Two girls stood outside the building, a large banner between them. The familiar red banner swung as they hoisted it above the large front window.

Coming Soon. Stone Book Festival.

His dry throat hitched as he tried to swallow. The book festival was at the end of the summer. The festival brought in much-needed revenue for the thinning downtown. Every few months another business folded up shop and moved to greener pastures in Auburn and Placerville.

Leo was gone. Molly was incapacitated. And Cassie was an unknown. Ben wondered if the woman would take care of her business here and wash her hands of Lake Willowbee once again.

Three

Her hand hovered an inch from the wooden screen door. Cassie's fingers shook as her thoughts raced. She bit her lip and exhaled deeply. Her knuckles tapped on the wood.

A woman came to the door and gazed out through the screen. A little thicker around the middle and more gray hair, but Amelia Johnson looked the same as she remembered her. Mrs. Johnson had been her second-grade teacher and the first person to show Cassie how to take the tumbled stories in her head and put them neatly down on paper.

Great, another person I let down.

"Cassie," the woman cried out as she flung the door open.

She found herself surrounded by warmth and the scent of cinnamon and spices. A sigh escaped her. Cassie would have stayed there all day if not for a familiar voice crying out from the depths of the house.

"Make her go away. I don't like strangers."

Her breath caught and her vision swam. She couldn't swallow past the lump in her throat. Maybe she could turn around and come back later and this would all be a nightmare she awoke from.

"Mom," Cassie said, her voice cracking.

A frail woman she didn't recognize stepped forward, her forehead furrowing and confusion swimming in her eyes.

"Cassie?"

Mrs. Johnson leaned forward and whispered in her ear. "She has some lucid moments, but they come and go."

The older woman stepped over to her mom and patted her arm. "Yes, Molly. This is Cassie. Your daughter."

In an instant, her mom straightened her spine and glared at Amelia. "Of course, this is my daughter. Do you think I don't know my own child?"

A shiver went down Cassie's spine. Even in her childish misadventures she'd never heard that mean tone of voice come from her mother's lips. Molly Stone was a kind and gentle soul. Her father had worried that his wife would bring home every stray; animal and human, so she could care for everyone.

Like a lightbulb switching off, Molly's gaze turned blank and she looked to Amelia for understanding. The elderly woman patted her mother on the arm again and turned her toward the back of the house. A nod of her head indicated Cassie should follow.

They stopped at a back bedroom. A pile of clothing was laid out on the gold bedspread. Amelia sat Molly down and started undressing her from a robe and nightgown.

With a rush of heat to her cheeks, Cassie turned away. Anger sliced through her. How could her father have said nothing of this? She called every weekend and he'd said nothing. Racking her brain, she tried to think when she'd last talked to her mother. Had it been last month or the one before? Had it been back in the spring, talking about the daffodils and new plants for the garden?

She was pulled from her thoughts by a tap on her shoulder. Amelia hugged her tightly and ran a hand down her hair.

"I'm so sorry, Cassie. I would help, but I can't keep up with her."

"Mrs. Johnson, I understand. This is my responsibility now."

The older woman cupped her cheek. "Still, you have friends here. Let us help, please."

"Of course," she murmured, knowing the woman meant her parents had friends. Cassie hadn't had a friend here since high school. Not since Renee. She buried all thoughts of her best friend. Those memories only led to anger, regret, and sorrow.

The drive back to the house was harrowing and terrifying. Cassie stopped the car in the driveway, her body trembling. She peeled her fingers from the steering wheel.

"Okay, rule number one. Mom sits in the back when I drive."

Twice the woman had tried to pull on the steering wheel.

Once so hard, Cassie still wondered how they hadn't ended up in Lake Willowbee. Now, her mother sat against the door, staring at her with tear-washed eyes.

She gentled her voice. "Let's go into the house and have some lunch. Would you like that?"

Her mom nodded and stopped crying. "I have a daughter named Cassie."

Her heart broke. She hadn't just lost her father. She'd lost her mother as well. The physical body was here, but her mind, her soul was gone. She choked on a sob and turned off the car.

"Yes, you do," she whispered.

Her mom undid her seat belt and pushed the door open. "Leo will be hungry from work. I really should get the food going."

Without a backward glance, her mother strode up to the porch and tried to open the door. Cassie had locked it when she'd left. Not missing a step, Molly reached under the planter and retrieved the key. Opening the door, she stepped through and shut it.

Cassie rushed to get out of the car and into the house before her mother locked her out. Turning the knob, she caught her breath as the door opened when she pushed.

"Cassie, you're home," her mother called from the kitchen.

She leaned her back against the door. For a split second, she imagined this was all a bad dream and everything would be fine.

Happiness lasted for an hour. Molly stayed in the moment. They made and had lunch. Even the mention of Leo's death didn't alter her mother's mind.

Molly patted Cassie's hand across the table. "Your father would want us to go on, wouldn't he?"

"Of course, he would," Cassie agreed, smiling at her mom. "He said we have to live each day and continue on."

"Oh, your father and his pithy sayings," Molly laughed. "Sometimes I think he kept his old fortune cookie papers and dug out a new one whenever he needed some deep thought."

Cassie laughed as they gathered the lunch dishes and carried them to the sink. It took a few seconds to realize her mother wasn't laughing along and had stopped talking. She turned from wiping the counter.

The water ran in the sink. Molly's hands were under the steaming water, turning red. Cassie rushed over and flipped the handle to cold, holding her mom's wrists. She breathed deeply as the skin turned pink and back to a light tan.

"Mom, what were you thinking?"

"Is my mom here? I want to go home now." A little girl voice trembled between Molly's lips as tears tumbled down her cheeks.

"We are home, Molly. We are home."

Four

By two o'clock, Ben was more than ready for the lunch he had missed. Putting aside the big flood of a few years past, not much of the big event variety happened in Lake Willowbee. Most days consisted of patrolling and stopping things before they started. But a lot of little things added up to time spent being the chief of police for the small town.

An alarm went off on his phone to remind him that he had an appointment this afternoon as Mayor Bridges with the Chamber of Commerce. A glance at his watch showed he had enough time to see if Cassie had Molly settled back at home before his meeting. Turning into the graveled driveway, Ben pulled in behind a gray sedan that was clearly a rental with tags in the window. Where was the sporty red number he'd seen the few times he'd spotted Cassie in town?

He stepped out of his car and closed his eyes as a rare breeze blew over him from the lake. Sometimes the conditions were just right for a cooling breeze on a hot, humid day. Opening his eyes, he strode up to the front door. His gentle knock was answered in a swift moment.

"Ben," she breathed his name as her eyes widened and she stepped back.

He would spend days wondering at the tone of her voice saying his name and the look in her eyes, but he didn't have time. Mores the pity.

"Hi, Cassie. I thought I would check and see if you picked up Molly and got her settled okay."

Tears brimmed over her eyes and washed down her cheeks. "I don't understand. Why are you checking?"

He took off his ball cap and turned it in his hands. "I came to check on her when Leo... when your dad passed. I could see she needed help and you weren't here."

The tears died as if they had never been. "I got here as quick as I could. As soon as Mrs. Johnson called me."

He reached out to take her hand, stopped in midair, and pulled it back. "I know you did. But your mom needed help right away and Mrs. Johnson is one of her closest friends. She offered to help, and I took her up on her offer."

Cassie wrapped her arms across her chest and rubbed them. "I don't understand any of this. My dad didn't say anything. What happened?"

"Can I come in?"

She moved back. "Of course."

Moving to the counter, Cassie took a barstool and sat. He grabbed the one beside her and settled in.

"Your dad had a heart attack at the bookstore. We got him to the hospital, but your mom didn't show up. We called and called. Finally, one of my deputies came here to the house and tried to get her to come to the hospital. He thought she was just confused. When he tried to help, she attacked him."

Cassie flung a hand over her mouth, but a gasp escaped.

"Doctor Adams sedated her, but we were aware pretty quickly that something was wrong."

Her brow furrowed as she glared at him. Her voice was low, but intense. "No one said anything. Mrs. Johnson just said to come home for dad's death and mom was having some confusing moments. Nothing about what I've seen so far."

This time he did take her hand and she let him. "We all figured you had enough to deal with, without hearing about Molly over the phone. I told Amelia to just let you know she was confused so you wouldn't come home knowing nothing."

"I had forgotten," she muttered, still glaring at him.

"Forgotten what?"

"Forgotten how everyone is in your life in a small town."

"You say that like you're not sure whether that is a good

thing or a bad thing," he said with a chuckle.

She laughed softly. "I'm not sure... yet."

Cassie enjoyed her hand in his warm one too much. She should move back. Let go. Anything but continue to enjoy it. Her face heated with a blush she hoped if she ignored, he would, too. She was thirty years old, not some schoolgirl with a crush. But Ben Bridges *had* been her high school crush. Only he hadn't known it. No one knew. Except her best friend, Renee, and Cassie's diary.

A squawk of his radio saved her from her inappropriate thoughts. He turned slightly to answer the call allowing her to glance at him without seeing those all-knowing eyes turned her way.

A peek through her lashes showed no wedding ring on the hand holding the radio. Not that that meant anything. She'd heard police officers sometimes didn't wear their rings to work. Yet, no tan line showed a ring worn sometimes. Still didn't mean anything. Some men didn't wear them at all. It wasn't as if she could just make conversation and say 'Oh, by the way. Are you still married to my best friend? The one who knew I liked you and took you anyway.'

Wouldn't that just sound petty, stupid, and childish?

She came back to the present as Ben finished his radio call.

"I'm at the Stone house. I have a Chamber of Commerce meeting in an hour. Then I'll check out the bonfire at the lake. Yes, they filed all the permits."

"Chamber of Commerce?" she asked as he turned back to her.

He grinned, and her heart skipped a beat it shouldn't as his smile brightened the room.

His gaze swept over his uniform. "One minute I'm the chief of police, the next I'm the mayor of our fair city."

He stood from the barstool and moved toward the door. Cassie followed and opened it for him. For what seemed an eternity, they stood there until a slight cry came from the back of the house.

She knew she had more important things to do than stand here mooning over a childhood crush.

"If you need anything, let me know. Or Mrs. Johnson."

She sighed. "Police chief. Mayor. Neighbor. I hope your wife doesn't mind all the time you give this town."

"My wife is dead. Renee passed away five years ago."

Without another word, Ben nodded, put his cap on his head, and walked to his car.

Five

Her mind skittered in a million directions as she contemplated Ben's last words. *How could she not know Renee had passed away? Years ago?*

"How could you be so petty to not let her know the past was the past?" she whispered to herself, tears running down her face.

A hole tore in her heart. One that had been filled with her best friend all through their school years. Later, anger left the hole in her heart for what she had seen as the ultimate betrayal. Now, the hole would remain with no way to make amends.

Another cry from the bedroom ripped her from her trivial thoughts. She didn't have time to wallow in what might have been. With Renee or Ben.

By the time she reached the bedroom, her mother had settled down and snored gently in the humid room. She turned and flipped the switch for the ceiling fan. A slow breeze wafted over the room.

She paused at the closed door next to her parents' bedroom. Her hand shook as she turned the knob and opened the door to her father's office. A whimper built in her throat. She pushed it down and stepped into the room. Opening the blinds flooded the room with sunlight.

The desk looked like Leo Stone had just stepped away to go to the bookstore. Papers were scattered across the immense oaken surface. She smiled at the lack of a desktop computer or even laptop. Her father had refused to have one. He always said he stared at a screen long enough at work. Home was for relaxing.

Relaxing. Cassie opened the drawers in the desk until she found her father's hidden bottle. With a clunk, she sat it on the desk's top. A crystal glass joined it. Not the best whiskey, that had a better hiding place, but her dad's second favorite.

"What could one shot hurt?"

The first went down smooth. Too smooth. Making it too easy to have a couple more. Her hand shook as she lifted the fourth to her lips. Or was it fifth.

She sighed as she threw her head back and gulped. The glass fell from her hand and thudded onto the carpeted floor.

Her face was wet. *When had she started crying?*

Her head swam, and her vision blurred as she laid her head down on the desk, papers crumpling under her cheek. *Could you call yourself an orphan if one parent was technically still alive?*

She awoke to darkness in the office. Papers fluttered on the desk and slapped against her face. Cassie sat up with a start. The room spun as she resisted the urge to lose her stomach's contents across her father's desk. Her tongue stuck to the roof of her dry mouth.

It took too long for her brain to catch up to the situation. Papers fluttering meant a door was open in the house. She flung herself out of the chair and across the room. The rest of the house was dark, a heavy breeze blowing through the rooms.

Curtains over the sliding glass door billowed like ghosts in the twilight. She grasped them and ripped them open. Her breath stopped at the frail figure sitting on the edge of the dock. Her mother's feet dangling into the lake.

She tiptoed down the dock to the end. With care, she settled down next to her mom and hung her feet over the edge.

"What are we doing?" she whispered, afraid to startle Molly.

"Cassie, dear. Just enjoying a cool night. Your father and I would love to sit here and dream of what we would do in the future."

Tears pooled in her mother's bright eyes and ran down her cheeks. "We were always going to do something. Go to Europe. Go on an Alaskan cruise. See the world. Someday."

She took her mother's hand.

"Live your life, Cassie. Someday never comes. It just never comes."

Molly's voice whispered away on the breeze. Her mother leaned her head on Cassie's shoulder. Wrapping an arm around her mom, she cried silently. Someday was never going to come for her mom. Her tomorrows had been stolen away.

Inwardly, she promised herself to never drink so much again. This evening could have ended so tragically. So differently.

Six

Ben sighed as the Chamber of Commerce meeting continued into the night. Half of the group wanted to keep doing things like they'd always been done, and the other half knew something new was needed or Lake Willowbee was going to continue its slow death. They'd all seen too many small towns become just an exit on the freeway for gas and a burger.

Too many times his mind wandered to that soft 'Ben' whispered from Cassie Stone's lips. Pink, luscious lips. He jerked his thoughts away from her lips and all her other body parts as he caught up to the raucous conversation in the conference room.

Evie Jackson stood from her chair, her face bright and animated. The woman had recently taken over the antiques store on Main Street when her partner, the elderly Mrs. Brown had died.

"I know we were all devastated by Leo Stone's death. The book festival brings in enough money for all our shops to be in the black until Christmas hits with the snow people vacationing. But it doesn't have to end with Leo's death. His daughter Cassie has come back to Lake Willowbee. With Cassie Stone highlighting the festival, we could double the size and income of the event."

Ben swallowed harshly through his dry throat. With Molly's condition, Cassie could find herself without a minute to spare for anything, let alone an event the size of the festival. The thought of Molly's health problem being made public stopped him from speaking. Gossip traveled fast enough without his help.

For all he knew, Cassie could put her mom in a nursing home and skedaddle away from Lake Willowbee again. Either way, he didn't see how she could help them.

Evie looked at him with those large, gentle eyes and he couldn't imagine how he was going to say no to whatever the woman suggested.

"Mayor Bridges, you went to school with Cassie. You can ask her to help, can't you?"

He wanted to ignore the plea in her voice, but he would do anything to help his town. Even if it meant begging, if it came to that.

Cassie would want to save her father's legacy. Wouldn't she?

Standing at the doorway to the town hall, Ben stared as the various cars left the meeting and people strolled across the town square to their homes and businesses. His gut still churned from the pats on the back he'd received. The others seemed to think getting Cassie to help was a done deal. An instant answer to a larger problem.

Crickets chirped in the sultry night air as he locked up the town hall and walked across the lawn to the police station. He opened the door to find his nephew, William, manning the front desk and the phones. As usual, nothing was going on and the young man was keeping busy with crossword puzzles and his laptop.

"Anything I need to know about?" he asked, pulling his tie loose and shrugging out of his suit jacket.

"All quiet in the town tonight," William said in a sing-song voice.

The deputy moved his puzzle book and papers fell to the floor. William jumped up to snag them but not before Ben spotted the logo for UCLA.

A blush shot across the young man's face as he shuffled the papers into a pile. "I was thinking of taking some online classes, Uncle Ben."

He pulled a chair over to the desk. As he sat, he undid his cuffs and rolled up his sleeves. "William, you can do anything if you set your mind to it. If you don't want to be a cop, that is okay. This job was just to help you get on your feet."

Ben leaned forward. "You don't have to stay if there is

something else you want to do."

A smile brightened William's face. "I filled out the papers. I didn't think they would accept me, with no community college and all. I got the letter today. They accepted me into the film school."

Ben smiled back as William's eyes shone and the young man ducked his head. "I know it's because of this job you gave me. Being a law enforcement officer helped so much, Uncle Ben. I couldn't have done this without you."

He stood and pulled his nephew into a hug. "You did this, William. Congratulations."

The young man sat back down as Ben continued to stand. "I don't leave until the fall semester. I'll still do my job until then."

Placing a hand on his shoulder, Ben squeezed. "Again, congratulations."

In the locker room, he changed out of his suit and back into his uniform. He sighed. Lake Willowbee always lost its best and brightest. The small town couldn't hold a candle to the great, big world.

He drove through the downtown, glancing at the shuttered stores and dim lighting from the corner bar and a restaurant still an hour or two from closing time. Everywhere else, it was the cliché of a small town rolling up its sidewalks at sunset. The town wouldn't bustle until the end of the summer for the festival. Then every business would stay open until the last customer left.

Thoughts of the summer event brought Cassie to his mind. He hoped her first day hadn't been too hard with her mother. He grimaced. Molly had been a vibrant woman. She'd helped Leo at the store. Done charity work at the Alicia Green Foundation Home. Been always ready to lend a hand to a neighbor in need. He settled his shoulders.

"I have to let Cassie know she can ask for help. It's Molly's turn to get something for all she's given."

He ignored the voice in the back of his head that said he'd just come up with a great excuse to see Cassie again so soon. It was town business. It had nothing to do with those soft lips whispering his name. Maybe if he said it enough in his brain, he would start to believe it. Yeah, like that was going to happen.

Leaning back in his seat, Ben drove to the lake. Lazy smoke trailed up into the dark sky from the water's edge.

As he drove across the field, the flickering lights shone on the beach and the sounds of rock music filled the air. A few words with the adults in charge and he left reassured everything was well in hand. Another hour and the party would wind down and the embers of the bonfire would be seen to. The danger of wildfire was ingrained in every resident of Lake Willowbee, from the smallest child to their ancient elders. The Sierras saw too many wildfires each year for anyone to get complacent about the dangers.

Seven

Cassie winced and grabbed her forehead. A migraine was the last thing she needed this morning. Tears filled her eyes as the sunlight bounced off the lake's surface. At this point, she wasn't sure if they were from the headache or the anguish of watching her mother huddling in a corner, softly banging her head on her knees and keening like a hurt child.

She'd prayed the closeness they'd shared last night on the dock would continue. That the memory lapses and childish behavior would disappear now she was home.

So much for prayers and wishes. Her mother looked up at her, confusion on her tear-streaked face.

"I want to go home," she cried.

Cassie plopped down on the floor in front of her mother. She grasped her hand gently and rubbed her arm.

"You are home, Mom."

Like a pale streak, Molly flung back her arm and slapped Cassie across the face. For a second, she sat there, stunned. Her mouth fell open. When her mother reared back with an ugly gleam in her eyes, she grabbed her arm and trapped it to her side.

"Mom, please. Stop this. I'm trying, but you have to help."

Her mother's face faded as the tears cascaded down her cheeks. She was drowning, and the shore was nowhere in sight. Molly's eyes widened as she stared at Cassie.

"Don't cry."

A laugh broke free. A sad, little laugh, but at least a laugh. "I'll stop if you will."

"Okay," Molly said, her face brightening like the meltdown had never happened.

Her phone rang. Her gaze shot between her mother and the countertop where her cell phone sat. Molly had pulled a magazine off the table and was leafing through the pages, humming to herself.

Pushing herself off the floor, she grabbed her phone. An unknown number showed on the screen, but it was the area code for town. Pressing the accept, Cassie put the phone against her ear.

"Hello?"

"Dear, this is Mrs. Johnson. I hope I didn't wake you."

"No, we're awake."

"Well, I called to let you know Molly has an appointment this afternoon. Doctor Adams referred her to a specialist in Auburn. Will you be able to take her? It's for three o'clock."

"Of course, Mrs. Johnson. Let me just get a pen to write down the address."

She swung around to find her mother right behind her. "Here you go, honey."

Her mom handed her the pen. Cassie just stared at her mom. "I'm going to take a shower and get dressed," Molly announced.

She would have stood there forever if a voice from the phone didn't keep talking to her.

"Is everything okay, Cassie?"

"I just don't know. One minute she's a child and the next—the next she is my mom." Her voice caught, tears burning her eyes.

Mrs. Johnson's voice comforted from the phone. "The specialist will do the tests and find out how far along she is and what your options are. Let me give you that address."

Cassie listened with half her attention, but she didn't need a doctor to tell her what she needed to do. She needed to be there for her mother, just like her mother and her father had always been there for her.

The sound of the running shower shut off and she heard her mother moving around in her bedroom.

Did she go in and help? Did she wait until her mom yelled or cried out?

She was clueless, and it hurt to not know the right thing to do. Cassie prayed the doctor would give her some information along with the tests. Glancing up as the bedroom door opened, Cassie swallowed her anger. Molly stood in the doorway, covered with every piece of winter outerwear she owned. From her pom-pom hat to the boots on her feet, the woman looked as if she was ready for a visit to the North Pole.

She bit her lip as sweat ran down her mother's face. This would be funny if it weren't so sad.

"Do you think I'll be warm enough?" Molly said, her eyes asking a sincere question.

She knew it was wrong, but the laughter built up until it exploded from her throat. Cassie clutched her side with the pain of a deep, belly laugh.

Her mother frowned. "What are you laughing at, young lady?"

This should be in a book. Except, no one would believe it.

Her mind skittered around like a squirrel being chased by a dog. How long had it been since an idea had sparked something in her brain? More than two years, that's how long. Two years without an idea, a spark, a page written. Now, with her mother's mental health on the line, the synapses fired, and her hands itched to type.

She sighed. "I don't have time for this," she muttered under her breath.

Crossing the room, she guided her mother back to the bedroom. Her steps stuttered to a stop at the clothes flung across the bed and floor. If it wasn't every piece of clothing the woman owned, it was close.

"Mom, it's the middle of summer. It's hot outside. We need to find you something cooler to wear."

The soft, calm voice must have worked, as Molly unwound her woolen scarf and dropped it to the floor. She plopped onto the bed.

"I don't know what I was thinking," she whispered. "It seems like I can't remember if it's winter or summer. Or even if it is

Tuesday or Sunday."

Cassie's eyes watered as her mother sat in her bra and panties, surrounded by her pulled-off clothing. "What am I going to do?"

She brought her arm up and hugged her mom to her side. "You don't have to do anything. Let me help you get dressed and we'll see what the doctor has to say about all of this."

Her mother leaned her head on Cassie's shoulder. "That sounds like a very good plan."

With her help, Cassie soon had her mother dressed and in the car. The drive to Auburn and Doctor Kincaid's office passed quietly.

Parking the car, she turned to help Molly undo the seat belt.

"I'm scared."

"Me, too, Mom. But we can do this."

"Why isn't Leo here?"

Cassie swallowed past the knot in her throat. She opened her mouth to speak, but no words could come out.

Her mother patted her hand. "Oh, I know your father is dead. But I wish he were here. He always made things so easy. He took care of everything."

Her heartbeat raced painfully in her chest. *Yes, he did. Now it's my job.*

Eight

Calmness had only reigned until they'd entered the doctor's office and the sight of the white lab coats set her mother off. She tore around the waiting room, careening off walls, and sliding to the floor. They'd sedated her, placed her on a gurney, and wheeled her down long, white corridors.

Cassie stood by the large, glass window as they settled her mother into the machine. Her fingers trembled as they arranged her mom, her limp arms sliding off the gurney. As they strapped the cage-like thing over Molly's head, Cassie had to look away. Doctor Kincaid had reassured her the MRI was painless, but it hurt to see her mom so confined.

She turned as the nurses exited the room and left Molly alone in the strange machine. A young man flipped a switch and a vibration she felt through the walls and into her bones filled the room.

On a computer screen, she watched as colorful pictures appeared. Science had been her least favorite class in school and the pictures meant nothing to her. A glance at the man at the controls showed her nothing. His poker face could have won championships.

"Can you tell anything?" she whispered.

"I just take the pictures," he replied as he flipped more switches and the vibrations died.

What was he going to say anyway? Your mom's brain is mush. So sorry.

She couldn't keep berating herself over what might be. She'd wait for the doctor's report and go from there.

Her phone rang in her purse. Retrieving it, her finger slid to the decline icon.

"You can take that in the hall, if you want," the young man spoke up. "They'll take your mother to a recovery room for the sedation to wear off. It's just two doors down."

"Thanks," she said. A glance in the machine room showed nurses pulling her mom out of the MRI machine and her mother still oblivious of what was going on.

Stepping out into the hall, Cassie spotted the door with a sign reading Recovery Room just like the man mentioned. She leaned against the wall and checked her phone. Ben Bridges showed on the screen for missed calls.

Her heart skipped a beat and raced painfully to play catch-up. She shook her head. Why did the tiniest thought of the man rip through her like a teenage girl with a crush? It wasn't as if she didn't have a million other things to worry about.

A career that was dead and buried.

A mother fighting the illness of her life.

A funeral to plan.

A family business to run. Or not.

She nibbled on a hangnail. Could her mind splinter under too much stress? She hoped not, because she feared it was only going to get worse.

There was one thing she could do right now. She pressed the call icon on her phone.

The phone rang as Ben was putting it back into his shirt pocket. Spotting Cassie's name on the screen, his fingers fumbled to press accept.

"Hi, Ben," Cassie's voice echoed through the phone.

"Cassie, I stopped by your house, but you and Molly aren't home."

Great job, Ben. Of course, she knows she's not home. No wonder they made you police chief.

"Yeah, I had to take my mom to the doctor's office for some tests. Mrs. Johnson set it up."

"What did they say, if you don't mind me asking?"

Cassie laughed, and the sound warmed his heart and sent his blood rushing beneath his skin. "I don't mind. You all took care of my mom until I could get home. Nothing yet. They just did the test.

"Ben, I have to go. They took my mom into the recovery room and the doctor is here now. Did you need something important?"

His assignment to ask Cassie to highlight the festival seemed so frivolous now she was dealing with everything else.

"Nothing that can't wait," he said.

"Okay. Thanks."

Her sigh of relief lingered in his mind long after the sound died on his phone.

Walking back to his patrol car, the phone rang again. His glance showed Henderson Funeral Home.

"What can I do for you, Mr. Henderson?"

"I was hoping to finish up Leo's services. Heard Cassie Stone was back in town, but I hadn't heard from her yet. Thought you might know if she is back or not."

Gossip might be faster than a hummingbird at a feeder in Lake Willowbee, but Ben wasn't adding to it. Although, he could guarantee, if Mr. Henderson was asking, then half of the town knew he'd already been out to see the woman.

"I'll send a reminder to Cassie. I'm sure it just slipped her mind with getting back into town and dealing with everything."

"But, of course," Mr. Henderson said. "The lady will have a lot on her plate, for sure."

Once the call ended, Ben shot a quick text to Cassie.

Henderson's Funeral Home needs some last-minute details. Call them as soon as you can.

He tried to stay professional, but he couldn't help adding—
Hope all is going okay.

Going as expected, she texted back. He gulped and tried to swallow with a knot in his throat. He'd so wanted to be wrong about Molly. But, just like with Renee, life didn't always turn out how you planned.

Or prayed.

Nine

From the near-Artic air of the doctor's office, outside was a blast from a furnace. Yet, the summer heat of the foothills couldn't penetrate the coldness of Cassie's bones and thoughts. Doctor Kincaid had explained as well as he could, but none of it seeped in.

She walked to the car with her arm wrapped around her mom's waist. Molly was dead weight as her feet stumbled on the pavement. Her mother's groan as she plopped into the seat shattered Cassie's calm. Tears ran down her face and she tasted the salt on her lips.

Where was the vibrant woman of her childhood? The whirlwind of the Molly Stone she knew and loved. Making cookies for the school bake sale while she helped Cassie with her homework and did the accounting for the bookstore all at the same time. She'd even managed her own hobbies in between being there for her husband and daughter.

As if that woman had never existed, Molly's fingers fumbled with the seat belt until Cassie reached and pulled it to snap it into the lock. Her mom's befuddled smile broke her heart.

Making sure she was all tucked in, Cassie shut the door and walked around the car to the driver's side. Getting in, she started the motor and turned the air to high. Her hand shook as she leaned over and took her mother's hand.

"We'll get through this," she whispered as she smiled.

"Of course, we will. We always do."

Her mom settled back in her seat and her soft snores punctuated Cassie's thoughts of aloneness.

Early Onset Dementia. Alzheimer's. Deteriorating brain function.

She swiped the falling tears, trying to keep the road in view.

Moving over to the slow lane, Cassie stared as the cars whipped by her. Like an analogy of her life. Everything was moving too fast and she couldn't keep up.

Her scattered thoughts traveled back to two years ago. To the argument with her agent and publisher. They'd wanted three more books from her for the new year and she'd known she couldn't produce even one.

"But, Cassie, dear. Everyone loves Mrs. Pumpernickel and Sassy." Her publisher, Jacqueline sat behind her behemoth desk, her hands neatly folded on a stack of papers.

The woman had seemed so nice and sweet all those years ago when she'd given Cassie her big break. A decade later, Jacqueline reminded her of a shark and she was the chum in the water.

"I can't write another Pumpernickel mystery. I want to write something else. Surely, twenty books are enough."

After twenty books, Cassie was ready to strangle Mrs. Pumpernickel and her orange tabby, Sassy.

"Maybe I could get back to them after I try something else?" Cassie knew she was pleading. Not that she had an idea for anything else. She hadn't written a word of any story in more than two months.

Jacqueline smiled, and Cassie was reminded of a shark once more. "I'm sorry. It's Mrs. Pumpernickel or nothing. As it is, you are over deadline for the next in the series." She flipped the pages of her day planner and looked up. "In thirty days you'll be in breach and could forfeit the next advance."

In the end, it hadn't mattered. The words wouldn't come, and Jacqueline and her company dropped her. Two years later, her agent, Anna, dropped her as well. She only had some money coming in because Mrs. Pumpernickel and her cat, Sassy still sold well around the world.

As Cassie turned onto the exit for Lake Willowbee, her mom muttered in her sleep. The nonsense words filled her with dread. Driving past Henderson's Funeral Home, she remembered the text from Ben. A glance across the car showed her mother in no condition to visit the funeral home and make plans.

She sighed. Calling Mrs. Johnson seemed such an imposition, but she couldn't see any other course of action. Details had to be worked out, and her mother wasn't going to be able to do it.

Refusing to let any more tears fall, she steeled her spine as they turned into the driveway. Her mother stirred and looked at Cassie with the lost eyes of a little girl.

"Where are we?"

"At home, Mom."

"Oh, good. I'm so tired. I think I need a nap."

Me, too. Only I'm not going to get one anytime soon.

In the end, it had been easier than she'd thought. Mrs. Johnson not only came over, but she'd offered to have dinner ready when Cassie got back. With nothing left to stop her, she'd headed to the funeral home.

Her father had had plans in place, so once Cassie sat down with Mr. Henderson it was just the little details to hammer out. Although he said them every day, his condolences seemed sincere and had Cassie reaching for the handy box of tissues. Now, the soggy mess was crumpled into a ball in her hand.

"I wish I could have seen him one more time," she cried.

"Leo's wishes were always for a cremation. And with the delay, perhaps that is best."

"I came as fast as I could get a flight and get here," she said. The well-meaning words stung more than she would have thought.

He patted her hand. "I didn't mean that at all. We all know you are dealing with more than just the passing of a loved one."

Her face heated. Years in New York City had made her forget the hazards of a small town. Everyone probably already knew she'd been to the doctor with her mom and what his prognosis had been. She took a deep breath. These people had been there for her parents and her mother when her dad died.

"Mayor Bridges let us know Molly was having a tough patch. We can have a service whenever you feel she is up to it."

"Mr. Henderson, I'm sure you will know soon enough. My mom isn't going to get any better." Her voice broke and she grabbed another handful of tissues.

"If you would rather do something quiet, we all understand."

She looked up at his gentle words. "No, Mr. Henderson. My dad loved this town, and I know, this town loved him. I want everyone to be able to say good-bye. Is this Saturday too soon?"

He smiled at her. "Saturday would be wonderful. Your mother..."

She sat up straight, the direction of his question obvious. "We'll get through this. We always do. Just like my dad used to say."

Ten

*B*en spent the rest of the week running around in circles trying to find time to talk to Cassie about the book festival. The first time he went to the Stone house, no one was home. A call to Mrs. Johnson got the information they were at a doctor visit in Auburn. A specialist for dementia and Alzheimer's.

He couldn't call her after what had to be a traumatic time. Ben didn't need a specialist to know Molly was headed in a bad direction.

The next time he'd tried again. A call from Mr. Henderson's funeral home let him know Cassie had made arrangements for her father's funeral. The whole town was turning out for the occasion. The businesses downtown would be closed, and the Chamber of Commerce would be in attendance. If he wanted to get to Cassie before someone said something, it would have to be before the service. That was how he found himself at the funeral home before anyone else had arrived.

He opened the door to the building and breathed a sigh of relief as the welcoming cold blast of air hit his sweat-soaked body. The overpowering scent of roses filled the waiting area. Quiet classical music wafted through the building as he searched for Cassie.

His quick glance stopped at the hunched-over woman to his left. She looked up and his heart ached at the sadness and tears in her bright eyes. He knew that lost look. It had stared at him from the mirror after Renee's death. The look of unfinished business. The begging for just a little more time to say a few more things. The belief there would always be a tomorrow.

He strode over and took the chair across from her. He reached for her hand and pulled back at the last second. His sympathy didn't entitle him to a familiarity he hadn't earned. Especially, when he would have to ask an enormous favor from her before the day was through.

"Where's Molly?" It seemed a safe question. He hoped.

She swiped her eyes with a balled-up tissue. "The doctor gave me pills to sedate her. Mr. Henderson is letting her rest in a back room until they kick in. Mrs. Johnson is with her. I just needed a few minutes for myself."

The look she shot him said she was waiting for his recriminations. He shook his head. She wouldn't get them from him. He'd beat himself up enough during his wife's last days to know no one berated you as well as you did it yourself.

"Have you been inside the chapel yet? Mr. Henderson and his staff do a great job for services."

"I'm — I'm afraid to go in."

"Why?" He gave her a small grin.

"Once I go in, it will be final. My dad will be gone. I've been telling myself for days that he is just on a business trip to get books. But when I step into that room and see the flowers and the box . . . it will be final."

She looked at him, her eyes red-rimmed, her mouth quivering, and his breath caught in his throat. Cassie Stone had been cute in high school, glasses falling down her nose as she sat with her face buried in a book. But the woman she'd become was so much more. He had a feeling her father's death and her mother's illness would only refine who she was even more. Something had happened in the years she'd been gone from Lake Willowbee and it had made her the woman she was today. A woman he'd liked to know better.

Ben took her hand. Her shaking fingers tightened around his. "You can do this. I'll go in with you, if you want. I know this is hard, but it gets better. I promise."

A blush raced across her pale cheeks. "I'm so sorry about Renee. I didn't know."

His thoughts raced. Today would be sad enough. He didn't want Cassie worrying about anything except her parents. Like closing a door and locking it, Ben determined to not let anyone discuss the book festival with her today. Not even him.

He turned to what he hoped was a safer subject. "She had all your books. She read them until the bindings broke. Renee would go to the bookstore as soon as your dad got a delivery."

Cassie's mind tumbled wildly at Ben's words. Why would her former friend read her books? After the prom, she'd never talked to Renee again. Not even during her infrequent visits home. She'd see her around town, but just ignore her.

She was saved from asking him a question she didn't know if she could handle knowing the answer to by Mr. Henderson coming out of the back. He walked toward them, his gentle steps muffled by the thick carpet.

"Your mother is ready to go into the chapel, Miss Stone."

"Is she okay?" She bit her lip and gazed at the man.

"I believe so. Mrs. Johnson has offered to sit with her, to assist if she can."

"Thank you. That would be wonderful."

He turned to Ben. "Will you be joining us, Mayor Bridges?"

She squeezed his hand and gazed into his understanding eyes. "Yes, please."

Keeping her hand, Ben pulled her out of the chair. He let go to help with her mother. Between him and Mrs. Johnson, they escorted her to a front pew.

Cassie gasped at the abundance of flowers around the altar. With her mother sitting silently, Ben joined her as she read the cards. She'd expected the arrangements and well-wishes from the businesses in town. Her father was a major member of the Lake Willowbee Chamber of Commerce and had helped many of the other businesses get started.

But her tears overflowed at the basket of his favorite carnations from the children at the Alicia Green Foundation Home. She didn't know they realized he was their secret benefactor and Santa Claus every year.

Ben handed her a giant poster of a redwood tree. "The high

school is planting a sequoia in his honor, in the courtyard."

"He touched so many lives," she said, tears choking her throat. "I should have stayed here."

Taking the poster, he put it back on the easel. "You've touched lives too, Cassie. Mrs. Pumpernickel and her orange tabby, Sassy helped dozens of people escape the pain of chemotherapy. I know they helped Renee, and all the people she gave your books to at the hospital."

"I need to sit with my mother now," she managed to whisper. Ben couldn't know how his kind words tore at her already-lacerated heart.

She'd let down her parents by not being there.

She'd let down her readers by not dealing with a Gibraltar-sized rock of writers' block.

She'd let down herself and her best friend by not dealing with her stupid jealousy and anger and waiting too long to make things right.

People came and went, and she hoped she said the right things. As the pastor started the service, Cassie stared at the small box with her father's remains. Such a small container for all the man had been.

Listening to friend after friend reminisce about Leo Stone, Cassie felt the weight of his legacy settle on her shoulders. When the last person spoke, the pastor looked at her.

Cassie nodded. She hadn't planned to speak. The words hadn't come for years now and she wasn't sure they would today. She had to try.

Standing at the podium, her jaw dropped. Sitting in the front pew she'd been unaware how many people sat and stood in the room. They lined the walls, two deep and crowded the doorway.

"To you, he was a businessman, an entrepreneur, a friend. To me, he was one simple thing. He was my dad."

Her knees gave out as she managed to stumble to her seat. Her mother reached and pulled her into a hug.

"Your father would be so proud today, Cassie. Thank you."

Eleven

"How do parents do this?" Cassie winced at the whine in her voice as she stumbled into the house.

The week after her father's funeral had been nonstop from morning to night. The only bright spot had been the visit to the lawyer for the reading of the will. Her father had taken good care of mom and her. The house was paid for and the bookstore was doing well enough to provide for them.

A moment of sadness had hit her at the office as Mr. Thomas had her sign papers putting her in charge of everything, including Molly. Her father obviously had known of his condition and made plans. Her mother had stared out the office window as if she hadn't a clue where she was or for why.

Bringing her thoughts back to the present, she tugged off her shoes and kicked them to the wall beside the door. Her head came up with the sound of footsteps across the wooden floor.

"I'm so glad you're home. She's been very fretful tonight. Keeps crying out for your father."

Cassie sighed as she eyed their angel. Abigail Williams stood in the hallway entrance, her pale-yellow scrubs as crisp and clean as they'd been this morning. The young, home care provider was a godsend.

The young woman handed her a note. "Uncle Ben called. He said to tell you thank you."

A blush heated her face. It should have been a simple request. But anything related to her writing and publicity was anything but simple.

Abigail's face lit up with a smile. "I can't believe the writer of the Mrs. Pumpernickel Mysteries is going to be the star of our book festival. Nothing this exciting ever happens in Lake Willowbee."

I'm such a fraud. For a second, she'd thought she'd said those words aloud. When the smile remained on Abigail's face, Cassie heaved a silent sigh of relief. Her heartbeat raced, and her shoulders slumped at the thought of all the work yet to be done on the festival, the care of her mother, dealing with the bookstore, and not letting anyone know she was a failure.

She raised her shoulders and took a deep breath. It didn't matter if she was a failure in her writing career. All that mattered was succeeding in taking care of her mother and saving her father's legacy.

There would be no retreating from life this time. Running away from her problems was not an option.

The phone's ringing saved her from her dark thoughts. She set her purse down on a barstool as Abigail picked up the phone, spoke, and handed her the handset.

"It's Uncle Ben. He wants to talk to you."

Cassie took the phone and turned around as far as the cord would reach. She bit her lip as the heat filled her cheeks. *It's probably business. Get over yourself, Cassie girl.*

"How's your mom?" Ben's deep baritone filled her senses and set her blood to humming in her veins.

"Abigail says she's having a bad day. But the doctor warned me about that. I just thought after the funeral went so well that she might stay that way for a while."

She heard Ben cough on the other end of the line.

"I don't want to heap anything else on your plate right now, but..."

A chuckle escaped her. "Heap away. What is one more thing?"

"I hope you still think that after I ask. The Chamber of Commerce has a dinner and auction each year to raise money for the festival."

"Oh, I remember that. Mom and Dad have pictures around here somewhere with them all dressed up. I love those pictures. They seem so happy."

He hemmed and hawed until she never thought he would get to the question. "I was wondering if you would like to be my date for the event."

Her breath caught in her throat and she gasped for air. Out of the corner of her eye, she saw Abigail rush forward and start pounding her on the back. She waved her away as she breathed deeply, and air flowed into her lungs again.

Cassie caught the tail-end of the conversation. "... I understand if you would rather not."

In that moment, she was a schoolgirl begging her best friend to ask the cutest boy in school if he had a date to the prom. Her heart skipped a beat as she remembered how that had turned out—with her best friend going with Ben and her sitting at home eating popcorn and crying into her pillow watching sappy romantic comedies.

Go for it, Cassie.

Tears stung in her eyes. She hadn't heard that funny, laughing voice in too many years. Even so, she would know Renee's voice anywhere.

Her heart raced. "I would like that, Ben. I would like that a lot."

Twelve

The ice-blue gown flowed over her skin like a dip in a cool lake. Her mother's dress was a classic. One that would remain in style year after year. Cassie reached behind and struggled to pull the zipper.

"Here, let me help," Abigail said, zipping her up. "You look wonderful."

She smiled at the young woman in the mirror. "Are you sure you're okay staying here with my mom? You've been here all day."

Abigail shook her head. "No problem at all. I have some studying to do. I'm taking a few classes from the college online."

Cassie turned around. "I thought you had all your nursing done."

The young woman blushed, red flooding her pale cheeks. "I'm taking some writing courses. I want to write a book someday about families dealing with Alzheimer's and dementia."

She nodded. "I think that would be a wonderful book. It's not like these illnesses come with an instruction manual."

"I know, right?" Abigail frowned, her sadness traveling to her eyes. "You get the diagnosis and you don't know where to start. I want people to know they aren't alone."

Cassie rushed and pulled Abigail into a tight hug. "You do that for me. For mom. Thank you."

The other woman stepped back and smoothed Cassie's dress. "Don't get wrinkled. You look perfect. Uncle Ben is going to be happy with you on his arm tonight."

She knew her face was as red as a fire truck. It felt like flames engulfed her cheeks. "This is just business."

Abigail laughed. "That isn't what my mom said. She said she

hasn't seen her brother this happy in, she didn't know how long. Probably back past when Aunt Renee died."

Her breath hitched. She was still caught unawares at the idea of her best friend's death. Finding out about it so recently made it seem like it had happened yesterday. She silently berated herself. She should have been here. For Renee. For her parents. For everything. All she'd ever done was run away. She'd even run away from New York and her obligations there.

"Was it terrible? When Renee died," she said, her voice dying down to a cracked whisper.

Abigail nodded, her eyes growing glassy with tears. She moved and sat on the bed. "It was awful at the end. Almost made me not want to be a care provider. The cancer ate her up. She was in so much pain. The morphine gave her some comfort, but it made her delusional a lot of the time. At the end, she thought I was you."

Tears swam in her eyes. Cassie tripped to the bed and fell onto it beside Abigail. Staring into the mirror, she could see how Renee could have confused them. Only a couple of years separated her and Abigail. Their hair and eyes were the same color.

"I'm so sorry," Cassie cried.

"That's what she said," Abigail replied.

"What?"

"She said she was so sorry for what she did to me ... I mean you."

"Did she tell you what she had done?" Cassie whispered.

"No. She didn't have time, but it must have been so terrible to give her so much pain."

Cassie took Abigail's hand and stared into her eyes. "It wasn't so terrible. It was teenage-girl stupid and if I had stayed to work it out, it wouldn't have been such a mess. I would have been here for her. I'm the one who should be sorry."

She felt the squeeze on her hand. "Don't be. Aunt Renee had a wonderful life with my Uncle Ben. Cancer sucks."

"So, does Alzheimer's," Cassie breathed back.

"Yes, it does."

"Oh, no," Abigail said with a gasp.

"What?"

"Your makeup is a mess and it's all my fault."

Cassie laughed. "It's fine. I'll get cleaned up."

She glanced at the clock as the doorbell rang. "Can you get that? Tell him I'll be right out."

Abigail left, shutting the door behind her as Cassie rushed to the bathroom. A fast glance told her a quick wash and redo and she could be ready in minutes.

Ben paced in the living room. His niece had let him in and then excused herself to look after Molly.

"Cassie will be right out," she said over her shoulder as she disappeared down the hallway.

He moved to the sliding glass door and gazed at the sunset-lit lake. The surface was like a mirror with no breeze tonight. A flicker of color in the glass had him turning.

"I'm ready."

He stared. All thought left his head. Cassie Stone was a siren rising from the sea. A pale-blue dress left her shoulders bare and hugged every curve. Her long hair flowed in wild curls to those bare shoulders. He licked his dry lips and tried to swallow.

"I thought I might be overdressed but look at you."

He tore his gaze away from her to stare at his tuxedo. He supposed he looked okay. He'd never been one to care overmuch how he dressed.

"James Bond eat your heart out," she said, smiling at him.

Sadness filled his heart. "Renee used to say that," he whispered.

A smile graced her face while her eyes glimmered with tears. "It was our favorite saying for the cute guys at school."

She frowned at him. "Don't make me cry again, Ben Bridges."

"Why were you crying?"

"Abigail and I were talking about Renee."

He strode over and took her hands. "She and Renee were good friends. Abby may be my niece, but age-wise we grew up as if we were cousins. Abby was there for Renee, especially at the end."

Cassie yanked her hands out of his. "And I wasn't."

He took her hands back and squeezed them gently. Moving in close, he stared into her eyes. "I know what happened. Renee told me everything. But we aren't going to discuss that tonight. We are going to this event and it will be you and me. No one else. You can't fix the past, you can only learn from it."

She pulled her hand from his and cupped his cheek. "When did you get so wise?"

The heat from her palm filled him with a tension he'd never felt before from a simple touch. "Just the passing of the years."

She smiled. "Not so many years. You look the same as you did in high school."

"I'm not that boy anymore."

"That's good. Because I'm not that girl anymore, either. At least, I hope so."

Thirteen

The lights. The music. The dancing. All Cassie had imagined a prom to be and more. When they stepped into the community center, the rose-colored lights flooded the room with a pale-pink haze. Soft music echoed in the room, bounced off the walls, and set her body to swaying.

Ben placed his hand on the small of her back. The heat from his skin warmed her. He led her to a table in the center of the room. A placard read Stone Books in the middle, next to a beautiful arrangement of roses and lilies. A couple sat in chairs at the table. The woman was model-beautiful with a copper-colored dress and her pale-blond hair swept into an up-do. The man was movie-star perfection. A true match for the woman at his side. The pair had eyes only for each other until Ben pulled her seat out for her.

He leaned down toward her. "You remember Lisa Miller. This is her husband, Todd."

Her mouth gaped open. Lisa was the manager for the bookstore, but she hadn't looked like this when Cassie had seen her at the store a few times.

Todd laughed and put an arm around his wife's shoulders. "She cleans up well, doesn't she? You should see her looking like a drowned rat after a flood."

"What?"

Lisa laughed and shoved her husband away. "Ignore him. One little natural disaster and he'll never let me forget it."

Cassie was sure her face showed her confusion as Lisa leaned forward to talk to her. "We were in the big flood. It's been a few years now. Not that anyone around here will forget it."

Todd reached out and took Lisa's hand. "My wife is forgetting about the part where she almost died."

Lisa leaned her head on Todd's shoulder. "I just choose to forget that part."

He kissed her forehead. "And I will never forget."

Cassie stared at them, envy gnawing at her heart. The older couple had to be in their fifties, but they gazed at each other like teenagers with their first love. Jealousy tried to rear its ugly head before she squashed it like the rude bug it was. Just because she'd missed all of that didn't mean she had to be envious of those who had enjoyed it.

The rhythm and words of Mariah Carey's *We Belong Together* started playing. She knew the song by heart. She'd sung it to herself, dancing in her room.

"Would you like to dance?"

Ben's voice whispered in her ear as he held out his hand to her. Her heart raced painfully in her chest. This night was all her girlhood dreams wrapped up in a gossamer fabric. Afraid it would all end at midnight like a fairy tale, she wanted, she needed, to seize every moment.

"I'd love to," she said, taking his hand.

His hand clasped hers as he placed her other hand on the nape of his neck. The warm skin there heated her palm. She shivered as his hand slid down her arm and wrapped around to her back. With a gentle pressure, he pulled her in closer.

The scent of his aftershave wafted over her. She leaned her head back and gazed into his dark eyes. She'd imagined this moment a million times in her dreams. It all paled beside the reality of her dancing in Ben Bridges' arms. She remained there, song after song.

She wanted this night to last forever, but all too soon the lights brightened slightly, and the scent of food filled the room.

"Oh," she said.

The pout in her voice must have bled through because Ben laughed as he took her hand and they walked back to the table. "Don't worry. There will be more dancing after dinner and the auction."

Her mood brightened at the thought. Back at the table, they took their seats. Todd and Lisa took theirs as well as they were joined by a few of the clerks from the store. She recognized Brett and Kimberly. The other couple introduced themselves as Chet and Connie. Chet worked at the store, but he had been out-of-town, looking at colleges, he explained as he introduced his girlfriend, Connie.

The younger couples made her feel positively ancient. They talked about music groups and teenage events she hadn't a clue about.

Ben nudged her arm. "Don't worry. I have no idea what they are talking about either," he whispered.

"She is, too," Connie said to Chet.

"No, she isn't."

"I'm asking her."

The dark-haired girl turned to her. "You're THE Cassie Stone, right? The one who writes the Mrs. Pumpernickel Mysteries?"

Cassie nodded, refusing to let a blush heat her face. "Yes, I've been writing them since I was probably younger than you are right now."

The girl leaned forward. "You haven't written a new one in forever. Please say you're going to write more, right?"

Her fingernails dug into her palm. "Of course, I am," she lied. "Just taking a break."

She was saved from lying to herself as much as the young woman by the arrival of dinner. Thankfully, eating meant she didn't have to talk.

Fourteen

*D*inner had been par for the course for these events, Ben mused. Nothing to write home about, but filling. Cassie had grown silent during the meal and it continued as they strolled among the tables covered in auction items.

Belle's Flowers had a table covered in enormous bouquets. Cassie's long fingers trailed over roses and flowing ivy before she moved on. They'd passed five tables and the woman had yet to place a bid, even though her lingering glances and sighs said she wanted to.

He strode to her side and placed a hand on the small of her back. Pleasure filled him as she leaned into his hand.

"Not seeing anything you want to try to win?"

She sighed. "No, the opposite. So many things I would love to have."

"Bid on something. The chamber members are expected to at least bid on a few items."

Her breath caught on a gasp. "What if I win? I can't—I can't afford these amounts."

He leaned close and whispered. "The bookstore is doing okay, isn't it?"

"Of course. But that's my mom and dad's money."

He placed a hand on her shoulder and turned her toward him. "Cassie, that is your money now. You are Stone Books. Even if that wasn't true, surely a New York Times bestseller can afford a few trinkets from the hometown businesses."

Her laugh and smile seemed false and he didn't know why. His cop instincts said something was off, but his friend instincts screamed to pull back. He let the friend win.

"Of course. What's a few hundred dollars?" Her words said it was a small thing, but her pale face said something different.

He followed along as she put her name and bid on several sheets. It wasn't hard to note she only bid on useful things like housecleaning services and meal-delivery services. The one frivolous thing was the vacation in the Napa Valley.

A quick glance showed her bid had no hope of winning a trip for four days to Napa and a ride on the Wine Train. As Cassie moved to another table, Ben wrote his name on the line below hers for four times the bid and easily double the value of the trip.

He joined her at the last table, the one for Stone Books. A giant basket sat on the table displaying classic books. Cassie straightened the big, red bow.

"Mrs. Miller did an amazing job, didn't she? I don't think there is anything the woman can't do. My dad was lucky to have her manage the store. I'm lucky she's willing to stay."

"Lisa and Todd, her husband, used to be summer people."

She grimaced. He had to agree. The locals didn't always look upon the summer influx as a good thing, other than the revenue it brought to the town.

"The only good thing the big flood did was show some folks' true meddle," he said. "The vacation people took their losses and the insurance money and hit the road. Those who stayed and rebuilt, put down roots, and became members of our community. They are town people now."

"Was the flood that bad? I was on a European book tour at the time." She ducked her head, but he still saw her flushed cheeks.

"That sounded awful didn't it? I asked my dad if I should come home, but he said the house was fine. I didn't see any damage."

The lights flickered on and off and then dimmed to a rosy tint again. The people around them meandered back to the dinner tables. She slipped her hand around his arm and strolled with him across the room.

"Todd and Lisa Miller, there? They were in their house, even though it was off-season. It had to be gutted to the frame and rebuilt. Todd and Lisa almost died when the dam went. A few others weren't so lucky. Nine people died that day."

Cassie stumbled. Ben pulled her in close against his side.

"I didn't know. Dad and Mom never said anything."

He grasped the hand on his arm. "Why would they? You were off in Europe and your parents were fine. The flood didn't reach the downtown, so all the businesses were fine, too."

After he pulled out her seat, Cassie sat. "Still, they should have said something."

He took her hand again and smiled as her fingers wrapped around his. "What, and worry you half a world away? That doesn't sound like Leo Stone to me."

Cassie warmed at Ben's words of comfort about her father. She could never have imagined sitting here with Ben Bridges talking to her, holding her hand, and looking at her as if he wouldn't mind doing more than just holding hands. Her thoughts had warmth spreading through her body. She tingled everywhere their bodies touched.

All the wonderful thoughts in the world couldn't completely tear her away from other not-so-wonderful thoughts. Dealing with her mother's illness was the least of her worries. And how sad was that?

I love my dad. He had been a shirt-off-his-back kind of guy. That made him great to those he helped, not so much for those depending on him. She bit her lip. It wasn't totally her father's fault.

A week of dealing with the other members of the Chamber of Commerce had been an eye-opener. Lake Willowbee was dying. They were all banking on the book festival being an overwhelming success. Her heart skipped a beat. They were all banking on her being a success, and she was all too aware — she was anything but.

As if he could read her mind, Ben took her hand and pulled her gently from her seat. "All your problems won't be settled tonight.

Dance. Have fun. Everything will still be there tomorrow."

Taking him at his word, Cassie savored every moment in his arms until the music stopped, the lights brightened, and the magical evening was over.

Fifteen

The drive back to the lake and her home passed in a comfortable silence. Fresh air, smelling of green things growing, and the scent of the lake wafted in her open window.

Fingers trailed over the side of her face and pushed her wind-tangled hair over her ear. "You look like a sunset-sky on fire."

She laughed as she gazed into his serious face. "That is the nicest thing I've ever heard about my not brown, not red, hair."

He took her hand and held it between them on the console as they pulled up the gravel driveway. He turned off the engine and all she heard was the chirping of crickets and the distant cries of bats roaming the nighttime skies.

"I should get in, so Abigail can get home."

"Of course," he said.

His hand moved away to open the door and she felt its absence instantly. The thought of turning back into a pumpkin at midnight seemed all too near.

She was dragged from her thoughts by the opening car door, and Ben's hands reaching for her. A slight tug on his part and a few steps on hers and she was flush against him. His hands reached and cupped her face.

The heat of his body enveloped her. She couldn't catch her breath and she didn't care. She'd wanted this moment since she was eighteen years old. Her hands gripped his arms and she held on as his lips found hers.

He tasted of the chocolate from dessert and so much more. The kiss deepened, and a moan escaped her. Her body pressed up against his and a moan sounded from deep in Ben's throat.

The sound echoed and stirred desire deep within her.

She wasn't an innocent. There had been several men over the years, but none of them stirred her the way Ben Bridges could, with just a kiss.

When they finally caught their breath, Cassie whispered, "Abigail."

"Right, Abigail," he muttered.

He gave her another quick kiss and wrapped an arm around her. Staying glued to his side, they reached the front door.

"Thank you for a wonderful evening," she whispered, raising up on tiptoe and giving him another kiss.

"Thank you," he whispered in that deep, husky voice that sent shivers down her spine and hot blood thrumming through her veins.

Cassie stood on the porch until Ben's car disappeared down the driveway with the crunch of gravel.

Opening the door, she spotted her mother and Abigail in the kitchen.

"Did you have fun?" the young woman asked as she poured hot water into tea mugs on the counter.

Her mother jumped off the barstool and rushed to her side before she could get a word out.

"That is my dress," she screeched.

Her fingers curved into a hook and grabbed the bodice of the dress. Cassie's hands flew up, but she couldn't stop her mom before the ripping of silk filled her ears.

Abigail rushed over, but it took both of them to untangle Molly from the tattered pieces of the dress. By the time they were done, Cassie and her mom were in tears.

"I'm sorry. I'm so sorry," Molly whined as Abigail got the older woman off the floor and headed down the hall.

Cassie sat there in a daze. Her fingers shook as she gathered the pieces of the beautiful dress. There was no saving it, it was gone. It took carrying the pieces to the garbage can in the kitchen to realize she was standing there in just her bra, panties, and high-heel shoes.

Abigail came back into the kitchen. "Let me look at that," she said, glancing at Cassie's chest.

She looked down and saw the line of blood running down her cleavage. "It's nothing, a scratch."

The young woman put the first-aid kit on the counter and moved Cassie's hand aside. "I'll be the judge of that."

She stared off into space as she allowed the woman to clean up the gouge and put ointment on it.

"It's not so bad," Abigail added, cleaning up the papers and putting the first-aid kit back in order. "If you let it air out tonight, it should be fine in the morning."

"At least something will be fine," she muttered, on the edge of tears.

Abigail took her hand. "These moments are going to happen, but they are just moments. One incident doesn't define a whole evening, or day, or lifetime."

Cassie felt a smile slowly stretch her cheeks. "You are too young to be so wise."

Abigail shook her head. "No, just seen a lot in a short time."

A shiver ran down her spine and reminded her she was standing there in next to nothing.

Abigail reached over to a barstool and handed Cassie a robe. "I grabbed it on my way back out here."

She wrapped the fluffy yellow material around her and belted it tight. "Thank you. Will my mom be okay?"

The young woman nodded. "I got one of the pills down her that the doctor gave you. She should be out for the night. I'm sorry I didn't grab her sooner."

A sigh escaped her. "It isn't your fault. I just don't know how to prepare for what might set her off."

Abigail stepped in and enveloped Cassie in a hug. "You can't prepare. Alzheimer's sucks."

She breathed out deeply. "Alzheimer's sucks."

The care provider gathered up her stuff and headed to the front door. "Get a good night's sleep. I can't be here until after lunch tomorrow."

"I'll handle it," Cassie reassured her as Abigail left and shut the door behind her.

It only took a few minutes to tidy up the kitchen and lock all the doors. A quick glance in her mother's room showed Molly sound asleep and snoring away. Cassie found her own room and bed, but sleep eluded her as the weight of her responsibilities pressed her into the mattress.

In the past, she would have gotten up and wrote until her mind cleared and she could sleep. But even that had been denied her. Mrs. Pumpernickel and her cat, Sassy had been abundantly clear. They were not coming out to play. They were not talking to her.

Sixteen

"Ben, this isn't going to work. I'm never going to bring in the numbers this event needs."

He started pawing through the papers on his desk. Amid the chaos, he remained calm and cool. Seeing him as Mayor Bridges was a surreal experience for Cassie. His dark suit and maroon tie had him looking official and sexy hot at the same time.

"Where is the press release Lisa Miller did?" He came up with a sheet of paper and a smile on his face.

"How can you say that, Cassie?" He started reading. "New York Times #1 bestseller with eight titles. More than five million copies sold worldwide. Available in more than one hundred countries and in twelve different languages. You're a star."

She shoved her chair back and paced the carpeted floor. "You don't understand, Ben. Those are just statistics. They look good on a press release. You're only as good as your last book. Readers can forget about you so quickly. They move onto the next book, the next author."

Cassie watched with dread as his finger scrolled down the page with her list of books. His frown told her he'd reached the end.

"I don't understand. Your last book was more than two years ago. I don't know publishing, but isn't that a long time without a new release?"

She swiped the angry tears off her face. "Not only no new release. No new words. I haven't written a word, a sentence, anything, in two years."

He dropped the paper on his desk, pushed back his own chair, and rushed to her side. His hands cupped her elbows and stopped her frantic pacing.

She swallowed past the lump in her throat. He needed to know the whole truth. "My agent has dropped me. My publisher has dropped me. I'm not a success. I'm nothing."

"Cassie, don't ever say that." His voice cracked.

She stared up at him, taking in the tightened jaw and angry eyes.

"You could never write another word and you are still a success. How many people say they are going to write a book and never do? How many write one or two and fade away? How many writers get to the bestsellers lists?

"You've lived the dream, Cassie," he continued, his hand coming up to wipe tears from her cheeks. "You've made millions."

"I've lost millions," she whispered.

It all clicked together as Ben caught her whisper. The rental car instead of the flashy sports car she visited in before. The comment about money for the auction. This woman had not had the easy time he'd imagined. Now, she'd lost her father, was losing her mother to a vile disease, and the town was putting its continued existence on her shoulders.

"We can do this," he said, giving her a smile and a kiss on her cheek.

"We?" she whispered, her glance unsure and troubled.

He helped her to her seat and took his own. His hands steepled and he stared at Cassie. He grabbed a pad of paper and a pen.

"Do you remember this town when we were kids? The summer visitors, the big events all summer long, the book festival being the biggest and the brightest at summer's end?"

She nodded, a smile growing on her face. "There was so much to do you didn't want to go to bed because you might miss something. Each day was something new and wonderful."

Cassie leaned forward and put her hands on the edge of his desk. "What happened, Ben?"

"I'll tell you what happened. This town got complacent.

They expected the book festival to be enough. To bring in enough people and money for everyone with your father doing most of the heavy lifting."

She sighed and leaned back in her chair. "We can't turn everything around overnight."

"No, you're right. But we can make this the biggest festival we've had in years."

"I told you. I'm not a big enough draw to bring in record crowds."

Suddenly, she sat up, a giant smile on her face. "I'm not. But I know lots of authors who are. The writing world is about connections, networking. I can contact a few friends and have them tell a few friends. Let's see how high up the chain we can go."

"There's that smile I remember."

"What smile?" she muttered, yanking the pen and paper off his desk and writing.

"The one peeking out from behind the ever-present notebook you were scribbling in. The one you had when you got the big publishing deal and left Lake Willowbee."

"This is better. Helping this town will last a lot longer than some publishing deal." She turned the paper around to face him. "And we can start with these five names."

His eyebrows rose at the name on the top of her list. "No way."

"Yes, way. We used to date. He'll do anything for me."

He slouched back into his seat. Not sure how he felt about meeting someone Cassie had dated, he quickly changed the subject. "Will they come on such short notice? We're talking about a few weeks."

She nibbled her lip. "Maybe not all of them, but enough. We won't know until we ask."

"So, do we contact their agents, or publishers, or something?"

She shook her head. "Nope. I'm going to call them personally. I'm going to call in every favor they owe me.

"If I don't know them personally, I'll find a friend who does. Or a friend of a friend. Or maybe the sister of a friend."

"Who else, do you think?" He grabbed the pad, prepared to continue her list.

"How about Lora Robins?"

Her mischievous grin set his heart to racing and wishing they weren't in his very public office, because he'd like to kiss that grin right now.

"You don't know Lora Robins personally, do you?" He didn't read the genre, but everyone recognized the name of the worldwide, top writer of suspense thrillers. Her books filled three to four shelves at any bookstore and greeted passengers at all the major airports.

She smiled at him, her eyes sparkling. "I was the maid of honor at her wedding five years ago."

His jaw gaped open, but he wrote the name down. He was beginning to believe they could make this happen.

Seventeen

Cassie tried to breathe shallow, stopping the hospital's antiseptic smell from clogging her brain. She smiled as she added checkmarks to the list of writers who'd agreed to come to the book festival. A few names were crossed out, but most of them had seemed thrilled to come.

When her downward spiral had hit the city newspapers, and then her scandal hit the tabloids, she'd thought her friends had abandoned her. Looking back now, from a safe distance, she could see where she'd pushed them away. It wasn't a time she was proud of, but she'd come through it.

Turning her mind away from waiting for her mother's appointment to be done and looking back on a bleak time in her life, Cassie called Lora Robins. She crossed her fingers as the phone rang in her ear.

"Hello?"

"Lora Robins, please. This is Cassie Stone calling."

"Oh, Cassie," a voice gushed. "Lora has been expecting your call."

Expecting my call? What?

"Cassie, darling. You, naughty girl. Why didn't you call me sooner? This is about the event in your hometown, isn't it?"

Tears welled up in her eyes. Lora's voice might sound like a movie star from Hollywood's Golden Age, but she was the most down-to-earth person she knew. When you heard her voice, you expected champagne for breakfast and a feather boa. Most times you got jeans and a T-shirt and a backyard barbecue.

"Would I sound terrible if I said I wanted some practice before I called you?"

"Yes, you would. But I love you anyway."

"How did you find out about the event?"

"Cassie, dear. Your event is the talk of the town. I've heard from dozens of people this morning. Some excited you called them, and some upset you haven't called."

She gasped. She didn't know what to say. "I thought after the mess I made, no one would want to talk to me."

"What mess?" Lora laughed in her deep, husky voice. "This town loves scandal. You were old news by the time you left town. Did you think you were the first woman to throw a glass of champagne in Burt Grumbly's face?"

"And knee him in the privates," she whispered into the phone, glancing around the empty room. "With a photographer taking his picture, no less."

"After what he did to Suzy Smith, I think you didn't hit him hard enough."

"What happened to Suzy?"

"Don't they read the newspaper in that little hometown of yours? He raped her. The man is in jail, awaiting a court hearing. His publisher dropped him like the scum he is, and his books were ripped off the bookshelves around the country. I don't agree with book-burnings, but in his case, I might make an exception."

She'd heard none of this. Granted, she'd been avoiding her old world since she'd returned, but she would have reached out to Suzy, if she'd known. The world-renowned children's author of The Adventures of Sammy Bootlebutt was a tiny pixie in pink minus the wings, with a heart bigger than herself.

Cassie didn't know whether to cry or throw the phone across the room. She should have called Lora ages ago, if only for the no-nonsense way she cleared everything up and made her see the big picture.

"So, you'll come?"

"Of course, I will. I wouldn't miss seeing your town." A silent pause filled the phone until Cassie opened her mouth to speak. Lora beat her to it. "Or seeing you."

She cleared her throat. "Can you do me a favor?"

"Anything, kiddo."

"Can you have your assistant contact those people you said were upset I didn't invite them? The more people we have, the better."

"I'll call them back myself. No one says no to Lora Robins." Her laugh brought a giant smile to Cassie's face. The woman got the biggest laugh out of her celebrity status and the fear it caused, only to those who didn't know Lora at well.

"Thank you so much."

"I'll see you soon, Cassie."

She pressed the end button and dropped the phone on her lap. Grabbing her red pen, she circled Lora's name half a dozen times. Her friend was bigger than life and would bring in hundreds, if not thousands, of fans to the festival.

Turning some blank pages over, Cassie started making notes. She had to call Suzy tonight. She had a long to-do list, but a call to her friend would be item number one.

Her pen moved down the list. They would need to get the publicity out as soon as possible. Fans couldn't come if they didn't know who would be at the festival.

A scrub-wearing nurse stepped up to her. "Miss Stone? Your mother is going to be a little longer. The doctor is waiting for the test results before he calls you back."

"Thanks."

She started doodling on the paper as the nurse walked back to the office on the other side of the wall.

> *Mrs. Pumpernickel sat impatiently in the vet's office. Sassy lay curled up in a ball on her lap, purring away like she was so innocent. Her plump tummy said otherwise. Sassy, the orange tabby, had gotten herself knocked up.*
>
> *Her sensible shoes tapped on the linoleum floor, but Sassy continued to sleep as if she'd done nothing wrong. One hand petted the cat, while the other worried at her beaded necklace. The cat wasn't the only one acting like she was innocent. So was Miss Harriette Peach, the prime suspect in little Fanny Button's kidnapping.*

"The doctor can see you now," a voice called across the room. The nurse stood in the open doorway.

"Thank you," Cassie muttered as she blinked her eyes and saw the words on the page. She sniffled and willed the tears back into her head. Two years — not a word. Everything on her plate right now and the writing bug decided to return. Someone up there had a wicked sense of humor.

She waited for the nurse to turn away and gave the page a fast kiss before stuffing the pad into her purse. Following the woman down the hall, she entered the doctor's office to find her mother already there, sitting in a chair in front of the desk.

Seeing the doctor's friendly, smiling face, Cassie took the other seat. The door shut behind her with a whisper.

"All of your mother's tests have come back the same as the last testing. I'm very pleased with that."

Her brow furrowed. "Why is that a good thing?"

"Her condition has not worsened. I'm hopeful it will stabilize at this point. At least, for a while. I would like to put your mother on Cetipal. We are seeing excellent results with it. In some cases, a slight improvement to the Alzheimer's symptoms."

"You mean I could get better?" her mother asked.

His gaze swung between them. "Not better, per se. But a marked decrease in the speed of the spread of the disease. In almost all the cases, the patient has stayed steady for twelve to eighteen months."

She gulped. It wasn't an instant cure-all, but it was hope. Sometimes hope was all you had, as Mrs. Pumpernickel said.

Eighteen

"Mrs. Johnson, thank you for coming on such short notice," Cassie whispered to the older woman at the door. "Abigail had a class she couldn't miss. She is here all day long, I just couldn't say no."

Amelia walked in and waved at Molly. Her mom seemed happy to see the woman. No one would know she'd been in a tantrum an hour ago. Cassie had tried to explain that Abby wouldn't be there tonight, but her mother had pouted and thrown a fit like a two-year-old over not getting their favorite toy.

The older woman patted her large sack hanging from her arm. "Don't worry about it. I have all the makings for cookies. Let me get started and you can slip away."

As soon as Molly turned her back to pour the ingredients into the bowl, Cassie grabbed her purse and went out the door. She shut it quietly behind her and rushed to her car. The city council meeting was starting in thirty minutes and Ben had asked her to not be late.

Yanking her keys out of her purse, she made sure her notes were tucked inside. With a reassured sigh, she turned on the car and headed down the driveway. Thankfully, the drive was too short to have time to worry about the meeting. Like most writers, she was a major introvert and public speaking was higher on a stress level than facing a firing squad. She'd said more than once; a firing squad would be preferable.

She slammed on her brakes at the city hall. The parking lot was full, with both sides of the street crammed with cars. Several groups of people hurried to the building. A cold sweat broke out down her spine.

Her fingers latched onto the steering wheel. All she wanted to do was turn around, go back home, and hide under her covers. *Was it too late to go home and make cookies with Amelia and her mom?*

"No more retreating," she told herself. "You can do this."

A car pulled out of a spot after dropping off a group of ladies. Cassie whipped her car into the spot and grabbed her purse. The high temperature of the day lingered and rose from the asphalt street in waves of heat. Once inside the old brick building, Cassie paused at the roar of voices from down the hall. A glance at her phone showed she had no time to lose. The meeting was scheduled to start any minute.

Pulling open the door, Cassie stepped inside. The room hummed with sound. There wasn't an empty seat to be had. People stood two and three deep, lining the walls. At the front of the room, Ben sat with the rest of the city council. His gentle smile and bright-blue tie drew her forward.

A young man stepped up to her. "Miss Stone?"

"Yes?"

"There's a seat up front for you," he said, leading the way to the front row.

Cassie swallowed and wished for a big glass of cold water. Her mouth felt like the Sahara Desert. Her nerves rose a thousand times higher as they reached the front row and the man directed her to a chair with her name on a sheet of paper taped to it.

Ben's voice filled the room from his microphone. "Let's get started. We all know why we are here. In six weeks, we need to host the biggest Stone Book Festival this city has ever seen. Here to help us is Cassie Stone. For those of you who don't know her, Cassie is the daughter of Leo and Molly Stone."

She walked up to the podium, glad of her pants hiding her knocking knees. "Thank you, Mayor Bridges." Her gaze swept the group at the front of the room. "And members of the city council."

Before she could continue, a voice rang out from the back of the room.

"We don't need her help. She isn't a part of this community."

Cassie whipped around and spotted the owner of the voice. An older woman, red in the face, glared at her.

She gripped her hands together in front of her. Mumbled voices echoed around the room. They seemed to be half for her and half against. Cassie hated confrontation with a passion, but even more, she hated being told what she wasn't.

"I am a member of this community. I was born and raised here. I may have been away for a while, but my mother and my father are and were a big part of Lake Willowbee." She glared back at the woman. "You don't need my help. I want to help."

Turning back around, she faced the council. "I want to help," she repeated.

Ben called for silence in the room. He smiled at Cassie. "Please, continue."

"We have six weeks to make this year's festival the biggest and the brightest this town has ever seen. And we can't do it."

A gasp echoed through the room. Cassie smiled as she turned. "We can't do it, without all of you. This isn't the Stone Book Festival. It is the Lake Willowbee Book Festival. Who knows who Mick Queen is?"

Almost the whole room raised their hands. "How about Jimmy Addison?" At the name of the most prolific writer on the planet, all the hands went up.

"They have both agreed to come to the festival." The level of noise rose in the room as they all looked to their neighbors with smiles on their faces and animation in their voices.

"More than two hundred other authors have agreed to come this summer to Lake Willowbee. Among them, my friends, Lora Robins and Suzy Smith."

The names of the best-known suspense writer of this century and the most-beloved children's author drew cheers and claps from the crowd. Cassie turned back to the council. "But, here is the hard part."

The council members smiled and looked to Ben. "I'm pretty sure I speak for the council when I say I think the hard part was getting all those big-name writers here," he said.

"Oh, no," she said with a smile. "The hard part *is* ... where do we put them all."

Nineteen

*B*en's smile died. *Where were they going to put all those people? Their entourages? The fans?*

He glanced at Cassie and her enormous smile. The woman had a plan for that, too. He could see it in her sparkling eyes and rosy cheeks.

She turned back around and started talking to the crowd. "This is where you all come in. You know from past years every hotel, motel, bed & breakfast will be full up for the festival. So where do we put all those writers? We build them a writer's retreat. Down the road from my parents' house is where the old Lake Willowbee Inn stood. The flood wiped it out and the Anderson's never rebuilt. It sits on fifty acres of beautiful Sierra forest.

"I spoke with Mrs. Anderson this week. If the land is used for the festival, the town can have it for one dollar a year. We will be responsible for upkeep, but it's ours to use."

"That's all fine, Miss Stone. But it is still only an empty plot of land," Mrs. Carrington said from the end of the table. "We can't build an inn in six weeks."

Erica Carrington had been a pain in his side since he'd become mayor. Everyone in town knew she'd wanted the job. She made no bones about the fact she was running against him in the next election.

Cassie turned around and faced the woman. "That is where the town comes in. We borrow every motor home and trailer we can get our hands on. If we all work together, we can have a writer's encampment in plenty of time for this year's festival and have all year to work on logistics for the next festival. Give a writer a bed and a place to plug in their computers and they are happy campers, as the saying goes."

"I guess that could work," Erica said with a pout on her face.

He'd wager his mayoral pay, small as it was, the woman would have herself in the middle of the planning committee for next year.

Miss Pippins spoke up. The elderly woman had been on the city council for decades. Her large, snow-white bun bobbed as she nodded at Cassie. "That takes care of the writers, but how do we get the word out. Even with thousands of flyers, we can only cover the nearest towns. The festival doesn't have the money for those fancy ads you had in New York City."

"Miss Pippins, you are absolutely right," she said in a gentle tone, looking at the elderly woman directly. "We don't need those fancy ads. We have something better."

Cassie turned her head to the left and the right. "We have a youth movement. I'm pretty sure the kids and young adults of this community are like their peers anywhere. Living on the internet. Chatpop, Fastagram, Chirp, and the other social media sites. We make them part of this event. Part of this town and community. In the publishing world, there is nothing; no ads, no publicity, like word of mouth. We do the same for the book festival. We spread the news, far and wide, as fast as possible."

"Thank you, Miss Stone," Ben said, watching as Cassie took her seat.

The room rumbled with murmurs and excitement. He looked to the council members at the table. He received enthusiastic nods down the line.

"Is the board in agreement to go with the suggestions made here tonight by Miss Stone?"

Miss Pippins raised her hand. "Only if Cassie Stone is in charge of the festival."

Ben watched as Cassie sat up straight with what could only be panic on her face. He spoke into his microphone. "Miss Pippins, that is a large undertaking for one person. I'm not even sure the usual committee of seven will be big enough for what this festival is shaping up to become."

The elderly woman sat up to speak again, but Ben forestalled her. "Perhaps we should take this into chambers?"

The council agreed, and he called a short recess. "We'll be back in fifteen minutes, people."

Cassie sat shaking in her seat. How did trying to help end with them wanting her to lead the thing? Sure, she'd made a few phone calls, but that wasn't anything close to running an event of this magnitude. Just like thinking up a new story. The initial idea was easy. The endless possibilities of what if? lay in front of her. Nothing was set in stone. She could change her mind. She could ditch the whole story if it didn't work. But the festival? They depended on the book festival to save the town.

She shuddered. Running away again sounded better every minute the council was meeting behind closed doors. Taking a deep breath, she closed her eyes and pictured Ben's face. He believed in her. If he thought she could do this, maybe she could.

Someone touched her shoulder. The angry woman from earlier stood beside her seat. "I should have known you would think of something. You are Leo's daughter, after all."

Her mouth moved, but words refused to come. She managed a 'thank you' as the door in front opened, the council took their seats, and the crowd quieted.

Ben reached over and flipped on his microphone. "Miss Stone, if you could come up to the podium?"

She walked over and placed her hands on the wooden surface. Amazingly, they didn't shake.

"The council has taken your suggestions into consideration and we are all agreed, as long as you are willing to spearhead the event, everything you noted will be put into motion. Immediately."

She didn't know whether to laugh or cry, and finally settled for a weak smile. "Thank you to the council members. I can—no, we can, do this."

Twenty

The days passed in a kaleidoscope of overwhelming heat and backbreaking hard work. The only thing that kept Cassie going was Ben at her side and Abigail being there all day with her mother. Molly sat in a chair in the corner, staring off into space as she stepped outside with their care angel.

"You don't look so good, Cassie. Do you need me to stay tonight? I can put off my finals until next week."

Cassie wrapped Abby in a hug. "Don't you dare. I'm not going to be responsible for you not finishing your class. You are here all-day long. I can handle the nights. Mom is asleep by the time the sun goes down. I'll be fine."

Her long, heavy yawn belied her confident tone. "Ignore that. It's just the heat. Took some begging, borrowing, and no-stealing, but we have enough trailers and motor homes out at the old Lake Willowbee Inn site for our author guests to lie their heads. Ben is even getting internet set up out there."

Abby laughed. "Can't have online withdrawals, can we?"

"Hey," Cassie said with a laugh. "They might have to do research on poisons or old legends or how to make a proper cup of tea."

She continued to smile as Abby got into her car and headed down the driveway. The smile died as fatigue caught up to her. Gazing at the setting sun, she knew a giant cup of coffee was in her near future. The elixir of writers everywhere.

Going back inside, she spotted her mother crying in her chair. She rushed over, sinking to her haunches at her mom's knees. "What's wrong?"

"I want to go home."

"Mom, you are home." She sighed. This happened every night. As if the encroaching darkness brought out childhood fears. The pills seemed to be helping during the days, but it was as if they wore off as the hours passed.

"Are you ready for bed?"

Her mom's mood perked up and she smiled. "That would be nice, dear."

Molly Stone was only in her fifties. Why did she sound like a little old lady, already? This disease stole everything. Memories, dreams, enough years to live a full life. It sucked.

Tucking her mom into her bed, the woman looked at her like a child at Christmas.

"I want my book."

Cassie reached over and pulled the binder off the shelf and opened it across her mom's lap. Abigail had made the book of photographs for Molly. Their family was in there.

The first one was a young Leo and Molly with baby, Cassie. She pointed to each face.

"Who is this?"

"That's me," her mother said with a smile. "And Leo. He was so handsome there. All that thick, dark hair."

She looked up at Cassie. "Just like yours."

Turning the page, a black-and-white photo filled the plastic protector. "What is this?"

"That's the bookstore your grandparents started. Then they gave it to Leo and me when we married."

"That's right." Cassie turned another page.

"Who's this?"

Her mother's face wrinkled up as her brow furrowed and her eyes stared until they watered, as if by sight alone she could figure out the puzzle through the fog her memories had become. "I don't know. Why don't I know?"

"It's okay, mom." She patted Molly's hand. "That's your parents. Jack and Ruby. The baby is you."

"I was a fat baby." She pouted.

Cassie laughed. "All babies are fat, Mom."

"Why don't you have a baby?"

She choked on her laugh. "I think I need a husband first."

"You don't need a husband. You just need a man."

"Mom," she cried out, her face burning.

"What about Ben? He seems like a hottie."

"Okay, Mom. That's enough. Definitely time for bed."

"Oh, dear. You do know where babies come from, don't you?"

She put the binder back on the shelf and smoothed the covers over her mother. "Yes, Mom. We had this lovely discussion many years ago."

"Oh, good," her mother murmured, her eyes closing. "I would hate to think you didn't know how to make babies with that hottie, Ben."

"Great," she muttered as she headed to the kitchen for coffee. "Now I'll have that image in my mind all night and I don't even write romance novels."

Once her coffee was full of the cream and sugar she craved, Cassie made her way to her room. Her desk overflowed with notes and index cards. She had a dozen calls to make tonight and a list full of people to check in with for the festival.

Her latest call to Suzy ended on a happy note. Her friend was doing much better and looking forward to the festival. That scum, Burt, was in jail and not getting out anytime soon. His assets were being seized by his publisher and no new money was coming in. He would sit in jail until the trial.

The rest of the calls went fast as she checked in with the chairperson in charge of each facet of the festival. Her next-to-last call was to Lisa Miller to make sure the bookstore was getting all the orders for books for the authors to sign.

"Just a couple more and we'll be set. Mick Queen's publisher called and said he has a new book releasing in a couple of weeks, but they will send an order if we agree to hold them until the festival."

"Cool. We can do that. I didn't know Mick had a new book coming out."

"Is it true?"

"Is what true?" Cassie asked.

"You dated Mick Queen."

"Did Ben tell you?"

"He might have mentioned it. I think he is a little jealous."

Her mouth dropped open. Now all those comments from her mother about making babies rushed to the front of her brain. She needed to wrap this up or she would get nothing else done tonight.

Or start writing a romance novel starring Ben as the hero, a role he could play no problem at all.

Her friend, Lora, had told her being a writer was a curse. The voices in your head never shut up for long, and if they did, you begged them to come back. Now, on top of everything else she had to do, Mrs. Pumpernickel and that stupid cat, Sassy, were begging for their next adventure to be told.

Cassie traded a few more banal comments and ended the call. Her mind skipped to thoughts of storytelling and plotting and different scenarios for how Mrs. Pumpernickel and Sassy could solve the kidnapping of little Fanny Buttons.

After the last call where she almost called Miss Pippins, Mrs. Pumpernickel, Cassie grabbed the kitchen timer and wrote for an hour and worked on the festival for an hour. She called people first, until it was too late to call them.

Ben had told her to phone him anytime, so at ten she called to update him on progress. His rich, deep voice filled her mind and set her blood to tingling through her body. He wasn't in the room with her, but she could see his dark, flashing eyes and his smile that lit up his whole face. The idea of him being jealous added another layer to the conversation. One she didn't broach but enjoyed holding secret inside.

She could have stayed on the phone for hours with him, but the dinging timer let her know she had a dozen more things to do tonight.

"What was that?" he laughed.

"Time's up," she said, laughing with him.

"Okay, I'll let you go. Don't stay up all night."

"I won't."

"Yeah, right."

"Night."

She pressed the end button and placed the phone on her desk. A glance at her clock and her list for the night showed her she needed one more cup of coffee. Back at her desk, Cassie fell into the cozy mystery world of Mrs. Pumpernickel until the timer dinged.

Her eyes drooped as the timer ticked in a monotonous tone. She checked off the last item on the list for the night and glanced up to see the sky turn from black to predawn gray.

Just one more thing, she promised herself as her chin fell to her chest and the pen slipped from her hand.

Twenty-One

The whiff of smoke tickled Cassie's nose as she stirred from sleep.

"Mom, did you burn the pancakes again?" she mumbled.

She sat up and cried out as her neck wrenched to the side. Sunlight filtered through the window. No smoke filled the room. Had she imagined it? A glowing brightness filled the window as she glanced at the clock. Six o'clock was too early for the overwhelming light from outside.

Cassie jumped out of the chair, tipping it over in her rush to the door.

"Mom," she yelled as she ran down the hall to her mother's room.

The taint of smoke and ash set her to coughing. She covered her nose and mouth as she scanned the empty bed. Rushing to the bathroom didn't turn up her mom either.

Frantic, she ran from room to room, calling for her mother. Smoke wafted into the living room from the open sliding glass door. She pelted onto the wooden deck, screaming into the gray-tinged clouds of smoke enveloping their home.

From the time she was a little girl, her parents had warned of the dangers of wildfires in their foothill community. Every year, dozens of homes and thousands of acres were lost to the ravenous flames.

The wind picked up, carrying the billows of smoke and the welcome sound of sirens. The sirens grew nearer as Cassie ran around the perimeter of their yard searching for her mother. The pall of smoke thickened until she couldn't see five feet in front of her.

A shape appeared through the dense smoke. It materialized into a firefighter.

"Ma'am," he said. "Anyone else inside?"

"I can't find my mom. She has Alzheimer's. I can't find her anywhere." She knew she was rambling, but she had to find her.

"Come out to the truck. Maybe one of my crew has found her."

She crossed her fingers and sent a prayer heavenward. They had to find her. She couldn't lose her mom. Not yet.

"Mom." Her voice cracked as she ran to the ambulance and fell to the ground beside a blanket-wrapped Molly. An EMT was putting ointment on her burned hands and wrapping them with gauze.

Her mother stared into space and mumbled to herself. "I'm sorry. I'm sorry. I'm sorry."

"Mom," she whispered. "What did you do?"

"I didn't do anything." Her gaze skittered away, unable to meet Cassie eye-to-eye. "Leo did it."

She put her hand on her mother's shoulder. "What did Leo do?" She had to ask, although she was sure she knew the answer before the words came out of her mother's mouth.

"Leo wanted to make s'mores down by the lake."

"Ma'am," the firefighter interrupted. "Should we be looking for someone else? The guys didn't see anyone but the old lady here."

Cassie looked up at the tall firefighter, tears blurring her vision. "Leo is my father. He passed away weeks ago."

The man said something before he moved away, but she missed it as her mother huddled into a ball and cried until she dry-heaved. Cassie rubbed her mom's back and fought to breathe without inhaling the soot in the air.

"Cassie," a voice yelled from the side of the ambulance.

"Over here," she called back, recognizing Ben's voice instantly.

His gaze swept over them both. "Thank God. I got the report over the radio and I came as fast as I could."

"We're fine," she said, taking in his uniform. *Was he here as her friend or as the police chief, coming to take in her mother?*

"She didn't mean to do it. It's my fault. I should have watched her better."

He squatted down in front of them. "Cassie, you can't think I'm here to arrest your mother. This was an accident. But, you must see you can't do this all alone. Molly needs more help than you can give her. She needs to be somewhere where she will be safe. Where others will be safe."

Cassie gasped, and her face heated with more than the high temperature of the day and the slowly fading fire. "A home, you mean."

"Don't say it like that, Cassie. There is a wonderful one a few miles up the mountain."

She stood, forcing him to as well. "You can't possibly understand. I'm watching the person I love fade away from me. Each day, she is a little more gone, until I'll be left with nothing."

Her anger faded like it had never been as she stared at Ben's white face and tight lips. Too late, she realized what she'd said.

"I'm s–"

"Don't. Just don't. I'm glad you and Molly are okay."

He turned and walked away.

She wrapped her arms around herself. How could she have said those things? The image of Ben's broken face would haunt her forever.

Dropping to the ground, she wrapped herself around her mother's frail shape. She wanted to ground her to this place and time, but her mother was slipping away right in front of her eyes.

"Cassie, I'm so sorry," Abigail panted out breathlessly as she rushed to fling herself around them. "I should have stayed."

Abby might be only a few years younger than Cassie, but in this moment, Cassie felt decades older. The young woman's red-rimmed eyes and wet cheeks made her appear barely adolescent.

"It's okay. I should have watched better. Locked the doors better. Something." Her voice trailed off as her brain circled around to a thought she didn't want to have.

Her gaze took in the blackened pilings of the dock and the

scorch marks up the side of the house. A shudder shot up her spine. She could have died. Her mother could have died.

Her heart broke. She was going to have to find a safe place for her mother to live. And it wasn't with Cassie.

Twenty-Two

Ben slapped the steering wheel with the palm of his hand. "Stupid idiot."

He should be the first to know you don't make decisions in the heat of the moment. Cassie was facing a life-changing moment, and he'd wanted her to make it sitting at the back of an ambulance, with her mother getting her burned hands taken care of.

Driving down Main Street, Ben spotted signs of the optimism Cassie had brought to Lake Willowbee. He waved at Mrs. Jackson, cleaning the windows at the antiques store, new merchandise laid out in colorful displays.

Lisa Miller stood in front of the bookstore as young men strung banners across the street proclaiming the Lake Willowbee Book Festival. He smiled and waved as he drove under the bright-blue banner.

Just one of the things Cassie had made happen. The festival was now the town's big event, not just the bookstore's. New paint sparkled on the diner and the cleaners and the hardware store. Downtown looked like a brand-new place. He hadn't seen it this lively and well-tended since he was a kid. All thanks to Cassie's drive and determination.

He swiped a hand over his sweaty forehead. All while dealing with her mother and all her other responsibilities. Wincing, he almost turned the patrol car around, but a call came over the radio.

He couldn't get the devastated look on her face out of his mind, but he had other duties as well.

"I'll go over tonight, after work," he told himself. Would give them both time to cool down and speak rationally. He hoped.

Like you thought rationally when they told you to let Renee go. Like you cooled down when you punched the car window and had to drive home without a window in the middle of December.

The squawk of the radio brought him back from a dismal past. He drove out to the writer's encampment, going slow as the firefighters finished cleaning up. He glanced at Cassie's house, but no one remained outside.

"Tonight," he promised himself.

Chaos reigned at the spot of the old Lake Willowbee Inn. Drivers were trying to get trailers and motor homes into the plotted spots without direction. Young men were stringing cable from tree to tree without checking height, and getting vehicles and people tangled in long, black wires.

He beeped his horn three long times and got out of the car. He had everyone's attention now. Miss Pippins trotted up to him, her winter-white legs exposed in shorts.

"Where's Cassie? No one will listen to a word I say." She huffed and put her hands on her amble hips.

"There was a fire at the Stone house this morning. We'll have to make do without her right now."

"Oh, dear," Miss Pippins muttered. "Is everyone okay? Is the town safe?"

He put his hands on her shoulders. "Everyone is fine. It didn't get far. It's already out and the fire trucks are headed back to the station."

In short order, Ben had the cable hangers directed, a deputy in charge of vehicle placement, and a sundry of other things cleared and taken care of.

Hours later, he heaved a heavy sigh and wondered, not for the first time, how Cassie accomplished so much, so fast.

Although, as he glanced around at the orderly rows of trailers and motor homes, the newly planted flowers around each plot, and the view through the pine trees to the lake, he thought they should all get a nice pat on the back.

Twenty-Three

Sierra Chateau
Alzheimer's Care Facility

bby, are you sure about this?" Cassie whispered as she gazed at the posh office. Walking into the place, they'd passed patients who looked as if they were at a day spa. The place reeked of privilege and seemed way more expensive than she could afford, even with the comfortable amount her father had left them.

"Oh, Miss Abigail, who have you brought us today."

Cassie looked up at the cultured, Southern voice. A statuesque blond stood in the open doorway. Her smile warmed her face as she came to their side and shook hands with Cassie and her mother.

She expected her to take a seat behind the spotless glass desk, but the woman pulled a chair over and sat beside them.

Abigail spoke up. "This is Cassie Stone and her mother, Molly. I've been helping with Mrs. Stone, but I think it is time for the Chateau."

A frown marred her perfect face as she took Molly's bandaged hand, gently in her own. "We've had a hard time, haven't we, Molly?"

"It was an accident." Her mother pouted and looked away.

"Of course, it was, dear." The woman said, glancing at Cassie.

"I'm Ms. Rose, the director of the Chateau, but everyone just calls me Clara."

"Well, Clara, I have to be honest," Cassie said. "This place is amazing, but I'm sure we can't afford it."

The woman looked at Abby and shook her head. "Abigail, didn't you tell them before you brought them here?"

She shook a finger at Abby like a schoolteacher and turned her gaze back to Molly and Cassie.

"Sierra Chateau is paid by the communities it serves and private donations. No patient pays a cent."

Her fingers shook as she raised them to her lips and her eyes misted over. She didn't know what to say. Everyone was making this so easy. Too easy. Shouldn't it be difficult to send her mother away?

As if she read her mind, Clara spoke up. "Just because there are no costs, doesn't make this any easier. It is a big decision to have a loved one stay here. Why don't we walk around, and you can see everything for yourself?"

Cassie was enchanted the more they saw. Clara didn't say a word, except to answer questions. She didn't need to. The place spoke for itself. From the physical therapy room that looked like an expensive day spa, to the dining room that wouldn't have been out of place in a five-star hotel.

When her mother spotted another woman playing with a doll, and rushed over, Cassie knew she'd found a safe place for her mom. Her heart broke when Molly looked up at her and said, "I like it here, can I stay?"

She felt better as Abby wrapped an arm around her shoulders. "You can do this, Cassie."

"Abigail, can you stay here with Molly while we take care of details?"

Abby nodded while Cassie let the woman drag her away back to the office.

"What if she doesn't like it here? She kept telling me she wanted to go home, and we were home."

"Miss Stone, Sierra Chateau has been doing this for more than twenty-five years and I've been here more than ten. Alzheimer's is a wicked disease, but we help our residents relax and feel comfortable here. And safe. I'm sure Abigail told you of our record or you wouldn't have come here today."

"Can I visit her?" she whispered.

"Of course," Clara said, reaching across her desk and patting Cassie's hand. "We have no set visiting hours. We have nothing to hide and family members can come anytime. You can spend the night on a couch in your mother's room if she is feeling unwell or you feel the need."

You did good, Cassie girl.

The tears came as her father's voice filled her brain. He'd known this day would come, he'd said as much in his will when he'd left everything to her, including her mother's care. She took a deep breath and slumped in the chair.

"Miss Stone, Cassie, this is harder for you than it will be for your mother. She will slip into a place where this is all she will remember. The friends she makes here. Her daily routine. You will have memories of the mother you had. Hold on to those."

"Thank you, Clara."

"No, thank you, Cassie, for trusting us with your precious mother."

She held it together through the paperwork, through getting her mother settled in a delightful, beautiful room. The walls were painted in a pale blue and the window looked out at a meadow capped by the majestic Sierras.

She held it together until they said good-bye and headed out to the car. Cassie slid in and spotted her mother's sweater cast over the seat. She snatched it up and her mother's floral scent wafted to her nostrils. Bringing it to her nose, Cassie breathed deeply, not noting the falling tears until she drenched the sweater.

She held it together until she broke.

Twenty-Four

Cassie grabbed her mother's sweater and got out of the car. Abigail had offered to be with her at home, but she knew she needed time alone to process everything. The idea of apologizing to Ben flirted with her mind, but she shoved it away. Her brain, heart, and body couldn't handle anything else today.

She dragged her feet to the front door, the heat of the day pounding into her head. Why did it feel like every decision she'd made in life was wrong? Opening the door, her breath caught at the silence.

This was a hundred times worse than when she'd come home a few weeks ago. The house would never be the same. The emptiness echoed and slammed into her.

She stifled her sob, an ache building in her chest. Half-shutting the door, she leaned against the wall and slid to the floor. Pressing the sweater to her nose, she cried until it settled down to hiccups.

Getting up off the floor took more energy than she had. In small increments, she grabbed the doorknob, pulled herself up, and pushed off to toddle down the hallway. She placed the sweater on her mom's bed, left, and shut the door.

Her head throbbed, stars swirling in the bright light. *When had she eaten last?* She couldn't remember. The fire. Abigail's call to Sierra Chateau. The packing of a suitcase. The drive there and back. It might have been last night. The idea of eating anything nauseated her. She roamed to her father's office and sat down at his desk.

Idly, she opened drawers and her fingers filtered through papers. A yellow envelope with her name on it caught her eye.

How had she missed this? She pulled it out of the drawer. Her father's fancy penmanship spelled out Cassie in large letters.

She placed it against her nose. The scent of her father's hand lotion wafted in the humid air. Her fingers shook as she opened it. Her vision blurred as the familiar handwriting filled the page.

> *My Cassie girl,*
>
> *If you are reading this, I fear I've passed away. I hope by now you realize how hard I tried to take care of you and your mother. I know you will take good care of my beloved Molly, my soulmate.*
>
> *I pray you will know that doesn't mean you have to do it all by yourself. Cassie, you and I are too much alike. Like me, I fear you will try to keep your mother at home, close to you. I've watched the woman I've known and loved for the past thirty-five years become someone I don't know anymore.*
>
> *If the worse comes to pass, I will have to place her somewhere that isn't home, and this letter will only be for me to clear my conscience. I almost wish I had the ability to do that, so you wouldn't have to, Cassie. But I haven't found the will yet. I pray if the time comes you will be able to do what is best for your mother and yourself.*
>
> *I know you will be strong. I know you will feel you didn't do the right thing. As I said, you and I are too alike.*
>
> *Be strong, my wonderful, loved child. Let us go and live your life.*
>
> *Love always, Dad*

The tear-stained paper fell onto the desk from her shaking fingers. Cassie covered her eyes.

"I can't take anymore today. Please, God. Let me be."

She shoved the chair back and strode over to the bookcases. Pulling books from the shelves she spotted the dusty bottle. Her father had thought she and mom didn't know it was there and they'd let him keep his little secret.

The bottle had a tiny bit missing. Leo would take a small shot whenever he had something to celebrate. A good month at the store. A great fishing day on the rare occasions he took a day off and sat out on the lake and relaxed.

She yanked the shot glass off the shelf as well and took them both back to the desk. Flinging herself into the chair, Cassie wiped the shot glass on her shirt and opened the bottle. Pouring the glass half-full, she raised her arm in a silent toast.

"Dad, maybe you should have taken more days off."

The anger in her voice startled her as she threw back her head and downed the drink. Leo had been fifty-nine and her mother only fifty-eight. Too soon to leave their only child. Why hadn't they taken better care of themselves?

After a couple more shots, Cassie moved from anger at her parents to anger at God, the fates, whoever was in charge.

"Why?" she screamed at the room.

The silent room had no reply. "Of course not. Just me and the shadows here."

By the time the amount in the bottle had gone down considerably, Cassie forgot what she'd been angry about. She tried to put the top back on, her fingers slipping and the cap falling to the desk with a metallic clatter.

"Screw it," she finally muttered, pushing the bottle and the shot glass away.

"I would say that's a pretty good idea," a voice said from the doorway, laughter in the tone.

She looked up and Ben stood in the doorway. "What are you doing here? I thought I'd never see you again. I'm sorry. I'm sorry about what I said."

"Don't worry about it. Abigail called me and let me know you took Molly out to the Chateau today. I wanted to check on you and see how you were doing. Your door wasn't shut. I called for you, but you didn't answer."

"My dad knew he was dying," she said, her words slurring.

"What?"

Her fingers found the pages. "He wrote me a letter. A beautiful letter."

Ben came over and slowly pulled her to her feet. "Let's get some coffee into you. I have a feeling you don't drink often."

She shook her head, and then grabbed his arm as the room spun. "And you would be right."

His warm arms wrapped around her, as they stumbled to the kitchen and he led her to a barstool. He moved around the kitchen, making coffee, as she settled into the seat.

"Why didn't you want to go to the prom with me?" she blurted out before she could stop the words.

Twenty-Five

*B*en stopped in the middle of pouring water into the coffee maker. "Do you really want to have this conversation now? I'm sure the day has been dramatic enough for you."

Those bright eyes pleaded with him, and he gave in with a sigh. He finished pouring the water, scooped the coffee, and pressed the brew button. Turning to her, he was startled to see her fingers tangled together, rubbing them over and over.

How could something that happened when they were eighteen still be so important? Why did she need to know how stupid and foolish he'd been?

"You said Renee told you everything."

"She did. Later. Much later."

Her mouth gaped open and he had to smile. "I didn't know back then that you were asking me to the prom. Renee asked for herself."

"How much later?"

"When she knew she was dying. She thought she had to clear her conscience. Twenty-five is too young to die. She thought hurting you and tricking me was the reason for her dying."

"She tricked you?"

He shook his head as he gathered cups and poured the coffee. He tried to hand Cassie hers black. She pointed to the creamer and sugar in a bowl. Handing it to her, he was happy to see her eyes clearing.

"She thought she tricked me. Two months after the prom, she thought she was pregnant. We thought she was pregnant. Turned out to be a false alarm, but by that time we were married."

"Did she lie?"

He heard no accusation in Cassie's voice, just a question.

"I've gone back and forth over the years, but in my heart, I know Renee was a good person. I think she thought she was pregnant."

"Were you happy?"

He searched Cassie's face. She seemed to want and need the truth. "For the most part. We were sad to not be parents. Then the cancer came. But, there were some happy times there, too."

Cassie finished her coffee and slid it over for more. She spoke as he turned his back.

"I hated her for so long that I forgot all the good times. She was my best friend in the world, and I lost her because I was so stupid jealous."

He returned with her cup and a smile. "You were jealous?"

She nodded, putting a ton of sugar and creamer in her coffee. "You bet. The cutest, hottest boy in school and my best friend snagged him. After saying she would ask him for me."

"Why didn't you ask me yourself?"

She bit her lip. "Right, Miss Buried in a Book was going to ask the captain of the football team and class president to the prom."

He leaned over the edge of the counter and slid his lips onto hers. She tasted of coffee and whiskey. He pulled back slightly and grinned as her eyes opened.

"I would have said yes."

That *I would have said yes* echoed in Cassie's still-befuddled brain. Along with that hot kiss, she was dazed and confused and wished she weren't.

Her body ached as if she been tossed through one of those old-fashioned wringers. Her mom. Her dad. Renee. Ben. Nothing was as she'd thought, and it hurt to think anymore today.

"Oh, no," she cried out. "I had things on my list today. Getting the encampment set up and cleaned up. The cable ran for Internet. Now we'll be behind, and it's all my fault."

"Relax, wonder woman. It's all taken care of. I was out there earlier, and the crew is on schedule. Get a good night's sleep and you can hit the ground running tomorrow."

"Are you sure?"

"Yep," he said. "The trailers are in place. The flowers are planted. The site is all cleaned up and looks ready for your inspection."

Her mind whirled with everything yet to be done, and all she wanted to think about was that kiss. Ben's grin said he was thinking about that kiss as well.

His gaze swept across the empty room. "Are you going to be okay tonight?"

She yawned. "I'll be fine."

"I could stay if you want. I'm off-duty."

Didn't that comment send her mind whisking to places it shouldn't?

She slid off the barstool and took his arm. Guiding him to the door before she could change her mind, she opened it and let him walk outside.

"Make sure you shut and lock it this time," he said, leaning in, and kissing her.

The kiss deepened until his moans vibrated through her. "Maybe you should stay."

"I didn't mean like that, and you know it."

She pouted as she stepped back. Cassie stood in the doorway until his patrol car drove out of sight.

With a sigh, she shut the door and locked it. Her fingers trailed over her lips, still tasting him. A big yawn shattered the moment. She laughed and headed to her bedroom.

All the drama of the day returned. The stench of burnt wood still lingered in the air. Her eyes ached from all the tears she'd shed. A slight buzz remained from the whiskey and coffee sloshed in her empty stomach.

Retracing her steps, Cassie returned to the kitchen for a snack and a glass of lemonade from the refrigerator. Goodies in hand, she went to her desk and booted up the laptop. She and Mrs. Pumpernickel would be spending some time together. It wasn't as if she would be sleeping anytime soon.

Not as much enjoyment as Ben's kiss, but still worthwhile.

As the sunlight peeked through her blinds, Cassie stretched and turned off the computer. A new day and a new beginning. One that started with a shower, breakfast, and a trip to see her mom.

She looked up and closed her eyes. "See, Daddy. I can do this."

Twenty-Six

Her resolve to manage her life was tested day after day as the deadline tightened and more things were added to her to-do lists. Cassie spotted Ben in front of the bookstore and rushed over. She handed him a blue sheet of paper.

"What's this?" he asked, his brow furrowing and his eyes squinting in the sun. August had settled in with a vengeance. Heat beat down on their uncovered heads and heat mirages shimmered down the black asphalt of Main Street.

"It's your to-do list for today."

He rubbed a hand over his jaw. "There must be twenty things on this list. I do have a job to do, you know. Two, actually."

"Twenty-two and a half, actually."

"How can I have a half of a thing to do?" He shot a fake mean glare at her before he burst into a big grin.

"Look at the bottom," she said, tapping on the black bullet point. "Dinner, with me. Two of us. Half a job."

He swept her into a hug and planted a kiss on her cheek. Her face heated from more than the sun. She glanced around, sure everyone on Main Street was watching. A relieved sigh escaped her as people hustled by, paying them no never mind.

"Dinner with you is not a job," he replied, giving her another quick hug, and then folding the paper into a small square he tucked into his pocket.

"Tonight's is," she replied back. "We have to finalize the transportation plans for getting two hundred authors from the airport, bus, and train stations here to Lake Willowbee."

"How do you keep your sanity?" he asked.

She held up her bright-red binder, close to bursting with papers. "To-do lists. Never leave home without them."

Cassie opened it up to a tab with today's date on it. "See. From the time I wake up, to the time I go to sleep."

"Get dressed? You need a to-do list to tell you that?"

"Laugh all you want. I put everything. I won't forget anything, and it is fun to make checkmarks."

He put his finger on one halfway down the page. "You forgot one."

"No, I didn't," she protested. Her gaze swept down the page and she glanced at her watch. "Shoot, I'm supposed to be helping Lisa catalog books."

"Good thing you're two steps away," he said with a laugh.

"See, this is why I need lists."

He put a finger under her chin and raised it. The long, lingering kiss he gave her sent chills down her spine in spite of the triple digits heat.

"Whatever helps," he whispered as she moved away and pushed open the bookstore's doors.

Waiting until she'd gone into the building, Ben pulled out the folded sheet and opened it. "One o'clock. Break."

He couldn't help laughing. She'd even added in when he didn't have something to do. Scanning further, he saw he had a free hour right now. He strolled to his car and turned on the air conditioner as soon as he sat. Hot air blasted him until it turned lukewarm a few moments later.

Glancing over his shoulder, he flipped a U-turn in the middle of the street and headed out to Sierra Chateau. He knew Cassie visited first thing in the morning, but he tried to visit Molly sometime in the afternoon.

Coming over the rise, the building sat nestled in the trees, calm and peaceful. He took a deep breath and let the hustle and bustle of the town slip away. It was only going to get worse before the festival came and went. Their sleepy community would burst at the seams, but in the end, the revenue dollars would see them through until winter snow and skiing brought the crowds again.

He got out of the car and the heat pummeled him instantly. What he wouldn't give for some snow and cold. The residents and staff greeted him as he took the cobblestone path to the meadow on the other side of the buildings.

He found Molly right where she was every day at this time, standing in front of an easel painting the gorgeous landscape. Her thoughts and memories might be slipping away, but she could still paint like a master.

"Ben, you came," she cried out, dropping her paint brush, and rushing to his side. Her hands gripped his T-shirt, leaving streaks of green and yellow on the blue fabric. He pried her fingers from his shirt and held them.

"I told you I would, Molly," he said in a low, calm voice. "What are you painting today?"

The hour passed quickly as Cassie's mother told him of her painting, she flirted with him, and complained about Clara making her stay at the Chateau.

"Not that it isn't wonderful, but I miss my own bed," she said, leaning forward to whisper. "I miss Cassie. She never comes to visit. Not like you do."

His heart skipped a beat. He knew Cassie visited every morning. Abigail talked about it constantly, how Cassie never missed a day, even in the middle of planning the festival.

He also knew Molly needed calmness, not questioning or confrontation. "I'll tell her to come see you soon, Molly."

"Okay." She brightened, her mood swinging back and forth just like that.

Back in his car, Ben took a moment to let the air conditioner cool the car and to settle his racing heart. He adored Molly, but looking into those vacant eyes, so like Cassie's, was hard.

Could he do this? Could he give his heart to another woman who might be taken from him too soon?

He laughed. It was already too late. He'd already given his heart to Cassie Stone.

Twenty-Seven

Ben's smile grew as he gazed at the woman walking toward him through the crowded diner. Every patron stopped Cassie to shake her hand and thank her. An eternity passed before she reached the table and he stood until she was seated.

"You didn't wait too long, did you?"

He locked eyes with her. "Not long at all. Well worth the wait."

A blush reddened her cheeks and highlighted the freckles scattered across her nose. He smiled as she glanced at her menu and tossed it aside.

"As if I don't get the same thing every time I walk into this place."

"Rosie's has the best burgers in town."

She grinned as the aforementioned Rosie placed glasses of water on their table. Cassie looked up at the older woman and smiled. "Best burgers anywhere. You better be ready for this place to be packed all day long."

"Honey, I am. There isn't room in the storage or freezer for another box or bin."

Rosie turned her gaze on Ben. "Anything is better than last year."

Cassie smacked her head. "Wow, I forgot to even ask what numbers you had in past years."

Ben took a sip of water. "Most years are thirty to forty thousand for the three days. Last year was colder than usual and I don't think we hit twenty-five thousand for the whole event."

Cassie turned pale and stared at them both. "We can't be sure until all the numbers are in, but Ben has been checking lodgings here and the other towns, and I've been helping Lisa with ticket sales."

Ben set down his glass and took her hand. "You tried so hard.

I was sure it was going to work."

"Is it going to be worse than last year, honey?" Rosie added, a frown on her face.

Cassie shook her head. "I think we're looking at three to four times as many."

"What?" Ben managed to get out, before gulping down half his glass of water to stop his gasping choke.

Cassie laughed as Rosie joined in. Ben caught his breath and they ordered. Once Rosie left, he turned his attention to the woman across the table. "You are amazing."

She blushed and ducked her head. "It isn't all me. Everyone has helped. I'm sure most of them are coming to see Lora. She only does two or three appearances a year."

"Cassie, why do you do that?" He took her hand. "Your books are popular all around the world. I've read them. You are an amazing writer, even if you don't write one more word."

She gazed at him. "I'm writing again," she whispered, as if to say it too loud would jinx it.

"That's wonderful. We should celebrate." He held up his glass and clinked with hers. "To Sassy the cat."

Cassie laughed and took a sip. "Stupid cat."

"I wish it was more than water, but we have a lot of work ahead of us."

"Yes, we do," she agreed.

Out from her purse came the bright-red binder. She turned pages until he spotted one with what looked like a million timetables.

"Okay," she said as the food arrived. "I've color-coordinated the schedules so each hour and location have a separate color. We'll need at least twenty drivers. Most of them will go to the Sacramento airport since that is where the main group of the authors are coming in."

He pointed to the page as he grabbed a few fries. "What is the small group in black? Don't they get a color?"

She took a sip of water. "Those are the ones who will need to be picked up separately. Their times and locations didn't match up with anyone else."

"How many is that? Five or six?"

Cassie glanced at the page and counted. "Seven."

"What if we send a minibus?" he asked. "We can design a route to get each person."

"You are a genius," she said, her eyes twinkling as she took up a purple pen and circled each of the black ink names.

Sitting back, he pushed his empty plate away. "I can't believe this time next week the town will be bursting with writers and fans."

"Do you get this excited every year?" Cassie pushed her plate to the side as well.

"I didn't help every year. Your father and his staff did all the work of the festival, with just a small committee of volunteers.

"Cassie, this is going to be more than just a book festival. There are craft vendors coming, entertainment, artists, food trucks. Heck, I've lost count of all you have arranged. You've worked a miracle."

"We've worked a miracle. This whole town. I can't believe it."

"Believe it. You did this."

Cassie glanced at her watch for the third time in as many minutes. Her to-do list was eating away at her brain, but she could have sat here with Ben all night. His praise meant a lot. For too long, she'd thought everything she did was wrong. First Lora, and then her dad, letting her know she was okay just the way she was. And now, Ben. Her nose burned as she held back the tears.

"Okay," she said, shutting her binder, and shoving it into her purse. "You, Mayor Bridges have a long to-do list yet tonight. I know, I wrote it."

"I'll go, Miss Bossy," he said with a smile. "But promise me dinner every night this week. Thursday night before the festival, I'll have a surprise for you."

"Oh, what?"

"It wouldn't be a surprise if I told you. Just know, you need a dress and fancy shoes."

He kissed her cheek and headed out the door. She looked over her shoulder as the bell jingled over the doorway.

Her step was light the rest of the day as she tried to imagine what the surprise could be.

Her dreams were filled with every memory of every moment they'd spent together.

Twenty-Eight

Cassie didn't know how she'd made it to Thursday night. Her nerves were wound as tight as a watch waiting to spring apart. She'd found a sparkly, dark-blue dress at the boutique downtown. She slipped on her heels and spun in front of the mirror. Curls framed her face and tickled her bare shoulders.

Tomorrow and through the weekend, she'd be at the festival's beck and call. Tonight was hers. Hers and Ben's. The sound of tires on gravel filtered through the open window. She grabbed a tiny purse and rushed down the hallway to the front door before the knock came.

She opened the door and her breath caught. Ben stood in the doorway, in a dark suit with a dark-blue tie.

Her eyebrow quirked upward. "Delilah told you what I bought."

His gaze swept over her and she felt the heat from the top of her head to the bottom of her feet. His dark eyes twinkled, and her heart raced.

"Ready?"

"Yes," she managed to breathe out.

Once in the car, she turned to him. "Where are we going?"

"The Lodge."

She didn't know what to say. Even after her years in New York City, she was still a small-town girl at heart. The vacation people went to the exclusive restaurant. They didn't post prices on their menu. If you had to ask, you couldn't afford it.

"Are you sure? There are perfectly good places in town or down in Auburn."

He reached over and took her hand. "I'm positive. You deserve this. I've never seen anyone work so hard as you have these past weeks."

The excitement in his voice set off her own. One night of indulgence wasn't too much to ask, was it? She settled back in her seat and relaxed as they wound up the long, winding road to the restaurant.

The valet took their car and Ben grasped her hand as they climbed up the flagstone steps to the log cabin style building. Stained glass filled the enormous door he opened for her. Once inside, the scent of lilies and steak filled the air.

Her mouth watered. She'd been looking forward to dinner all day and grazed instead of eating a full meal.

Ben spoke to the *maître d'*, who led them to a cozy table in a corner. The man pulled back her seat, and Cassie found herself in front of a china plate with a bloodred rose laying across a damask napkin.

She picked it up and breathed in a deep, rich rose scent. "It's beautiful."

Ben winked. "Not as beautiful as you."

Course followed course in a meal that was as delicious as it was exquisitely presented. By the time dessert arrived, Cassie wasn't sure where she was putting it, but the sliver of chocolate cake with raspberry sauce called her name.

She sat back in her chair as the waiter cleared the table and brought tiny cups of coffee. Sipping the rich mixture, she sighed.

"I don't want this night to end."

Ben took her hand. "I don't either. I think I'm falling in love with you, Cassie."

"What?"

She must have looked confused. His fingers rubbed against hers and he stared at her with a smile on his face.

"You don't have to say anything. I just wanted to let you know how I feel."

"Ben, you know I had a crush on you in high school, right?" She laughed as a blush rushed across his dark cheeks.

"I always assumed so since you wanted to ask me to the prom."

She leaned closer, her face inches from his. "I could fall in love with you so easily, Ben Bridges. You were the object of many a schoolgirl fantasy."

His fingers trailed over the shell of her ear, down her neck, to rest on her bare shoulder. The heat of his hand warmed her from the tips of her fingers to the ends of her toes.

Leaning closer still, Ben whispered in her ear, his breath tickling the tangled curls there. "They don't have to remain fantasies."

All she could do was nod. He raised his hand, got the *maître d'*, and paid the bill. Outside, he wrapped an arm around her waist as they waited for the car.

She tapped her foot in impatience. *Stop it,* she admonished herself silently. You aren't a kid anymore. You aren't going to be groping in the back seat. You can wait to get to a bed.

Her mouth went dry.

A bed.

Ben.

Her.

Her mind skittered in a million directions. It wasn't until she realized the car had stopped that she looked through the windshield and saw her house.

"I hope this is okay. I have a tiny apartment on the other side of town, and to be honest, I don't even remember if I made the bed."

She adored his stricken look. Leaning over, Cassie kissed him. He tasted of the rich coffee and delicious chocolate cake they'd had at the restaurant. Coffee and chocolate and desire. She ran her fingers through his thick hair and reveled in the groan he emitted.

Her mind in a daze, they managed to get out of the car and into the house. Her lips stayed plastered to his as they stumbled and found the way to her room.

Ben Bridges in her bedroom. She couldn't help it. She giggled.

Cassie had imagined this moment since she was eighteen years old, sitting on the couch with popcorn and a sappy movie while everyone else was at the prom. She'd fantasized how this moment would play out.

For a woman who made a living using her imagination, her fantasies hadn't even been close.

He kissed her, and she melted.

He touched her, and her entire body tingled.

He joined with her, and the world stopped spinning.

Twenty-Nine

A weight pinned her to the bed. Cassie cracked an eyelid open and winced as sunlight pierced her vision. Still half-asleep, her brain took a moment to compute the fact the sun was up and bright enough to filter through the blinds.

"No, no, no," she cried out, Ben stirring beside her.

Glancing at the clock, she knew they'd screwed up. She reached over and shoved his shoulder. "Get up."

She ran around the room, trying to find the clothes she'd picked out for the first day of the festival. "There's not enough time," she said, tears choking her voice.

Ben's head came up and he glanced at the clock. "It's only seven thirty. We have thirty minutes before we have to be downtown. Plenty of time," he mumbled, turning over and slowly throwing back the covers.

"There isn't plenty of time," she bit out, yanking her shirt on. "Now, I don't have time to see mom this morning before everything starts."

She started crying, tears rolling down her cheeks. "I see her every day."

He rushed over and pulled her to his chest. His very naked chest. Conflict boiled inside over whether to be angry or turned-on. That she was conflicted only made her angrier.

"This is all your fault."

"Whoa, how is this my fault?"

"If you hadn't been so amazing, I wouldn't have been so worn out, and we wouldn't have overslept."

She stared at his big grin and fought to not slap him upside the head.

"I was amazing?"

How could she stay angry? He looked like a kid who just found out he'd aced the spelling test.

"We can't do anything about this morning, except get our butts downtown, but this afternoon, we'll take an hour and go visit Molly. She's usually painting by one or two, so we'll visit her then."

"How do you know she's painting?"

Ben started pulling on his clothes. "I go visit her every day," he mumbled as he attempted to do his tie.

"You go visit my mom?"

"Sure, she's my friend, your mother."

She started crying in earnest. Cassie had always thought Ben was a hot guy, a nice guy. She'd never known he was a great guy. A keeper as all her writer friends called them.

Walking over, she moved his hands and did his tie. She gazed up at him. "I love you."

"Just remember who said it first."

"I will, if you get us to the festival in time."

"No problem."

Ben was as good as his word. By the time they parked behind city hall and walked out to Main Street, her committee was putting the finishing touches on the booths. Kissing quickly, Ben headed to the hardware store as Cassie made her way to the bookstore, binder in hand.

A crowd swarmed the Stone Bookstore, spilling out onto the sidewalk. She moved steadily to the front of the line.

"Excuse me. Thank you. Excuse me."

"Darling, I made it," Lora Robins said, wrapping her in a giant hug.

When she could breathe again, she pulled back. "What are you doing in Lake Willowbee? You aren't supposed to be here until late this afternoon. You aren't signing until tomorrow."

"I couldn't wait to see your little town, Cassie." Her gaze swept the store. "I love it. I can't imagine why you left it."

Thinking of Ben and all the people helping with the festival and everyone helping her mother, Cassie couldn't imagine why she'd left it either.

"Hello, tall, dark, and handsome," Lora whispered, her gaze going to the doorway.

Cassie turned, spotting Ben, head and shoulders above the crowd. A blush heated her cheeks as Lora stared at her.

She leaned over and whispered in Cassie's ear. "This must be Ben."

All she could do was nod as he reached them by the bookshelves. "Cassie, they need you at the bakery. Something about the wrong cookbooks."

"Oh, no," she cried. The coordinated books at each business down Main Street had been her idea. Wood project books at the hardware store. Business and exercise books at the yoga studio. Antique appraisal books at the antiques store. And cookbooks at the bakery.

"Lora, I have to go."

"Do what you have to do, sweetie." She gazed up at Ben. "I'll just get to know your friend here."

Oh, she really didn't want to leave Lora here with Ben, but she had a job to do.

"Fine, Lora, this is Ben Bridges, our mayor and police chief. Ben, this is Lora Robins."

He looked starstruck. "The Lora Robins?"

"In the flesh," she purred as she wrapped a hand around his arm, her femme fatale persona in full force.

"Play nice," Cassie gritted out, turning, and pushing through the crowd.

Ben gazed down at Lora, realizing the writer he'd thought of as bigger than life was a petite woman, barely reaching his chest.

"Cassie's told me a lot about you," Ben said.

Lora gazed up at him, worldly knowledge gleaming in her

dark eyes. "She's told me a lot about you, too."

He swallowed harshly as Lora laughed.

"You hurt her, and you die."

From anyone else, the comment would have made him laugh. From the small dynamo at his side, he found her deadly serious.

"Now that we understand each other, show me this delightful town of yours, Mayor Ben."

He walked her down one side of Main Street and up the other. She listened as he told her stories of the town's founding and the people who made up the businesses on the street.

He listened as Lora told him of Cassie's trials in New York City and how harsh things had really been. "She's lucky to have you as a friend, Lora."

"Ben," she said, squeezing his arm. "I'm lucky to have her as my friend."

The woman dropped his arm as they approached Cassie at the front of the bakery. Ben stepped slightly away. Lora laughed. "Oh, you've got it bad."

Her words barely registered as his gaze shot to the woman he loved and all he saw was her. How she bit her lip when she was nervous. How she thought tucking her curls behind her ears would make them stay there. How the sunlight caught her hair afire. How her imagination and hard work had made all this possible.

An elbow jabbed him in the side. He turned to Lora.

"Keep her in the moment. Don't let her retreat; from life, from you, from anything."

He looked Lora straight in the eye. "Don't worry. Her retreating has been interrupted."

Ben stared at Cassie until he caught her eye. She smiled at him, her face brightening.

"Permanently," he whispered.

The End

About the Author

Jill James didn't start out wanting to be an author. Along the way she wanted to be an astronaut, President of the United States, a lawyer, and a doctor. Once married with children she realized she could be all those things; in the pages of the stories she wrote.

She lives in Nevada with her husband, who is the inspiration for all her romance novel heroes.

Jill writes contemporary and paranormal romance, with a dash of urban fantasy thrown in from time to time.

Find Jill online:
Twitter - @jill_james
Facebook – facebook.com/Jill.James.author
Website – www.jilljameswrites.com
Newsletter – http://eepurl.com/hvtn-/

Other books by Jill James
The Lake Willowbee Series
Divorce, Interrupted
Dare To Trust
Defend My Love
The Reluctant Bride – a Lake Willowbee novella
Shifters of San Laura
Dangerous Shift
Time of Zombies
Love in the Time of Zombies
The Zombie Hunter's Wife
A Time to Kill Zombies

Beached

Jude Knight

One

The road home wound through the hills until the sudden last corner before the coast. Nikki had known the way by heart since she was a small girl, returning from a shopping expedition or a sports event.

In recent years, the little fishing settlement had been discovered by weekenders. Land Transport New Zealand had been hard at work during Nikki's decade overseas, widening and straightening, cutting through slopes and filling hollows. The first time she'd driven out here a few months ago, the alterations made it unfamiliar.

But she'd been twice more, checking on the beach house for Gran and Poppa, and the landmarks beyond the road remained the same. A clump of native bush still screened Murphy's Pond, a favorite summer swimming hole. They'd built a lookout with a picnic spot over Pleasant Valley, but the view of farmland, bush, river, and hills remained as beautiful as ever, and the hill known as Two Heads was still as impressive, even if an aesthetically-challenged cretin had somehow obtained permission to quarry on one side.

The road dropped down again from the hillside into the river flats. This time, the long row of massive willows at the river's edge signaled the difference, growing steadily smaller as they approached the tidal reaches. No more hills, and in a moment she would have her first glimpse of the sea.

"There, Nikki," Poppa used to say as they rounded that last corner, "the sea. Nothing else between us and South America."

The numbness lifted for a moment, pierced by a shaft of pure joy. The wall between Nikki and her feelings had helped when the second funeral followed only a week after the first, and through all the aftermath of sorting the estate. She would not need it where she was going. She could mourn Gran and Poppa properly in the lands of her childhood: not the diminished frail pair she had nursed and cared for these past few months, but the vigorous couple of twenty and thirty years ago; the only parents she had known or needed.

The car, Poppa's little hybrid, seemed as eager as she to eat up the last five miles, gaining speed on the curves around the little coves and over the small promontories between her and Valentine Bay. Gran and Poppa had left most of their estate to be split between their three grandchildren—her and the half-siblings she barely knew. But the beach house at Valentine Bay was left to her alone, and the decision to keep it had never needed to be made. She had been born there; had spent her early years in that community; had left only for high school in Barnsley, the regional hub the locals called 'Town', and later for university in the United States. The beach house was home.

Beks, her dearest friend from school and a faithful correspondent in all the years away, had promised to air the place and make up a bed with fresh sheets. She would undoubtedly stock the cupboards, too, though she'd insisted that Nikki join her and her family for a meal tonight. Nikki found she was looking forward to it. Beks had married her high-school sweetheart, and she and Dave had both known Gran and Poppa.

She began to hum the song Gran always sang as they finished this last stretch of the coast. "Our house, is a very, very, very fine house…"

Soon. Soon she would be home.

"Casual? Or super casual?" Zee asked, lifting up the open-front cotton-weave shirt in one hand and the tee in the other. Oliver waved his tail hesitantly, looking from one garment to the other and then into his master's eyes before deciding no game was in the offing and slumping back down on his rug.

"Super casual," Zee decided. Tee and jeans. Becky, his landlady and wife to Dave, his employer, had told him to treat it like any family meal, and that's what he usually wore when he joined the Mastertons for dinner.

"I won't be going to any fuss," Becky had assured him, which was demonstrably untrue, since she had been buzzing like a bee on steroids for the past week. The other guest tonight would be Becky's oldest friend, back in Valentine Bay after years on the other side of the world. Becky was over at the friend's house now, having left detailed written instructions for Dave on what needed to happen with the dinner.

"You don't have to invite me. You'll want to spend time with your friend," Zee had protested, and Dave had grinned. "Too right, Zee, and that's why I want you there. Be a mate and give me someone to talk to when the Niks and Beks gossip train leaves the station. Those girls chat every day on FB, but you won't know it when they get together."

So instead of taking Oliver for his evening walk, Zee had showered and changed into clean jeans and a t-shirt with a slogan that said, "Be yourself. Everyone else is already taken."

Trainers? Flip-flops? It was well after five, but the day was still hot and humid. Zee compromised on sandals to dress the jeans up a bit, and sat on the edge of the bed to put them on. Oliver sat up, his tongue lolling from one corner of a doggy smile, his tail thumping the polished floor beyond the edge of his mat.

"Sorry, fellow," Zee told him. "Not tonight. I'll make it up to you tomorrow."

He closed the door on the disappointed animal, and descended from his studio apartment in the loft over the garage.

In the kitchen of the main house, Dave was stirring something on the stove, his arm at full stretch so he could peer round at the game show on the television in the family room.

"Ah, Zee," he said. "Great. Here, stir this, will you?"

Zee took over the spoon. Some sort of stew? He took the

fragrant air deeply into his nostrils: onions, bay leaf, something he couldn't quite identify. Dave removed a tray of herbed roast vegetables from the oven, and replaced it with a casserole dish from the fridge. "Apple crumble," he explained. "And custard. And probably ice cream, too, if I know Becky." He turned off the gas to Zee's hob. "We can turn that pot off now. Becky said to make sure the gravy didn't catch. Can you put the veg into this dish while I start the cleanup?"

Zee picked up the bowl Dave indicated. "Sure. Where are the kids?"

"Being quiet?" Dave suggested.

"Yeah, right," said in a voice heavily laden with scorn, was as much a Kiwi-ism as an Americanism.

Dave laughed. "Mum has them. She's keeping them overnight, too, in case Becky wants to sit up late. At least, that's Mum's excuse." He finished stacking the cooking pots and began to run water into the kitchen sink.

Zee grinned back. He'd been the Mastertons' tenant for a year, after all. "They're off to Thailand for their river cruise in a week," he commented. Dave's parents, Jill and Bruce, had built another house on the large Masterton property and surrendered the main house to Bev and Dave when their youngest left for university. They adored stealing the grandchildren—and never more than when they were about to indulge the wanderlust they'd repressed while raising their own large family.

"There." Dave turned off the tap, and dropped a handful of dirty implements into the soapy water. "I'll boil a kettle to give the silver beet a head start when the girls arrive. A river cruise could suit you, Zee. No waves."

Zee used the dish mop he'd just picked up to flick some soap suds at Dave. He'd never live down the condition in which he'd landed in Valentine Bay, but the teasing from his workmates was good natured.

At the sink, he had a good view of the big turning zone outside the triple garage. He glanced up idly when the Masterton people mover drew up, then froze, his hands hovering above the hot water. Nicola Watson? What was Global Earth Watch's gun attorney doing in Valentine Bay? He'd last seen her on television, leaving the courtroom in which she had just lost her case against O'Neal Hotel Corporation. A loss aimed at destroying GEW's credibility and that had been orchestrated in a plot between Miss Watson's colleague and fiancé and Zee's brother, Patrick O'Neal.

Discovering the machinations had been the final straw that precipitated Zee's flight from his career, his family, his trust fund, his name, and the United States.

"She's a stunner, isn't she?" Dave said, and Zee accepted the excuse for looking as if he'd been bashed across the side of the head. Though he'd known the lovely Miss Watson was a New Zealander, he'd not known she was here in her home country. He had certainly not known that her family owned a house in the fishing village where he'd come ashore.

"She sure is. A lawyer, I think you said?" He finished scrubbing the brush across the base of the pot and put it on the rack for Dave to dry. Would she know who he was? They'd never met, and he didn't court the camera the way his father and half-brothers did. Nor did he look like the other O'Neals, red hair to their black, finer boned, with his mother's grey eyes. Any family resemblance needed another O'Neal for comparison.

If she realized who he was, he would tell her he was not an O'Neal anymore, if he ever really had been. One of his last acts in repudiating the family had been to legally change his surname back to the one on his birth certificate; his mother's name. And if Ms. Watson didn't know who he was, he wouldn't say anything that would sour the evening for Becky and Dave.

He'd made his decision just in time, as the two women came into the kitchen from the mud room—back porch, the New Zealanders would say.

Becky went straight into her husband's arms for the kiss with which they always greeted one another, turning her head to make the introductions from that safe harbor.

"Niks, this is our lodger, Zee Henderson. He lives above the garage."

Ms. Watson showed none of the hostility she owed an O'Neal, offering instead a friendly smile and a hand to shake. "Pleased to meet you, Mr. Henderson."

"Zee, please," Zee begged. "If anyone calls me Mr. Henderson, I look around for my grand-dad."

Nikki crossed the room to greet Dave with a hug and a kiss on the cheek, Becky having left her husband to check on the status of the dinner. "You're an American," she observed to Zee.

"Guilty, as charged."

"Niks works in New York," Becky observed. She touched the kettle, decided it was hot enough, and poured some water into the waiting pot. "Or, at least, she used to. Have you ever been there, Zee?"

"I sailed from New York." Zee grimaced. "Turned out to be a bad idea."

Nikki looked from Zee to Becky. "Why? What happened?"

"He gets sea sick," Dave explained. "By the time the boat berthed in Valentine Bay, he'd been sea sick for six months. He staggered off onto the wharf, took hold of a bollard, and swore he was never leaving land again."

Becky took up the story. "So Dave brought him home, and the New Zealand Immigration Service gave him a new name, and a year later here he is."

Nikki raised one elegant brow. Close up and in person, she was even more gorgeous than on television, her face devoid of makeup and not needing it, her long hair caught back casually with a couple of hair slides and a clip. "Gave you a new name?"

"My name is Zachary Henderson, ma'am. Only the immigration officer thought I said Thackeray. When I told him 'zee' for 'Zulu ', Dave thought it was hilarious." New Zealanders called the last letter of the alphabet 'Zed'. "Around here, they've been calling me 'Zee' ever since."

"Except when we call him Drift," Dave corrected.

Nikki's eyes sparkled. "Short for driftwood?"

"Right," Zee agreed, as he let the water go and wiped out the sink. There. Becky liked to start a meal with a clean kitchen, and

Dave liked her to be happy. "I'm beached, and that's the way I plan to stay."

"There are worse places than Valentine Bay to be beached." Nikki had taken the drying cloth from Dave's hand, had dried the last of the pans, and was putting them away, clearly familiar with Becky's kitchen.

"There are few better," Zee said. And the place was improved by having her in it. New Zealand had a worldwide reputation for scenic wonders, and she was certainly that!

They carried the food through to the dining room where the table was already set for four — Dave and Becky at either end, and Zee facing Nikki between them. Dinner conversation at the Mastertons' was always wide-ranging. The couple had lived all their life in Valentine Bay. They'd married young and started having babies almost immediately, and Dave had apprenticed for his father straight from school, then taken over running the family firm. But they were both intelligent people with an active curiosity about the world, and a determination to leave at least their corner of it a better place for their growing family.

Zee had soon found his opinions needed to be well founded, and had changed his mind on quite a few things after a few polite but incisive questions from Becky or friendly derision from Dave.

The first course passed quickly as they talked about the current whereabouts of people Nikki had once known.

"John Fallon and his family have gone to be missionaries in Vanuatu, Niks," Becky said about one of their former classmates. "John was president of the AOG youth group, Zee, so it was no surprise."

"He married a Wellington girl," Dave offered. "Met her at Vik." Vik was Victoria, one of the big New Zealand universities.

"Pokey Kenworth is still around, though," he added.

"More's the pity." Becky wrinkled her nose. "That's uncharitable, I know, but he is just the same, Niks. Anything for a dollar, and nothing unless he gets something out of it."

In Zee's opinion, that summed the man up, though it was

a surprise that he'd been a classmate of these three; he looked much older. Too much of the drink taken, Grandma O'Neal would have said.

"He's behind this hotel project you wanted me to look into." Nikki made it a statement, rather than a question. "Or," she amended, "he is the New Zealand front man for the project."

"Can we go somewhere with that?" Dave asked, but Nikki was shaking her head. "Maybe under the new Act, but the paperwork all seems to be correct. And if the council has approved it..."

"Because Pokey's father is a councilor," Becky groused.

"Nothing we can do about that. He's only one councilor, and proving undue influence would be a problem, I reckon. Even if we all know it's true," Dave said.

Nikki put her knife and fork neatly together on her empty plate. "I need to brush up on the New Zealand legislation and regulations, and I haven't had time yet."

"Well, we're not giving up." Becky gave a sharp nod of the head. "But no more about that tonight, Niks. I'm not spending your first night home making you work." She stood and began collecting the plates. Dave and Nikki both made as if to help her, but she waved them down. "I've got this."

Nikki turned to Dave. "I haven't thanked you for intercepting Snoopy and Pokey at Gran's funeral. I don't think I could have borne to hear them pretend compassion. In fact" — she held out her hand to Becky, who put down the hot bowl of apple crumble and disentangled her own hand from the pot mitt in order to clasp her friend's — "thank you for coming to both funerals, and so close together."

"Of course we came to the funerals. Best friends forever, remember? I wish we could have stayed more than the day, Niks. I hated having to leave you there with them."

Nikki clearly knew who 'them' referred to. "It wasn't so bad. Sarah is nervous around me. I never realized that but, now I know, I find her much easier. And I enjoyed spending time with Julia and Xander. My family, Zee. My half-sister lives with my mother Sarah in Brisbane, and my half-brother is in Sydney."

"Australia, right?" Zee confirmed. He knew perfectly well that both cities were Australian state capitals, but New Zealanders persisted in believing that Americans were ignorant of anything beyond their borders.

"Julia is a sweet girl, and Xander has a sensible head on his shoulders for a twenty-one-year-old. I'm sorry, Zee. You can't be interested in the complicated relationships in my family."

Zee doubted Nikki had anything to teach him about complicated relationships. The O'Neals took them to new heights, with his grandfather's three marriages, his father on his fourth and two of his siblings on their second. And that didn't count assorted uncles, aunts, and cousins.

He told her what Grandma O'Neal had told him when he arrived in the O'Neal family as an eleven-year-old, grieving for his mother and bewildered by his change of status and name. "You get one year off from caring about what anyone thinks. When you lose someone close to you, I mean. We all need to make allowances for you, Nikki."

Becky approved. "I like that. One year to grieve and to bite everyone else's heads off if they don't let you. You've eleven months to go, Niks. Are you going to visit them while you're out here? Your brother and sister?"

Nikki was silent for a moment, intently studying the dessert Becky had just passed to her. "I don't know what I'm going to do. I might not go back."

"You're going to stay? Here in New Zealand? In Valentine Bay?" Beks waved her hands in spontaneous celebration, and the serving spoon in one hand flicked a spot of apple crumble crust onto Zee's cheek. Dave sent him a commiserating grin, but Becky was intent on her friend and didn't notice. "But you love what you do."

"I loved it. But..." She trailed off, clearly searching for the words to explain.

"Is this about Tyler Russo?" Becky directed a glare at the spoon in her hand, then served Zee his bowl of dessert. *The fiancé, and Pat's accomplice.*

"Perhaps a bit," Nikki agreed. "The ex, Zee," she explained in an aside. "He's part of it, Beks, but only because he is typical of what people become in that pressure cooker. Anything to win. Anything to get what they want."

Zee nodded. "I know what you're saying. That's what drove me out. I don't believe—I don't want to believe—that the only way to win is to make someone else lose."

"Too much of law is like that," Nikki said, "but I thought we were working together as a team; trying to catch the corporate robber barons who don't care what they break or who they hurt as long as there is money to be made."

Zee had a sudden urge to plant his fist in Tyler Russo's face to make him pay for the regret that shadowed Nikki's voice.

"So what will you do here in New Zealand?" he asked, hoping to bring the lightness back into her voice.

"I don't know. I don't even know if I'll stay. But there must be some way to use my skills that doesn't involve trying to win at all costs."

"Cook at the takeaway," Dave suggested.

"Ptomaine poisoning," Becky teased. "You know Niks doesn't cook. How about gardening, Niks? We could do with a landscape gardener for our spec homes."

They made several more suggestions, each more ridiculous than the last. Laughing took Nikki from gorgeous to spectacular, Zee decided, as he helped carry the plates through to the kitchen where Becky filled the dishwasher and Dave topped up their glasses.

In the comfortable Masterton living room, Zee resumed the conversation on a more practical note. "You're a lawyer? There must be plenty of work for a lawyer."

Nikki shook her head. "I'm not registered here in New Zealand, though they'd recognize my qualifications if I applied and did the appropriate courses."

"Even without that, I imagine a lot of employers would want someone with your training," Zee insisted.

"Her degree is from Columbia," Becky told him, her pride in her friend evident. "Anyone would be lucky to have her."

"My legal training has come in handy the past six months," Nikki admitted, "while I've been looking after Gran and Poppa. Start a sentence with 'In my experience as a lawyer,' and the healthcare funders suddenly find they can do what they've just been saying they can't do. But enough about me. What do you do, Zee?"

Zee shrugged. "Dave gave me a job. I potter about here and there." He and the Mastertons had kept his investment in Masterton & Son under wraps, but it had let the company expand their design side, with Zee supervising a couple of draughtsmen and building relationships with contractors and suppliers all over the region.

"He's too modest," Dave told Nikki. "He is qualified in architectural and interior design — just not here in New Zealand. He's none too bad a builder, either, but mostly we use him to measure up and plan the work."

"I need to talk to you about a measure and quote some time, Dave," Nikki said. "Whether I stay or not, keep the house or sell it, it needs work."

Becky lifted her glass of lemonade — the next little Masterton was harbored within her, so wine was off limits — in a salute to her friend. "A lot of work."

"You're not wrong, Beks," Nikki agreed, "but it could be fun to bring it back to life again."

Two

Nikki walked along Beach Street, arm in arm with Becky, who had joined her on a cupboard-stocking expedition. "One last day of freedom before Jill leaves for Thailand," she explained.

The shape of the harbor had given Valentine Bay its name: a heart on its side. A gap at the eastern point provided entrance to the harbor. On the western side, directly opposite, the wharves and moorings of the fishing port occupied a rocky promontory between two gently curved beaches. North Beach was currently undeveloped farm and bush land, though the planned hotel would change that. On the shores of South Beach, the settlement spread from the fishing port around the curve of the southern lobe of the heart and beyond, stretching partway along the road that led to the historic lighthouse at the harbor entrance.

Most of the shops in Valentine Bay lined one side of Beach Road or the other. That hadn't changed. The shops themselves had—in her childhood, there'd been half a dozen businesses offering services and products to the locals and the rare visitor. A dairy, a fish and chip shop, a general store, a bakery, a book shop that also sold stationery and gifts, a garage with petrol pumps out the front and a workshop out the back. If any of those survived, they had gone upmarket to match the twenty or so others that now extended the shopping area far beyond the boundaries she remembered.

On the coast side of the road, the shops, cafes and restaurants backed onto the beach reserve, a wide stretch of lawn with picnic tables and public barbecue stations scattered among the pohutukawa trees and plantings of tough flax and ornamental grasses.

The businesses on the other side backed into the hill, no longer half farmland, but split up into residential lots with an eclectic mix of houses: Victorian villas cheek-by-jowl with modern beach extravaganzas and little square mid-20th century holiday houses, or baches as they were known here in New Zealand's North Island.

"There's been a lot of building," Nikki observed.

"Business has been good," said the builder's wife, with satisfaction. "When Dave and I first married, he and his Dad used to travel all over the district to get work. Now, we have three times as many builders, and as much as we can handle right here in the Bay."

"How many of them are holiday homes?" Nikki wondered.

"Around two-thirds, I'd guess, but half of those are weekenders. With the new road, we're close enough even for people up from Wellington. We've got three weekenders on the fundraising committee for the school, and a lot of them made submissions against Pokey's development. Let's go in here, Niks. They make a seed loaf to die for, and you should try their focaccia."

'Here' was Maggie's Bakery and Tea Shop, with several tables inside and more on the extended skirt of the footpath. Nikki stopped just inside the doorway to absorb the visual and olfactory impact of basket after basket of baked delights. "What to choose!"

"One of everything," Becky joked.

Nikki grinned, recalling their mantra when they were children at the sweets counter of the dairy. "Not hardly. Just what one woman can eat in a few days. I don't have a freezer yet, remember."

"Best to buy fresh, each day," offered the shopkeeper. She was a comfortably padded woman in her sixties, her lilac gingham dust jacket with lace-trimmed collar toning beautifully with the wisps of purple hair that had escaped the confines of her white cap.

"Margaret," Becky said, "this is my friend Nikki Watson."

Sympathetic hazel eyes met Nikki's. "You're the Watsons' granddaughter. They used to speak of you, Ms. Watson. I am so sorry for your loss. They used to come here to buy their bread when they were in the Bay. Your grandfather loved my cheese rolls, and your grandmother always bought an apple and cinnamon bun. She said she could never get them the same anywhere else."

"Well then," Nikki decided. "I'd better have one of each."

Margaret bagged Nikki's selection, while Becky hovered over the display case full of delicate cakes and robust slices.

"Go you halves on a custard square?" Nikki suggested. They ordered a pot of tea to go with the treat, and took their plates to one of the outside tables.

"What's next?" Becky asked, craning to look at the notebook in which Nikki had written her shopping list. "Fruit and veg we can get at the superette. Just enough for the next two days, Nikki, because the weekend market is the best place for that. We'll leave the meat till last. In this heat, you'll want to get it home as fast as you can."

"I don't have a lot of confidence in Gran's old fridge," Nikki mused. "I should probably do what Margaret suggested for the bread; shop for the day."

"Nicola Watson! Thought you'd have headed back to the bright lights of New York by now." The speaker grabbed a chair from one of the other tables, and turned it back-on to Nikki's and Becky's table before straddling it. "Checking out the old home town, eh? Quite a bit bigger than when you were here last."

Pokey Kenworth. Sunglasses hid his eyes, and a cloth sunhat masked his bald patch, but if she hadn't seen him at the funeral, she still would have recognized the raspy voice that hadn't changed since he'd done his best to make her life miserable in high school.

Thank goodness for dear friends, who had turned tables on him. When she'd refused him a date, he'd told the whole school that she'd been abandoned by her mother and didn't know her father. She'd laughed that off—it was true, after all—but only until she heard his outrageous claim that he'd dated her back in Valentine Bay, had sex with her, and then dropped her because she cheated on him with anyone who would pay her fee. That story was around the school before she heard it.

Becky and Dave took the lead in the revenge. Becky came up with some creative storytelling about the origin of Pokey's nickname, linking it to the size and function of an appendage most male teenagers don't want to have questioned. Dave, the captain of the first XV rugby team, enlisted his team mates to spread the tale in a whisper there and a snigger here. Since Kenworth was not much liked, people were happy to spread the tale and soon most of them believed he'd lied about Nikki in order to cover his own inability to perform.

By the end of the school year, she almost felt sorry for him, and she was relieved when he did not return the following year. He joined his father's real estate firm and their paths didn't cross again. She'd heard he spent considerable effort over the next few years finding females with whom to demonstrate the falsity of the rumors.

Thirteen years later, he headed the firm since his father had retired to focus on duties as a district councilor, so Nikki was not surprised when he said, "I guess you need to sell the old house before you leave. Put it in my hands, and I'll get you a good price, for old times' sake. Of course, it needs a lot of work, but I'm sure I can find someone in the market for a fixer upper."

"Thank you for the offer," Nikki told him, "but I doubt I will sell."

"Keeping it for a rental, are you?" Pokey nodded, pursing his lips, his eyes narrowed as he considered this. "Not a bad idea. Valentine Bay is on the move, and the new hotel is going to put it on the map. You'll need to do some work before it's fit to live in, even if the rent's cheap. Here, take my card. We manage property rentals. No need to worry your pretty little head about the place while we're looking after it. In fact, I have some builders you can use—much cheaper than the Masterton & Son."

Becky enquired sweetly, "Cheap like the apartments in Brayden Street?"

Pokey ignored her, continuing to address himself to Nikki. "You just give me a ring, Nicola. Or drop me an email." He dropped his voice and leant towards her across the back of the chair. "I'm happy to make myself available to you at any time." He waggled his eyebrows to underline the suggestive nature of the offer.

Thirteen years had not improved the man. It had, however, taught Nikki the futility of arguing with people like him. "I haven't made a decision, Mr. Kenworth. But thank you for the card. Good day to you."

"Mr. Kenworth? No need for such formality between old friends." Pokey went to pat Nikki's arm, caught her glare, and changed his mind. "Call me Pokey, like you used to."

Margaret emerged from the shop with their tea on a tray: a teapot under a knitted cozy, two cups on saucers, a small jug of milk, and a bowl of sugar.

Pokey sneered. "You won't appeal to the young crowd with that old fashioned stuff, Maggie. You need decent sized mugs and a good barista. Yes, and a coat of paint to brighten the place up. If you'd accept my offer —"

"Thank you, Margaret," Becky interrupted. "That's perfect."

Pokey tapped Margaret on the arm. "You might as well fetch me a cup."

Nikki decided to be firm. "I am sorry, Pokey. Becky and I were having a private conversation, and we'd like to continue it. Thank you for stopping by."

Reluctantly, the man accepted his dismissal, cancelled his order for tea, and strode off down the footpath, hitching the belt that curved under his belly as he went.

"The apartments in Brayden Street?" Nikki prompted as she watched him walk away.

"Pokey's investment and a builder he brought in from the South Island. They cut corners from the first. Designed to use minimum materials, built on the cheap, breached code when they could get away with it. Within two years they were being sued by purchasers."

"Serves them right," Nikki said. "I suppose they walked away with a slap on the wrist with a wet bus ticket."

Becky shrugged, her focus seemingly on the tea she was pouring, only the grim set of her jaw indicating her irritation. "The builder went bankrupt and started up again under another name. Pokey managed to slither out from under—convinced a judge his only role was funding the project, and he was as much a victim as any of the house owners."

Nikki accepted the cup Becky passed. "Slippery as ever. What's he still doing in Valentine Bay? You'd think somewhere like Auckland or Wellington would offer him more scope. Or over the ditch in Sydney or Brisbane."

"He spent several years across the Tasman," Becky confirmed. "The story is he came home because his father needed him. There are other stories, but let's not waste a perfectly nice day thinking about Pokey Kenworth. Are you really thinking about staying? And what do you plan to do with the house? It isn't as bad as Pokey says, but it does need work."

"Dave is sending the Luscious Lodger over to take a look," Nikki said. "I'll have a better idea once I know what needs to be done, and how much it might cost."

Zee turned the tight u-bend into Cliff Road, which was as precipitous as the name implied, narrow and winding, with cars parked half up on the sidewalk that hugged the side of the hill, so that he had to edge uncomfortably close to the concrete lip and a few inches of grass bank that topped the steep slope to the houses below.

The place he was looking for was nearly at the end of the road. Only the letter box with a painted number hinting that a dwelling waited at the top of the stairs running in a zig zag up the hill. That, and the bright yellow Kia hybrid car nosed into a parking space cut into the hill.

Zee parked the Masterson & Son van as close to the bank as he could get, blocking the sidewalk but leaving plenty of room for passing vehicles. He took a clean notebook from the stack on the back seat and tucked it into his briefcase with his tablet, pencils and laser measure. The rickety gate looked as if it might disintegrate if he opened it, but he was tall enough to just step over. The path climbed steeply between overgrown banks where a few summer flowers struggled to compete with rampant grasses under straggly bushes. The remnants of a garden remained, obscured but still discernible. Beyond the first turn, the path devolved into steps, and the pattern continued, each turn almost level and then the path climbing steps across the slope. The third turn had a bench seat, its support posts rotting so it slumped to one side. Zee didn't risk sitting, but he did stop to take in the view — the whole heart shape of Valentine Bay laid out before him, with a glimpse of the ocean beyond the heads.

Three more bends had their own seats, two other rotting wooden benches and one in rusting wrought iron. After that, the slope gentled, and he was not surprised when it led him out onto a broad platform where a once grand old house dozed in the sun.

It was wooden — the most common building material in New Zealand. At a glance, he'd guess it had been built in several stages, the second story a more recent addition with windows that did not quite match the ground floor. Very likely the large verandah that wrapped the front had been added later, too. Even from the top of the path, twenty yards away, he could see the place was in need of some loving care, with the paint almost worn off in places and one corner of the verandah drooping below the rest.

He'd not know the worst of it standing here. He took the path across the lawn and mounted the three steps to ring the brass bell that hung beside the front door. Nikki must have been close by, because he barely had time to step back before the door opened.

"Hello, Nikki." In cut-off shorts and a tee, Nicola Watson looked even more delicious than she had in slacks and a knit top on the day she arrived, or in the light summer dress she'd been wearing when he spied her out to lunch with Becky while he'd been walking his dog.

"Zee. Nice t-shirt." Today's had been a Christmas gift from the Mastertons — the words 'Keep calm. I am a builder' topped by a crown.

She moved to one side, smiling as she waved him inside. "Come in. Come in. I'll show you 'round."

The hall was dark and narrow, with little natural light and shelves piled with books and bric-a-brac lining both sides. He tried to take it all in while still listening to Nikki. "It's quite run down. Gran and Poppa haven't been out here in five years, since the slope grew too much for them."

"Nothing that can't be fixed," *so far, anyway. Depending on how big a budget she had.* "How long since you were last here?"

Nikki led the way into a sitting room, generously proportioned but cluttered with furnishings and ornaments. "I've been out three times since I came home, but just quick trips to check on the place. To stay? It must be twelve years. We spent Christmas here, me and my grandparents, before I left for Columbia. It was getting a bit run down even then. Poppa said he'd have to get some repairs done, and some painting before next time I was here. I guess once his health deteriorated..."

A door led to a kitchen that had not been updated since the 1970s, except for some new appliances on the sorry excuse for a bench top. Nikki was clearly eating whatever could be cooked in a microwave, a bench top grill, or an air cooker.

"I am sorry for your loss," Zee said. "Bev said they died within a few days of one another?"

"Yes." Nikki stopped to run a finger across the table — metal legs and Formica top, with matching metal-framed chairs whose vinyl upholstery was cracked and peeling. "Nobody expected Gran to go first. She seemed well, and she never complained. It was an aneurysm in the brain, they said. And Poppa just slipped away a few days later. He has been having heart problems for years, so that wasn't a surprise."

Zee made a commiserating noise, and she rushed to reassure him. "It's a good thing. They would not have wanted to be parted."

"I like that." He smiled. "It's reassuring to know that some people get their Happy Ever After." Certainly no one in his family, but he liked that it was possible. He followed her back through the sitting area, where she stopped to point at a photo that took pride of place on the wall.

"That's them. And me. I'm the scrawny kid."

"You spent a lot of time with them," Zee said, more a statement than a question.

Nikki nodded. "They raised me. My mother... she was just a kid herself. Sixteen. She gave me to Gran and went off to her own life. And I don't know why I imagine you might be interested in such ancient history. Let me show you the rest of the place and tell you what I want to do." Suddenly crisp, she led the way back out into the hall and waved for him to precede her up the stairs.

Zee took the hint and backed away from family history, but wasn't quite ready to stop finding out more about this fascinating women. "So this is your home town, then."

"Back when I was a child, it was still a fishing village, with just a few summer folk like ourselves coming here from Barnsley."

"There's still a thriving trade in fish, but tourism is the big thing now," Zee commented.

Zee somehow managed to look piratical in his jeans and joke t-shirt. He was far less kempt than the men she knew in her New York days, with hair long enough to be tied back and the heavy workers boots he wore scuffed. The t-shirt clung in all the right places, as did his jeans. Following him upstairs had induced all kinds of naughty thoughts, which she firmly repressed. She didn't need those kinds of complications.

After they'd visited every room in the house, and Zee had poked around in cupboards and climbed up through hatches into the ceiling, he'd taken his laser measure and his notebook outside and subjected the walls, foundations, and roof to the same careful consideration.

"I'm limited to what I can see on the surface," he warned as he put his figures into an app in his tablet. "In a house of this age — or ages more like, since it has been added on to a number of times — we can expect unexpected problems to show themselves when we start demolition for the repairs and alterations."

"The original two-room cabin is over 100 years old," Nikki told him.

Zee nodded. "I believe it. Has it always been in your family?"

"Only the past fifty years. By the time my grandparents bought it, the first verandah had been built, extended, and enclosed as a living room, and two bedrooms and a bathroom added on the side. Poppa put a new verandah right around, and later built the upstairs." Rooms for their two children: Philip, who died young, and Sarah, Nikki's mother. "He was the local builder, till he retired." Dave's father had once been his apprentice.

"So they lived here year round?" Zee was taking another measurement in the sitting room and typing the results into the tablet. "Not just in the summer?"

"Yes. Until I started high school. They moved into Barnsley to be close to me, and after that we only came home in the holidays." She was blathering again. But this man was remarkably easy to talk to. "They knew I loved it here."

He put his measure into the briefcase he carried, and looked at her, his head tipped slightly to one side. "What do you want to see happen to the house? Repairs, you said? But how far do you want us to go? Clear out any rot? Repile, rewire, and replumb? Bring the kitchen and bathroom into the twenty-first century?"

She should have an answer to those questions, but somehow she hadn't thought that far. "I haven't decided."

He accepted that without any sign of impatience. "I guess the key question is what do you plan to do with it?"

Another excellent question she had not thought about. "Would you like a cold lemonade? Fresh made?"

"Lemons from that massive tree out the back? Sure thing."

Nikki sent him out to the verandah beyond the kitchen while she found two glasses, and filled them with ice and lemonade. If she was staying, she'd need to get rid of the old fridge and replace it with a new one.

Zee was leaning against a post looking out over the north curve of the bay where regrowth bush grew almost to the beach.

Nikki came up by his shoulder. "That's a lovely spot. Bev and I used to go skinny dipping down there."

She laughed when he waggled his eyebrows. "What! We were ten! You. Here," she shoved his glass into his hand, "have your lemonade and cool down."

A moment later she could feel her cheeks heat as she realized she was visualizing this near stranger naked. Thankfully, he ignored her blush, still looking out over the bay as he sipped his drink.

"What do you think of the plan to build a hotel there?" he asked.

She thought any project with Pokey behind it was likely to be terrible for the town. "Beks and Dave say the place needs accommodation for tourists, but this development worries them."

"As it stands? The developer's track record is for sloppy work and bad relationships with the locals. It's a bit of a worry." He shrugged. "Shouldn't much affect your view, though. So where do you want to go with your house?"

She sat down on the edge of the verandah, letting her legs swing in the weeds where Gran used to have a rich productive herb bed. "How much does it matter?"

Zee dropped to sit beside her. "Look at it like this. If you're planning to sell, most of your value is in the land and the view. So we pack up anything you want to keep, ditch the rest, pull down what is going to cost more than its value to fix, repair anything that'll improve your return, slap on some paint, and buy some bright furniture."

That sounded awful. A shoddy job on the place that was Gran's and Poppa's pride and joy? "Let's behave as if I'm not going to sell."

Zee gave a short nod. "Fair enough. Then decide whether

you're going to holiday here from time to time, maybe renting it out when you're not here, in which case you'll want to set it up to suit yourself, with secure storage for stuff you don't want tenants to have access to. Or maybe you want to rent it all year round, in which case we set it up for tenants, which means durable finishes, maybe not top-of-the line in quality or price."

Nikki considered the two options, but there was a third, of course. "What if I want to live here myself? All the time?"

"Really?" Zee turned to look at her. "You could do worse. It's a nice town." With his eyes back on the bay, he went on, "In that case, think about what you need in a home, and what sort of money you want to spend, and we can make it work."

That was the problem. Nikki had no idea what she needed in a home, or even whether she planned to stay in New Zealand. "I don't know," she admitted. "I was just thinking of making it back the way it used to be when I was a child. But no. You're right about the kitchen and the bathroom. They're old fashioned and inconvenient. And if we're having to rewire and replumb, we might as well make other changes, too."

He clearly sensed her ambivalence. "You don't have to decide straight away."

But the more she thought about it, the more she wanted to bring the house back to what it could be. "According to Beks, Dave is run off his feet. If I don't get into the work schedule, this job is toast."

His smile warmed his eyes. "True, but I'm sure he'll make an exception for his wife's best friend."

"What would you do with the house?" Nikki asked. "If it was yours?"

It was the right question. Zee pulled out his notebook and opened it to a fresh page.

"I'd push the kitchen back to the end of the verandah to take advantage of that view." A few lines with his pencil transformed the space where they sat into the outer wall of a new kitchen. "Open concept to dining and lounge," he continued, his pencil turning his words into a sketch on the next page, "and a big hall that doubles as circulation space when the pocket doors are open. Leave the stairs where they are." A few lines and some shading miraculously turned into stairs disappearing into shadow on the far side of the hall. "Make one of the downstairs bedrooms into an office and leave the other as a guest room. Upgrade the Jack and Jill bathroom."

"I like that," Nikki commented. New appliances in the kitchen, some more modern furniture and certain pieces from her childhood refinished.

Zee kept sketching, turning from page to page to illustrate his ideas, and Nikki moved up closer so she could see more clearly, her head almost touching her shoulder.

"Upstairs, you could consider cutting off this side of the house and making it a separate apartment. Bedroom, sitting room, bathroom, verandah here over the new kitchen, with an outside stair to give access."

He turned his head to smile at her, his eyes warm. "That way, you can have a tenant or a holiday let, but they don't come into your space or you into theirs."

"If I wanted to do that," she mused, "I could make the entire upstairs a separate let."

"You could," he agreed, turning to another page. "In that case, I'd turn this other bathroom around and make it an ensuite for this bedroom. Three bedrooms and two bathrooms and views to die for. You might want to take that one and let the downstairs!"

"More room downstairs."

"True," Zee agreed and sketched the floor plans they'd discussed on facing pages.

Nikki reached over to take his pencil, and he held the notebook for her while she added a kitchenette to the upstairs sitting room, and a second upstairs verandah across the front of the house.

"Yes. Nice," Zee agreed, taking the pencil from her hand to wrap the downstairs verandah all the way around the house. "Folding doors from the kitchen, so you can take your coffee — or your lemonade" — he indicated their empty glasses with a tip of the head — "into your outside space."

And what is all this going to cost? "Is this the Rolls Royce version?" Nikki asked.

"The top of the line?" Zee was getting to his feet. "I'll tell you what. Why don't I do a bit of assessment of the work required on the basics like fixing rotted timbers and replacing electrical and plumbing, and give you an estimate for that, then work out the upgrade costs above and beyond that basic work?"

"Could you give me a breakdown for the different parts of the house?" She rose, too, scooping up the empty glasses before Zee could. He followed her through the house.

"Yes, sure," he said. "I'll set it out for you. Downstairs, upstairs, verandahs? Three stages?"

The phone in her pocket buzzed. She ignored it, seeing Zee to the door and confirming that his suggested division of the estimate would work for her. Already, though, she was imagining the house as sketched by his creative pencil. Too big for one person, but she could rent out part of it, as Zee suggested. And what better purpose for the money Gran and Poppa had left than to put it into restoring their home?

The message was from Beks. "What did you think of Hot and Handsome?" it read.

She thought for a moment. "Might be bad sailor, but not bad builder. Seems to know his stuff."

"Hot stuff!" said the return message.

Nikki sent back a winking face, and moments later the phone buzzed again. "Get over here and tell Beks all. Have biscuits. And cake."

"Had lemonade with Z," she sent.

"No excuses," came the reply. "Have coffee with Beks."

At the big old Masterton house down by the beach, Nikki was greeted by the smell of warm vanilla and spice, and followed it into the kitchen where Beks was sliding cookies off an oven tray onto a cooling rack. No. Not cookies; biscuits. She was back in New Zealand now. Nikki snagged one then tossed it from one hand to the other when the hot melted chocolate burnt her finger.

"Serves you right," her friend scolded. "You're as bad as the kids."

Come to think of it, the house was surprisingly quiet. "Where are the kids?"

"Jill has them," Beks explained. "She's going to pick Stace up from school, too, so I have until dinner time to finish."

Nikki took a deep breath to better enjoy the luscious smell, before taking a tentative nibble, cautious of the heat. Yum. Chocolate dough with lumps of chocolate, and undoubtedly Beks intended to ice them with chocolate icing. "You've baked enough for an army," she said between bites.

"Big Dig this weekend, to raise money for the school and the kindergarten," Beks reminded her. She stacked the empty oven tray onto several others that waited next to the sink, and picked up a piping bag with a large cookie head on it. "Have you forgotten? You promised to be on the ticket booth." She began piping rosettes of mixture onto another oven tray. They were going to be vanilla kisses from the look of it—melting moments, Gran used to call them.

"Shall I team you with the Sexy Redhead?" Beks asked.

"Beks!" Nikki laughed. "You're a married woman."

Beks winked. "Looking isn't a sin, sweetie. I'm just admiring God's handiwork."

"I'm just admiring Beks' handiwork," Nikki told her. "I was promised cake. It isn't all for the Big Dig afternoon tea tent is it?"

"In this house? There'd be a revolt, led by my dear husband. Here." Beks whipped a cloth off a large chocolate cake, cut two slices, and carried them across to the kitchen dining nook, where mugs and a plunger of coffee waited.

She poured them a mug each, and said, "You have cake. Now give. What do you think of our Zee? Truth, Niks. BFF, remember?"

Nikki surrendered to the inevitable. "He's smart, funny, talented and good-looking. What's not to like? Not my type though. Ginger? And with a beard? Besides, I'm not in the market, Beks. Recently burnt, remember?"

"Not that recently," her friend pointed out. "It's been nearly eighteen months since Russo the Rat! Time to get back on the dating horse, girl."

Nikki didn't think so. She had been within weeks of marrying a man who was lying to her; who would cheat on her and expect her to forgive him because 'it was for the job, Nicola. It didn't mean anything', as if having sex with the wife of a member of the opposing legal team didn't make the whole betrayal worse. "I have had one or two other things on my mind."

Beks softened immediately. "Of course you have, and I am a beast to tease. I worry about my friends."

"And you want everyone to have what you and Dave have," Nikki agreed, understanding what motivated her friend, but Beks shook her head.

"Well, no, because that would be impossible. Because Dave is special." Her smug grin faded and she leant forward to emphasize her point. "But I want my friends to be happy. Zee is lonely, you are lonely, and you are both nice people. It couldn't hurt to keep an open mind." She took a sip of her coffee. "And that's all I'm going to say on the subject."

Yeah, right. "I'll believe that when it happens, Beks. I know you." The woman had more tenacity than a bull dog.

"Yes," Beks admitted, "but you love me anyway. More cake?"

On Big Dig day, Zee was up with Dave's team at the crack of dawn marking out a numbered grid on the North Beach sand with tape and flags and burying numbered tokens — a guaranteed four tokens per square. People would purchase one or more squares at the ticket booth and claim the prizes associated with the tokens they dug from their temporary territory. By 10am, half an hour before start time, the queue of hopeful diggers stretched from the temporary barrier around the Big Dig site all the way back to the car park behind the fishing port.

When Zee reported for duty at the ticket booth, he found

himself paired with Nikki Watson, one of four teams appointed to cope with the rush when the booth opened. They watched a brief demonstration of their job: one to handle payments and the other to hand over the ticket and map, and explain the rules of the Dig.

"Money or explanation?" Nikki asked. She was dressed for the weather, in cropped shorts that hugged her buttocks and hips and a loose cotton shirt, tied at her tiny waist. Her outfit displayed long gorgeous legs that had Zee jerking his imagination back from a salacious fantasy, and a vee of skin at the neckline that hinted at, but did not show, the breasts he'd spent over-hot nights trying not to visualize. Not a sexual object, he growled at his baser self. But certainly a work of art, and easy on the eyes.

He'd been woolgathering, and Nikki called him on it. "Zee? Money or explanation?"

"Money," Zee decided. In his family, rich kids worked for their spending money, and several of his summer jobs during college had involved handling card and cash payments. "If that suits you, Nikki."

She shot him a grin, as the barrier came down and the eager treasure hunters flooded onto the sand. "No worries, partner."

For half an hour, they were flat out, each team dealing with a long queue as expeditiously as possible. The mobile EFT-POS machines hiccupped as they competed for bandwidth so the four money-handlers had to co-ordinate rather than collide with one another, but most of the patrons waited cheerfully enough. Zee and Nikki soon developed a patter, Nikki talking to the kids about what they hoped to find and Zee focusing on the adults, leading with asking them where they'd come from that day. Most were weekenders or holiday visitors, but quite a few had driven out from Barnsley just for the day after seeing the adverts online and in the community papers.

"Not many locals," he said in an aside to Nikki as the rush slowed.

"That's because Beks has roped most of them into the work crew," she replied. "Volunteers with kids get their tickets in an envelope when they arrive. She uses a randomizer to pick the numbers, so the only advantage they get is not having to line up, but they seem to like it."

People continued to trickle in as the day wore on, but an hour after the Big Dig opened the beach was crowded, most squares in the grid occupied by eager children with spades, sieves, and buckets.

Beks and Dave were everywhere, keeping an eye on all the activity and moving volunteers to make sure that the whole day ran smoothly. "Everything okay here?" Beks asked, at the ticket tent.

"We're getting quiet," she was told, and Zee and Nikki found themselves reassigned to the marquee where successful diggers were exchanging numbered tokens for prizes, donated by businesses in Valentine Bay, Barnsley and even further afield. Everything from beach toys and wooden blocks to bikes and kick boards crowded the marquee, which was enclosed on three sides by plastic mesh to ensure that no child pre-empted the process by helping themselves. On the open side, winners were channeled into queues, each bringing their token to a volunteer who would call out the number so another volunteer could fetch the associated prize.

"Hurrah," the woman running the show responded when Nikki said that Beks had sent them. "Take a quick look around to figure out what's where, and then start finding prizes for the callers."

In the close confines between the rows of prizes, the fetchers couldn't help but bump into one another—a sweet torture for Zee when Nikki squeezed past him with an armful of plush bunnies, or when he had to lean over her to fetch a board game from a high shelf. *If you let her get close, you'll have to tell her who you are, and that'll be the end of that,* he warned himself. But his body didn't care.

A few kids were disappointed with what their tokens got them and joined the group in the next tent over, negotiating exchanges under the supervision of several adults. For the most part, though, the thrill of winning and the fun of the day prevailed, and the occasional major prize was greeted with cheers and goodwill.

So the loud argument that erupted as the crowd thinned came as a surprise.

"You stole it from my square," a shrill voice proclaimed.

"Did not, did I, Dad?"

Two children faced off, each with fists clenched; one a skinny girl of around nine or ten, and the other a stocky boy of a similar age. An adult stood behind each child, both glaring: Pokey and a woman Zee didn't know.

The girl turned to her mother. "I saw him, Mum. It was in my bucket when I tipped out the sand, and he grabbed it before I did. He stole it."

"My son is no thief," roared Pokey, jutting out his chin.

The woman was not impressed. "My daughter is not a liar," she shouted back.

"I'll get the maps," Zee whispered to Nikki. "You stop them from killing each other."

In moments, he was back, with Dave as backup. They'd brought the book into which they'd drawn the grid, taking up 10 pages from north to south along the beach. Each square had its ticket number written in red and its token numbers in blue.

"We'll be able to sort it out," Nikki was saying to the two children, as Zee and Dave arrived. Two of the other volunteers had separated the adults and were talking earnestly to them, but Pokey brushed them aside as soon as he saw Dave. "Masterton. Good. Sort this out, will you? This woman and her daughter are trying to take my son's prize."

The girl burst into tears, her fist clenched as she stamped a foot in frustration. "It's my prize!" she yelled, and her mother came charging into the conversation with a description of Pokey that Zee privately thought accurate, though inappropriate in front of children.

"Everyone calm down, and give Mr. Masterton an opportunity to check his records," Nikki ordered, managing to project so much authority that the watching crowd stopped muttering and the main combatants shut their mouths and turned expectant attention on Dave.

Dave squatted so he wasn't looming over the two children. "Can you show me your tickets and the tokens you found?" he asked.

A few minutes later, the girl was the proud owner of a new

bicycle, as well as a lunch-box, a kit of acrylic paints, and a soft toy. Pokey's son was still grumbling about losing out on the bike, and refused to touch the prizes he had won — a school backpack, a kick board, a voucher for a computer game, and a bucket of biscuits.

"I wanted a bike," he whined, just as Pokey's father arrived, one eye on the journalist from the local paper who was taking a photograph of the happy girl.

"Smile nicely and congratulate that girl, and I'll buy you a bike." Zee only caught the district councilor's words because he had come close to scoop up the biscuits, which Pokey had dropped. Snoopy Kenworth was smiling broadly at the crowd, waving and nodding to people he knew, the hand on his grandson's shoulder tensing in a squeeze.

"A bike and tickets for the movies," the boy bargained, then manufactured a warm smile when his grandfather nodded. "Look what I dug up, Granddad," he said loudly, and began to take his prizes one by one from his father's arms.

"A chip off the old block," Nikki observed, as three generations of Kenworth males plastered on identical false smiles and crossed to congratulate the wary bike winner. "I didn't even know Pokey was married."

"He isn't," Dave said. "But that never stopped biology from doing what biology does. The mother lives on the Gold Coast, in Australia, but the kid comes over a couple of times a year in the holidays."

"Huh," Nikki commented. "I thought the man was gifted with the perfect contraceptive."

Zee remembered the old joke. "His personality?" That won him a quick smile from Nikki and a short laugh from Dave, who said, "No accounting for taste. Well, I'd better get back on patrol. We close in another half hour, and by now most kids know which numbers get the big prizes. We might have a few more border incidents."

They didn't, though, perhaps because word quickly spread about the records that prevented cheating. People continued to arrive to collect their prizes, then move on to the drink and food stands.

Soon enough, the dig was over and the clean up began; taking down the barriers around the dig site, rolling up the tape that marked the squares, raking the sand, passing out the last of the prizes to those who could show their ticket number but had not found all of their tokens.

"Right," Dave announced to the volunteers, as the last of the tents was rolled and loaded onto the back of a pickup truck—a ute, they called it here in New Zealand—"barbecue at my place."

Nikki came up beside Zee. "And I happen to know that Beks kept a lot of baking back for dessert."

"Sounds good," Zee agreed. "That girl can cook!"

Perhaps the memory of that comment led Nikki to invite Zee for lunch on Wednesday, when he phoned to say he had the estimate and wanted to come by to discuss it. Nothing complex, she decided. Grilled salmon and a salad of mixed greens, with a side of kumara chips and a lime and mustard dressing. Maybe summer berries to follow. She had a tub of ice cream from one of the boutique manufacturers she'd missed while she was overseas; vanilla and pistachio, which would complement the mix of berries nicely.

Keeping in mind his delight at the view, she set the wrought iron table on the back verandah. It really needed a new glass top to give a good surface for dishes and glasses, but she made do by covering it with a tablecloth.

Was he interested or wasn't he? Beks thought he was, citing the way he watched her as evidence. Certainly, she had caught his gaze several times and felt her own heat rise in response to the inferno she sensed in him.

He hadn't made a move, though. Perhaps because they'd only met in the company of others. Perhaps because he wasn't interested, which would serve her right for denying her own interest to Beks.

They wouldn't be in the company of others today.

The bell at the front door rang. He was here, his broad chest once again setting off a slogan. 'Nothing is impossible with the right attitude and a hammer', the t-shirt read.

"Can I come in?" he asked.

How embarrassing. She had been gawping at his chest instead of inviting him inside. Best carry it off with a laugh. "Nice tee," she said, stepping out of the way and waving him through.

"I've got a collection. I do the slogans on my laptop and a lady in the village prints them on transfers and irons them on for me."

Nikki raised her brows as she showed him through to the back verandah. "Multitalented! I like that. Take a seat, Zee, and I'll bring out the food."

He put his briefcase down by the leg of the table. "Can I help?"

"No. I have it all ready." She left him pulling out his chair and went to set the salad and salmon on the waiting tray. An oven cloth to pull the bowl of chips from the oven. *Anything else?* No, that was it.

On the verandah, Zee moved the salt and pepper mills to make more room for the tray and nodded with satisfaction at the contents. "That looks great."

"Serve yourself, Zee. Don't stand on ceremony. Water?" It had been chilled, and she'd added slices of lemon and sprigs of mint to the jug.

"Please. The view doesn't lose its impact, does it?"

She looked out across North Beach. "No, it doesn't. I hate to think of the bush being cut down and the place being made off limits to the locals. Oh, they say it won't happen, and we'll fight it if it does, but I don't trust Kenworth. At all."

Zee nodded. "For three generations. Did you know he had a son? I didn't. A girl he shacked up with in Sydney, apparently. His big overseas experience; a couple of years with a property development company across the Tasman."

Yes, Beks had told her the story. Pokey told his drinking mates that the girl was just someone he flatted with, and the boy had been conceived on a night of lousy television when the pair were looking for other entertainment. He had been indignant at her refusal to have an abortion, but—now that his son was older— seemed to enjoy having him to visit. "I didn't until we had the pleasure of meeting the little darling last weekend. Three of them. The mind boggles."

"I can't figure out how Snoopy keeps getting re-elected," Zee complained. "And what kind of a grown man puts 'Snoopy' on his campaign ads?"

"He thinks it refers to the dog," Nikki guessed, "not his habit of poking his nose in where it isn't wanted."

They continued to talk easily, moving on to discuss the Big Dig, the housing market and job prospects in Valentine Bay, and the nearby vineyards and other attractions. Nikki took the remains of the first course out to the kitchen and came back with the berries and ice-cream, which Zee accepted with an appreciative hum. Did he make that sound when indulging other pleasures, she wondered, then admonished her mind to keep it clean.

Enough of this. He was here to talk about building, not for her to salivate over. "Coffee, Zee? Or tea? Or a cold drink?"

"Another lemonade, if you have it. Shall I help you clear the table? And then I can spread my plans out on it."

Nikki waved Zee off when he would have helped with the dishes. "I'll do them later," she said. "And I hope you have a dishwasher on your list, Zee."

"Sure do." He stacked the papers he'd brought into a preplanned order and put the tablet on top. Nikki returned with a lemonade each, sitting in the chair he'd pulled around so they were on the same side of the table.

"What's first?"

"I thought we'd start in the middle." He handed her the estimate. "This is the plan that does the essential structural work and adds the extra rooms, but leaves off the deck extensions and uses middle of the road appliances and finishes. Not rubbish, but not top of the line, either."

He'd intended to spend fifteen minutes showing her the plans and explaining the calculations, but it expanded into an hour as she asked incisive questions and made notes of her own. In the end, after he'd been through all three scenarios, she furrowed her brow over her own tablet. Heck, she was stunning when she was thinking. Zee had always been a sucker for a clever woman, and this one was as smart as they came.

She was all business, though. He'd thought of nudging closer, but she'd shown no interest in him as a male; no hint that she'd welcome an advance. Oh, she was friendly, but no more than she'd be to any other near stranger. He'd heard her address random Big Diggers with the same warmth and interest.

She sat next to him completely oblivious the effect she was having, inches from his shoulder, turning his brain to mush with the sweet scent of whatever soap she used — something floral with a hint of spice.

Just as well. If she finds out you used to be an O'Neal — Vice President of Interior Design for the whole O'Neal chain, no less — she'll hate you. Evisceration will be too good for you, you idiot. You should have told her from the beginning.

She turned her beautiful eyes Zee's way and he lost himself in them, and then found himself trying to catch up with what she had been saying.

"...and keep the verandah upgrade from the more comprehensive estimate, but leave the nice, but not extravagant finishes, that would bring us in around here, wouldn't it?"

She tilted her tablet so he could see her calculations, and he bludgeoned his brain into concentrating. Ah yes. Very practical.

"I've allowed a twenty-five percent contingency," he warned. "That's high, but parts of this house are a century old."

"Yes, and though Poppa was meticulous, no major work has been done for forty years, and little beyond essential maintenance for at least fifteen. Not even that, recently." She pointed to the sum at the bottom of her calculations. "That's my budget, Zee. If anything cuts into the contingency, I want to know about it. If we use up the contingency and need more, we'll probably need to take things off the list. When can you start?"

"We can file permit applications tomorrow for the bits that need permitting, but there's stuff we can start on while we wait for approval," he told her. "We could start demolition next Monday, if you can move out in time. We've had a job cancelled, so there's a crew free. And Dave is letting you cut in ahead of others on our work schedule, which I didn't tell you and you don't know." He grinned. "But he'd rather keep Beks happy than the out-of-towners who've been bumped down the list."

Nikki was frowning. "Move out? Do I have to? I thought maybe I could live in the bits you're not working in."

"You could, of course." And then he would see her every day, because he was going to work on this renovation himself. He forced himself to give her the best advice, instead of what suited himself. "But if we have to work around you, it will take longer, and you'll have to put up with the noise, the dust, the mess, and the inconvenience."

"Hmm. I'll think about that. It's a big renovation, Zee. How long will it take? If I move out?"

He pursed his lips as he did some swift arithmetic in his head. "Three months? If it all goes well and the weather is kind."

Nikki grinned. "We're coming up to the end of the summer holidays. Traditionally, we get our hottest weather after the kids go back to school."

Zee returned the smile, but warned, "Dave reckons this heat could break at any time."

"True," Nikki agreed. "We've had frost and even snow before at this time of year. No accounting."

We'll just have to do as much as we can while we have the good weather," Zee said. "It is certainly hot enough today."

"It is. After this, I'm going down to North Beach for a swim." She had been examining her tablet, but now she looked at him without moving her head, her sidelong glance turning his innards molten. "Do you want to come?"

He had another estimate to do, but he could catch up this

evening, after Oliver had his walk. His 'yes' was out of his lips before he had finished the thought. "I have some swim trunks in the truck. I'll get them."

"Wait down there. I'll get changed and join you, and we can take the bush path," Nikki said.

The path began one turn of the road around the hill, plunging steeply towards the bay through typical New Zealand regrowth forest. Bush, the Kiwis called it, though Zee could not have said why. Ferns, both ground ferns and tree ferns, predominated, with the native manuka and kanuka trees interspersed with young rimu and beech that reached high overhead to form a canopy.

The track came out on the road a couple of times, and then continued on the other side, before veering away to the north in a long flight of rough steps carved into the hill and edged with rounds of wood.

Nikki and Zee came out onto a less wooded area, which would have been a meadow except for the baby gorse plants that had Zee hopping and wishing he'd left his work books on instead of changing into thongs. On the far side, a row of pohutukawa trees marked the boundary of the beach, the ground underneath still red with the remains of the flowers that had covered the gnarled twisted trees in glory for a few brief summer weeks.

"I love these trees," Nikki said, patting the tree they passed as they made their way down to the sand. "I've missed them while I've been away. You should see them in flower, Zee."

"Glorious," he agreed. The thinly spread pohutukawa along South Beach had been lovely enough in the weeks leading to Christmas, but North Beach had been incredible.

"I'll be here for them next year." Nikki laughed. "And will undoubtedly be roped into the Big Dig, again."

They draped their towels over a pohutukawa branch dangling over the beach. "Hard to believe this beach had hundreds of people here a few days ago," Zee commented. The cleanup had been thorough, wiping all signs of the invasion, and today a mere dozen people enjoyed the long curve of the beach and the gentle waves beyond.

Nikki stripped off her shirt, and Zee stopped half way through removing his, struck by the sight of her in her bikini. Who knew that the severe suits and the loose blouses concealed such perfectly molded breasts?

She noticed him gawking, but the small smile that played around her lips hinted she wasn't taking offence. Still, he looked away and took off his own shirt, then risked a glance. He worked in a physically active profession, and a walk with Oliver usually turned into a run, a wrestle, and (at this time of year) a swim. She clearly appreciated the results, and the swim trunks would do nothing to disguise his response to her interest. He shouted, "Last one in is a rotten tomato," and took off across the beach.

The sun-heated shallows weren't cool enough to quench Zee's ardor, so he struck for deeper water as he heard her hit the waves behind him. Two buoys marked a swim lane that boats and sail boards were meant to respect, and he swam from one to the other. On his second lap, she caught up, and after that matched him stroke for stroke for another six laps.

Eight laps done, he paused to tread water, and she stopped beside him, grinning. "When you say 'swim', you mean swim," she commented. Zee raised his brows, wondering what she meant.

"Yes?" he ventured, hoping she would explain.

"It's frustrating going to the beach with people who don't want to get their togs wet."

Ah. The old boyfriend had a bit of a reputation as a Narcissus. "Stripping off as an excuse to show off the body beautiful?" he asked.

"You know the type," Nikki agreed.

"I had a girlfriend like that." Iria, who, he'd met as his translator in Cyprus where he was working on a project. After six weeks, he'd taken her home to New York, promising her a job in the O'Neal empire, planning to turn their affair into something more permanent. Within days, she had turned her sights on Pat, his brother. "She married my brother," he disclosed. Another in a long line of betrayals by Pat. Anything Zee had, Pat wanted—

and usually got.

He expected a sympathetic comment, but Nikki surprised him again. "A lucky escape then."

"You're right." She was a self-absorbed, cheating bitch, and she and Pat deserved one another. "I hadn't thought of it that way." In fact, if he was right about her being involved with Nikki's fiancé Russo, he should be feeling sorry for Pat, unfamiliar though that emotion was.

"That's what I've been telling myself about Tyler Russo, my ex. Come on. I have some lemonade in the chiller bag." Nikki struck out for the shore, and he followed her. They spread their towels on the sand under the pohutukawa tree and sat to let the water evaporate from their skin, each sipping from a plastic goblet of lemonade.

Comfortable with the silence between them, Zee contemplated the beach and the bay beyond, enjoying the view and taking in the sounds. Distant shouts from some people playing beachball, the calling of gulls, the constant susurration of the waves. And beside him, a beautiful woman lying on her back with her eyes closed. She had spent the last six months in a sick room, according to Beks, but she'd found time for exercise. Hot didn't begin to describe it.

A conversation started up behind the trees, in some distant part of the gorse-strewn meadow. Three voices, coming closer. "...and we'll have to have these trees down," one said. "The mess in the drains!"

Nikki sat up. "That's Pokey Kenworth," she whispered.

Another person spoke in what Zee thought was Mandarin, and then a third voice, this one female. "Mr. Chow wishes to know where the housing for his workers will be built."

"His workers? Come this way," Pokey said, "I will show you."

Chow? Zee knelt, then lifted himself higher so he could see over the bank to the three people walking away. One of them was Pokey. One was a small woman in a pastel suit and heels unsuitable for the terrain. The other? It could be Chow, the Taiwanese hotelier, whose worldwide empire had frequently clashed with the O'Neals, mostly when a local agency went for his cheaper development plans rather than their more up-market and environmentally-sound options.

Indeed, Chow should have been the target of World Global Watch's landmark court case, and Zee was certain that Russo and Patrick had conspired with Chow to turn the activist group's attention to the O'Neals instead. And specifically to a project Zee had been responsible for building.

But what was Chow doing here? He was certainly not on the investor list that the Mastertons had acquired from the Overseas Investment Office. Zee should tell Nikki. But that would mean explaining who he was, and he didn't want to spoil the afternoon.

"What is it," Nikki asked.

"It might be something..." he temporized. "I'll have to check it out. I should be getting back now, I guess. I have another estimate to do, and I need to take Oliver for a walk."

Pokey and his guests were out of sight when they crossed the meadow; somewhere in the bush, which the vandals no doubt also intended to destroy. Cutting down the row of pohutukawa? That certainly wasn't in the plans that had been submitted to the district council.

They climbed the hill, not talking, saving their breath for the steep path, and parted at the truck.

"Thank you for lunch, and the swim," Zee said, wishing he'd been brave enough to kiss Nikki while they were on the beach. He'd lost his chance now. As soon as he confessed who he was, she'd cut him.

For now, she was warming him with her smile. "Thank you for your advice on the house. Tell Dave it's all on. I look forward to starting."

Three

The next few days, Nikki had no time to think; no time to do anything but pack up the house and have all the furniture and other belongings she wanted to keep moved to a storage facility. By Sunday afternoon, when she arrived at Becky's place with two suitcases, she was exhausted.

"Come on through," Beks said, trying to take one of the cases.

"Not in your condition," Nikki scolded, as she pushed her friend's hand away and grabbed the handle of the case herself. "Lead on to this granny flat, Beks."

When she'd told Becky of her need for accommodation, Becky had offered a one-bedroom apartment that Dave and Bruce had built for Jill's mother. "It has never been used; not even quite finished, because she decided to go and stay with Jill's sister first, and she died before she could move on to us."

In the last few days, they'd painted the bedroom, put a door on the wardrobe, and made a trip to Barnsley to buy a dish drawer, which Dave had installed by one of his plumbers. With Nikki's bench top cooking appliances, and a few pieces of her furniture, it would be a pleasant haven for the next three months.

"You have your own entrance," Beks was explaining as she led the way through the house.

"Aunt Nikki!" That was Stacey, Beks oldest daughter, barreling out of the playroom to give Nikki a huge hug, as if they hadn't seen each other two hours before. "Aunt Nikki, now that you are living with us, will you hear my reading?"

"Aunt Nikki is living next door in the flat, Stacey Masterton," Beks scolded. "And you will not scare her away her very first night." She unlocked the door from the Mastertons' living quarters to the living room of the flat. "Niks, here are the keys. I've given you both sets to the internal door, which I suggest you keep locked unless you want to invite my little monsters over."

Nikki smiled at Stacey. "I expect I will want to do that sometimes. Where are the other two, Stace?"

"Having an afternoon sleep," said the six-year-old with scorn, then excused them in a confidential whisper. "They're just babies, you know."

Becky had filled a vase with summer flowers and a basket with peaches and plums from her orchard, and the bed Nikki had had delivered yesterday afternoon was now made and ready to get into.

"Make yourself comfortable, sweetie," Becky said, giving her a hug, "and don't worry about a thing. You'll have dinner with us tonight, and after that you have an open invitation, and no hurt feelings if you'd rather not."

A shower dealt to the grime of the packing and moving, and an hour's sleep—which might sink her forever in Stacey's eyes if she found out—took the edge off her weariness and set her up to go looking for her friend.

Becky was sitting at the island between the kitchen and the family room, peeling vegetables while watching the children play. No. Not just the children, Nikki realized as she rounded the island. Dave and Zee were on the floor, too, surrounded by the largest wooden train set she had ever seen.

Four-year-old Will saw her first, and sent up a shout: "Aunt Nikki, Aunt Nikki," which was echoed by his older and younger sisters. Nikki knelt to receive an enthusiastic hug from each of the children, who then dragged her over to admire the construction.

"Zee is helping me build the biggest, bestest railway ever," Stacey explained.

"No, ours will be biggest and bestest," argued Will. "Daddy is helping me and Emma, Aunt Nikki, and Daddy is a builder."

"Zee is a builder, too," Stacey retorted.

"It's great to have builders helping," Nikki said, pacifically.

"But I have just had a wonderful idea."

She sat herself down on the rug with the others, and waited to be asked to explain.

Sure enough, Will and Stacey both came and sat beside her, cuddling in. "What is your idea, Aunt Nikki?" Will asked.

"Aunt Nikki has good ideas," Stacey informed him.

Nikki swept her gaze around from person to person, including the toddler Emma and the two men. "If we all built our own railways, but made them go over and under the other railways, wouldn't that be the biggest and the best wooden model railway in the whole entire world?"

They thought about that for a moment, then Will got up and spread his arms to race around the room shouting, "In the whole entire universe!"

"Two railways that co-operate." Zee nodded. "Team work!"

"Three," Nikki suggested. "Will, how about you and I build one of the railways?"

Will stopped his plane imitations and looked at the two layouts already on the floor, and then at Nikki. He wanted to work with Nikki, his face said, but he didn't want to start again.

Zee read the message as clearly as Nikki did. "Stacey, Dave, and Emma, I propose we all help start Will's railway track. We will work for," he narrowed his eyes as he thought, "seven minutes. That would be fair, wouldn't it? Becky, will you keep the count once we start? Will, where do you want your train to run?"

Clever Zee. He had invoked the childhood diety Fairness, and Stacey could not find an objection in time to derail the new plan. Soon, all six of them were clipping tracks together as fast as they could, and hunting through the boxes in the corner for bridge supports so that Will's new railway could fly over or under the other two. Becky called out the seven minutes, and the three teams returned to their own work, the competition now muted but no less fierce.

Becky finished putting the dinner on and sat down to watch, laughing at suggestions she should get down on the floor with the others.

"You build your railways and I'll knit," she said.

With nothing more than two minor incidents — when Emma knocked down Stacey's bridge while trying to step over it, and when Stacey got to the last six-way crossing seconds before Will — the next hour was happily beguiled, until Becky declared it was time to wash for dinner.

The six builders obediently picked themselves up and headed towards the hall and the bathroom, but stopped at a low whistle from Zee, who was bringing up the rear.

"Wow," he said. "Look what we did!"

The large family room was almost completely covered by track in complex interlocking curves and straights, climbing block mountains and down the other side, diving through tunnels and under bridges. They clustered just this side of the doorway, and Nikki imagined her grin was as goofy as those she saw on the others. Will, leaning against her with an arm around her leg, put their feelings into words. "The biggest and bestest in the universe. Isn't it, Aunt Nikki?"

Tonight's family dinner made no concession for guests. Nikki had attended others and knew the drill, and Zee — who was seated next to her — obviously did too because he held out his hand for her to take when Dave asked them to bow their heads. "Tonight it is Will's turn to ask God to bless us and this food," he said.

Will, his face grave, recited, "Thank you for the food we eat. Thank you for the friends we meet. Thank you for the birds that sing. Thank you, God, for everything. Amen."

Nikki joined the Amen, and heard one from Zee, too. When in Rome do as the Romans do? Or was he a believer? She had fallen back into the way of going to church in the months with Gran and Poppa, finding comfort in the familiar prayers and songs. Was she a believer? She supposed she must be. She certainly wasn't an unbeliever.

The next part of the family ritual was for everyone at the table to say the best part of their day. Will said it was building the train track. Stacey said having Aunt Nikki arrive to stay was her best thing, and Nikki agreed. Emma, in enthusiastic appreciation of her mother's cooking, proclaimed the lamb roast in front of her to be best, and Dave shook his head. "It's tough deciding between the train track and lamb roast," he complained. "But I'm going to pick the train track." Will held up a palm and Dave high-fived it, then hunched his neck at a glare from Becky, which made Will laugh.

"Train track," Zee agreed. "It is the biggest one I've ever seen." He leant closer to Nikki as the attention moved to Beks, and whispered, "Having you to stay is pretty neat, too."

Nikki expected Beks to side with her and Stacey, but her friend surprised and topped them all when she put her hands on her belly with eyes that looked at a private vision and explained, "The best part of my day was feeling the new baby move."

That stopped the meal for a few minutes, while Stacey and Will ran around the table to check, and Emma demanded to be lifted from her chair to put her own hands on her mother's abdomen.

Zee and Nikki exchanged glances, and stayed silent to allow the family this special time together. Nikki found herself yearning for the kind of closeness the Mastertons shared. From his fond but wistful smile, Zee was having similar thoughts.

He was good with children. She'd seen it at the Big Dig, and witnessed it again as he chatted to Will after Will returned to his chair. She'd never seen Tyler Russo with children. They moved in a circle of lawyers, scientists, and marketers, all committed to the cause of calling corporates to account when they damaged the environment. None of them had children. Indeed, not having children was almost a requirement—the world had too many people already, they told one another. People had a duty to consider the results of their actions, they insisted, over a glass of wine shipped from Spain, while wearing designer shoes from Italy and eating French cheese and Greek olives.

Nikki hadn't questioned it, had thought sacrificing a family life was something noble, until Beks sent a message with an ultrasound picture of child number three, the baby who would be Emma. Delighted, Nikki told her fiancé the good news, and was hurt and dismayed when Tyler ranted about narrow-minded selfish provincials who absorbed the world's resources and gave little back.

"Will you think that way about us having children?" she asked him.

He had laughed. "Come on, Nicola. We have years to think about having a child. If we decide to go that route at all. We're still young."

She shook off the memories and joined in the conversation around the table — a general free-for-all of ideas for baby names, with Dave and Zee competing to choose the most ridiculous. "Mum," Stacey said at last, "Daddy and Zee are being silly."

"They are, darling," Becky agreed, "and for that they can do the dishes, while Aunt Nikki and I help you with your baths and get you off to bed. If that's okay, Niks. If you're too tired..."

"I'd love to," Nikki assured her friend.

Zee was in deep trouble. Nikki was a top environmental litigator, working for a fanatical activist group. She was meant to be tough-minded, hard-hearted, and competitive. Not funny and sweet and clever and sentimental. He'd come out from the kitchen to find her cuddled up with Stacey, reading her a story while Beks put the younger two children to bed. Nikki had her cheek resting on Stacey's head, and was rubbing it back and forth, her eyes soft.

He'd excused himself to go take Oliver for a walk before dark, but he couldn't walk fast enough to outstrip his thoughts.

She had been wonderful with the children at the Big Dig, managing even Pokey's little brat, and look how she'd turned today's competition into a co-operative venture, getting all of them on board, including Stacey! What a mother she would make.

"Not my children," he told Oliver. "I won't be having any after she emasculates me for not telling her who I am."

Oliver drooped his head and whined, responsive to tone.

"If I'd told her straight up, though, I wouldn't have got to know her," he argued, and Oliver barked eagerly. Zee decided to take that for agreement. "Do you think I can convince her of that?" he asked.

At least the information he'd been collecting about Mr. Chow might soften the impact. He'd tell her that first, he decided. Stopping the development was more urgent than progressing his courtship. Perhaps he could save his own personal history until she was celebrating the win? "I'm being a coward, aren't I, Oliver?" he asked.

But the dog had stopped to investigate a power pole and didn't respond.

"I'll tell her about Chow, then lead up to telling her the truth by talking about my family," Zee decided. "I'll go over when we get back."

He let Oliver back into the flat and crossed to the main house. The kitchen and family room were dark, but he could see light under the lounge door and hear gun-fire and then a swell of theme music from the television. He knocked and went in; Dave and Becky were on the couch, Becky with her head on Dave's lap.

Dave lifted one eyebrow. "Didn't expect you back again tonight, mate."

No sign of Nikki. And Zee had clearly interrupted a bit of marital canoodling. "I wanted to tell you two and Nikki something. But it can wait till tomorrow."

"Nikki's gone to bed. She was worn out," Becky told him.

"She looked tired," Zee realized. "She's been working pretty hard. Tomorrow, then."

He backed out and returned to his flat and his dog, taking his last sight of the Mastertons with him. They'd turned their attention away from him and back to one another before he was out of the door—Dave's hand gently cupping his wife's face, Becky's hand sliding under Dave's tee-shirt. It was the loving connection in their gaze that haunted him. They were living proof that true love was real and reachable. But was it reachable for him?

Four

The following evening, Zee told the Mastertons and Nikki that Pokey had a financial backer whose name did not appear on any of the papers filed with the Overseas Investment Office. Interested in exploring the ramifications, they brushed over Zee's vague explanation for his knowledge: 'I crossed paths with the man while doing some work as a hotel designer'.

"We'll have to prove the connection," Nikki warned. "That conversation we heard would just be our word against Pokey's."

Dave promised to talk to the rest of the impromptu committee formed to co-ordinate opposition to the development and Becky remembered a couple of school friends who worked in the Ministry of Everything who might be able to suggest lines of investigation.

"The Ministry of Everything?" Zee asked.

"The government department made up of all the bits and pieces left after they finished the reorganization a few years ago. Among other things, they're in charge of immigration and tourism. Ministry of Business, Innovation, and Employment," Dave explained.

Nikki offered her research skills. "I have the time free, and you guys have excellent broadband. Pictures of them meeting, connections between this Mr. Chow and the named investors. If it is out there, I'll find it."

"I can help in the evenings," Zee offered. "I may know some of the names or faces. And Dave, don't you have a copy of the plans that were filed with the council? Maybe I could go over them and see where an unscrupulous person might cut corners? If he could pull the wool over the eyes of the building inspector?"

Zee Henderson was all business the following evening, and looking far too sexy for Nikki's own good as he focused on plans and specifications spread across his share of the table. Every now and again, he would ask her opinion about the meaning of legal terms and phrases used in the conditions, and every now and again she would call him to look over her shoulder at his laptop.

After two hours, she pushed the laptop away. "Would you like a drink? I have a local Pinot Gris in the fridge, and you don't have to drive."

"Sure," he agreed. "No luck so far?"

"Not yet, but I have a couple of leads to follow. You?"

"Possibly. I might need to do a trip into Barnsley to check a couple of things at the Council offices. I want to give them a polite shake along on your permits anyway. I thought—there's a home show at the Events Centre this weekend. Everything from building materials to plumbing supplies and light fittings. Opens at noon on Friday. Do you want to come for the drive, and we'll have a look around? See if there's anything that strikes your fancy?"

They went in Zee's ute—his pickup he called it—leaving after breakfast. Nikki had offered her car, but Zee said he had some stuff to pick up for Dave, and needed the pickup's bed.

Nikki decided not to call him on being a typical male, hating to be driven. Besides, she enjoyed watching his competent hands on the wheel and not driving meant she could enjoy the scenery—both inside and outside the car.

"We've gone as far as we can with the demolition," Zee explained, as the truck skirted the foreshore. "I've got the crew tidying up today, and I've a few jobs lined up for next week that don't need permits, but we'll run out pretty quick. No problem if the council sticks to their ten-day timeline, but if anything is holding them up, I want to know about it ahead of time. If I let

Dave take the team off your house and get involved in another job, who knows when we'll get them back?"

"I thought you worked for Dave?" Nikki teased, prompting a broad smile and a sideways glance.

"Believe me, Nikki, I'm working for you on this one." No misinterpreting that, although all week he'd been blowing hot and cold. She'd manufactured several opportunities for them to be alone, and any other man would have made a move by now. Showing an interest had always been enough and she'd done that, surely? Perhaps he was shy. Or she hadn't been obvious enough.

They had the whole day together today; time enough for things to develop.

The road made its turn from the coast, running beside the estuary before turning to climb into the hills.

"Is this anything like where you grew up?" Nikki asked.

Zee laughed. "Not much! Me and my mom lived with her dad up on a mountain in Wyoming. They call it off the grid these days. To me, it was just the way you lived. Fishing in the lake for lunch. Hunting to put meat on the table. School was lessons with mom or grandpop, not just out of books but in our everyday lives. I learnt design hands-on, making things with grandpop."

"It sounds idyllic," Nikki commented.

"I remember it as idyllic. At least until..." He trailed off, his hands on the wheel clenching then releasing.

Should she ask or let it go? Before Nikki could decide, Zee spoke again.

"My mother was having dreadful headaches. Grandpop insisted on taking her into town; dug up some money for some tests. Inoperable brain cancer. We moved into Cheyenne while she had chemotherapy, but in the end she begged to go home. She would have liked you, Nikki. She was a brave strong woman, too."

The compliment warmed Nikki's heart, softened by the thought of the orphaned child. "I am so sorry, Zee. How old were you when you lost her?"

"Just turned eleven. That wasn't the worst. Well, it was. It was the center of all that happened. But it wasn't all." He was silent again, calm competent hands on the wheel, eyes on the road, mind far away in that long-ago childhood.

Nikki waited for Zee to be ready to speak, and after several miles he did. "She was on morphine for the pain—couldn't be left on her own. It was my turn to be with her while Grandpop did the chores and a bit of fishing. He didn't come home."

He worried at his upper lip with his teeth. "I radioed one of the neighbors. Took him half an hour to walk from his place to ours and another twenty minutes to find Grandpop. He'd had a massive stroke. They airlifted him out, but he died in hospital later that night."

"Oh, Zee." Nikki didn't know what else to say. So young, and so much tragedy.

"That's when Mom sent for my father. It was that or Child Welfare. With Mom so sick and no other adult in the house, they wanted to take me straight away, but she insisted that my father would come and look after us."

"That must have been a relief. Your own family. Someone you knew."

Zee shook his head. "I'd never met him. I had no idea he was still alive. All I'd been told was that he and Mom came from different worlds, and it didn't work out. Not his fault, Mom said. He was a nice man, and I would like him. I'd enjoy getting to know my brothers and sisters, too. I didn't even know I had brothers and sisters."

A hint of the devastation he had felt as a young boy survived in the bleak even tones of his voice.

"Zee, that's terrible," Nikki objected. "How could your parents do that to you?"

"I imagine Mom meant it for the best," Zee excused, "but at the time, I felt betrayed. I couldn't even be angry, because she was dying. So I was angry with him, instead."

A herd of dairy cattle on their way back from milking filled the road, and Zee stopped to wait for them to trail their way through the gate to their field. He turned to look at Nikki.

"You know, I never talk about this. I've only just realized

how horrible it must have been for my father. I found out later that he hadn't seen her or spoken to her since she walked out on him three months after they married; didn't even know I existed. But when she phoned, he dropped everything, crossed the entire country, and arrived within a day."

"He still cared?" Nikki asked.

"I don't know." Zee shrugged. "He's a great man for doing his duty. Maybe Mom and I were a duty. It can't have been easy, though. She was dying; I was angry and plain nasty. I sulked because he paid for nurses to come and look after her, instead of doing it himself."

Nikki put a comforting hand on his. "More strangers in your house. No wonder you were cross."

He turned his hand over to squeeze her fingers. "You're kind. I was also furious that he kept on running his business. He was always walking up the mountain to a spot where he could get cell phone reception. I hated that. I didn't give him any credit for staying. It didn't even occur to me that he could easily have whipped us both down into town, or even back to New York, to his own home. Or taken me and left Mom to the nurses. He's — he's a complicated man, but that was a good thing to do, letting Mom die in her own home, and letting me stay till the end."

"It was a good thing. It would have broken her heart and yours to separate you too soon. And then he took you back to New York?"

"Yes. To the family I didn't know I had. Three half-brothers and two half-sisters, from his first marriage and his third. They were nearly as disgusted at having to welcome me as I was to be there. I'd promised Mom I would try; that I wouldn't fight my father and my brothers and sisters. I tried, but I just... I guess I was depressed. I wanted to sleep all the time, and since I couldn't fight or yell, I just kept walking away, shutting myself in my room."

The last of the cows lumbered through the gate, followed by several dogs and a man on a four-wheeler bike. Zee lifted Nikki's hand to kiss it before turning back to the wheel and starting the ute again.

"Thank you for listening. I didn't mean to get all maudlin on you. I've never talked about this."

Nikki said what was in her heart. "I'm honored, Zee. Truly. And I really want to know what happened to that poor grieving boy." Or was she intruding? "Only if you want to say."

"Grandma happened," he was relaxed again, now, hands at ease on the wheel and whatever memories ran in his mind putting a gentle smile on his face. "My father's mother. She used to live with us, and she wouldn't let me keep her out. She said the same as you, Nikki. She told me I was grieving."

"The one who said 'You get one year off from caring about what anyone thinks'," Nikki remembered.

Zee's smile broadened. "Yes, that was Grandma. I don't know what she said to the others, but even Pat stopped teasing me, and after a few months I realized New York wasn't such a bad place, and living with my father was certainly preferable to a foster home."

"Or more than one," Nikki agreed. "Angry kids tend to be moved around a lot."

"So that's my long answer to the question." Zee waved one hand in a circle, indicating the landscape. "Is this anything like where I came from? Not even a little bit. Not the mountains nor New York City."

Nikki laughed. "Definitely not like New York City. The Big Apple was a real shock to this little Kiwi girl. I'd been to Wellington on a couple of school trips, but Barnsley was the biggest place I'd really known till I arrived at Columbia."

They had come out of the coastal hills and were approaching the intersection with the main highway north through vineyards and olive groves interspersed with fields where animals grazed.

"This country is nothing like where I came from, but I love it. I envy you growing up here, Nikki."

"It was pretty special," Nikki agreed. "It's like you said. At the time, it's just the way you live. I wasn't the only kid at school being raised by grandparents, and I took them pretty much for granted. They were the best, though. And it sounds like you had some pretty awesome grandparents, too. Is your Grandma still alive?"

Zee took the turn onto the main highway, heading south towards Barnsley. "She isn't, no. She died two years ago."

"Just before you left the United States."

Nikki was right to make the connection, though Zee hadn't done so himself. He'd been restless for a while, feeling increasingly alienated from the endless drive for *more* that motivated his father and siblings. He'd buried himself in his own projects, ignoring as best he could the occasional niggles when the board blocked or diverted budget for one of his proposals.

There was satisfaction in designing and building luxury hotels in exotic places. And it wasn't just about wealthy tourists. Unlike Chow, O'Neals made a practice of hiring and training locals to staff their enterprises. Zee thought they could do more, and put together a proposal for investing in the local communities: in schools, infrastructure, health centers, and small enterprises. To his surprise, his father and eldest brother backed it, and now every O'Neal hotel in a developing nation put part of its profit into The O'Neal Development Foundation, to be dispersed in consultation with local leaders.

And the O'Neal women ran the foundation, leaving Zee to get back to making money for the business.

"I was in a job that meant I was travelling all the time. I was tired of it. The work had got to be pretty meaningless, and living out of a suitcase sucked. I needed to put down roots, I guess. Grandma—I guess she was the only thing holding me to New York and my father's family. When she died, I was free."

Nikki chuckled. "So you went to sea to put down roots?"

When she said it like that, it was pretty funny. "A slight miscalculation. But it turned out well, because here I am."

"What did they think of you leaving?" Nikki wondered. "Your father and your brothers and sisters?"

Zee slowed down as they crossed the bridge that marked the northern edge of Barnsley to drive between a long ribbon of houses and businesses on the way to the commercial center. Could he disclose just a bit more of his story, for her to remember when he finally admitted who he was?

"There'd been a blow up. One of my brothers had been involved in some shady dealings to win a court case. More. He'd taken money to manufacture evidence that absolved a guilty party and accused an innocent one. I found out, assumed my father was involved, and faced him with it at a family dinner."

Nikki was silent, and he glanced sideways to see her face intent, her eyebrows raised.

"The whole family got in on the act." He went on, "Most of them — or so it seemed to me at the time — defending my brother. And his wife, who was in it up to her ears. I walked out. I haven't spoken to any of them since."

Nikki picked up on the doubts that had slowly seeped through his self-righteous judgment. "It seemed to you at the time?"

"My father didn't say much, and my brother Brendan — he's the eldest — just asked questions. Thinking back, cheating isn't their style. They can be ruthless, and I don't always agree with their priorities, but they're honest men. I'd love to know what happened after I left."

He took the turn for the district council buildings, and found a parking space nearby.

"So that's my whole sorry story," he finished. "Shall we go and charm your permits out of the Council?" He armed himself with his briefcase and a roll of backup plans he could substitute to meet probable objections.

Zee had made an appointment with the chief planning officer, leaning on the number of dealings Masterton & Son had with the district council to go straight to the top. He and Nikki came out of the meeting after an hour of discussion and negotiation with the necessary permissions to begin the work, but without everything they wanted. Someone had put in an objection to the extensions to the verandah, complaining that it would change the skyline view from the two Valentine Bay beaches. They'd need to go through a review process on that part of the build.

"Thank goodness you made a separate application for the verandah," Nikki said, as they moved down to the public workspace to look at the filed plans for the hotel project, the next job on their list. "We'd be stalled if you put the whole build under one permit."

"We'll get it through," Zee assured her. "We just have to prove that the new build is within the aesthetic of the village. You and I both know who the objection came from, don't we?"

"Pokey. Or his father, maybe."

Beyond a doubt, Zee thought as he nodded. *The councilor probably had a tag to alert him about building projects in his son's territory.*

"What are we looking for?" Nikki asked.

Zee pulled some pages from his briefcase. "Anything on the plans that isn't in the specifications and vice versa. I've written a list of the most likely things to watch for. Here. You take these, and nudge me if you think you've found something."

Another hour passed, as they went carefully over the plans, zooming in on the touch screens to examine the detail, murmuring to one another as they discussed anomalies. Drainage far larger than needed for the proposed buildings and running under the protected reserve area. Visuals that showed the view from the hotel with no pohutukawas (also protected) between the hotel swimming pool and the beach. Several parking areas that extended beyond the land the developers owned, into the surrounding bush.

"Do we have them?" Nikki asked, but Zee shook his head. "It's indicative, but not conclusive. If we raise these things now, they'll just claim the draughtsman got it wrong and change the plans. If they were building these things—but by then it would be too late." He took a deep breath and sighed it out. "The undisclosed ownership relationship with Chow is still our best bet, if we can prove it. I think we've done what we can here, Nikki. Come on. I'll buy you lunch."

Nikki put her tablet back into her handbag, along with the notebook and pen she'd also been using. "Let's eat at the Event Centre. They have a good cafe, and these shows usually have food stalls, too."

The Event Centre was a public building that provided a range of different-sized meeting and exhibition spaces, currently completely given over to displays by suppliers of building materials, home appliances, and construction services.

They bought a hamburger each, and wandered around looking at the exhibits as they ate, circling all the rooms and deciding on which products and services to investigate further once they'd finished their lunch.

Kenworth Real Estate had a booth, with photos of houses for sale in Valentine Bay and a 3-D model and visuals of the proposed hotel. "No pohutukawas," Zee murmured in Nikki's ear.

Nikki took the last mouthful of her burger and wiped her fingers on a paper napkin before dropping it in a bin. "Let's take a closer look," she suggested, entering the booth. A rack of colorful brochures extolled the virtues of the development. "Loving a Holiday in Valentine Bay," said one. "Tourist Boost to Local Economy," claimed another. Zee snorted, then jumped when a voice shouted in his ear.

"Who asked you? You Americans. Coming in where you aren't wanted. Think you own the world."

Pokey Kenworth, attempting to loom over him and failing because Zee was taller. His father stood at his shoulder, glaring at Zee.

"He and Ms. Watson were over at the Council looking at your plans," the older Kenworth said.

Pokey sneered. "Maybe you want to invest? Of course not. A bit rich for a two-bit drifter. Why don't you go back where you came from?"

"That's a bit rude, Pokey," Nikki scolded. "Hardly what one expects of a man who intends to bring tourists into Valentine Bay."

Pokey ignored her, turning instead to listen to his father, who asked, "How did a washed-up sailor get a work visa? A man has to wonder."

"Good point, Dad," Pokey agreed. "We don't like people coming here taking jobs from genuine New Zealanders."

Zee winked at Nikki. He'd easily met the New Zealand

Immigration Service's points system, with qualifications and experience in a needed skills area, a job to go to and a place to live, good health, and funds he was more than happy to bring to New Zealand—his own savings from his salary, not O'Neal family money.

Pokey caught the exchange and reddened still further. "You stay out of my business, Henderson, and I'll stay out of yours."

Zee spread his hands and smiled. "I'm an open book, Kenworth. Come on, Nikki. Let's go look at bathroom fittings."

Five

The email took a long time to write. Zee knew what he needed to say, but the words didn't come easily. Twice, he deserted his laptop to do his Saturday chores—take Oliver out for a walk, clean the studio, catch up on his laundry, set dinner simmering in the slow cooker. In the end, he thought he had it. Reading it over carefully, he adjusted a few words here and there, went to send, then changed his mind and resaved as a draft.

Stop procrastinating, you idiot.

It was as good as it was going to get. He opened the draft and clicked on the send button before he could have second—no, nineteenth or twentieth thoughts.

> *Hi Dad,*
>
> *It's Drew here. I should have been in touch long ago. In fact, I shouldn't have stormed off without first talking to you. And I'm going to admit straight up front that I'd still be putting off writing if I didn't want something.*
>
> *First, the apology. I knew fairly early on you couldn't have been involved in Pat's deal with Russo at Global Earth Watch. It just isn't your style, or Brendan's either. I'm sorry I didn't figure that out before I blew up.*
>
> *That wasn't why I left, though it was the trigger for the timing. I'd been thinking of trying something else, outside of O'Neal Hotel Corporation, for quite a while. I needed to see if I could make it on my own. I should have talked to you about that, too. Looking back, I can see that you've always supported all of us to do what we thought was right for us. You might have*

argued – probably would have. But just to be sure I'd thought things through, and then I would have had your blessing to make my own decision.

I'm sorry for judging you and getting it wrong.

I've been living in New Zealand, which I expect you knew. And I'm guessing you knew I've gone back to my old name. Zachary Henderson, not Andrew O'Neal. When Grandma and I decided to change my name when I first came to live with you, you understood it was part of me trying to fit in. I hope you'll understand that I needed to be that guy again, and see what he could grow into without the corporation and the O'Neal history behind him.

But, as Grandma always said, family is family. I like being Z. Henderson of Valentine Bay, New Zealand. But I'll also always be an O'Neal. I needed some distance and the good friends I've found here to understand that.

Which brings me to my request. There's a developer here who is building a hotel in a beautiful spot not far from where I live. Not a bad idea. The local economy would benefit from a properly designed and targeted project, one that respected the local community and the environment.

I have fears about the project as it stands, especially since Chow Hsin-hung seems to be involved. I overheard him talking to the developer about bringing in his own labor, but the investors in the publicly-available documentation, which is attached, are all New Zealand residents or New Zealand-registered companies whose directors are New Zealand residents.

I have tried following the trail from the named investors to Chow. I'm sure he's holding the purse, but I can't prove the connection. Would you put some people on to it? I'm happy to cover any costs.

Dad, I'd like to keep in touch. Give my love to the rest of the family, and feel free to pass on my email address.

How to sign off had bewildered him for a while. Just his

name seemed far too cold. 'Kind regards' was too business like, and 'Love' was a step too far. He did love his father, and he knew his father loved him, but a male O'Neal didn't talk about such things. In the end, he settled on 'I miss you all, Drew'.

He hovered over the laptop, berating himself for expecting an instant reply. His father was a busy man, and might—in any case—need some time to come to terms with an out-of-blue contact from the prodigal son. But in less than fifteen minutes, the laptop dinged for an incoming message.

> *Drew, it is good to hear from you. Or should I call you Zack now? Or Z, as I'm told your friends do. Don't give the past another thought. I'm glad you've found what you were looking for, and very pleased you've got in touch. Yes, I'll look into the Chow connection. As you know, the family owes him a disfavor. I will be in touch. Your stepmother sends her love.*
> *Dad.*

Zee grinned at the 'as I'm told your friends do'. He'd assumed his father was keeping tabs on him, and he'd been right. And 'the family owes him a disfavor'. *Interesting. Did Dad have evidence that linked Chow to Russo and Pat?*

The walk around the north coast to the heads had taken longer than Nikki had expected. It had been every bit as spectacular as she remembered. The trail ran along North Beach, and then dived in and out of the regrowth bush, climbing saddles between mini bays, dipping to skirt tiny beaches or meander between rock pools, ascending hills and running along cliff tops then plunging back to sea level again.

It was deserted—the weekend crowd wouldn't attempt such a walk on a Sunday, and the local youth had been back at school for a week and probably had homework.

The day was one of the hottest of the summer, but she had

plenty of sun cream and a broad hat. She could wade in the sea or linger under trees to cool down. And she had no reason to hurry.

Somewhere along the way she had resolved her doubts about doing the courses to register in New Zealand — more, to sit and pass the courses she needed to set up her own law practice in Valentine Bay. 'Resolve' was the wrong word, for she had not been going over the arguments for and against that had been plaguing her since the idea first raised itself in her head. Instead, between one cove and the next, she revisited the notion and found her mind made up.

It would be mostly wills and property conveyancing, she supposed. The occasional neighborly dispute about noisy roosters. Maybe relationship breakdowns.

But not if Nikki walked off a cliff in the gathering gloom. The sun dropped behind the coastal hill leaving her still on the switchback trail north-east of the beach. She hurried her steps, peering at the path just in front of her feet, skirting shadows for fear they concealed dips and holes in the path.

Thankfully, before the path comprised nothing but shadows, she crested the hill that sloped down to North Beach, where white stones marked either side of the trail. In minutes, with only a minor stumble, Nikki was safely on the sand.

It was now full dark, stars providing the only light. She hoped Beks wasn't worrying. She hoped no-one else was out and about, or at least no-one with unsavory intentions.

The tide was retreating, leaving a stretch of wet sand that made for easy walking, and another ten minutes would see her almost to the ridge between the beaches; fifteen minutes and she would be back at the Mastertons.

A shadow ran out of the dark, straight for her, and she almost shrieked before she recognized the bark of greeting, the joyfully wagging tail, and lolling tongue.

"Oliver! Down, boy." She used both hands to rub the ruff that collared his neck, bending over to praise him, while keeping an eye out for his master. "Good Oliver, good boy." Thank goodness. She would admit to herself, if not to him, she was pleased to have Zee's escort home.

"There you are," he said, one shadow among the others resolving into a human being as he approached. "Beks was concerned you might have had an accident or been delayed and got stuck in the dark. She sent me with a torch and a phone."

"Uninjured," Nikki said, standing and holding out her arms to show she was whole. "But it took longer than I thought. I would have let Beks know, but my phone ran out of battery."

"Good walk, though?" he asked.

Nikki nodded. "The best. I'm almost reluctant to go home. It's so peaceful out here."

"What's the hurry?" Zee asked. He turned to look out to sea. "The moon will be up in half an hour, and it's near full. How about a swim?"

Nikki laughed. "We can't swim. I don't have my togs with me, and anyway, Beks will worry."

"Half a mo'." Zee pulled his phone from his pocket and hit a couple of buttons. "Beks? I met her on North Beach. She's fine. No, no problems. But we're going to stop and have a swim, and watch the moon rise. Yes, we will. Thanks. Bye."

Nikki tried to frown, but the grin kept breaking through. The heat from the day lingered, and a swim sounded wonderful. If she kept on her shorts and bra, she'd be decent enough, and no need for a towel when the air was so hot.

She unbuttoned her shirt, and looked around for somewhere to leave it that they'd find again in the dark.

Zee switched on his torch, driving back the shadows but making everything beyond the circle of light seem darker. He turned in a slow circle, then said, "We can leave our things there."

Yes. Perfect. A rocky outcrop that had captured a large tangle of driftwood, centered on a log with an upright branch.

They hung their shirts on the branch, white shapes in the night. Her hat and their shoes went underneath with her little backpack, the shoes inside the hat so it didn't blow away. Zee stripped off his jeans, too, but Nikki kept her shorts — for modesty or as a barrier against her secret longings, she could not have said.

Oliver ran around them, whimpering with excitement.

"Yes, Oliver," Zee assured him. "Swim."

They ran down the beach, following the dog, who splashed through a couple of waves then stood hock deep, looking back at them. "Last one in is a rotten tomato," Nikki said in imitation of his challenge last time they'd been here. She took a dozen swift steps forward, before diving under a wave and coming up on the other side, waist deep, shaking her hair to send drops flying.

Oliver barked, and Zee was nowhere to be seen before he surfaced a few feet away, the water around his hips and his hands reaching to restore his underwear to its proper place. "Oops," he said cheerfully. "The elastic wasn't as tight as I thought. Just as well it's dark."

Nikki dived again, swimming further out and further away, but Zee easily kept pace, even swimming one-handed with the other keeping his sole garment in place. He kept his distance, though; close enough to be seen, but far enough away she didn't feel crowded or threatened. Rushed. Rushed was a better word than threatened.

On just such a night, in a hotel swimming pool in the Caribbean, she and Tyler had first—no, tell it like it was. They had been on assignment, there to interview witnesses, and Tyler had made a move on her without warning or encouragement. She had been so surprised she had not resisted. Later, she had rationalized that she must have done something that hinted interest, and felt guilty for being a tease, however unconsciously. Or had that been Tyler's suggestion?

At the time, she had just felt—rushed. He had backed off when she protested, but not before they nearly… No. Let the thought go. Tyler was ancient history, and he and Zee were chalk and cheese.

"Toad."

She realized she'd said that out loud when Zee asked, "Me? Have I offended you?"

"Not you," she reassured him. "My former fiancé. He was a toad."

"Which is, I take it, why he is a former fiancé," Zee said. Her dark-adjusted eyes managed to make sense of the grey shape of

his body on the almost-black waves. He was floating on his back, looking up at the stars. Nikki stopped paddling in place and lay back. "Hold my hand so we don't drift apart," she suggested.

Linked, they floated, letting the sea cradle them.

"Did you love him?" Zee asked, then corrected himself. "You must have. You planned to marry him."

Nikki thought about it. "You know, I don't think I did. I loved who he convinced me he was. But he lied. He didn't have the character or the ethics he pretended. He didn't like the things he said he liked. He wasn't the mask he wore."

"I get that." From the meditative quality in Zee's voice, he had a toad or two in his own history. "It's still a loss, though."

"True," she agreed. "And grief for loss is no easier when mixed with anger at betrayal and embarrassment at your own stupidity. But when you get over it, you're over it."

They floated in silence.

"What happened?" Zee asked, after a while. "If you don't mind me asking, that is."

"Slow disillusionment, I guess. I knew something was wrong for ages before I had my nose rubbed in evidence he was a liar and a cheat."

Zee was half sorry he'd raised the question, and half wanted more. Who rubbed her nose in the evidence and why? Was it to do with Global Earth Watch vs O'Neal Hotel Corporation? He couldn't think how to ask and then she answered so he didn't need to.

"I got an anonymous packet of papers proving he had conspired with opposing council in a court case we'd just lost. It was meant to be a showcase trial. He'd picked the target, done the research, found the witnesses. All lies. All to make Global look like idiots and to divert us from going after the real culprits, who were paying them both."

An anonymous packet. His father? And what happened to Pat

and Iria? Zee had resolutely avoided looking up anything to do with his family or the corporation, but now he was wildly curious.

Oliver interrupted. They heard him approaching, panting as he went, and then he was trying to clamber aboard Zee's chest, breaking Zee's hold on Nikki and sinking him under the waves. He rose again, spluttering, and grabbed the dog by the collar before Nikki suffered the same fate. She was laughing. "He thinks it time we went in," she said, and took off for the beach, just the white wake of her kick visible as she slid down the far side of a wave.

He followed but stopped in the shallows to release the water that had caught in his whitey-tighties, adding weight that warred with the elastic that barely held them up. There. Plastered to his form, which he could do nothing about, but at least firmly in place.

Oliver stopped where the water was only a few inches deep and shook himself vigorously, then raced up the beach after Nikki. Zee followed more slowly. She'd put her blouse back on and it had turned transparent where it clung to her wet shoulders and bra.

Zee struggled into his jeans, the fabric refusing to slide over his wet legs, but didn't bother with his t-shirt. Instead, he spread it on a handy log that provided a seat a few feet further along the beach.

"Your moon-watching throne awaits, my lady," he said, bowing with a flourish.

They sat, side-by-side, almost but not quite touching, Oliver recovering from his excursions at their feet, his nose on his paws and his eyes shut.

The moon rose over the heads, slowly climbing until the full globe sailed free in the sky. Bit by bit, Nikki gravitated towards him. Or perhaps Zee drifted towards her. Certainly once their shoulders touched, it seemed only natural to put his arm around her shoulder, and she didn't pull away. Far from it. She shifted slightly so she could lean against him. Her damp shirt against his naked chest should have been cold, but it would take more than that to quench his heat.

"Beautiful," he said, and he didn't mean the moon. When she

looked up he bent his mouth to hers. She greeted his inferno with her own, so that what he had intended as a respectful salute became a feverish exchange of promises; a prelude to intimacies his every fiber demanded and his soul craved.

Merciful heavens, I'm in trouble. He wanted to stay on this beach forever, exploring the potential her lips and her tongue offered. He wanted to take her home to his apartment and wash the sand and salt from every inch of her skin with loving hands before spreading her on his bed and exploring her with his mouth before joining his flesh to hers. He wanted to wake up beside her and do it all again, not just tomorrow but every day of his life.

She doesn't know you're an O'Neal, his conscience warned him, and the hand he'd slid up under her shirt stilled on her breast. Fighting the insistent demands of his body, he forced the hand around to her back, gentling the kiss and eventually easing back, until they were no longer kissing, but still locked together arm-in-arm, body-to-body, his cheek resting on her head.

"We should go home," he said, but he didn't let her go.

Oliver woke at the word, and leapt to his feet, panting eagerly. When neither of his humans moved, he barked — one short sound, and then expectant waiting.

Nikki shifted, and Zee released her, but once they were walking along the beach, she slipped under his arm, and he matched his stride to hers.

Tell her, his mind screamed. Not yet, his heart insisted. Tomorrow. Tell her tomorrow. Or the day after. But definitely this coming week.

Six

Nikki was humming as she chose what to wear out to lunch. She'd had a busy week so far. She'd talked on the phone to the New Zealand Council of Legal Information about her overseas qualifications and then hunted through boxes to find the certificates, diplomas, and testimonials they required to make the necessary assessment. She'd contacted her boss at Global Earth Watch to tell him she wasn't coming back, and asked for a reference to use in her application to practice in New Zealand. There'd be exams to sit and courses to study, but the decision she'd made on Sunday still felt like the right one. She was happy here in Valentine Bay, and the man she was on her way to meet was part of the reason.

She was going up to her house to have lunch with Zee. He needed her to make some decisions, he'd said last night at dinner, and there were a couple of things he had to tell her.

All the heat of their kiss last Sunday was in his eyes. He hadn't touched her since that night, except with his look, but there was no mistaking his desire.

"You're inviting Niks to have lunch with you and the gang?" Beks had asked.

"I've loaned the gang to Dave for the day," Zee said, not taking his gaze off Nikki. So they would be alone. And he'd gone to some trouble, for Beks had confided that he'd consulted her on a picnic menu, including wine. Yes, and strawberries for dessert.

She dabbed a bit of perfume behind each ear, and some more on the pulse points of her wrist. Then she opened the jar again and put a couple of dabs in between her breasts.

There. Ready for anything.

Almost to the door, she stopped to turn her laptop to sleep mode, first rescanning the email she'd left on the screen these last few days. Her mother and half-sister were going to be in Auckland for a week, and wondered if she would like to fly up to join them.

That helicopter sounded close. Nikki had heard it approaching, but now it seemed to be right overhead. She looked out of her window in time to see it flying low over the roof of the house, but the noise continued. Surely it hadn't landed here? And if so, why?

Nikki opened the door between her apartment and the main house. She could see the length of the house and out through the kitchen windows to the parking space in front of the garage, and sure enough, there was a large helicopter, a man in a suit descending from it, his clothing and hair blowing in the wind from the blades.

Nikki was drawn by her own curiosity down the hall to the front of the house, where Beks was opening the front door while holding a struggling Will by his wrist. "Want to see the helicopter."

Will insisted. Presumably Emma had managed to sleep through the racket, which was diminishing now since the helicopter pilot had turned off his machine.

"Can I help you?" Beks asked whoever was at the door, raising her voice to be heard through the last of the noise.

"Mrs. Masterton?" An American accent. Nikki couldn't see the man from her position, but she had a bad feeling about this.

"Yes, I am," Beks confirmed.

"I'm Michael O'Neal, and I believe you can tell me where to find my son."

Zee took the drive to the Mastertons in record time. Becky's call had been brief and horrifying. His father was there. Niks, on the other hand, never wanted to see him again, and Becky tended to agree with her. "But whatever," she said. "Get your butt down here and deal with your father. I'll deal with you, after."

Whatever her opinion of Zee, Becky had made his father

comfortable in her living room. On the table in front of him, Zee could see the remains of a cup of coffee and a plate with the crumbs from a slice of Becky's chocolate cake. And the hotel magnate had a child on either side of him, to whom he was reading Dr. Seuss's *One Fish Two Fish*.

"Excuse me," he said politely to the toddlers. "Drew. I'm sorry son. I seem to have upset the ladies."

"My fault, Dad. I… There never seemed to be a right time… I was going to…" Zee trailed off, looking helplessly at Becky, who narrowed her eyes in a glare.

"I'll be another minute or two," Michael O'Neal said, turning back to the book and the children, and Zee shifted uncomfortably while he waited, not wanting to sit on Becky's furniture when she looked fit to murder him.

"It isn't what you think," he murmured.

"It's what Niks thinks that you should be worrying about," she retorted. "There," she said to her children as Dad finished the book. "Come and play in the family room. Mr. O'Neal needs to talk to…" she left the sentence dangling with another glare.

"I'll take my Dad over to my place." Zee had known his deception would infuriate Nikki, but he hadn't thought about how Becky and Dave would feel. Had he lost his friends as well as the woman he loved?

"Can I play with Oliver, Zee?" Will begged.

"Not now, Will." Becky's voice, edged with her irritation at Zee, propelled the little boy out of the room.

"This way, Dad." Zee ushered his father across the driveway and up the steps beside the garage. "No car?" he asked.

"I flew into Wellington then came out here by helicopter. I sent the pilot down to the village when Mrs. Masterton called you; figured you could take me down to the motel later."

"Barkers? They'll make you more comfortable than you'd be on my sofa. If I even have one after Becky has finished with me." He opened the door to his flat and stepped aside to let his father in first.

"I'm sorry about upsetting your friends," Zee's father

repeated. "I should have let you know I was coming. I just...
I have the information you need, and I wanted to see you. Will
Miss Watson let you explain?"

Zee shook his head. "I don't know. She doesn't like the O'Neals
much. Blames us all for..."

"For Patrick's stupidity. Yes. I'm sorry about that, too, son. I
should have kept a closer eye on him. He has always been one
to cut corners when he wanted something."

Zee did his best to subdue his anxiety about Niks. "Tell me
about the family. Is Bethany well?" She was his father's fourth
wife—not the trophy wife that the mass media expected of a
billionaire, but a relaxed and loving woman, comfortably
upholstered, who returned her husband's adoration, had added
another daughter to the O'Neal clan and mothered all of her
stepchildren, even those close to her own age.

"She sends her love," the older O'Neal said.

For several minutes, they talked about Bethany and her
daughter Rosemary, then Zee's other brothers and sisters, and
their spouses or partners and children. Zee had missed them
more than he expected. If nothing else good came from his
reaching out to his father, at least they'd broken the ice. He could
keep in touch now, though he'd have exchanged his entire family
to have Nikki back.

O'Neal didn't mention Pat or Iria. In the end, Zee asked. "And
Pat? Iria?"

"Divorced." Zee's father grimaced. "That's part of the reason
I could get your answer so quickly. We already had some of the
connections."

Zee stopped pouring the coffee he'd just made, and frowned.
How did his brother's divorce relate to the ownership of a New
Zealand hotel?

But his father was explained. "Iria talked both her husband
and the Global Earth Watch man, Russo, into working together.
Global already had a target in mind for their class case, but Iria
persuaded Russo to go after O'Neals' instead, and she was the
conduit for communications between Russo and Pat."

"So who was the original target?" He added milk to his father's cup, handing it over and collecting his own.

The older O'Neal nodded. "The correct question. A hotel chain owned by Iria's paymaster. I'm sure you can make an accurate guess."

"Paradise Holidays." A statement, not a question. "Iria was taking bribes from Chow?"

"Once we had the target, we went digging for links. Iria said her money was old family money. We never questioned it. But when she arrived in Cyprus not long before you did, the name on her passport said Marija Vladislav."

Vladislav? Not from Cyprus? "She played me?"

O'Neal shrugged. "She played us all. But once we knew who to look at, we uncovered a trail of shell companies, bitcoin operations, and the like that led back to Chow. And those same links, when we followed them in the other direction after your email, led to the known investors in your hotel project."

That was good news, then, but Zee couldn't focus on it at the moment. "I'm having trouble fathoming it." He sank onto the sofa, cradling his cup in both hands. "I brought her back to New York with me. I introduced her to Pat."

"Pat was pretty upset. Mostly about being played for a fool, I think. Not just the Chow involvement, but her cover story for seeing Russo was that she was having an affair with him, and that turned out to be almost the only point on which she told the truth. Russo was your Miss Watson's fiancé. Is that right?"

Zee nodded, staring into his coffee. Feeling sorry for Pat was not a familiar emotion, but the poor sod must be bleeding.

Outside, Dave's truck pulled into the parking bay beyond the garage, and Dave descended, glared up at the loft above the garage and strode in the direction of the house. Becky had clearly been talking to him.

Zee stood. "Dad, my boss is home. Will you come and tell him and his wife about Chow?"

O'Neal picked up his briefcase. "I have the evidence here. The investors have broken New Zealand law. And the developer, this

Kenworth, too. You're a witness to the fact that he knows Chow is his ultimate backer.

Zee knocked on the Masterton back door, uncomfortable with letting himself into the house where he had been welcome for a year. He made the introductions when Dave answered his knock; his friend was wearing his poker face. "My father has the information we need to stop the hotel development," Zee told him, and Dave stepped to one side and waved them in.

Zee let his father lead the conversation, summarizing the evidential path that led from Chow Enterprises to the New Zealand residents and New Zealand-registered companies that appeared on the investor list for the Kenworth hotel development. He stood at O'Neal's shoulder, uncomfortable under Becky's glare and Dave's more contemplative look.

"So we have them," Dave said to O'Neal, when the last piece of paper had been spread out and explained. "We report this to the Overseas Investment Office, and the development is dead in the water."

"Unless your developer has other sources of funding," O'Neal agreed.

Dave turned to Zee. "Now we have our other problem," he said.

O'Neal stood, putting his body between Zee and Dave. "My son has a problem," he countered. "Partly, I understand, of his own making. But he knows that." He looked over his shoulder at Zee. "Son, how important is Miss Watson to you?"

Zee met Becky's eyes while he thought about what to say. *The truth, of course, to these three.* "She is the woman I want to spend the rest of my life with. Here in Valentine Bay, if that's what she wants. But anywhere that works for her, if she'll have me after this. Becky, I was going to tell her about my connection to the O'Neals today, at lunch."

"Rather late," Becky grumbled. But her eyes softened.

"Then tell her," his father urged. "I should have gone after your mother when she left. Should have made the changes she needed to live with me happily. I buried myself in work, instead. Got the annulment. Married again. Pat never recovered from losing two mothers in five years, and I… Well. It doesn't matter. Don't make my mistake, Drew."

Zee would certainly try, if she would listen to him.

"That's okay, then," Dave said, with relief. "Mr. O'Neal, I hear you're booked into the motel for a couple of nights. Why not stay here instead? We have plenty of room."

"He's sorry," Beks reported when she phoned Nikki in Auckland. "He was going to tell you today."

"I'm not talking about it," Nikki retorted. "I've had more than enough of liars in my life. I don't need another." She was being unfair, and she knew it. On the long drive to Auckland she had replayed Zee's revelations about his family and matched them with what she knew of the O'Neal dynasty. Except for the matter of his identity, he had told her the truth.

"How close would you have let him get if you'd known he was Michael O'Neal's son?"

Nowhere near. "A rather large omission, claiming a false name," she argued.

"Zachary Andrew Henderson is the name on his birth certificate, apparently," Beks told her. "He changed it to O'Neal when he turned 21, and changed it back when he broke with his family."

"When the O'Neals bribed Russo." Nikki's anger rose again. She could accept that Zee had been an O'Neal, given he'd left them. But they had cheated and lied, and even so, he'd stayed in touch with his father.

"When one of his brothers bribed Russo. Mr. O'Neal told us all about it. And Nikki, Zee contacted his father to track the links between Pokey and Chow. And he's done it. He came to give us the evidence."

Nikki managed half a smile. "That's good, then." *Now Zachary Henderson O'Neal can hop onto the helicopter with his mega rich father and go back where he belongs, and leave Nikki Watson alone.*

"Niks, how important is Zee Henderson to you?" Beks asked.

Nikki could feel tears rising, and blinked rapidly to chase them back. "I thought he was The One, Beks."

"Then don't be a fool," her friend said. "Hear him out and give him a chance."

Nikki tipped back her head and took a deep breath before speaking. "Whose friend are you? His? Or mine?"

Beks laughed. "Best friends forever, darling. That's why I want you to be happy. Say hi to your Mum for me, and give me a ring when you're ready to come home."

Nikki closed the phone app, looking thoughtfully at her phone. She then lifted her head to meet her mother's gaze. "Your friend thinks you should forgive your young man for deceiving you," the older woman said.

"She says he was going to tell me."

Sarah huffed. "They always say that. Or is she right?"

"Possibly. Probably. I think she is. But what if I'm wrong?" She'd been wrong about Russo, and look how that turned out?

"I trust you." Sarah patted her hand, then withdrew again, cautious about overstepping. Nikki reached out and gave her mother's hand a squeeze. Last night after Julia went to bed, they had talked for hours, partly lubricated by a bottle of wine, forging the beginnings of a friendship.

"I don't trust me," Nikki confided.

"You should. You're a smart woman, and you learn from your mistakes. But more to the point, do you trust Zee?"

Dave made a couple of phone calls to find out who they should be talking to, and on Thursday morning Dave, Zee, and O'Neal took the helicopter down to Wellington for an appointment with several serious officials, who heard their story, accepted the paperwork O'Neal had collected plus the background material he supplied on a thumb drive, and took Zee's statement about the conversation he and Nikki had overheard.

"And is Ms. Watson not with you," asked the woman in the pastel blue suit.

Zee, after the shocks of the day before and a night without sleep, had a mad impulse to claim that the bearded Dave Masterton was actually Nikki in disguise, but he suppressed his sarcasm and left Dave to reply.

"She went to stay with family in Auckland yesterday morning. We're not sure when she intends to return, but I can give you her mobile number and email address."

Does she intend to return? Zee had wanted to go after her yesterday, but Beks told him to stay put and give Nikki time, and he would. But not forever. He was not giving up until she told him, with her own lips, that she never wanted to see him again; that he'd killed any chance of a future together.

If she went back to Brisbane with her mother, he'd have to go to her in Australia. By plane, though. He got airsick, a little, but nothing like his reaction to the ocean.

The civil servants were closing their tablets, putting them into a pile with their notebooks, slipping their pens into pockets. "Thank you, gentlemen," said the one who had mostly taken the lead. "We may be in touch with further questions, and there may be charges to be laid, in which case you may hear from the police. Mr. Henderson and Mr. O'Neal, you do intend to stay in the country in the next week or two?"

Zee assured them that he lived here, and O'Neal said he would stay for at least the next week and check with them before he made any plans to go home.

Sure enough, in the following days, they had several phone conversations and a Skype call with various officials. O'Neal had taken a two-week vacation for this trip, which meant leaving to his assistants anything that didn't require his personal attention: even so, his mornings were given over to reports and emails, and he attended several long-distance business meetings.

Zee worked up at Nikki's house while his father was busy. When Nikki came back — if she came back — she'd find the framing up for the new rooms, and wiring and plumbing well begun.

In the afternoons, he took his father around to see Valentine Bay and further afield, and they talked as they never had before.

A week after Nikki left, Zee and O'Neal were returning to where Zee had parked his pickup after having afternoon tea at Maggie's. A raised voice drew their attention to the front door of Pokey's real estate office; Pokey, complaining loudly. "Mr. Chow is my guest, and a very wealthy man. You can't come in here and start throwing accusations around."

O'Neal raised his brows as he glanced at Zee, and Zee answered the unspoken question.

"Unless I am much mistaken, Dad, our friend Pokey has just discovered that he's in trouble with the law."

The tall well-built men who surrounded Pokey shifted a little, and the much smaller Mr. Chow came into sight for a moment. "And how fortunate for the forces of good that Chow was with him at the time."

At that moment, the Taiwanese billionaire looked their way, and O'Neal smiled broadly and waved. "I enjoyed that," he said to Zee.

Quite a number of locals had stopped in the street or come out of the shops to watch as Pokey and Chow were escorted to waiting cars, so dozens of witnesses saw Snoopy Kenworth emerge the small office that provided a few minimal council services in the beachside village.

"I expect to enjoy this," Zee murmured, gesturing to Snoopy with his head and eyebrows.

The elder Kenworth stopped, his head jerking backwards, when he saw the cluster of men surrounding Chow and his son. His face flooded with red, and he hunched his shoulders forward, his fists clenched, as he strode towards the group.

"What's going on?" he demanded. "Barrington! What's happening here?" Barrington was the local constable, and an old school friend of Dave's and Becky's. Zee had met him and his family often when the Mastertons entertained. Confronted by Snoopy, he managed to turn the broad grin he'd been wearing into a concerned frown.

Zee couldn't hear his reply, but he heard Snoopy's shouted response.

"What! That can't be true. Someone has lied to ruin the Kenworth's good name. Jealous of success. It's disgusting."

One of the other police officers moved in, and by now Zee and O'Neal were close enough to the group to hear the end of his polite request to "accompany us to Barnsley to answer some questions about a fraudulent breach of this country's overseas investment regime."

The color drained from Snoopy's face with the bombast, and it was a much deflated bully that allowed himself to be put into one of the cars, with Pokey in a second and Chow in a third.

The timing of the arrest was good management rather than good fortune, Barrington told Dave later. He had been notified of the arrest as a courtesy to the local station. "The Wellington lads," as he called them, "saw that the overseas person of interest was still in the country, and figured arresting old Pokey in front of him would help sew Pokey up, and maybe let them tag the overseas person as not welcome in New Zealand."

But the final injury to the insult of the arrest came in the local newspaper the next day, and on national news in print, online and in broadcast the day after.

'Councilor repudiates son' screamed the local headlines. Snoopy had denied all knowledge of Chow's ownership role in the hotel development, claimed he'd only put money in as a favor to his son, and contradicted Pokey's statement that he'd taken an active role in the project.

It would be played out in the courts, which could take months, and Chow meanwhile was walking free, though never again in New Zealand. But the Mastertons' *ad hoc* hotel committee met to celebrate with a glass of wine, and agreed that they'd won. The development was dead in the water, Pokey would at the very least need to pay an enormous fine — which would not be covered by insurance because he'd broken the law — and Snoopy had lost enormous support with the local voters. Even if he didn't have to face charges, he could at least expect to lose his treasured role as a local district councilor.

Zee tried not to dampen the general merriment with his own anguish, but after a while he touched Dave on the shoulder to attract his attention. "I'm going to make an early night of it," he told his friend. "I've got an early start at the house tomorrow."

Dave examined him, eyes narrowed. "You're looking tired. Not sleeping, I imagine."

Not much. He tossed and turned, replaying his time with Nikki over and over, trying to make it come out differently.

"Becky! Zee's off to bed. Walk him out, will you?"

Zee muttered that he knew the way, but Becky had already handed off the tray of cheese and crackers she was carrying and was heading his way. He'd been avoiding her as much as he could, feeling her judgment of him in her thoughtful gaze, and ashamed of disappointing her. She was as formidable a matriarch as Grandma O'Neal, though less than half the age. The thought let him steady himself before she reached him.

"I wanted a word, Zee," she said. "Come on. Let's go see Oliver."

Zee caught his father's eye, hoping the man would offer to come too. Another person would ease the tension. His father raised a wine glass in salute, then turned back to a conversation with the chairperson of the local marina.

Outside, the sun had gone down, reminding him of that last evening with Nikki. He stopped, looking up at the darkening sky, his throat tight.

Becky stood several steps up the staircase to his studio loft, examining him carefully. "You miss her," she said.

He spoke before he could censor himself. "Do you think she's coming back, Becky?" It sounded plaintive, but he didn't care. Becky, of all people, knew how he missed her.

"Tomorrow, actually. I spoke to her this afternoon."

Zee's mouth dropped and his mind whirled. "Tomorrow? She's going to be here tomorrow?"

"She is. That was what I wanted to tell you."

"Did she...? Did you talk about...?"

"You? I can't tell you, Zee. She is coming back to Valentine

Bay and the house her grandparents left her. Any more, you'll have to find out for yourself." She descended the steps she had just climbed. "That's it. That's what I wanted to say." She stopped next to Zee and patted his cheek.

"I wish you luck, if that's any consolation. Goodnight, Zee. I'm going back to my guests. I hope you manage to get some sleep tonight."

He watched her cross the turning circle and reenter the house. *Sleep? Not likely.*

Nikki returned to the Mastertons' house on Valentine's Day, crossing the driveway to let herself into her apartment. She knew Zee had seen her park her little car; he was standing at the studio window. Beks said he wanted to talk? Let him come and talk.

Even so, she jumped when a knock came at the outer door a few minutes later. She put on her bland 'I hear you but none of it affects me' lawyer face, before she opened up to find Zee on the doorstep. He was holding out a dozen red roses. She ignored them, folding her arms.

"May I explain?" he asked.

She opened the door wider and stepped out of the way.

"I'm listening." She walked through to the living room but didn't sit. He followed, putting the roses on the kitchen bench as he passed.

"I'm sorry, Nikki. I know I should have told you. At first, I didn't think it would matter. As I got to know you better, I kept putting it off. Then I fell in love with you and I was afraid you would hate me when you knew I was an O'Neal. But after that Sunday night on the beach… I was going to tell you the day I invited you to lunch."

Fell in love? "That's unfair," she grumbled. How was she meant to stay cross with him now?

"I know," he agreed, hanging his head. "I should have told you."

"You hurt me, Andrew O'Neal, or Zachary Henderson, or

whatever your name is. I thought we were friends. I thought I could trust you. And then I found out I didn't even know who you were. How could you have let me find out like that?"

He spread both hands. "I didn't know my father was coming." And then, hastily, as if to forestall the words she wasn't about to say, "But I should have guessed."

"It shouldn't have mattered. It wouldn't have mattered if you'd told me at the start."

He nibbled nervously at his lip. "What do I need to do? I'll do anything."

She narrowed her eyes at him, struggling to hold on to her anger. "How am I supposed to trust anything an O'Neal says? Your brother bribed a member of my legal team. You O'Neals made Global Earth Watch—and me—look like idiots."

"It still burns me, too." He looked sincere. But so had Russo, when he assured her he only had Global's best interests at heart.

"If it helps, my brother Pat lost his wife over it."

"She left him because he was a liar?" She probably left him to move in with Russo after Nikki threw him out. "Good on her."

But Zee shook his head. "He divorced her because she was working for Chow, who was behind the whole scheme."

Nikki sat down, the news too unexpected for her indignation to keep her upright any longer.

"Chow? The same Mr. Chow who was the secret investor in Pokey's hotel?"

"My father says he sent you information about the conspiracy, but he didn't know about Chow at the time."

More revelations. "That was your father?"

Zee nodded. "He thought you had a right to know. Yes, and Global Earth Watch, too. They've had the decision overturned. I guess you knew that."

So the patriarch of O'Neal Hotel Corporation had given her the information that Global Earth Watch needed to recover their reputation and go after the real offenders. The idea that he was one of the good guys was going to take some getting used to.

Zee was waiting, sad and watchful, his gaze never leaving

her face. Dark bruises under his eyes hinted at lost sleep, and he had cut himself trimming his beard.

"You said you would do anything," she reminded him.

"Anything." It was a heartfelt sigh.

"Leave Valentine Bay and never come back?" she suggested.

Zee paled and swallowed. "That's what you want?"

"No, it isn't." She twisted the screws a bit tighter. "Would you leave New Zealand if I told you that was what I needed from you?"

He bit his lip, but nodded.

"Good. But it isn't that, either."

"Nikki, you're killing me," he protested, and Nikki relented.

"Do you really love me, whatever your name is?"

Zee lifted his hanging head, hope flaring in his eyes. "With every particle of my being, and my name can be anything you want."

"Beloved, then. My beloved."

She was in his arms, being thoroughly kissed. "You forgive me then?" he asked at last, when he could speak again.

"I suppose I must," Nikki told him. "I love you, Zee."

He bent his head and kissed her again, and very little was said for some time.

Epilogue

On Valentine's Day a year later, Zee and Nikki were eating lunch where they'd had many an outdoor meal, in both rain and shine, enjoying the cover of the upper verandah and the view out over North Beach. That view would soon be changing. With Zee's application for permanent residency finally approved, they'd submitted to council the proposal for the latest hotel in the O'Neal hotel chain. Not that it was owned by the O'Neal Hotel Corporation. Dad and Brendan had agreed to try a franchise model, and had persuaded the board; local ownership and a licence payment to the international company. If it worked here in New Zealand, they might try it elsewhere, helping local communities own their own luxury hotels.

The primary shareholders all lived in Paradise Bay. Zee, Nikki, the Mastertons, and a number of other smaller investors from the village. The district council would undoubtedly put them through the wringer to make sure the plans were robust, but Zee could hardly complain about them acting on the lessons they'd learned from the failed Kenworth development.

His wife followed Zee's train of thought without difficulty. "It'd be great to at least clear the ground and make a start on the foundations before winter," she said.

"Dave says it could take months to get through approvals. We'll have our pohutukawa to ourselves for a while yet." The trees she loved; the trees that had witnessed their courtship.

When his wife went inside to put the desert dishes into the dishwasher and fetch them both a glass of her lemonade, Zee moved as swiftly as was compatible with silence, using a gesture to order Oliver to stay put in the shadow of the table. He rounded the corner of the house and let himself into his study through the bifold doors that opened onto the new verandah.

In the study waited the Valentine's Day tokens he'd hidden there earlier. A dozen red roses, a box with the logo of the finest manufacturing jeweler in Barnsley, and a card he'd made himself, painting the cover picture and writing the sentiment inside. "To Nikki. Yesterday, Today, Forever."

Nikki was coming out through the French doors from the kitchen as he returned to the table. She laughed, holding up her own sheaf of red roses. "Two minds with but a single thought," she quoted, and put her floral offering down at his place at the table. He did the same with the bunch for her, freeing one hand to take the wrapped box she gave him.

In companionable silence, they each opened their present. She had merely to ease the lid off hers, which she quickly did, giving a low crow of delight when the pendant within was revealed: a pohutukawa in full bloom, a gold tree against an iridescent paua-shell background, with enameled red flowers.

"How beautiful, Zee. Here. Help me put it on." She held the pendant out by its gold chain, and half her back, lifting her hair away from her neck.

He put his half-unwrapped present down and fastened the clasp for her, staying close for a kiss before resuming his seat. "We are wealthy, you know," he reminded her. "I could cover you with diamonds and it wouldn't make much of a dent."

Nikki had helped him come to terms with accepting his share of the O'Neal money but was more frugal than him about spending on frivolities. "I love this," she insisted now. "You designed it yourself, I know you did. And the pohutukawa is our tree."

She colored suddenly. "You helped me make my present, too. The real present, that is. The one you haven't unwrapped yet is just to give you a hint."

Curious, he ripped the last of the wrapping, and frowned at the box. A silver rattle? A moment's thought had him looking up at Nikki, his mouth open. "A baby? You're having a baby?"

He caught her in his arms and swung her around, then stepped back and patted her arms. "Are you alright? Should you sit down? When are we due?"

"End of September, early October. He or she will be with us in time for pohutukawa flowering, Zee. And I'm fine. I feel wonderful. I haven't even been nauseous."

"Don't knock being nauseous, my love," said the man whose seasickness had beached him in Paradise. "It worked for me."

The End

About the Author

Jude Knight's writing goal is to transport readers in time and space to where they can enjoy adventure and romance, thrill to trials and challenges, uncover secrets and solve mysteries, delight in a happy ending, and return from their virtual holiday refreshed and ready for anything.

She writes novels, novellas, and short stories, contemporary and historical with strong determined heroines, heroes who can appreciate a clever capable woman, villains you'll love to loathe, and all with a leavening of humor.

Find Jude Online

http://judeknightauthor.com
https://www.facebook.com/JudeKnightAuthor
https://www.twitter.com/JudeKnightAuthor
https://nz.pinterest.com/jknight1033/%20

That Song in Patagonia

Kristy Tate

One

*I*n a hazy room filled with flashing lights, throbbing music, and hundreds of beautiful people, Adrienne felt like a mallard surrounded by swans. And she longed for a peaceful bit of swamp. A woman in a silvery dress resembling plastic wrap pushed past her, leaving behind a stench of perfume. Adrienne sought out a corner where she'd be less likely to be touched or bumped into, but the best refuge she could find was a bar stool. She hiked herself onto it and checked her watch. Was it too early to go home? Meanwhile, a man wearing a floral shirt brushed up against Adrienne and sloshed his drink on her.

"Oh, clumsy me," he said. "So sorry!" After setting his drink on a nearby table and grabbing a handful of napkins, he patted her down.

Adrienne shied away from the man with his lingering fingers and overpowering cologne. Silently she cursed Sebastian because somehow this was all his fault—even though he wasn't there. She didn't know where he was. And she didn't know why she'd ever agreed to attend this awful party. She slid off the bar stool and, weaving through the laughing and smiling guests, made her way to the restroom.

In the hall, Steph snagged her wrist. "You're not escaping."

"This was a bad idea." Adrienne pulled her wet blouse away from her skin and the warm scent of wine wafted over her.

"And you think moping at home is a better one?"

Adrienne's phone buzzed. She scrambled to open her sequined clutch bag.

"Huh-uh." Steph snatched the purse. "No! He doesn't get to talk to you."

"How do you know it's him?"

"I don't. But if it is, he's the last person you should be talking to." Steph turned her voice into a purr. "Come on, sweetie, have some fun. You don't need him."

Adrienne blinked back tears. "He's my husband."

"But he hasn't acted like it in months… maybe even years." Steph opened the purse and sighed when she checked the phone.

"It was him, wasn't it?"

Steph handed the purse back to Adrienne. She slipped her arm around Adrienne's waist and tried to urge her back into the thick of the crowd. "Let me introduce you to my friend Geoff. He's an artist, too."

"Graphic design?"

"No, video games."

Images of violent computer graphics flashed in Adrienne's mind. A creature carrying an automatic weapon crashed into the room and began firing. Blood spurted. People screamed. Adrienne shook the visual from her mind. "I have to go," she said. "I really need to talk to Sebastian."

After thanking the hostess and following her directions to the bedroom where the coats had been gathered, Adrienne stepped into the room, closed the door, leaned against it, and battled tears. She took a deep breath and glanced at the coats and jackets heaped on the bed. Ninety percent of them were black — like hers. But wait, why was there a shoe amid the jackets? Two shoes. No, four shoes.

Oh dear, what was that couple doing on the bed, buried beneath the coats? And how would Adrienne ever extract hers without interrupting? She quickly left, sans coat.

Outside, away from the party's noise and crush of people, Adrienne breathed a little easier. The misty air blurred the headlights of the cars splashing down the shiny black roads. Reflections of the store's neon advertisements glistened on the slick sidewalk. The cold damp penetrated Adrienne's blouse and the mean breeze twirled around her legs. Why had she let Steph talk her into going to a party full of strangers? Because it was better than spending another evening alone.

On the drive home, Adrienne tried to rehearse all the things she needed to say to Sebastian, but instead, she choked on all her tears.

Nick stared in horror at the computer screen. "How did this happen?" His voice, usually so deep and melodic, came out in a croaky whisper.

"Come on," Steph elbowed him, "you have to admit this is amazing for business!"

Nick pulled his gaze away from YouTube to give her what he hoped was a terrifying glare. She was like a sister to him. He had backed her when her parents had thrown a fit about her purple hair and multiple piercings. He had chased off her loser boyfriend. He loved her and thought the feeling mutual, but all those warm fuzzy feelings were evaporating as he watched himself singing on the internet and realized she was the one to blame.

Steph grinned back at him, wiped her hands on her apron, and pointed her chin at the line snaking around the counter of Bar de Música. "They don't just come here for cocoa, you know." She patted his shoulder and practically skipped out of the office.

He watched her join Jon behind the counter and say something to the guy next in line, who threw back his head and laughed.

Nick told himself they weren't laughing at him. Were they? He glanced at the computer. According to the views counts, so far about a thousand people had watched the video of him singing at his cousin Pedro's wedding. There had to be millions of amateur videos of people singing at weddings—why would a thousand people choose to watch him? Of course, it didn't help that his cousin's bulldog, Lester, dressed in a tux, gave Nick his rapt attention, his big head swinging in time with the music. How had Nick not noticed this at the time? He replayed the video, curious about what else he'd missed.

Jon strode into the office. "Are you still obsessing over that?"

Nick shook his head, closed the laptop with a sharp click, and pushed away from the desk. "Nah."

"I don't know why you want to hide your talent beneath a bushel." Jon was studying to become a youth pastor and liked to spout Biblical phrases. "You have a gift. You have to let it shine."

Nick interrupted before Jon could start singing *This Little Light of Mine.* "No, I don't. What I have to do is keep this shop afloat." Nick thought about going out and wiping down tables—his standard go-to when his accounts were all caught up—but the fear that some of the guests had seen the video froze him. He paced across the room.

Concern flashed in Jon's eyes. "We're doing fine, right?"

"Well, yeah." Nick stopped and clapped a hand on Jon's shoulder. "I'm sorry, I didn't mean to scare you. We're doing great." In fact, they were doing much better than he'd projected when he'd opened the café. He'd patterned the shop after his uncle's in Uruguay. Like any standard coffee shop, they served hot beverages and a smattering of baked goods, but what set them apart from a Starbucks was their open microphone for musicians, poets, and comedians. They also sold vinyl records and vintage sound systems.

Nick's thoughts drifted to Jose and he fought a wave of homesickness. But moments later, the sound of his own voice jolted him back to the here and now. He glanced at the closed laptop before bolting out of the office.

He halted behind the counter and stared at the TV screen in the corner of the room. All the patrons in the shop turned to stare at him before bursting into applause and cheers. Stunned, Nick backed away. Moments later, without any real recollection of how he'd gotten there, he found himself in the service closet wedged between a shelf of cleaning supplies and a hamper of dirty aprons. He pulled out his phone, sank into a squat, typed in YouTube, and found the video of himself and Lester.

Five thousand views.

How is this happening? His head spun. There weren't even five thousand people in Jose's entire village. He let this process before he climbed to his feet. So, five thousand views. Everyone was watching Lester. Not him. And as Steph had said, this would be good for the shop. Publicity was publicity.

He checked his reflection in the mirror and smoothed his thick dark hair, before squaring his shoulders and heading back into the fray. The number of patrons had at least doubled. The shop had an occupancy capacity of three hundred, and while they were nowhere near that number, they still had twice as many guests as was typical for a Thursday afternoon.

He glanced outside at the weak January sun attempting to singe the edges of gray clouds. The rain was good for business. But so, apparently, were musical dog videos.

A blinding light flashed, making Nick blink. Had someone just taken his picture?

Adrienne gripped the steering wheel as she pulled up at a light and stared at the building in front of her. She had driven to 44 East Elm on auto-pilot. There stood the offices of Cavallero Land Development. Her eyes traveled to the top floor. Sebastian's office. She imagined him sitting at his big desk. She could go in and talk to him. Confide her worries. Reveal her insecurities about how they rarely talked. How seldom they touched. When had he stopped calling in the middle of the day? When had her company become an obligation to fulfill?

The driver of a Volkswagen behind her bleeped its horn. The light had turned green. When? How long had she been parked there — not really coming or going, stuck in neutral?

The Volkswagen horn bleeped louder and longer. After raising her hand in apology, Adrienne turned onto High Street, away from Seb. Irrationally upset, angry with herself for being overly emotional, she pointed the car toward her own office. But then she saw him.

Her husband had his arm flung around the shoulders of a tall, dark-haired beauty wearing a cobalt blue coat and a pair of red stiletto heels. Who dressed like that to the office? The woman turned and answered Adrienne's question. Therese Acosta dressed like that. And Therese Acosta kissed Seb on a Seattle corner.

A Honda in front of Adrienne stopped suddenly, forcing her to slam on her brakes. The hood of her BMW came dangerously close to the Honda. A large, furry dog in the back seat of the other car stared at her. Adrienne's heart hammered at her near miss. Had Seb seen the almost-accident? Was Therese laughing at Adrienne's clumsy driving? Adrienne tightened her grip on the steering wheel and sped away to anywhere else.

Adrienne woke in the middle of the night to find Sebastian asleep beside her. Sitting up, she stared at his inert form and for the first time considered a life without him. He slept with his back to her, his dark head just poking out of the blankets. Gray light filtered in through the slats of the window blinds and cut stripes across the rumpled bedclothes.

Picturing the bed empty was easy enough. Lately, Sebastian had been gone more than he'd been home. Traveling. Business. Even on weekends. How could she have been so stupid?

She glanced at the clock. 3:00 a.m. Lying back against her pillows, she stared at the ceiling and, like a chess master, she began to plan out her next move.

"What are you doing?" Sebastian mumbled.

"Leaving you." Adrienne rolled from the bed and padded across the room in the dark.

"You can't." Sebastian pulled the quilt over his shoulder. He didn't even seem surprised by her pronouncement.

"Watch me." She threw the words over her shoulder.

"It will kill Abuelo," Sebastian said.

Adrienne had thought of this, and while she loved the old man, she'd long grown tired of Sebastian's family's hierarchy and manipulating ways. Inside her closet, she flipped on the light, pulled down her suitcase, and began to fill it. She glanced at her sweaters and jeans—Seattle winter wear—and instead chose shorts, T-shirts, and sundresses. She was going to find summer.

Three Weeks Later

"What would you like for dinner?" Aubrey asked.

Adrienne shrugged her response without looking up from her *Argentina Now!* magazine. There was an article on Iguazu Falls, and Adrienne promised herself she would go. Soon. Although, she'd been in Argentina for one week already and had only left her sister's apartment once.

Aubrey blew out a sigh. "Will you stop already?"

"What?" Adrienne stared at her sister. Despite their ten-year age difference, they were similar in appearance—tall, blond, willowy. Neither wore much make-up. The major difference was that Aubrey was usually spattered in mud.

"You're an attorney, for pity's sake. Arguing is what you do!"

Adrienne turned her attention back to the magazine and tried to ignore Aubrey. "You want me to argue about what we have for dinner?" she said after a beat of silence. When Aubrey didn't answer right away, she looked up.

Aubrey, who stood in the kitchen surrounded by terra-cotta pots filled with rosemary, basil, dill, oregano, and lavender, shook her trowel at Adrienne. "I want you to do something!"

Adrienne looked back at her magazine and flipped through it until she found pictures of the most luxurious bookstore she'd ever seen. "I'm going to go to El Ateneo Grand Splendid."

Aubrey looked at her through slit lids. "When?"

Adrienne swung her feet off the sofa and planted them on the wooden floor. "Now?"

Aubrey fixed her fists on her hips. "And what about dinner?"

"I said I didn't care."

"No, what you said was"—Aubrey mimicked her exaggerated shrug.

"Do you want me to go?" Adrienne asked.

"To the bookstore, yes," Aubrey said, her voice softening. "Back to Sebastian, no."

"Thanks for letting me stay here." Adrienne went to find her shoes.

"Of course," Aubrey said, sounding contrite.

Adrienne shared the guest bedroom with a shelf holding dozens of glass jars full of herbs and spices and pots filled with various trees. A warm light shone on a tray of seedlings in the corner. These plants were the love and passion of her sister's life and Adrienne knew she was lucky that Aubrey would carve a space out for her, but still, she secretly wished for a room less junglesque. Adrienne found her shoes wedged between a potted grapefruit tree and a watering can. She slipped them on before padding back into the living room.

Aubrey stood in the entry with her coat on. She'd removed her dirty apron, but a smudge of dirt remained on her forehead.

"Are you coming with me?" Adrienne asked.

This time it was Aubrey that answered with a shrug.

"Well, then you might want to wash your face," Adrienne said with a smile.

"Have you heard from him?" Aubrey asked once they got outside.

"No." Adrienne turned her face to the sun. Although Buenos Aires was a much larger city than Seattle, they both sat on the water and shared similar climates. But they were polar opposites. When Seattle was gray with winter, Buenos Aires enjoyed the summer sun and vice versa.

"I don't think she was the only one," Adrienne said in a small voice.

"What makes you so sure?"

Adrienne's thoughts skittered over the years and lingered on all the prolonged business trips that had filled her seven-year marriage. "Did you know some say that the seven-year itch is a real thing?"

Aubrey nodded. "Divorce rates show that on average couples tend to divorce around seven years. Statistics say there is a low risk of separation during the first months of marriage. After the 'honeymoon' months, divorce rates start to increase. Most married couples experience a gradual decline in the quality of their marriage — in recent years, around the fourth year of marriage. Around the seventh year, tensions rise to a point that couples either divorce or adapt to their partner."

"So says the woman who never married."

"And never will," Aubrey said. "Did you know that human cells are replaced every seven years? So, it's like you're a brand-new person every seven years. Although the linings of your stomach and intestines are renewed much faster."

Adrienne kicked a pebble down the sidewalk, thinking of how much her sister sounded like their father. "Have you talked to Dad recently?"

"No. Have you?" Aubrey skated her a glance. "I assume you told Mom."

"Hmm," Adrienne muttered.

"Let me guess what she said: I told you so?"

Adrienne elbowed her. "You're so smart." She paused on the corner of Avenida Indepencia and stared at the University of Argentina. "Which building is the science building?"

"My lab is on the other side of campus. You should visit."

"I think I will." It felt good to change the subject. She asked about Aubrey's work, her colleagues, and her sabbatical from the University of Washington as they walked down the street until they reached Avenida Santa Fe. Once they passed through the doors of El Ateneo, Adrienne murmured, "I may never leave." And she didn't know if she was talking about the bookstore or Argentina.

Sebastian pushed through the doors of Bar de Música. If the crowds in the shop surprised him, he didn't show it. Nick took a deep breath and braced his shoulders for the encounter with his cousin and best friend.

Seb waved to Nick. Like all the Cavallero men, he was tall, broad, and handsome. And impatient.

Nick motioned for Seb to join him in the back office.

Seb nodded before attempting to weave through the patrons without spilling anyone's coffee. "This place is a zoo," Seb said. "Are you going to expand?"

"Nah. Things will calm down soon." At least, he hoped so. Nick took the chair behind the desk.

Seb settled on the cracked leather sofa. "What if they don't?"

"They will," Nick said with more certainty than he felt.

"Not if Steph has anything to do with it."

"Your sister," Nick said, "is a godsend."

"Is she a blessing or a plague?" Seb asked, grinning.

Nick beat his fingers on his desk, waiting for his cousin to get to the point of his visit.

"Have you heard from Adrienne?" Seb finally asked.

"No, why? Haven't you?"

Seb frowned and looked out the rain-streaked window. "She's gone to visit her sister."

"Right." Nick knew that.

"It's been a few weeks…"

"Yeah."

Seb leaned forward and put his elbows on his knees. "Abuelo can't know."

Nerves tingled down Nick's spine and the palms of his hands started to sweat. "That she's gone to visit her sister?"

"That she's gone." Seb didn't fill in any of the blanks, but Nick's thoughts rushed to answer all his questions.

"She left you?" Nick tightened his grip on the pen he was holding, realized what he was doing, and set it down quickly in the hope that Seb wouldn't pick up on his visceral reaction.

"Nah." Seb stood and went to the window to stare out at Seattle's busy sidewalks. "I mean, she'll be back."

Nick fought the urge to clamp his hand on his cousin's shoulder, spin him around, and pelt him with questions first and his fists second.

"How's Tio Jose?" Seb asked.

Nick gripped the arms of his chair, feeling slightly dizzy and ill. The sudden change in topic didn't help. "He's good… aging, but… why?"

"Well, it's just, you know Aubrey is in Buenos Aires on sabbatical, which means that Adrienne is also in Buenos Aires." He paused as if waiting for Nick to connect the dots.

"You want Tio Jose to check in on her?"

"No." Seb turned around and frowned at Nick. "I mean, it probably won't come to this. She'll be back… but I thought, maybe you could go and get her if Abuelo starts to ask questions. Maybe drop by and see Tio Jose, swing past Aubrey's."

Nick narrowed his eyes at Seb, trying to read him. They had been raised as brothers and had shared a room since Seb was thirteen and Nick ten. Instead of resenting a young, fresh-from-Uruguay cousin foisted on him, Seb had taken Nick under his wing, made him his protégé, introduced him to his friends, coached him in sports. Nick had adored him. But their relationship had changed the moment Seb brought Adrienne home.

"Come on, you know she loves you," Seb said. "If you ask her to come back, she will."

"Why would I do that?" Nick asked. "Why ask her to come back to an unhappy situation?"

"Who says the situation is unhappy?"

Nick folded his hands to keep him from strangling his cousin. "If she was so happy then why did she leave?"

"She wanted to see her sister."

"And why would I need to persuade her to return?"

"Because I'm her husband."

"That's an argument that should be made by her husband. What are you not telling me?"

Seb pushed his fingers through his black hair, making it stand on end. "Abuelo can't know."

"Can't know what?" Nick pressed.

Seb turned back to the window. "As soon as Abuelo dies, the company will be mine. But if he finds out… It's in her best interest to stay married, you know, for the time being. I'll be worth a lot more and the divorce settlement will—"

"Divorce?" Nick stood. "You're talking divorce?"

"Well, not until Abuelo is gone."

"You make it sound like he's going to the grocery store. We're talking about the end of his life. And that business and his family are his life!"

"Exactly. You know how he is. You understand his feelings on divorce."

"You want to divorce Adrienne?" Nick tried to tamp down the incredulity and hope in his voice, but he still heard the rise of timbre. Thankfully, Seb, always so self-centered, didn't pick up on it.

"Not while Abuelo is alive. It's not even an option!"

Nick choked back his questions.

"Look, I'll pay for the flights."

"You should go," Nick said. "You said she loves me, but she loves you more. You're her husband."

Seb opened his mouth just as the floor rolled under their feet. His face filled with astonishment.

Nick braced his feet and held onto the shaking desk. "Earthquake," he murmured.

Commotion came from the next room — a woman screaming, a child crying, a dog barking.

"Did someone bring a dog in here?" Nick asked, astonished.

Jon ran in. "You okay, boss?"

"Yeah," Nick said. "I better go and make sure everything is — " He cut his sentence short as another tremor rolled through.

"The Cascadia Subduction Zone." Seb laughed, but still sounded nervous. "They say everything west of I-5 is supposed to break off into the ocean."

"I'm good," Nick said with a grin because his shop and home were on the Eastside.

"But I'm screwed."

"Yeah, you are," Nick said, and he wasn't thinking about earthquakes.

One Week Later

Adrienne sat at a waterfront café nursing a cup of hot cocoa while she watched an artist paint the sunset. "We're in the same sort of field, you know," she told the old man wielding a paintbrush and wearing a straw hat. "We probably took the same classes in college."

"I didn't go to college," the man told her.

"Oh. Well, you're very good," she told him. "I was in graphic design."

"But now you're not?" He didn't look at her, but kept his attention flicking between his canvas and the fading sun. His long beard was spattered with paint.

"I'm an attorney."

The man chuckled. "I didn't go to law school either."

"I wish I hadn't."

The man didn't say anything but lifted his eyebrow.

"Have you ever wanted to change everything about your life?"

"No," he said. "What do you want to change?"

"I just said: everything."

"You cannot mean that. There must be people that you love."

"Of course, but… not everyone I love loves me back."

"*Claro.* It's unreasonable to expect them to."

"Is it?"

"It's not only an unrealistic expectation, it's also unfair."

Adrienne blew out a sigh. "But if you've pledged your life to someone…"

"Ah, but that is different."

Nick stood on the embankment near the Río de la Plata watching the fading sun. He had lost both his parents to the river. The memories, long faded, were nothing more than a dull, gray ache. Of the actual accident itself he had little recollection, and for this he was glad. Everyone had told him his survival had been a miracle. Why had the freak storm that had capsized their boat not taken him as well as his parents?

Familiar laughter cut through Nick's painful memories. He turned, searching the crowded plaza, then spotted her bright yellow hair. Adrienne sat at a bistro-style table, her chin propped on her cupped hands as she gazed out at the dying sun. The light breeze ruffled the hem of her cherry-strewn sundress. She appeared to be chatting with an elderly man who was painting the sunset. The sound of her voice reeled Nick closer.

"But you still love your husband?" the man asked.

"Of course. Just because he no longer loves me doesn't mean I can just turn off my feelings."

Nick froze, unsure how to approach her.

"I mean, it's not like my emotions come with an on or off button," Adrienne told the man.

"But you're happy here, now, without him."

"Absolutely. But this isn't real life. This is a vacation."

"A vacation." The man dipped his brush into a smear of blue paint on his palette and carefully drew a streak along the upper edge of his canvas. "But why must life be more or less than a vacation? Should we not be happy all the time?"

Adrienne blinked at him. "We have to work."

"Is that why you went to law school instead of pursuing art?"

Adrienne made a noise that coming from anyone else would be a snort. Nick edged closer and a twig snapped beneath his shoe.

Adrienne lifted her gaze and met his. Her cornflower blue eyes widened with surprise. "Nick!" She stood and launched herself into his arms.

He caught her and inhaled her vanilla-scented shampoo. But there was something different about her, too. She was thinner, brittle, breakable.

She pulled away to look into his face. "Oh my gosh, what are you doing here?"

"My Tio Jose," he began.

The worry lines around her eyes faded. "Of course. How is he?"

"He's good. Aging…"

The man behind the easel pointed his paintbrush at Nick. "This man is not your husband."

"No. This is his cousin, Nicolas."

"Ah," the man said as if he could see what Adrienne could not. That Nick was, and always had been, completely in love with her.

Two

Adrienne laced her fingers through Nick's, abandoned her cup of cocoa, and gazed into his eyes. "I'm so glad to see you. I've been getting bored and lonely. When she isn't cooped up in her lab, Aubrey spends all her time talking to her plants."

Nick squeezed her hands, knowing that this was his opening—where he needed to say, why not come home? But he couldn't make himself say the words.

As if she had read his thoughts, Adrienne asked, "How is everyone at home?"

Her everyone, he knew, meant Seb. "Hmm, good."

"And the shop?" Adrienne pressed. She had helped him navigate all the legal documentation and permits when he'd first opened Bar de Música, so she had a vested interest in it. She hadn't let him pay her, so unbeknownst to her, he deposited a small percentage of his monthly earnings into an account Seb had set up for her for just this purpose.

Nick ran his fingers through his hair. "It's…crazy."

"Crazy, huh?"

So she hadn't seen the YouTube videos. He swallowed, debating whether to show them to her.

Concern flashed in her eyes. "Is something wrong?"

"Define wrong."

"Nick, what's going on?" Panic tinged her voice. "Did you really come here just to visit your uncle, or is—"

"Business is booming."

She breathed out a small laugh. "Good."

He made a decision and dug his phone out of his pocket. "In

fact, I have to show you something." After pulling up the video of him and Lester, he scooted his chair so close that his shoulder brushed against Adrienne's.

She watched, clearly enchanted.

"Almost a million views," Nick said.

She laid her head on his shoulder. "I always forget how talented you are."

Nick bit his lip to curb the urge to kiss her hair. "There's more."

"More?"

"It seems that Steph has been secretly recording videos of me performing for a while."

"Whoa," Adrienne breathed.

Nick sniffed and scrolled to the next video. "Not only did she record me, but she had the videos professionally edited." He swallowed. "They're actually pretty good." He handed the phone back to her and watched her face. The sound of his songs filled the air.

She squeezed his arm and blinked back tears after the second video ended. "That was beautiful," she said, her voice thick with emotion. "There's more?"

He nodded. "Quite a few more." He cleared his throat. "To quote Steph, I am an 'Internet sensation.' I had to leave."

"Leave?" She twisted so she could see his face. Her nearness took his breath. "Why would you need to leave?"

"The tavern is… as I said, crazy. Standing room only even during the mid-day when we should have a lull. I need some guidance from my uncle. He doesn't know I'm here. I'm going to surprise him tomorrow. Would you like to go with me?"

"I would love to, but if your business is as busy as you say, how can you afford to be gone?"

"I hired three more people. Steph and Jon can run it as well as I can."

"So you're hiding?"

He had come to seek advice from his uncle and to see Adrienne but he didn't feel the need to share the latter of those things. He decided to turn the tables on her. "Are you?"

"Ah." She pulled away from him as if he'd stung her, and then changed the subject. "How is the family?"

Should he tell her about his conversation with Sebastian? No. "Abuelo is as crazy as ever. Tia Maria's Sofia died."

"I always hated that cat, but Tia Maria must be sad."

"You would think, but within a week she replaced Sofia with a really mean chihuahua she picked up at the shelter."

Adrienne wrinkled her eyebrows. "Why does she like mean animals?"

Nick shrugged. "Why do we love who we love? Who can say?"

The man with the paintbrush raised his eyebrows and met Nick's gaze. Nick looked away, afraid to let his feelings show.

Tio Jose still lived in the apartment behind his beachfront music café. Every evening, guitarists, bands, and solo vocalists gathered for their chance to perform on his makeshift stage, but the afternoons—especially during the siesta hours—were quiet. Nick was counting on this.

He met Adrienne at her sister's apartment the next morning. "The ferry crossing to Colonia del Sacramento is less than an hour," he told her. "And it should be calm, given the weather. Do you get seasick?" He would rather die than admit to his own weakness in that area.

"I don't think so." Adrienne cast a glance at the cloudless blue sky.

Nick's thoughts skittered back to Seattle, where it would be gray and drizzly. "Do you want to bring a sweater, just in case?"

She shook her head and wrapped her hand around his arm. "I'm loving this weather. It's like I was so cold and lonely in Seattle, but here... I'm finally beginning to thaw."

He put his hand over hers. "I'm glad. Come on." He urged her to move faster down the sidewalk. "We need to be at the dock an hour before our boat leaves."

She wore a pair of espadrilles and an embroidered sundress

that skimmed the tops of her knees. With her hair pulled back in a ponytail that bounced when she walked, she looked like a different creature than the black-suited attorney she'd morphed into after she'd graduated from law school.

Nick didn't want to talk about their life in Seattle, but curiosity drove him to it. "What's happening at Crenshaw and Meeks?"

"I had just finished up a big case and told Crenshaw I needed a leave of absence."

"And he just let you go?" That didn't sound like the Crenshaw Nick knew.

"I think he knows about Seb and Therese." She skated him a glance. "Do you know about Seb and Therese?"

Nick stopped at a flower cart and without saying a word, he purchased a bouquet of wildflowers and handed them to her.

"I don't want your pity!" She pushed the blooms away.

"Well, if you won't accept these, will you please just hold them?"

"Why should I?"

"Well, for one thing, they match your dress, and for another, I feel it's a slight to my manhood to carry a floral bouquet."

"That's silly." But she took the flowers while he paid the florista.

"Not as silly as Seb having an affair." Nick draped his arm around Adrienne's shoulders. He was wading into dangerous waters by trying to comfort her without exposing his heart. "Any man who would choose another over you would be... silly to the extreme... like Mr. Bean." Adrienne loved British comedy, but Seb hated it. "Right now, I'm so mad at Seb, I can't even say his name without feeling incredible rage, so I have a suggestion."

She slid him a glance. "What's that?" she asked, her voice full of suspicion.

"We will not say the name of... your husband, my cousin. From now on, his code name will be Mr. Bean."

A smile tugged at Adrienne's lips. "He would hate it if he knew."

"Then we have to tell him!" He dug his phone out of his pocket.

Adrienne took his phone from his hand. "Hmm, not yet. Maybe when the thought of him no longer hurts."

"Do you think you'll get there?"

They arrived at the dock. A cluster of people crowded around the gangplank. Nick pulled his wallet from his pocket and went to purchase the tickets.

"You're helping," she told him as soon as he returned. "Before you showed up, I was just hanging out at Aubrey's watering the plants—not with my tears, but a watering can—okay, sometimes with my tears... I was beginning to hate myself. No, stop. If I'm honest, I'll admit that I've been hating myself for a while."

As if to argue, the ferry blew its horn. The sound struck a chord in Nick's chest. He wanted to help Adrienne, but he also didn't want to get seasick. "I can't imagine anyone, even or especially you, hating you."

The crowd surged up the gangplank and Nick and Adrienne moved with the tide of people.

"You're sweet," Adrienne said. "And you're only saying that because you're such a good person you can't hate anyone."

"Right now, I'm hating S—Mr. Bean for making you feel that way."

She lifted a shoulder in a defeated shrug. "He fell in love with Therese."

Everything that sprang to Nick's mind couldn't be said. "I'm sorry," he told her. "I can only think of profanities right now."

They made their way to the deck and Adrienne pressed against the railing. "Would it be wrong if I just shouted out a whole bunch of naughty words at Mr. Bean?"

"Right now?"

She nodded.

"I'm not sure if it would be wrong, but I don't know if it would help. Not really."

"Then what would you suggest?"

"Not thinking about him. Let's pretend he no longer exists." He held up his finger. "I have an idea. I'll be right back." He went back into the cabin, pulled a napkin from the dispenser near the snack bar, and returned to the deck just as the boat pulled away from the dock. The horn sounded again. Nick took a deep breath. For the moment, the boat held steady, but he knew that soon it would leave the harbor's protection and the rolling tide would be more pronounced. Could he travel without getting ill? He would try, for Adrienne.

"Here," he said as he handed Adrienne the napkin and a pen from his pocket.

"What's this?"

"Write down Mr. Bean's real name—and any other names you want to call him."

She looked at the napkin in her hand and hesitated.

Nick turned his back to her. "Use me as your hard surface."

"What if the ink leaks through onto your shirt?"

"Then I'll take off my shirt and toss it into the sea as well," he said without looking at her.

"Are you sure?"

"Absolutely."

She held the napkin against his back and scribbled for a few minutes. When she stopped, he turned and asked, "Are you done?"

She gazed at him with tear-filled eyes. "I'm not sure I'll ever be really done."

He placed a finger under her chin. "You will. I promise. Now, throw him away."

She tossed the napkin into the air. The wind picked it up and carried it toward the Argentine coast. It fluttered and swooped before hitting the water, then disappeared in the boat's churning, foamy wake. Nick swallowed the bile rising in his throat.

Nick sighed and rolled his shoulders as the Uruguayan coast loomed ahead. The palm trees swayed in the warm, humid breeze. The stretch of beach welcomed him like long-lost love. He could already smell his aunt's *budín de pan* even though he was still miles away from Tio Jose's café. He gripped the railing as homesickness rocked through him.

Adrienne wrapped her hand around his arm and leaned against him. For a moment, he let his imagination carry him to a forbidden future, one that included Adrienne and their children, the beach, a warm tide, laughter. He longed to recreate for his own family the idyllic childhood that had been ripped from him with his parents' deaths. And he wanted Adrienne to be a part of that… but she was the wife of his cousin and best friend. He edged away from her, frightened by his own hunger.

If Abuelo could read Nick's thoughts, Nick would be hauled by his ear to see the priest.

If Abuelo could know of Seb's infidelity, Abuelo would cut him off from the family and leave him for dead.

No matter. Nick couldn't let Seb's sins justify his own. He loved Adrienne as she loved him, as a friend. And nothing more. Someday, he would find a wife of his own and together they would bring their children to the beach to build sandcastles and bonfires.

"It's such a relief to be here," he told Adrienne.

"To see your uncle?"

"Yes," he replied, "but mostly because no one here has seen those ridiculous videos."

After a few toots of the horn, the ferry pulled alongside the dock. Nick guided Adrienne down the crowded gangplank and onto the sidewalk of Colonia del Sacramento. He spotted a taxi, hailed it, and placed his hand on the small of Adrienne's back, urging her toward the yellow car.

Jose lived in a small fishing village about twenty minutes north of Colonia del Sacramento. Their driver, Manuel, a middle-aged man with a handlebar mustache, knew it well.

"Your wife is very beautiful," Manuel told Nick in Spanish.

"Yes, she is. Although she is not my wife, but my cousin's," Nick replied.

"Too bad," Manuel said.

Nick cut Adrienne a sideways glance. "And she speaks Spanish fluently."

Manuel glanced at Adrienne in the rearview mirror and gave her a flirtatious smile.

"*Gracias*," Adrienne said.

"'Tis but a truth," Manuel said.

"Manuel, if you had millions of dollars, what would you do with it?" Adrienne asked Manuel.

"We're back to that?" Nick asked.

"Yes," Adrienne said. "I think that if God gives you the resources to do a tremendous amount of good, you have a responsibility to use it to make the world a better place."

Manuel laughed. "I suppose I would send my children to the university and pray that they would do the world some good, but what if they didn't? What if I paid for them to gain an education, but they did nothing more than become taxi drivers?"

"But would that be so bad?" Adrienne asked. "What if they really enjoy being a taxi driver? Shouldn't they be free to choose a profession that makes them happy?"

Manuel snorted. "You're right. I do not need a million dollars. I don't want the responsibility."

"That's an interesting way to look at it," Nick said as he watched the familiar landscape flash by his window. His thoughts drifted to Tio Jose and the life they'd shared before Tia Martha's death, before Nick had been sent to the States. For the millionth time, he wondered if that move had been to his benefit. His aunt and uncle in Seattle had loved him and given him a good home, a wonderful education, and a stable upbringing, but maybe, like Manuel's children, he would have been just as happy working with Tio Jose in Uruguay.

Manuel pulled the taxi alongside the curb in front of Jose's café. After paying, Nick climbed out, and reached for Adrienne's hand.

But once on the sidewalk, he froze. Immediately, he knew something was terribly wrong.

Three

The sound of Nick's singing floated out to the street through the café's open windows. Adrienne didn't even try to hide her grin.

"Oh no," Nick muttered. He stood rooted to the sidewalk with horror and shock written on his face.

"Is everything all right?" Manuel stuck his head out the taxi window.

"Everything is just fine," Adrienne told Manuel as she elbowed Nick.

Nick shook back to life. "Just peachy," he growled.

"Then what is the matter?" Manuel asked. "You look as if you have seen a ghost."

"The ghost of the future," Adrienne said.

"Not if I can help it." Nick slung his bag over his shoulder, captured Adrienne's, and marched into his uncle's café like a soldier ready for battle.

Grinning, Adrienne tripped after him. The café patrons burst into applause and cheers as soon as Nick passed through the doors. A handsome middle-aged man standing behind the counter threw down his washcloth and approached Nick with outstretched arms. A TV the size of a pool table stood in the corner playing the YouTube video of Nick and the dog Lester at Pedro's wedding.

"What's all this?" Nick asked before hugging his uncle.

The two men slapped each other on the back. Tio Jose kissed both of Nick's cheeks.

Nick pulled away first and pointed at the enormous TV with a shaking hand. "When did you get that?"

"Don't think that this is all about you!" Jose placed his palms on both sides of Nick's face. "We have to keep your head from swelling! All this internet fame is bad for the soul, but good for the bank, hey?"

"Tio Jose," Nick muttered.

"Who is the *rubio* you have brought with you?" Jose turned his attention to Adrienne.

"This is Adrienne, Seb's wife."

"Seb's wife?" Confusion flashed in Jose's eyes.

"It's a pleasure to meet you," Adrienne said in perfect Spanish and offered her hand. "I happened to be in Buenos Aires visiting my sister. When Nick told me he was visiting you, I jumped at the chance to come with him. I hope you don't mind."

"Mind?" Jose nearly shouted. "Why would I mind that a beautiful creature comes to my humble café? Come." He took Nick's arm. "I have to introduce my famous nephew to my friends."

Adrienne settled into a chair at the bar and watched while Jose steered a clearly embarrassed Nick around the café and introduced him to nearly everyone. It astounded her that Jose seemed to know them all by name. Despite his obvious discomfort, in time, Nick visibly relaxed, and by the time he joined her at the bar, his smile appeared genuine and warm.

"Now," Jose stepped around the bar, "how long can you stay?"

"Indefinitely," Nick said. When he caught the surprise on Jose's face, he added, "I hope that's okay."

"Of course," Jose stumbled. "But are not... don't you need to go back? Your café—it can't run itself, can it?"

"Actually, yes. It is fine without me."

"And you?" Jose turned his gaze to Adrienne. "Surely you must wish to return to my other, less talented nephew?"

Adrienne didn't know how to answer, but finally came up with, "I'm here to visit my sister in Buenos Aires. She's on sabbatical from the University of Washington." She gazed around the room at the variety of potted plants that decorated nearly every corner. "In fact, she would be fascinated by some of your ferns." Adrienne sucked in a deep breath and decided she needed to make Jose her accomplice. Propping her elbows on the bar, she placed her chin in her hands. "I need your help."

Jose's eyebrows shot up. "My help?" He flashed a curious glance at Nick.

"Yes. You need to help me convince Nick that he needs to share his talent with the world."

Nick pointed at the TV screen. "I am!"

"Willingly," Adrienne added gently.

"Ah," Jose said, "yes, I see that you do need my help." He brushed his hands together. "Chiquita, you have come to the right place. I am your man for this very difficult task. It will be hard. Nick has always been a shy boy, but perhaps together, you and I, we will coax him from his shell, no?"

"Yes!" Adrienne said. She wanted to clap her hands.

"No!" Nick shook his head. "Look, I don't want to be a rock star. There are a million dogs chasing after that bone. Speaking of dogs, where is *Viejos*?"

Sadness washed over Jose's face. "Gone to be with my beloved Martha."

"Oh no, I'm sorry," Nick said.

Jose braced his shoulders. "This is why I play your videos all day long. It's to keep me company. Well, that and it's also good for business. You really could be a rock star."

Adrienne felt Nick tense, and she placed her hand on his arm. "Sweetie, you don't have to be a rock star. Not that you aren't terribly talented, but you aren't cut out for a life on stage."

"I'm glad you see that," Nick said, sliding a reproachful glance at his uncle.

"But you don't have to perform in front of a crowd," Adrienne said. "In fact, I have a much better idea."

"Whatever it is, I don't like it," Nick said.

"How can you know that?"

"Because I don't like the look on your face."

"She has a beautiful face!" Jose said.

"Thank you," Adrienne said.

"Of course she does, but that doesn't mean her ideas are as lovely!" Nick said.

"You haven't even heard me out."

Nick cocked one eyebrow, which Adrienne interpreted to mean, go ahead, I'm listening, but I will dislike everything you say.

"I did a little research last night." Adrienne leaned in and raised her voice because she knew many of Jose's friends sitting in the café were interested in what she had to say. "One music-business source estimates that acts can make fifteen hundred dollars per one million streams on YouTube via advertising. Top stars can make even more by signing up sponsors."

"That's a whole lot of streams for not a lot of money," Nick said.

"But it's passive income," Adrienne argued. "You put it up and it works while you're sleeping or surfing. Plus, look how many views your videos have garnered without you doing a thing!"

"She's beautiful and brilliant!" Jose exclaimed. "How did Seb get so lucky?"

"Plus—" Adrienne began.

"Another one ?" Nick mumbled.

She nodded. "I really like this idea, and I think you will too."

"Why would you think that?"

"Because this will be fun."

"I like fun," Nick said grudgingly.

"Then this is what we'll do. We'll travel to cool places in South America and you'll sing—"

"Wait. No." Nick stood, but Adrienne grabbed the back of his shirt as he turned away.

"Just listen," she pled, "you don't have to perform in front of a crowd."

"Okay, so you're saying we'll just go to Machu Picchu when no one else is there? Like when does that happen?"

Adrienne grinned. "Midnight." She shivered with anticipation. "It'll be so cool."

"Why am I doing this?" Nick asked, slowly returning to his seat.

"Listen, I didn't say anything at the time, but you should know, I really disagreed with Manuel's answer in the taxi."

"Who is this Manuel?" Jose asked.

"Our taxi driver," Nick told him.

"Just because you don't want or need money doesn't mean that there aren't a lot of others you can help who do," Adrienne said.

"This is true," a man at a nearby table said. "My sister's family lost their home in a fire last week. Her six children are now sleeping on my kitchen floor."

"We could hold a benefit concert!" a woman at his table chirped.

Nick's grip on the table tightened.

"But," Adrienne said, reading Nick's nervousness, "this is exactly what he can't do."

"But maybe we could do something like I saw on an old Flintstones episode," Jose put in.

Nick sucked in a deep breath, and Adrienne feared he was gathering steam before exploding.

"Barney Rubble couldn't sing in front of a crowd—he could only perform in the shower," Jose said. "Maybe you could try singing in the next room. We could set up a microphone so everyone could hear you."

Adrienne watched indecision flicker through Nick's eyes.

"It would be pretty cool to go to Machu Picchu at midnight," he said.

Jose slapped his hand on the table. "Let's try it!"

"Machu Picchu?" Nick asked.

"No!" Jose stretched across the table so he could slap Nick on the side of the head. "You sing in the next room." He nodded in that direction. "Everyone will listen out here."

"I don't know..." Nick drew out the words.

"One song," Jose wheedled. "A short one," he added when Nick didn't respond right away. "Two to three minutes tops. Anyone can do anything for two minutes."

"So not true," Nick said. "You can't hold your breath for two minutes. You can't stand in a fire for two minutes or swim in icy waters for two minutes. Did you know that if it's twenty below and you spit, your spit will freeze before hitting the ground?"

"No one is asking you to brave fire or ice," Jose said.

"The café will be less crowded than the weddings where you have performed," Adrienne said. "I'm wondering what's the problem."

Nick swallowed and shook his head. "You're right, it shouldn't be a big deal."

"Hooray!" Jose exclaimed. "I'll set up the microphone."

"And I'm going to the beach." Nick pushed to his feet.

"Fine, but be back here at eight," Jose said before standing and announcing to the crowd, "All of tonight's proceeds will go to the Hernandez family!"

They spent the day playing at the beach. Several times, Adrienne felt like pinching herself to make herself wake from an amazing dream where there was nothing but warm water, hot sand, and a clear blue sky. It was as if Seattle and Seb belonged to a different world—a soggy and rain-drenched universe where she had to wear black suits and make arguments for other people's problems while her own concerns festered beneath the surface.

She watched Nick swimming in the tide, moving away from her with strong, sure strokes. The first time they'd met, she'd been twenty and he sixteen—almost seventeen, but still just a kid. He'd looked like Seb, but less confident, less substantial. He'd been wiry then, with a shock of dark hair that fell over his forehead. He'd jerk his head back to keep the hair out of his eyes. He'd been quiet, watchful, reserved, but a surprisingly fierce competitor when it came to a game of any kind—cards, soccer, or basketball. Not that she had ever played the latter two with him, but she'd seen him go toe to toe with Seb many times on the basketball court. Seb, being bigger and stronger, had usually won, but Nick had put up a challenge. Idly, she wondered who would win if they should play today.

A shudder passed through her as her thoughts turned to Seb. She had promised herself and Nick that she wouldn't think about him, but at some point, she would need to reach a decision. She couldn't hide out at her sister's indefinitely. Briefly, a cloud shrouded the sun and the air cooled. Could this phase of her marriage be like the passing cloud? Cold and dark momentarily?

Sunny and warm in the future? Or would there always be another Therese on the horizon?

Adrienne dove into the tide and tried to let all thoughts of Seb go. Closing her eyes, she swam hard, enjoying the rush of water against her skin. She stopped when she bumped into someone.

"Hey," Nick said. "I caught you." He stood before her, the water glistening off his tanned skin, his hair slicked back, his dark eyes shining.

Adrienne's feet sought solid ground, but she couldn't find it. Nick reached out, snagged her wrist and pulled her closer to the shore.

"I've been thinking about your idea," he told her. "Come on, let's go back to the café and make it happen."

Nick set up his laptop while Adrienne took a shower. Because Tio Jose lived in an apartment behind the café, Nick could hear the shower running while he waited for his computer to boot up. He steered his thoughts away from Adrienne. That way lies madness, he told himself as memories of the slippery smoothness of her skin as they played in the tide tormented him.

His phone buzzed and he pulled it from his pocket.

Seb. "Hey, I was just thinking about you," he told his cousin. In a roundabout way.

"How's it going?" Seb asked. "Are you two coming home soon?"

"In a roundabout way," he said, echoing his thoughts.

"What does that mean?"

"It means we'll get there, eventually."

"That's good."

"What do you mean?"

Seb cleared his throat. "Listen, I know I told you that I wanted you to bring her home, but I was wondering…"

Nick's throat tightened and his breath caught. "Spit it out."

"Well, do you think you could try and keep her down there for a while?"

"Why?"

Seb grunted. "Abuelo is going to Rome for a month."

"Rome? That doesn't sound like something a dying man would do!"

"He said he wants to see the Vatican before he dies."

"Okay, but what does that have to do with Adrienne, or me?"

"I have some things I need to work out. They require some… finesse."

"What sort of things? Therese-type things?"

"Ah, so you know about her?"

"I think everyone does."

"Not everyone," Seb said grimly.

"Seb, tell me, if it wasn't for Abuelo and the business — " Nick had a dozen questions he wanted to ask, but he pressed his lips closed when Adrienne appeared in the doorway, backlit by the afternoon light. Even with her hair wet and her face scrubbed clean of make-up, her beauty took his breath. A faint sunburn touched her cheeks and nose. Her dress clung to her damp skin. "I gotta go," Nick told Seb in a strangled voice.

"Wait, will you keep her down there?"

"It might be expensive."

"Whatever it costs."

"I'm glad to hear you say that," Nick said before ending the call. He turned his phone to silent and put it back in his pocket.

"So you've come up with a plan?" Adrienne settled into the chair across the table from him.

"Iguazu Falls, Machu Picchu, Punta Arenas — "

"Punta what?"

"It's near Antarctica. There's a penguin colony. Patagonia. The Glacier National Park."

"Wow. This sounds expensive."

"Don't worry about it."

"I can't let you pay for me."

"Why not?" He grinned. "Consider it a business expense."

"I'm going to make videos of you singing in all these locations?"

"Hmm, I'll be a Where's Waldo with a guitar."

"I love it! But…"

"But what?"

"I need to start thinking about going home."

"Why?"

Her eyes welled with tears. "Oh, Nick, what am I going to do?"

"You are going to travel South America with me."

"I'm going to make you a star is what I'm going to do," she said, "but we don't need to travel to do that."

"But it'll be more fun this way," Nick told her.

She tipped her head, hiding her eyes. "True," she murmured. When she looked up, she looked more hopeful. "Where do you want to go first?"

"I thought we'd make a circle," he said, turning his laptop and showing her his proposed map. "Iguazu Falls, Machu Picchu, Patagonia, the glaciers."

"Why not Brazil?"

"We'd need to get a visa, but we could stop in Venezuela, maybe Costa Rica and Cancun on our way home."

"It all sounds so… incredible."

Nick wanted to tell her that the most incredible, unbelievable part of the whole thing was that Seb, always so smart, had turned into an idiot of a husband. "But it'll take a few days to get our flights set up, so until then, tell me — are you afraid of ghosts?"

"Why?"

"I want to sing in the Recoleta Cemetery before dawn."

"Did you say ghosts?"

"Quite a few, actually," he said.

"Yeah?"

He nodded. "They say Rufina Cambaceres was mistakenly buried alive near the turn of the last century. Local workers heard screams a few days after her burial, and when her coffin was disinterred, they found scratch marks on her face and on the insides of the coffin. It was later thought that she had been in a coma when they buried her."

"That's terrible, but what makes you think she haunts the

cemetery?"

"Well, I would if I were her."

Adrienne snorted at this logic.

"There's more. David Alleno worked for years as a gravedigger, carefully saving his money for his own plot and a statue of himself. It is said that as soon as the architect he had commissioned for the statue finished the work, Alleno went home and killed himself. Apparently, you can still hear his keys jangling as his ghost walks the cemetery's narrow pathways at dawn."

"And that's when you want to go?"

"I can't think of a better time. Can you?"

"Is it open?"

"We'll sneak in with the gardeners."

Adrienne laughed and shook her head.

"What?"

"You're incredible."

So are you, he thought, battling back images of Adrienne in her swimsuit.

She cocked her head, studying him. "You're willing to break into a cemetery, brave security that may possibly be armed and ghosts wielding who knows what weapons, but when it comes to singing for a crowd of strangers, even though you have an amazing voice, you want to hide out in the next room."

"That's right," Nick said without hesitation.

Four

Three days later, Nick arrived at Aubrey's before dawn and guided Adrienne to a waiting taxi.

"Is all this cloak and dagger stuff really necessary?" Adrienne pulled her jacket around her shoulders. Without the sun to warm it, the moist air felt brittle and cold. She glanced up at the cloud-shrouded moon before stepping into the taxi. "It's still nighttime."

Nick settled in beside her, pulled the door closed, and gave the driver instructions.

"Five a.m., technically morning," he corrected her. "A.m. stands for ante meridiem, which is Latin for before midday." In his wool pea coat and dark jeans, he blended into the monochromatic cityscape. "P.m. stands for post meridiem, which is Latin for after midday. But in Uruguay, madrugada is the early morning before sunrise."

"Well, right now it is definitely B.A.W.," Adrienne argued.

"What's that?"

"Before Adrienne Wakes."

"But you are awake," Nick argued.

"Only because you asked me to be here." Adrienne slid her hand around his arm, more for warmth than for companionship. "I don't know why we have to record you singing in the dark. You were great at Uncle Jose's."

"This was your idea," he reminded her. Nick had sung only one song in the back room, and five on the stage. Adrienne had worried Nick would be angry when Jose pulled down the partition between the two rooms, leaving Nick and his guitar exposed to the bursting-at-the-seams mob gathered in and around the small café, but Nick had smiled and taken it all in stride. He had moved from one song to another with grace and had even taken requests from the crowd.

"There's a difference between singing in the café and in a cemetery. Besides, I think the Recoleta will be amazing at this hour."

They traveled the quiet city streets in silence until the taxi driver pulled up beside an enormous pair of wrought-iron gates.

Once they paid the fare, climbed from the taxi, and peeked through the cemetery's giant white marble pillars, Adrienne decided the Recoleta would be amazing at any hour of the day.

Nick steered her past the entrance.

"Where are we going?" Adrienne asked.

"This way," he whispered.

She followed him wordlessly, their footfalls loud in the early morning stillness. A few cars rushed up and down the nearly deserted street. Dogs without leashes or owners prowled while cats watched from their perches on windowsills. A sleeping man lay curled on the sidewalk beneath a collection of broken-down cardboard boxes.

"Here." Nick led her through an open wooden door in the stone wall. They tiptoed past a gardening shed and a wagon plied with shovels, a weed-whacker, a leaf blower, and other yard tools.

"Any idea where we're going?" Adrienne whispered. On the boat ride home from Uruguay, Nick had been quiet and then she hadn't heard from him again until last night when he'd told her to be ready at 5:00 a.m. Now, she wondered if he'd spent yesterday scoping out the cemetery, looking for the perfect stage. The tombs came in all shapes and sizes, from grandiose mausoleums to Gothic chapels, Greek temples, fairytale grottoes, and elegant mini-mansions.

"We're traveling the labyrinthine city of the dead," Nick whispered. "Be quiet though. We don't want to get arrested for trespassing."

Adrienne's steps faltered as she thought about spending time in an Argentine jail. She paused for a moment, watching Nick move away from her, then hurried after him, because she was quite sure she'd be lost without him and he seemed to know where he was headed. She argued with herself that soon the cemetery would be open to the public and no one would realize that they had entered earlier. After promising herself that she would make a large donation, she felt better about their breaking and entering.

The farther they wandered into the cemetery, the more muffled the city noises became. The faint moonlight glinted off the marble. Adrienne paused in front of a tomb that looked like a doll's house bedroom.

Nick read from the plaque. "Liliana Crociati died on her honeymoon in Austria in the 1970s. Her parents reconstructed her bedroom within her tomb, and at the entrance placed a bronze statue of Liliana in her wedding dress, with her beloved pet dog at her side."

A chill that had nothing to do with the cold passed through Adrienne as she thought about her own wedding dress.

"I thought I'd sing over there," Nick said, pointing at a portico resembling a Greek temple. He sat on the steps, set his guitar case at his feet, and unlatched the case. "You might want to check the lighting."

Adrienne pulled out her phone and pressed the camera app. The gray morning light and accompanying mist made an eerie backdrop. It really did look amazing, as did Nick.

She froze when she heard it. Jingling.

The expression on Nick's face told her that he heard it, too.

The story of the suicidal gravedigger floated back to her. *You can hear his keys jangling as his ghost walks the cemetery's narrow pathways at dawn.*

"Do you hear that?" Nick whispered.

She nodded.

"You don't think…" she murmured. "Do you believe in ghosts?"

"What do you think? I'm Catholic."

She thought about pointing out to him that she was too, but this miffed her. She'd always felt that Seb and the rest of his family considered her faith not as solid as their own because she'd converted. She hadn't been born into it, baptized as an infant, and schooled in the catechism. Part of her wanted to shake her finger and scold Nick. As the jingling drew closer, another part of her wanted to run and hide behind his strong back.

A fuzzy gray dog emerged from the shadows. He poked his head around a monolith and studied them with dark eyes. With his matted fur and apologetic expression, he reminded Adrienne of a dust bunny that skitters to hide beneath furniture with every breath of wind.

"Aww." Adrienne dropped to her knees to bring herself to the dog's level. "Come here, boy."

The dog bolted and the jingling, once loud, faded.

Adrienne slowly stood. "I always wanted a pet."

"Yeah? Why don't you get one?"

"Seb's allergic."

"Oh, that's right," Nick said.

"Besides, I work, Seb works. Neither of us is home very much. It wouldn't be kind."

"Maybe I'll get a pet and he can live with me at the Bar. You can visit." Nick balanced his guitar on his knee and plucked a few strings, tuning it.

"I wonder what the health department would say about that." Adrienne didn't take Nick seriously. He was always making over-the-top generous gestures that no one in the family ever took him up on. Adrienne sank back to the ground and sat cross-legged on the frigid concrete. She pointed her phone at Nick. "Ready?"

Nick strummed his guitar and the tune floated through the air. Gently, he began to sing.

"But the summer faded, and a chilly blast,
O'er that happy cottage swept at last:
When the autumn songbirds woke the dewy morn,
Little 'Prairie Flow'r' was gone."

The dog crept out from behind a monolith and inched toward Nick as if afraid of being run off. Adrienne widened the scope so she could include the creature in the video. The sun too edged out of hiding and tinged the morning air with pink.

"For the angels whisper'd softly in her ear,
'Child, thy Father calls thee, stay not here.'
And they gently bore her, rob'd in spotless white,
To their blissful home of light."

Beside Nick, the dog rested his head on his outstretched paws, and closed his eyes as if in prayer while the sun cut through the shadows.

"Though we shall never look on her more,
Gone with the love and joy she bore,
Far away she's blooming in a fadeless bow'r,
Sweet Rosalie, 'The Prairie Flow'r'."*

The sad music swam around Adrienne. She was so caught up, she didn't notice the tears washing her cheeks until Nick stopped playing. She sniffed and wiped her cheeks with the back of her hand. "That was beautiful. I'm not the only one who thinks so," she said, nodding at the dog.

Nick smiled. "It's nice to be appreciated."

Someone behind her applauded.

Adrienne twisted around so she could see the groundskeeper. He had his wide straw hat pushed back off his forehead and a grin on his face. "Encantadora!"

Nick stood and gave a little bow.

Adrienne wagged her finger between the two men. "You had this set up, didn't you? All that 'they may send us to jail for trespassing' business wasn't true, was it?"

"Would you like me to hold you captive in my gardening shed?" the man asked.

Adrienne held up her hand. "No, of course not." She balled her fists and planted them on her hips. "But you lied to me," she said to Nick.

"I was teasing," Nick said.

But this still bothered her and she tried to understand it.

"Do you know who owns this dog?" Nick asked the gardener.

"The Lord, for God made all creatures, no?" The gardener

frowned at the dog. "This dog is one of the many who live on the streets and fend for themselves."

How sad not to have a home and someone to care for you, Adrienne thought. She froze when she realized the same could be said of her. She had a home, but no one was there, and Seb, who should have been there, had proved himself incapable of caring for her the way she had cared for him. Was this Seb's fault, or her own for expecting too much from him? Not that loving just one person was too much to ask of most people, but maybe it was too much to ask of Seb. Maybe she'd been wrong to assume that he could keep his vows. Maybe he was incapable of devotion.

"I know someone who will love him," Nick said. "He just needs to be cleaned up."

"Tio Jose?" Adrienne dropped to her knees beside the creature. "She's a girl. Aren't you beautiful." She stroked the fur between the dog's ears. "You should name her *Ximena*."

"Why's that?" Nick asked.

"It's the Spanish female equivalent of Simon, which means 'listener' and she was listening to you." She addressed the dog. "That's what everyone loves to do, huh, sweetie? It's not just you. By the time we're through, everyone is going to be listening to Nick."

"Let's go. I want to clean Ximena up and maybe take her to a vet before giving her to Tio Jose."

"I want to come," Adrienne said.

"Of course," Nick said as he scooped the dog into his arms. *Ximena* snuggled against him.

"Well, no one asked me, but I would love to come, too," the groundskeeper announced. "But, sadly, I must stay here and protect the Recoleta from trespassing musicians and stray dogs."

"You're doing what?" Aubrey's trowel froze midair and she stared at Adrienne.

"It's going to be like a musical tour of Latin America," Adrienne explained as she went for her suitcase in the bedroom she shared with the plants.

"And Nick agreed to this?" Aubrey trailed after Adrienne and sat on the bed to watch Adrienne fill her bag.

"Amazing, right?" Adrienne frowned at all her warm-weather clothes. It would technically be summer in Patagonia, but it would still be chilly. She hugged herself briefly, thinking of the penguin preserve and the midnight sun. She would need to buy some rugged shoes for hiking, a jacket, and a couple of sweaters.

"Something's not right," Aubrey murmured.

"Why do you say that?"

A scowl settled over Aubrey's brow. "Why would Nick do this? It's so out of his character."

"But it's good for business." Adrienne finished her packing and studied her sister. Aubrey wore the same expression she always wore while playing chess and considering her next move.

"Nick isn't that interested in business. He needs it to support his music, but it's a means to an end — not an end to a means."

"I'm not even sure I know what that means." Adrienne didn't like to admit that her sister's reasoning often left her confused.

Aubrey blinked at her. "How can you not see this? You know him better than I do. He's not like Seb."

"I know he's not like Seb."

"You should have married Nick," Aubrey said.

"He was just a kid when I met him."

Aubrey arched her eyebrows. "He's not a kid anymore."

"I know that."

"So don't toy with him."

"Toy with him?"

"Don't break his heart."

Adrienne clicked her suitcase closed. "This trip isn't a romantic getaway. It's business."

Aubrey stood, gave her sister a parting glance, and stomped back into the living room. "You're not even listening," she grumbled.

Adrienne gathered up her bag, double-checked her purse for

her passport, phone, and credit cards, and deposited everything by the front door. She glanced at her watch. Nick would be arriving in just a few minutes. "Nick knows I'm married."

"He also knows you're unhappy."

"I'm still married."

Aubrey wrinkled her nose as she pinched spent blooms off an African violet. "Are you still married if your spouse has broken his vows?"

"Yes. That's his choice, not mine. His behavior shouldn't dictate or excuse my own."

Aubrey nodded as if she understood this logic. "You wouldn't have an affair with his cousin for revenge."

Aubrey's words stung. "Of course not. You know me better than that."

Aubrey didn't look up from the violets, but she bit her lip as she always did when concerned. "I really like Nick. He's a sweet kid."

"As you said, he's no longer a kid."

The doorbell rang.

"He's here," Adrienne whispered before opening the door to let Nick in. She studied the planes of his face, the set of his broad shoulders, the strength in his hands. She could still see traces of the boy she'd first met all those years ago, but Aubrey was right. He was a man. A good one.

"Ready to go?" Nick asked.

She nodded.

He glanced across the room. "How are you, Aubrey? It's good to see you."

Aubrey put down her trowel and swept a glance over Nick. She was almost fifteen years Nick's senior, but her frank assessment sent a warning shiver down Adrienne's spine. With a start, she realized that she'd never known Nick to have a girlfriend. Why was that?

"It's good to see you, too," Aubrey said with sly smile.

Adrienne flashed her gaze from Nick to Aubrey. It was as if they were communicating a secret that only they shared.

Adrienne mentally shook herself. "I have something for you," she told Nick.

He quirked an eyebrow at her and she answered by pulling a red and white striped shirt out of her bag. Her heart lifted when he laughed and she waved it at him like a flag.

"Now you'll look like Where's Waldo. I thought about getting you the hat, but that seemed like a bit much. Do you want to try it on?"

"Later," he said, checking his watch. "Right now, there isn't time."

"You two be good," Aubrey said with a smirk.

Adrienne crossed the room in a few strides and hugged Aubrey goodbye. "You are totally misreading the situation," Adrienne whispered in her sister's ear.

"Am I? Or are you?" her sister quipped back.

Once settled on the plane, Aubrey's insinuations settled like an itch between Adrienne's shoulders and refused to be ignored. Nick couldn't be interested in her like that. He was more Catholic than she was. She'd converted shortly before her marriage. Her parents, both scientists, had little use for religion and joked about their heathen status. But despite her agnostic upbringing, Adrienne had immediately fallen in love with the Catholic services. She enjoyed attending mass and loved the heavy choral music and liturgy. When she'd married Seb, she had thought she had made a commitment before God that bound them beyond the grave.

She had thought he had shared her commitment.

Now, she stared out the window at the clouds and endless blue sky and wondered why Seb hadn't honored his promises and why God hadn't heard her prayers.

Nick sat beside her with earbuds tucked in his ears. She could tell he was listening to music because his fingers tapped to an inaudible rhythm. He caught her glance. "Excited?" he asked with a smile.

She nodded. "I've been thinking about seeing a priest."

He raised an eyebrow.

"About a divorce."

Nick's expression sobered. "I'm sorry."

"It's not your fault."

"Still, I'm sorry you're going through this."

"I know we said we weren't going to talk about Seb," Adrienne said.

"Mr. Bean," Nick corrected. "And we're not, or at least we weren't. We're talking about you consulting a priest."

"I know divorce is still really frowned upon."

"The church has a more lenient view of divorce than it does of adultery."

"That's good to know." Adrienne fingered her wedding ring, wondering if she should remove it. "You don't think God would judge me for leaving Seb?"

Nick thought for a moment. "God loves you," he said. "He wants you to be happy. If you can be happy with... Mr. Bean, I know He would want you to stay and honor your vows."

"I can't be happy with the way things are," Adrienne said.

"Of course not."

"You wouldn't think less of me if I divorced... Mr. Bean?"

"I wouldn't want to, but the truth is, I would think less of you if you stayed. I'd try to understand and support your decision, but..." Nick shook his head. "If you stayed in a marriage that allowed Mr. Bean to continue his affair, that wouldn't be good for you or Mr. Bean and the bimbo."

"Therese isn't a bimbo," Adrienne said. She wrinkled her nose. "I sort of wish she were." She dropped her voice to a whisper. "I really wish I could hate her."

"I'll hate her for you," Nick said.

"That's not fair. Do you even know her?"

"I know she's hurt you. I know she's going to hurt Mr. Bean."

"How do you know that?"

"Someday, Mr. Bean is going to wake up and realize his mistake. Losing you will be the biggest regret of his life, and he will die a broken man."

Adrienne blew out a small laugh. "Maybe he'll be happier with Therese, happier than he could have ever been with me. Maybe we were just poorly matched and we're better apart than we could have ever been together."

Nick gazed at her. "Do you really believe that?"

She wilted beneath his scrutiny. "I don't know what I believe anymore."

A stewardess appeared beside Nick. "Anything to drink?" she asked.

Nick ordered a Pepsi and Adrienne a water. They both waited for the stewardess to hand them their drinks before resuming their conversation.

"Is that why you want to meet with a priest?" Nick asked.

"I want someone to tell me what God wants me to do," Adrienne said.

"You don't need a priest to tell you that. And you don't need to make any decisions right now."

"No?"

He grinned at her. "Right now, we have an amazing trip planned through South America. We don't need to think about anything other than chasing monkeys in the jungle, running with llamas in the Andes, and counting penguins in Patagonia."

The air cloaked Adrienne like a warm, wet, heavy blanket and smelled of rain and jungle. Strange animals that looked like a mix between a cat, a raccoon, and a monkey swung in the trees.

"Coatis," Nick said, answering her unasked question.

"They look like cartoon animals," Adrienne said, glancing around at the long lines forming around the park's entrance. "And there are so many people here. How will we ever find a private place for you to sing?"

Nick consulted the map on his phone. "The park is supposedly huge with several trails cutting through the jungle to the water's edge. We'll be fine."

"Everything's so green," Adrienne said. "Like Seattle, but different."

"Do you miss it?" The tone of his voice made her wonder if he was asking about Seattle or Seb.

She squeezed his arm. "I'm glad I'm here. There's really no other place I'd rather be."

Her answer softened the concerned wrinkle between his eyebrows and he briefly put his hand over hers.

She waited while Nick bought the tickets to the park, her worry mounting. After he returned, she said, "The price tag of this trip is climbing."

He gave her a smile that seemed full of secrets. "Don't worry about it."

"Are you sure?"

He raised his eyebrows. "What are you saying? We came all this way! You want to back out?"

"Of course, we have to see the falls now that we're already here, but…" She paused before adding, "There are a lot of cool places where we can take videos in Buenos Aires. We don't have to—"

"Stop." He placed his finger on her lips. "I know what I'm doing, okay? Don't worry about the money."

She stared at him. He looked so much like Seb, but despite the fact that they'd been raised as brothers, they were so very different. Seb never said don't worry about the money, even though he had plenty of it.

"Where's your guitar?" she asked, noticing for once that he was empty-handed.

"I checked it."

"But the whole point of our being here—"

"Stop! Please." He sighed. "We'll see the falls, explore the park, and after we've found a private place, I'll retrieve the guitar."

"Are you sure?"

"Yes. I'm surprised we can't hear the falls from here," Nick said, clearly in an effort to change the subject. "We have to take a tram to the trailhead."

They shuffled through the line with all the other passengers waiting to board the tram. Sweat beaded on the back of Adrienne's neck and rolled between her shoulder blades. Nick's damp shirt clung to his chest. She had to look away as memories of them playing at the beach, and guilt, swamped her. She chided herself for being attracted to her husband's cousin. What would Seb—or any other members of his family—say if they could read her thoughts?

"What are you thinking about?" Nick asked.

Adrienne started. "You don't want to know."

He touched a spot between her eyebrows. "You get a wrinkle right here when you're concentrating on something."

Had Seb ever looked at her the way Nick was looking at her right now? For the last few years, he'd hardly noticed her at all. It was as if she were invisible.

"It's back," Nick said. "It disappeared for a second, but—oh, it's gone again."

Adrienne laughed. "You're making me self-conscious." She wanted to ask him to stop looking at her, but she didn't know how. Instead, she tucked her hand around his arm and whispered, "So, which of our fellow passengers will be the first to try and feed the coati-creatures?"

Nick scanned the people in the crowd as they filed onto the tram. "The man wearing the cravat?"

Adrienne settled onto the seat. "Hmm, that's a good guess."

Nick sat beside her. His thigh briefly touched hers before he scooched away. "Why? Because he looks ridiculous?"

"Yes. It's a hundred degrees out here." Adrienne lifted her hair off the back of her neck and longed for a hair-tie.

The tram's engine rumbled and barked before lurching into gear, then gathered speed as it pulled away from the park's entrance.

"Maybe he has a good reason for covering up his neck."

"Like what?"

"A rash? Scars?"

"Hickies," Adrienne put in. She rolled her hair into a long cord and attempted to tie it up as she watched the jungle flash by.

"I cannot believe you just said that," Nick said in a mock self-righteous tone. "Besides, this man is probably the sort who would want to flaunt his hickies. Who is your choice?"

Adrienne glanced around at the few children. They were the obvious choices, but because she really hoped it wouldn't be one of them, she nodded at a woman with a mane of chestnut-colored hair wearing a pair of silver stilettos.

"She's pretty," Nick said.

"Yes, but she didn't make a wise footwear choice."

Nick fell quiet. After a moment, he said, "I can feel the falls."

Adrienne listened and a quiet thunder vibrated in her chest. "So can I."

The sound grew heavier and more distinct once they disembarked from the tram.

"Amazing," Nick said as they followed the crowd. "Should we take the upper or lower falls trail?"

"Both?"

"Are you interested in riding the boat?"

Nick's grin deepened as his stride lengthened. After a few moments on the trail, the fall's roar drowned out all other noise. Nick stayed directly beside her, and sometimes his shoulder brushed against hers, but he didn't try to speak to her. They followed the path to the water's edge.

The boat service was nothing like Niagara Falls' Maid of the Mist, where people wore ponchos and stood on the deck of an enormous and sturdy ferry. The Iguazu Falls tour included an inflatable boat and lifejackets. A man with a bullhorn encouraged them to quickly find their seats.

"Welcome, everyone. My name is Jorge, and our captain here is Leo."

Leo, who manned the engine, smiled and waved.

"We are your escorts today," Jorge continued.

Adrienne's attention wandered to Nick's muscles that seemed to be bursting out of his lifejacket during Jorge' lecture on safety precautions, but she tuned back in time to hear about the legend.

"Folklore claims a big snake called Boi lived in the river,"

Jorge said. "To calm its vicious hunger and lust, the natives sacrificed a virgin every year as an offering. But once a brave guarani aborigine kidnapped the woman and saved her from the traditional rite. They escaped through the river. Boi burst in anger, literally exploding the river into the cascading waterfalls that forever separated the man from the woman."

Interesting that both the Iguazu Falls and Niagara Falls legends had snakes, virgins, and human sacrifice, Adrienne thought. She wanted to ask Nick if he was familiar with the Niagara legend, but since she didn't have a bullhorn, she knew he wouldn't hear her. She tucked it away to share with him later.

When everyone was settled in, the boat sped across the water. The closer they came to the falls, the choppier the waves grew. Jorge ditched his bullhorn and began recording the boat's passengers with a large video camera.

The water sloshed over the sides and the fall's spray soaked the passengers. Repeatedly, the tossing tide threw Adrienne against Nick's side. Every time, he responded with a smile. Water droplets glistened in his dark hair, clung to his eyebrows, and ran down his face.

The power of the falls shook through Adrienne, making her feel small and insignificant. In a good way. Yes, her marriage wasn't what she'd thought it would be. Seb wasn't who she'd thought he'd be, but then she wasn't who she'd thought she'd be either.

In the courtroom, she was strong. In law school, they had called her Audacious Adrienne. So why was she such a sniveling coward with Seb? Why did he make her feel like she was something stuck on the bottom of his shoe?

A wave of shocking cold water washed over her. She was too surprised to even scream. After she blinked, her sight returned. Jorge had his camera pointed at her and a grin on his face, waiting to see what she'd do.

She plastered on a smile and leaned against Nick, trying to absorb some of his warmth. Nick draped his arm across her shoulders and pulled her closer.

A few minutes later, the boat returned to quieter waters. Adrienne eased away from Nick and tried to tame her hair.

Once they were on solid ground and away from the roaring falls, Adrienne asked Nick if he'd ever heard of the Niagara legend. He hadn't, so she tried to recall it as best she could as they followed the path up the steep bank.

"A young bride was so distressed over the death of her husband that she paddled into the middle of the roaring Niagara River. Singing a time-honored death hymn, the girl allowed the canoe to be caught by the rushing current, and soon she and her boat were thrown over the edge of the enormous falls."

"And she died?" Nick asked.

"No. She wanted to, but the god of thunder caught her mid-descent. He brought the girl to his home behind the falls, where she and the god's son nursed her back to health. The girl fell in love with and married the god of thunder's son, and together the family lived behind the falls."

"Aww, a happy ending," Nick said.

Adrienne pulled at her wet clothes. The sun had warmed them, but, given the humidity, she worried that they'd never dry and she'd be soggy for the remainder of the trip. "You would think, but no. The girl, although happy in her magical life behind the thundering water, missed her people. The god of thunder, knowing how much she still loved her family, warned her that a giant snake planned to poison the river, hoping the people from the girl's village would drink from the water and die so he could feast on their bodies."

"Oh, grisly."

A woman shrieked somewhere ahead on the path.

Adrienne paused her story while Nick sprinted up the path and disappeared around a corner. Following at a slower pace, Adrienne came across Nick and the woman in the silver stilettos a few minutes later. The woman sat on the road with her legs splayed out, cradling her bleeding hand in her lap.

Adrienne bit back the I told you so on her lips and instead asked, "Is there anything I can do?"

The woman ignored Adrienne, gazed into Nick's face, and stuttered in Spanish, "The c- critters, they looked so cute and h-harmless."

Adrienne answered in Spanish, "Even cute things can be dangerous." She tried to dismiss the mental image of Seb flickering in her mind.

"Come on," Nick said, taking the woman's elbow and helping her to her feet. "I bet they have bandages at the ranger's station."

"Do they even have a ranger's station here?" Adrienne hoped her voice didn't sound as testy as she felt, but she didn't like the way the woman was leaning against Nick.

"I'm sure they have a first-aid kit where we bought the tram tickets," Nick said in a soothing voice.

Adrienne trailed after them, fighting her irritation. So what if that beautiful woman in ridiculous shoes was making goo-goo eyes at Nick? Someday he would marry a lovely woman — because he was so wonderful, he deserved nothing less — and he and his wife would make gorgeous babies. And he, because he was so good, would adore his wife and his children. He would never be tempted by a Therese. He wouldn't flirt with the girls in the office or the interns.

Adrienne's pace slowed. Even though Nick and the stiletto-she-wolf weren't galloping up the hill by any means, Adrienne lagged behind as fatigue caught up with her. What am I doing here? she wondered. What am I doing with my life?

She reminded herself that she was supposed to be helping Nick shoot YouTube videos. Looking around, she spotted a trail that led into the jungle. "Huh, Nick? I'm going to see if this is a good place for your video."

He shot her a glance. "Okay, but don't wander too far off the trail. I'll pick up my guitar at the station and be right back."

She nodded, wondering why it hurt so much to have Nick leave her behind, especially since it had been her idea. On a small knoll, she spotted a boulder protruding from the ground. She sat. Her clothes and hair, still damp, clung to her. The rock was hard. She wondered how she had come to this place in her life.

What had made Seb look outside their marriage? Had she spent too much time at the office? Would it have been different if they'd had children?

Thank goodness they'd never been blessed… but why hadn't they even tried? Would a child have melded them together? Or would she now be a single mother? Or would she have been a single mother from the very beginning, with or without a divorce? She suspected the latter. And if her suspicions were true — as Seb had proved them to be with a hundred percent accuracy so far — why was she even trying to hold onto something that he had let go of a long time ago?

I made a vow before God.

God will understand, Aubrey and both of her parents had argued. But none of them believed in God. Not really. Not like she did. Not like Seb. A small sob broke from her lips and she brushed away a tear. Giving up Seb was like giving up her faith, because he was the one who had introduced her to religion.

"Adrienne?" Nick called out.

She stood and dried her eyes. "Over here."

Nick pushed through the ferns and jungle leaves. "This is a perfect spot!"

"Really?" She glanced around. The tree's canopy was so thick only snatches of sunlight filtered through. "It's a smidge gloomy." Or were those just her thoughts? "Do you think it would be better if we could get the roar of the falls in the background?"

"We could try it here, then find another place if you want." He studied her and she flinched away from his gaze. "You okay?" he asked. He swore softly. "I'm being selfish, aren't I? Dragging you around, making you shoot videos of me."

"No, not at all!" She put her hand on his arm. "It's not that. I love that we're doing this."

He stepped closer. "Are you sure? Because we don't have to do this." He waved his arm. "We can go home, or at least you can. I need to stay in Uruguay. I promised Tio Jose I would help him train *Ximena*."

"How long will that take?" Why had she assumed Nick would go home when she did?

He shrugged. "I'm not in any hurry to get back. The Bar is doing fine without me."

But would she? To hide her confusion, she fumbled in her bag for her phone. "So… are you ready to sing?"

Nick glanced over his shoulder toward the trail. "Just a sec. Let me check." He brushed through the foliage and returned a few minutes later. "There's people out there. Let's give them a few minutes to disperse. Hey, you never finished your story."

"My story?" she echoed blankly.

"Yeah, the girl who went over the falls. I assume there was a happy ending."

Adrienne sucked in a deep breath and shrugged. "Sort of. The girl was able to warn her village, but the snake was enraged to find the people had fled to higher country. It searched for them, but the god of thunder rose from the crashing water and struck the beast dead with a single lightning bolt. The snake's body blocked the river's flow, and water began rushing directly into the god of thunder's home behind the falls. The god evacuated his family, including the girl, and they created a home in the sky. Now the girl can watch her people every day, but she can never again visit."

"Bittersweet," Nick said.

"Yeah," Adrienne agreed, thinking of parallels to her own marriage. She could love again, create a new home, but she could never go back to the person she'd been before she had loved— and lost—Seb.

"Are you ready?"

The question startled her, then she realized he was talking about his video. "Sure," she said, matching his grin. "Let's do it."

Patagonia has a windswept beauty. Even in the height of summer, the clear air held the promise of frosty nights and crisp days. Nick chose the Seno Otway colony because it didn't require a boat ride but it was a nearly fifty-kilometer drive from the Punta Arenas airport. He didn't mind, though. Not as long as he had Adrienne beside him.

They passed a few cars, herds of alpacas, and flocks of flamingos. The birds' startling pink was almost as surprising as the crystal blue sky.

"I can't get over the flamingos," Nick said.

"I know. Me neither," Adrienne said. "I always think of them being tropical creatures." She glanced at the tour book they'd picked up at the airport. "It would be amazing if we could see their mating ritual, but according to this, it's really unlikely. Seems they like their privacy."

"I get that," Nick said, his gaze leaving the narrow track of road and sweeping over the undulating, barren terrain.

"What are you going to sing at the preserve?" Adrienne asked. "'Birdland'?"

"Like from Manhattan Transfer? That's a change for you, isn't it?"

He shrugged. "Sing it with me?"

"I don't know the words!"

"Just repeat after me." Nick loved listening to Adrienne sing. She didn't have a strong voice, but it was clear, sweet, and naturally high—all adjectives that could be used to describe her as well as her voice.

Anger and frustration rushed through him. He tightened his grip on the steering wheel, wondering how long he could perpetuate this charade. He poured his heart into the song, singing one line at a time, listening to her echo before providing the next line. Slowly, they pieced the song together, an awkward duet in the beginning, but by the end, they were belting out the words and even occasionally harmonizing.

If only life could be as easy as a song.

Nick pulled the car into the nearly deserted gravel parking lot. A wooden fence surrounded the heath. They hadn't walked very far along the trail before Adrienne clutched his arm. "Oh look! There's one!"

A black and white penguin stood on a small bluff staring at them.

Adrienne dug her camera out of her bag to take his picture. "This might be the only one we see," she told Nick.

He waited while she snapped about ten photos of the patient bird. The creature stood so regally, it was almost as if he were posing.

They followed the path to the top of the hill where they both hesitated, overcome by the sight of hundreds of penguins. The birds paid the human visitors little attention, but waddled around, doing their thing.

"Amazing," Adrienne breathed.

"Yes," Nick agreed. He loved the expression on her face much more than he appreciated the birds.

They stayed on the path, wandering through the bluffs and tufts of tall grass. After a short distance, they found a bench overlooking the beach and sat to watch. Nick drew his guitar case onto his lap, unlatched it, and pulled out the instrument. He tuned the strings and plucked out a tune.

One penguin let out a squawk.

Nick twisted around to look at the bird as it stood on a small rise, barking.

Adrienne laughed. "That sound is why they're nicknamed jackass penguins."

Nick's hand hovered over the guitar. "He doesn't like my music."

"Don't take it personally."

"Everyone's a critic," Nick grumbled as the bird continued to complain.

Suddenly, hundreds of birds began to bark.

"Oh look." Adrienne pointed at the water. "I think they're calling their mates. See, the other penguins are returning."

Nick laughed. "I think it's the changing of the babysitters."

"It's so cool that they just know what to do," Adrienne said. The tone in her voice made Nick wonder if she was like him, wishing someone would hand out a guidebook on where to go next.

"I can't sing with all this noise," he said.

"But it would be really cool if you could find some way to use it."

"They'll probably stop in a few minutes," Nick predicted. He picked out a song on his guitar, waiting for the cacophony to die down. And eventually it did. He sang a couple of songs, including "Birdland."

The next day they drove out to the Torres del Paine National Park. It was even more isolated and desolate than the penguin preserve. The Towers of Paine loomed in the distance.

"The Towers of Paine," Nick murmured. "Who thought of that name?"

"Mr. Paine, probably," Adrienne said, checking her guidebook. "We'll stay tonight in the hostel?"

Nick nodded but cast a worried glance at the clouds gathering over the mountain peaks as they drove deeper into the park and further from civilization.

After they parked near the trailhead, Adrienne didn't have any hesitation but tucked the guidebook into her bag and strode down the path. With every step he took, the temptation to kiss her grew. The need to share his feelings swelled inside him.

Thunder boomed in the sunny sky.

"What was that?" Adrienne asked over her shoulder. "It can't be rain."

The guidebook had warned that the weather in Patagonia could change in an instant. Even during the summer when the days were warm and endless, the winds could reach up to a hundred and twenty-five miles an hour.

Thunder crashed again.

"I think it must be the sound of the glaciers cracking," Nick said.

Adrienne's eyes lit up and she increased her pace. Nick followed. The path meandered through forests of trees he didn't recognize. As the way grew rockier, he felt less sure about nearly everything. His pretense of being a brotherly friend became increasingly hard to shoulder.

Ahead of him, Adrienne sang a love song. She was waiting

for him to join her, but he couldn't make himself do it. His boots grew heavier until he felt like he had bricks strapped onto his feet. His guitar, which normally felt like an extension of his arm, seemed to weigh a hundred pounds.

The hike went on forever, but eventually they reached the crest that overlooked a surreal blue lake.

"I've never seen anything that color before," Adrienne said, her eyes almost as bright as the glaciers. "This has to be the most beautiful thing I've ever seen."

He wanted to tell her that she was the most beautiful thing he'd ever seen, but he bit back the words, knowing that if he ever dared to cross that line, their camaraderie would tumble into awkwardness.

But just then a giant condor sailed above them with a loud cry.

Startled, Adrienne jumped and landed against Nick's chest. His arms instinctively went around her and they each bobbled for balance. He found his feet first and steadied her.

She twisted so that she faced him and grabbed his arms. For a moment, they stood inches apart, her eyes laughing and looking up at him. He took a mental picture, knowing that her proximity was fleeting and rare.

"I love you." The words seemed to burst out of him, unbidden and unplanned. But once they were said, he didn't regret them. He knew that he should, but he couldn't.

Confusion flickered across her face.

"It's wrong, I know, but I can't help it," he said.

"No." She pulled away. "You can't mean that."

"It's true," he said, letting her go.

"Traveling like we have, maybe you've developed—"

"It's not new," he interrupted her. "And yes, these last few days have been amazing, but I loved you long before all of this." He waved his arms at the glacial lake. "I think I fell in love with you the first day I met you. When Seb brought you home."

He hated himself for mentioning Seb, but he had to.

"Nick—"

He interrupted her again. "I get that you don't feel the same.

It's okay."

"Is it really?" The crease between her eyebrows that he loved so much returned. "Because I don't think so. You've spoiled everything. This isn't fair to either of us."

"I know this is where I should say I'm sorry, but I'm not." She moved to walk away from him, but he took her arm. "I'm tired of lying and trying to hide my feelings."

She whirled back to face him, her eyes sparking with anger and unshed tears. "We were having such a good time!"

He cupped her face. "Don't you see? We could have a lifetime —"

She wrenched away from him, stumbling down the hillside.

He went after her.

Five

Adrienne hadn't noticed the gathering clouds. She mistakenly thought the first raindrop was her own tear. Anger rushed through her as she stormed down the hill. She knew Nick with his long legs could overtake her in minutes, but the fact that he kept his distance reminded her that he was a good person. But she was still angry that he'd ruined their easy camaraderie.

She reached the trailhead but halted when she spotted the car's flickering dome light. "Oh no," she breathed. The passenger-side door hung slightly ajar because the seatbelt had gotten caught in it. And she couldn't blame this on Nick, because she had been the one on that side of the car. "Oh dear," she murmured.

Nick caught up to her and quickly assessed the situation. He pressed the fob, but the doors remained locked. "Bad sign," he muttered.

Adrienne climbed in through the passenger side and unlocked the driver's side door for Nick. He settled behind the steering wheel and inserted the key in the ignition. The dome light went out.

Nick turned the key and the engine made a weak growling noise.

"Can we call anyone?" Adrienne asked.

Nick took out his phone. "I don't get reception. Do you?"

Adrienne checked hers. "No. Maybe someone will come by."

"It's hard to tell because of the midnight sun," Nick said, "but it's actually close to ten o'clock. Besides, we're like a hundred miles from anything."

Adrienne shivered. "Maybe not. I thought we passed a cabin."

Just then, lightning flashed. Fat raindrops fell. Thunder crashed and the wind whipped the trees' branches.

"Which way?" Nick asked.

"I'm not sure I'll be able to find it," Adrienne said. "And, for all I know, it was a porta potty."

"Which would be disgusting, but not as bad as spending the night in a storm."

"We could sleep in the car," Adrienne suggested, but she knew she would be much more comfortable than poor Nick, who was at least eight inches taller than her.

"I'll go and see if I can find it," Nick said.

She grabbed his arm. "I don't want to be separated."

"You'll be fine."

"They have pumas here!" Panic caught in her voice.

"Then come with me. We'll look for fifteen minutes. If we haven't found it by then, we'll come back to the car."

She silently agreed and stepped out of the car to face the elements. How many miles to the next town? Twenty? Alone, dark, cold, a storm—this was the stuff of nightmares. She tromped up the trail and was relieved to spot the roofline of a small building poking up out of the trees' canopy.

Nick spotted it, too, and jogged toward the porch. He rattled the door. "Locked." He threw the word over his shoulder before trying the window. It slid open.

Adrienne let out a sigh of relief and hurried to take shelter on the cabin's small porch while Nick climbed in through the window and came to the door to let her in.

"We're trespassing." She stood in the doorway, surveying the small cabin. A large bed dominated the single room. She took one of the two chairs at the lone table. Someone had stacked firewood and newspapers near the hearth, and a jar of matches sat on the mantel. The kitchen consisted of some wooden shelves stocked with canned foods and a few utensils. Glancing at the bed, she saw that it was as clean as the rest of the room. A large quilt, fat pillows… She looked away quickly and met Nick's eyes.

Nick plucked the jar off the mantel and muttered, "Thank you," to whoever had come before them as he shook a couple of matches into his hand.

"I wonder who owns this place," Adrienne said.

"Maybe the park department," Nick suggested without turning around. He wadded up some newspaper and shoved it between the logs in the grate before striking a match. Minutes later, a flame glowed.

Nick peeled off his wet shirt, but not his drenched, mud-splattered jeans. She'd seen him in a bathing suit countless times, but somehow, this time was very different. His hair was longer and curled along his neck. Watching his back muscles work as he poked at the flame, she wondered if he'd been working out.

"I'd rather be trespassing than wet." He gazed into the fire. "My feelings aside, you really should hang up your clothes to dry. You must be cold."

She ignored his suggestion and shifted her gaze to the fireplace while he coaxed the tiny flame into a roaring fire. A pot hung from a hook.

"Soup?" she asked.

"I'm not hungry."

"Me neither, but I thought maybe you'd be." Adrienne cleared her throat. "This all belongs to someone."

"We'll leave money and a thank-you note on the table."

She didn't doubt that Nick would be generous. "What if they find us here?"

Nick looked out the window at the now-raging storm.

Lightning lit up the small room, momentarily blinding Adrienne. After a moment, the room returned to a cozy glow.

"Your pants are wet," she said.

Nick turned from the fire, rifled through his bag, and pulled out a large T-shirt, the sort of thing he slept in when they stayed at hotels. He tossed it to her and she caught it. It smelled of his cologne. He had thought to bring his bag, but she'd left hers in the car.

She quickly stepped out of her jeans and pulled the T-shirt over her head, hypersensitive to him, wondering if he was watching her. Her skin tingled. She heard him moving behind her and turned to see that he'd taken off his jeans and now wore only his boxers. He pulled back the covers on the bed.

She folded her arms protectively across her chest and frowned at him.

Nick sighed. "As much as I'd like to, I'm tired and cold. You're swaying on your feet. Tonight, I think you'll find sharing my toothbrush to be as much intimacy as you'll be able to stand."

He knew her too well.

He gestured at the bed. "Would you like the right or the left side?"

Adrienne shifted. She couldn't find a comfortable place. The bed groaned every time she moved. Staring at the embers smoldering in the fireplace, she willed herself to sleep. The colors in the grate shifted, and she turned her attention to the much more boring and static ceiling.

Beside her, Nick lay on his side with his back to her. She knew by his breathing that he wasn't sleeping. It'd taken her weeks to get used to sleeping without Seb beside her, and now she couldn't sleep because of Nick. He didn't seem bothered at all, whereas she had morphed into a collection of protruding, restless bones. She tucked her knees into her chest, lying on her side, her arm pinned beneath her, its circulation cut off, slowly growing numb. She eased onto her back and the bed groaned again.

The sheets smelled musty, but they seemed clean enough. No obvious stains. She didn't think she could have tolerated that. As far as beds went, this one wasn't so terribly uncomfortable. Just noisy.

She considered the mound in the blanket beside her. Why was she so ridiculously aware of his breath, his smell, the warmth of his body? Adrienne tried to make herself as small and still as she could. Huddling in the fetal position, she wondered how they'd get out tomorrow. No cell service — they'd have to walk to the main highway and then hitch a ride into town. Of course, being with Nick would be much better than being alone. Safer.

Her neck hurt. She rolled over and punched her pillow. She had down pillows at home. This pillow must have been made from shredded cardboard. It smelled like oatmeal. Maybe it'd been made from a recycled cereal box. Why wasn't she asleep?

"Adrienne?"

She went still. Played dead.

The blankets rustled as Nick rolled over. Adrienne scooted to the edge of the mattress.

"Why are you awake?" he asked.

"How could anyone sleep? This bed is noisy. The pillow is made of gravel." She didn't like the sound of her voice. She knew she sounded petulant, and she hated being the spoiled princess. "I'm cold."

Nick hitched himself onto his elbow. "Here," he said, enveloping her in his arms and pulling her against him.

She nestled against his warmth.

His arm draped across her, holding her against his chest. Nick adjusted so his chin rested on her head. He smelled of cologne and of the fire, a mixture of the familiar and the primitive.

"Adrienne," Nick murmured into her hair.

Adrienne woke with the sun on her face and quilts tangled around her legs. She watched Nick sleep for a minute. She'd forgotten what this was like, watching someone in unguarded moments. He looked different. Older. He hadn't shaved and his hair had been mussed.

Stirring, he flung his arm over her. In his sleep, he pulled her close and she let him draw her to him.

She had so many questions. A night in a cabin didn't answer any of them. In fact, their night together just seemed to highlight all her questions in red. Had he come to South America to visit his uncle, or her? Did he really love her? His hold on her tightened and his breath fanned her cheek.

At this moment, should she turn away? Sanity told her she must, but she closed her eyes, seduced by the warmth, quiet, and comfort.

She had so many questions, but they could wait.

Cold. The smell of doused fire drifted from somewhere. Instinctively, she reached for Nick's warmth, but found only icy sheets. Realization washed over her, and she sat up. Her eyes felt gritty, her teeth fuzzy. She needed a bathroom. A real one. One with white porcelain and running, flushing water. She wanted bath salts, body gel and a loofa. Lying down, she pulled the quilt over her head.

She'd spent the night with Nick.

Her husband's cousin.

Nothing had happened.

That, at least, was good. Right? Sex would only have complicated things.

She'd cuddled up to him. For warmth.

Peeking out from under the quilt, she wondered where he'd gone. And why.

Outside the window, a bleak sun shone in a steel gray sky. Adrienne sat up and looked at all the damage the storm had caused — downed branches, bent trees and thousands of pinecones scattered on the ground. Just yesterday, it'd been warm. Or was it two days ago? She couldn't remember.

Where had Nick gone? She knew he wouldn't leave her alone. Adrienne climbed from the bed, taking the quilt with her. She spotted his bag in the corner.

He'd left the bag but taken his wallet.

Twinges of guilt pricked her as she went through Nick's things. She told herself he wouldn't mind.

She gathered what she needed — toothbrush, toothpaste, and comb. Her hair, a snarled curly mess, resisted her efforts, and she twisted it up into a bun. She went outside in search of a privacy tree or makeshift potty. Lots of trees, but no Nick.

She returned to the cabin and put Nick's toiletries back in his bag. Her fingers hit something smooth and the light from Nick's phone flashed at her.

A text from Seb lit the screen.

After a quick glance over her shoulder, she drew out the phone. *Thanks for keeping her away.*

Adrienne had always thought the cliché the headlines screamed ridiculous, because how could printed words be at all vocal, let alone scream? But Seb's words tore through her and thundered in her mind. Her thoughts skittered back to yesterday's hike to the glaciers and the sound of the splintering ice breaking and falling into the lake. That was how she felt. She was breaking and the sound of it was deafening.

Sitting on the bed, she cradled the phone in her lap, longing to read the entire text message chain. But she couldn't. The only text showing was the one. To access the others, she'd need Nick's password.

But this one was enough, wasn't it? Seb wanted her out of the way so badly, he'd sent his cousin to keep her entertained.

And Nick. What exactly was his role? He'd said he loved her, but did he really? And how could he, when she was so broken?

She threw on her jeans and sweater, slipped into her shoes and stepped out into the bleak sunshine.

Up the road, she saw Nick talking to a man in baggy pants standing beside a truck. A thick yellow tow rope attached the truck to their rental car.

Adrienne didn't know what to say. Should she tell him she'd found his phone with the text message? A part of her wanted to tell him she was sorry, but she didn't know exactly what for, and she didn't know if he would misconstrue her apology as something she didn't mean. She didn't know what she meant. She didn't know what she wanted.

Should she go home?

Should she try to fight for her marriage?

Should she ask Nick to open his phone so she could read all the messages from Seb? No. Definitely not. She was tired of being pathetic, and even though she didn't know what she wanted, she knew exactly what she didn't want. She didn't want to wait around anymore for someone who valued her company so little that he would employ someone else to keep her occupied. She felt like a puppy in need of a dogwalker or a child requiring a nanny.

"This is Mario," Nick said, motioning to the mammoth man sitting behind the wheel. "He's going to give us a ride into town."

Mario wore a straw cap and a polo shirt with gray chest hair poking through the buttonholes. His skin had weathered to a wrinkly rawhide, tanned to the middle of his biceps but paler beneath the sleeves of his shirt.

Nick held the truck door open for Adrienne. "I'll sit in the back."

But the back was full of chickens—dozens of them. They clicked their beaks against the wire cages and clucked and shook their downy feathers at Nick.

"Where?" she asked. "You need a beak to sit back there."

"There's plenty of room up here," Mario called out, smiling at Adrienne.

Nick and Adrienne looked at each other. It'd be a squeeze. She'd have to wedge between Nick and Mario. Nick would never fit in the middle, not with the gear stick.

Adrienne climbed into the cab. It smelled of mud and grease. Nick clambered in beside her, put his guitar case between his legs and rested his arm across the back of the bench seat. To keep from touching Mario, Adrienne pressed herself against Nick's side. He felt warm and solid against her goosepimply skin. By necessity his thigh ran alongside hers.

"Are you selling your chickens?" Adrienne asked, attempting small talk.

"Yep," Mario said, looking her squarely in the eye. "Tomorrow being the Lord's day, I do all my trading on Saturdays." His big beefy hand rested on the gear stick inches from her knee.

"Are you a commercial chicken farmer?" she asked.

"No." Mario shifted from second to third gear and his hand grazed Adrienne's thigh. She scooted closer to Nick. "I just raise a few chickens on the side and trade my leftovers to the Gallo Pasada over in Puerto Natales. He looked from Adrienne's legs to Nick's face. "You two married?"

Neither replied for a moment. Finally Nick said, "No."

Mario chuckled and shifted into fifth. Adrienne crossed her legs, trying to avoid contact with him and the gear stick.

"Bet you will be soon," he said.

What is that supposed to mean? "Nick is my husband's cousin and best friend," Adrienne put in.

Mario's grin didn't fade. He shot a quick glance at Nick's thigh pressing against Adrienne's. "Not for long, I'm guessing."

Was Mario a Dr. Phil in overalls? He knew nothing about either of them. Adrienne tried to pull away from Nick, but that brought her knee closer to Mario's hand resting on the gear stick.

"So how is it you're traveling together?"

You don't have to answer him, Adrienne mentally told Nick. We need a ride, not a counseling session.

"This is a business trip," Nick said. "Of sorts."

Mario snorted and threw Adrienne a quick glance. "Some hanky-panky business."

Adrienne stiffened. Again, what is that supposed to mean? She'd just been insulted. She didn't speak until they pulled up at a stop signal next to a tavern called El Toro Enojado.

"Thanks, Mario. We'll get out here," Nick said, opening the door and pulling Adrienne out with him. He slammed the door as Mario got out to unhook the rental car from the tow line.

"Wait, why here?" she asked Nick's retreating back. He was already climbing onto the porch of the tavern.

"I didn't like Mario," he said over his shoulder. He stopped beside the tavern door. "Did you? Were you comfortable with him pressing against your thigh every time he shifted gears?" He waited a beat. "I didn't think so. We'll get roadside service. But first, I need a human moment."

While Nick went inside to use the restroom, Adrienne settled onto a wooden bench on the porch. Wondering if she might finally have reception, she fished her phone out of her bag.

Her pulse quickened when she read a text from Aubrey that said, *Call me now.*

Six

ad's in the hospital," Aubrey said. "Where are you?"

"Patagonia." Adrienne glanced around at the windswept, barren landscape. "Literally the middle of nowhere, but I think Puerto Natales must be close because we have reception. Tell me what happened."

"They think he had a stroke."

"Is he going to be okay?"

"They don't know. My flight leaves tomorrow, but I can't stay for more than a few days." Aubrey's unuttered question hung in the air. "Mom is… well, she shouldn't be alone."

"I'll be there as soon as I can," Adrienne promised.

The sound of a clicking keyboard came through the phone. "I found you a flight from Punta Arenas to Seattle." She softly swore. "The fastest flight is more than twenty-four hours. Want me to book it?"

"What's going on?" Nick sat beside her, his breath tickling the back of her neck.

"My dad has had a stroke," Adrienne told him.

Aubrey swore again. "The cheapest flight is thousands of dollars."

"Doesn't matter," Nick said. "I'll pay for it."

"No," Adrienne protested.

"You're here because of me," Nick said. "Let me get you out of here."

"I'm here because I want to be here."

"And now you want to be home."

"I'm not arguing with you," Adrienne said.

Aubrey laughed.

"What's so funny?" Adrienne demanded.

"You sound just like Mom and Dad," Aubrey told her.

Aubrey made the arrangements using Adrienne's credit card, but Adrienne only half-listened to the particulars. Her thoughts were already with her parents.

"This time with you has been amazing," Adrienne said to Nick as they stood on the curb of the Punta Arenas airport. She leaned in to kiss his cheek. "But this is goodbye."

"For now," Nick put in.

She had so much more to say, but she had no time. He drew her in for a quick hug. Briefly, she allowed herself to sag against him.

"Are you sure you don't want me to come with you?" he asked.

She shook her head. "Keep to the plan. Sing your songs. You never really needed me, you know? Get yourself a tripod—"

"I can't replace you with a tripod," Nick told her. "You were my cheerleader. No, more than that. You were my catalyst. You made everything happen for me."

"And I can still do that, but from a distance. I need to be with my parents."

Nick nodded, hugged her again, and turned away. Adrienne's heart twisted as she watched him walk through the airport . He looked naked without his guitar bumping at his side. She felt torn between wanting to stay with him and burning anxiousness for her mom and dad.

It dawned on her that for Seb she felt nothing at all.

A day later she arrived in Seattle to find a weak sun struggling to break free from a shroud of clouds. She shivered in the misty gloom as she waited on the curb for Aubrey to pick her up. After several minutes, she spotted her parents' aged Oldsmobile puttering through the line of cars.

Aubrey steered the Olds alongside Adrienne. Moments later,

Adrienne was slowly thawing beneath a blasting heater.

"How are they?" she asked.

Aubrey nodded. "Good, but try not to be shocked when you see Dad. He's lost use of his left side. The doctors are hopeful, though. He's in amazing condition for his age."

"And Mom?"

"It'll be hard. He's always been large and in charge. He's not going to surrender his dominance just because half his body refuses to work properly."

"Do you think" — Adrienne swallowed, hating the thought and not even wanting to know the answer — "that this could be permanent?"

"They've scheduled a brain scan for tomorrow. We should know more then."

Adrienne nodded and looked out the window. Her parents had always been such brainiacs. It was impossible to think of them in any other way, but she supposed it could happen. In time, one or possibly both could lose their mental capacity. Maybe her dad already had.

"Are you going to see Seb?" Aubrey asked.

"Yes."

"What are you going to say to him?"

Adrienne sucked in a deep breath. "What do you think about divorce? In general."

"That it's a whole lot easier if there aren't children involved."

Adrienne thought about this. Of course she agreed, but it wasn't really the answer she was looking for. "I made a vow before God."

"So did Seb."

"I can't let his behavior determine mine."

"You've told me this before," Aubrey said through tight lips. "Who are you trying to convince, me or you?"

"You don't like him." This wasn't a question.

"I never have."

"Why?"

"He was always smarmy. Trying too hard to be something he wasn't."

"Why didn't you tell me this before I married him?"

"Would it have stopped you?"

Adrienne thought about pointing out that Aubrey, who had never been married, was unqualified to be handing out marital advice, but since she didn't want to start an argument she bit her lip.

"Where are we going?" Aubrey asked. "Will you stay at your apartment or at the house?"

"With Mom." Adrienne slid her sister a glance. "My being here has everything to do with Mom and Dad and very little to do with Seb."

Aubrey smiled. "Of course. Why would you stay with your husband when you can stay with your parents?"

"One more word and I promise you I'll start ripping out the plants in Mom's garden."

Aubrey braked hard at the street signal and fixed a glare on Adrienne. "You don't mean that!"

Adrienne nodded and snapped her fingers. "Make me mad and the lilacs are out of there."

"Mom won't let you!"

"I'll do it while she's sleeping."

"You're evil."

Adrienne just grinned.

"Man, I'm glad you're here," Aubrey said.

"Me, too."

"The dogwood tree is off limits."

"There are no promises," Adrienne said. "Nothing is safe."

They stopped at the hospital to visit their parents, but both her father and mother were sleeping even though it was the middle of the day. Her father lay on the bed with an IV strapped to his arm. With his shock of white hair and graying skin, he looked corpse-like. Her mom dozed in the chair beside him, her hair hiding her face.

"Let's not wake them," Aubrey whispered.

Adrienne nodded. "Take me to my apartment."

"Are you sure?"

"Seb will be at the office. If I want to pick up some clothes and my car without drama, right now is the perfect time."

"Seems cowardly," Aubrey said.

"Keep talking and your tomato plants are toast."

Aubrey pressed her lips together as they headed down the hall.

"I know I need to talk to him," Adrienne conceded, "but the thing is, I don't know what to say."

"Why can't you tell him his corn has been shucked?"

Adrienne elbowed her sister.

Aubrey's grin faded as she nodded at a man in scrubs with a stethoscope striding toward them. "Dad's doctor."

Adrienne wondered how a man dressed in baby blue could command such presence.

"Dr. Lazlo." Aubrey went to meet him. "Can you tell me any more about my father?"

Dr. Lazlo consulted his tablet. "I'm sorry, no. We should know more after his brain scan. He's sleeping now, which is good. Sleep is when our bodies heal." He smiled at Adrienne, prompting her to put out her hand and introduce herself.

He took her hand and held it a minute too long, making her wonder if he'd noticed her wedding ring. Maybe she should have had him shake her left hand.

"He'll be glad you're here," Dr. Lazlo said as he shot a glance at their dad's room over his shoulder. "They'll both be."

"I'm glad I'm here, too," she said, although just then she heard a familiar voice and her heart stopped for a moment. "Excuse me." She followed Nick's voice to an open door.

A tiny woman sat propped up on her bed with a lunch tray in front of her. When she caught Adrienne staring at the TV screen, she waved her fork at Nick's image. "They call him the Where's Waldo of Music. I call him dreamy."

"He just follows you around, doesn't he?" Aubrey asked from behind her.

"He's everywhere," the tiny woman said as she attacked her dessert. "Kind of like the holy spirit," she said through a mouthful of cake.

"Wowzers," Aubrey said. "Nick just got elevated to deity."

"There's my car." Adrienne nodded at her Camry when Aubrey pulled the Oldsmobile into the apartment complex's parking garage.

"Are you sure you're going to be okay?" Aubrey asked.

"Absolutely. I have a set of car keys in my purse." She winked at her sister. "So I can make a quick getaway if needed."

"What if he's there?"

"Then we'll talk."

"But you said you don't know what to say!" Aubrey's voice lifted in panic.

Not knowing what to say or do was probably what Aubrey, as a professor, feared the most. But as an attorney, Adrienne was used to thinking on her feet.

Although, not when it came to matters of the heart. In that area, she was almost as inept as her sister.

"I'll see you back at the house," Adrienne promised.

"I'm going back to the hospital," Aubrey said.

Adrienne nodded. "Call me when either Mom or Dad wakes."

"Are you sure you don't want to rest after your long flight?"

"I'm sure."

Adrienne supposed she could claim the apartment as hers and force Seb out, but that would require a lot of emotional energy she didn't have.

Strangely, she didn't feel sad as she moved through the rooms she used to consider hers. Seb had picked out most of the furniture and the art on the walls. It looked like a spread from a magazine, but one she didn't particularly enjoy.

She took pity on the dying plants on the kitchen windowsill and found a box so she could take them to her parents' house, knowing Aubrey would approve. The basil appeared scraggly and the dill had wilted but the rosemary seemed hardy, if prickly.

Most of the apartment wore an empty and abandoned look, but a discarded pair of black socks lay on the floor next to Seb's side of the bed. She tried not to look as she headed for the closet and her clothes, but then she saw a hair. A long, straight black hair lay on the fluffy white pillow.

That hair said more to her than Seb ever could. It was the final statement in her long debate. Of course, she'd known about Therese. Why hadn't she ever considered her—the other woman—in Adrienne's bed?

Adrienne stomped into the kitchen, pulled the roll of trash bags from the cupboard and began to fill one bag after another with everything she considered her own. In her closet, she considered her business suits. She hated them—not only their boxy shoulders and slim skirts, but because they represented the person she'd become. In the end, she left all but the most expensive one hanging in her, make that Seb's, closet.

On her way to her parents' house, she called Crenshaw and told him she quit.

"Life it too short," she told her mom as they sat side by side in her dad's hospital room. "Watching you take care of Dad made me realize I have to let Seb go. It's not fair to him, or to me, to try and stay."

Her mom patted Adrienne's hand. "If you think you'll be happier without him, then of course that's what you have to do."

Adrienne frowned at the raindrops streaming down the window. "But I made vows before God. Those should count for something, right? I know you and Dad aren't religious, but..."

"Actually," her mom interrupted, "it might surprise you to know that I've been doing a lot of praying these last few days."

"Really?"

Her mom nodded. "But don't tell your dad. I'm not sure he'll understand."

"Oh, I understand," her dad said, uttering his first words in a week.

"Harvey!" Adrienne's mom bounced to her feet.

"Dad!" Adrienne called out, then, "Nurse! Nurse!"

Minutes later, the room was full of doctors, nurses, and the buzz of excited and hopeful conversations. Adrienne stepped back to watch while tears clouded her vision. Her dad caught her eye and winked.

The day her father was released from the hospital, something snapped in Adrienne. She put on her expensive business suit, pulled her hair back into a tight chignon, picked up her nearly empty briefcase, and marched into Seb's office.

The secretary raised her eyebrows as Adrienne strode past the reception desk. A few people in their cubes looked up. Their gazes followed her into Seb's office.

"Adrienne," Seb said, leaning back in his chair. "This is a surprise."

"Really?" She shut the door with a loud click and turned to face him.

"What's this about?"

"You didn't even call when my dad had his stroke."

"So?"

"I thought you loved my dad. He loves you."

Seb ran his fingers through his hair. "I'm sorry, Adrienne, but I haven't read the handbook on how to navigate family relations with your ex."

"You shouldn't need a handbook on how to be a decent person." She put her briefcase on the desk and clicked it open. "But I'm not here to reform you. I've brought the divorce papers."

Seb stared at her. "I thought we agreed to wait until after Abuelo's death."

"I don't want to live a lie, nor do I want to wait with bated breath for the passing of a sweet old man that I happen to love before I can get on with the rest of my life."

"What sort of life is that?" Seb asked with a smirk. "I heard you left Crenshaw and Meeks."

"That's right, I did." She placed her fingers on the papers and edged them toward him. "And now I'm leaving you, too."

"Listen, it's in your best interest, you know, to wait. When Abuelo passes, this company will be mine, which will only increase your alimony settlement."

"The company is yours already, and you know it. You should settle with me now and save yourself potentially millions." She watched him calculate the risks. "If we can go through arbitration amicably," she pressed, "we won't need to incur unnecessary legal costs."

"I'll think about it," he said.

"I wish it wasn't like this," she said. "I wish we could be friends."

"We can be friends," he said with a smile Aubrey would call smarmy.

She gazed at him, wondering what had happened to the boy she'd fallen in love with. "Sure," she said, all the while hating herself for perpetuating another lie.

Later that night as she tried to sleep in her childhood bed, her phone buzzed with a text from Seb.

Can we talk?

Sure. Call me, she responded.

I'm on your front porch.

Adrienne slipped from the bed, pulled on her clothes, and although she hated herself for running as soon as Seb called, she pulled open the front door within minutes.

The moon, peeking through a haze of clouds at the zenith, provided little light, but even in the dimness Adrienne could see Seb's distress.

"Abuelo's d-dead," Seb stuttered.

Adrienne, fearing that he would wake Aubrey, or worse, her mom and dad, took Seb's sleeve and pulled him off the porch, down the front walk, through the gate, and onto the sidewalk. She shied away from the streetlamp's glow. The last thing she wanted was her sister to see or hear her talking to Seb. She dreaded her sister's lecture more than whatever Seb had to say.

I thought that was what you wanted came to her lips, but she bit the words back, and said instead, "I'm sorry. I know you loved him."

He nodded and ran his fingers through his hair. He looked like a lost child. "I don't know what to do."

"Do? I'm not sure what you mean. You've been running the company for years."

"The business is fine. That I know how to manage." He toed a pebble on the ground, not meeting her gaze. He breathed out a sigh and looked up at the bleak stars. "I'm sorry. I'm not sure what I'm doing here."

"I can see that."

He swallowed. "Do you still want the divorce?"

"Of course. Don't you?"

"I'm, hmm, not sure?"

Adrienne stared at him and an image of her Uncle Josh weeks before his death flashed in her memory. He'd died after a long and painful battle with cancer. *I always said that if I ever had a terminal illness I would drink, smoke, take drugs, and eat whatever I wanted, but now that I'm here, none of that forbidden fruit is interesting to me.* Was that how Seb was feeling? Had Therese just been forbidden fruit? Poor Therese. Poor Seb. Adrienne felt nothing but release and even though she'd loved Abuelo, elation and a sense of freedom swept through her, as cleansing as the night air.

"Seb, go home."

"There's no one there." His voice bordered on panic.

"You'll be okay. When's the funeral?"

"We're burying him in Italy."

"Oh, that's nice. He'll like that."

"And having a memorial here in a few days." He lifted his eyes to her. "Will you come?"

"Will Nick be there?" She tried to tamp down the excitement in her tone.

"No one's been able to get ahold of him," Seb said. He returned to toeing the pebble. "Steph thinks he's either on Easter Island or in the Andes. We can't wait for him," he added defensively. "I'm leaving for Italy and the interment in a few days."

"I'm sure Nick'll understand."

"Adrienne!" Aubrey called from the porch. She'd turned on the light and stood beneath it. Clad in a ratty, fuzzy red robe and a pair of men's black socks, she looked comical, but there was nothing funny about the fury on her face.

"I have to go," Adrienne said.

"How's your dad?" Seb asked. "You were right, I should have asked about him."

"He's getting better."

"That's good. Maybe I can visit him? We could play chess like we used to."

"I don't know, Seb," Adrienne hedged.

"Adrienne!" Aubrey barked.

"You're not very popular around here," Adrienne said with a sad smile.

"I get that," he said. "I deserve that."

"I have to go before Aubrey wakes the neighbors." She leaned in to kiss his cheek and for just a moment inhaled his warm, familiar scent. "Goodbye, Seb."

Seven

Six Months Later

Adrienne pulled her Camry into the art academy parking lot. Excitement and nerves stirred in her. She didn't know a lot about kids, but the thought of sharing her love of art filled her with a sort of joy her career in law never could have. She parked her car, gathered her paints and brushes from the trunk, and headed for the wide double doors.

Artie, the owner of the school, stopped her. "Yeah, congratulations!"

"On what?" Adrienne asked.

"I heard your divorce was final!"

"It's not much to celebrate," she said. "It's more of a failure."

"No!" Artie punched her finger into the air. "It's a liberation celebration."

"That might be how my ex sees it."

"But how do you see it?"

Adrienne thought back over the past few months, on how she'd refused to continue their marriage charade just so Seb could keep his share of Abuelo's business, how Abuelo had died while still in Italy and never learned of the pending divorce, her stilted conversations and negotiations with Seb, and the job opening at the art academy. "It's all good," she said with a smile. "It's not the story I thought I was going have, but it's all good."

"Hey, someone told me that you know the Where's Waldo musical guy."

"That's right, I do."

"So, what would you think of asking him to perform at our school fundraiser?"

"Oh, I don't know. Nick is almost pathologically shy. He very rarely performs in front of people."

Artie scoffed. "You could have just said no. You don't have to make up stories."

"I'm not making up stories," Adrienne said.

"That guy and his dog are all over the internet!"

"I know but—"

"Just think about it, okay?"

Adrienne nodded and followed Artie down the hall. She stopped when she got to her classroom door. Exhilaration rushed through her as she stepped into her own studio. She drew in a deep breath, loving the smell of turpentine, paints, and freshly sharpened pencils. Just like her students would create their own masterpieces, she was creating her new life one day at a time.

On her way home, she decided on a whim to drop by Bar de Música. "Home" was still at her parents' house, but as her dad was slowly regaining his health and the use of his arm and leg, she was looking at bungalows to buy in their neighborhood. Close so she could help if her parents needed her, but far enough away to enjoy her privacy.

She pulled into Bar de Música's parking lot, pleased to see a throng still lining up out the door. Lingering on the sidewalk, she hesitated and debated. She hadn't come for a cocoa, but still it seemed wrong to cut through the crowd.

Jon spotted her and waved her inside. "It's like a miracle you're here!" he called over everyone.

Steph also noticed her and looked like she wanted to vault over the counter. "Get back here," Steph said. "He'll be thrilled to see you."

"He? You mean Nick?"

And that was when she saw *Ximena* lying on a cushion just inside the front door. Her heart lifted. "Nick's here?"

Matt nodded. "Heard your divorce was final."

Nick heard or Jon heard? Slightly confused, Adrienne

maneuvered through the crowd, passed the counter, and headed for the office.

Nick jumped to his feet when he saw her. "Adrienne! I wasn't expecting you!"

"And I wasn't expecting you."

"What are you doing here?" they both asked at the same time.

"I just came to ask about you," Adrienne said.

"And I came to ask your help," Nick said.

"Yeah? With what?"

He pushed some papers toward her. "With these."

"What are they?"

"Contracts. I've been offered a deal with Urban Records."

"Wow, Nick! That's awesome."

He blinked. "You know more about contracts than I do, so…"

"Do you really want to do this?"

He took a seat behind his desk. "I do. I saw a lot of things while I was traveling and some of them were hard. It's not right that there's so much grinding poverty while, well, I have a lot I can give." He waved at the crowded café before pushing the contract closer to her. "As you can see, the Urban folks are offering a lot of money. A whole lot." He lifted his gaze to hers. "And if I have a chance to help others, don't you think I should take it?"

"Of course, but Nick, they're going to want you to sing in front—"

He nodded. "I'm working on it. I think I can do it, with a little of your help." He pushed another paper toward her.

"What's this?"

"It's a contract."

"But for what?"

He stepped around the desk and took her in his arms. "For you, when you're ready. I want you to be my legal counsel. But not just that… I want you to be a part of my life."

"And we need a contract for that?"

"And a license—when you're ready." He lowered his lips and kissed her long and deep. "Remember how I told you this was just the beginning?"

Two Months Later

Olympic Avenue and Main Street were both insane. Traffic moved like turtles. Finally, Adrienne parked her car and got out to walk to the school. Nerves fluttered in her chest. Could Nick really handle all this attention?

The closer she got to the school, the crazier the mobs. A helicopter flew overhead. And then another. Helicopters. Really?

Someone, somewhere, played with the microphones, and a high-pitched squeal tore the air. Where had all these people come from? She found it hard to pick out the locals from the visitors, but she suspected everyone knew exactly who she was. People would look at her, their eyes would widen, and then they'd look quickly away.

Adrienne spotted her mom and dad near the makeshift stage that the faculty had set up on the school's playground. Her dad huddled in his wheelchair while her mom sat in a metal folding chair beside him, holding his hand. Both of their faces radiated excitement. People made room for Adrienne—most of them wore knowing smiles.

"Hey, Mom, Dad," Adrienne said. "Is today a good day?"

"A very good day," Dad said, his speech only slightly slurred.

"We got the best seats in the house," Mom said with a wink.

"Thanks to me and Old Ironsides here," Dad said, giving his wheelchair an affectionate pat.

"Oh, I think Adrienne could have gotten us prime placement even without you," Mom said.

"This crowd…" Adrienne shook her head. "I hope Nick will be okay."

Mom bit back a laugh. "Of course he will. This is just the beginning."

"Wait! What?"

Louise nodded. "They're calling it the Caritative Concert Tour—first stop, the Art Academy Fundraiser."

"Seriously?" Adrienne shook her head and fought back a smile. "And Nick didn't tell me? Why didn't you tell me?"

"I thought you knew."

Adrienne felt as if the ground beneath her feet had turned to quicksand, and all her thoughts tumbled in a freefall with nowhere to land and nothing to stop her. She pressed her fingertips to her temples. "I didn't know."

Artie looked a little more presentable than on a typical school day because she'd swapped her paint smock and jeans for a clean white shirt and crisply ironed black pants. She took the stage, and the crowd erupted in wild cheers. Artie held up her hands, asking for quiet. The microphone squealed like an electric pig with its tail caught in a vise.

The crowd hushed.

Artie puffed out her chest. "Friends, students and teachers, thank you for joining us. Your participation here today demonstrates not only your generosity and thoughtfulness, but also your dedication to the arts."

"Or their desire to see a hot rock star in the flesh," someone called out behind Adrienne.

Rock star? Nick?

Morgan, a middle-aged woman who dressed like a 1980s teenager, poked Adrienne in the ribs. "I heard you got to touch his flesh. What was that like?"

As always, Adrienne tried to ignore Morgan. But Morgan, with her bouffant hairdo, bright makeup, and neon-painted nails was usually hard to ignore. Still, Adrienne turned her back on her and searched the makeshift stage.

If Nick was here, he had to be close by. Where could he be? She ruled out the porta potties, and the cars lined up behind the stage. Her gaze lingered on an RV. Maybe.

How was he feeling? She ached with worry for him. What if he couldn't do this? What if he didn't show up as he'd promised?

"As you know," Artie said, "one hundred percent of your generous donations and ticket sales will go to the academy." She paused and sucked in a deep breath. "We have a great show planned for you today, with some local talent." Her grin widened.

"Where's Nick?" someone in the crowd called out, interrupting her.

"Nick! Nick!" Someone else tried to start a cheer, but her voice died out when no one joined in.

A deafening cheer went up. Cameras flashed and women and girls screamed.

Adrienne had to stand on her toes to watch Nick climb from the back of a horse trailer. What if he saw the crowd and turned and slunk back into the trailer? She wouldn't blame him — at all — if he turned and ran. But if he did, would he take her with him?

Her mom grabbed Adrienne's arm so tightly it hurt.

He looked good but different. He moved with an easy grace that spoke of quiet confidence. His jeans sat low on his hips and he carried an acoustic guitar in one hand.

The crowd roared when he waved and smiled. His gaze swept over the park, searching. His smile deepened when his gaze met Adrienne's.

Everyone looked at her, and she felt as if they were all holding their breath with her.

Grinning, Artie ducked her head and relinquished the microphone to Nick.

"Hello!" Nick said.

The crowd's clamor died down.

"Where you been, Nick?" someone called out.

"Haven't you seen the videos?" he called back.

Laughter rippled through the crowd.

"But today isn't about me," Nick continued. "It's about lending a hand to a school that provides more than just an introduction to the arts; it opens up a world of expression, paths to creativity, and a vision for a better world. For the past few years, I've done a lot of hiding. Well, I'm done with that. I want to spend the rest of my life giving." He sat on the stool and swung the guitar into position. "This first song is for the woman I love."

Adrienne's breath caught. Her mom's grip tightened. Morgan nudged her in the ribs.

"Is this about Adrienne?" someone in the crowd called out.

"Yeah," someone else chimed in. "Tell us about you and Adrienne."

Nick smiled and his gaze met Adrienne's. "I wouldn't be here today without her."

He winked at her, picked out a few notes on his guitar, and began to sing.

His voice and music floated through the air. Silently, the crowd fell under the spell of his song.

> *"Tho' I may range in foreign lands, beyond a dreary sea,*
> *The home I leave in Uruguay shall still be dear to me.*
> *And as the river seeks the sea, my thoughts to it shall flow,*
> *To rest on scenes I dearly loved, in the days of long ago."* **

Her mom wrapped her arms around Adrienne and whispered in her ear, "Love really is all that matters. Love can change all of us. It makes us stronger, braver, and better."

Adrienne spent the remainder of Nick's performance wrapped in a haze of hopes and bewilderment.

He joined her during a juggling act.

"Why didn't you tell me you were going on a concert tour?" she whispered.

A sheepish look washed over his face and he cast an apologetic glance at the stage. Mr. Hancock, the P.E. teacher, must have noticed, because at that same moment, he dropped the oranges he'd been juggling.

"Do you mind if we go somewhere to talk?" Nick whispered.

"You want me to miss Miss Lemon's water glass song?" Adrienne whispered in false outrage. "That's the best act, other than yours, of course."

He just nodded, took her hand, and led her through the crowd. They stopped at the swing sets. He kept hold of her hand but stepped in front of her so they were face to face.

"Honestly, I didn't tell you about the tour because I didn't know if I could go through with it."

"Then why did my mom think it was a sure thing?"

"Because Steph found the proposals in my office and she told everyone she knows. Although, I'm surprised your mom heard about it before you. I hadn't agreed to the tour. I told them it was conditional on today."

"Today?"

Nick nodded. "Will you marry me? I can't go on the tour without you by my side. I need to be able to see you when I take the stage. I need to know that you're there."

She laid her palm on his cheek. "Oh Nick, you don't need me."

He captured her other hand so that he now held both. He held her tightly, as if afraid she would slip away. "I don't think anything is ever a sure thing," he said, "excerpt for this—I love you. I've loved you since I first met you. I'm pretty sure that I'll always love you."

He paused, as if unsure.

"I love you, too," she said. "But…"

"Is it too soon?" Nick pressed.

"I just got this job. I just barely started rebuilding my life."

"I'm asking you to share your life with me."

"And I want to do that. So much. But—" She broke off. "I guess I'm scared."

He pulled her into his arms. "I get that. I'm scared too. But with you, I can be brave. Can you be brave with me?"

And just then, her mom's words floated back to her. She leaned into Nick and pressed her cheek against his chest and repeated what her mom had told her. "Love really is all that matters. Love can change all of us. It makes us stronger, braver, and better."

The End

*The original music for Rosalie has the author as G. F. Wurzel, which was a pseudonym for George F. Root (1820-1895)

**Old Irish Folk Song

About the Author

USA Today bestselling author Kristy Tate--writing her own happily-ever-after one day (and sentence) at a time.

She's the author of more than twenty books, including the bestselling and award-winning Beyond Series and the Kindle Scout winning Witch Ways series. She writes mysteries with romance, humorous romance, light-hearted young adult romance, and urban fantasy.

When she's not reading, writing, or traveling, she can be found playing games with her family, hiking with her dogs, or watching movies while eating brownies.

50 Miles at a Breath

Lizzi Tremayne

Acknowledgements

To Elizabeth, wife of my vet school classmate, Bob~

Thank you both for being a part of our class. No wife, husband, or partner of a veterinary student gets out unscathed, or unloved. You lived it as much as we did, maybe more. As mentioned in the story, Bob, with his extensive life experience, added so very much to the flavor of our class. Elizabeth, I appreciate your letting me include his name and a little of his story in mine, as well as correcting the parts of the Bob's history where my memory was just plain wrong.

To Bob~

Thank you for all the smiles, the encouragement, and the caring.

RIP. xx

To Matthew~

I've said this before, and I'll say it again. As you keep saying, I may be doing the writing, publishing, promo, and the everything else to get my stories out there... but I couldn't do it without your support, love, and care. Yes, maybe I could do it on my own... but I'd be just as 24/7-frazzled as I once was. (Sorry, boys.) Thank you from the bottom of my heart for making my life not only reasonable, but exquisite. Xx

To Melinda Hughes of Hughes Photography~

Thank you for your permission to use the wonderful cover photo (as yours always are) of my step-grandmother Trudy Petersen riding up Cougar Rock in the Tevis Cup, so very long ago. It's been hanging on my wall for years and I've always wanted to share it, so here it is.

And to my wonderful beta readers, Kirsten Davidson, Marjorie Jones, Jude Knight, Kate Le Petit, Matthew Mole, and last but not least, Sharon Smith.

Without you this story would have been just the one-eyed blather that comes out of my pen sometimes. And at short notice. You're all gold. Thank you so much.

Dedication

To Muriel Eston and Trudy Petersen

My grandmother and step-grandmother, and all those other breast cancer warriors who held up their heads and fought valiantly to the end.

We will remember you.

To Nonna Trudy, I loved the festive, elegant holidays you created; my favorite stable playplace; your lovely mare Tilla; the keen polo ponies and endurance horses; and your magnificent home. While I may have worn drab colours next to your Swiss butterfly brilliance, the autumn shades were my colors. I remember with pleasure the day you finally recognised it too — it made such a difference to us both. I'm so glad you finished the Tevis and earned that buckle, which you wore so proudly.

To Ma Muriel, from "Miss Clean 1972": I actually scrub up okay, you'd be pleased to know. Thank you for: Easter egg hunts in you massive front yard; swimming in your pool overlooking the College of Notre Dame; letting this little three-year-old make biscuits in (all over) your kitchen while wearing my Sunday best; your splendid yolkies and waddies; potato latkas; bagels and lox with red onions; the biggest thanksgiving turkeys I've ever seen to this day; and the back half of my first pony ("The half that doesn't eat," you said.); but especially, your love.

Lena finished this race for both of you.

Praise for Lizzi Tremayne

A Long Trail Rolling

"vivid, light and fast-paced...it will appeal in particular to anyone interested in American...history, and in general to those looking for a ripping good read. I'm looking forward to reading The Hills of Gold Unchanging, the next volume in the Aleksandra and Xavier saga."

–Deborah Challinor, #1 bestselling author and historian

"The mystery, adventure, and danger of life in Utah in the 1860s is beautifully described...an authentic, emotional story of one woman's fight for survival in an unforgiving landscape. I couldn't put Lizzi Tremayne's book down."

–Leeanna Morgan, USA Today bestselling author

"An impressive debut from a New Zealand (ex-American) author...a romance, a western, and an adventure story, all rolled up into a compelling read...I devoured this one and am hungry for more."

–Booksellers NZ

With this, her debut novel, Lizzi was: Finalist 2013 RWNZ Great Beginnings, Winner 2014 RWNZ Pacific Hearts Award, Winner 2015 RWNZ Koru Award for Best First Novel, Third 2015 RWNZ Koru Long Novel, Finalist 2015 Best Indie Book Award

The Hills of Gold Unchanging

"The pace is fast, there's plenty of action and adventure and a few twists I didn't see coming. Lizzi Tremayne writes good characters, and that definitely includes the horses. For me, though, it's the history that's the star in this story. Good characters plus excellent history equals a great read, which is what this is."

–Deborah Challinor, #1 bestselling author and historian

"... superb storytelling. As Aleksandra and Xavier faced and survived human malevolence, natural disaster and accidents, and their own doubts and insecurities, I kept turning pages to find out what happened next. I love books in which adversity sculptures character and where challenges to relationships bend them to breakpoint and rebuild them stronger. This is one of those books. I can't wait to read the sequel."

–Judy Knighton, editor

"Aleks has a stubborn streak and a determination to survive, no matter what. Both inspired me to cheer them on as they faced one problem after another along the way from Utah to California. The plot is well developed, and I particularly liked the attention to historical detail... This is an author who does her homework, and it shows... this story ... is a cracking good yarn."

–Shelagh Merlin, NetGalley Reviewer

A Sea of Green Unfolding

"As usual in this series, the historical research is excellent...well-integrated into the narrative. The description of the environs through which Lizzi Tremayne's characters travel are particularly good—lush and vibrant. In the New Zealand section of the novel she makes our country sound like paradise. Which it is. There is one more volume to come after this, Tatiana, and I'm looking forward to it."

–Deborah Challinor, #1 bestselling author and historian

"A lovely combination of historical accuracy and adventure... beautifully researched and engrossing story... kept me on the edge of my seat throughout... [it was] interwoven with New Zealand's turbulent mid-19th century history as European settlers and Maori tribes battled. Most of all, though, I loved travelling... through the Waikato countryside in her bid to be reunited with Xavier. Lizzi Tremayne has stamped her mark as an excellent story teller who does her homework well and puts her knowledge to good use in her writing. I look forward to seeing what she comes up with next."

–Shelagh Merlin, NetGalley reviewer

"Loved this book. The characters draw you in on a story filled with interest and suspense. A great read and I love how I always learn some thing from reading Lizzi Tremayne books."

–Kate Le Petit, reader

One

Southern California, 1986

ou'll regret you refused me," Gareth Barnett-
Payne menaced, reaching for me, but I spun and ran
until my legs—

"Lena... *Lena*." Raywyn, the head veterinary technician,
waved her hand before my eyes.

I blinked, shaking my head and willing my heart to stop
pounding in my chest.

"Are you okay?" Her brows knitted together.

I gripped the edge of the desk before me. "Yes, fine," I
mumbled, wondering how anyone could be so vicious. "So"—I
swallowed hard and dragged myself back to today— "what's
the surgery schedmostule for tomorrow, Ray?"

She looked at me sideways, then turned to the schedule
before her.

I took a deep breath and let it out slowly, trying to release the
tension stacked up from three weeks of flea allergy dermatitis,
hotspots, anal glands and catfight abscesses. Through those
stinking hot Santa Barbara summer days, I yearned for the touch
of a velvet nose, the solid muscle and bone, and the scent of a
horse. *Any* horse. It wouldn't be much longer before I could go
home to my own roan. I bit my lip and scanned the small animal
clinic, my eyes and nose running as freely as they'd been since
the moment I first walked in through the practice doorway. Cat
allergy in a vet—great. Thank god I was going to be an equine vet.

"Let's see..." Ray's finger ran down the page. "Two dogs

spays, a cruciate surgery, four cat neuters, and… hmmm… I can't read it. I'll need to ask Dr. Franco." She flashed a grin at me. "With your handwriting, you should make a fantastic veterinarian, too. I can't read a thing you write."

"I really do try," I said, with a rueful grin.

"Could have fooled me."

"Not too many cats for tomorrow, then," I sighed, "that's a good thing."

"We don't have many appointments, so Dr. Franco will be free to supervise and you should be able to do most of the surgeries."

"I'm pretty lucky." I nodded. "I get to do so much surgery here. I've been speaking with some of my classmates. They just don't get the opportunities I've been handed. I'll be forever grateful to you and Dr. Franco for that. I'm going to be a horse vet, but I'm sure there'll still be other animals in my life."

Ray looked at me, brows narrowed, until I began to squirm with an overwhelming urge to cover myself. "What?"

"It's a man, isn't it?"

I gritted my teeth and held my breath. "Maybe."

"No maybe about it. Who is he?"

"Some creep with a control fetish."

Ray blinked and shook her head. "Tell me he isn't your problem anymore."

"He's not my problem anymore."

"Truth?"

I nodded. "Never was, much, though he encouraged the idea… rather forcefully."

"You need to come out with us to a few clubs tomorrow night. Just the girls."

"I'd rather stay away from men, but thanks all the same."

Ray's smile faded. "It'll be fun, Lena. It's a group of women. We'll dance, have a blast, and go home. Alone. Can you think about it?" Her smile was hopeful.

"I'll think about it," I said, biting my lip. "Can I tell you tomorrow?"

"Sure, but we'd love to have you along."

"I don't know… I'm truly over men," I swallowed hard. "They're just not worth the angst."

"All you have to do is come out with us. You don't even need to dance with them. You can dance with the rest of the girls."

I was far from certain, but I had no other plans for my hot Friday night. "Okay," I finally said.

The electronic music throbbing across the dance floor jangled in my head. It was so loud, my heart thumped in shock along with the beat. With a deep breath, I forced my butt to stay on the barstool. And tried to smile. And look pleasant. Hard when everything about the place made me want to run screaming out the door. The men either plastic and young in their shiny, synthetic shi—

"Aren't you glad you came with us, now?" Ray's voice cut into my thoughts during a momentary lull in the noise.

I bit my cheek and nodded. No use wrecking her night, too. There certainly wasn't anyone here with whom I'd want to wake up, much less spend the rest of my life. Maybe I was just too serious.

"That guy"—Ray nodded her chin—"the one who looks like he never leaves the beach, has been eyeing you up for the past half hour. Why don't you go put him out of his misery?"

I rolled my eyes as the music started pounding again. "Come on, Ray, you know I can't shoot guys in here," I shouted over the music and smirked. "Someone might object."

Ray closed her eyes and shook her head. "You really are a tough case, aren't you?" she yelled back.

"Okay, I'll go. I don't imagine he knows how to dance Western Swing," I said into her ear as I hopped from my perch.

"You go girl!" Ray barked, her eyes twinkling.

Mr. Lifeguard may have been eyeing me up, but he looked ready to bolt at my approach.

"Hi, my friend thought I should come ask you to dance."

"Hello," he said with a heavy accent and I blinked.

"A Danish hello?" A smile cracked my visage.

This *could be interesting*.

His rabbit-in-the-headlights look dissolved and he laughed.

"*Hvordan har due de?*" he said, in my mother's native language.

"*Fint tak*," I replied. That made me smile. My mother would be pleased.

He started off on a stream of rapid-fire *dansk*, and with a laugh, I put a hand on his arm to stop him.

"Whoa there. You've already heard most of my Danish. From my mom, I learned hello, thank you, you're welcome, and stand up. Baby words."

His smile melted and he bit his lip.

"It's okay," I smiled. "Want to dance?"

"*Tak*, thank you. That, I would love," he said, as he put a hand on the small of my back and guided me to the crowded dance floor.

"You wouldn't know how to dance properly, would you?"

With a smile that lit the whole room, he took my hand and whirled me around the floor. The man could dance — and I was thankful once again for my many years of Latin and ballroom lessons. I never knew when they'd come in handy, like now.

"What are you doing so far from home?" I asked, after we'd been dancing for what seemed like hours.

"I've been at University here, studying marine biology."

"Really?" So, the lifeguard guess was close. "I almost did that. I love to dive — I started when I was an undergraduate here," I shouted, "but I'm in veterinary school up north now. Maybe we could go for a dive before I have to go home."

"I would love to" — he bit his lip, his brow furrowed — "but I fly back to *Danmark* tomorrow morning. I wish we'd met sooner." He genuinely looked wistful and my heart twinged at the thought of the friendship we might have had.

"Believe me when I say I'm gutted to hear you're leaving." That'd be right. I finally meet someone with the same interests… and he's heading halfway around the world the next day.

"Gutted?"

"Sorry, very sorry." My mouth twisted.

"Me too," said the Viking. He took my hand and made a little bow over it, then he kissed it. I had to take a deep breath and lock my knees to keep from melting. I love Europeans.

"It seems your friends are ready to leave." He nodded at Ray's table full of women. They looked at us over their empty glasses, purses slung over their shoulders. "*Mange tusind tak*, and goodbye for now," he said, as he turned away toward his own friends.

Many thousand thanks...

My heart sinking, I rejoined Ray and her friends as they walked out the door.

Outside on the street, Ray and I split from her friends and turned toward our apartment over the clinic. Ray stared at the retreating back of the blonde Viking as he and his friends headed away from us and tripped over a crack in the pavement. She recovered and turned back to me. Her mouth twitched in the light of the streetlamp. "Well, you've certainly found yourself a live one," she said, with a wink. "When will you see him again?"

I snorted. "Probably never. He flies home to Denmark tomorrow."

Ray's face fell. "You can't be serious."

"Story of my life." I nodded. "Told you it's not worth it" —I couldn't repress a smile—"but the dancing was spectacular."

"You two were awesome out there."

"It was all him. I just followed."

"Could have fooled me," Ray muttered.

"Truth be told, it's easier, or safer, anyway, than dancing Western Swing, where the only rules are to try to stay on your feet while they fling you around. It's fun, but Jesper's dancing was… so much more subtle. It was easy, like… like… *dancing*." I beamed at my friend. "Thank you for dragging me along. I really enjoyed myself."

"You at least have each other's contacts, right?"

My mouth dropped open and nothing came out.

"I can see," Ray sighed, "I'll need to take you under my wing. You clearly lack training."

We both laughed, but mine was a bit self-conscious.

"I'll be okay." I gave her a half smile. "My focus needs to be veterinary school now. I really don't have the time or the energy for anything other than that. The next two years are going to be hard enough just taking care of me and my animals, without worrying about the ups and downs of a relationship."

"I see," Ray said, though she looked like she did no such thing.

"It's really true," I said firmly, wrapped an arm around Ray's shoulders, and gave her a squeeze. "I have friends like you. What more could a vet student want?"

"I guess you're right, and you have your precious horse waiting for you back at home." Ray stopped dead and stared at me. "Oh my god, horse...." She slapped her palm to her forehead and jerked her head toward me. "How could I forget about you?"

"Pardon?"

"A vet tech friend of mine asked me last week if I knew anyone who could help at an endurance ride next weekend."

"Like a *horse* endurance ride?" I goggled at her.

"No, you goof, they're racing *penguins*. Of course, it's a horse endurance ride." Ray's eyes sparkled. She'd grown up with horses, but with her head tech position at the clinic, she didn't have time for them now.

"Where do I sign?"

"Have you ever helped at an endurance ride?"

"I've been on the 'P & R Team' at the vet school and my family's done endurance since before I was born—I've been on my family's Tevis Cup crew since before I could walk."

"Boy, am I glad to hear that." Ray let out a breath and shook her head. "Sarah's desperate for some helpers." She turned to me, brow furrowed. "What's a P & R team?"

"P for pulse, R for respiration. It's a team of vet students that helps at local endurance rides by taking heart rates and respiratory rates on the horses before they go on to the vets at the control checks. It frees the vets up to focus on lameness and metabolic problems."

"Oh, of course."

"Where is it?" A tingle of excitement ran up my back.

"It's at Los Lomitos, about an hour and a half from here. I'll make you a deal: if you go help Sarah, you can leave on Friday at noon and needn't be back at work until Tuesday morning—you can take some time for yourself up there."

The weight, the tension sliding from my shoulders made me want to dance the rest of the way home. I was grateful for the opportunity offered by this summer preceptorship, but I wasn't sure if I'd survive a whole two months down here, away from home and my animals, with only patient dogs and cats for company. Ray was offering me not only respite, but horses, too.

"Sweeten the deal," Ray said at my continued silence. "I'll send you with my tent, sleeping bag, and everything you'll need to camp in luxury. Including poison oak medication."

I laughed, afraid my cheeks might split from smiling so widely. "I'm in. You had me at hello."

It was still early afternoon on Friday when I arrived at the endurance race campground and found Ray's friend Sarah, the ride manager.

I'd beamed at myself in the rearview mirror for most of the drive. Four days of horses, camping, and outdoor life after the desert of life in a city. I'd owe Ray forever.

The somewhat frazzled Sarah managed a welcoming smile for me. "There's nothing you need to do until later, Lena," she said, handing me a lanyard and passes. "Ray told me your history, and I can't say how glad I am to have a volunteer of your experience and training."

"Happy to help," I said. "I just want to touch some horses."

"Plenty of opportunity for that." Sarah's eyes twinkled. "The P & R team briefing starts at 7 p.m. and there's another session afterward to practice taking pulse and respiratory rates. You wouldn't want to help with that, would you?"

"Of course," I said. "I'm at your disposal."

"I'd hoped you'd say that. Most of the team are experienced horse people, but only a few have taken vitals before."

"I'd be happy to help them." I smiled.

"Thanks so much." Sarah's eyes glinted. "Go ahead and set up your camp. There's a nice swimming hole in the creek, just down there," she pointed, "if you feel so inclined. I need to run," she said, as a man wearing an OFFICIAL badge touched her on the shoulder, an expectant look on his face. "I'll see you at dinner." Sarah and the man headed off at a trot.

As my meals were supplied by the ride management, setting up camp took only minutes and I was soon free to enjoy my afternoon.

A luxury I haven't had in long months.

Inside Ray's tent, I dropped my jeans and slipped into my shorts and bikini top, grabbed a towel, and headed for the proffered swimming hole. I hadn't gotten far when the throaty rumble of an Arabian caught my attention. He stared at me intently from his wooden tie stall and I approached him, looking around for someone connected to this magnificent creature, but no one was near. His blood bay coat gleamed over a faultlessly muscled body. He whickered again as I neared him. With his body carriage, he had to be a stallion, so I peeked under his belly. Yep, a stallion.

I reached out a hand to him and he lipped gently at my palm.

"Ooh, aren't you the most handsome man?" I murmured.

I jumped when he answered.

"Why, thank you," came a deep voice, tinged with humor.

I chuckled into the laughing gaze of the man who raised himself from the ground behind the short wall at the stallion's feet. "I thought he answered me for a moment."

The man's face creased into deep laugh lines around his gorgeous blue eyes. He was as handsome as the horse, to be sure.

"He talks, this boy," he said, as he slid one arm over the bay's back and gave him a scratch on his withers, then stuck out his other hand. "Blake, Blake Sagan. Pleased to meet you."

I smiled and introduced myself. "Just admiring your stallion. He's a beaut."

"Thanks. He's pretty special. His name's Prince. Prince Witeż, after his grandfather. My pride and joy. Are you racing tomorrow?"

"Not this time. I'm here to help, P & R team."

"Ever been to an endurance ride before?" He looked sideways at me while he waited for my answer.

"Oh, a few. My grandfather's done the Tevis Cup numerous times, my mom and stepdad a few more, and I've done some shorter rides plus ride & ties. I usually get to crew, though."

"Ah," his eyes glinted, "you must be the vet student from Santa Barbara."

I blinked. News traveled fast.

"I knew Sarah was looking for helpers." He smiled. "Thanks for coming along."

"Glad to help. I was in serious need of a horse fix. I've been working in a small animal clinic this summer."

"Not keen on the smallies?"

"I love them, but my heart's with the horses."

"You off for a swim?" He nodded at my towel.

"Sure am. Sarah told me to go down by the bridge."

"It's a nice spot, but there's an even better one a little way upstream. I'm taking Prince down there for a swim shortly."

"I'll see you down there, then."

"Be there soon," he said, and waved at me as I walked away.

Blake's gaze — there was more light in that man's sparkling eyes then I'd seen in ages. I wondered what he did besides ride horses — with that quick, intelligent spark, it must be something special.

What can I be thinking?

The next two years are not about having more devastating relationships. It's time to finish my doctorate and establish my career.

I cannot go there.

I simply cannot.

Two

The clip-clop of hooves on stones let me know Blake and Prince were finally here. I shaded my eyes against the sun, looked up the hill, and blinked.

Did the man have to look like that in a pair of swim trunks? Really?

You found the place, I see." Blake's honeyed voice slid over me as I lay back down in the sun, trying to ignore the bronzed god coming down the hill toward me. He negotiated the last steep portion of the bank and stood before me. We both turned back to watch the magnificent bay nimbly pick his way down the narrow trail.

The stallion practically dragged him straight into the water and Blake hopped up onto his back as the stallion waded in deeper, laughing as the horse struck out across the deep part of the river, swimming for the other side.

"Not many horses would do *that* by choice," I called out.

He's different, this guy," Blake said, his deep voice carrying across the water. He grabbed at the bay's mane as the horse shook the water out of his coat, nearly dropping him.

"He doesn't look scrawny, like most of the fit endurance horses I've ever seen…" I hesitated, then cringed a bit as I continued. "Are you sure he's fit to race tomorrow?"

Most riders wouldn't appreciate a comment like that, but I was, frankly, concerned. The stallion looked ready to walk into the arena at the Arabian National Show or into a breeding shed, not race fifty miles over rough mountain trails.

"Vets!" He laughed. "They're always worried about that. I guarantee you, he'll be in the same condition at the end of the race. Better yet, I'll bet you a nice steak dinner that he'll finish in perfect health."

I glanced sideways at him. He was *not* helping my resolve. "I'll skip on the bet, thanks, but I can't wait to see him at the finish line."

"You're on." Blake slid from the horse's back. Holding the end of the stallion's long lead, he swam lazily back to where I sat on the bank.

His quick appraisal of me in my short jean cutoffs and a string bikini top couldn't truly be considered an ogle, but it was enough to warm my cheeks. Fair's fair. I'd done more at the sight of him while he was occupied clambering down the riverbank. Best get my head out of the gutter.

"Have you been in the water? Your hair's still dry."

"Thought I'd warm up first, after dipping my foot in." Under his frank perusal, I decided I was definitely warm enough to swim, stood up, and looked for a spot deep enough to dive in.

"Lost something?"

"No, I'm just a wimp about getting into cold water. Easiest if I dive in."

He cocked one brow at me and quirked his mustache. "I'm a bit of an all-in/all-out kind of guy, too. Dive in head first, usually."

I frowned, my heart clenching a bit. A shadow crossing his face said he might be talking about more than hopping into a pool of water, too, but then it was gone.

I dived. And came up sputtering. The bay drank deep from the water two yards away, ears pricked, his liquid eyes gazing into mine. I glanced back at Blake.

"He's okay. Call him."

"Prince," I murmured.

He lifted his head, muzzle dripping water, and sniffed the air between us. The stallion seemed to come to a decision and strode through the water toward my outstretched hand, then came closer and lipped gently at my fingers. I scratched under his forelock, then atop his withers, while he preened. Prince took a sideways step closer, shook his head then reached around to nuzzle me.

"You can hop on and he'll bring you back. He won't mind." Blake chuckled. "You're his, now. He's a true man."

I hadn't swung up on a horse with such a round barrel in years, much less from a position knee-deep in water. Prince stood like a rock while I clambered on, then he carefully picked his way into the deep water and swam me back to Blake.

"This horse is magical," I breathed, stroking his sleek neck, then barely stayed on when he shook again. "What a shake!" I grinned. "Haven't had such a shaking since my first pony, 'Lady' used to try to lose me when I was little."

"Something else, isn't he?" Blake turned his gaze to the dripping stallion. "Never had a horse like him, and I've had some good ones."

"How long have you been riding endurance?" I slid to the ground and hugged the horse. "Thank you," I whispered into the stallion's mane, and stepped away.

"About ten years. Prince has been racing with me for the past four. He's unstoppable. Just have to be aware of who's around when you're riding a stallion."

"Have you always ridden stallions, then?"

"No, he's my first. I'm just used to having to be aware of everything around me, anyway, because of my work."

"Work?"

He sighed. "I'm a pilot."

"Ah." His can-do attitude and watchfulness fit with that. I waited for elaboration, but there was none. "You fly for…?" I ventured, looking at him sideways.

"Short-haul commuters for Western Sky, out of Bakersfield. Not exciting, but it pays the bills."

"Any flying" —I winked at him over Prince's back— "is exciting."

A smile spread slowly over his face. "I guess so." Reluctantly.

"What's wrong with being a pilot?" I stared at him. "It sounds like one of the best jobs in the world, after being a vet."

"Well, there is that, but… people seem…" he considered for a moment, "to think you're a good catch. Attracts the wrong sort of women. The money-grubbing kind."

"Really?" I'd never considered anything of the sort.

"Must be. I'm done with that."

"Me, too." Our eyes met, and we smiled, then I looked away for a moment. "My goals right now" —I turned back to him —"are finishing my degree and building the next step of my career."

"Good plan." He nodded. "Do you have any duties here before tomorrow morning?"

I told him, and he nodded.

"Prince and I are going for a little ride to loosen up, but we'll be back soon. If you'd like, I'll introduce you to some people tonight before dinner.

"I'd like that," I said, and meant it. I enjoyed talking with him… more than I should, probably.

"Come on by the truck when you're ready," he said with a smile, as he gathered up the stallion's long lead.

"Will do." With a last pat for the bay, the horse climbed up the bank behind Blake. I watched as the pair disappeared from sight.

If only…

But no. Goals were goals and it was crunch time. The culmination of six years of college, with two more to go. Out of the question.

But couldn't a girl have a little fun?

No. Just no.

Prince was back in the corral attached to his trailer when I arrived at Blake's camper. The stallion whuffled softly to me and lipped at the grass I'd found for him. I may be a disaster with men, but I know how to make horses love me.

"He'll leave me for you if you keep that up." Blake's eyes glowed down at me from the open door of his camper.

I grinned.

"Come on in and have a drink with me but leave Prince out there. He'd wreck the camper, so he has to stay outside, but you look like you have better manners." He waved me in. "Beer? Juice? Whiskey?"

I thought the juice might be safest in my present state of mind.

The comfortable cab-over camper looked well used, but well cared for. Blake caught me looking it over.

"It's not fancy, but it's gone a lot of miles. We take it camping in the high Sierra and to a lot of endurance rides."

We?

I gulped. Getting ahead of myself again. Of course, a man so vivacious and fun would have a wife. I swallowed the bitter disappointment and accepted the juice with thanks. "High Sierra?"

"Yes, we take the horses and camp up high, near the tree line, and take day rides out from the camper."

I grinned at him beneath my brows. "That's not real camping, in a camper."

He snorted. "Have you ever done it?"

"I've camped for years."

He lifted a brow. "In the high Sierra?"

"Well, no."

"Wait until you try it. You won't think I'm such a tenderfoot, then."

That got me. I had no idea what he meant. And I probably wasn't going to find out. Surely, he was married. Probably to one of those money- grubbers he'd mentioned last time we spoke.

"So, you've finished your meeting?"

"Sure have. I know where I need to be, and when. Stethoscope in hand and secretary assigned. One Janelle Knight."

"Nice girl, Janelle. Known her parents for years. She wants to be a vet."

I shuddered, then grinned. "I'll try not to put her off vet school."

"That tough?"

"Let's just say the course is designed to be passed, but it's tough. Their selection process is strong, so the retention rate is pretty high. So far, out of 134 classmates, we haven't lost any, but we've been lucky enough to gain one from the previous class." I smiled. "Bob had to deal with a pretty steep learning curve when he returned to school after retiring from his naval career—

twenty-two *years* after his last college course."

"Most of you weren't even born" — Blake stopped and his amused look disappeared, then he continued with some hesitation — "when he last studied, then."

What was that about?

I nodded, eyeing Blake sideways.

"Bob's career as a merchant marines engineer was cut short by the Viet Nam draft. Seems the Navy needed marine engineers, so when he was offered a commission in the Navy as an officer, or alternately, to be drafted as an ordinary Army soldier, there wasn't really a choice. The Navy life appealed, so Bob stayed until retirement, but afterwards, he pursued his old dream of becoming a vet of another kind."

"Wow, what dedication."

I smiled. "Yes, he adds so much to our class, every day."

"Let's go or we'll miss dinner." Blake held the door for me as I climbed down the steps.

Gentlemanly.

I didn't see much of that these days. I grinned over my shoulder as I thanked him, then promptly tripped over the trailer brake.

Pull it together. A guy's nice to you and you melt.

I managed to hit the ground with my feet, rather than my head, and stood waiting beside Prince while Blake climbed down — carefully, I noticed.

We headed in the general direction of the cookhouse. Blake stopped at this trailer and that to introduce me to his friends.

The on-duty ambulance rolled slowly to a halt near us, the driver looking around and talking on his radio.

"What's up?" Blake asked someone.

"Faye Waters took her horse out for a ride and her horse came back alone. Not sure what happened, but they found her on the ground, her head against a rock. She had her helmet on, but she was unconscious." He nodded his head at the ambulance. "They've radioed for a chopper and it's on its way. They're finalizing a landing spot now."

The other ambulance attendant hopped out. "Can you all

please clear the area? The chopper is on its way," he called out in a loud voice.

We moved to the edge of the clearing and searched the sky for a helicopter. Blake saw it before I could even hear it.

"He's going a pretty good clip." Blake raised an eyebrow at the chopper racing toward us. Suddenly, it was right above us, coming faster than I could have imagined, dropping like a stone into the clearing before us. It was only twenty feet above the ground, too close for comfort. A graying man walked past us, struggling to lead a gray Arabian as it danced sideways, snorting and tugging at its lead. The man glanced around, and then up to see what was frightening his charge. Suddenly, his horse galloped past me, so close I felt the wind from its passing. I turned back to see if the man was okay, but he'd vanished.

Blake dashed off to catch the horse and I ran over to where the man had been. Where had he gone? I peered over the riverbank near where I'd last seen him. There he was. Ten feet down, hunched into a ball on the rocky riverbed, hands and arms cradling his head. His whole body shook.

"Are you all right?" I called out, but he didn't respond. I scrambled down beside him and reached a hand out toward his shoulder.

"No!" Blake's voice rang out from high above me.

I froze, but not before I'd touched the hot skin of the man's shoulder and my world went ballistic. I tried to scream past the fingers digging into my face and covering my mouth, and then a band of flesh-covered steel clamped tight across my throat.

Three

Blake leapt off the wall, even as the stranger lunged toward Lena and put her into a chokehold, his fingers reaching for her wildly rolling eyes.

"It's OKAY," Blake yelled at the top of his lungs, jumped down to a patch of sand beside the pair and grabbed for the man's scrabbling free hand. He captured it and held on for grim death, spun the pair around, and twisted the man's arm behind his back.

"No!" The man's voice came out as a sort of a strained croak.

"Let go of the girl, you're both safe," said Blake in the calmest, most level voice he could muster. The man must be mostly deaf.

Lena's captor took one deep breath and then another, then his grip on Lena seemed to loosen.

"Lena, don't move." Blake whispered. "Just stay still."

The girl shook, but she remained frozen, her back to the two men. The only movement was the chopper's vibration of the air, and of the very ground.

"I'm back," the stranger said, his voice cracking and rusty.

He released Lena and she stood like a rock, frozen in place.

"You're a returned serviceman?" Blake's loud question was more of a statement, and the man gave a faint nod. "Okay, I'm letting go now. Do you want to talk about it?"

He shook his head and glanced up from the ground toward Lena. "I'm sorry, ma'am." His gravelly voice was barely audible.

She turned to the man and reached out her hand. "Nothing to forgive," she said, as tears filled her eyes. "Was it the chopper?"

He flinched, then squared his shoulders. "I'm okay now."

Blake placed his hand firmly on the man's shoulder. "Can I do anything for—"

"MARK!" A blonde woman, tears streaming down her red,

sweaty face, jumped down the embankment in two hops. Pulling him into her arms, she rocked him like a baby. "Are you all right?" She fairly shouted into his ear.

He nodded, slowly. "I thought it was a Snake," he barely got out.

"I saw the chopper show up and got here as fast as I could," she puffed. "Lord knows what they think back at the registration desk, but I don't care. I had to find you."

"These nice people," Mark grated, "helped me. I'm afraid I scared the young lady when she surprised me—"

"No harm done," Lena barked and turned to the woman. "Anything we can do to help?" she continued, in a softer voice. "Shall I go get your horse?"

"Nothing anyone can do," the woman growled softly, "except be there for him. It's the choppers. The horse will be back at the trailer with his buddy by now. He knows the score—and he's less scared of choppers than Mark is."

Blake assessed the man's age—about the same as his own. "Was he in Nam?"

The blonde nodded and kept rocking.

"I was there, too. I understand. If you both feel like it, come find us later. We'll be at the white trailer with the attached corral and the bay stallion. You're both welcome."

The sound of the chopper's rotors changed. The woman gulped and gripped Mark even more tightly.

"Thank you for being there for him." She took a deep breath and backed away from her man, just far enough to lock eyes with him. "You're okay. Hold on to me, that chopper's heading out now. The ambulance crew already had Faye strapped into the stretcher, so they'll just head straight out." She gripped him to her with what looked like all her strength as the chopper blades whipped the air and dirt around them into a gritty cloud, then it was gone, the intense noise fading into the trees like it'd never been.

Mark filled his lungs and turned his face to Lena and Blake, though he never let go of his woman. "We'll see you tonight," he said, and let the blonde lead him away.

Lena stared at Blake after they'd gone, her pupils so wide that her green eyes looked black.

"You okay?" Blake said, his voice sounding rough to his ears. He wanted to reach out to her but held back.

"I've never experienced anything like…" Her voice trailed off.

"And it's a blessing you've never had to," Blake cut in, letting himself reach for her hand. She gripped it with surprising strength.

"Will you tell me about—"

"No." It came out more brusquely than he'd meant, and she inhaled sharply, glancing up from the hand he still held.

"I'm—"

"No. I didn't mean it that way." He filled his lungs and slowly let the air drain away. "The fact you've never been exposed to anything like that, as I said, is a blessing, and please god you never will. It marks you for life. You're never the same again"—he glanced at the retreating backs of the blonde and Mark—"mentally or physically."

"Poor man," she murmured. Her tears flowed freely now. With a sort of grim admiration, he watched the girl who'd held up under pressure yet still had the depth of feeling to crumple when the threat was past.

If only…

He shook himself.

No. She has too much life to live yet.

But… he hesitated… she needed comfort, anyway. "Come here." Blake pulled her into his arms for a hug but released her as she stiffened. "Let's go, eh?" He found an easy way up the bank and climbed up, then put a hand down to her. "Let's find some supper before the rest of them eat it all."

His thoughts jumbled as they walked toward the sounds of clanging pots and clinking silverware. She was fun, bright—and just starting out. He sighed as his heart squeezed tight in his chest. And she was young. Probably too young for him. He glanced down at the top of her shining brunette head. It would just end up like last time… in tears. She was far too pretty for it to be otherwise.

Nice thought, Sagan.

He shook his head to clear it and walked on, packing more stuffing around his heart in the hope that would keep it safe.

I leaned forward, closer to the light of Blake's campfire later that evening to make sure my marshmallow was browning and not turning into a flaming torch.

"Haven't had marshmallows in years." Blake's satisfied murmur warmed me. "Thanks for bringing them. Great idea."

"Hello," came a gravelly voice from the edge of the firelight.

"Hey, you two, pull up a stump," Blake said, as Mark and his blonde ladyfriend walked into the light of the campfire.

"How's your horse?" I shouted, with as much warmth as I could muster. "He didn't find any trouble running around camp by himself, did he?"

"No," Mark said, looking down at the ground with a little smile, "and I'd like to introduce you to Wendy. I wasn't much of myself earlier today."

We both greeted Wendy, talking until Mark spoke again.

"I wanted to thank you both. They really throw me, the choppers. Doesn't matter what kind—they all feel like Snakes to me." He fell silent and Wendy took his hand, then moved her log seat closer.

"Do you want to talk about it?" Blake's voice was gentle.

Mark nodded, but didn't speak for long moments.

"Would anyone like something to drink?" I looked around the circle. "I've brought homemade chocci-chip cookies, too."

"We brought our drinks, but thanks, I'd love a cookie," Wendy said, as a smile broke out on Mark's face.

"Yes, thanks," Mark said, as I leapt to my feet for the container of munchies.

Mark took a deep breath and let it out slowly. "You sure you don't mind my talking about it?" He looked at Blake, who smiled and reached out a hand to pat him on the shoulder, then sat back down beside me.

"I fought in the jungle in Nam... for too long." Mark winced, and went on after a few moments. "Lucky to have survived. The Vietcong were like wraiths, appearing where there'd been no one a moment before. That was terrifying enough, but it was the choppers that got to me. There really weren't frontlines defining 'us' versus 'them' most of the time, so our fighters couldn't just go in and bomb everything. They had to fly in low — just over the treetops or the elephant grass — in their little Loaches to see exactly who it was on the ground." He stopped and took a sip of his bottle of beer. After another deep breath, he went on. "When the pilots of the Loaches saw a target, or some men they wanted to bomb, they'd drop a smoke flare and clear out. Within seconds, a Cobra" — he glanced up at Blake — "we called 'em Snakes, would fly over and rocket the crap out of the area." His voice quavered to a halt and he shook his head.

"You don't have to go on," Wendy murmured.

"Yes, I do," he hissed, then squeezed her hand and kissed it. "I want to get over this... not talking about it hasn't worked either, but thank you, anyway."

Wendy swallowed hard. Her knuckles over her man's fist glowed white in the firelight as Mark continued.

"A Loach went right past me and suddenly the air was full of smoke," he mumbled. "I knew what was coming, but I couldn't get away fast enough." He fell silent again. "The bomb hit — too close, *way* too close. I got burned pretty badly. They sent me on one of the R & R flights the airlines organized for us — took me and a bunch of the other boys to Australia. When they said I was 'fit to return to service', back I went." He swallowed hard and took another sip.

"How long were you there?" I finally asked into the gap in the talk.

"When most of the troops left in the '73 withdrawal, I stayed behind as security for the embassy. How long? Seemed like forever, but it didn't much matter." He fell silent, and it stretched out to minutes. "Didn't have any family to go home to," he said, with abrupt finality.

No one moved a muscle until he spoke again.

"Just before the North Vietnamese took over a couple years later, I had a girlfriend who worked for Pan Am. Seems Pan Am had promised they'd get all of their people out and she tried to get me onto a special volunteer mercy mission they flew — after the airports were already shut down — but I was a guard for the ambassador at the US Embassy and the ambassador'd been good to me…" Mark stopped again and stared into the fire. "I don't think I'll ever hear 'White Christmas' again without tearing up.

"When the NVA were nearly at the gates of the Presidential Palace, we pulled out for good. Thousands of Americans and South Vietnamese wanted to get out before the North Vietnamese took over — they were afraid of being executed or sent to one of the famous NVA 'reeducation camps'. The airstrips were all destroyed, so a mass evacuation by plane was out. Air America and the Marines flew all night through thunderstorms and evacuated seven thousand people by *chopper*. I was guarding the embassy building that night, quaking in my boots at the sound of the choppers flying in and out. They landed on whatever roofs would hold them and hovered over the others, loading up all the refugees they could carry. Ambassador Martin was a good man. Yep, a good man." He nodded vehemently. "A Marine in a chopper landed on the embassy roof helicopter pad and asked for him, but instead of coming up himself, the ambassador sent up Vietnamese and other non-U.S. evacuees, and the Marine guards had to load *them* into the chopper and fly them out to the USS Blue Ridge. Not once, but again and again. Every time they landed, the ambassador kept sending his staff and other Vietnamese. He knew the flight he left on would be the last one out, so he stayed in the building.

"Around five in the morning, when the same pilot landed for the umpteenth time, he called the embassy sergeant over while the guards were loading his chopper with refugees again. He told the sergeant the chopper wasn't leaving until the ambassador was aboard." Mark looked up at all of us. " 'Get these refugees off and bring Ambassador Martin either freely or under arrest' the pilot said. I remember it like it was yesterday, and he added 'the president sends', which probably wasn't true, but it worked.

"So how'd you get out, Mark?" Wendy said, gripping his arm.

"The ambassador took me with him, but if he hadn't grabbed my jacket and held on, I wouldn't have gotten anywhere within 100 yards of that chopper. I heard the pilot saying he'd been flying for over eighteen hours straight — including fourteen trips to the embassy." A faint smile played upon his lips. "Later that day, I took great pleasure in helping everyone push choppers off the USS Blue Ridge into the sea."

"Pushing choppers off?" Wendy stared.

Mark shrugged. "With all the refugees on board, there wasn't enough space for more choppers to land."

He leaned back and shared a long look with Wendy, then turned back to Blake and me. "So you see why I don't do helicopters. I lived, but anytime I hear a chopper, or see one..." He gave a sigh so massive I could almost see the tension flow out of him. "When I have some warning, I can hold on, but otherwise... as you've seen, I can't."

I let out the breath I didn't know I'd been holding and reached for the hand Wendy wasn't already gripping for dear life and squeezed.

Mark gave us the hint of a smile. "Thanks for listening, all... maybe... this will help."

"You're alive, man." Blake reached out to place a hand, almost in benediction, upon Mark's shoulder.

Mark looked around our circle in the firelight and lifted his bottle. "I give thanks for that. Most of those from my units aren't. Don't know how or why I've been spared, but sometimes I wonder. Lots of better men than me died."

"Who's to say?" Blake said softly. "All you can do is live your life well."

"The horses have been good for me — they make up for a lot." Mark looked sideways at Wendy, who flushed when he said, "and so do you."

"Don't I know that." Blake's eyes in the flames' flickering light were haunted for a moment, then the look was gone.

What was that about?

They sat in silence for a few minutes, only the sound of crackling flames consuming wood, the stamp of a random hoof against the ground, and the steady rhythmic chomp of horses chewing their supper.

"We'd best get off to bed, folks," Mark said with a smile. "Not as young as I used to be. Thank you again for the hospitality and the friendship."

"Any time. We'll be seeing you tomorrow," Blake said, standing to see them off. I waved and sat back down.

"You okay?" I murmured, when he'd sat back down.

Blake didn't answer for a moment. "Yep. Fine." Abruptly.

I swallowed hard. He didn't sound it, but who was I to pry where it wasn't wanted?

He looked up at me and smiled, but it was more of a grimace. "Best I head for bed too, much as I'd like to stay up and talk. Rain check for tomorrow? Four a.m. feeding for Prince will come early."

"It sure will." I twisted the tail of my shirt in one hand. "Thank you for the campfire and the talk, Blake. I enjoyed it."

"Not the most pleasant of topics, but..." Blake's gaze was lost to the fire. "It's all fine." He tightened his jaw and stood.

"Don't get up, enjoy your fire." A niggle of discomfort at his unease ran up my spine and I shivered.

"Hard to walk you back to your tent if I don't." His eyes shone in the light of the lantern and his luminous smile lit up the night brighter than any artificial lantern.

"You don't have to do that," I protested.

Lowered brows and a look of confusion. "Of course, I do. My mother raised a gentleman and I don't intend to change."

I smiled. This was a first. "Thank you then, kind sir." I gave him a half bow and preceded him from the camp.

"Thanks for listening tonight..." Blake hesitated, then went on. "I'm sure it made a difference to Mark. It did to me." He took my hand and squeezed it, then with a whispered "goodnight," he left me.

Blake had looked so sad tonight. My heart squeezed in

my chest just thinking of it. His campsite was within view of the open door of my tent, and I couldn't help watching as he returned to his temporary home. Blake's outline, highlighted by the campfire light, disappeared into his camper for only a minute, then it returned to stand alongside his horse for long minutes, his arms wrapped around the bay's neck. It was still there when I let the tent flap drop, leaving him to his thoughts. I hoped he'd get some rest—he looked like he needed it, and he had fifty miles to ride tomorrow. I was thankful he had Prince.

Four

ena," said the head ride veterinarian, Seth Latimer, the next morning, "I know you're only here to do P & Rs, but can you please keep an eye out for metabolic problems?"

"Sure can, no problem." I nodded.

"Specifically, we'll be watching for dehydration, capillary refill time, and decreased gut sounds," Dr. Latimer said, "and we've only got two vets here today, so we're a little understaffed. With your Large Animal ICU experience, you're a godsend."

I smiled, right down to my heart. With two more years of vet school left, my dream of actually becoming a veterinarian still seemed a long way away, but his comment helped me believe it was all real and *would* actually happen. It had taken such a very long time.

Finally.

"Here's your radio," he said. "If you need me, I'm on number one and Dr. Grant is Vet Two. You're Vet Three. You have my permission to hold and check any horse that concerns you. Try to contact me with any concerns, but if you can't find me, pull in Dr. Grant. This race is running under AERC rules, so the vets are the control judges and we, or I, anyway, have the last word.

"Sounds good. Do you expect trouble?"

"With this heat"—he wiped his brow, already sweating in the early light—"we're bound to have problems if the riders get too competitive and don't take care of their horses."

My jaw clenched. In a human sport, people could make their own decisions, but riders could easily push an animal beyond its fitness level or capabilities. That's why vets are in charge here. To keep the riders from pushing their horses, or to keep the keener horses from killing themselves during the fifty miles of the race. It wasn't a hundred-miler, but fifty miles wasn't exactly a walk in the park. The horses would need to be well-conditioned to have a chance of staying well.

"Now you know the weather conditions, what will the P & R criteria be today?" I asked.

"I'll go over that in" — he glanced at his watch — "ten minutes at the pre-ride talk, but their pulses have to be down to 60 after a trot out within half an hour of coming into a vet check, and of course, they have to be metabolically stable and sound at a trot." He turned toward his truck, then spun back. "You have a thermometer? Everyone remembers stethoscopes, but the thermometers often get left at home."

"Always." I patted the EMT belt pouch at my side.

"Then let's head over to the meeting. It's nearly time."

The meeting passed uneventfully, then the riders headed back to their trailers for their final preparations. As we left in Dr. Latimer's truck for the first vet check, horses and riders were already assembling near the starting line.

The big Ford with a vet pack on the back bounced over the ruts and bumps of what passed for a road, jarring bones at every pothole, on the way to vet check number one.

"Would've been a smoother ride" — I glanced at him — "on a horse."

"Yeah, well, you're right, but we might need some of the gear in back. Hopefully not, but... you never know your luck. The meds might look like a milkshake, though."

"Activated." I grinned.

"So, have you got a job lined up for after graduation?"

I shook my head. "Haven't started looking yet, but I had a great preceptorship in the Santa Ynez Valley in a big surgical practice. They cut a lot of colic surgeries and did plenty of orthopedic and stud work."

"Which did you prefer?"

"I enjoyed the surgery and the stud work, but I'm leaning

toward a practice where I can work with individual owners and their horses—horses they'd like to keep going for many years."

"Racetrack and stud work don't appeal to you? It's a much more glamorous life." He raised a brow at me.

"I'll do them if I must"—I shook my head—"but I prefer pleasure and competition horses on a smaller scale—glamour doesn't do it for this small-town girl, I guess."

"I like the way you think, Lena. Private owners need good vets too. Don't ever let anyone tell you you'd be wasted on them." He smiled at me as he parked the truck, then pointed out the P & R area. "Sarah will get you set up. First horses should be in"—he glanced at his watch again—"right about now."

Within five minutes, a big rangy bay mare with a dark-haired woman aboard trotted in, first through the gate.

The timer consulted his stopwatch, then wrote her number and time down on his clipboard and on her rider card, then she continued on to her crew who'd set up a temporary camp near us.

The man quickly sponged the horse while the other crew member, a teenaged boy, swapped a full water bottle for the rider's empty one and checked the bay's legs, then the woman's saddle and bridle.

"Going well?" the boy asked.

"She's flying. Left the others way behind." The rider glanced up to see the second horse come past the timer, then glanced at the stopwatch she wore around her neck. "Check her heart rate, please, love?" she asked the man as the boy handed her a paper-wrapped packet and she stuffed it into the neckline of her shirt. "Thanks darling, I'll eat it on the trail."

The man produced a stethoscope from around his neck and slid its head behind the mare's left elbow while the woman stroked the horse's head and neck. His lips moved as he multiplied the rate. "She's good to go. Head on over to P & R."

My brows raised. She must be fit if she was already ready to go through.

"Well done, crew. We're off." The rider smiled at her team. "P & R, please?" she called, as she walked the horse toward us.

"Over here, thanks," I said. When she reached us, she handed her card to my secretary, Kim. "She's recovered quickly." I closed my eyes to listen to the mare's heart.

The rider laughed. "It's funny to see everyone close their eyes to listen to a heart rate."

"Fifty-four," I said, to Kim, and grinned at the dark-haired woman. "But we all do it—it helps me focus on the quality of the sound, but it *is* funny, you're right."

While I counted her respiratory rate, I pulled a bit of skin out and watched it retract over the point of her shoulder to check for dehydration, then lifted her lip to press a finger against the mare's gums for her capillary refill time. "How's she going out there?" I asked the rider, who couldn't be more than a hundred pounds soaking wet. This big mare wouldn't even notice her weight.

"54/16," I said to my secretary. She jotted it down and handed the card back to the rider. "She's looking great, and you're good to go. Have a nice ride."

With a cheery smile and a wave of thanks, the girl walked the horse away a few steps, then clucked her tongue. The mare pricked up her ears and set off at a lope from a standstill as the woman vaulted on and they disappeared at a canter.

"She's serious about this, isn't she? What a team," I said to Kim as I glanced at her crew. They'd already packed up and were halfway back to their truck.

"They're going for AERC Top Ten Award for the year. It's certainly not out of their reach."

I shook my head with a smile. "Lovely to see that sort of care for a horse."

"It's their trademark," Kim said.

"Time to get busy," I said as more horses came through the gate.

"P & R," called the second-place rider, and our teammates headed to take care of him.

It wasn't long before the horses were coming through hard and fast. There was no time for idle chit-chat, but having ridden plenty of these races, I knew how much riders appreciate a smile and a well-wishing upon their exit. The day progressed like that — quiet periods of joking around with the P & R teams, then rushing to get everyone checked.

"Lena, let's go on to the next check," called Dr. Latimer, and we headed for his truck. "How have the horses been?"

"So far," I said, "they're looking great."

Doc Latimer grinned, probably at my rampant enthusiasm. "What did you think of that first horse?"

"She's a stunner, and what a crew!"

A slow smile. "They're in my practice. A better crew you won't find. Her son has a very good six-year-old he's bringing on. He'll be ready to compete next year... and he'll give Karen, his mom, a run for her money. Best thing is, Karen'll love it."

"Does his dad ride? I take it that's him?"

"Jake doesn't ride, but he loves to crew. He can't wait to crew for them both... but as he tells them all the time, they'll have to both be top notch or he can't be there for them both."

"He's got a point," I said, with a wry grin.

"Nice family. They take fantastic care of their horses. The best. They deserve to win races... and they do win."

It was all on at the next vet check. Horses came and went as fast as we could check them and sign them off.

Blake and Prince stayed within the top ten throughout the morning. At the first check, our group checked them and at the next, one of the other teams had the chance to listen to his heart and lungs, but everyone agreed, Prince's recovery times were astonishing.

"And I have to admit," I said to the others, after Prince trotted out the gate, "I thought he was too out of condition to race. I was *so* wrong." I chuckled.

"Those Polish Arabs are the best," said Vanessa, a girl on my P & R team.

"P & R?" another rider called.

I could only nod as we hurried over to the next horse.

Mark and his gray Arabian were about the thirtieth team to come through the second check. Mark looked so ecstatic, I could hardly reconcile him with the distraught man beside the campfire last night.

"How's your horse going?" I asked him.

"Doing great, and so am I. Thanks for last night, Lena, and please give my best to Blake, too, from both of us."

"Any time. Hope to catch up with you later," I said as I placed the stethoscope over his horse's heart.

I pulled the stethoscope out of my ears and told the secretary the horse's heart rate.

"Sorry, but we have to head out as soon as we're finished, so we probably won't see you, but let's get together sometime?" Mark said, as he led his gray away. "Thanks again," he called, beaming around at the world.

We were about to pack up and head for the third vet check when Jared, one of the other P & R team members, tapped me on the shoulder.

"Lena," he said, as I looked up, "number 79 is due to come back to be checked and hasn't shown. Should I send someone to look for them?"

"Yes, thanks." I turned back to the horse I'd just clamped a stethoscope on. "60/18," I reported. Kim noted it down as I thanked the rider while checking the skin turgor and refill, then wished her well with a wave.

"I found number 79," Jared said, beside my ear. "I think you need to check him. He doesn't look so good and his rider says his pulse isn't coming down."

"Okay, Jared. Can you take over here please?" I waved goodbye to him and Kim, throwing back over my shoulder, "there aren't any vets at this check anymore, are there?"

Jared shook his head with a grimace. "Doc Latimer had to go on, but he said to find you if there were any horses needing to be checked."

"I'll go see the horse. Call if you need me." I pulled out my radio. "Vet Three to Vet One, come in Vet One."

"Vet One," Dr. Latimer's voice crackled over the speaker. "What've you got?"

I told him.

"Okay, let me know. I'm ten minutes away, out."

"Out."

The bay Morgan gelding drooped, his head hanging low, and he didn't even glance up as I approached. His eyes were dull and incurious, as if he didn't care what was happening around him.

I introduced myself to the middle-aged female rider. "How has he been going?"

"He was fine until an hour ago, then he seemed tired all of a sudden."

"Are you his rider?"

"Yes." Shortly.

"Has he done this before? In your training rides?"

"Ummm... haven't had much time to trail him lately," she said, her eyes everywhere but my face.

I gulped and tried to unclench my jaws. Unfit and still racing, on a 104-degree day? I forced myself to stay calm.

"Is he drinking? Eating?" I looked around the area to see an untouched hay net and no water bucket in sight.

She stared at me. "What is this, *20 Questions*?"

"I'm trying to ascertain the condition of your horse" — I placed the stethoscope on the horse's chest and shut my eyes — "and anything you can tell me would help."

"You're a vet?"

"Vet student."

"Get away from my horse," she squeaked.

I blinked and stepped back. "Dr. Latimer asked me to evaluate your horse and let him know what I find. He's at the next vet check, ten minutes away."

She eyed me sideways. "Okay, check him. He didn't want any water at the last stop, so my crew didn't get him any this time."

I tried not to shriek as I moved back to the horse's girth. His heart rate was way too high, 72 beats per minute. Fast and thready.

"He can't be dehydrated," she snapped. "He stopped sweating

miles back."

My heart stopped in its tracks. It didn't get much worse. I tented the skin over the horse's shoulder and the skin took several seconds to slide back. I swallowed hard. Moving my stethoscope to his flank, I listened in vain for gut sounds, but the regular, progressive gurgling sounds of borborygmus were absent and his capillary refill time was three seconds. I'd seen better CRTs in a nearly-dead horse. This one was in trouble. I slid the thermometer into his backside and waited while I stroked his dull coat with my other hand. When I pulled it out, I blinked. 39 degrees. Off scale.

"He's not looking so good," I said to the woman. "I'm going to radio Dr. Latimer. Can you see if he'll drink some electrolyte water, please? How much electrolyte water has he had today?"

No answer.

"Yesterday?" I was close to pleading now. "Salt block?"

"I don't use any of those things. Look, what's the matter with the lazy sod?"

"I'll let the vet speak with you about this, if you don't mind," I said, trying not to growl at her. Ignorance was no excuse in this game, and I didn't trust myself to not deck her for abusing and neglecting this horse.

"Vet Three to Vet One, come in," I barked as I walked away. I had to get far, far away from the rider.

"Vet One here. How's the horse?"

"Any worse and he'd be dead," I muttered as soon as I was out of hearing range of the rider. "Heart rate 72, depressed, dehydrated, no gut sounds, not eating or drinking at last check, so didn't offer it at this one. I've sent a girl for water, but his eyes are glazed and he's past caring. His temp's 39 degrees." We need you back here, Doc. You have fluids?"

"Yes. On my way," he said. A truck door slammed and an engine revved as he signed off.

"Dr. Latimer's on his way," I said to the woman and spun to borrow a bucket and sponge. This horse needed a cool-down.

So did I.

Five

*M*y professional opinion?" Dr. Latimer's voice, as he spoke with the irate owner of the exhausted horse, was so soft as to be barely audible, but the thinly-veiled fury was unmistakable.

"Yes, what's the matter with my horse?"

"I'm glad you asked. Plain and simple, he's been pushed past his fitness level and you're in very real danger of losing him, especially if we don't pull off some heroics here. Do we have your permission to begin?"

The rider of horse number 79 threw up her arms and stalked away. "Do what you need to," she threw over her shoulder. "I'm going to take a nap. It's been a long day."

The young teenager crewing for her stood looking at the retreating woman's back, tears in her eyes, then she ran to the bay and wrapped her arms around his neck, sobbing as if her heart would break.

Dr. Latimer turned to me. "You go see what you can do for the girl, I'll get the truck."

I nodded and approached the pair. "We'll do whatever we can for him. What is his name, and yours?" I said softly.

"Sara," she said, between sobs, "and Sabado." She reached for the bucket to offer him water again. He lipped at it listlessly, but didn't drink, and just leaned his head against hers.

"Is that your mother?"

"My *step*mother," she spat from between gritted teeth, then stepped back to slip the girth and pull his saddle off. She grabbed the towel tucked into the back pocket of her jeans and began to rub him down.

"Does she do much endurance with her horse?"

"Sabado is *my* horse," she growled, reaching for the halter to replace Sabado's bridle. "Tracey" — she thrust her chin in the direction of their camper — "heard about this ride and wanted to enter, so she did. My dad is away, and she wouldn't tell me his new phone number." Sara stood still, her eyes staring into the distance as she spoke. "This horse is my everything. He's only fit for the show ring and trail rides with an empathetic rider. My mother and I broke him in together. I was the first to ride him. The *only* one to ride him until Tracey came along — and Dad won't do a thing about it. I begged her not to take him in this race, but you see how she is." Her face was set.

Dr. Latimer backed his vet truck right up to them and the horse didn't even lift his head.

"Sara, do you have some clean water in a clean bucket?" I asked her, and she stirred.

"My first aid kit has a new garbage bag to line a bucket, *and* electrolytes."

"Great," I smiled at her, "Can you get it right away?"

With a kiss on her horse's forehead, she bolted.

"If you get me a cutthroat razor and some scrub, I'll prep him for a catheter — two, probably, 14 gauge?"

His brows shot up, then his grimace cracked into a smile. "I forgot you're an ICU tech. Fantastic. Go for it — I'll get the fluids set up." He handed me the scrub supplies and set up a folding table beside me.

I told him what Sara had said.

"The lying…" He clamped his mouth shut in a hard line as he placed catheters and a T-port onto the table top.

"Some suture and an 18 gauge needle is all I'll need," I said as he prepared to open a surgical pack.

"No needle holders?"

I shook my head and glanced up at the sound of running feet. "Oh, Sara, do you have some braid bands?"

"Sure thing," she said with a tortured look at her horse and spun away again.

I quickly scrubbed and shaved over Sabado's jugulars on both sides, the hair slicing cleanly away under the straight-edged razor.

"I've got them." Sara held out the bag of small black rubber bands.

"Can you make some long braids, one down each side, just behind his bridle path?"

She looked askance at me, but she did as I'd asked and tied the ends off with her bands while I prepped the catheter sites.

"Can you get some tape from Dr. Latimer?"

She was back in a moment and I told her how to make loops from the main braids to hold the IV lines. As she completed that task, I blocked the catheter areas and four points surrounding them with a fine needle and local anesthetic.

"Poor Sabado." Sara bit her lip. "He never even moved when you stuck him."

I bit my lip, then returned my focus to my table. I gloved up and soon the first catheter slid into place.

"I have your fluids ready, 'Doc'." He nodded up at the fluid bags tied high on the side of Sara's horse trailer.

I smiled. "Thanks. Some suture please, and that needle?" I screwed the T-port snugly to the catheter and held it against the horse's neck, then glanced up to see Dr. Latimer watching closely, holding up a suture cartridge and the needle. With a pair of forceps, he drew some suture out till I nodded, cut it, and handed it over. Looping the material in one gloved hand, I asked him to open the needle case. I grabbed the needle hub, while he held on to the cap, and I slid it into the already-blocked skin beneath the T-port.

"Ah, that's how you do it. I've always used needle holders and a cutting needle."

"Easier this way, and they stay in better. The sutures don't cut through the skin so easily. We do them like this in ICU."

"Very tidy." Dr. Latimer nodded his approval then threaded one of the IV lines through Sabado's top halter ring, looped it twice through one mane loop, and attached it to the T-port. "I pulled some blood while you were busy here, so we have a baseline, anyway. I have a microhematocrit in the truck, so we can at least check his PCV."

Reaching up, he turned the drip set to full and it flowed like a little river, delivering life-giving fluid to the dehydrated horse.

"Go ahead and run the bloods while I put the second line in, if you want," I said.

"I can help with the IV line," Sara said, from my elbow. "I watched Dr. Latimer do it."

"Sure." I smiled down at her face, all big eyes and worry lines. "I'd love the help."

"And just for the record," Sara said, "he wasn't well at the last stop and didn't want to drink, so she wouldn't *let* me give him any this time—said she'd teach him… and now she's probably *killed* him." She finished on a wail, then collected herself.

My heart ached for the girl. "When is your father back home?"

"He should be home tomorrow," she whispered. "I miss him so much. He'll be heartbroken. Sabado's mother was Mom's pride and joy."

I didn't dare ask any more about either of them. The girl was holding together, but by her shaking hands and quivering lip, it was a near thing.

By the time we ran fifteen liters into Sabado, he started to perk up and his gut sounds returned. Sluggish, but returned, and his temperature had dropped. When his PCV fell to something near normal range, we slowed the fluids. After twenty liters, he ate the handful of grass Sara picked for him and looked around for more.

Dr. Grant radioed to say Blake and Prince came across the finish line first, followed closely by the second to fifth-placed horses. All else was well.

My heart leapt at the news.

"Nice horse, that Prince," Dr. Latimer's face relaxed into a grin. "Lives for him, does Blake."

"He seems an awfully nice man." I smiled inwardly. "We met yesterday. Do you do his regular vet work?"

"Sure do, though he's nearly an hour away from me. No other

equine vets up that way." He looked sideways at me but didn't say more.

We capped his T-ports and flushed them, then watched Sara lead him away to pick at any grass they could find.

"He's still not as alert as I'd like to see," Dr. Latimer said, "but he's alive."

I nodded.

"One of us has to stay here and run Sabado more fluids, at least until he starts to urinate again" — he hesitated — "and I don't want you subjected to that woman on your own." His lips tightened as he glanced toward the silent camper. "It's a blessing Sabado happened to crash here, rather than somewhere inaccessible."

"He's a lot brighter," Sara said, as she led the horse up to them, "and he's eating… do you… do you think he'll be all right?" The pleading in her voice made me want to cry.

"Honestly, Sara, he's not out of the woods yet, but when he's fully hydrated, I'll give him some anti-inflammatories to try to ward off any potential complications, but he *is* looking a lot better."

"Potential complications" — the girl swallowed hard — "like…. like colic and… laminitis?" This last was said in a whisper.

Dr. Latimer's eyes narrowed at her and his jaw clenched. After a deep breath, he spoke. "Yes, Sara. You sound like you've seen this before?"

"Yes." Flat. Final. She tied Sabado back to the trailer. "You're giving him more fluids now?"

"Yes… Sara, I've got him here, why don't you go with Lena to the finish line for awhile?"

She looked at him with horror. "Leave Sabado?"

"I'll be with him… I want to speak with your stepmom alone."

"Oh." She shivered. "Okay, then." With another hug around Sabado's neck, she walked to the front of their truck and grabbed a jacket. I got mine and put it on as we walked. With the evening's approach, the temperature was dropping rapidly.

"Lena!"

I turned to see Blake leading Prince toward me, his head and back swinging. Beside me, Sara sighed.

"What?" I asked her.

"What a beautiful horse." She smiled.

"He is."

"He's just finished the fifty miles?" She stared at Prince as he neared them.

"He's just *won* it."

Sara blinked. "But he looks so... so *well*." She swallowed hard and tears filled her eyes.

"Yes, he's fit for it, and a stallion to boot," I said. "Doc's taking care of your boy. It's all we can do right now."

She took a deep breath and looked at Prince. "He's lovely and looks full of life."

"Congratulations, Blake," I said, and wrapped my arms around Prince's neck. "And to you, Prince." Lifting my head, I met Blake's gaze squarely. "And I have to give it to you, you're right. He looks like he's been for a trot down the road to the store and back. No different from the way he looked yesterday." My grin was so wide I thought my face would split.

His eyes glowed at me for a moment before he turned to Sara. I introduced them while I rubbed Prince's forehead, or rather, he rubbed his forehead on me. I finished with, "I normally wouldn't let a horse rub on me like this, but he's earned it today."

"He sure has," Blake said, then turned back to the girl. "Sara, your dad's first name isn't Kent, is it?"

She narrowed her brows at him. "Yes, why?"

"I used to fly with him. How's he going, and your mom? Haven't seen you since you were just a little tyke."

"Dad's away, but mom's... mom's...."

"Blake," I stared hard at him, "Sara's horse was in the race, ridden by her *step*mother."

He took the hint. "How did the horse do?"

A stony silence met him.

"Dr. Latimer's been treating him. Heat exhaustion, dehydration..." I fell silent.

"Lena has been helping a lot," Sara said proudly, with an ineffective swipe at the tears in her eyes and I smiled at her.

"Where *is* the good doc?"

"He's still with Sara's horse," I murmured. "And hopefully talking some sense into Tracey."

"Tracey…" Blake froze.

"She was Tracey Brownlea."

Blake let out his breath and looked at Sara. "So, is your horse going to be okay? Which horse is it?"

"If you remember my mom, it's the son of her mare. Sabado."

Blake smiled at her. "He was a beautiful and trusting foal. But why did you let Tracey…"

"Blake, don't you need to get ready to go back for Best Condition judging? They'll be starting"—I glanced at my watch—"soon," I said pointedly, with a sideways look at Sara, who looked like she wanted the ground to open up and swallow her.

His brow lowered as he flicked a glance my way, and then toward the girl. "Yes, do you two want to come?"

Sara's hopeful gaze fastened on him and she glanced at Prince. "Do you have a towel? He needs a tidy-up first."

"We'll get one when we go past the truck. It seems"—he smiled at me—"we have a team member who knows how to pretty up a horse."

After they arrived back at the trailer, Blake sent Sara for a small bucket of clean water.

"But we have a tank on board," I said, after the girl had trotted off with her bucket.

He glanced at Sara's retreating back. "Tracey, her stepmother, is one of those money-grubbing ones I mentioned. I wondered why she finally got the message I didn't want her hanging around. She found herself another pilot."

"Poor man, and poor Sara… and Sabado," was all I could say.

"And so," I said to Raywyn with a grin, which of course she couldn't see beneath my mask while I prepped a dog for surgery on the following Tuesday, "not only did Prince win the race, but he also won Best Condition."

"So, tell me about Blake," Ray said, with a sly sideways look, and handed me another disinfectant-soaked gauze with her gleaming steel forceps.

"What about him?" I hedged.

"I can't see your lips, but your eyes are glowing." She watched my motions as I swabbed the dog's abdomen from my planned incision line in a circular outward motion and made a little correction.

"Is this right?" I asked.

"Yes, better."

"A good vet tech is worth more than a hundred textbooks in true learning value."

"Good to know I'm appreciated but stop changing the subject." I snorted behind the blue fabric.

"So, when will you see him again?" Ray was relentless.

This should stop her.

"Next weekend."

She blinked. "Truly? Where?"

"At his ranch." Smug.

"But where?"

"Elk Valley Springs, Tehachapi."

"But that's over two hours away!"

"Just seeing his *horse* is worth it—Blake's a bonus." I giggled. It'd been a long time since I'd felt so good.

"It's wonderful to see you happy"—her brows lowered—"but are you sure you know what you're doing, I mean, you just met the guy, and… you're going to his place for the weekend? What do you really know about him? He could..." Ray gulped "Be a—"

"It'll be okay, he's an old-fashioned gentleman," I interrupted.

The little voice inside my head said it too…

Yeah, you don't even know the guy.

"I'll be fine. I always am."

"Famous last words." Ray cocked a brow at me. "Ready to start this surgery? I'll get Dr. Franco and he can observe you."

"Thanks." I smiled at her. Good friends weren't easy to come by and Ray was one in a million. But was Ray right? What could life be like with a gentleman like Blake? Surely, I'd not done anything to deserve that kind of care and attention.

But maybe, just maybe…

Six

Somehow, the week flew by, a million dogs and cats, plus the occasional bird and reptile. Before I knew it, it was Friday. I threw the last bag, full of riding clothes, helmet, and boots, onto the back seat and waved goodbye to Ray.

With Gordon Lightfoot and me blasting out songs from *Gord's Gold* on the truck stereo, windows all the way down, the tension of the week just slid away. As much as I love cats and dogs, I could never be a small animal vet. Horses are it for me. Always have been and probably always will.

My excitement grew as I climbed from the valley floor into the Tehachapi Mountains, heading away to play with horses and get to know a new friend. Despite whatever I seemed to be thinking, that's all it could be... for now.

I turned onto Elk Valley Springs Road and blinked. Blake told me there was a gateway... but a gated *community*? I stopped before the big metal sliding gate beside a guardhouse, with "Elk Valley Springs" lettered on its front.

The uniformed guard looked up from his desk and sauntered out to meet me. "Hello, may I help you?"

"I'm here to see Blake Sagan."

His brows shot up briefly. "One moment, please." He returned to his post and, half a minute later, he spoke into the phone mouthpiece and chuckled.

"Mr. Sagan awaits," he called to me, apparently struggling to keep a straight face, and motioned me forward. "Enjoy your stay, Miss," he added with a wave, before he ducked back inside again.

Now the road curved upward in a graceful arc until it disappeared from sight between two hills. I drove over the top and caught my breath, then pulled off the road into a turnout to get a good look at the stunning panorama... and if I were honest, to compose myself.

View first.

I slid out of the seat and stumbled, legs half-numb from the drive, then took a deep breath and stretched my arms up over my head, my cramped muscles protesting at every movement.

Hawks played on the air currents high above Elk Valley as it spread out before me. Dark, pine-rimmed mountains encircling the tan, dry-grassed valley floor with occasional houses and small ranchettes around the perimeter. Other than the rustling in the dry scrub nearby, channeling images of rabbits and squirrels, the only other sound was the breeze whispering through the nearby pines. A taste of heaven for this country girl, especially after a month spent in the city.

Another big sigh.

What was I doing here, really?

My attention needed to be on my school, my career I'd pursued so diligently for all these years. Couldn't I wait?

Maybe he just wanted a friend...

Who are you kidding?

I screwed up my mouth and allowed myself a little grin.

No one.

With another deep inhalation, I climbed back into my car, no less resolved than I'd been upon my arrival at the gate.

A mile on, Prince stood in a field on my right, and I turned into the next driveway. Blake and the stallion stood silhouetted against a two-storied log cabin with dormer windows and a big, covered front porch. I shivered, shaken. Now was not the time to have my romantic dreams all come true at once. What the hell was I going to do with *this*?

I squelched the feelings and swallowed hard, then returned his wave, shifting my attention to the three dogs hurtling toward me from the front door of a barn on my right. Thankfully, they flowed around my old pickup as I continued up the drive, accompanied by Blake's futile shouts for them to leave off.

I parked in front of the house and schooled my face to neutral friendliness, but one glance in the rear-view mirror, showing Blake coming toward me, confirmed that yes, my cheeks were as red as they were hot.

Opening the door, I was attacked by three laughing dogs, with tongues lolling. I talked with them and tried to pet all three at once.

"Dogs, leave her alone!" Blake hustled up to save me.

"I was getting seriously concerned I might get licked to death," I told him as he gave me his hand and drew me from the cab of my truck into the middle of the melee.

"Welcome. So glad you could come." His smile went all the way to his eyes and there was little question he meant it with all his heart. "I'd like you to meet Jake LaRue Sagan, the boss."

I held a hand out to the gray-bearded Labrador and he planted a forefoot in it for a shake. The fat black dog beamed and shook for all he was worth, then came closer for a lick.

"And Kelpie Anne Sagan." Kelpie was, not surprisingly, a red Kelpie. She wriggled around my legs and nearly knocked them out from under me. Solid, keen, and very friendly.

"And this little one is Sara Lee Sagan. She's the baby." The black and white cocker spaniel looked up at me with soft, sorrowful eyes and I stroked her head gently. Blake laughed. "She acts like a softie, but she sets these two back on their heels when her supper's threatened. She's just waitin' till your guard's down. She's a lot tougher than she looks."

"I'll be sure to watch her." I laughed, then glanced back down the drive to see Prince standing at attention. He called out to us in a loud, demanding, stallion-like voice.

"He wants you come down there, now, obviously, but you'll see him in a bit."

"Hello, Prince," I returned.

He shook his head, mane flying in all directions, and wandered away to pick at weeds in the dust of his pen.

"Can I get your bags? Then I'll show you upstairs."

"Yes, thank you." I smiled and handed him my overnight bag. *A gentleman. I could get used to this.*

I told my insides to stop melting.

"Did you have a good drive up?" Blake led me toward the house.

"Beautiful," I sighed, gazing upward at the front of the cabin, with pretty calico curtains in the paned windows, "and you have a lovely home."

He winked at me. "Glad you like it. Took me years to build."

My jaw dropped. "You *built* it?" It was the biggest log cabin I'd ever seen, and the loveliest.

He nodded.

"Yourself?"

"Nope, Jake helped." He glanced at the grinning Labrador. "Kelpie Anne tried, but she was just a pup — always in the way, and Sara Lee wasn't born yet."

I shook my head and gazed around as he led me into the house. The old-fashioned, floral pattern of the wallpaper complimented the mellowing pine of the trim and the rustic logs of the outer structural walls.

He was the perfect gentleman, but as he led the way upstairs, my heart was in my throat... I'd volunteered to come, but... like Ray said, I didn't know him from a bar of soap. Would he expect me to be staying in his room — his bed?

I swallowed hard and put my foot on the first step. I had a mouth, and I could say no, if I had to. Maybe this wasn't such a good idea, but now was a little late to be getting cold feet... wasn't it?

Stop being a fool and get on with it.

I took a deep breath as my fingertips slid smoothly along the hand-carved banister. I walked behind Blake, my heart squeezing tighter with every step upwards, then we were on a landing and he stood aside to let me precede him through a door into to a little room under the eaves. One look into the room and I let out the breath I'd been holding.

Its walls, with delicate cream flowers on a pale blue background, and the ruffled natural calico curtains framing the view of the mountains made me feel I'd just stepped into a fairy tale.

"It's beautiful," I breathed.

"Like it?" His smile stretched from ear to ear. "And out there," he pointed across the valley, "are trails around the whole valley."

My heart stopped for a moment. "Riding trails? Around the whole valley?" I flicked my gaze to his face and our eyes met.

He smiled and slowly nodded. "Ready to go for a ride?"

"We can go, now?" No five-year-old could have been more excited. I shook my head with a rueful smile at myself.

"Why do you think I invited you up here? You brought your riding gear, didn't you?"

My face flamed. He was being honorable and I'd just been thinking… no, better not to even think of that. I looked up and our eyes met. "Sure did. Breeches and boots okay?" I didn't think my grin could stretch any further. "You sure know how to make a girl happy."

"My specialty. Go change and I'll get drinks to take along."

I was ready in two minutes flat and met him outside in the brilliant mid-afternoon sunshine. As we turned the corner of the barn, a beautiful gray Arabian mare came into view.

"Her name is Miss Witeża, Tessa for short, Prince's wife. He adores her. They've had a few nice foals together, but they're still young yet."

"Are they here?"

"No, they've gone to good endurance homes."

Handing me a grooming kit and pointing out the mare's tack, he left me to make friends while I groomed and saddled her.

We mounted, and Blake pointed out the different trails around the valley while we rode down the drive and crossed the road circling the valley.

"It's too late for a long ride today, but I'll show you around what the brochures *call the amenities Elk Valley Springs has to offer,*" he said, with a smarmy radio-announcer voice. "The fancy bits down here—the clubhouse, tennis courts, bar, gym—I don't use. I'm here for the dedicated horse trails and the fact I don't need to trailer to go for a good, long ride."

"If you're trying to convince me, you're wasting your breath. I saw all that when I topped the rise coming into the valley from the entrance gate. Oh, by the way, I was wondering something. The man at the entrance gate."

He grinned. "Yes? What about him? He's a friend of mine, of sorts…"

"Why the quirky smile on his face when he was speaking with you?"

"I told him quite some time ago that I was staying away from women. "

"So, why the grin?"

"You're a woman."

"And?"

He sighed and looked straight at me. "You're the first female younger than sixty-six who's arrived alone at that gate — looking for me — since I was married. A good six years ago."

My mouth opened, but nothing came out. I slapped it shut and bit my lips together. Not a playboy, then. That had to be good… I think.

But then, was I ready to try again?

Blake pulled another piece of firewood from the basket beside the log wall and set it carefully on top of the already-stacked kindling in his wood stove.

Lena was a hoot. Not only that, she was a dream with the horses and dogs, and was simply… a pleasure to be around.

That doesn't mean I can trust her with my heart.

He lit the newspaper twists at the base of the stack, opened the flue and sat back.

That's probably never going to happen again.

Blake looked around and tugged the sheepskins off their stand and onto the floor in front of the fire, sat down on one, and leaned back against the sofa base.

Just what is my intent?

He wouldn't think of that for now. He planned every other

part of his life to death. Maybe he could just let this one ride.

A board creaked on the stairway and Lena came into view, hair wet from her shower.

His intent got a little messed up, looking at her with her hair and her guard down. "Good shower?"

She smiled. "Good ride, good company, and a hot shower. What more could a girl want?"

"How about dinner before the fire?"

"Now you're talking." Her eyes lit up. "Can I help?"

"It's done. I hope you like steak and potatoes."

"Love them."

"Your steak?"

"Medium rare, please."

He grunted and headed to the kitchen. The barbecue out the back door was hot and ready to go. The steaks were ready in minutes and Blake returned with full plates to find her bent over, swinging her long hair before the fire to dry it. He gulped and nearly turned around. This "friendship" would get taxing if he had too many views like that. Clenching his jaw, he carried on and set their meals down on two trays.

"Already? You're quick."

"Quick, but not fast," Blake said, pleased she was now right side up with her bottom buried in the sheepskin.

Appetites piqued by their day in the sunshine, their meals disappeared in minutes, and Blake leaned back against the sofa again.

"So, what do you want to do tomorrow?" he asked.

"Whatever you need help with around here, and then maybe," —she looked up at him with her big green eyes—"we could go for another ride."

"My kind of girl," he said, then clamped his jaw shut as his heart squeezed in his chest. He'd have to watch his mouth if he were—somehow—going to stay out of trouble.

But... why stay out of trouble?

Beside him, Lena lay back on the sheepskins, a sleepy smile on her face. So close. He could reach out and—

She leapt to her feet, terror in her eyes, then swallowed hard and looked at him.

He hadn't moved.

"Lena, what's the matter?"

She shook her head as the fear slowly melted from her visage and sat down again beside him, but a foot farther away. "It'll be okay," she murmured.

They were silent for long minutes, only the crackling of the fire and a dog snoring from its bed in the corner.

"Are you sure? Want to talk about it?"

She only shook her head in answer.

It clearly wasn't okay, but she wasn't talking about it tonight, that was for certain. "Where would you like to ride tomorrow?"

Her pale face was regaining some of its color and she made an attempt to smile as he told her of the trip around the rim to the south and west. He'd save the northern branch for her next visit.

It was special.

Seven

"And," I said to Raywyn as I sprayed the inside of the dog cage with disinfectant and climbed inside to wipe it down, which gave me time to think about how much I was going to tell her, "we spent the rest of the weekend sitting on Blake's front porch with the dogs, working with the horses, and riding."

"Riding?" The tone in Ray's voice was unmistakable, though it came from inside another kennel.

I shook my head, which of course, she couldn't see. "Riding *horses*, Ray. Get your mind out of the gutter. This guy isn't like all the college studs you keep telling me to avoid, my history notwithstanding. The man's a gentleman." I crawled out of the cage and reached for a stack of old newspapers.

"But what do you know about him?" She sat back on her heels, paper towels wadded up in one hand. "I mean, what do you really *know* about him? Is he some shyster on the make for a vet to support him? Criminal convictions? Is he an ax-murderer?"

I laughed outright and peeled off layers of newspaper to line the cage. "If you worried half as much about the men *you* find, I'd be happy. He's everything I've ever wanted: kind, loving, independent... I mean, you should see his eyes glow, and that smile... mmm."

"You're in trouble."

"He's gutsy, and he rides the stallion I adore." I hesitated, seeking just the right argument. "Okay, this should get you. Every animal I've ever seen him near adores him. His dogs have three names. Each."

Ray spun around, her eyes bugging. "Pardon?"

"You heard me." Smugly.

"Three?"

I told her. "And Jake LaRue Sagan helped him build his log cabin. They built it on their own."

Ray twisted her mouth and was silent.

"See? He's okay."

She drew in a big breath and let it out slowly. "That doesn't answer the question of his just looking for someone to support him. What does he do?"

"He's a short-haul pilot."

She blinked. "Really?"

I nodded and let a grin break through. Victory was sweet.

Ray must have been thinking hard. She was silent for long enough for me to clean, paper, and fleece three more cages while she finished one, and she was usually twice as fast as I was. "So, tell me about these horses," she said in quite a different voice.

I'm afraid I gushed, rather. "The horses are a hoot. Prince I've already told you about" — I smiled at her eye-rolling — "but he's so funny at home. When he's bored, he bites the near side of his feed bucket — one of those big, flat-bottomed rubber ones? Then he flips the thing over his head. He stands there, peering out from under it, his wild mane and forelock everywhere. When it finally falls off, he does it again and again until he finds something else to do."

"Those things weigh a ton," Ray said, with the first grin I'd seen on her face all morning.

"He's one strong boy. And the mare, Tessa, she's a Polish Arabian like Prince, but gray. Nearly as stocky as Prince, though. They're awesome horses. They both have Witez II for a grandsire, at least once."

"Isn't he that Polish Arabian stallion Patton's army rescued along with the Lippizaners during World War II?"

I nodded. "Disney made a movie about them. I loved it."

"Me too" — Ray raised a brow at me — "but you didn't ride horses all night, or maybe you di—"

"Ray," I cut in, "we very properly played Scrabble and chess in front of the firepl—"

"Excuse me, Ray," cut in Nancy, the receptionist. "We just had a cat come in. Can you please come check him out? Dr. Franco is on his way, but he'll be awhile."

"I'll be right there," Ray said. "We're done here, anyway. Let's go see this cat, but don't think" —she raised a suspicious brow at me and shook her head—"that you're getting off this lightly. I'm not done with you yet."

I laughed. "I hadn't imagined you were. Let's go see this cat."

Our new patient had to be one of the tallest cats I'd ever seen. Fred was a long, lean, and lanky gray two-year-old male. He looked far from all right, though, with the lower half of one hind leg from hock to toes lying flush with the examination table. His owners, a harried young couple with a herd of three under-fives, were in a panic.

"I've just lost my job." The young man flushed and swallowed hard. "And we have to move into an apartment… today."

They clearly loved the cat, and it was easy to see why. Despite the pain in his leg, he was still rubbing his head on the youngest child's grimy hand while another pulled lightly on his tail.

"I'm sure we can get him fixed up for you, but we'll have to wait for the vet. I'm only the vet student," I said, stroking the cat and surreptitiously picking up his paws one at a time. A gentle squeeze of the pads of his front feet showed his frayed claws—probably hit by car. "Is he an outside cat?" I asked, while I palpated the rest of his body with gentle touches of my fingers.

"Yes, we live—lived—a little way back from the road, but he's a bit of a wanderer," said the woman with a sad smile.

I'd seen it in textbooks, of course, the hock and metatarsals horizontal in the standing animal. Ruptured calcanean, or Achilles, tendon. The tendon had somehow been torn or else ripped off of the top of the calcaneus, analogous to our heel. It would require surgery, and not a minor one, at that. Fred seemed all right, otherwise.

His color was fine and his heart and lungs sounded perfect.

"Problem is…" — the man went on, his knuckles white on the table — "or the problems are…. we can't keep him where we're going, and we've been trying to find him a new home… and… we don't have any money." He finished on a whisper and glanced at his children, his brow furrowed as he bit his lip.

I made comforting noises about the vet coming soon, but he stopped me.

"We have just enough to put him out of his pain."

I swallowed hard and clamped my jaw shut, trying not to let my feelings show. These people were barely hanging on, in more ways than one.

With only a surgery, this sweet and loving cat could live a long and happy life.

It's one of the hardest things about being a vet.

The choices are not always our own.

"I'm sorry," I said to Fred's owners, "but Dr. Franco won't be in for another hour. Do you have time to wait?"

The woman looked at her husband, then back at me. "We could run our errands and bring him back then, if it's all right with you."

"We'd be happy to keep him here for you, if you like," Raywyn said.

Her eyes lit up. "That would be very helpful," she murmured. "Thank you. We'll see you soon." She swallowed hard and kissed the cat on the head. "Come on, children, Fred's staying here but we'll return."

Fred's family came back half an hour after the vet arrived and waited for the doctor in the reception area. By then, Dr. Franco, or James, as I'd known him since I was a child, had caught up with the already-accumulated backlog of patients. I cornered him before he went out to see Fred's owners.

"You can't save everything, Lena." The vet closed his eyes, then opened them and looked hard at me. "And this is no exception."

"But look at him. He's a fantastic cat.... loving, kind, and so *young*."

"They want him euthanized."

"They don't want him euthanized, but they don't have the money to have the surgery... and they can't keep him."

He glanced up from the gray beast rubbing his head on his hand to see the hopeful look on Ray's face and then his eyes narrowed at me. "What have you two been cooking up?"

"Well..." I couldn't help wincing. "We—"

"Don't get *me* into trouble, Lena. It was *you* who cooked up this hare-brained scheme," Ray cut in.

"*I* thought," I corrected, "maybe if I did the surgery and paid for the materials and drugs, I could find him a home... that is, if the owners agree."

He rubbed his hands over his eyes, silent for a moment.

"It'd be... in the interest of my training." I said, in a rush. Not the truth, but if the shoe fits...

He took a deep breath and let it out slowly, then raised a brow at me. "You're determined to save him, aren't you?"

"He's such a lovely cat. You should have seen him with his children. This cat deserves to live."

James considered for a minute, then shook his head with a rueful smile. "Okay, if they agree to sign him over and you can find him a home this week, we can do this. And," grudgingly, "you won't be paying me anything. You're more than earning your keep."

I hugged him and raced from the room.

"The doctor will see you now," I said to the family, somehow stifling the whoop that begged to be let out. They filed silently into the room and flocked around the gray ball of fluff Ray held on the table.

When Dr. Franco explained the offer, both adults burst into tears and agreed with everything. They signed on the dotted line with watery smiles and I was now the proud owner of a very large, loving, cat. Now I just needed to do a good job of the surgery... and find him a home.

The cat's previous family left, planning to return to visit him after his surgery. They were sad to be losing him, but happy he could have the life they could no longer offer.

My heart swelled that we could give them and the gray cat some happiness, but my happiness was shadowed by thoughts of all the other animals in similar situations… who didn't get this option.

As it turned out, we had time to do the surgery the same afternoon Fred was left with us.

My heart squeezed tight in my chest at the thought of performing this surgery on my own as I pored over the surgery textbooks on the practice library's shelves. I made notes and drew diagrams of different options, depending upon what we found on X-rays and further examination, to lash the tendon back in place. I finished with a surgical plan for James' approval.

"What's your first step?" the vet said and took a bite of his ham and Swiss on rye.

"Radiograph the leg."

"Looking for…?" he said after he'd finished chewing.

"Determine whether it's a simple gastrocnemius tendon rupture or an avulsion fracture of the end of the tuber calcanei." I popped the last bite of donut, not an ideal lunch, into my mouth and awaited his next question. Despite being quizzed, lunchtime discussions were less stressful than vet school pre-surgery rounds.

"Good. And if it's a tendon rupture or an avulsion fracture?"

"Surgery as soon as possible, before the tendon has a chance to shorten. If it's a tendon tear alone, suture with polypropylene in a Bunnell pattern."

"How likely is a pure tendon rupture in the absence of a wound?"

"Unlikely. It's probably a chip or avulsion fracture, though I suspect he's been hit by a car, so it could be anything. With his youth and large size, I'd be looking for an epiphyseal avulsion — separation at the growth plate. I'd repair that with 4-0 stainless steel in a Bunnell pattern again, and... let's hope it's just a chip fracture and not the epiphysis, then we can just fix the tendon to the remainder of the calcaneus, and pins and tension band wire won't be needed, as they would if the growth plate has been pulled off."

"Very nice. Good plan. We'll make a small animal vet out of you yet," he said, and stood up from the lunchroom table. "Let's take those films."

While I slid the cassette beneath the lounging cat, my mind was ticking over. I could keep Fred, but what to do with him until I returned home?

Cats can be tricky to X-ray, but not Fred.

"Here?" he seemed to say, when I positioned him. He must've meant, "I like the feel of that sandbag on top of one leg and under the other," by the purrs vibrating through the table.

"What a cat," I said, to James. "You can leave, I've got this. He's not going anywhere." As soon as he cleared the room, I started up the rotor and clicked the button.

"All clear," I called, and he returned.

"You're right, that cat's really somethin'. Let's just start with that one before we try for an AP."

I smiled smugly and took the cassette and label into the developing room, locked the door, reached for the developing frame by rote and set it down before me. I checked for light leaks around the door while my eyes adjusted to the red light in the room's dark interior, then snapped open the cassette. Carefully removing the film, I clicked it in the labeler and scrabbled for the almost-invisible steel frame. After manhandling the film into the frame, I dropped it into the first tank and gave it a swirl, then refilled the cassette with a fresh film.

"I can take over here," Ray called through the door.

"Ok, let me get the lids on and it's all yours."

"Thanks, Ray," I said a few moments later as I exited, blinking in the brightness. "It's just gone into the developer and the timer's set.

"I'll be out to do Fred's anesthesia in a few minutes," she said with a smile, and sent me on my way.

Ray had already set up for his surgery, bless her soul. The unopened sterile pack, scrub kit, drapes, gowns, and gloves lay neatly on the trolley in the scrub room adjacent to the surgical suite.

I'm glad the surgery was today, so I didn't have too much time to think about the effect this surgery could have on Fred's life.

The x-ray was perfect. Even better, it showed no displaced piece of bone, indicating it was just a rupture of the tendon itself.

With James, silent on the opposite side of the surgical field, acting as my vet technician, the procedure went like clockwork. The polypropylene behaved and knotted only when I wanted it to, and the injury must've happened just before they brought him in, because I was able to draw the long fragment of the gastroc tendon down and reattach it to its partner with a minimum of fuss.

Before Fred woke up, we placed a splint on the leg to keep him from tearing our work apart before it healed. It would take some time—tendon healing is slow.

"Now you just need to find him a home," James said, later that afternoon.

"I'm working on it," I said. "And James, thanks for giving him, and me, a chance."

"I'm not as crusty as I want people to think," he said and ruffled my hair as he left for the day.

Ray saw the exchange and watched the vet walk out the front door. "He could be up for harassment with that."

"It's okay. I've known him and whole family since I was little. They lived next door while he was an undergraduate student at Stanford."

"Really? I didn't know that."

"Yep. I tagged along with him on our 'fix the neighborhood animals' rounds when I couldn't have been more than seven or eight. When he moved on to veterinary school, I took over his rounds."

"You've wanted to do this for a long time," Ray shook her head.

I nodded and raised my brows at her. "Well, what's left to do? I've cleaned all the instruments and have a hankering to clean some kennels and go home."

"You're on. Besides, I have more questions for you."

I smiled. "Hey, you know, small animal medicine isn't so bad. I could get to like it."

"Doing surgery usually turns people around. Either you love it or you hate it. You did a great job today."

"It helped that I don't seem to be allergic to Fred."

Ray laughed.

"And your anesthesia, as always, was perfect. I hope someday I'll find a vet tech as good as you." Ray really was good at what she did and I appreciated her no end.

"So, when are you" — Ray handed me a bucket of cleaning materials and turned toward the kennels — "going to hear from him again?"

"Probably… on Friday night."

"He's calling you then?"

"Ah… no. I'm going back."

Eight

"*B*ack." Ray turned away from the row of cages in the kennel to face me, hand on hip. "You're going back there already?"

I looked at her sideways. "Something wrong with that?"

"You just met the guy. He's going to think you're too eager and drop you."

"I *am* eager" — I twisted my lips for a moment — "but trying not to look like it."

"And going up to his place again isn't eager?"

"Look, Ray, I love that he lives in a beautiful place, that he has a career that lets him train and compete his horses, that he's excited about my becoming a vet, and most of all, that he's a genuinely nice guy who had me in his home for the entire weekend — and didn't try to jump my bones. If that's not a match made in heaven, I don't know what is."

"I just" — Ray scrubbed her fingers through her hair — "don't want to see you get hurt."

"Tell me about it. I don't either." I gave her a sheepish grin. "Thanks for giving a damn."

She shook her head, then turned toward the first cage, armed with her spray bottle of disinfectant.

"Anyway, I have to go see my mom," I said.

"But she lives up north, doesn't she?"

"Not anymore. She's halfway between here and Blake's, in a roundabout fashion. I miss her — I haven't seen her since Christmas. It'll be nice to see her."

Nice, as long as she doesn't hear about Blake.

"I'm not sure how that guy managed to get her in here," I said, absently stroking the Irish Setter's long, soft ears as James and I sat by the red dog's cage late on Wednesday night. "He carried her five blocks after he saw that car hit her."

I'd come downstairs to help James when the emergency call came in and had met the man at the front door.

"He'd had a few too many," James said, with a smile.

"He was potted, all right," I said.

The vet smiled. "And she isn't even his dog." He adjusted the drip and lifted the bitch's lip to check her color again, then looked at me. "It's a bit like old times," he said.

"From the emergency clinic?"

He nodded, with a smile.

"Good thing you and your wife talked me back into aiming for vet school after my ridiculous high school counselor told me it was 'hard to get into vet school and maybe I should think of something else'." I finished on a growl.

"Idiot. She should've known better. You had the highest GPA in your high school, played in band, did cheerleading and pom pom, rode that big chestnut horse of yours, worked part time, and graduated a full year early."

"I'm going back to visit her someday. I promise you, she won't do *that* again."

He laughed. "And when you first found us down here, you were studying English, history and Spanish at the UC."

"Complete with a humanities student's fear of science, by then."

"But you took that job in my emergency clinic and studied hard, and now you're in vet school." He smiled at me. "But I was thinking about the bar next door to the emergency clinic."

I snorted. "The customers always peered in the front windows when the bar closed at two. I'd be alone there, scrubbing floors," I said, with a shudder. "I'd always leave the back rooms for their closing time, so I could hide. And then the phone would start to ring. All emergencies, whatever the problem."

"Drunk callers." He shook his head with a rueful grin.

"Good thing they didn't tend to show up," I said, with a smile. "You'd never have gotten *any* sleep." I returned my attention to the setter's silky coat. "Thanks for taking her in. You probably won't get paid for this one, you know."

"Has that stopped me before?"

"Nope," I smiled, "it sure hasn't. And you've been a good role model. Thanks, James."

Sarah, the part-time receptionist, put her head around the door into the treatment room early the next morning. "Lena, has Dr. Franco arrived yet?"

"No, sorry, he hasn't." I gave the countertop a final swipe with the cloth. "Is there an emergency?"

"Well, sort of," she said, and bit her lip. "Shall I show them into the exam room?"

"Yes, thanks. I'll come take a look."

A few minutes later I stopped just outside the exam room and froze. Whatever it was, it was quite possibly demonic. I waved Ray over to listen.

"Do you want to go in there or shall I?" I whispered.

"It might take two of us." Ray glared at the door. "Dr. Franco keeps promising to put a peephole into this door." She took a deep breath and opened it just a crack, then held it open for me. The beast must be securely contained.

I peered into the room. A plastic cat cage sat on the floor beside the feet of a tousled young man. I use the term "sat" loosely. Very loosely.

The container was doing anything but sitting. It bumped from side to side. It even bounced a little. From the howls and yowls, I assumed it was a cat. Frankly, I wasn't game to duck down and have a good look until I needed to.

With an apologetic look upon his face, the young man stood and offered a scratched and bleeding hand for me to shake.

"Thomas. Thank you, Doctor, for seeing me so quickly. I hit it"—he nodded at the dancing cat carrier—"with my car." He shrugged. "I couldn't leave it there by the side of the road."

A heinous combination of a growl and a hiss came from the box. Something I'd expect from a rather pissed-off tiger.

"Can you please put the cage onto the examination table?" I said, then flinched as a ginger claw shot out and sank into the hand he was using to steady the carrier while he lifted it with the other.

With amazing presence of mind, Thomas somehow got the cat's nails out of his hand without shrieking or dropping the plastic handle and set the semi-contained beast on the table. He did leap away, however, when the cat's paw hooked the wire front door and yanked several times, threatening to tear it from its mounting and decapitate everyone in the room.

An eerie howl filled the room as we all took a step back from the hidden monster.

"Thank you for bringing him in." Ray ducked down to peek into the cat box, but didn't get too close. "Or her, as the case may be. Is this your cat?"

"No," he said. "I've never seen it before. It's got to be the biggest cat I've ever seen. Do you think it's a Maine Coon? I've always wanted one."

"Hard to say," Ray raised a brow and shook her head at me behind the excited young man's back.

"The receptionist had me fill out my details," he said helpfully, and straightened up. "She left it on the countertop over there." He pointed.

"So she did, thanks." I took it up and glanced at the neat lettering. "*Stray HBC*".

"So when was he hit by the car?" I asked.

He glanced at his watch, which was smeared liberally with blood. "Half an hour ago."

"How did you get him into the cage? He doesn't seem very happy in there." Ray commented, keeping her distance while trying to see the animal in the dark interior.

"He was pretty out of it. I carried him home. He just woke up on the way here. He's been yowling ever since. Do you think he'll be all right?"

"I'm just the student," I said, thanking my lucky stars. "We'll have to wait until the vet gets here to do a full exam. Thanks so much for bringing him in."

"Of course. Couldn't do anything else, right?" He gave me an anxious glance.

"We have your information, so you don't have to wait."

"I'm headed for work, but I can come get him on the way home. Just before five?"

"Does he have a collar on or anything? Anything to identify him?" Ray said, her eyebrows nearly touching her hairline.

He shook his head. "No, sorry."

"It's okay. SPCA will come pick him up, so you needn't worry about him anymore. It was really nice of you to bring him in."

He gave me a horrified look. "I hit him, I'll take full responsibility. And I'll come get him tonight. He might belong to one of my neighbors."

I shot him a sideways glance, which he thankfully missed.

He wanted to take that *home?*

Ten minutes later, Thomas stepped out the front door, his wounds cleansed, disinfected, and bandaged in the back room to the accompaniment of Ray's admonitions about tetanus vaccination and cat scratch fever. "Look at it this way," she said, "maybe the cat just hates the carrier. I'm sure he'll be fine once he gets out."

"Out?" I stared at her blankly. The only "out" I could see for that cat was general anesthesia. This was one of those days I was glad to be the student, and not the vet.

It was an eventful morning, and I counted myself truly blessed to see just what a true master of a vet and a gem of a vet tech could do together to get that—wild—cat out of the cage and into an anesthetic induction chamber to repair the lacerations on two of its legs.

"I'm only thankful for absorbable sutures and that we don't

have to do bandage changes," I said with a shudder. "Do you think he's truly wild?"

Ray nodded. "No doubt about it. I'm not sure what Thomas is going to do with him."

Just before five, the sleeping cat lay oblivious in the cat carrier as Thomas carried him out of the clinic.

"Thank you so much," he turned in the doorway to beam at us. "I was so upset when I thought I'd killed him."

"Are you sure you don't want SPCA to come pick him up? We think he's truly wild," Ray said.

"No, we'll be fine," he said, smiling. "I think I'll call him George."

I winced. "Please take care. I'd hate to see you even more scratched up."

"Oh I think we'll be fine," he said, and he walked out the door.

We both waved at his back as he disappeared around the corner.

I looked at Ray, who was still waving. "Promise me," I said to her, "if we read of his death by cat scratch fever at the hands of a cross between a rabid Honey Badger and a cat, you'll go with me to the funeral."

She took my hands in hers and nodded solemnly. "But we won't be searching the papers too hard," she said and shuddered.

On Friday evening when I drove up in front of the log cabin, Blake looked as happy to see me as the dogs were... and that was saying a lot. He took my hand to help me out of the pickup as if I were a princess.

I could really get used to this.

"Hard week?" He leaned toward me, then swallowed hard and straightened up.

I pretended not to notice.

Blake reached for my bag and led me toward the house.

"Busy, but good." I hesitated for a moment, then asked the all-important question. "Blake, do you like... cats?"

"Yeah, why?"

While we headed up the stairs, I told him Fred's story.

"Can't wait to see him. He sounds like one cool cat. 'Fred'. Even his name sounds like he's a character." Blake grinned as he set my suitcase on the bed in my little room under the eaves.

"He's been keeping us entertained in the treatment room when we let him out for some exercise. Talks up a blue streak."

"If you love him that much already, he's welcome to live here, no problem." Blake's eyes were warm on my face.

"So, that's me unpacked." I glanced out the window at the sun-kissed valley. "What's next? Ride? Feed?"

"It's a little late to ride and the feeding's all done, but nachos went into the oven when the dogs went nuts at your arrival. We just have time to go say goodnight to the horses before the cheese melts."

The dogs went nuts again outside and I looked out the window to see a pickup with a vet pack on the back revving its way up the drive. "It's a vet."

"It's Doc Latimer." Blake took the stairs two at a time. "Jake might lick him to death. Best we go save him."

"Where's his practice?" Lena asked.

"It's down in Inyokern. I talked with him the other day and he said he'd come by if he was up here."

Blake dragged the dogs off of his legs. For a vet, dogs sure loved him.

"Good to meet you, Lena, call me Seth."

"Okay, Seth."

"I hear you've only got two years left at school." Seth smiled.

Lena nodded. "Seems like forever, but I'm sure it'll feel like the blink of an eye when I don't have anyone to hold my hand anymore when I'm out in practice."

"You got that right" — he laughed — "but hopefully you'll get a good boss to guide you along."

"I'm aiming for that, sir."

"So, Seth" — Blake looked at him sideways — "you wouldn't still be looking for a vet up this way, would you?"

"I just might be." Seth smiled at Lena. "Especially since I hear there's an up and coming equine track student who's been hanging around the valley."

Lena shot a look at Blake. Surprised, yes, but was she pleased or annoyed? She turned back to Seth, her back a little stiffer than usual.

Hard to tell.

Blake hoped she was happy about it, because right or wrong, and most likely too soon, he was already getting used to the idea of Lena in his life.

Seth must've noticed, because he changed the subject, asking if certain of the vet school instructors were still there. "Seriously? Old Lucas is still in charge of the barns? He was there when I was a student!"

"He's still my favorite out there. That man's full of knowledge." Lena was smiling again, and Blake breathed a sigh of relief.

"Seth, will you stay for some nachos?" he asked. "Speaking of which —" he dashed back into the house and rescued the only slightly over-browned platter.

"Sorry, Blake," Seth said when Blake returned. "But I've got to get a move on. We have company for dinner tonight, but another time soon? Lena, I look forward to seeing you again. Come on by for dinner when you're down our way."

"I know that one" — Blake laughed — "but you're never there. We'll take our chances of seeing you up here."

"Smart man," Seth said, and tipped his hat at Lena. "Ma'am."

The dogs trailed him to the truck and gazed at him mournfully as he closed the door and waved, then headed down the drive.

The nachos were good, and the dogs soon forgot their favorite vet was gone, wriggling and grinning ingratiatingly beneath their feet at the big picnic table on the deck.

I awoke to the sun through the windowpanes etching a lattice pattern over the profusion of tiny white flowers on the wall and stretched. Even this single bed was heavenly after sleeping on a sofa bed for a month in Ray's apartment over the clinic.

Blake's voice came from outside and I peeked over the window sill. The dogs ran from the far side of the field toward him, where he was grooming the mare. Was it still ogling when you gazed upon a man in a skin-tight tank top out the window of his own house? My face warmed at the thought.

I dressed and looked out the window again.

Blake turned and looked up toward my window. He must've seen me then, and he waved.

I opened the casement and leaned out, hoping the cool air would do its job on my face. "Good morning! I'll be right down."

"No rush," he called and resumed his efforts to make Tessa's coat look something closer to its normal gray, and not dust-brown.

"What are you up to in here?" Blake said, when he found me in the kitchen a short time later.

"I brought breakfast, seeing as you've been spoiling me so much."

"What is it?" he said, peeking over my shoulder as I broke eggs into a bowl.

"Cottage cheese pancakes. Nearly 100% protein." Cottage cheese and a handful of flour followed, plus a pinch of salt, then I whizzed them with my stick blender. "Bacon's nearly done out on the barbecue, and I'm ready to do the pancakes on the griddle."

"Home-cooked breakfast" — he beamed — "and the eggs are already in it."

Blake loved them, especially when I brought out the applesauce.

"I could get used to this," he said, leaning back and taking a deep breath. "There's no room for more, and those were great, thanks. Are you ready to ride?"

"As ever." I hopped up.

"How about you get your gears on? I'll throw these in the dishwasher and pack us a snack," Blake threw over his shoulder as he and our plates disappeared toward the kitchen.

Blake's humming wafted up the stairs as he tinkered in the

kitchen while I dropped my shorts and tugged on breeches and boots, then raced down the steps two at a time until I came up short before an older woman standing at the foot of the stairs.

"Oh, hello," I said, shrinking a bit at the disapproving look she aimed at my form-fitting breeches.

She pursed her lips and glanced up at my face but didn't say a word.

Nine

The humming from the kitchen ceased and Blake stuck his head around the corner. "Oh, I see you've met Myrtle." He looked sideways at the woman. "Myrtle," he said, "this is Lena. She's here for the weekend."

"Oh," she said, and the corners of her lips turned up in a caricature of a smile in my direction. "Hello," she said to me, then turned back to Blake with a beatific smile. "I was just about to put your dinner on."

Blake blinked. "As I said yesterday, that won't be necessary, thanks. Lena and I will be out for dinner."

Now it was Myrtle's and my turn to blink. Blake hadn't said anything to me about wining and dining. I'd have so set some boundaries.

Like you're setting boundaries now? Spending another weekend with a man you don't even know… and you're worried about a dinner date and a two-legged watchdog?

"You ready?" Blake glanced at me and hefted a set of full saddlebags over his shoulder. He held the door open, said goodbye to Myrtle, and ushered me out and down the driveway toward the barn.

I held my silence, wondering just who Myrtle was.

I didn't have long to wait.

"Oh, and about Myrtle, don't worry about her. She's just a boarder, but she takes good care of the animals when I'm away."

"She lives with you all the time?" I didn't think I acted

surprised, but must have, because he laughed.

"Yes. She was away visiting her daughter last weekend, so you didn't meet her before. Myrtle thinks she needs to guard me against all comers, but she's all right. And the dogs love her."

"A lot to be said for that." With a lighter heart, I beamed in his direction. Spending time with this pleasure of a man and horses *too*…

"Trees or wide-open spaces?" he asked, pointing one way and then the other. "Your choice."

"Trees, most definitely."

"Your wish is my command, milady." He grinned and turned Prince toward a thick belt of pines running along the base of the steep mountains rising from the valley floor. "This trail circles the whole valley and meets up with the trail we took last weekend."

I stared around the perimeter. "That's got to be fifty or sixty miles!"

"Sure is, fifty miles of dedicated horse trails. That's why we can hold our fifty-miler here."

"Here? An endurance ride?"

"Yep, later in the year, or rather, early next."

"What a place to live," I breathed. What I wouldn't give to live in a place with this sort of riding… it'd been my dream forever.

Blake glanced at my face and nodded, as his smile grew. "Yep, it's always been my dream, too," he said, as if reading my mind. "That's why I bought land here."

I shook my head, gazing around.

Heaven to a horsey-girl.

"So, I get to ride and train these horses three days a week." He gazed off into the distance. "Life doesn't get much better."

"I'd say it wouldn't," I said with feeling, then glanced his way. "Three days a week? How do you manage that?"

He gave me a cheeky grin. "I was fed up with trying to get two horses fit to race on two days a week. It was okay before, when I was marrie"—he stopped like he'd been shot, his visage masked for a moment, then he resumed smoothly—"doing it on my own was too hard. It took all the pleasure out of it. What's life for, if you spend your whole life working and don't take any time to enjoy it?"

"I understand," I murmured, though at my current position in life, I lived with constant work — every day.

"So, I told my boss I was going to quit, retire early."

"Just like that?" I stared at him, a sinking feeling in my chest. Security issues panicked me.

"Just like that."

"And... what did you do?

"I guess when you've been flying for a company for as long as I have, they get used to having you around. He wanted me to stay and asked what I wanted. I told him I wanted a four-day work week and no overnight trips away."

"And they bought it." It was a statement, rather than a question.

"Sure did. And they gave me a raise." He quirked his mustache.

"Well done," I said, with a chuckle, as I guided the mare between some rocks. I needn't have bothered, she knew this trail better than I ever would. I stroked her shiny neck. "Tessa's lovely. Never puts a foot wrong, does she?"

Blake shook his head. "Nope. She's amazing, and you ride her well. She's happy with you up there."

My heart glowed. There was no finer praise from a horseman of Blake's caliber. Riding partner he may be, but something inside me was liking the sound of Blake... probably too much.

We'd been riding for a few hours, alternating walking and trotting through treed gullies and open hillsides of low brush and rock, keeping an eye out for rattlesnakes, when Blake indicated a rise up ahead.

"Just up there," he said.

"What is it?"

"My picnic ground," he said, his eyes shining. "Nobody's usually up here, so we should have the place to ourselves."

Sounded fine to me. We walked the last mile and by the time we got to the spot, marked by a tinkling stream running delicately past it, the horses were completely cool and dry. A thick cushion of pine needles dampened the sound of the horses' hooves as we rode off the trail and stopped beneath the overhanging branches.

After we dismounted and unsaddled, Blake pulled out halters, leads, and a picket line, which I helped him fix between two trees.

"If you want to water them, I'll get our meal out."

"Sounds fine," I said and took Prince's lead from him, pleased the mare wasn't on heat and once again grateful Prince was such a well-behaved stallion. The sharp, astringent scent of pine needles crunching underfoot filled my nostrils as I led the horses to drink, then tied them both to the picket line.

Turning away from the horses, I filled my lungs and finally looked down the hill at the view. It took my breath away. Our other rides had mostly been down on the flats or in the lower slopes of the hills encircling the valley. We'd climbed so gradually I'd barely noticed the change in elevation, but now I saw how high we'd come. Elk Valley spread out before us. It was similar to the panorama I'd seen from near the entrance gates, but from this height, everything was spread out and so much clearer. The ring road, flanked by occasional houses with their own barns and corrals, surrounded a central cluster of buildings and several arenas. Higher up, stands of pines topped the high ridges surrounding the valley, continuous with the one in which I now stood. One last look and I turned back to where Blake had already set out his "snack".

"When you said" —I sank down onto the forest cushion beside him on an actual *tablecloth*, wincing as my abused muscles contacted the ground— "you were bringing a snack, I thought cheese and crackers and a beer, or something…"

He grinned with triumph across the tablecloth. Blake knew how to make friends. Out of the saddlebags had come a sumptuous meal. Succulent chicken, ham, cheeses, sourdough French bread, and wonder of wonders, a *salad*.

"How" —I shook my head, staring at the veritable feast— "did you manage to get all of this here in one piece, much less a salad?" The crispy greens and tomatoes were in perfect condition. "I couldn't manage that in my kitchen, and this has travelled for two hours on a trotting horse."

He laughed. "Magic, I guess. I've been packing a long time. It grows on you."

By the time our hunger was sated, I was starting to stiffen up. I'd barely ridden, even on my own horse, in six months and while it didn't affect my riding ability, my muscles weren't used to it. Tomorrow would be hellish, and I wouldn't let myself even consider how I'd feel the following day. The horses, however, were fine. Used to this life, they'd nibbled what wisps of grass they could reach, then dozed, one hind leg cocked, tails lazily swishing at the ever-present flies, while Blake pointed out more trails and landmarks.

The ride, the sun, the horses… and the man. Kind, generous, keen to share his time and place with me, and handsome—summed up, it was deadly… and downright sexy. Along with the good Danish Blue and Swiss on delicate, fragile (how *did* he do it?) crackers, the combination was a heady mix and I feared if I looked into his eyes, he'd see how affected I was. And that was far, far away from even resembling a good idea. I had goals… and dreams… but the hard edges around these seemed to be softening.

I lay back and covered my eyes with one arm, hiding. A few minutes later, I sighed and sat up. "I can't imagine a more perfect place to live with your horses. Nice and quiet. Just the way I like it."

"Yeah, well, it's quiet," he said. "I hadn't meant to live all al—" he broke off, his jaw set.

I turned away to give him some space in the pregnant silence.

"Dessert," he announced with a quick sigh and the flash of a grin I was coming to love.

"Thank for inviting me," I said, then blinked as he spooned whipped cream onto one side of a bowl packed full of dark chocolate-dipped strawberries. I stared, open-mouthed, at the extravagance, then I frowned at him. "This was not an impromptu lunch you whipped up this morning."

"Ya think?" He handed me the bowl, one eyebrow raised.

"I *know*. This was premeditated." I accepted the bowl with a smile. The man might have ulterior motives, but I couldn't blame him. My resolves were slipping further and further by the wayside.

"I aim to please, ma'am." He smiled off into the distance for a moment, then turned back to me. "I *do* plan—I can't help myself. Remember, I'm a pilot. But… this is just what I'd do for a friend."

I doubted the latter, but who was I to look a gift horse in the mouth when he was such a stunning specimen? I tried to tell myself I was just thinking of Prince, but even I wasn't fooled.

I handed the bowl back. Even before our fingers touched, the surge of something—electricity? —between us made me shiver. "Static," I said, shakily.

"Mmm…" he said, with a glance at me as he took a strawberry from the bowl. He hesitated, his hand straying toward me, as if he'd offer me a bite, then with a little shake of his head, lowered his arm and took a bite of it himself, his attention locked on the glided fruit.

I swallowed hard. I'm afraid I'd have accepted the proffered bite from his fingers, if he'd continued. I was starting to think those resolutions of mine might be silly, after all.

"They're filled," Blake said, just as the sweet almond scent hit me.

My teeth sank into the crimson flesh and chocolate melded with amaretto to send my already-heightened senses skyrocketing. Damn good thing he hadn't offered me a bite of his strawberry; I'd probably be in his lap by now.

Get your mind out of the gutter, girl!

I straightened my spine. "How'd you get the chocolate to stick?" was the first thing that fell out of my mouth. It stopped us both, anyway.

He chuckled. His voice rumbled deeper than I'd ever heard it, or was I just on another planet?

"Dip them first, then inject them with amaretto after the chocolate has set."

My mouth formed a silent "O" as I nodded, and Blake gazed across at me.

"Of course. The amaretto would leak out all of the little pinholes in the berry's surface. I haven't tried making them," I rambled at random, "but my sister complained she couldn't get the chocolate to stick. I'll definitely make them now." I fumbled for something witty to say — and failed, then tried to think about something… something safe… *anything* other than the thought of Blake's strong fingers molded around a big, luscious strawberry, feeding the chocolatey goodness to me, then tracing a line down my throat—

Stop it!

There were far too many deep sighs coming from my direction. It was high time for desperate measures. If my brain wouldn't work, maybe my body would. I jumped to my feet. "So, the trail, it goes right the way around?" I said, my voice too deep for the question.

Blake smiled up at me lazily from his horizontal position, lying back with his folded arms for a pillow. A fleeting glance at his jeans told me he wasn't as unaffected as he seemed. I shook my head and shut my eyes for a moment. He just controlled himself better than I did.

A thought finally flashed through my brain. "Did you do all this?" I pointed at the closed, empty containers, "or Myrtle?"

He sent me a smug grin. "It was all me. Myrtle'd like to mother me, or worse, get me to think she's thirty years younger and marry me, but it just ain't gonna happen. She likes to throw her weight around when there are other women around. I don't think she wants her place here threatened, but as I said" — he twisted his lips — "I can't do this alone — the horses, the dogs." He filled his lungs and breathed out slowly. "So it works, for now."

I smiled down at him. "I'm glad you're making it work."

"Me too." He heaved a great sigh. "Things are about to get even busier with the ride we're running in January."

"Oh yeah." I blinked. "In the winter?"

Blake gave a short laugh. "Remember? We're in the high desert." He scraped free a little of the gritty soil from beneath the pine needles and let it run through his fingers. "It doesn't rain much, so conditions up here are perfect for a post-Christmas ride." He turned those gorgeous baby blues straight into mine. "You should come down."

I think I sputtered something about clinic rotations or some such nonsense and he cocked a brow at me.

"Just after Christmas? Cripes, girl, they need to let you have *some* time off."

"Oh, they do… it's just…" I floundered, but I finally couldn't help letting a smile break through. I took a deep breath. "Frankly, I probably won't have the money. I barely make enough to feed my horse, the cat, and me."

He looked at me sideways. "You forget. I'm a pilot, and we fly into Sacramento."

My face heated. This man didn't just think of getting his rocks off for today. January was half a *year* away. I gulped and sat down beside him again. The thought was terrifying, but somehow, despite the barriers I'd so carefully built, it was also comforting. "I'd like that," I said, with caution. "Let's see how we go."

"Another strawberry?" His voice was slow, deep, and syrupy, like the chocolate he'd nearly tried to feed me before.

Something tightened down deep inside me at his words and I looked up to see him holding the largest, most beautiful berry in his fingers. Its surface glistening with droplets of liqueur and capped with brown gold, he held it up this time toward my lips, and in his intent gaze lingered an expectancy.

Ten

I swallowed hard as Blake moved the gilded strawberry toward my lips. I froze, then slowly opened my mouth to accept the fruit and bit down. The juicy, aromatic goodness melted into my mouth, and we both laughed as the amaretto dribbled down my chin. As one, we reached to catch the drips before they hit my shirt, our fingers colliding in a tangle.

With a sharp inhalation, Blake sat back and handed me the rest of the berry, his face as flushed as mine no doubt was.

I took a shaky breath, along with the stem of the strawberry, and focused my attention on it.

Neither of us was unaffected. That was patently obvious now.

But where to go or not to go?

That was the question.

Somehow, we fumbled our way through packing up our lunch and mounting up again.

Once we were safely on the trail, I dared to look at Blake. Our eyes met, then slid away again. Best take the bull by the horns here.

"That was a wonderful lunch, thank you, and especially" — my gaze lifted to his face — "dessert."

The tight lines around his mouth melted a little and he smiled. "Liked that, did you?" His Adam's apple bobbed a few times, then he reached forward to stroke the stallion's neck.

He did that a lot, the stroking.

I think I might be starting to get a little jealous.

I snorted and attempted to change the circular track beginning to wear its way around my brain. "So, how long will the ride be, the January one?"

The tension in his hands upon the reins, the only place I dared to look, softened, and a look of excitement replaced doubt. "It's a fifty-miler. We're not having a twenty-five, don't want to mess with people who don't bother to train for it, then use up all our resources because their horse crashes. We're light on vets around here and we need them to take care of all the horses, not just the unfit, crashing ones. It's only fair."

"Good thinking. It'd sure be nice to come down."

"Keep it in mind. I can get you a cheap flight. They might let you fly jump-seat, if I ask the right person."

I grinned. This could be a fun friendship.

Friendship, ha. We'll see how long it stays at that.

I shook my head to clear it.

"You know" — he flicked me a glance — "we *are* short on good horse vets in this valley."

"Don't tempt me. My uncle's already put in his dibs. He wants my help on his stud farm and he's dangling carrots, like an on-site clinic."

Blake's brows shot up. "Generous offer."

Tessa stopped short, her body rigid. I swung around to face forward… toward the yawning gap in the trail not two yards ahead of her planted forefeet.

"Good girl, Tess," I murmured, and slowly backed the mare, afraid our movements might let even more of the trail slip away, taking us with it.

I stared across the gap of nearly six yards-worth of trail. A massive pile of dirt and rubble — the remains of the trail — rested in the valley far below.

"What is it?" Blake barked from his position behind us.

"There's a landslide up here. Looks like a new one," I threw over my shoulder, my voice and the rest of me shaking, and kept backing the mare until I was level with Prince.

I slid to the ground and into Blake's arms. "That was close," I mumbled into his shirt front.

He let out a big breath. "I'm so glad you're both okay." He shook his head and we both gazed up at the top of the slide, nearly a hundred feet up.

I took Prince's rein from Blake and stayed well back while he inched forward, a step at a time, to assess the damage to the trail. "We'll have to go bush to get around this," he said when he returned to where I stood with the horses. "It'd be dark long before we get home if we went back the way we came."

I nodded and handed him Prince's rein, then followed him and the stallion's bunched hindquarters straight up the bank beside us, leading Tessa. For nearly the next hour, we scrabbled our way up and far around the slip, finally returning to the trail just opposite where we'd been stopped.

"You all good back there?" Blake peered around Prince to check on me.

I nodded, then mounted Tessa. "I hope we don't see any more of these today." I shivered. "It's getting late."

"That's the first one I've ever seen up here." Blake frowned, then swung up onto the stallion. "Lena, the trail's wide enough for us to walk side-by-side."

I nudged the mare and she walked up beside Prince and kept pace with him. "Good thing Tessa was paying attention, because I sure wasn't."

"You were talking with me." He winced. "Sorry, Lena. Anyway, before we were so rudely interrupted by a mere slip, you were talking about your helpful uncle," he said, with forced cheerfulness.

"Ah, yes. My uncle." I tried to smile — I could at least try to return the cheerfulness, and with the dropping temperature, after our climb, I was at least warm.

I considered for a moment. "He's convinced himself it's for my benefit, but he'd get every cent out of it, and then some. I'd have to pay it off in blood."

"It's got to be better" — Blake raised a brow — "than having no job."

"True, but I'll be putting out job applications as well.

"Of course. Where are you looking?"

"A few equine practices down east of LA and some in the Santa Ynez Valley always take a bunch of new equine track grads."

"You're determined to stay equine?"

"Yes."

"Then you should probably do it." He hesitated for a moment. "But if so, why the small animal preceptorship?"

"I wanted more experience with small animals, in case I chose a mixed animal practice after graduation, and as much surgical training as I could get. Unless you're in a big equine surgical practice, other than suturing wounds and castrations, a general equine vet wouldn't do much surgery."

"And is the practice with small animals really so bad?"

"Not really." I looked down at my hands on the reins. "Truly, it's not. It does put me out of my comfort zone, though, which probably isn't a bad thing. I understand horses' health problems so much better than I do those of small animals—it seems more intuitive to me."

"And have you been allowed to do much surgery this summer?"

"I sure have," I said with a grin so wide it stretched my whole face. "Dr. Franco's given me more opportunities than most preceptors ever get. He supervises me on surgeries a new small animal vet would rarely see, much less perform, for several years in practice." I gave him a sheepish look. "I really shouldn't complain—I'm actually quite lucky."

He nodded in agreement, and we rode on down the valley, reaching home just as the sun set.

Myrtle stood watching in one of the upstairs dormer windows as we walked in the gate and up the drive. I waved half-heartedly and turned back to Blake.

"She's not likely to go away tonight," he murmured. "Would you like to go out to dinner?"

"That would be lovely, but first, I don't think we could top our lunch, and second, I don't think I could eat another bite. That was truly an amazing meal. Thank you again."

"You're so welcome." His smile warmed me to the tips of my cold toes. "Let's get these horses to bed and get you inside."

After the Arabs were fed and groomed, we loitered around the barn, hanging up tack and tidying.

"It's surprisingly cold tonight, for summer." I rubbed my arms to warm them up.

"If we're not going out, maybe we could make a fire and play scrabble, or chess?"

I grinned. Chess with him would be fun. "You'd probably kick my butt if we played chess, but if we played Scrabble, Myrtle could play, too."

"Thanks for that," Blake said, with a big sigh, and he looked straight at me, his eyes glowing. "I think it'd make all the difference to her."

"She *was* here first, after all" — I gave him a twisted grin — "and she keeps your life in one piece. That's important."

"We do, however, have more strawberries." He hesitated, his gaze locked onto mine. "Would you… like one?"

I froze, swallowed hard, and took a deep breath. "How about we eat them with Myrtle while we're playing Scrabble?"

"You're right, you know," Blake said softly, a short time later as we walked up to the house, "to keep things slow between us."

I flicked a glance up to his face, just visible in the darkening gloam.

"I have issues to work through," he murmured. "It'll take time."

I reached for his hand and squeezed it. "I'm starting to think you're everything I've ever wanted… and I'm scared, too. It'll take time for me, too." I filled my lungs and closed my eyes for a moment. "Strawberries and Scrabble? Maybe we can play chess after Myrtle goes to bed."

"You've got yourself a deal." Blake lifted my hand to his lips and pressed a kiss lightly upon my knuckles. "I've got time. All the time we need."

"You know" — I brushed the hair back out of my eyes, and my breakfast, then shook my head at myself — "Myrtle was hilarious, once she figured out I wasn't a threat."

"Three dogs and two horses can't be wrong. Myrtle's okay," Blake whispered as the sound of a door closing at her end of the house echoed up the hallway.

"Good morning, you two." Myrtle smiled. "I haven't had such a fun evening in years." She glanced at me. "You'll give him a run for his money, I'll bet."

"I'll do my best, ma'am," I bobbed my head at her, "but I don't know if it'll be enough."

"You'll do, you'll do just fine. Can you children stay out of trouble for a whole day? I'm heading out, so be good."

"What are you up to, now?" Blake grinned at her.

"I happen to have a hot date out on the golf course with a new resident, and don't you mind which." She stuck her nose in the air and walked out front door. "And he's paying for breakfast at the clubhouse," she threw over her shoulder before it closed behind her.

"Don't do anything I wouldn't do!" Blake called after her, just before the door slammed.

My eyes met Blake's and he reached out a hand across the table. I took it and the spark tingled up my arm and warmed my heart.

"She'll probably talk him into dinner, too, just watch," I said.

"How about we ride down to the manager's office and tell them about the slip in the trail? They'll take care of it — that's why we pay exorbitant association fees."

"So, all this is managed?" I stared at him. "I've never seen anything like it."

"Think you might like to spend some time here?"

"Would I?" I took a deep breath. "Sounds like heaven."

Blake started to speak, then stopped. I waited in silence.

"Would you… would you like to stay for the rest of the summer after you're done in Santa Barbara? Maybe you could get a part-time preceptorship in Tchachapi?"

I blinked. That would take some thought.

Wasn't it a little soon to be planning life together?

He left me to my considerations for long minutes as we neared a massive covered arena, corrals with a few horses, and a dressage arena.

"Before you make up your mind, perhaps you'd like to see the equestrian center they're developing. I'm sure you'd have some good ideas for them."

I eyed him sideways. "Now you're just trying to coerce me," I said, but I smiled to myself.

"They're making a big arena, Olympic carriage driving size."

"How did you know I've always wanted to drive?"

"Just a guess. It's always been my dream."

We meandered over the grounds and found even more arenas and some little mare motels. Most people we met stopped to say hello and chat, but we finally made it to the corporate office and told the burly manager about our find.

"Thanks for letting me know, Blake," he said. "Most people don't get that far up the northern trail. Good thing nobody was hurt."

"This good mare stopped just in time," I said, with a scratch for Tessa on the withers.

"I haven't seen a slip up there before, certainly not one that size," Blake said. "It's big—might take a while to fix. We'll definitely need access by this winter for the endurance race, though."

"Consider it done," the manager said with a smile, and shook Blakes's hand and mine. "When you get time, come down and have a look at the plans for our equestrian center. You might have some ideas to improve them. There might"—he winked at me—"even be a spot an equine vet might like to set up a little practice."

I flicked a glance at Blake, my eyes narrowed, but he shrugged and held up his hands.

"Honest, I said nothing to the man." Blake defended himself as they walked down the steps of the office. "But you've been seen here for going on two weekends now... and you know my history."

"Conspiracy, I say!" But I grinned all the same as the manager waved from his office.

"What do you say?" Blake asked when we were alone again. "When you're done in the big city, want to come up here? Ride and relax until school starts again?"

I took a deep breath, held it, then let it out slowly. "My heart says yes, but my head says no. Like I said before, I can barely feed myself and my animals on my part time wage, much less make school fees."

"I could help."

I stared at him. "You barely know me. You're certainly not responsible for feeding us." I was silent, my mind racing, then I continued. "I'm lucky Frank at ICU held my job for me while I was down south. During the summer, the full-time techs get their vacation time and we get the extra work. These summer hours, combined with my part-time hours during school, will be enough to pay my bills. And then there's my own horse, getting fat in a big pasture, and a cat to think of. I'm not being a very responsible mother to them."

Neither of us said anything for a long time.

"Maybe we could bring them down," Blake finally said, into the silence.

I gawked at him. "You're not on an airplane now, Toto. We're talking a seven- or eight-hour trailer ride. Each way, for a few weeks' visit."

"And? I travel that far to a ride."

He had a point. "But…"

"It's not a big deal."

I reached out a hand to him and he gripped it as we rode along together. "I'd love to, I seriously would, but I need the work."

"But I can—"

"No, you can't. I have to have some pride, too, Blake. Let's see how it all goes, and we can talk about this later, ok?"

"Sounds good," he said, but he didn't sound convinced. "You have to leave tonight?"

I sighed. "I probably should. I need to be at the clinic at 7:30 to open up. If anything should happen on the road over…"

"You're right. Wish I had a plane."

"You do. Planes that someone else pays for."

"True, the best kind."

"Also, I'm going to leave a little earlier today. I want to visit my mom."

He blinked. "Your mom? Where is she?"

"Mariposa. By looking at the maps, it should take me an extra hour or so to get home."

He grinned. "On a fine day with no motor homes. You never said she lived down there."

"I've been so excited about… everything." I swallowed and tried to smile guilelessly. "Guess I forgot."

"We'd best get back, then."

"We're not in that much of a hurry. What else do you want to tempt me with?"

He looked at me from the corners of his eyes. "Not so sure that's a good idea, but I can—"

"That's not"—I gave him a stern look, which cracked after a few seconds—"what I meant." I shivered at the tingles lighting up—down where I shouldn't be feeling them.

His lazy smile let me know he had a pretty good idea about my thoughts. Good thing I was heading home soon. Lord knows what might happen otherwise.

"It's good to see you, Mom," I said, and I meant it, as we clung together in the doorway of her little house in Mariposa.

"I feel like it's been years, but it's only been since Christmas," she said and wiped the tears from her eyes. "I miss you, girl."

"You did have to move all this way south. That's actually one of the reasons I took this preceptorship, so I could see you."

"You're such a darlin' girl. But where have you just come from? You've been, if I'm not mistaken, cuddling"—she picked several white hairs from my shirt—"a gray horse?" She looked askance at me.

"Yes, I went to help out at an endurance ride a few weeks ago and made some new friends. Horse friends." I beamed.

"The best kind, but come on in. Dinner's just ready. I'm so glad you're here and that you gave me *some* notice," she said, with a grin.

We got dinner on the table and sat down on her back deck. The sun, in its final throes of setting, blazed a full spectrum of purples, yellows, and oranges across the sky.

"It's beautiful," I breathed.

"One of the reasons I like it so much here. And it doesn't rain." She looked up from her fork, loaded with my favorite, lasagne. "So where have you been today?"

"Up in the mountains" — I flung one hand airily toward the east — "riding with my new endurance friends I met at the ride." I jumped into the details of the ride, treating the sick horse, and this very cool stallion I'd met.

I soon finished and jumped up to clear the table, quickly adding, "But Mom, what have you been up to?"

From the look she gave me, she knew I was hiding something, but I had good reason. Mom had been into endurance racing for years — and she still knew everyone in that world. That didn't help me much — I'm sure she'd know Blake. After she updated me on her life, Mom looked at me, point blank.

"So, any interesting men in your life?"

I mumbled something into my crème brûlée and thankfully, she didn't push me.

She'd find out eventually, but I wasn't ready to talk about Blake. Not yet. I wanted to be sure there was something real there before I made waves. And there would be waves. After all, he was... a little older me.

Well, a lot older.

Fortunately, my mother is very patient and understanding.

My father, however, isn't. Neither patient *nor* understanding.

And that doesn't bear consideration.

Eleven

"How was your weekend?" Ray waggled her brows at me as she grabbed a horribly burnt pot and dunked it into the sink in our apartment the next morning.

I smirked. "Not like that, but it was lovely."

"And you expect me to believe that? You two holed up together all alone in a log cabin before a fire… you *did* say something about sheepskins on the floor, didn't you?" She shook her head. "How stupid do you think I am?"

I moved her sideways and took over at the sink. "What *did* you do to that saucepan? I swear, I can't leave you alone for a weekend."

She quirked her lips. "I was outside flirting with the new neighbor and forgot it was on. I don't think he was impressed by the smoke coming from our doorway."

"I'll bet not." I shook my head. "And it wasn't like that. Sure, we like each other, but we're waiting… till we're both ready."

"For what, Christmas? Lord, girl! You're both consenting adults."

She had a point. "But this one's worth waiting for… and it seems, when I sleep with men too soon, they drop me. I'm not willing to risk losing Blake when a little patience might make the difference."

"Hmmm… you have a point. They want it well enough, and when they get it right away, you're labeled easy. Haven't been able to figure that one out, myself."

"Me either. That's why I'm trying something different this time. Besides…" I smirked. This would finish her. "We were properly chaperoned. He has a watchdog."

Ray stared at me, incongruous with the superman-emblazoned

dishtowel she held. "A what?"

"He has a sixty-five-year-old female housemate."

It was her undoing. We laughed until we cried.

"A sixty-five-year-old roommate?" she finally got out, between giggles. "Is it his grandmother?"

"No." I was still giggling. "And not his mother, either."

"Just how old is this guy?"

"Ummm…" I couldn't tell her. She'd go nuts.

Ray stopped laughing and her eyes narrowed. And she waited.

"Well, he's… a little older."

"How little?"

I bit my lip. "A year older than my father?" I winced. "But he acts much younger… and he's a gentleman. I don't think I could find a guy my own age that's a gentleman like Blake is," I said. I sounded a bit defensive, even to my own ears.

"Can't you? What about your Dane, Jesper?"

She had me there. "Well, not one in this country."

"You obviously know Blake better than I do, but… you're twenty. He's what, forty-five? If you're as serious as it looks from here, have you considered just how old he'll be when you're fifty? When you're still bouncing around having the time of your life?"

I shook my head. I hadn't gotten that far yet. He was still just a gentleman to me. "We'll see how it goes. Other than his age, from *here*, he's the perfect man for me. Time'll tell, Ray."

She swallowed hard and shook her head slowly. "I hope you know what you're doing."

"Me, too, but I'm sure loving it now."

Ray glanced at the kitchen clock. "And we're going to be late if we don't run now," she said, grabbed her lunch off the counter and bolted. I raced on behind her.

We were late for work.

The week flew by at the clinic and Fred the cat seemed happier with every passing day.

Blake called on Wednesday night. "The horses and dogs send their love, and I can't wait to meet Fred. You're bringing him up this weekend?"

I smiled, my heart warming to this man who didn't look like he was giving up on me, despite my chicken-like behavior. "If I get the go-ahead from James, I sure will. You'll need to fix him up a little room, so you can contain him and keep him in the house until his splints come off. I warn you, it'll be awhile."

"No longer than a broken leg, though."

"Yes, longer. Tendons heal slowly because there's not much room for blood vessels between the tendon fibers."

"Good to have a vet around."

"Is that the only reason you want me? Your own private vet? Isn't there a female vet already over there you can keep?" I was only half joking. I'd wondered about it before but hadn't been game to mention it.

"She's already married," he teased, but it was true. He'd told me.

I just want to be loved and wanted, truly wanted. Did he want me or just his own vet?

I nearly missed his next comment.

"It's you I want. The vet part is just the icing on a very, very nice cake."

I couldn't help smiling at that.

"And I'm starting…" I admitted, in a whisper, "to want you." At a clatter of pots from the kitchen, I wished the phone had a longer cord—like long enough to reach into my bedroom.

On Friday, I got the official word on Fred.

"He's free to go, as long as Blake brings him down next month for a checkup"—James counted off on his fingers—"takes good care that he doesn't get rubs or sores under his splint, and keeps him confined."

"I promise. I won't leave him there until I'm sure he can do all that. Besides, he has a watchdog."

He looked at me strangely, his brows nearly touching, as he headed into his first consult of the day.

I grinned at his back and returned to wrapping up a surgical pack.

"You away again tonight?" Ray bumped me with her hip as she passed.

I grinned at her and placed the pack in the autoclave, added water, cranked it shut, and pushed the red "on" button.

She twisted her lips at me. "I take it that's a yes."

"Yes."

"I was hoping you'd come out with us again." Ray's lips turned down at the corners. "You're going to be leaving soon."

"How about we go out midweek next week sometime? We don't have to stay out late."

"Sounds decadent, and good." Bouncing back, she smiled and carried on her way.

My ancient pickup seemed to be learning its way to Blake's.

"I couldn't wait to get here," I said out the open window to Blake as I pulled hard on the parking brake on Friday evening.

Blake pulled open the car door and fought the dogs off as he pulled me out of the truck and into his arms.

Though we'd only been together a handful of days, with all the midweek phone calls, (I shuddered to think what they'd cost), it felt we'd been together for ages.

"The horses missed you." He leaned back to look into my eyes, his arms still around my waist. "Especially Tessa. She much prefers you. Your hands are better, and you weigh"—he picked me up against his hard body—"definitely less than I do."

"You'd better let me down before you embarrass yourself," I murmured. "Where's your watchdog?"

"She volunteered to make dinner tonight if I went out and got a chocolate banana cream pie."

"Why is she bothering with dinner, then?" I grinned.

"That's what I asked her. Seems to think we need our veggies, so the pie's in the fridge."

I shook my head. "That's *so* wrong."

"So, you up for some riding tomorrow?"

"When wasn't I?"

"So, where's my cat?" he demanded.

"Bossy, bossy." I grinned up at him, just as an annoyed "meow" came from the cat carrier on the back seat.

"He's *beautiful*," Blake said, cuddling him close after we'd taken him out in his new laundry room kennel. Fred rubbed his head up against Blake's chest.

"Looks like he's known you for years." My heart swelled with happiness for this almost-dead cat who had a second chance at life. "Traitor," I added and rubbed him between his green eyes, where he liked it best.

"Thank you for saving him. I'm sure you did a fantastic bit of surgery." Blake gazed into my eyes and I reached up and kissed him lightly on the lips. "Did you see that, Fred?" he asked the cat. "I'll keep you around if you can make her do that more often."

I laughed and went to get some cat food.

"And so," Blake went on, shouting to make himself heard above the wind as we trotted down the trail, "I spent a lot of time on my own out running around the mountains. My mother always knew how long I'd be gone by the number of cans of mushroom soup that were gone from the pantry."

"Didn't you get lonely?" I screwed up my face.

"Nope. It was bett—I was happier that way."

"I was always a bit of a loner, too, I guess. Spent a lot of time out in the fields alone at school, hiding out. If I went far enough, they wouldn't tease me."

"About what?"

"Whatever. It didn't matter. That's where horses come in. I could be alone for hours or days, but never lonely." I smiled, remembering.

Blake grinned. "You pegged it."

We spent half of that Saturday riding, cleaning tack, and mucking stalls. That evening, we barbequed steaks and ate out on the porch while the dogs wriggled at our hips, before the big wooden rocking chairs called to us and we sat and rocked like an old Appalachian couple.

"Come here." Blake jutted out his chin at me and my face heated. His big chair had room for two and he reached out for me.

I sighed and went to him. He enveloped me in his arms and just held me... for so long, I nearly fell asleep.

"Am I boring you?" he mumbled.

"Absolutely not," I whispered, half asleep. "I can't remember feeling safe in anyone's arms in years." My heart clenched and I stiffened, but I fought it, forcing my muscles to relax. Then I began to breathe again.

"Who was he?" Tersely.

"He?" I turned my head away.

"The man who wouldn't let you feel safe in any man's arms."

I hesitated until he gave me a little jiggle.

"He... he was a student. A few years ahead of me. Thinks he's god's gift.... but he's just a bully."

"What did he do?" Blake growled, tension locking his every muscle.

"Wined and dined, then proceeded to get demanding. When I resisted, he got rough. When I wouldn't go out with him again, he threatened me. I still have nightmares."

"What's his name?"

"It doesn't matter. He's graduated and gone. I'll never see him again."

"Did you report him?"

"What's there to report?"

"You're that scared of him, eh?"

I nodded and stared off into the distance. "It would be his word against mine. Just drop it, please. I'm happy now. I didn't think I'd let a guy near me again, but your patience won out." I looked into his eyes and his lips lowered to mine, softly, gently, in a kiss, then he lifted his head.

"Okay?"

"Better than okay. Fantastic," I said and sought his lips myself this time.

His body stiffened and hardened against me as the kiss deepened and somehow spread between us. I opened my lips to his soft request and he asked for more. I gave it willingly and soon forgot my surroundings in the rolling wave catching us up, until a wet nose worked its way under my armpit, and I giggled.

Jake LaRue grinned into my face.

"Jake, you know just when to show up, don't you?" Blake said, shaking his head. The other two dogs crowded around, now Jake had broken the ice. We patted them and looked up to see Myrtle coming out the front door.

"We're screwed now," I whispered.

"No, we ain't," he replied.

I'd learned his mantra last week. It broke the tension when things weren't going quite to plan.

"Off again, more golf," Myrtle said, not looking down at us. "Don't wait up."

"She's getting cocky," Blake said.

Myrtle turned and shook her head. "Just leaving you two alone, or you'll never get together." She stomped off.

We stared at each other.

"Are we really taking too long?" I whispered, joking.

"Maybe. If Myrtle thinks so, we might indeed be."

"Do you think we should do something about it?"

"Got any bright ideas?" He raised a lazy brow at me.

"A few…"

"I'd like to see them… shall we go inside?"

My heart pounding, I slid to the deck and stood, reaching a hand out to him. He took it and rose, then kissed my hand, picked me up and carried me over the threshold and up the stairs.

We didn't awaken until the dawn peeked through the east-facing windows and spread its light over Blake's big four-poster log bed.

"Good morning," he whispered, his arms snug around me.

"Mmmm… I don't think they get any better," I said and rolled over, still in his arms, to face him.

"No, surely they don't. And it's only Sunday morning. We have another whole day more." He took my lips with his and pulled me hard against him.

"But what about the horses?" I leaned back and looked into his hooded eyes. Eyes that were anything but sleepy.

"Found a note slipped under the door an hour ago. Myrtle's feeding everyone. Complete with threats." He held it up and read it aloud. *"If you come down those stairs before ten, I'll murder you both."*

"I'd sure hate to see her get arrested for a double murder," I murmured.

"Me too. See? She even brought up a breakfast tray."

I shook my head and chuckled under my breath. "Wonderful woman."

"After you, the best," he said. He sat up and twisted sideways to reach his bedside table and my mouth dropped open at the ragged white scar zig-zagging its way across his back. I shut it hastily as he returned to face me, a bright red berry from the plate between his fingers. "Now about those strawberries…" he whispered. "I seem to remember…"

I forced my attention away from my vet student mind's automatic classification of "the severity of a wound required to leave a defect of that size"… the *pain*… and onto his gaze, hot and molten above me. His eyes gripped me in their sway as he lowered the berry to my lips and I bit into it, my insides once again pulsing fit to burst. He put the rest of that delectable bit of sweetness into his own mouth. After that, fruit became the last thing on my mind for quite some time.

After I had forgotten the horror of the ridged pale mark that jagged its way across his torso.

"About time, you two," Myrtle barked, when we finally stumbled down the stairs later that morning.

Blake frowned. "But you told us not to get—"

"About time you got *together*." She grinned like the cat who ate the cream. "I had to take things in hand, but you've finally done gotten on with it."

"Truth be told," I said to Myrtle, with a twist of my lips, "we didn't want to shock you."

She shook her head. "Girlie, when you've been around as long as I have, you learn not to waste love when it's offered. You never know when you might not have the chance anymore." A shadow passed over her face, then it was gone. "I'm off," she said.

"Another golf date?" Blake's brows shot up.

"So many men, so little time. They'll just have to take their turns. And today, I'm putting them all off to play golf with the girls," she said as she slammed the door.

Sunday passed in a sleepy haze. The horses even obliged, their paces slow and relaxed. I stayed Sunday night, barely able to drag myself from the warm bed before the dawn's first light.

"You drive safely, you hear?" Blake said, concern in his voice. "You're not too sleepy?"

"No," I smiled. "I'm fine. I'll talk with you tonight, eh?"

"Promise. I'll ring after I land in Bakersfield."

He leaned in my window for one last kiss.

"Bye bye." I waved, and headed back to the coast.

Twelve

he phone!" Ray dashed up the last few steps and scrabbled for the apartment keys in her purse while balancing two big bags of groceries on her hip.

Like a tag-team member, I raced after her and dropped my bags on the deck, then fished in her bag until I hooked the recalcitrant keys and opened the door. Ray followed up by trotting into the living room, abandoning her bags on the sofa, and reaching for the phone.

"For you," she called from the living room. When I reached her, she covered the mouthpiece. "It's a man," she hissed. She wiggled her eyebrows and headed into the kitchen.

"Hi darlin'." Blake's voice coated my heart with chocolate with just words.

"Hello there, yourself," I said, my voice melting, along with the rest of my body.

"Just wanted to hear your voice. Got home okay?"

"Sure did. *And* made it to work on time."

"So what are you doing on Wednesday night?"

"What's Wednesday?"

"A certain favorite girl of mine's birthday."

"Oh!" I blinked. "I'd forgotten. Probably nothing, since it totally slipped my mind."

He laughed. "Well, I wanted to say 'Happy Birthday' for tomorrow. I hope your day is special. I just landed in Bakersfield and wanted to call before I headed home."

"Thank you... for thinking of me... and for another lovely weekend," I whispered, as a fist curled pleasurably down deep in my abdomen.

"There'll be many more, I hope. Well, bye for now, and have a great birthday tomorrow," Blake said. "Sleep well."

"That was" — I wiped the sweat from my brow with the back of my wrist after my last surgery on Wednesday — "particularly nasty." I surveyed the surgery room. It looked like a battle scene, with blood drying sticky over drapes, instruments, and me. The metallic smell of the blood still tingled at the sides of my tongue.

Ray shuddered. "It would have been nice if we'd seen all those fractures on the x-rays."

I sighed. "Sometimes they don't displace enough to see them on the films right away. Without a few days of bone resorption to show us the fracture lines, I guess that's just the way it is."

"Lucky we had a K-E apparatus to fit him." Ray picked up a few of the clamps and half-pins, plus the two stabilizing bars we hadn't used, scrubbed them, and dropped them into the ultrasonic instrument cleaner. "We'd never have been able to stick together all the fragments we screwed and plated without it.

"Lena, someone here for you," said the receptionist, as she opened the door.

In walked a man hidden behind the biggest bunch of long-stemmed roses I'd ever seen. "Ms. Lena Scott?" he asked.

"Yes?" I stared, searching for his face behind the blooms.

"Delivery for you. Please sign here."

"Let me take those." Ray reached for the crystal vase containing the stems so the flower man could hand over his clipboard. He fumbled for a moment and nearly dropped the vase before Ray could grab it. "That vase nearly went into our purses," she said with a laugh.

"I can't believe this," I breathed, and scrawled my signature. "Thank you."

"Have a nice day." He nodded, spun, and disappeared.

"Wow, just wow." Ray handed the bunch to me and my heart swelled so much I could barely breathe. I fossicked amongst the thornless stems but couldn't see a card. "No card, but no matter.

There's only one man who'd send roses like this." My smile was so wide, I thought my face would split.

Ray leaned over and inhaled their scent. "Mmmmm... yep, that man's a keeper, all right. A keeper." She beamed over her shoulder and went back to scrubbing the blood off the remaining instruments.

I was still beaming an hour later, just on quitting time.

"We haven't planned anything for your birthday." Ray frowned. "Would you like to go out?"

"Really, after the afternoon we've just had, a bath and crashing on the sofa sounds good, but let's see how it goes."

"You've got me there." Ray smiled. "I didn't want you to feel neglected on your special day."

"Not a chance of that." I chuckled. "Not a chance."

Blake opened the door of the veterinary hospital and the bells hanging on their cord jangled, stilled, then rang madly again as the door clicked shut.

"May I help you?" The redheaded receptionist gave him a sunny smile.

"Yes please, I'm here to see Lena."

"Do you have an appointment?"

"No. She doesn't know I'm coming." He moved closer to the front counter. "In case you don't know, it's her birthday."

"And you must be....."

"Blake. I don't want to disturb her, but do you know what time she's finishing tonight?"

"Should be soon. More flowers?" She beamed at me. "She's a lucky girl. Come on back, I'll take you through. She's straight through here."

Lena saw him in the doorway and took three steps toward him, beaming, then her eyes dropped to the flowers in his hands. She stopped like she'd been shot and her mouth dropped open.

"Tell me you're not allergic to lilies?" Blake raised a brow at her and handed her the flowers with a smile. "Happy Birthday, darling."

Lena smiled and accepted the flowers, cradling them as if they were a baby, then gave him a big hug around the flowers. "No, I love lilies, thank you so much. They're beautiful, and even my favorite colors." Her voice quivered, and she almost looked embarrassed for a moment. "And you're *here*!"

"Couldn't miss my favorite girl's birthday!"

"Hello," Ray said, and introduced herself. "Lena is too awestruck to remember."

"Sorry, Ray," Lena said, and bit her lips together.

"Nice to meet you. I've heard all about you," Blake said, as Lena stepped back and reached down into a cupboard for a vase.

"Likewise." Ray laughed.

"I've come to take you out to dinner, Lena, if you wish. I came early so I didn't miss you, but don't let me get in the way. I'll just sit out in the waiting room—"

"You can sit in here. We're almost done."

"Are you sure?" He frowned.

"No problem," said Ray. "We should be about ten minutes. We'll just finish up the kennels, then we'll be right out." She stuffed a handful of magazines into his hands. "Here's some reading material for you."

"Nice clinic," he said as Ray walked away. It'd been built from an old house, modified to feature the best of the old as well as the new. Maybe they could use some of these ideas in Lena's new clinic at Elk Valley—if it all worked out between them. He glanced around the treatment room, taking note of the deep tub under the treatment table, the lab in the corner, and the flowers—

The flowers.

Not only flowers, but nearly two dozen long-stemmed, thornless blood-red roses.

"More flowers…"

He shuddered and forced himself to walk over to the blooms.

His heart constricted in his chest when he found the florist label. They were for Lena, all right, but no card. A surreptitious glance around the room revealed no little pink or white card.

Maybe they were from her father.

Yeah right, Sagan. How smart are you?

He tried to breathe deeply to keep his vision clear.

Lena is nothing like Jana.

His ex-wife had never looked at him like Lena already did.

Or had she?

He swallowed hard and tightened his jaw. With a glance at the lilies, he picked up a National Geographic and forced himself to turn the pages, one after the other.

This wouldn't alter his plans for tonight.

Lena was worth keeping.

I raced after Ray into the kennels, flung the door closed, and pillowed my head on my forearms against the back of the closed portal… as if that would keep Blake from seeing the roses. "Oh my god. What just happened?" I whispered.

"We need to find that card," Ray murmured, with a shiver.

"I have *no* idea who sent those roses… and they're in there with Blake," I hissed.

"You must have *some* idea. No man you haven't told me about?"

An uncomfortable niggle raced up my spine. *Tim?*

"There was a guy I was going out with, but it wasn't serious. I've only spoken with him once since I came south. Just before the endurance ride."

Ray winced. "Your father perhaps?"

I winced right back. "He's overseas, in the middle of nowhere. No phone, probably not even a telegraph. And he certainly wouldn't have sent roses."

We stared at each other.

"We need to find that card," we both said at the same time.

"Let's get done here. We've got a man waiting," Ray said.

My chest tightened further, but there was nothing we could do now.

Fifteen minutes later, the three of us walked out the back door of the clinic and climbed the stairs to Ray's apartment.

"I'm Ray's roommate while I'm in Santa Barbara." I smiled up at Blake. "We can get changed here. How fancy are we getting?"

"As dressy as you want. We're going to *Le Chez Soir.*"

Ray inhaled sharply. "Lena, we'll raid my closet, okay? You didn't bring anything *remotely* suitable for *Le Chez.*"

"'One's Own Backyard', and it's that dressy?" I blinked.

"Trust me. I've been there once. You know which forks to use at a place like that?"

I nodded. "Sure do. Mom taught me to survive anywhere, from a big international dinner to the hippie house next door." I looked up at Blake with a smile. "I won't embarrass you. Promise."

"I'm not worried about that." He kissed me lightly on the lips. "We're paying them to serve us dinner. Our manners are the least of their concerns."

"I like the way you think," I said.

This evening would be fine. Maybe he hadn't even seen the flowers.

Men didn't tend to notice things like that.

Did they?

The few remaining pieces of *Le Chez Soir's* sterling cutlery and the silver Victorian under-plates glittered in the light of the million-faceted crystal chandelier. I sat back. My tummy was too full for the sequined, strapless black gown I'd borrowed, and I wasn't at all sure how I was going to teeter back to the truck along the waterfront's brick walkway on Ray's six-inch heels.

"Happy Twenty-First Birthday, Lena." Blake lifted his champagne glass to me once again. "Enjoying your dinner and the restaurant?"

I smiled at the gentleman seated across from me. Blake looked comfortable in his tux and it suited him. "Yes, though I don't think I want to make a habit of it. I haven't seen such opulence since my grandfather's passing several years ago."

"I'm sorry." Blake frowned. "I didn't mean to remind you of sad times."

"It's okay. He lived a full life—more than a full life." My fingertips caressed the ridges of the fine gadroon borders on my under-plate, so like those in my grandparents' home and their Scandinavian fine furniture import stores. "He packed more into his life than most men ever dream of. Did you know he finished the Tevis nine times?"

Blake blinked. "You mentioned he'd done it several times, but you didn't say how *many*-several. That's nearly a record."

"I think that was one of his only regrets." I twisted the narrow stem of my champagne flute in my fingers. "He didn't earn his 1000-mile buckle."

"If he's anything like you, I'll bet he gave it a good shot."

"He did, and his wife, a lovely Swiss woman, rode the Tevis as well. I have a wonderful photo of her climbing Cougar Rock on her gray Arab."

"I'd like to see that sometime." Blake's voice was warm, his eyes dark in the candlelight as he reached a hand across the table to take mine.

"I'm sure you will." I smiled at him and glanced around the room. "This reminds me of the World Trade Club, my grandfather's club and *the* businessman's club in San Francisco. It's in the Ferry Building on the waterfront, much like this." I looked out the window at the glittering Pacific Ocean."

"I've never been there."

"It's lovely. It has wood-paneled walls and floor to ceiling glass sliding doors opening out to balconies over the water, and they carve a new ice sculpture every night for the buffet centerpiece. The last one I saw was my favorite—a magnificent dolphin playing in the waves."

He shook his head. "Sounds wonderful."

"It was pretty exclusive—and personalized." I couldn't help smiling. "The *maître d'* always remembered to bring out my grandfather's burnt toast when dinner rolls were served."

He laughed.

"Thank you, Blake. This is an amazing birthday surprise. Dinner was exquisite."

"Would *mademoiselle* like dessert and coffee?" Our waiter appeared out of thin air, the napkin folded over his arm as snowy and crisp as the shirt beneath his dinner jacket.

I looked across at Blake. "You go ahead. I'm too full, but thank you."

"I'm done, too. Prince'll toss me if I eat any more." He glanced up at the waiter. "No, thank you, but our compliments to the chef."

"I will convey that to Chef. Thank you very much."

I excused myself to go to the ladies and teetered back afterwards. I'm not sure if the champagne helped the shoes or hindered them.

"The men are watching you," he remarked.

I quirked a brow at him. "It's the dress."

"It's what's *in* the dress." His eyes glimmered in the shadowy room.

I glanced around at the men. Some turned their heads away, but others glared at Blake with hostility. I shook my head. "They do seem to be watching, but they're frowning at you."

"They're just jealous. How many men my age have a gorgeous twenty-one-year-old on their arm?" he said, but his smile melted just a little after that.

Blake gazed around *Le Chez Soir*, quelling the sideways looks of the other male diners with just his eyes.

Lena smiled, but she bit her lip and turned her gaze away, out over the bay. The men had looked on indulgently while he and his date had dined.

The man and his daughter.

Once he and Lena finished their dinner and moved closer to each other, holding hands, they'd seen the truth.

What the hell.

She was mature, bright, lovely, and fun. And he was only twenty-five years older than her. Heck, she was older than his son.

A shiver ran up his spine.

It'll be okay.

He took a deep breath and glanced across at her, glad the smile had returned to her face. He wanted to see her happy forever. "Lena?"

She met his eyes, one eyebrow raised.

"Would you like to take a turn on the balcony with me?"

"My mother warned me about men like you," she smirked, "but, yes, please."

Under the moon, the ocean was a glittering sea of stars as he took her hand and kneeled before her.

Lena looked at him strangely, then her mouth dropped open.

"Lena, would you do me the honor of becoming my wife?"

She stared, swallowed hard, and thought for a moment.

Blake's heart was in his throat as she began to speak.

"We've known each other for such a short time, but… I think we were made for each other." She bit her lips together for a moment, took a deep breath, and gave him the answer he wanted. "Yes, Blake, yes. I will marry you."

He leapt to his feet and took her face in his hands. The kiss was sweet and lasted forever.

Thirteen

"I'm sorry I have to leave so early," Blake said the next morning, craning his neck to watch as I struggled to button his pilot's four-bar gold epaulette into place for the first time.

"You came all the way down here to take me out for my birthday, midweek." I smiled and smoothed my hands down his brilliant-white pilot shirt. "And you even asked me to marry you. Who am I to complain?"

He laughed and kissed me atop the head as I buttoned the second epaulette into place. "So now that you can feel more secure about school for the next two years, you'll stay down here the rest of the summer?"

I stared up at him in silence, a thousand thoughts racing through my head.

He looked sideways at me. "What?"

I took a deep breath. "I still have a life up north, Blake... animals, a house, and a job I've promised to return to. I can't drop everything, just like that." I snapped my fingers. "Can you give me a little time to get used to the idea? You've had time to think about it, but it's all new to me."

"But you don't *need* to work this summer, or during the rest of school, for that matter. That's the whole point. That's why I asked you to marry me now."

"The other point" — I tried to keep my voice steady — "is that every day in my ICU job, I'm practicing to become a better vet. I wouldn't get that opportunity as a student, even as an equine track student."

Blake glanced at his watch and his jaw tensed. "I've got to

go, but can we talk about it this weekend? You're coming up?"

"Of course" —I smiled at him—"I'll be there Friday night."

"I'm sorry, but I've got to run. I'm flying jump-seat and they won't wait. There's money on the table for a taxi back home."

"Thanks again for last night, and this morning, and..." My face heated, and he smiled. "I'm glad I'm going to be your wife. We'll make a good team. Fly safe, my love."

"Don't let the little dogs bite. Love you."

We shared a quick kiss, then he ran down the hallway for the waiting taxi.

I locked the door and let myself fall back onto the bed for a few minutes, gazing around the lovely honeymoon suite Blake had reserved for us, shaking my head. This man was well on his way to spoiling me for anyone else, ever.

I finally rose and stepped out the French doors onto the balcony overlooking the ocean. This sort of luxury hadn't been in my life for many, many years, if ever.

The student life just didn't quite compare.

"Ahhh... that feels good." I smiled at Blake as I sank backwards onto the sofa in his log-lined living room, late the following Saturday afternoon. I'd managed to drag myself into the shower after slithering from Tessa's saddle half an hour ago. And we'd only trotted for four hours up hill and down dale.

"And you want to ride a fifty-miler?" Blake raised a brow at me. "Sure you're fit enough?" He chuckled.

"I assume I'll have ridden a bit more regularly to condition myself," I shot back, and laughed. "But I promised to help you with the new dog bed. Let's get to it."

"Don't you sound excited." Sarcasm. He opened a bottle of juice and poured a glass for each of us.

I roused myself and sat with him at the kitchen counter. "Blake." I looked him squarely in the eyes. "It's my last weekend here, and I promised I'd help."

"You *promised* to discuss that. The part about it being your last weekend here." His words were steel-tipped.

"True. You know I'd love to stay and ride, play with horses, and you, of course," I added, trying for a smile, "but it's impossible right now. I've asked my house-sitter if he can stay on longer, but he's committed elsewhere, and I can't just dump my animals."

"We can go get them."

"Blake, I have work that I need to do to live, and it's part of my education. Don't you want me to be the best vet, ever?" I wrapped my arms around him, wheedling now.

He gave me a look, something between a twisted grin and a frown. "But…" He let out a big breath. "I wanted you to feel secure, that you're loved, and that you didn't need to worry about money."

I bit my lip. "I appreciate all of that, but there are, and always will be, some things I need to do for myself. It doesn't mean I love you any less."

Blake was silent for long minutes. "What if your uncle succeeds in talking you into working at his place? That's a pretty good offer," he added grudgingly.

"Yours is better. All of yours. And you." I reached my fingers up to slide through his hair and brought his lips close to mine. "I'm not going anywhere away from you, if that's what you're worried about. All of this" —I waved my hand around the house, encompassing him, the dogs, and the horses out the window" —has all made my uncle's actions so much more clear. He never really believed I'd get into veterinary school in the first place. Wouldn't surprise me if he figures I won't graduate. I have little to no interest in a broodmare or racetrack practice. I worked at a track awhile, and that world isn't for me." I couldn't help an involuntary shudder.

Blake kissed me then, and the peck deepened into a driving desire. I clung to him.

"Just because I'm not staying down here doesn't mean I don't want you, Blake," I murmured, on the verge of tears. My voice sounded deep and throaty to my ears. His eyes darkened as he held me hard against him, then picked me up and headed for the stairway to a place we could let our tensions out in a more constructive way than fighting.

A long time later, Blake slowly sat up. He moved to the window, where he stood for long minutes, just staring out over the valley. When he turned back, his face was ashen.

"What is it?"

"Nothing. I'll just miss you."

I reached for him and he slid into bed beside me. "I will return, and I will marry you. Just see me through the rest of my school, will you? Please?"

He nodded and held me close. My fingers ran over the scar and he flinched. I swallowed hard. He'd never mentioned it and I hadn't had the guts to ask. It was time.

"What happened?"

He was silent so long, I thought he hadn't heard me. Finally, he spoke.

"One of my mother's men friends."

I pulled myself away so I could focus on his eyes. "Your mother's what?"

"She had a steady stream of men—most of them drunks. They didn't appreciate a boy in the way. This one used a piece of firewood to see I stayed away."

"Didn't your mother do—"

"She didn't care enough to stop it and I learned to love mushroom soup from a can, out in the woods on my own. No one hurt me out there. I'd rather not discuss it further."

I clung to him like a limpet. "Thank you for telling me," I mumbled into his chest.

"You're the first I've ever told," he whispered.

"Maybe it'll help. You couldn't have done anything to deserve that, you know."

"Just drop it."

I swallowed hard and was still. We held each other for what felt like hours before he rolled away and reached a hand up to wipe the hair from my face.

"Thank you. Just for being you," he said.

"I'm not so good at being anyone else." I was silent for a moment, then, "Blake?"

"Mmm?"

"Can I ask you a question?"

He nodded, turning a wary look upon me.

"What happened to your previous marriage?"

Blake was silent for a long time, then he looked away. "We grew apart, I guess."

I wasn't fooled. Something had happened, and I can't imagine it was good.

He held me tightly and then looked me in the eye. "You hungry?" he asked.

I nodded.

"I thought after we feed the horses, we'd go get a bite from down the road."

I gazed around and out the window at the peaceful valley, devoid of restaurants. "Down the road? Where?"

He smiled. "There's a charity dinner tonight at the clubhouse and I thought you might enjoy it. Dinner and dancing."

"You had me at the dinner, but the dancing'll get me there for sure."

"A lovely dinner, that." I sighed and patted my belly, gazing around the golf club reception hall, which had been converted for the evening into an impromptu dining room. "Thank you, Blake. I'm so glad I brought over my little black dress."

He arched one elegant brow. "So am I. You're always gorgeous, but"—he reached his fingers toward my long braid hanging over one shoulder and tugged it lightly—"you're particularly lovely tonight."

A man dressed in black passed by our table and headed for a table covered in black boxes near the stage.

"A DJ, even?"

He grinned. "I already put in a list of requests. Do you have any?"

"Whatever he plays will be just fine. Do you dance?"

"Only a little."

That made me smile. Some of the best western swing, Latin, and ballroom dancers I've ever met told me those same words.

And yes, as we started, he showed me just how "little" he could dance. Waltz, foxtrot, quickstep and western swing, to be exact.

"Yes," he admitted, when I cornered him after the first few sets. "I've done a bit of dancing. Two step?" He nodded at the floor.

"Thought you'd never ask," I said with a laugh. " 'A little', you say... more like, you probably competed."

"Only a little," he conceded.

"As a vet school class, our only vice is dancing. My classmates Dane and Toni and I knew how to dance western swing before vet school and we taught the rest of them."

He was silent for a moment, a shadow passing over his face. "And where do you dance?"

"Usually at *The Classroom*, a bar with a big dance floor, lights, you know the sort of place. We go as a group, so it's not a pickup situation." I smiled up into his face.

But he didn't return it. "I wouldn't think you'd have time to dance," he said tersely.

I raised my eyebrows at him. "We usually don't. But when you're studying twenty-four-seven the rest of the time, a couple hours a week could be considered allowable?" I ended on a question, with a hint of a challenge.

He took a deep breath and spun me along the line, around and around, as he two-stepped behind me. When we reached the end of the dance floor, he spun me to a dizzy halt as the music ended, then placed a hand on the small of my back to guide me, wobbling a bit on my high-heeled cowboy boots, to my seat.

"Drink?"

"I'll just have water, thanks. I only have one drink when I'm dancing."

He nodded and disappeared, returning with two waters and a better attitude.

What was that about?

I bit my lip and looked across at him, staring off into space. He was usually so happy and positive... but I was starting to realize there were still many things I didn't know about this man.

And I'd just promised to marry him?

I hoped the darker ones wouldn't amount to much.

I must have imagined the shadows on his face last night, because this morning, there was no room for darkness in the bright spark that was Blake as he whirled me around the kitchen in his log house before breakfast.

We finished that dog bed, my normally bossy self probably irritating him more than a bit, and took the horses for a — slightly shorter — ride.

"I'm going to miss you terribly, Blake," I said, for the umpteenth time, as I shoved Prince's supper hay between the rubber straps of his hay barrel. The horse was a Houdini for dragging his hay out and strewing it over the gritty ground, perfect conditions to wind up with sand colic.

"Not half as much as I'll miss you," he returned, "but you'll be too busy to miss me. I'll keep myself occupied with getting two horses ready for us to compete in January. You *do* want to race Tessa, don't you?"

"Wouldn't miss it for the world," I said with a smile. "I'll get as much riding in as possible and start running again. Wouldn't want to embarrass you or Miss Tessa."

"You could never embarrass me half as well as I do myself."

"Un-likely," I said, and bit my lip. "I have to go pack. My mom's expecting me for dinner, and it's the last time I'll be able to see her before I go north."

He gave me a twisted smile and took my hand to lead me back to the house.

We packed my bag and he grabbed the snack he'd put together for me from its place on the kitchen counter, and together we walked out into the cooling evening air.

"I'm going to miss you," I said again, "and this place." He kissed me, then opened the passenger side door.

"Oh hell," I growled, as my purse tipped out into the gravel. "It must've been sitting against the door." I shook my head and ducked down to gather it all up. "I really shouldn't pack everything but the kitchen sink into a bag designed for a wallet."

"Sorry, I should have looked before I opened the door."

"Not your fault." I smiled and returned to picking everything up, knocking the dust off, and shoving it back into its place.

A pink card lay half-covered with gravel. I frowned and shook it off.

Blake looked up. "What's that?"

"I don't know. Never seen it before."

"It's a florist card." He pointed at the logo. "FTS"

I turned it over.

> *Happy Birthday, Lena! Miss you! Can't wait to go back to Kirkwood again, this time in the summer. See you when you get back, Jeff*

Fourteen

I blinked and stared at the pink bit of trouble in my hand. "Oh my god. *That's* who sent the roses. You remember the roses at the clin…" my voice trailed off at the look on Blake's face.

"I remember the roses." His voice could have cut steel.

"I thought… I thought they were from you. There was no card."

"Clearly, there *was* a card. You're holding it."

"But I never saw it," I whispered as my heart squeezed in a vise. "It must have fallen into my purse. Truly, I never saw it before this moment," I managed as tears filled my eyes.

"Who is Jeff?" He spat each word.

"A guy… just some guy I was going out with… but it wasn't anything serious."

"Red roses? Were you sleeping with him?"

"Sometimes, but…" I stopped, searching for words, then straightened up and clamped my jaw tight before I went on. "Blake, he means nothing to me. He was a friend. Sometimes we had sex. It was casual. We weren't ever together in the way you and I are. I told you I'd marry you—that means you'll be the last man in my life. That's what marriage means."

"Not to everyone."

"Well, it does to me," I growled. "When I give my word, it stands. Period. If you don't trust me, tell me now and you won't see me again."

Blake closed his eyes, his lips moving silently. When he opened them, he reached for me. "I'm sorry. Trust doesn't come easy for me. I didn't learn it when I was a child and my ex-wife certainly didn't help me learn it, either. I swore I'd never trust anyone again, and then, look what happened?" He gave me a watery smile, then pulled me hard against him. "I want to, but it's... hard."

I took a deep breath, trying to let go of my anger. I'd never given anyone cause to distrust me and resented my word being questioned... but, and it was a *big* but, he had his reasons. I needed to have some patience with him...

I'm blessed sure he'll need patience to deal with me plenty of times in the future. This is just paying it forward.

"Honestly, Blake, about the card, neither Ray nor I ever saw it. When you came to the clinic" —I bit my lips together and gave him a little smile—"we were desperate to find out, after you brought flowers, too. When you walked in, I was about to thank you for the roses."

"That's what the hesitation was." He tried for a smile, too.

I nodded and squeezed him around the middle. "That's what it was. I had no idea who they were from. Can we agree to trust each other?" I said in a small voice.

He nodded and held on tighter.

Our upcoming separation by distance stretched out in my mind clear to eternity.

It was bound to be a long, long wait, but it'd be worth it.

Mom's smile stretched from ear to ear as I parked my old truck before her house. I really needed to tell her tonight—this was the last time I'd see her before I headed north next weekend.

I managed to delay until we'd nearly finished the peach cobbler.

"So what's his name?" Mom said, out of the blue.

"Who?" I played dumb, fingering my fork.

"The guy you don't want to tell me about." She smiled and reached out a hand to pat my arm. "This is a long way from Santa Barbara, so there must be some real interest. Is he a nice boy?"

Silence. "I don't think you'd call him a boy... more of a *man*."

I hadn't cared about Blake's age, but I had an idea Mom would. I had no plans to even *tell* dad, who was a year younger than Blake. I can't imagine him understanding.

"'Man'," Mom tried again. "Did you meet him at school?"

"Nooooo…" It was now or never. I took a deep breath. "We met at an endurance ride," I said, as brightly as I could manage.

"Oh? Nice! What's his name?"

I gulped audibly, cursing myself for my cowardice. "It's Blake Sagan."

"Blake… Sagan." She tilted her head, her brows narrowed over a little smile. "Nice family. I know them from our endurance years. But surely, you mean his son, Jordan."

I cocked a brow at her. "No, Mom. Blake."

She blanched, then swallowed hard. "If it's the same man I'm thinking of, isn't he a little old for you?"

I took a deep breath and tried to get my heartbeat to slow a little. "We don't think so and we've been having the most wonderful time. I'm *so* over the guys my age. I'm tired of being hurt."

She blinked. "And you think an older man won't hurt you? How do you figure that?"

"Well, he's a gentleman."

She waited.

"He doesn't try to get into your pants at the slightest provocation. I spent three weekends up at his house before he even—" I broke off, my face burning.

Mom closed her eyes and gripped the table edge before her. "Have you thought just how old he'll be when you're—"

"Yes, Mom," I interrupted. "I've thought of all that." I think I might have growled that last bit.

"How does he feel about your new career as a veterinarian?"

This one, I could handle. I smiled and breathed again. "He's excited at the idea of having his own vet." I laughed.

She considered for a moment. "Yes, I can see he'd be happy for that… and how will he feel about his young wife out at all hours working on horses for young, virile men as he gets older and older?"

I blinked.

"One last thing… have you thought about children?"

"Children? I'm only twenty-one, Mom!"

"And if you decide to have them, just how old will he be then? And when the children are teenagers?" She was silent for long moments. "I'm not asking you for answers, darling" —she took my hand—"but I want you to consider these questions… before it's a done deal. If your mother doesn't ask them, no one will."

I gulped and gripped her fingers until my knuckles turned white. "I love you, Mom, but he's really very special."

"I know he is. He's a wonderful man. You'd like Blake's son Jordan, too, and he's just your age. All I ask is that you go into it with your eyes open."

I got up and went around the table to hug her. I was lucky to have her, even if she wasn't saying what I wanted to hear.

I didn't have the heart to tell her about the engagement. Time enough for that later.

A lot later.

"Engaged?" Ray gaped like a fish out of water.

"Well?" I raised both brows at her.

"But you barely *know* the man! And, have you thought about what I sa—"

That wasn't the response I expected and my face heated as I struggled for words. "Of course I—"

"Lena," the receptionist interrupted from the doorway, "there's a dog in the exam room for you to see. Here's the record. Go ahead and check it out. The doctor will be in soon."

"Thank you," I said as I took the file and tossed a look over my shoulder at Ray.

The spaniel's people were pleased the rash on their pet's tummy was probably just a response to fleas and the hot, steamy weather we'd been having. They trotted out the door with their flea control and some medication to sooth the itch, waving as they left.

Ray was waiting for me in the kennels, eyebrows lowered and her lips a hard, firm line.

I took a deep breath and looked at her.

"So you've said yes? Where's the ring?"

"We'll worry about that later."

"What's his rush?"

"He'd hoped…" I winced, and tried again. "He had in mind to support me… because then I'd no longer have to work… and he hoped I'd change my mind and stay down south with him for the rest of the summer."

Ray looked at me sideways, her forehead furrowed.

"I told him I had to go back to work, and continue learning at my ICU job."

"And…"

"He wasn't impressed, but he got over it… *I think.*"

"Do you really? How many men that age do you know? How many that have a woman in the work force, with an actual *career*?"

I was stunned. Something I hadn't remotely considered.

Ray took a deep breath and seemed to give up. "Well, anyway, it's your last week here," she said, grumpily, "so we're going to have some fun before you go."

I tried to smile, but I'm not sure I made it. Our ideas of fun didn't always coincide, but I'd do a lot for my friend. As she said, it was my last week.

"Oh, and Ray," I swallowed hard, "I, or we… found the card."

"The car — oh! So there *was* one?"

I closed my eyes, unable to speak.

"That bad, was it?"

I just nodded. "That bad."

Ray put an arm around my shoulders and sat me down on a shipping crate. "I want to hear all about it," she said.

After I drove home to Northern California and played with my animals, my next stop was the vet school. I headed for the ICU office, and was pleased to see Frank, our hunk of an ICU supervisor.

"Lena," he said, in his most wheedling tone, "can you work full time for the next month until school starts?"

"Full time, I don't know… what hours?" I said casually, just to wind him up.

His brows narrowed and his mustache twitched. "I thought you wanted—"

"I'm just having you on, Frank. Of course, I'll work." I laughed. My friend Jess had already told me he was scrambling desperately to cover shifts. "Gotcha." I gave him my cheekiest grin.

"Brat." He shook his head. "Thanks."

"In case you hadn't heard, I just got engaged. Blake wanted me to stay down south with him until school starts, but I told him I had to return to work, so I'd best make good use of my time."

"Engaged, like, to be *married*?"

"Yes, that kind, and pick your jaw up off the floor, Frank." I laughed. "I'm not *that* bad a catch."

Although he was the worst flirt in the world, and a good dive buddy to boot, he managed to evade even the most ardent and beautiful pursuer. I don't know how he did it.

He shook his head. "Better you than me."

"I think Blake would agree," I said, with a chuckle. "When do you need me?" I pulled out my calendar and proceeded to fill it with dates.

"How's your horse doing?" he asked when we were done.

"Fat, bored, and happy to be out on the hills. I thought of letting him stay there for the rest of the summer, but I'd miss the riding and need to get fit for an endurance race later in the year."

"Which race?" he asked, and I told him all about Prince, Tessa, Blake, and the Elk Valley Springs 50.

"Hello, darling," Blake said when I picked up the phone that evening. "How was your day? Glad you got that long drive out of the way yesterday."

"Hello yourself," I said. "It was good. I start work again tomorrow."

"In ICU?"

"Yes. Frank needs me."

"Frank? Who's Frank?" He almost, but not quite, growled.

"He's my boss, remember? Yes, he's handsome, and yes, he's a friend. No, I'm not sleeping with him and never have. Any more questions?" I was only half-joking.

"It's okay. I get it." He laughed a little. "So how's that horse of yours? Did your cat miss you?"

"Horse is good, but I think the horse and cat would rather I stayed away. The cat's probably gained two pounds and has been spoiled to death. She now disdains cat food."

"Oh no." He laughed. The tension broke, and I could breathe again.

"Did you get to work the horses today?"

We spoke of his animals until it was time to get off. He told me Fred was being a good cat and goodbyed me with a kiss in my ear.

I sat, looking around my little old house until my eyes fell upon the stack of board exam study notes I'd begun compiling. With a sigh, I pulled the top one onto my lap, opened it, and began to read.

This would be my life for the next few years: eat, study, clinical rotations, work, and if there was time, sleep.

When I got home after working the next night, or the wee hours of the following morning, to be exact, there were five messages from Blake on my answerphone. Their tones became more testy as the call times progressed.

"Hello?" came the groggy voice on Blake's end.

"Hi, sorry it's so late, I just got home from work."

He was silent for a moment. "Where have you been? I've been worried about you."

I blinked. "I've just got home from work."

"In the middle of the night?"

"Yes. ICU runs 24/7. Right now, I'm on swing shift, four to midnight, so I'll be home at this time for most of the week."

"Ah, okay. Well, I'm glad you're home." He still sounded grumpy.

"It'll be a bit tough to talk, other than early mornings before you leave for work. I won't be home this week until one a.m., if not later."

"Okay. Sorry I growled. I miss you already. I'm not sure how I'm going to do this, but I will."

"Good night. I'm shattered," I said, still more than a little put out.

"Goodnight, sweetie," he said, and hung up.

I was well-awake now, so I went to bed with my study notes on my lap to make the most of the time until I felt like I could get to sleep. Another morning coming up with a book on my face and the light still on. My nose must be flattened from all the books that landed on it during my college years.

I arrived home the next day in a howling summer gale to find a message from Ray. I called the clinic to talk with her at lunchtime.

"How's it going up there?" she wanted to know.

"It's great up here, but I don't think Blake's very happy. Our work hours aren't coinciding, so we'll talk this weekend."

"That's tough. Everything is fine down here, we miss you. Just a mo —" A muffled conversation, then, "Hey Lena, I have to go. A patient just came in."

"Okay, great to talk. Give my love to all."

I was just a little bit lonely after that. Empty, even, as thunder shook the little house. The lightning came soon after... too soon. I glanced outside to see how the horse was taking it. He had a full hay net and didn't seem to care. He only cared when we were out riding in it. I smiled, thinking of our last exciting stormy ride.

A car revved its way up the gravel road to my little farmhouse and turned my gaze that way.

And closed my eyes, leaning my head against the window, heart going a mile a minute. Now was not a good time.

A broad smile on his cherry visage, Jeff hopped out of his

fancy blue car. It was different from the fancy red car he had last year.

I swallowed hard and went to the door. I tried to smile as I opened it.

"Well hello, Lena. Missed you something awful," he said and gave me a hug. His arms still around me, he leaned back and looked into my face. "You okay?"

I nodded slowly and he let his arms drop from my stiff body.

"So, did you have a good summer? I just got back." He reached for my hand and began to drag me toward his car. "Come on and see my new wheels"—he glanced up at the roiling gray clouds—"before it pours. We can take her to Kirkwood before school starts."

I tried to breathe while he rattled off the specs of his new blue car. I missed the whole thing. Not a huge surprise. If it didn't have four hooves and a mane, it simply didn't compute.

"Lena?" He stopped and turned me around to face him. "What is the matter? Where's my girl? Have you lost her in Santa Barbara?"

I didn't have the faintest idea what to say. Had I?

"Ummm… thank you for the roses." I frowned, but gave in to a giggle. "They dropped me into dog poo, though."

"You're welcome." Jeff smiled. "I thought you'd enjoy them, all on your own down south."

"That's just it. I have a boyfriend now," I blurted out.

"Oh."

I peeked up to see him looking down at his feet, disappointment lining his face. My heart twinged in my chest.

"What's the matter, now?" I said, giving him a little shake. "It's not like we were ever together so this isn't splitting up, or anything. He's a *real* boyfriend."

He blinked. "Like, a real, *real* boyfriend?"

"Like a real, *real* boyfriend."

"A forever one?" He didn't seem to be getting it. He'd never wanted commitment in the entire time I'd known him.

"A forever one," I said, with a laugh.

"I didn't think... like..."

"What? Don't you think I could get someone who actually wanted to stay with me, not just sex?" I said, probably more hotly than I'd meant.

He chewed the inside of his cheek then straightened up and looked me in the eyes. "And how exactly did my beautiful, I imagine they were beautiful, roses dump you in the proverbial?"

I closed my eyes and finally opened them, looking at him from beneath my brows. "The card must've fallen out of the bouquet, into my purse, so I didn't know who sent them..." My face was steaming. "I nearly thanked Blake for them... then nearly died when he carried in his own bunch of flowers."

"Oh no..." He was shaking his head, his lips pressed into a tight line holding back the laugh.

"And we found your card a month later... as I was driving out to head home. It wasn't't" —I quirked my lips—"my finest hour. He's a little jealous." Now it was my turn to bite my lip.

"I won't apologize for sending flowers, because I'd still send them tomorrow," he said flatly.

I winced. "Hopefully without the Kirkwood reference."

"Are you going to invite me in?"

"Of course." I smiled and led the way. I got him a drink while he sat down on the sofa.

"So where did you find this Casanova?"

"We met at an endurance ride."

"Makes perfect sense, for you," he said, then fell silent. The only horsepower he liked had wheels, not legs.

"He's a pilot," I added. "He has lovely horses and he built his own log cabin. A big one."

Jeff pursed his lips, his brows touching. "That's a lot to do by the time you're thirty."

"Did I say he was thirty?" I blinked. "He's older than that. More like his forties."

"Forties? Isn't that a bit old for you?"

"Some men mature like a fine wine," I said tightly.

"By the time you get to his age, your fine wine'll be getting a bit vinegary," he said, with a twist of his lips. And he didn't look like he was joking.

"Why Jeff, I do believe you're jealous!" I shook my head. "You never wanted more than a casual sexual thing. You made that clear long ago," I said with a frown.

He looked away as I stared at the side of his face.

"I knew you were busy with school and couldn't commit, so I never... asked." He finished on a whisper just before the thunder and lightning hit simultaneously and the skies opened up so loudly we couldn't hear each other talk for a full minute.

I looked outside to see rain already overflowing the gutters, then turned back to him in time to see him looking at me with sad puppy dog eyes, which he wiped with the back of one hand.

"Don't do this. Not now, Jeff."

He shook his head and stood to go as my own eyes teared up. I'd wanted him to care for me, too, for a long time, but he'd made it clear... It was too late now. Simply too late.

I asked him about his car and stood to get him a wet cloth. Talking about his cars always cheered him up.

He sat up and scrubbed at his face, talked for awhile, then soon stood to leave. In the doorway, he bit his lips together for a moment.

"Thank you again for the roses," I said, "and thanks for stopping by."

"Look, Lena, I'm sorry I don't get the chance to really be together with you, but I'm... glad you have someone to love." He touched my hands with his, and shot out the door into the storm while I watched the rain drip down the windows. The blue car turned and disappeared down the drive the way it'd come.

My imagination ran away with me, as it does. Things that would never be.

Even the house was crying.

It was a long week. Blake and I didn't manage to talk much that week, between his leaving at five for Bakersfield to fly out and my getting in at one. Our talks were short, at best.

"How about we just talk on Saturday?" he said one morning

when he'd just woken me up to talk at 4:45 a.m.

"Sounds like a good idea," I slurred. I'm not sure what else I said, but I think I fell asleep while he was still talking.

Fifteen

So, how's Lena getting on back up north?" Myrtle looked at Blake, one brow raised.

He twisted his mouth and said nothing for a moment.

"I haven't heard you talking on the phone for days.

"Yeah, well, she's never there," he said, with a scowl.

"Is she out partying?"

"No." Blake squirmed. "She's working. And studying. And lord knows what else, but she's on swing shift and we can't manage to talk." Myrtle knew just how to trip him up from a good pity party, and he had an idea what she was about to say.

"Well, boyo, that's to be expected. She already has a life up there. I'm sure she'll fit you in as best she can."

"I know that, but…"

"No buts about it," she said, with a frown. "That girl's been working more than hard for most of her life to get where she is right now. Cut her some slack," she said, and she stomped off.

Great. Another pushy woman. Just what I —

He cut off his thought and tightened his jaw. She'd done nothing wrong and he was just going to make himself, and her, miserable.

Good job, doofus.

He made himself a sandwich and headed out for a ride. At least he had that.

School started again, and rather than getting easier, everything got that much harder. Clinic rotations started early, with treatments to be done before rounds with their rotation service clinician, then depending upon your service, treatments, surgery, seeing patients and clients, or running around barns all day. And always the incessant records—S.O.A.P.s, surgical records, anesthetic records, treatment records, and research and preparation for rounds presentations. And then there were sometimes still classes.

Yes, this was what I came to vet school for, but I'm being buried alive here.

There were lonely animals at home, and training for the upcoming endurance ride. I fit in a run whenever I could, most days.

And then there was Blake.

Meant for each other or not, there was not much left of me to give.

He came up on the occasional weekend, and we trained together—in the few minutes I could spare. He worked on his pilot updates while I studied.

"You know?" he said with a wry grin one Sunday as he pulled the last of his outdated airstrip maps out of their binder and replaced it with the current one, "I've never been as current in my updates as I am now. I have so much time while you study. There's got to be a plus here." He put his book down and came over to my desk. "Are you ready for a break? You've been at it for three hours."

I blinked and set my pen down, then rubbed my eyes. "I have so much to do, I can't stop, but I can't do any more, either."

"Let's go out for some dinner. I'll feed while you get a shower."

I smiled my thanks and stumbled off the bathroom.

When I emerged from the shower, I felt almost human. And ravenous.

Blake came in the door just as I finished dressing. "Better now?" he asked and hugged me.

"Yes, and dinner sounds fantastic. We need some time to ourselves, from" —I took a deep breath—"somewhere."

"Let's go," he said, and held the door.

"Would you like to drive?"

He reached out a hand for my keys and handed me into the passenger seat. "Sure. You need a break."

"I wish I could find more time to spend with you when you're here on the weekends," I said. The guilt was getting to me.

"The time's just not there," he said as he buckled his seatbelt. "I don't like it, but short of you quitting school, there's not much you can change, other than stopping work."

I gritted my teeth. "You know why I won't quit."

"Just sayin'." He stuck the keys in the ignition and held up his hands. "As I said before, I can support you."

"I don't feel right about it."

"Don't you trust me?"

"Don't you trust *me*?" I flung back at him. I didn't have enough patience for much right now, and certainly not this.

He sighed and clamped both hands on the steering wheel.

I closed my eyes and held my peace until we got to the restaurant, then I tried again. "I've been training as much as I can fit in."

"That's good," he said, automatically. "I'm busting myself every moment I'm home to get two horses ready to race."

I swallowed. "I'm not sure what I'm going to do about the animals over Christmas. My usual house-sitters will all be away. I might have to bring them down with me. That should create chaos with yours."

"We'll do whatever we have to." Short.

"Look this isn't getting us anywhere." I covered my face with my hands. "I'm sorry, I'm being terrible, but I'm past exhausted. Can we just eat and go home, then cuddle till we fall asleep?"

I looked up to see his gaze softening, the hard lines melting a little. He reached for my hands and I gripped them for dear life. "I just need some rest," I whispered.

"We both do," he said. "We both truly do."

That night, he held me wrapped tight in his arms until we dragged ourselves from bed and I dropped him at the airport at five a.m. the next morning to fly to Bakersfield—to work, and home.

Blake picked up the phone one Sunday morning, a month later, to hear Lena's voice.

"Hello?"

"Well hello there, busy girl. Missed you yesterday. What did you get up to?"

"Worked a shift and a half, came home and fell asleep. Sorry I didn't ring."

"That's okay."

"Whatcha' doing?" The wistful sound in her voice tugged at his heart.

"Well"—he paused—"sitting on the porch in the morning sunshine with Fred and the dogs."

She was silent for a moment. "Don't you have anything better to do? Stuff to learn?" Her voice raised a bit.

He blinked and took a deep breath, considering, while trying to be understanding… instead of simply snapping at her. "I'm sure I do, but… isn't it okay to enjoy life a little?" You were fine sitting here on the porch with me when you were here."

"I just… " She fell silent. "I'm sort of… stressed, but that's no excuse, really."

"If you'd seen the things I have, darlin', you'd understand." She didn't answer.

"I know you're tired. You're burning the candle at both ends. I am too, getting Prince and Tessa fit, working, and worrying about you. No small feat for either of us."

"I guess so," Lena said, and she sniffled, then began to cry.

"It's okay, sweetie. God, I wish I were there to hold you."

"But then I wouldn't have time," she wailed. "I don't have time, I push you away, you cling, and I feel trapped.

"And then, and then," she sobbed, "my stupid uncle is pressing me for a decision, and a loan… now he wants me to finance it. Whether I tell him 'no, thank you', or 'go to hell', the whole family is going to go ballistic. I don't know what to dooooo…" her cry broke off and stopped. All he could hear is her breathing and the occasional sniffle.

"Look, Lena, I'm coming up this weekend. I want to see you and talk. We're going nowhere like this. Is it okay?"

Silence.

"Is it okay?"

"Sorry, I was nodding 'yes', and of course, you couldn't see me. Yes, I'd love to hold you. But do you have time?"

"No, but I don't think we can wait."

"Me either," she whispered.

"I love you," he murmured. "Can you get something to eat and go to sleep?"

"Yes, I will."

"Now?"

"Okay. Love you. Bye."

The phone clicked dead and he sat there for long minutes, staring at it.

He couldn't go through what he had with Jana.

And she was even younger.

He wouldn't.

But if he didn't let himself trust anyone again, he'd be as lonely as he had the past six years… and most of the rest of his life.

And that didn't bear thinking about.

At a knock, I opened up my front door to Blake's concerned visage. "Oh Blake!" I cried, and lunged into his arms.

"Whoa, whoa, girl. Are you okay?"

I shook my head. "Everything's too much."

"Well, we'll do what we can to help that this weekend, okay?" Blake picked me up like I weighed no more than a child and carried me to my big old overstuffed chair. He set me in his lap and held me while I sobbed, his fingers stroking my hair until I quieted.

"Well, what's first?" Blake said, after I'd run out of tears.

"Eat, probably," I mumbled.

"When was the last time you ate a decent meal?"

"Mmmm… not sure."

"Well, that's first, then."

We were fine until halfway through Sunday.

"Lena," Blake said, "you said something the other day on the phone. It was the only thing that really stuck, and I have to say it worried me."

I stared at him.

"You said you felt trapped. I don't want anyone to feel trapped by me."

I was silent for long moments, then finally managed to whisper, "When you cling or get jealous, or make snarky comments if I tell you I've done something with someone else, male or female, I think you don't trust me…"

He gulped. "I trust… I trust you."

"I don't think so," I said, my voice becoming stronger, "and I wonder"—I hesitated for what felt like a lifetime—"if it'll always be like this. I tried, when we were down at your place, to let you know you could trust me, that I'd be there for you, but it seems like… when we're apart, that trust disappears. That's what jealousy means to me. That you don't trust me. And I can't, no—I *won't* live with that." I finished on a whisper.

He took a deep breath and let it out slowly.

"And it makes me wonder…" I said, "what really happened in your marriage."

"That was nothing like us."

I looked hard at him. "Are you so sure?"

"Of course," he growled.

"Okay…" I still couldn't believe it, but that was his story. I'd accept it, for now.

"What else do we need to air?" he asked, and gritted his teeth, his jaw as tense as the rest of him.

"Other than your serious prep for the big fifty miler coming up, I don't see you wanting to go anywhere with your life. You work, and you're 'gettin' by'. Is that all you want from life? I mean, you're just happy to sit on your deck and look at the view. Is that important?"

He stared at me. "I fly jets. Do I have to keep striving for something? Just because you chose to become a veterinarian and kill yourself for eight years of straight-A study, does that mean I'm a lazy so-and-so? I used to tease you about your intensity and serious pursuit of your dreams and goals, but other than school, your flightiness and unpredictability remind me more and more of Jana—" he broke off.

"Jana." I swallowed hard.

"My ex-wife," he finally bit out.

I waited for him to tell me about it, but it looked like it wasn't going to happen. I reached a hand out to him, but he didn't even look at it. He wasn't done.

"More *importantly*, have you ever had experiences that let you see what life is really about? Strive and strive, so you can fly men, in the hundreds, home in body bags? Boys going to R & R with bleeding stumps of arms and legs? Young men… *young* men, in the thousands, who'll never see the light of day again? Don't talk to me about what's important, if you don't think celebrating *life* is."

I froze. "What?"

He looked away, his face like stone. "Nothing," he finally muttered and began to walk away.

"It's important," I whispered as I grabbed his jacket, chastised. "Please tell me about it?"

"Never mind," he growled. "You could never possibly understand. Just leave it."

I closed my eyes—unable to look at the pain in his—my fingers still gripping denim, and then our arms were around each other.

"I knew you struggled with self-doubt," he continued on, "and so I encouraged you to go past it, knowing I'd probably lose you when you had more confidence. It terrifies me. I don't think I can do it… again." He finished on a whisper and I clung harder. "It makes me want to clutch you to me and never let go."

"And it makes me feel," I whispered, "like I'm drowning."

"What are we going to do about it all?" he said.

"I don't know, just hold me, Blake, just hold me, please. I don't know if I deserve you, but I'll try to understand."

"I will, too," he said, into her hair.

I began my small animal rotation the day after my argument with Blake. I was determined to enjoy my time upstairs in the small animal clinic, although it was away from the beloved horses I understood so well.

After only a few days of scrambling to learn the systems up there, I ended up with a nasty respiratory infection. The stress of school and our relationship must have wiped out my immune system completely.

"I haven't had one like this in years," I told Blake on the phone, then had to hold the phone away from my ear as I hacked, my lungs rattling. "When I try to run, I can't do anything but gasp for air and my eyes are streaming all the time."

"Lena, you've got to stop. What did the doctor say?"

"Doctor?"

"You know, that person you go to when you're sick? Sort of like a veterinarian for people. Come on, Lena." He finished on a growl.

"I don't have time to sit in Student Health."

"You're sick. Go tomorrow, please. Promise me?"

"Okay," I croaked, then coughed my lungs out again.

"Look, I'm getting off the phone so you don't keep talking. Take some cold meds and get to bed."

"I don't have time. I have to study for rounds in the morning. In rounds every morning, Dr. Sing looks at me and starts spitting questions at me full speed while he frowns at me like I'm an idiot, and I break into tears."

"Oh, Lena."

"It's got to get better. Maybe if I study even more, I'll have the confidence to stand up to him. I've heard he thinks people who go equine track are too narrow… he probably" —I broke off, with more coughing— "thinks he's broadening my horizons."

"Lena, go to bed, now. Please," Blake begged. "And go to the doctor tomorrow, or I'll have to come up there and drag you in. I don't have time, but I'll make it."

The doctor at Student Health didn't take long.

"Severe allergy to cat dander," he said, with a wince, knowing I was a vet student.

"Thank god I'm equine track," I whispered. "I knew I was allergic to cats, but it's never been like this — only sniffles and congestion."

"Be thankful for small favors," he said, with a smile. "You're twitching, though, Lena. I know what med and vet school are like. You look awfully stressed, and it won't help your immune system."

I tried to take a deep breath and coughed some more. "Yes," I squeaked.

"Try this inhaler," he said as he pulled a box out of a drawer in his desk. He opened the container and showed me how to use the plastic and metal contraption.

I breathed in the medicine, coughed a few times, then did it again. As my hand containing the inhaler lowered to my lap, I took one tentative breath, and then another, and I stared at him. I closed my eyes and just sucked air in and out of my lungs for a minute, smiling. It was like magic. I could breathe again… and I didn't cough at all.

He grinned. "Like magic, eh?"

My mouth dropped open, and I breathed again. I nodded. "Thank you," was all I could say.

"Some anti-allergy tabs should help, as well." He grinned widely as he scrawled a prescription on a white pad. "Try them and let me know how it goes. And see what you can do about the stress levels, eh?"

I thanked him profusely and headed back to the teaching hospital. It was good I'd gotten the breathing problem sorted, because the news there was all bad.

Sixteen

o I made it to the doctor," I told Blake that night on the phone.

"I knew you could do it. You sound better." He sounded so pleased, I could hear his smile through the line.

"The inhaler works like magic, but…" I swallowed hard, not sure how to say this. Failing wasn't in my vocabulary. "Unfortunately," I barely managed at a whisper, "it's too late for the rotation."

"What does that mean?"

"It means my small animal medicine clinician, Dr. Sing, has decided I'm not mentally up to it, due to my performance of falling apart in response to his grilling in rounds, and he has failed me for the rotation." I finished on a sob.

"Lena, Lena. Hold on. What does that mean?"

I couldn't breathe, my chest was so tight.

I couldn't say the words.

"I don't know," I hedged, "I've been called into the Dean's office… tomorrow."

"I'm sure it'll be all right," he said, his voice soft.

I gulped. "It won't be all right. It means… it means… I won't be able to graduate on time."

There was a stunned silence on the other end of the phone. I had some idea what might be racing through his mind… and it wasn't going to be all right. Not now. Not ever.

"It'll be okay," Blake whispered. "Call me as soon as you know, okay? Do you want me to come up?"

"No, it…" I struggled for words. "I wish I had some cherry pie," I blurted.

Silence.

"Pardon?" Blake said.

"Cherry pie." My voice was stronger. "But they're out of season."

"What, in heaven's name, does cherry pie have to do with anything?"

"Mom used to make it for me when I wanted to die," I sobbed.

He made comforting noises. "I love you. Now… can you try to get some sleep, please? I realize I sound like a broken record."

After a deep breath, I agreed, and we hung up.

Tomorrow would be a test.

I don't know how I made it to the dean's office. I'd thought I was a mess before, but by the time I got there, I might have been a murky puddle, for all the sense I could make of my brain.

"The dean will see you now," the secretary said with a smile that I suspect was meant to put me at ease.

I mumbled something to convey gratitude and stumbled through the door she held open for me. Right in front of me sat the frightening man himself.

Pull yourself together.

I was only *in* this mess because I couldn't handle my emotions when a man snapped at me. I'd best buck up or turn around and walk away from the dream I'd held close for as long as I could remember. I filled my lungs and forced my jaw to tighten.

"Miss Scott?" He raised a brow at me.

I nodded and flicked a glance at the Class of 1988 photo on the desk before him. He knew it was me. Just a formality before he…

"Would you like to sit down?" He indicated the comfy chair across from him.

As I sank into its leather-bound depths, I knew why he'd offered. The chair was like a cuddle, and it warmed my heart so much I was able to smile at him. "Thank you," I murmured. "Please call me Lena."

"Lena, then." He smiled. "I understand you had some difficulty in your Small Animal Medicine rotation."

I swallowed hard and nodded.

"Would you care to tell me your thoughts on the situation?"

"I'm sure Dr. Sing has told you everything."

He raised a brow at me. "He has. However, I'd appreciate your thoughts on the matter. You're nearly a full-fledged veterinar—"

How could he be so cruel? So close, and now he was going to rip it away?

My lungs didn't seem to belong to me and I gasped for breath for a few moments before I remembered my inhaler. I whipped it out and sucked on its plastic nozzle. After a moment, I was composed again, my jaw clenched tight.

"Are you okay?" His brows nearly touched. At my nod, he continued. "As I was saying, you're nearly a full-fledged veterinarian. What, and I'm sure there are many, are the extenuating circumstances I need to know, from your viewpoint?"

I stared at him for a moment.

I was going to get a chance?

I straightened my spine. "Well, sir, within a few days of starting the service, I came down with a serious respiratory complaint. A rattling, croup-like cough and draining sinuses which seemed to progress to bronchitis. When I finally went to Student Health, I was diagnosed with severe allergy… to cats." I winced at the dean. "That didn't help. I understand the medicine of cats and dogs, though that of horses comes more easily to me, so I put a lot of extra time into researching and working up my cases. I'm sure my sleep suffered. I was trying my very hardest and it seemed Dr. Sing was determined to push me to, or past, the edge. I became terrified even thinking about his rounds. After awhile, all Dr. Sing had to do was look at me with his frightening frown for the tears to start, but when he derided me or snapped at me, it was all over.

"I realize vets have to deal with all sorts of people, but this is the first person in this entire school, or in any of my previous schools, with whom I have had such a problem. I'm an ICU tech and work with clinicians and owners day and night. Never a problem. I don't know what else to say." I gazed into his eyes as I bit my lips together. I forced my fingers to release their grip on the side of my Pierre Cardin suit skirt. The wool would never be quite the same again.

"Well, Lena, I can understand your problems. I'm glad you've sorted out your allergy, and for your sake, I'm glad you want to become an equine vet." He smiled at me. "However, Dr. Sing is an experienced clinician and if he's concerned about your ability to perform as one of our graduates, I can only bow to his decision."

Tears welled, but I *would not cry*.

"It would mean you may not be on track to graduate on time and could potentially be required to repeat a year. However" — he looked directly at me, his visage rigid in the face of impending tears — "if you can find a clinician or resident in the Small Animal Medicine Service who would be willing to take you on during a break, you'd have another chance to prove yourself."

My mouth dropped open as my mind raced. I hastily slapped it shut and struggled to think. "So you mean," I hesitated, getting my head around it, "I could still graduate?"

He smiled and shook his head. "Your record here, from your previous clinicians and teachers, is exemplary, as is your work in ICU. Small Animal Medicine is a major rotation, but I'm sure you'll do fine in a makeup rotation."

I jumped from the seat and reached across to shake the dean's hand. I wanted to hug him, but that seemed a bit far-fetched, so I left it. "So I just have to find a clinician to take me during Christmas?"

"That's right." He added in an aside. "I happen to know an excellent resident from New Zealand who might be short-handed over that time and could use another pair of willing hands. He's a very thoughtful and kind man, as well."

Ah, that would be Brant.

I smiled. The dean had pegged him. If I had to describe the Kiwi, I'd have used the same words. With the weight of the world sliding off my shoulders, I thanked the dean again and ran to the teaching hospital, and Brant.

"I'm so glad you can repeat the rotation and complete your course this year, honey," Blake said. He couldn't tell her how relieved he was. She wouldn't have to wait an extra year and this hell they were living through would be over.

"Me, too. Thanks so much for your support."

"So when can you repeat it?"

Lena sighed. "I'm so happy. I can make it up right away. Over Christmas, if the resident he mentioned will have me."

"How long is the rotation?" Shards of ice began cutting into Blake's chest.

"It's three weeks. I should be able to start as soon as school is out."

Now Blake's heart froze solid in his chest. "That's through Christmas... and the ride."

Not a sound came through the phone.

"Lena?"

"I'm here," she whispered.

"What is it?"

"I was so relieved, I... I forgot."

Blake bit his lips together. He wouldn't, he *couldn't*, say the things screaming to get out.

"Blake? Talk to me?" Lena said on a sob, her voice sharp with fear.

"We'll just have to make it work, won't we?" he said, between clenched teeth.

"I guess we will," she murmured. "I should be able to talk with the resident shortly. Brant wasn't there when I stopped in earlier. I'll see what we can work out."

"You do that."

"I have to leave for work, but I love you."

"Love you too. Goodnight."

Blake sank into a seat at the table. His thoughts spun in ever-widening circles. Finally, after what seemed an eternity, his gaze snapped to the coffee mug sitting in front of him. The veterinary school mug Lena had given to him.

Would it ever end?

He'd had enough. He picked up the mug and flung it with

all his strength at the solid oak door. Score: Door-one, Mug-zero. He scowled. It should have helped, but it didn't.

"What the hell?" Myrtle shouted from the top of the stairs.

"Nothing," Blake growled, starting to feel a little bad.

"What are you doing, Blake?" Myrtle eyed him sideways when she saw the shards of pottery from the foot of the stairs.

He ignored her, his head in his hands.

"How long have you been sitting there?" demanded Myrtle. He shrugged.

She clattered around the kitchen for awhile while he contemplated his fingers against the tabletop.

"Tell me," Myrtle said, as she plunked two mugs of steaming hot cocoa on the table. "I'm listening."

I looked up from the record I was writing in the ICU office. Surgery residents Kit and Robert, along with the anesthesia resident Sarah Morton, faced the ICU stall, where a black Thoroughbred stood, its belly wrapped in rolls and rolls of Elastoplast over its abdominal suture line. They'd performed colic surgery on it last night.

"Lena" — Kit turned to me — "do you have this horse's record?"

I nodded and stood to hand it to him as he came into the office.

"Thanks," he said. "The referring vet will be here soon, and I suspect he'll be in a right snit if anything's not perfect. I remember him as a student."

I'd only been listening with half an ear while I searched for some equipment in the back of a cupboard. I shut the door with a frown and turned to the clinicians. "Kit, can you possibly keep an eye on him for a moment? He keeps trying to rub out his catheter so I need to find some sort of a cradle for him. It's sutured in, but mere suture is no match for this boy, and tape's not cutting it, either." I smiled at him as my face heated. He was something else. I don't know how they pick the residents — they all have exceptional CVs, that goes without saying, but somehow they manage to find the most gorgeous men and women for our surgery and medicine services.

"No problem, we'll be here for the next fifteen minutes."

"Great, thanks," I said, and slipped out the back door, heading for the storeroom.

Behind me, Robert's Texan drawl echoed through my head. "He ought to be here soon. He called the front desk fifteen minutes ago and gave the girls at the desk a hard time. We'll have to talk with him about that."

"You have some idea it might make any difference? We're too close in age to him—not official enough. Thank god he's moving to Southern California."

"Now if we could get Dr. Rye in here," Kit said, "he'd listen to him, but mere residents like us? Or a woman? Not a chance in hell."

"So he doesn't like women, eh?" Sarah said. "What did you say his name was?"

"Barnett-Payne," Robert muttered. "And he doesn't like much of anybody. Be sure it's reciprocated."

I stopped like I'd been shot, and didn't wait to hear more. I bolted to the storeroom and locked myself in. Thank god there was a phone in here to call the front office. "Mary? Could you please page Frank for me and ask him to meet me in the storeroom?"

"The ICU storeroom?"

"Yes, thanks."

"No problem," her sweet voice said, and she hung up.

I froze at a knock on the door and sat in silence in the darkness, behind a shelf for good measure.

"Lena, are you in there?" Frank asked. At the sound of jangling keys I ran to the door and opened it before he could even get one into the lock.

I stood behind the door while he came in.

"What the hell? What are you doing in here in the dark?"

I shut the door and locked it, then turned on the light. "Thanks for coming, Frank," I managed, my voice and the rest of me shaking, "but I need your help."

"Are you okay?" Frank's brows narrowed.

"Can I swap anyone anywhere else in the barns to work for the afternoon?"

He stared at me. "What's the matter?"

"You know that colic in ICU?"

"The black Thoroughbred?"

I shuddered. "The horse is not the problem, but the referring vet is."

"Who is it?"

"Remember a student from last year, Gareth Barnett-Payne?"

He winced. "Sure. Hard to forget."

"Well, he's here."

"And you want to be out of ICU, why?"

"We have a history... a scary one." I swallowed hard.

"Very scary, by the looks of it. Are you sure you don't want to go home?"

"No, but if I can stay out of the way, I can still work."

He took a deep breath. "I don't like seeing you like this, but if you want to stay, they can use you over in B-Bar. Go ask Betty to come on over here."

I shook my head. "Thanks. I'm sorry to do this to you."

"No problem," he said, and patted me on the back. "I'll keep an eye out for him, and you."

I went the long way around and found Betty. She was happy to go into ICU and she was tough. If anyone could stand up to the jerk, it was her.

I kept my head down and worked hard for the next hour.

"Arggghh!" Betty growled, as she walked up to the stall I was working in. "What a jerk!"

"Who?" I asked.

"That jerk of a referring vet on the colic horse in ICU. Thinks he can push me around—and the residents, too. I don't know who the hell he thinks he is, but he's a real special case. He had Janette in tears after five minutes of perusing the horse's record. That's when Dr. Rye showed up—right in the middle of it all. He kicked him out, while the cretin groveled and brown-nosed him and Dr. Salisbury."

I swallowed hard. "He has respect for somebody?"

"Only the top-level senior professors."

"So glad he's gone," she threw over her shoulder, as she continued on her way to get some meds from the pharmacy.

I took a deep breath and glanced around, my heart constricting in my chest as I realized he could be… anywhere. One hand in the pocket of my scrubs, I fingered my blunt-blunt bandage scissors and an extra pair of sharp-sharps that had found their way into my hand as I scrabbled around in the storeroom.

I turned back to the little appaloosa in the stall beside me. "How did you"—I capped her catheter off and proceeded to untwist the hopelessly tangled mess—"manage this?"

She gave me a nudge and rubbed her head against my side. I couldn't help but chuckle at her, thankful she'd allayed my terror for a few moments, anyway.

"Little ratbag. I think you did this on purpose to get some attention. You're far to well to be here," I said, and kissed her spotty nose.

She would have done justice to a fine bit of Celtic knot work, but I finally managed to untangle the IV lines, reconnect the catheter and get the life-giving fluids going again.

I gave the appy a final pat and stepped backwards out of her stall, looking once again over her drip set, then reached for the latch. Two hands gripped my shoulders.

Seventeen

Heart in my throat, I spun and jerked away from my attacker, then froze, my sharp-sharps against his abdomen just beneath his ribs — staring in horror. It wasn't Gareth at all, but my boss.

Frank stared right back and didn't move a muscle. "Oh my god, Lena! You're that scared of him?" He gently took my hand with the scissors and moved it out of the way, then wrapped his arms around me.

We'd been friends for a long time and I basically collapsed against him, muttering something that even I couldn't begin to decipher.

"I came to tell you he's gone, and that you didn't need to worry. He's *persona non-grata* here for awhile."

I managed to fill my lungs and my brain started to work again. "Thank you, Frank," I murmured, and lifted my head. "I'm sorry" — I nodded at his tearstained shirt — "and I almost stabbed you."

"Having a little experience with the guy, I'd have understood. You were *involved* with him?"

"He's good at hiding it. Or used to be."

"Glad you're away from him, then. Look, it's a little early, but you head on home now. Someone's there?"

"Nope."

"Well then, head on over to my place. Leslie will be there by now. You can have dinner with us. I'll ring her."

I put everything I had left into the smile I gave him. "Thanks, Frank. I owe you one."

"You owe me nothing. Just stay away from him."

"You've got that promise. Forever would be too short a time. I'm off."

"Blake!" I whipped open the door of my little house and flung my arms around him. "I wondered why you wouldn't answer the phone. I thought something had happened." I couldn't stop the tears that rolled down my cheeks.

"What are the tears for?"

"I'm glad you're here," I said, and kissed him.

"I'm surprised to find you at home," Blake said, his voice tight. "I couldn't find you this afternoon or tonight when I landed, so I got a jump-seat to Sacramento and just came up." His jaw was twitching.

"I had a terrible day," I said, with a shudder.

"Mine hasn't been so great, either."

"Come on in, I'm so glad you came. How did you know I needed you tonight?"

He held me at arms length and really looked at me then, his eyes narrowing. "You've been crying."

I'd washed the tears off my face, but doubtless I was still blotchy from bawling with Leslie on their sofa until Frank came home.

I nodded and told him the whole sordid mess.

As the story progressed, his demeanor changed from annoyance to anxiety, and on to pulsing anger with Gareth. I'm not sure which worried me more, but it was good to be held all night.

So good.

"And so," Lena told Blake the next morning, "Brant, the Small Animal Medicine resident said if I start my rotation as soon as school finishes and work through the shorthanded Christmas time, I can finish a little early. Frank will let me off for my ICU shifts, and I could come home a few days after Christmas and have a week before the ride."

"That must have taken some work to figure it out." Blake was still annoyed with the whole thing, but just hearing it was exhausting. Lena *was* trying her best.

"So I'm sorry, but I'll miss Christmas." Her brow wrinkled and she worried at her lip. "At least I can get the animals taken care of, since it'll be after Christmas," she said, hope in her voice.

"*Grrrrr…* I'm so frustrated, but if *I'm* frustrated, I can't imagine how you feel," Blake said. "I'm sorry, Lena. I just want us to be together."

"I do, too."

"So," Blake took a deep breath, "have you and your classmates been doing any dancing?"

She pulled back and stared at him, her face rigid. "Seriously?"

"You said you all did it to blow off steam."

"Yeah, well, these days I need to hold on to all the steam I can, and we're all scattered to kingdom come."

He couldn't help feeling comforted at that. The thought of Lena dancing with other men… no matter how innocent… it just didn't improve his attitude. "What do you have going on tomorrow?"

"Work and study," she said, automatically. "It's Sunday."

"Can I take you out to breakfast?"

She inhaled and let it out slowly. "I have a study group in town at eight and start work at four. Can we do lunch?"

"Is that all the time I get? Lunch?"

Lena closed her eyes for a moment. "Look, you didn't tell me you were coming up. Don't get me wrong, I'm glad you're here, but I'd have made different plans if I'd known."

"When you *do* know ahead of time, you're still too busy. Face it, you don't have time for me," Blake growled.

"I don't have time to breathe or sleep, much less do fun things. I have ridden my horse *twice* since I got home. *Twice*." Lena's eyes blazed.

"You were so upset, I couldn't just let you deal with all this on your own," Blake snapped. "What do you think I am?"

"I don't know!" Lena yelled. "You know I don't have any time, you show up and get mad at me for not making more of it! If I knew how to make more time, I wouldn't be such a nutcase." She slumped to the sofa, head in her hands.

Blake sat down on the coffee table, just in front of her knees, and reached out for her hands. She was limp. "Lena," he whispered, "Lena, look at me."

"I'm too tired to even open my eyes," she murmured.

"I'm sorry. I know we're both exhausted. It's late. Let's go to bed."

She nodded, but didn't move.

Blake picked her up and placed her carefully in bed, tugged her clothes off and then his own. She was asleep even before he pulled her close and curled himself around her.

"So how are you doing, Lena?" Blake's voice crackled over the line.

"I'm missing my mom. She's back east and with the hours I'm keeping, I can't get hold of her when she's awake, either."

"She'll be back soon, anyway, right?"

"Mmm-hmmm. Thank you for sending the ticket. It came in the mail today."

"I'll pick you up in Bakersfield when you fly in on Sunday."

"It'll be good to see you. Feels like forever."

"How's the rotation going?"

"It's good," I said, smiling.

Blake was silent. "Good to hear you're getting along well. You didn't sound so good last week."

"Brant's amazing. His diagnostic skills are nothing short of miraculous, and he's so helpful. Anything I need, he's always there for me, no matter how late it is. After the previous rotation," I sighed, "it's such a pleasure." My smile stretched my face so wide, I chuckled. I'd forgotten what if felt like.

"What's this guy like?"

"Pardon?"

"What's he like? Is he married?"

"What the hell kind of question is *that*? He's my resident. He's helping me. I'm getting through and it's not like having my teeth pulled every day."

Blake didn't say anything.

"You're jealous?" This was too much. Way too much.

"Damn straight, I'm jealous." Blake's voice was rough. "You never have time for me and you're spending plenty of time with other people at school."

"Studying? That's spending time?"

"And you haven't sounded so happy in months. Certainly not when I've been with you."

"Is that any surprise? You're jealous all the time, no matter what I do. Is our whole life going to be like this? I've never done anything to deserve this."

He said nothing.

"If this is the way you feel, like you can't trust me, you might as well not bother anymore." I struggled to hold back the tears. If I started crying, I'd just blubber and wouldn't be able to ask my next question. I gritted my teeth. "What I'd really like to know is, what happened to your marriage? Did you wife leave you or what?"

Silence rang through the phone lines for long moments, then Blake took a deep breath and started, his voice raising with every word. "No, I left her. She screwed around on me with my best friend. And yes, she was younger than me," he said, and hesitated, "though she was still older than you. Does that make you happy? What else do you want to know?"

I didn't know what to say. Neither of us spoke for long minutes. My anger fell away and all I felt was sorry. "No," I whispered. "I'm sorry. Nothing else."

"I'm sorry, too, Lena," Blake finally said with a groan like his guts were being wrenched out. "You're not Jana, and I have no right to put my anger with her onto you... a million times, sorry."

"Me too. There's just nothing left of me," I whispered.

"I'm afraid to lose you and I'm afraid to shut down. I just don't know what to do."

"I love you, Blake. Thanks for telling me."

"You deserved to know." Grudgingly.

"Will you be home tomorrow?" I asked.

"Not at the times you'll be home. I thought I'd try to to catch up with Jordan for Christmas."

"Jordan, your son? You know where he is?"

"I found him last week. He's willing to meet with me."

"Oh Blake, that's wonderful." I hadn't heard anything so good in days.

"So Merry Christmas for tomorrow," he said gruffly.

"And to you. I'm sorry not to be there for our first Christmas."

"Me too. You go to sleep and I'll try to catch you tomorrow, okay?"

"Okay. Love you. Night night." I said as I drifted off to sleep.

"It's so good to be outside, and finally back here," said Lena, staring off across Elk Valley, as she stroked Tessa's neck.

Blake glanced at her face. Lena's tan had faded to nothing. She'd clearly spent the past several weeks indoors. He'd never seen her look like this. Happier than after her first small animal rotation, but she still hacked, even with the inhaler. "Happy to be home?"

She swallowed and didn't look back at him from her seat atop Tessa. "Yes," she said.

"Are you okay?" Blake had to ask.

She took a deep breath. "I think we just need some time to get used to each other again. Get some trust back."

"You might be right." Blake looked down into the valley beside them. "We'll have plenty of that soon, as soon as school's done."

I hope.

"What's your training schedule been for the horses?" Lena finally looked over her shoulder at him.

"We've only got another" — he counted on his fingers — "six days before the race. Today we'll go twenty miles, and tomorrow —"

Tessa whinnied frantically over a great rumbling and slithering sound, then Prince was scrambling backwards as the trail beneath his feet crumbled. When he stopped, snorting, the trail, Tessa, and Lena were gone.

Blake leapt to the ground. "*Lena!*" he yelled. "*Lena!*"

A few rocks still slid and bounced downward where the trail had been. Blake stepped toward the edge and dropped to his belly, then inched forward.

A hundred and twenty feet below, on the valley floor, Tessa was just getting to her feet and gave a great shake. As Blake watched, the mare limped through the loose rocks and boulders toward Lena, lying still as death ten yards from her.

"Lena!" he called again, but she never moved.

Eighteen

*B*lake shook his head, fear for Lena rising by the second as he searched the area around the slip for a safe place to get down the hillside.

No way down.

He'd have to find another way. Mounting Prince, he spun him around. From memory, there was a fire trail… yes, there. They turned onto it and scanned the valley for any movement, any help, as they raced down the trail. Nothing moved at the bottom but the gray mare, grazing wisps of grass near Lena.

Within minutes, he was at her side.

"Lena?"

She didn't answer, but she was breathing. She lay curled up on her side, covered with dust and grit, but the only blood he could see ran from a cut over a rapidly-swelling egg on her head. The helmet she'd been wearing was nowhere in sight. He made sure there was nothing in her mouth and wrapped his coat around her. "Oh my god, Lena?" he said again, but she still didn't respond.

He quickly checked Tessa. The mare was covered with dust and very lame in one forelimb but seemed otherwise intact. Blake slipped her bridle from her head, put on her halter, and tied her to a nearby tree. With another look at Lena and a hug for the mare, he swung up on Prince and galloped to the closest house to call for a chopper.

The people were kindness itself and called the ambulance, then drove behind him back to the slide with blankets and hot water bottles.

Blake had only just dismounted and tied Prince beside Tessa when the throbbing sound of the chopper's rotors filled the air. Untying their leads, he held tightly to both skittering horses as the chopper came down.

"Blake?" shouted his friend Marcus, the chopper pilot from Bakersfield.

"Didn't waste any time, did you? Thanks for coming. She's not good at all," Blake said, biting his lip as he helped Marcus carry the stretcher towards Lena while his partner gathered more gear.

"Is this your girl?" Marcus ducked down beside her and began checking her out. Blake gave her details, as much as he knew, and Marcus introduced his partner. Together they got her strapped onto the board, and then into the stretcher. "I'm not feeling any fractures, and she appears stable, but she's got a pretty good knock on the head. Hopefully she'll be back with us soon. You coming?"

Blake glanced at the horses. The helpful neighbors had just driven away. "I need to take these guys home, then I'll drive to the hospital."

"Okay," Marcus looked dubiously at him. "See you soon. Drive safely."

They hopped into the chopper and she lifted, leaving a cloud of dust, as Blake rode the stallion and ponied the limping mare alongside them.

Blake had just finished bandaging Tessa's injured legs when the beat-beat of a chopper came over the hill behind the house.

"Oh no, not another one," Blake said to Myrtle.

"Horses aren't the safest habit," she said, putting the sad mare's bucket down. "I hope Lena's okay, and Tessa, too." She turned to watch the chopper. "I'll finish up here. You've got to get going."

"It's Marcus, and he's landing." Blake said, recognizing the chopper. "I wonder why he's come back?" The horses snorted, but left their noses in their buckets.

"Thought you might need a ride," Marcus shouted from the chopper.

Blake gave him a thumbs up and raced to grab some clean

clothes for himself and Lena. He was back in moments.

"I'll see you when you get back," Myrtle said. "Don't you worry about anything here, I've got it."

He smiled at her and gave her a quick one-armed hug, then bent over and ran under the rotors.

Marcus waved away his thanks. "If it was my woman, I'd be driving like a mad thing to get down to her. Thought it'd be safer to pick you up here than out of a crashed truck."

"Thanks, man," Blake said, shaking his head. "I owe you one."

Blake shivered at the hospital disinfectant scent as he walked in through the emergency entrance from the chopper pad. He'd spent more time than he liked within their white walls, but he was still alive.

Lena was still unconscious. He swallowed hard when the nurse showed him into Lena's curtained-off cubicle.

"We're pretty sure she has no spinal injuries," the young emergency room doctor said, "but she's had a pretty nasty knock on the head. We've sutured it, but now we just have to wait. She's young and strong. How did she do it, by the way?"

Blake told them.

"Rough. I'll be back to check on her. If there are any changes, could you please use the call button? We'll be here right away."

"Thanks, Doctor."

Blake sat in silence beside her for what felt like hours, holding her hand. Finally he had to say something.

"I'm so sorry, Lena," he whispered, gripping her fingers for grim death. "I should never have let you take the lead, not after that last landslide. I was skulking behind, letting you go ahead on a trail you barely knew.

"Please wake up. I promise I won't make you crazy anymore. I know you love me, I just need to get a handle on this jealousy. I'll love you forever. I won't be jealous of you anymore, just wake up, please?"

She stirred, the hint of a smile on her face.

"Lena?"

She opened her mouth, then shut it again. "Oh, my head... who hit me?" she finally murmured.

"A rock or a horse, not sure which," Blake said, and stood up beside her. He bent over and gently, oh so gently, kissed her lips. "The trail slipped out from under you and Tessa."

"Is Tessa okay? Prince? You?"

"We're all fine. Tess is lame, but she'll be okay."

Lena closed her eyes again. "I heard that, what you said…" Her lips shaped into a faint smile.

"And I meant it," Blake said.

"That's good… because… I'm not going… to fall down… a mountain just to hear you say that again." Lena squeezed his hand and closed her eyes. She slept.

Sleeping in the chair beside Lena's hospital bed wasn't great, but it had to be better than being in her position. By the next morning, Lena was well enough to leave.

"Excuse me, Mr. Sagan, but there's a phone call for you," a nurse said from outside the cubicle.

It was Marcus. "I'm outside. I was just coming off shift, and asked the doctor about Lena. He said she'd probably be released soon. Your chariot awaits."

"I was wondering how we would get home." Blake shook his head. "Thanks, Marcus. We'll see you in a half hour or so, as soon as they let her go."

Lena was walking around the room when he returned.

"Before you say anything"—she held up one hand—"the doctor wanted me up and walking around while they prepared the discharge papers."

"Are you sure?" he growled.

"Quite. So, Blake, no more fears, right?"

"Yes. No more stressing, right?"

Lena smiled. "Nope. And we can work on everything together?"

He nodded. "No more misunderstandings. Talking."

Blake enclosed her in his arms and held on, thankful to be given a second chance to prove his love.

Always and forever.

"I'm so sorry Tessa's hurt. That tendon should heal, but it'll take awhile," I said.

"I'm sorry too, but you're in no condition to ride in the race, anyway." Blake looked at me sadly.

"I'm fine. The doctor said I could ride. I've had no ill effects since the first day."

Blake shook his head. "I imagine he thought you were talking about a little walk around an arena, not fifty miles over rough terrain."

"I suspect I didn't make myself" — I rolled my eyes — "completely clear."

Blake brushed the hair back out of his eyes and blinked at her. "You look good... better than good, as usual." He reached for me and I melted into his arms.

"I'm even more sorry for your injury," he said, "but it let me realize just what we mean to each other and helped us resolve some issues, anyway."

I nodded and reached up to kiss him. "I'll go make us some breakfast while you move that hay."

Ten minutes later, a crash came from the direction of the barn and both horses stood, ears pricked, staring at the barn, before they trotted over and disappeared into their stalls.

I smiled. They were probably going in for a treat. When they didn't come out again, I called down to the barn, but there was no answer.

The horses' ears were still pricked, watchful over their half-doors, all attention on the man sitting on a hay bale, swearing the sky down as he held his ribs, his face white as a sheet.

"What have you done to yourself?" I said, as I trotted to him. "Are you okay?"

"The gutter," he winced. "It blocked up a few weeks ago when it rained. Thought I'd clean it out." He wouldn't look at me.

I closed my eyes and I waited while he stalled. "What happened?" I finally asked.

"Nothing," he mumbled.

"Let me see," I said past gritted teeth, and gently pulled him to his feet. Something was clearly not right. I slowly peeled his shirt up. And gasped.

"Damned ladder tipped over," he muttered.

"Don't you know you're—" I started to berate him about old men and ladders, but I shut my mouth when I saw the line of red marks overlying several ribs, and alongside them, the hint of blue, already spreading.

"Can you breathe in for me, gently?" I asked him.

He grimaced. "Probably not." But he tried. And blanched further.

They were clearly fractured, and the race was in three days.

"It'll be better tomorrow. Fine for the race," he said, with a gasp. "They're just bruised. I've done this before. I have three more days."

I blinked.

Over my dead body, he'll be riding.

He'd *not* be riding, no matter what excuse he could find.

Blake's chest looked much worse in the morning, but he wouldn't let me take him to the hospital.

"They'll just tape me up and tell me to rest. They usually do."

"Some X-rays would be a good idea," I growled, for the tenth time since we'd woken up.

"They're all out where I can see them. I'll take it easy," Blake argued. "We don't have time to go down there and it won't make any difference.

I quirked my lips at him.

"What?"

"Well," I said, "that was my argument last time I broke five ribs, so I guess I don't have much to say about it."

He started to laugh, stopped with a wince, then just smiled. He *carefully* pulled me closer, then let go. "It hurts too much to do even that."

I nodded, remembering how much my own ribs had ached, especially while bending over, so I kissed my fingers and touched them to his lips.

"Blake, I'm fine."

"I know you are." He looked at me sideways, his eyes narrowed, and waited for it.

"You've worked so hard getting both of these horses ready to race."

"Nothing doing, girl." Blake shook his head. "You've just come out of the hospital with head trauma, remember?"

"But I feel fine. I even called the doctor… and this time I told him what kind of riding I had in mind." I went on, as fast as I could go. "He said as long as my vision was fine and I had no dizziness or pain, I was fine to race."

He started to sigh, but froze instead, and stood still, biting his lip, then turned concerned eyes on me. "You've never even been *on* Prince."

"I could ride him. He knows me."

"He's a stallion. Anything could happen.

"I've handled plenty of stallions."

"In a race, with a hundred other horses, on narrow trails?"

"I promise, I'll keep him away from everyone."

"It'll only end in tears."

"It'll be fine. And if I don't feel fine, or if I get worried, I'll pull him."

He stood leaning against the kitchen doorjamb in silence for long minutes. "Okay," he finally murmured. "I don't want to risk you again, but if you're dead set on doing it and truly feel fine, it may be possible to switch Prince's rider with the race committee."

Blake was as good as his word. He called and left a message for Leslie, the ride manager, and she rode up to talk with us soon afterwards.

"Sure, we can switch Prince's rider, and I already have your details, Lena." She smiled at me. "I'll pull Mis Witeża. I heard about what happened, and she's clearly lame now," Leslie said, with a glance over her shoulder at the mare, "so you don't even need a vet certificate."

That was rather decent of her. "Thank you for that, Leslie."

"I don't know what's going on but everyone's getting broken. Have you heard about Dr. Morton?"

"No, what's up?" He frowned.

"She fell off her horse yesterday."

"Is she okay?" Blake cringed at his sharp intake of breath.

"She broke her leg, but otherwise, she's okay. She won't be vetting the ride, though. We're hustling to find another vet in time, but we'll manage. Luckily, we still have Seth, our head vet, but he can't do it alone." She backed her horse away from the porch. "I'm off. You take care of yourself, eh? See you at the race."

I looked up at the sky, clear blue without a hint of cloud, as I finished checking Prince's shoes for any loose nails one final time. "Lovely day for the race. I'm sorry you can't ride Prince today," I said as I walked over to Blake, "but I'll do my best to take care of him for you."

"Well" — Blake grimaced as he picked up a bucket, swallowed hard, and straightened up — "at least I can crew for you two."

I shook my head. "Marcus said for you to leave the buckets. He'll be right back." I kissed him on the lips. Gently. "Are you sure you want to do this? We could get you a job pushing paper at one of the registration desks. I don't know how you're going to stand the drives between vet checks."

"Easy." He twisted his lips. "I'll drive. The ribs are better with a steering wheel in my hands."

He had a point. From experience, I knew it was a good one.

"Blake," called a girl on a bay Morgan, "have you heard about the pre-rides?"

"We did it last night, Maria," he said. "Didn't you?"

"Yes, but for some reason the head vet says the new vet they just pulled in wants to see the horses himself, so they're doing another pre-ride vet check."

"Can they do that?"

"I don't know" — the girl shrugged — "but they're doing it."

I looked at Blake. "Well, do we front up for it?"

"If Maria says that's what they're doing, I guess so. Can you bring Prince along?" he said, and stiffly made his way toward the vet check area.

Prince was good at his job, and he knew it was race day. All ready to start the race, he danced on the end of his lead until Blake growled at him, then he settled.

The new vet stood talking to one of the competitors. Something about his stance niggled at my brain, sending a shiver up my spine, but I shook my head and looked down to negotiate some rocks in our path. We were nearly to the enclosure when the vet turned around and I saw his face — and froze.

"Lena, are you okay?" Blake's voice seemed to come from far away. "Lena, what's the matter? You're white as a sheet."

My world was going gray and I gulped air like a guppy. "Blake," I whispered, as his arm came around me, "it's him."

Nineteen

W ho?" Blake's brows narrowed, and he stared at the crowd assembled at the gate to the vet check.

"The new vet—he's the one from school"—I breathed against his shirt—"my nemesis—"

Blake spun toward the vet with a sharp intake of breath. He locked his jaw and slowly breathed out. "So, that's the jerk."

I nodded. "Gareth Barnett-Payne. I wouldn't put anything past him. He's the devil incarnate," I said, as I frayed the end of Prince's leadrope with both hands. "Can you keep your eyes peeled for me, please?" I tasted bile in my throat and swallowed hard to keep it down.

"Hold on, Lena. He can't do anything with all these people here."

I raised a brow at him and tried to stop shaking as I led Prince forward.

By the stare he sent my way, Gareth expected me, no question about that. There wasn't a hint of surprise in his steely eyes. I could have sworn I heard Blake growl from behind me.

Just before I reached the in-gate, Blake called out to me. "Lena, the head vet needs a ride to the first stop right now. You going to be okay?" He turned a baleful look toward Gareth.

I nodded, though I knew it was impossible to be okay with Gareth Barnett-Payne in the same county.

Blake winced over his shoulder at me but followed the official who was practically tugging at his sleeve. "See you there," he shouted, and his brow furrowed as he waved.

"Lena Scott?" Gareth said, checking his secretary's clipboard, then handing it back to her. "What have we here?" He looked Prince over, then asked me to trot him out.

His eyes burned a hole in my back as I jogged away, Prince

bouncing along beside me, stopped, turned, and trotted back toward him, my eyes on a spot somewhere beyond him. Looking at Gareth wasn't helping my sanity.

"You're nearly a vet, Lena. How could you do this to a horse?"

I blinked. "Pardon?"

"He's totally out of condition."

I shook my head. "He's a stallion. I thought the same the first time I saw him, too, but it's all muscle."

He raised a brow at me and shook his head. "He's too fat. He'll get into trouble in the race. You should know that." Flatly.

"There's not an ounce of superfluous fat on this horse. It's all stallion muscle. Truly." I closed my eyes for a second. "Please? Let us start, and you'll see. He already passed the pre-ride last night. Dr. Latimer didn't have a problem with him."

"Well, I do."

"Please?" I was pleading now, and something changed in his eyes—he almost smiled. *Bastard*. Pleading women, his favorite. I gritted my teeth.

Gareth stood in silence for a moment. Finally, with a glint in his eye, he agreed to let Prince start. "I'll be waiting at the second vet check to pull you if he's not in perfect health." His jaw tight, he took a step toward me, evil in his eyes, but Prince snaked his head around toward him, teeth bared. Gareth stopped in his tracks and glared at the pair of us.

"He'll be okay," I murmured. Damned if I was going to thank him.

"Passed," he said, through clenched teeth, to his secretary. "Next?" he called out, and we bolted.

I looked for Blake, but all I saw were his tail lights heading off toward the first vet check.

My vision cleared again as I bridled Prince and told Marcus what was up. The chopper pilot offered the horse another drink of electrolyte water and saddled him. I made sure Prince's hoof boot was lashed firmly to his saddle, retrieved my rider card and ID from the trailer, and stowed them in my pack. I smiled as I returned to the fidgety stallion, looking at our competitor number. Thirteen, my lucky number, was marked in a fluoro-orange livestock paint stick on his left hip. It suited him — the horse might just get a saddle pad of the same color for his birthday. With that color marking his flank, at least they could find us if he was unlucky enough to slide down the side of a mountain.

Then the five-minute warning was called, and everything was a flurry. Marcus gave me a leg up and sent me on my way. "I'll see you at the vet check," he yelled after me.

Per Blake's instructions, I held Prince, the only stallion in the race, off to one side of the starting line. No use creating a scene or getting anyone hurt. He quivered as he waited for the gun to go, and then we were off.

Thankfully, I knew the course fairly well, after riding the start area for several days. Knowing there was plenty of room for several horses abreast in the first few miles helped. I let Prince settle into his long trot that ate up the miles. When he was out moving, he tended to think of his work, and not of the girls around him. Several horses took off at a canter and passed us, but Prince, other than a brief flick of his little ears, ignored them. I suspect he knew he'd pass them soon.

Five miles out, we did. He trotted along, looking neither right nor left, and already, we were passing horses which had started out too fast. By the time we reached a narrower trail, there were only a handful of horses in front of us.

My heart sang. To be blessed with riding such a horse... he seemed to be in his element in competition. All I needed to do was think "forward", and he flew.

Like all good endurance horses, especially on the longer rides such as the Tevis, Prince drank when there was water and nibbled at any available grass he could reach while trotting past. The horses that stayed well-hydrated and kept their guts going stayed well — and performed well.

We must have been nearly to the ten-mile mark when a trough showed beside the trail ahead. Prince headed for it and plunged his whole muzzle beneath the surface, then lifted his head and shook it. When he returned his lips to the surface and began to drink, I counted the swallows going down his esophagus. Good drinker he was, but I wouldn't founder him by letting him have too much water.

One, two, three, four, five, six – one liter, two, three, four, five –

Prince flung up his head and spun around, every muscle tense as he tested the air. A little brown Arabian sporting four white socks with an older woman aboard planted her feet and whinnied shrilly to Prince. The filly backed up a few steps, but her rider kicked her on and pushed her forward.

"Is she on heat?" I called to the woman and took a firmer grip on Prince's reins.

"Yes, she is," she said.

"This is a stallion. Could you please take her around to the other side, or wait? We'll be done in a moment."

The woman glared at me and jerked the filly hard to the left, and around toward the other side of the trough, but the filly began backing again, then stopped, spread her hind legs, and urinated in little squirts.

Prince's throaty stallion whicker vibrated through his whole body, and out to my legs, but he remained obedient to the reins.

The woman prodded her forward again, this time toward the trough and us, snarling at her horse and, I suspect, at me. The filly stepped forward, then leapt into the trough with both forefeet to get to Prince, whinnying at the top of her lungs as the woman started to shriek.

I backed Prince away, which didn't impress him. He stuffed his head down to buck, but I managed to drive him on, pushing him hard to the right, away from the floundering filly. When we reached the edge of the clearing, I glanced back at the ruckus to make sure they were okay.

The rider had dismounted and tugged the filly out of the plastic trough. Thankfully, I saw no flashes of red on her white stockings.

"Stallions and people who ride them shouldn't be in races," she ranted, at full noise.

Funny, she hadn't added in-heat mares to her list.

"Sorry," I called, just for good measure, and we bolted.

"Good boy, Prince," I said, shakily, and patted his neck. That could've ended badly. If Prince were any less well-behaved... it mightn't have been pretty at all.

Soon we were into the first vet check, and Blake was beside me in an instant, gripping my leg. I slid from Prince's saddle and handed him to Marcus to walk cool. Blake wasn't impressed when I gave him the lowdown on Gareth and on the lady at the trough.

"That man needs to be reported." He didn't even mention the trough incident. Clearly, it was a lesser concern.

"He's evil, Blake. Let's see if we can get through this without a direct confrontation," I begged.

"Thankfully, he's not at this check. He'll be at the next one, though. We'll stick close, never you worry, darlin'."

Prince passed through the check with flying colors when his hold time was up and we were away again.

As I had been from the start of the race, I hopped off and ran the downhills to save Prince's legs. It was easy for me and would probably make a big difference to him over time. It *was* a beautiful day, and I wasn't about to let that creep Gareth destroy it for me, no matter how hard he tried.

With the morning's progress, the temperature rose. It was going to be a scorcher. I kept hydrated from my water bottles and Prince drank from every small spring we passed.

At the second vet check, Blake and Marcus flanked me as Gareth checked Prince's vitals. The vet scowled and gritted his teeth, but he couldn't find fault with the horse beneath his stethoscope, even if he didn't like the rider. He looked at Prince doubtfully, but by his recovery, he had no real excuse to pull him.

With a kiss of Blake's lips, I mounted up again and was walking toward the exit gate when I glanced in Gareth's direction just in time to see the filthy look Gareth flung in Blake's direction. I expected that. It wasn't a surprise.

What *did* bother me, though, was the grin of malicious delight that followed, as he continued to look at Blake.

Not a good sign.

I nearly lost my seat when Prince was bumped from behind. He leapt forward and spun toward whatever had just hit him. A flash of brown and white and the heavy thud of two hind hooves meeting flesh, and my world exploded in a flash of pain.

Through a blur of tears, I pulled Prince back and away from the direction of whatever horse had just blasted us and glanced up to see the brown Arab filly. Again. I swore a blue streak at shriek level and reached down to grip my ankle. Her silly owner, red-faced, had just caught up the horse's leadrope. She tugged for all she was worth while the filly pulled to get away and back to Prince.

"Get that filly out of here, you idiot," Blake yelled at her as he raced toward me, his face stormy. "Holy crap, Lena, are you okay?" He made it to my side in seconds and pulled me out of the saddle, ribs or no ribs.

I didn't trust my voice to do anything but swear some more, so I only nodded.

"Is that the cow with the filly from the trough?" he demanded.

"Yes," I spat, with a glare in her direction.

"Marcus, can you pick her up and take her back to the truck? I'll take the horse and go get some ice," Blake said, and added his own string of curses.

"I'll be okay," I said, as I tried to put weight on the leg, and quickly jerked it off the ground.

Blake frowned at me. "You're done. I heard that kick. You'll be a toast by the next check. I'll be right back. You're done," he repeated, and hurried on ahead.

Marcus picked me up like a small sack of—breakable—potatoes and made his way back to the truck.

"Marcus, can you get me the bandages in the tack box?" I said softly in to his ear, wincing as my bad ankle bumped into the other one. "And a bigger boot? There's a pair in the camper."

He turned his head to me. "What do you have in mind?"

"I'm going on."

"Can I watch?" he whispered dryly. "Blake won't take it sitting down."

"I'll be fine. I'll wrap it up snugly and it'll be okay. I'm sure it's not broken."

"And how, miss vet, do you know that?"

"When I move it around, there's no *crepitus*."

"In English."

"It doesn't crunch and gronch."

He shuddered.

"Will you help me? I probably could use something rigid, like a bit of flat wood? Two pieces?"

"He's not going to let you."

"If it's bandaged before he gets back, he will."

"Your funeral, girl."

Marcus stalked off, shaking his head, but he found what I needed. I had the already grossly swollen and blue-green tinged ankle wrapped up with elastic sticky bandage, sticks cunningly padded and wrapped in place, long before Blake returned with the ice.

I stood and put some weight on the contraption.

"If you get any whiter, you'll pass out," Marcus observed. "Here he comes."

"What are you doing on that leg? Sit down and put it up," Blake growled as he reached us.

"It's okay. Just bruised. I've wrapped it up and I'm ready to go on. I don't have much time." I glanced at my watch. "I was supposed to leave two minutes ago." I bent to pull my tights down over the bandage and strap on the half-chaps, grateful I was riding in them, rather than breeches.

"You can't be serious," Blake said with a frown.

"I've had worse. I can live with it." I bit my lips together. And the anti-inflammatories I'd just tossed back should kick in soon, too.

"I heard that impact. Prince is okay, thankfully, but—"

"I'm okay to go, really. Look, I'll even tape that ice onto it," I said, as I reached for it.

Blake stood glaring. "You can't possibly ride like that."

"I can. Please? We're late already."

He shook his head and looked at me doubtfully. "If you really think it's okay…"

"I do. Can you give me a lift please? This leg's a bit heavy." A grin cracked through my tight lips.

"I really don't feel good—"

"I'll be fine. Kiss me so we can get out of here," I said. His lips, tight, met mine, and I spun the horse around and we headed off at a trot, watching all around for wayward fillies.

It wasn't long before I had to drop my stirrups and flip them over Prince's withers. Like just around the corner from the vet check, out of Blake's sight. There'd be no running the downhills for me for the rest of this race. Trotting wasn't a good option, either. For all my assurances, I had no idea if there was a fracture. I just knew I had to finish this race… for my Nonna. She didn't get to finish her big race… and would never have the chance again.

Ever.

Twenty

The day just got hotter and hotter.

"I'm worried about Lena," Blake said, to Marcus, as he wiped the sweat from his brow. "Not only can she barely walk, and that's bad news if something more happens out on the trail, but that guy's cruisin' for a bruisin', messing with her like that."

Marcus gave him a wry grin. "And you're not the one who's going to give it to him. Lena'll have to do that herself."

Blake glared at his friend. "She's in no way big enough, and she's hurt."

"She has another way to do it. One we can't touch."

Blake took the deepest breath he could without screaming in pain and turned back toward the gap in the trees through which the horses would come. "They're sitting on third place. I wonder if she knows?"

"I doubt it. She's just focused on taking care of your horse." Marcus smiled. "She's a good girl, that."

"Don't I know it," Blake murmured and frowned at the leadrope he held in his hands.

"What's the matter?"

"You know about Jana, right?"

Marcus nodded.

"I can't let it go."

"Let what go?"

"Believing it's not going to happen again. And I'm driving Lena crazy with it."

"Is she messing around on you?"

"No," he said, and closed his eyes. When he opened them, Marcus was frowning.

"Then what's the problem?" Marcus said, his brows nearly touching.

"I can't seem to get over it and trust her. But soon it'll be okay. She'll be down here, and I won't have anything to worry about."

The chopper pilot was silent. When Blake turned to face him, Marcus was slowly shaking his head at him, incredulity in his eyes.

"What?" Blake demanded.

"Location makes no difference."

"Of course, it does," Blake said, glaring.

"Did it make a difference last time?"

Blake barely heard the whispered question from his friend, but he pretended he hadn't. It would be fine.

It had to be.

"Are we all ready for Lena to come in?" he asked Marcus. "I feel useless, not even able to carry buckets."

"That's what I'm here for, remember?"

He nodded. "Thanks for listening. I'll get through it, and it'll all be a —"

"Number thirteen!" the gatekeeper shouted.

They spun toward the gate to see Lena trot in.

"How's the leg?" Blake asked, as he reached out to pull her from the saddle and winced even before his hands got to her waist. He gritted his teeth and stepped closer.

"Blake, I can get down myself, you're going to hurt your —"

"Let me help," Marcus said, stepping closer.

"It's not gonna kill me." Blake ignored Marcus. "But watching you hit the ground and scream might," he growled and wrapped his arms around my waist.

"Blake, let Marc —" Lena snapped, as Blake, not as gently as he might have, tugged.

She bit back the scream as her ankle dragged over Prince's saddle and Blake swore as Lena clawed the heck out of his arm with her fingernails, and probably wrecked what was left of his ribs, but she was finally down on *terra firma*.

They both glanced back at Marcus.

The chopper pilot stood, one brow raised and mustache quirked to one side. He raised his hands. "I'm not sayin' anything. You clearly have it all under control." He chuckled and turned to walk Prince away for a drink.

Lena and Blake looked at each other.

"Sorry," they both said at the same time, and both winced their way back to the trailer.

"It's tough, trotting this far without stirrups, I let him lope as much as he felt like," Lena said, swallowing hard. "This horse is magic, though."

Prince pushed his nose against Marcus, who gave him a scratch while he drank. The stallion munched a few mouthfuls of hay while Lena had a drink of water and a snack bar.

"You can't go on like this," Blake said past gritted teeth.

She ignored him. "There's plenty of water out there," Lena said as Blake checked Prince's membranes and pulled the skin over the point of his shoulder. "He's drinking well at every chance and he's still nibbling any grass or bushes within reach. He's the best endurance horse I've ever ridden."

Blake looked at her. "He looks fantastic, but you don't."

"It's probably all the dirt." She gave him a cheeky grin.

Blake sighed. She wasn't going to give an inch. "Prince's probably glad not to have to lug me around. I'm sure I've got fifty pounds on you," he said, "stirrups or no stirrups." He ducked down beside her. "Lena, I'm serious. If that leg's broken—"

"It's not broken. I can stand on it."

"If it were a spiral fracture, you might still be able to."

"But I'm okay."

"Why are you so dead set on staying in the race? There'll be other races, but if you wreck that ankle now, you might not *get* to do them later."

She looked at him, her jaw set in frustration and tears in her eyes. *Whoa. What have we here?*

"Remember," she whispered, "when I told you about my grandma? The one who was training, but didn't get to do that Tevis because she was so sick from cancer?"

Blake gripped her hand tightly and nodded.

"Well, this is for her. After I was kicked, and I thought I'd quit, I realized I couldn't. This is for Nonna."

"She wouldn't want you to go through this much pain."

"This is for *her*. Unless you pull the horse, I'm going through with it," she said, through clenched jaws.

"Well then," Blake said, "guess you're goin' on."

Marcus came over, probably seeing we'd stopped growling at each other.

"Should we tell her, or should we make her wait?" Marcus grinned at Blake.

He took a deep breath and glared at Marcus.

Lena brushed at her leaky eyes and frowned. "Tell me what?" She looked from one to the other.

"You're holding third place," Blake muttered, "but it's not worth risking yourself for."

Her eyes bugged. "*Really*?" She struggled to her feet and threw her arms around Prince's neck. "I knew you were magic," she mumbled into his long mane.

"Now just because you're placing, don't go gettin' cocky, just *try* to take care of yourself and your horse and... I hope everything'll be fine." Blake tried to smile, but he was past it. All he could do was roll his eyes and clamp his jaws together.

Letting go of the horse, Lena held Blake by the shoulders and kissed him. "Good thing I can hug the horse. You'd be screaming if I tried to hug you," she said, as she slipped the girth and started to slide Prince's saddle off. "Really, Blake, I'll be okay," she murmured at him as he took her hands off the saddle and removed it himself.

Blake fed her while Marcus walked Prince, and then they were back in the vet box with Dr. Latimer. Marcus ran beside Prince for the trot-out, and soon Prince and Lena were trotting out of the rest stop.

She was worth getting a few things sorted in his head... if they both lived through this race.

He'd do it.

He had no other choice.

"Woo hoo!" Lena shrieked, as she passed the finish line! "We did it, Prince!"

"You sure did, honey," said the woman taking her number and her rider card. "Well done. You just go on over there and the P & R team will write down your numbers."

"Thank you," she called back.

"Congratulations, Lena," Blake said, held his breath, gritted his teeth, and hugged her, then let his breath out slowly. Despite her excitement, Lena's face was white as a sheet.

"Thank you so much for letting me ride him. He's a gem," she said as Marcus helped her off again. He buckled his halter around Prince's neck and slipped his bridle off, while Lena reached for the carrot Marcus held out to her.

"Congratulations, girl! You took good care of that horse. He looks like a million bucks," Marcus said.

Prince bit the carrot and munched contentedly, then took the rest of it and played with it in his water bucket.

"We passed someone," Lena said excitedly, as she hopped a few steps to hand Prince's bridle to Blake.

"You sure did. You're second."

Lena gazed between him and the horse with stars in her eyes. "I just can't believe it. What a horse. I'm sure you'll get tired of me saying that for the next few days." She grinned.

"Never. He *is* that good. Now let's go get him ready for the post-ride check."

With another hug around the stallion's neck, Lena led him away to nibble grass and cool down. Blake handed her a stethoscope and she checked him.

"He's coming right down and his color's great. Not a lick of dehydration."

"Proud of you, girl," Blake said as he took her hand and walked along with her, "but you need to get off that leg. The horse looks great, but you" — he glanced down to see her grimace — "look like crap." He kept Lena turned toward him, so she never saw

Barnett-Payne walking toward them. Over her shoulder, Blake challenged the creep with his best stare. The vet must have decided he didn't really want to torture her… not just yet.

Soon, their time was up, and they headed for the vet check.

"Thank you, again, Blake, for everything," Lena said, her eyes aglow. He squeezed her hand and let her and the stallion go, her limping, but him looking fantastic, off into the taped-off post-ride control vet check.

An official asked Lena her name and glanced at her watch, then noted something on her clipboard. She indicated where Lena and Prince were to wait then moved on to the next horse.

Blake turned his attention to the first-place horse, currently being examined by the vets. Two members of the P & R team were walking away from the horse toward the vets, frowning. Even from here, Blake could see the gray was lame at a walk in one foreleg. There were hard, gaunt lines over his flanks and rump and his coat was staring. Even when he stood still, he appeared a little unsteady on his feet. When he trotted out, his head bobbed over his left fore. Blake bit his lip and shook his head.

"What's going on?" Marcus murmured.

"That rider's not in a good position. AERC's motto is 'To Finish is to Win'. The corollary of that is that unless a horse is deemed 'ready to go on', it isn't a finisher, much less a winner."

"Oh. How disappointing for him. I suspect he went too fast to try to win."

"I wasn't out on the trail, so I can't comment, but it's a possibility."

They watched as the vets both took turns listening to his heart and lungs, then they stepped away to confer. The P & R team joined them.

"Not fit to continue," Dr. Latimer called out to the official, whose brows narrowed as she wrote on her clipboard. "Disqualified."

The P & R team approached Lena and Prince and started taking his vitals. They'd just turned to their secretary when Gareth interrupted them and seemed to take over. They watched the vet glare at the team and they slowly backed off, while he turned back to Prince and started examining the horse.

"What about the P & R team?" Marcus turned to Blake with a frown.

"I don't know. I don't like the look of this." Blake swore beneath his breath.

Lena said something to Gareth and her face blanched even whiter than it already was, as white as Blake's knuckles on the fence rail.

"The bastard. I'm going to help her."

"No, you aren't," Marcus growled low. "She can handle it."

"No, she can't," Blake muttered. "You should have seen her before. She can't handle him, and she can barely walk on that blasted leg. You've never even been to an endurance race."

"I'm here to help you both," Marcus said, past clenched teeth.

"I'm going in to—"

Marcus grabbed his arm, just as he was about to climb over the fence. "I may not have been to an endurance race, but I know how competitions work. Leave it. You'll just get her disqualified," he hissed. "Back off and let her handle it."

My heart sank for the rider at the announcement disqualifying the previously-winning pair, but tingles started up in my spine, just the same.

The P & R team came over to us and one counted Prince's respiratory rate while another placed her stethoscope against Prince's chest to listen to his heart. They'd counted, and one had opened his mouth to give the secretary his results, when Gareth walked up with a smarmy look on his face. I glanced up to see Doc Latimer walking away toward the other end of the trot-up area, and my guts knotted up.

"I'll take over here, thanks," he said, and took my rider card from the secretary, who frowned.

She stood there, as did the P & R pair, but he gave them a cold smile and turned his back.

"He's looking pretty tired," Gareth said casually, when they were all out of earshot. "Doesn't look fit to go on."

Prince snorted at him and backed up, ears laid back. The horse never forgot an attitude.

"The P & R team didn't get a chance to record Prince's parameters," I said.

"That's okay. I'll do it. I have time."

The world began to spin around me, but I gritted my teeth and forced myself to stay focused.

This isn't about me.

I took a deep breath and held it, and my ground.

He's like this with all women.

"This horse is fine." My voice sounded loud to my ears and the crowd hushed. "I had to hold him in for the past mile because he knew he was coming into the finish." I shifted my weight off of my bad ankle, hoping no one would see it.

"I don't know," Gareth, shaking his head.

With some hesitation, he stepped up to the horse's shoulder and placed his stethoscope against the Prince's girth.

I ran my fingers up to the stallion's jugular and counted while he listened to his stethoscope.

Under forty-eight beats per minute.

No way was he going to pull this horse.

"His heart rate is still pretty high. He's not fit to go on and I'm going to pull him," Gareth said, with that awful look I knew so well. His "control look".

"Look, Gareth, we went to the same veterinary school." I spoke softly, but he flinched at the edge of steel I managed to put into it. "Since when does a heart rate of fifty-six equate to 'over sixty-four'?"

He glared at me. "I don't see a stethoscope on you."

"Who needs a stethoscope? Any untrained person can count a pulse," I said, then added, more softly. "Your personal life has nothing to do with this horse's fitness. Please let it go."

He spun and stomped away toward his truck.

I turned to Doc Latimer, who looked from Gareth to me, and back again, with a frown marring his face. I motioned to him to come to me, while I chewed at my lip.

"Now look, Lena, I don't know what you said to him, but the control judges are the last word on this ride, you know that. I'm sorry, but the fact you're nearly through vet school doesn't hold any water here."

I *Twenty-One*

took a deep breath before answering the head vet. "Doc Latimer, I understand your position, but would you please check Prince's heart rate and tell me what it is?"

"Hasn't Gareth already done that, and the P & R team?"

I gritted my teeth. "He disregarded the P & R team and made them go away after they'd assessed Prince. Then he took my card away from them." I took a deep breath to steady myself. "I'm counting fifty-six. Gareth is counting it as 'over' and wants to disqualify me, though he didn't say what heart rate he'd actually counted." I gulped.

His frown deepened. "Now why would he do a thing like that? That's crazy talk, Lena."

I shuddered. I'd have to say it. "We, unfortunately, have a history... and not a salubrious one, at that."

The vet's visage softened, and he let out a breath.

And counted.

"Fifty-four." His eyes narrowed at me. "You're telling me the truth?"

I nodded. "Never been more truthful," I murmured.

Doc Latimer set his jaw and turned toward Barnett-Payne.

We all watched Gareth as he returned from his vehicle, his face thunderous.

Doc Latimer turned toward him and headed his way, then stopped and returned to Prince. He listened to his heart and lungs and noted the parameters to his secretary. "Can you trot him?"

I bit my lip. "Does the rider have to be 'able to go on' for us to complete the race?"

His mustache quirked. "Nope." He turned toward the P & R team which had just left me. "Jeff? Can I see you for a moment please?"

One young man from the P & R team came at a run.

"Jeff, can you please trot him out for us? Lena's had a bit of an injury."

"No problem, Doc," he said, and smiled at me as he took Prince's lead.

"Jeff's shown Arab stallions. Prince won't give him any trouble," he said, in response to my worried look. "You go get off that leg," he whispered.

I took a few steps away, but I wasn't going far. Jeff trotted him, turned him on his hind end, then tried to trot him straight back, but he was so full of himself that he bucked and bounced all the way back to the vet, or vets, now. Jeff came toward me with the stallion as I watched Gareth, who stood beside Doc Latimer not saying much, his jaw clenched.

As the vets began to converse again, Gareth's face grew redder and redder, then he turned away completely.

"SOUND," Doc Latimer barked, with a huge smile. "Congratulations to our new first-place winners, Prince Witeż and Lena Scott!"

From force of habit, I couldn't help watching Gareth from the corners of my eyes. He flinched as the crowd erupted and his whole body went rigid.

I dragged my attention away from him and limped Prince back toward the truck, amidst congratulations from all around. Blake made his way to my side, took Prince's lead, and kissed me, while Prince nudged at his back.

"Well done, Lena! I'm so proud of you. Not only for the ride, but especially for standing up for yourself to him." He flicked a glance in Gareth's direction. "I thought I needed to save you, but you and Marcus proved me wrong." He pulled me against him to take some pressure off my bad leg, while somehow managing his ribs. "You can thank Marcus for keeping me on the other side of the fence."

I smiled at the beaming Marcus and returned my attention to Blake. "It's true," I said. "I couldn't have done it before. I guess I'm stronger than I was. Certainly, stronger than I thought."

"Now let's go pretty up this horse," Blake said, and kissed me again.

An hour later, a crowd had assembled for the Best Condition trot-out and Prince and Marcus led the parade around the fenced-off area.

"That horse looks the same as he did before the race this morning," I heard one woman say to another as I stood behind the tape with Blake. "And that vet tried to pull him. No accounting for taste."

I smiled and looked up at Blake. The woman was right. Prince looked so ready to go on. "Pity about the rider," I mumbled into Blake's shirt, and he chuckled and held me snugly against his side.

My heart pounded as they worked their way through the lineup from tenth place toward us, both vets examining, and then watching the horse trot away and back. Finally, it was Prince's turn. Prince nuzzled Doc Latimer but kept one wary eye upon Gareth whenever he was near.

"I hope Marcus can keep him from biting or kicking Gareth. He tried, you know."

Blake's brows narrowed. "That'd be a disaster."

The vets examined him thoroughly, listened to his heart and lungs twice, and then went away to confer. I squeezed Blake's hand and nodded at the three P & R team members whom Gareth had sent away from Prince and me. As one, they stalked over to the vets and Doc Latimer turned to talk with them, while Gareth's face turned stony. The trio soon retreated, and the vets resumed their discussion.

A ripple of sound spread through the assembled spectators as the two vets, voices raised, conferred back and forth. They eventually returned, both grim-faced, and handed their clipboards to the ride manager.

"Well, that's us," Blake said, one arm over Prince's back as he led him back to the trailer. "We couldn't have made him look any better than he already does."

"Thank you both for crewing today. It's a big job, lugging

everything around from one stop to the next. I appreciate it from the bottom of my heart," I said after we'd put Prince into his pen. I hopped over to pick up a rubber grooming mitt to give the stallion an extra scratch.

"No problem," the guys both said, smiling at me, as Marcus took the mitt and Blake placed me in one chair and put my leg up onto another one. I had to be the luckiest girl in the world. The horse, the man… life was good.

"Congratulations again, Lena," Blake said, as they curled up together on his big bed in the top of the camper for a rest while they waited for the awards ceremony. "Despite neglecting yourself" — he frowned at her — "you took good care of the horse."

"Mmmm…" she murmured, nearly asleep. "Thank you again, but you know what?"

"What?" he dropped a kiss on the top of her head, probably one of the only places that didn't hurt.

"Remember when I thought you were a softie for having a camper?"

"Mmmm?"

"Well," she mumbled, "it's okay. Camping like this would be fine with m…"

Blake smiled. Tucking her arm beneath the covers, he pulled her against him and let sleep claim him, too.

Despite the anti-inflammatories and the nap, my ankle was worse by the time the Best Condition award was to be announced.

"I wish I could carry you, Lena," Blake said, frowning.

"Well, you can't," I said. "And Marcus has been dragging buckets for me all day. I can walk a few hundred feet." I smiled at them both.

Half an hour into the ceremony, I was called up for First Prize.

"I feel like a little kid," I said with a grin, showing Blake and

Marcus the trophy.

"You earned it, sweetie," Blake said, with a smile.

The air hummed with excitement as the Best Condition prize was announced.

"And for our last prize of the day, a prize I value more than even First Place," said Doc Latimer, "because this is the prize for the person who has trained their horse carefully and taken the best care of their horse during the ride. Today I'm pleased to present this to a team who's been plagued with injuries but has done what it took to make it happen."

Blake looked over at me and my face heated.

"This horse was to be ridden by its owner, who broke his ribs three days ago, so his partner, who'd never even been on him, took the ride."

Now I was grinning fit to split. Blake squeezed my hand so hard I thought he'd break it.

"And today, after she was kicked by an on-heat mare who'd taken aim at the stallion, she bandaged her leg up and rode the rest of the race without stirrups. And still took fantastic care of this horse. If this team doesn't deserve this award today, I don't know who does."

The crowd was on its feet, facing us and applauding.

"Best Condition goes to," Doc Latimer shouted over the crowd, "our first-place winners, Lena Scott and Prince Witeż!"

Blake, wincing, gave me a big hug, then released me so I could go up front to pick up my, or rather, *our* trophy, and a hug from Doc Latimer.

Gareth was nowhere to be seen.

"Let's load up and get you to the hospital," Blake said, and drew me to my feet after the last of the riders and crews had offered their congratulations and headed for their own trucks.

"I'm okay. We need to get Prince home and bandaged, then we can go.

Blake stared at me in stony silence. "Hospital."

"Horse."

"Lena, how *about*" — Blake glared at me — "I take you to the hospital, leave you there to get X-rayed, then *I'll* take him home, get him bandaged, then come back to get you."

I sighed. I was too tired to argue anymore. "Okay," I said, and we packed up, or rather, the men packed up after they managed to get me to sit down and put my leg up.

Somehow there was no one else waiting to see the doctor at the emergency room, so Blake stayed outside to keep an eye on Prince while I saw the doctor and had my ankle X-rayed. The doctor spoke soothingly about sprains, keeping my leg elevated, and staying off it for several days.

"And please get it re-checked in a few weeks to make sure there aren't any spiral or other undisplaced fractures."

"I can do that, thank you, Doctor Parker," I said.

"I'm still astonished at how swollen it is, for not being fractured," he murmured, looking sideways at me as he held open the front door.

I smiled at him and waved as I kept walking.

"He was surprised at the amount of swelling," I said to Blake, as he helped me into the truck.

"I'm so glad it's not broken. I'd feel even worse for letting you go on with it." Blake sighed. "And I'd imagine you didn't tell him just why there was so much swelling."

"Well," I winced, "no, but it'd have been worse if I hadn't bandaged it."

Blake pursed his lips and shook his head. "I'm glad you're okay, anyway, you little minx."

Blake padded the dashboard with some towels. "Here, you settle back and get comfortable. I'm sure you could use some shut-eye, after the day you've had."

I must have dozed, and when I looked up, Blake glanced

across at me and took my hand in his. I smiled lazily at him across the cab. "If I feel this stiff, I can't imagine what Prince feels like, but it's worth it. That was a fantastic—"

Blake hit the brakes as he glanced in the rear-view mirror and I struggled toward an upright position as he eased the camper and trailer off the side of the road on a sharp corner in the four-lane highway. "Pray no one hits us. I'll get some flares," he said.

"What is it?" I sat up and my mouth dropped open at the sight of the piled-up carnage spread out in the road ahead.

"Accident." Blake's jaw was set and his face pale. "I'm not going to park any closer. Let's go. If you can, grab some blankets from the camper, and don't get hit," he barked.

I slid down from the truck just as he flicked the seat back forward and scrabbled behind it, then limped to the camper, climbed in, and dragged out the bedding.

Blake had lit a flare and set it on the road. He handed the rest to another motorist then grabbed most of my bundle and my hand, and I hopped beside him at a run for the disaster.

We split up, calling out to the people in the cars, but few answered. Those who did were already screaming. I nearly screamed myself at the pools of blood and body parts scattered on the pavement. We gave wide berth to several cars, already fiery infernos—nothing we could do to help there. The wreckage, the screams, the reek of burning rubber, and the pervasive metallic scent of blood. We struggled to pull people from their cars without damaging them further and get them away from the vehicles, vehicles in danger of catching fire along with the others, and hand them over to others who'd stopped to help.

"Has anyone gone to find a phone?" Blake shouted over the fracas. "Has an ambulance been called?

"I've radioed for help on my CB," one man shouted, as he passed, a crying, bloody child in his arms.

The night seemed to go on forever, out on this lonely stretch of twisting road.

I couldn't find any more people to pull from the non-burning cars. My throat ached, my ankle throbbed, and my eyes burned. The smell of burning plastic and the coppery scent of blood was almost unbearable. I turned to find Blake, but he wasn't there. I limped from one end of the crash site to the other, but he was nowhere to be seen. Trying desperately to stem my panic, I realized I couldn't actually remember the last time I'd seen him.

"Blake?" I said. "Blake!" Now I struggled to move from person to person, asking if they'd seen him. My heart constricted in my chest and I couldn't think straight as I hopped at a run, calling his name.

Where could he be? He wouldn't have tried going into a burning car?

I wasn't far from hysteria now, and then I remembered Prince, all alone in the trailer, with the smells, the sounds. I bolted for Blake's truck as the scream of sirens came closer, and flashing lights heralded the arrival of the fire trucks and ambulances. I stopped when I got to the trailer to get my breath and some sort of calmness, then spoke softly to Prince through the side door. At the continued silence, I peeked inside. Standing like a rock, his nose against Blake's face, the stallion stood guard, his ears laid flat back and nostrils flaring with every breath.

Twenty-Two

Blake was curled up in a fetal position in front of the horse's forelegs, shaking and mumbling.

"Prince, will you let me come in?"

The stallion's ears slowly slid forward and he reached his muzzle toward me and whuffled softly as I climbed in, my ankle screaming with the effort.

I stroked his muzzle and he lipped at my fingers and I inched toward Blake. I slowly reached a hand toward Blake's shoulder, then froze, remembering Mark and the chopper. Backing up a step, I softly called out his name. He flinched, then took a breath.

"Blake, are you okay?" A little louder.

He nodded briefly, then reached a hand out to me. I took it and gripped it for all I was worth, dropped carefully to my knees and wrapped my arms around him while Prince nuzzled my hair.

"Can you tell me?" I whispered.

He shook his head, silent.

"What is it?"

"Too many memories." He shivered.

"About what?"

"Like I told you before, you'd never understand."

"I love you. Try me."

He remained motionless for long moments. "Okay, okay, I'll tell you."

I squeezed him tight, but he straightened up and I released him. His voice was soft, nearly inaudible, and cracked as he spoke.

"I was in Nam too, like Mark... but I flew soldiers from the

USA to Viet Nam and back with Pan Am. Many, many trips. We flew soldiers from there to R&R over the next many years—to Australia, the islands… you name it. We flew them, these men, boys, to their deaths. We flew some there and brought only some back… some in"—he swallowed hard—"in bags, or covered with bandages over missing body parts, missing minds, missing sanity. What would they suffer for the rest of their lives?" He stopped and took a deep breath. "We thought we were picking up soldiers. The girls, the stewardesses, they were shocked… at the bags and the injured men, but they talked with them." He looked up at me, almost pleading. "They held their hands, gave them the love they needed so badly. For crying out loud, they were only kids…"

He broke down and I clung to him, trying not to bump his ribs.

"They were only kids," he began again, "fighting for what? In an unpopular war…. we flew men there, hundreds at a time, and half of them were dead by the time they got back… if they went home at all."

"You did what you could," I tried again.

He went on like he hadn't heard me. "I was flying on that mercy mission Mark told us about at the ride, you know"—he glanced up at me for a moment then dropped his eyes again—"when I met you. We flew one last trip in after the airports were closed, no tower, crashed planes on the runway, you name it… to rescue the airlines' personnel from Saigon. Pan Am had promised, so along with a few volunteer air hostesses, wonderful girls… we did it."

I hugged him closer.

"But the futility… the futility of the struggle, and afterward, what did those boys, the ones who got to come home, what did they come home to? After that war, there was no respect for being one of the ones left living. Hell, it makes no sense, no sense…" His voice faded off and he lay limp in my arms, finally out of fuel.

I held him for long minutes, trying to breathe my soul into him to comfort him.

I needed to get him and the horse home.

"The ambulances are here, Blake," I whispered into his hair.

He took a deep breath and picked up his head with a wince.

The emergency services vehicles were everywhere. He struggled to a sitting position and leaned back against the wall of the trailer. Together we watched out the trailer side door as the firemen and EMTs did their jobs, and the volunteer motorists slowly filtered out, amidst thanks from the firemen. The screams quieted down to nothing as the traffic began to pass them, slowly resuming its dull roar.

Prince shuffled his feet a little, but otherwise never moved as we finished talking, wrapped in each other's arms.

Blake blinked. "We've got to go. You'll miss your plane."

"My plane." I stared at him. "If you think I'm leaving you at a time like this, you've got another think coming. I'll get another flight."

"But—"

"No buts about it," I said, and let him painfully turn over onto all fours and stand, holding onto my hands.

We both wrapped our arms around the stallion's neck for a moment and climbed out.

"Oh my god, the place looks like a battlefield," Blake whispered and hunched up again, hugging his arms tightly to his body as a tow truck drove past us and stopped.

"Come on," I said, and walked him forward to the truck.

"What are you doing?" he said, looking at me with blank eyes as I handed him into the passenger seat of his own truck.

"I'm driving," I said. When I hopped into the other side, I added, "And you"—I pulled him over into the middle and strapped him in—"are going to sleep on my lap."

It didn't take long.

The house was lit up like a Christmas tree when we drove up the driveway. Myrtle appeared in the open doorway, while Prince's muffled and Tessa's shrill neighs filled the night.

"I heard you guys won, but where have you been? I was starting to get worried! Everyone else drove past with their trailers hours ago." The dogs scurried around our feet for a few minutes, then went off to look for rats in the barn.

"Thanks. Long story, Myrtle," I whispered. "Can you get him into bed? I've got to get Prince out and bandage him, then I'll be up, too."

Blake lifted his head. "I'm helping with the horse." His voice was hoarse. "You're in no condition—"

"Neither are you," I retorted.

"We'll do it together," he said, and I didn't have the strength to argue. My leg was throbbing again.

"Why are you limping?" Myrtle peered at my face in the dimness.

"That's a long story, too," I said.

Myrtle shook her head. "Everybody's been fed, and I'll draw you both a bath," she said. Turning on her heel, she headed back to the house. "Come on, dogs, back to bed," she called, and they followed, looking longingly back at the barn.

"Bless you," I said, meaning it with all my heart, as I hopped to the back of the trailer and unlatched Prince's ramp. I didn't think I could take dogs bouncing off my leg tonight. Blake and I got the stallion out of the trailer and led him to his dinner in the barn. Tessa raced into her stall from her attached pen and stood staring at us over her half-door.

"You have some under-quilts and track bandages, Blake?"

He nodded.

I eased myself on a low stool, my bad leg straight out alongside the stallion and, untwisted the cap on the liniment. My tongue curled at the alcoholic menthol fumes as I rubbed a few generous handfuls onto Prince's first leg.

I cringed at the sound of clanging cupboards and swearing from the tack room but it resulted in an armload of bandaging that Blake laid out on a makeshift table of hay bales beside me.

I bandaged one leg while Blake moved on to the next with the liniment, and soon we were somehow done with them all.

All the while, Prince never moved a hoof or picked up his head from his feed bucket. After greeting his mate, of course.

"He's a good horse," I said, after one last hug. "Thanks, Prince, and Blake."

Blake gave me the ghost of a smile as he wrapped an arm around me and helped me limp my way up to the house.

The answerphone was blinking red when we walked in.

"Your supper's on the table," Myrtle called from upstairs. "Let me know if I can do anything to help, otherwise, I'll hear your news in the morning. Good night."

I punched the button on the flashing machine as I took a bite of the steaming quiche Myrtle had left for us.

"This is a message for Lena Scott from the veterinary school. Lena, I called to tell you you've passed your Small Animal Medicine rotation and are on track to graduate on time. Enjoy your last few days of vacation. Goodbye."

My eyes met Blakes and he reached for me. I closed my eyes and sank onto his lap.

"Congratulations, girl," he whispered into my hair, "on all counts, today."

As if winning the race wasn't enough.

We shared our last bites of pastry with the dogs, wished them goodnight, and then I limped towards the stairs.

Blake sighed. "Wait for me," he said. "You have to be the most impatient little brat I've ever met," he murmured, as he kissed my lips and reached out his arms to pick me up and froze.

"With broken ribs?" I couldn't help a giggle as I shook my head.

"I was going to carry you up to bed, but—"

"Thanks for the thought. Next time, maybe?" I said, and we struggled up the stairs like a couple of oldies that smelled like they hadn't bathed in weeks and tried to cover it up with liniment.

Couldn't wait to get into that tub.

"And so, Raywyn," I said into the mouthpiece of the phone,

lazily lying back in a rocking chair on Blake's deck, my foot up on a box, "I wanted to thank you."

"For what? Just a sec," Ray said, and her muffled voice gave some go-home instructions on a blocked cat to the new technician. "Sorry, it's my lunch hour, but the Doc is out. Now, where were we? You wanted to thank me? For what?"

"Yes. If not for you, I wouldn't have ever met Blake."

"So, are you truly so happy?"

"I am, we are."

"And you don't think the age difference is… going to be a problem? Truly?"

"Nope. We're doing fine. Really. And he's supportive, mostly. He just misses me."

"And do you miss him?"

I was silent for a moment. "Sort of, but really, I only have time for school right now, and he understands that. We see each other when we can. That'll have to be enough for now."

"Well, if you're sure."

"I am."

"Okay, then you have my blessing. When's the wedding?"

"Sometime after I graduate, I think. We haven't planned it yet, but there won't be time until then."

"Well, I'll be there, holding your hand."

"Love ya, Ray."

"You too, Lena. You take care, okay? Congrats on the win with that stallion. I've got to go, but we'll speak soon, okay?"

"Bye, and thanks again."

The phone clicked in my ear.

It would all be okay. Jake plopped his head onto my lap and I patted him in the warm sunshine until I melted into sleep.

"Your jealousy, though, Blake, it makes me feel you don't trust me," I said the following night as we sat on the sheepskins before a roaring fire, my bad foot elevated on the sofa. "I've given you no reason to distrust me. We've talked of this so many times before…"

"I was afraid of losing you from my life." He fell silent for a few moments. "You remember wondering how I was content to just live a quiet life, content to sit on my porch with you and the dogs, no ambitions?"

Wincing, I looked him fully in the eyes and nodded.

"Think about last night," he said. "Really think about it for a second."

I closed my eyes and shivered, remembering the carnage… the carnage on the road, and in Blake's heart. I swallowed hard. "I think I begin to see," I finally murmured. "I'm sorry, Blake, I never saw it before. The 'what's important'. I've been struggling so long to succeed — to get into vet school, and now to get *back out* of vet school… I guess everything doesn't have to be full-on, every minute, to stay on track for my dreams… and life."

"It's taken me just as long to see you're not going to disappear." Blake took my hand. "When you've seen the things I have," he stared blankly out the window into the darkness, then turned back to me, "you're thankful for the life you've created and the special animals and people you've been given. Like you." He sat in silence for a moment. "I'm willing to give you the time and space you need to complete your lifelong dream, and I want to be there beside you to share the finis—"

At a knock upon the door, the dogs set up a cacophony as they raced toward it and flung themselves against the groaning wood.

"Whoever could it be at this hour?" I stared at Blake.

He climbed to his feet and grabbed Kelpie Anne's collar, then opened the door.

In the doorway stood Seth Latimer.

"Come on in, man, what are you doing out at this hour?"

"Thanks," Doc Latimer said, as he swept his hat off and hung it on the hatrack. He came over and sat down on the sofa across from me. "I saw your lights on and figured you were still awake."

"Like the welcoming committee would've let us sleep through that," I said dryly, then laughed.

Seth grinned at me. "I'm on my way home from a colic and wanted to see how that ankle was. I see you're behaving, Lena." He nodded approvingly at my raised foot.

"It's good, thanks. They said it was a sprain, but they want to x-ray it again in a few weeks to make sure there aren't any fractures. It's a little swollen."

With a growl beneath his breath, Seth said, "What a surprise, after riding with it like that for half of the ride, or so…"

"I took my feet out of my stirrups…" I twisted my lips and shrugged.

"Probably because you couldn't *ride* in stirrups, you cretin," Blake muttered.

"Well, it was splinted."

"What about elevated?"

"Children, children…" Seth said, "I also wanted to let you know I read the riot act to our good Dr. Barnett-Payne and put in a formal complaint to the Veterinary Medical Board. I told him, but it doesn't seem to register that it's not someone else's fault." He shook his head. "Never seen anything like it."

"He's a special one, all right," I mumbled. "I was a bit slow to learn his true nature."

"Good thing you figured it out," Seth said, nodding. "Anyway, I'm sorry for the difficulties he's caused and I wanted to congratulate you again on your win, but especially on your Best Condition award."

"Thanks," I said, "but it's Blake who conditioned that horse. It should by rights be his."

Seth stood, then faced me with a smile. "We really do need an equine vet up in this valley. Goodnight to you both," he said as he walked out the door into the chilly night.

After he closed the door behind the good doctor, Blake carefully lowered his sore body down to the sheepskins again, only wincing a little, and looked into my eyes. "I'd say, compared to the past two days, the chances of you and I making a serious go of it will be easy as pie."

I smiled at him and sniffed. "What's that smell?" I asked as the sickly-sweet scent of burning sugar invaded my nostrils. "Something's burning."

"Thought we both deserved something special." He winked at me. "While you were napping, I went to the bakery."

"Cherry pie!"

Blake's smile lit his whole face and I stretched up to kiss his lips, then he groaned as he pulled himself up to full height once again and headed off to save the pie.

Life would be good, together.

The End

Cottage Cheese Pancakes

Lena and I love both of these high protein, quick, healthy, and yummy pancakes.

You can make them with either rolled oats or flour.

Cottage Cheese Pancakes with Oats — GF*

2 large servings

7 large or 8 smaller eggs

1 c (250 g) cottage cheese

1 c (100 g) rolled oats, uncooked

or

Cottage Cheese Pancakes with Flour

  2 moderate servings

(double this for two hungry teenagers and you)

3 eggs

1 c (250 g) cottage cheese

2 T (30 ml) Oil

1/4 c (30 g) flour

Instructions for either recipe:

1- Break eggs into bowl or blender first, then add cottage cheese. Blend in a blender, food processor or with a stick blender. Alternately, whisk or beat them with a spoon.

2- Add the other ingredients and mix until smooth — as little or as much as you like.

3- Using about 1/4 c (60 ml) per pancake, fry in a hot pan or on the hot flat plate of a barbecue (we use our barbecue) with a little butter, oil, or drippings over a medium heat.

4- Turn when bubbles appear, then cook until both sides are

golden.

The pancakes from the first recipe stick together a bit better, in case that matters to you.

Serve with:

applesauce, cooked up fruit (great way to use up overripe fruit), fruit syrup, bananas, yogurt or sour cream, maple syrup, honey… you name it.

Our favorite here is to drop banana slices into the just-poured batter… and if mum isn't looking, the boys add chocolate chips.

Bon appétit!

*Oats themselves are gluten free but check the label in case gluten products are made on same equipment.

About the Author

Lizzi grew up riding wild in the Santa Cruz Mountain redwoods, became an equine veterinarian at UC Davis School of Veterinary Medicine, practiced in the California Pony Express and Gold Country before emigrating to New Zealand. When not writing, she's swinging a rapier or shooting a bow in medieval garb, riding, driving a carriage or playing on her farm, singing, or working as an equine veterinarian or science teacher. She is multiply published and awarded in special interest magazines and veterinary periodicals, and has served as secretary and as president of the Romance Writers of New Zealand.

Awards for her debut novel include: Finalist 2013 RWNZ Great Beginnings; Winner 2014 RWNZ Pacific Hearts Award; Winner 2015 RWNZ Koru Award for Best First Novel plus third in Koru Long Novel section; and finalist in the 2015 Best Indie Book Award.

Also by Lizzi Tremayne

The Long Trails Series

Lizzi Tremayne Sampler

In Plain Sight

Leigh Morgan

Dedication

For Ewa –
A woman of passion, strength,
and an inherent sweetness that
radiates into whomever
she meets.
Summer O'Hara is almost
as wonderful as you.

Prologue

2002, the Museon Museum of Science in the Netherlands is burgled while housing an exhibit showcasing several royal jewels valued over 7.4 million pounds. No alarms sounded during or after the theft. Shattered glass housing the jewels was the only damage done to the museum (not counting the theft). Local and international newspapers used the word "baffled" to describe the mindset and progress of the local authorities searching for jewel thief or thieves.

2003, over 62 million pounds (British pounds sterling) in diamonds is stolen from the Antwerp Diamond Center in Belgium. The Antwerp Diamond Center holds 160 underground vaults used to house diamonds. Of the 160 vaults, 123 were emptied. Although one man with mafia connections was arrested and convicted (based on circumstantial evidence) for the crime, the diamonds were never recovered.

2005, 73 million British pounds sterling worth of diamonds is stolen from a cargo truck on its way to the Schiphol Airport.

2008, the Damiani showroom in Milan is broken into by slowly drilling a hole into the shop basement from a basement next door that was under construction. Thieves, dressed as security, entered during a private showing. They walked away with over 12.4 million pounds sterling of gold and jewels.

2008, the Harry Winston store in Paris is robbed. This robbery, of over 68 million pounds sterling worth of jewelry, made headlines not just for the sheer volume of jewelry stolen, but because the men who robbed the store did so dressed as women. No arrests have been made.

Jack Smith—not the name given at his birth, nor the name he used for any of his previous incarnations which were many—retired from active jewel procurement a decade ago. By any measure, he was an unmitigated success. He'd never been detained. He'd never been questioned. And, most importantly, he'd never been suspected in any of the robberies or burglaries he'd committed.

No one suspected him. No one butted into his business. No one questioned who or what he pretended to be.

Jack's criminality had been ridiculously easy. Not the theft part. That had been hard. It required planning for every contingency while maintaining the flexibility to improvise. It took every skill in his metaphorical toolbox to pull off each and every job.

Every job—until the last one. That one he enjoyed. Dressing as a woman to commit robbery had its own appeal, but it was holding the terrified and trembling employees at gunpoint that stirred his soul in a way Jack hadn't thought possible.

He didn't want to kill anyone. Not really. But making someone tremble with the need for self-preservation was a uniquely heady experience. One that, had he let it, would become addictive. That kind of power filled him with heat.

Provocative. Arousing. It gave him the kind of high that bordered on invincibility.

That's why he quit the acquisitions end of the business. Aside from the fact that he'd acquired far more than he could spend in a lifetime, no one was invincible. No high was worth the inevitable loss of control it bred. Acquisitions was a young man's game, and he hadn't been young a decade ago when he'd done his last hands-on acquiring.

Acquiring was hard. Selling, or rather underselling, by contrast, was proving ridiculously easy.

Jack had spent years alternating between shops in Chicago and Door County selling his "replica" line of jewelry without so much as a whisper or a raised eyebrow. No one questioned who he was or the authenticity—strictly speaking, a lack-thereof—of his product.

No one questioned.

Until Summer O'Hara came back to town.

Summer O'Hara had seen something she wasn't supposed to see. She waltzed right into his Ephraim store one morning while he and his assistant were still doing setup. It was the first big tourist weekend, Memorial Day weekend, and he was still unloading from his Chicago shop.

He had one of the Harry Winston rings out, a small one by Chicago standards, but big enough to capture the notice of the Ephraim prodigal flower child who fashioned herself a jewelry expert. He'd meant the ring to stay packed until his client came to pick it up, but his assistant placed it in with the vintage rings for sale.

Amateurs—the bane of those in the know. That held true for both Summer O'Hara and his assistant who was still so eager to please.

Summer O'Hara asked to see the ring. She noticed the distinctive Harry Winston hallmark, and her pulse picked up a beat. She wasn't good at hiding her excitement, but then normal people didn't hide their excitement the way thieves and organized criminals learned, by necessity, to hide theirs.

Jack had to tell her that the ring (a three carat, D color, Internally Flawless, brilliant cut center flanked by two tapered baguettes totaling .30 carats) had already been sold to a customer who was due to pick it up that very day. It was just bad luck that his "customer" arrived in time to meet Summer.

Summer O'Hara got a good look, not only at Jack's client but her car—complete with Illinois plates. His client's car was parked in Jack's small car park in front of his small house-like shop. No way Summer could have missed it. It was the only car in the lot besides Jack's decade-old Porsche Boxer and Summer's late model sub-SUV.

Summer stayed in his shop, eavesdropping through the entire exchange while pretending to window shop as the cases were being set up. Once she looked at every partially completed case, Summer left. But not before taking another long glance at Jack's client.

That was strike one.

Strike two came three weeks later, the third week in June, when Summer again came into the shop when it opened, this time with one of her adult sons. Just like last time, Summer honed in on the case that housed the only stolen items in the store. His "replica" case.

The "replicas" included three original coins from the Atocha, each mounted as pendants in 24k yellow gold; an Art Deco Asscher cut 9.34-carat diamond engagement ring set in platinum with tapered bullet-cut diamonds totaling .40 carats that had been part of his safety deposit find; and a broach he'd made after taking the 60-carat vivid pink diamond, previously known as the "Flower of Scotland," from the tiara a Japanese billionaire had made for one of his daughters. Another of his safety deposit box finds from Antwerp's Diamond Center, the tiara housed colored diamonds of impeccable quality, ranging from 14 to 19 carats. His favorites included vivid yellow diamonds, more pink diamonds, a small blue diamond, and three green diamonds that appeared to change color due to their florescence.

The Asscher ring was from 1925. Jack knew that because he'd gotten rid of the dated inscription and the initials that accompanied it. He'd also eradicated the GIA certification number—no easy feat but one he had the expertise and the access to accomplish.

The 60-carat pink diamond Jack got as part of the same Antwerp job. He'd gotten far more than expected from that job, including the Atocha coins.

Jack took the Zoe Tiara apart, setting the center piece pink in a sterling silver broach. It galled him to put such a collector's gem—a gem that rivaled any collected by Graff or Winston—into anything but platinum, but he did it. The best place to hide something of potentially limitless value was to put it in plain sight. His clients loved that. It made them feel like they were flaunting theft and getting away with it.

The Art Deco diamond ring he placed in his *Immaculate Imposters* case. Most people wouldn't have raised a brow at the ring if they had reason to believe it wasn't real—it was rather gaudy in his opinion. Lovely in the way perfectly cut step cut diamonds are lovely, but gaudy. He'd seen many created diamonds, cubic zirconia and other diamond substitutes, made into rings this size. Not his preference, but then he'd rather steal diamonds than wear them.

The pink, the former Flower of Scotland, simply didn't look real. That was the beauty of what he'd accomplished. Jack Smith, jeweler extraordinaire, had made the real and exceptionally rare appear fake.

Genius.

And it had worked flawlessly for over a decade.

Until the morning Summer O'Hara walked into his store and zeroed in on the pink.

Her hand went to her chest as she inhaled deeply. Honestly, Jack thought he saw tears in her eyes as she asked to see it. It was the one piece in the case that didn't have a tag indicating that it was a "replica" of whatever it actually was. It was the one piece that looked like cut glass. Ostentatious set on its own, but the light hitting it refracted brilliantly, shooting out mesmerizing rainbows of color.

"Oh, Gus, look," Summer said to her son, who appeared bored but feigned interest because it seemed important to his mother. Summer pointed toward the broach. "It looks exactly like the Flower of Scotland in the Zoe Tiara."

To Jack's knowledge, the Zoe Tiara had appeared in trade magazines and in British Vogue only once. It wasn't well known. No princess had been photographed wearing it. There wasn't even a photo of Zoe wearing it. She'd been only seven years old when it was commissioned, and Jack had stolen it shortly after. It had never come up for auction, so there wasn't great opportunity for gem collectors to see it or for those who wrote about rare gems and jewelry to report on it.

Summer looked up at Jack as he stood behind the case, fingers curling into fists at his side, thankful the case hid his rising anger. He never expected anyone would recognize the Flower of Scotland. He certainly believed no one entering his Ephraim shop would have ever heard of the Zoe Tiara.

But then, Summer O'Hara wasn't ordinary. She was a flake. Today, Summer was dressed in a tie-dyed peasant blouse, jeans, and sandals that looked like they cost fifteen dollars at the local Wal-Mart. She had a high-quality emerald cut diamond she wore on her right hand. It looked like a replica of Grace Kelly's engagement ring, only much smaller.

If he didn't miss his guess — and he didn't — Jack estimated that the ring was worth about $35,000. Why a woman with the wherewithal to wear a ring like that didn't wear better shoes was anyone's guess.

And that attempt to pigeonhole Summer O'Hara into a box that clearly didn't fit was Jack's mistake. A mistake he'd already made once and was about to make again.

Summer gestured toward the broach expansively. She was definitely interested and just knowledgeable enough to be dangerous. "Can I please see that broach, Mr. Smith?"

Deflection. Jack tried that first. He'd learned long ago that the key to offending someone enough to make them leave was the kind of polite effusiveness that walked the razor's edge of being insulting but not insulting enough to get punched in the face.

Jack ignored Summer's request to see the pink and grabbed her waving right hand instead, giving her his best smarmy smile. "This is a lovely ring, Mrs. O'Hara. If you're interested in selling it like the other pieces of jewelry from your late husband, I'll give you eighteen thousand for it."

Summer went pale halfway through his question.

Summer's son turned mean before that.

Jack hadn't expected the violence of Summer's son's intervention. Gus Murphy grabbed Jack by the wrist and squeezed so hard Jack had no option but to release Summer's right hand. Jack, a man of quick reflexes and even quicker response to aggression, hadn't even seen it coming. One second, Gus was standing stock still. The next, he'd manacled Jack's wrist.

"You, and everyone else in this county, know my mother sold everything Geoffrey gave her to keep our family business afloat after Geoff's death. He wasn't the only one to lose everything in '08, but he managed to lose more than most." Gus gave one sharp nod toward his mother. "That ring is all my mother has left of Geoff. I'd sell the gallery before I'd let her sell that ring."

Gus still had ahold of Jack's wrist. His grip got tighter as his voice got lower and infinitely more threatening. "That ring is worth twice what you just offered and you know it." Gus's blue eyes shifted from angry to lethal. "Don't touch my mother again without her consent."

Just as Jack thought the bones of his wrist might snap, Gus Murphy released him. Gus stepped back, and when he spoke again the ice had left his eyes, and his tone was politely neutral. "Now, please show my mother that broach."

Jack's miscalculation of Summer's knowledge and her children's determination to protect her was Summer's strike three.

Jack was sorry for that.

Not because Summer O'Hara would have to die, but because her death would mean increased interest in the small Door County town of Ephraim, which meant increased traffic in his shop. Just the kind of attention that could complicate the constant funnel of funds he'd grown to rely on from the sale of his "replicas."

Without a word, Jack retrieved the broach from the locked case and handed it to a now subdued Summer O'Hara. Summer's enthusiasm for the piece had been deflated by his offer to buy her ring. She wasn't comfortable with her son's leashed aggression either. That was obvious by the way she looked down and away when Gus grabbed him.

Summer examined the broach critically for half a minute then turned the broach over in her hand, assessing everything over again from the back.

Gus noted the stamp Jack had used in the metal. "It's sterling, Mom. No one would set a pink diamond in sterling. Not even a small one."

Summer said nothing.

She reached into her purse with her free hand and pulled out a small 10x loupe. She held it to her eye, then brought the broach to it like a pro.

Jack had underestimated Summer O'Hara. And her son's devotion to her.

Summer lowered the broach away from her eye, put the loupe away, studiously avoiding Jack's gaze as she held out her hand, palm up with the broach cradled in it for him to take.

Before Jack could take it, his client walked through his front door, walking directly to Summer O'Hara. The woman took off her sunglasses, threw Gus, then Summer, a blinding smile that warmed her eyes and lit her face with the ethereal beauty only those blessed with good genes and supreme confidence could pull off. It was an *I'll-always-be-richer-than-you* smile. Every one of Jack's clients kept that smile in their arsenal.

His client held out her gloved hand to Summer. "I believe that," she said, nodding toward the broach nestled in Summer's outstretched palm, "belongs to me."

Summer O'Hara handed the broach to the woman. She'd seen the woman in Jack's store before, last time picking up a Harry Winston original. The woman was all long legs and straight long blond hair that looked like a wig, with an affecting smile that rose the hair on the back of Summer's neck. Summer had a knack for spotting people who were not who they pretended to be. Dangerous people.

She'd ignored the feeling with Jack Smith. She'd chalked it up to the affected superiority those living and working on Michigan Avenue in Chicago embodied. Oddly enough, it wasn't usually displayed by those working at Tiffany's or Georg Jensen or even Graff's in Chicago. Yet Jack had it.

Summer wasn't ignoring the warning signs any longer.

As soon as the broach left her hand, Summer grabbed Gus's hand and left Jack Smith's store. She'd never visited his sister store in Chicago. Now she never would.

"Thank you for your time, Mr. Smith." Summer pulled her twenty-nine-year-old son, who was a foot taller and nearly eighty pounds heavier than her, over the threshold and down the stairs toward the lot where she'd left her car.

Summer was in a hurry.

Certainty burned through her like boiling magma breaking the earth's crust. There was no time for half measures. As Hamlet would say, "Something is rotten in the state of Denmark." Ephraim, for all its Scandinavian roots, wasn't Denmark. Still, something *was* rotten in Ephraim and Jack Smith reeked of it.

"Why the rush, Mom?" Gus asked, extracting his hand from his mother's. For a small woman, Summer O'Hara had one heck of a grip when she was on a mission. Which, more times than not, had something to do with her children. This time was different. Whatever was bothering Summer, it had to do with Jake Smith's shop. Gus shook his head. His mother had let her overactive imagination run amok with her crazy theory that Jack Smith was fencing jewels stolen by international jewel thieves. Gus didn't like the man, would have preferred to punch him in the face for trying to play his mother, but that didn't mean he was buying into his mother's fantasies.

Summer O'Hara needed a hobby. Gus would talk to his brother about having her take a more active role at the gallery. Maybe they could start selling a line of affordable jewelry. That might take her mind off Jack Smith. It may also take her mind off all the beautiful jewelry she'd been forced to sell after her second husband's death.

Summer stopped outside the door of her car. "Sorry, darling, I didn't mean to pull you out of the shop."

She had meant to do exactly that, but Gus didn't call her on it; he simply raised a brow and waited for her to finish.

"I'll have to skip lunch today." She looked at her watch. She'd replaced the Cartier that Geoff had given her for her fortieth birthday with a Citizen Eco-Drive which she claim to love just as much. Now for the first time, Gus felt the heat of helplessness flare. Someday he planned to get back every damned piece she'd been forced to sell, but for now, he had all he could do keeping the orchard, winery, gallery, and the house payments in check.

"Mom, don't do anything radical. Please."

His mother smiled. "Aside from the belly-dancing classes and the watercolor tattoo, when have you ever known me to do anything radical?"

Gus had a list. Instead of detailing it, he kissed his mother's head and said, "Drop me off at the winery then?"

"Of course," Summer said.

Her phone call could wait the thirty minutes it would take to get back home.

Little did Summer O'Hara know that the phone call she was about to make would be her last in this lifetime.

One

"Max, that crazy Irish lady from Door County is on line one for you," Jason, Max Scott's onetime partner and friend, shouted from across the room. "Main routed the call to me, but she's all yours, buddy. You made the mistake of calling her back the first time. Now you keep her."

Max waved Jason off with a shooing gesture that said, *yeah, I got it, you think I'm crazy too, now go away.*

Jason lifted his chin in acknowledgement, then went back to his desk.

Max wasn't sure if the call was good news or bad news. The first call he'd gotten from Summer O'Hara concerned a moderate to large Harry Winston diamond. There were plenty of legitimately purchased three to four carat diamonds available in shops that sold vintage jewelry, including e-Bay.

Max Scott had known his fair share of crackpot tipsters. Those who managed to be credible or crazy enough to make it past the tip-line screening, claiming some sort of information on high-value jewelry thefts, usually landed on his desk.

He should have learned his lesson about following questionable leads when he got transferred from the Miami field office back to Chicago. Miami didn't do questionable, which he'd done one too many times. That was how he found himself back in Chicago, where June hadn't figured out it was supposed to be warm.

Max was part of the FBI's Jewelry and Gem Theft Team of investigators stationed in various cities across the nation. In his career, he'd worked with Interpol to investigate and ultimately arrest a ring of thieves who committed heists from Milan to London to Miami. International criminals traveled from country to country, generally covering their tracks. That was part of the allure and a big part of the problem in trying to identify, and ultimately, apprehend them. That was the high point.

The low point was where he found himself now—fielding calls on local thefts, waiting for the phone to ring with that big case that would get him back into the game.

He'd been kicked out of Miami for chasing leads on a closed case from Antwerp. They arrested and ultimately convicted one man in Belgium for the 2003 Antwerp job, but the diamonds were never recovered. Max knew they were out there somewhere. He suspected at least one member of the ring was still active. He suspected that same member was involved in the Harry Winston theft in Paris, in which twenty percent of the haul was never recovered, and in the 2009 theft of over 40 million pounds sterling worth of diamonds and jewelry from the Graff store in central London.

He'd chased every real lead that came his way.

None of them turned into anything solid.

Then he chased every iffy lead that came in. Some of which he thought were purposely planted to watch him spin his wheels. Frustrating, since he'd been chasing those leads since he inherited the case six years ago.

Again, his leads led to nothing.

His superiors hated the wasted time. More than that, they liked closed cases and hated that he continued to chase phantom leads that led nowhere, making the field office look bad. That's when he got shipped out of Miami and back to Chicago. Even Interpol didn't want to hear from him any longer.

He'd been assigned to an investigation on an organized theft ring out of Columbia that did business across Western Europe and a good portion of North America when the first call from Door County came in. He'd listened to Summer O'Hara. He'd been polite. He even took down the name of the shop and the proprietor and ran checks on both. No hits. Not even a civil complaint.

Still, something nagged him about Summer O'Hara's certainty.

He couldn't define it, but it wouldn't go away. So he started a file. And he filed it away, doing nothing more on it. Following his personal promise *not* to go down the rabbit hole again. Worried they'd send him to Alaska next time.

Knowing he shouldn't, Max pushed the button next to the blinking light and put the receiver to his ear. "Max Scott," he said, more curtly than he should have.

A familiar, not-so-crazy voice said, "Agent Scott, I've found the lost Flower of Scotland."

Max said nothing.

He couldn't formulate a response before his heart stopped beating and his breath caught painfully in his chest. The fact that the Zoe Tiara, which contained the Flower of Scotland as its centerpiece, had been part of the jewelry stolen in Antwerp was never made public. Only those agents assigned to the investigation, the owners of items stolen, and those who had access to the Jewelers' Security Alliance database of stolen jewels, knew the Zoe Tiara had been stolen. Damn few people knew it existed. The only other group who could have known about the theft was the people who stole it.

Max swallowed hard and asked, "Is this Summer O'Hara?"

"Yes."

"Are you calling from your home?" Max asked, knowing she was. Her number and address came up on his screen. He also knew this call was being recorded, which he didn't need or want. He needed to get to Summer O'Hara and interview her in person.

"Yes."

"Stay where you are," Max said. He looked at his watch. "I'll be there in six hours. We'll talk then."

Max didn't wait for Summer O'Hara to confirm she understood. He wanted no more details recorded that could send him from Chicago to some place even colder. He disconnected the call.

Then he got up, walked to Jason's desk and said, "If she calls back, tell her I'll get back to her after the weekend. I'm heading out."

Jason looked at his watch. "It's barely noon."

"It's *after* noon on a beautiful Friday. I've already logged fifty hours this week. That's twelve more than you, partner." Max smiled what he hoped was an appropriately lascivious smile. He was out of practice on that score. It had a long time since he'd had cause to feel anything approaching lasciviousness.

"I've got a date," he lied.

A date long past due and a long drive to catch my white whale.

What Max didn't count on was that his whale attacked preemptively.

Max pulled into Ephraim later than he expected. Road construction and state troopers up and down I-94 had seen to that. It was 7:06 when he pulled into Summer O'Hara's driveway. Almost an hour later than he'd told Summer he'd be.

The first thing Max noticed as he approached the two-story Victorian-style house was how welcoming it appeared. There were bright flowers lining the sidewalk and around the home. Hanging flower baskets on the covered front porch appeared to wrap around the entire home. Windows stood open on the second floor, letting in the breeze off the lake that cooled the warm evening air.

As he walked up the curved concrete sidewalk, the idyllic image changed. Max couldn't define what worried him, but he sensed something was very wrong. That sense of dread magnified with every step he took, propelling him forward as he quickly scanned the yard and surrounding area. The house and adjoining backyard nestled into a tree-dense hill that shot up at a steep angle, ending at the road about a hundred or so feet above. Max scanned the hill. Anyone could have been there watching him, but he couldn't make out movement in the trees.

Max stepped up onto the porch, noticing the camera high in the corner shooting video of him as he approached Summer O'Hara's door. Many people he knew had a doorbell app that took video and sometimes stills of anyone ringing their doorbell and notified their cell phone in real time with the video.

Hopefully, Summer O'Hara knew he was here and wasn't dialing the local police about a stranger on her doorstep. Max didn't need that headache on top of his continuing an investigation he'd been ordered to leave alone.

When the doorbell wasn't answered, Max knocked.

No response.

He knocked again, this time longer and harder.

Nothing.

Max looked toward the large window to his left. It was open and there were no shades or drapes blocking his view into the house. He moved closer, looking through the glass, knowing as he did something was very wrong. Summer O'Hara wanted to speak with him. She should have swung the door open the second he pulled into the drive. She hadn't struck Max as the kind of woman who would hide her enthusiasm for anything that spiked it. It was clear the Flower of Scotland spiked Summer's enthusiasm.

Max scanned what looked to be a living room or some large sitting area. Neat. Clean. And empty. The kitchen lay beyond, and he couldn't see the entirety of it from where he stood. He looked to the staircase that wound up at an angle and ended directly about ten feet short of the front door.

The first thing Max saw after the tile at the base of stairs was a sandal. The slide in kind, without a back.

Then he saw a bare foot attached to a leg bent at an improbable angle.

He went to the door, knocked again, saying loudly, just in case the camera had an audio feature, "Federal agent," while turning the knob. He didn't pull his sidearm until he was through the front door. He went immediately to the woman. It was Summer O'Hara. No doubt about it, she looked just like the picture on her driver's license.

He swept the house, finding it empty. All the windows on the first and second story were open. Screens attached. No obvious sign of a break-in.

Max quickly made his way back to Summer. Her breathing was shallow, but steady. Her heartbeat slow, yet discernible. She was unresponsive when he called her name. Max kept his fingers at her neck, feeling her pulse as he said, "Ms. O'Hara, tell me what happened."

Max had found through trial and error that most people respond, or do their best to respond, if given a command rather than being asked a question.

"Summer, squeeze my hand if you can hear me," Max said, gently wrapping his hand around hers, letting his fingers touch her palm.

She responded with a feather light squeeze.

Emergency services would take close to an hour to get to Summer's house from Sturgeon Bay. Max passed a naturopathic clinic on his way from Fish Creek. He knew little about naturopaths other than they don't use herbs to cure emergency situations.

He did a quick inventory of Summer's injuries. He didn't want to wait for an ambulance—there wasn't time for that. Her left wrist may have been broken, but he didn't think her arm was. Her legs had the beginning of bruises but didn't look broken.

He stepped back, took a quick series of photos, then picked Summer O'Hara up and carried her to his car. The doorbell app caught it all on tape. No help for that. She needed medical attention and there didn't seem to be any obvious reason she was unresponsive to his questioning. There was no scent of alcohol on her, no bottle of pills spilled on the steps.

When he leaned down to pick her up, Summer moved. She was half sitting, half slouched, supporting her weight on her right arm.

She opened her eyes. "Drugged," she said. Not clearly, but Max understood.

She opened her opposite hand, which had been tightly clamped, revealing a small ring with a domed surface. "In the ring," Summer said. "Tea is in the ring."

Max put the ring in his pocket. "If I support you, can you make it to my car?"

Summer nodded.

Max lifted her under her arms, placed his shoulder under her left side, the side where her wrist was injured, and stood for a moment. Summer O'Hara leaned into him, giving him most of her weight. She was a small woman, maybe a buck twenty soaking wet. Her weight didn't affect Max. "Let's see if you can walk."

She could but not well. He lifted her down the steps and kept her to his side until he reached the passenger side of his car.

Max took her straight to the back parking lot of the naturopathic clinic. Three things happened rapidly from there.

First, the naturopath knew immediately what had been given to Summer O'Hara in her tea from the sample Summer stored in her ring—a clever contraption that opened, revealing an inner compartment that sealed completely when closed.

Second, after diagnosing and treating Summer with the antidote, Summer formally died.

Third, Max sought and received, permission to investigate Jack Smith, not only for theft, money-laundering, and trafficking in stolen goods, but also for attempted murder, from his boss's boss. His investigation was eyes only, so no one on his team was advised. Max was simply relocated from Chicago to Milwaukee, where he needn't actually present himself.

It was the fourth thing that happened that would change Max Scott's life forever. He met the Murphy triplets—Summer O'Hara's children.

One knew his secret, which gave them a bond of sorts and made liars of them both.

One he'd learn to tolerate but not before blood was shed.

One would prove to be to be his undoing.

Two

Her mother was dead.

Fallon Murphy took the news first with shock, then with denial, and finally with an abject sorrow that left her numb. She and her brothers lost their father so young. Death didn't seem real then. Their father was there one day, then he went to work like always, then he was gone forever. Just like that.

Commercial fishermen on the Great Lakes took risks people not part of the industry didn't understand. The Great Lakes — massive bodies of fresh water — do not allow all who venture there to come home. To this day, every time Fallon stared out onto Lake Michigan, she felt her father's presence. She smelled his drugstore aftershave in the breeze off the water. She imagined her father's hand in hers when she ran her hand over the lake's cool surface. Fallon felt peace rather than sorrow when she was on the water. It didn't make sense to her that she felt whole on the water rather than fearful or angry. In the sentimentality of her heart, Fallon imagined that was her father's parting gift to his children.

They all loved the water.

It took years after losing their father for their mother to find love again. Geoff had been kind, funny, and so easy to love. He'd also been twenty years Summer's senior. When the housing market crashed in 2008 and the stock market followed, Geoff lost most of the capital he'd invested in both. He would have survived it; he certainly had the will and the knowledge to start over. Unfortunately, Geoff's heart had other ideas.

Losing two fathers had been hard on Fallon.

Losing her mother was unthinkable.

Fallon couldn't quite believe Summer was dead. Nothing about it felt right.

It didn't feel real. Not yet. Not when Fallon was so far away in a land so different from Door County, Wisconsin, yet so similar.

Life in Key West was lived in tune with the water. The same was true of Ephraim. One was less than one hundred miles from Cuba. The other had more in common with Canada than the tropics. Fallon escaped to Key West. Now, it was home. Going back to the Door for any extended period wasn't something Fallon thought she'd ever do. Under these circumstances, it sucked. That simple. That crude.

Her brother Gus called to give her the news. Ever the blunt one, he'd simply said, "You need to come home. Mom's dead. She's been cremated. The funeral is in three days." Four sentences. Gus turned her world upside down in fewer than twenty words.

When Fallon asked Gus what happened, all she got in response was a clipped, stoically brutal, "She slipped coming down the stairs. Then her heart just stopped beating. It was an accident, Fal. Just a tragic accident. Come home."

Fallon disconnected the call without asking who decided to have their mother cremated or why. Was her face that damaged that she couldn't have an open casket? Had mom changed her will adding the request to be cremated? Why wouldn't she be buried next to Geoff? Nothing made any sense. Fallon packed her one black dress, her heels, and a few odds and ends as she mindlessly made her way through her apartment. She hopped on the first nonstop flight to Milwaukee.

The first thing she planned to do when she made it home was hug her brother Fingal. The second thing she planned to do was punch Gus as hard as she possibly could. The third thing she would do was take her mother's ashes to the lake shore and sit with a bottle of Chardonnay. She wanted to watch the sunset with both her parents.

She'd cry when she made it back to her room in her mother's house. When she was alone. When she had the solitude, surrounded by her mother's things, to contemplate that in a very real sense she was now an orphan.

After Fallon arrived in Ephraim, she went directly to the funeral home to pick up her mother's ashes. She'd texted her brothers — both of them — with a statement that read more like an arrest warrant than a request. She wanted her mother's ashes, and she wanted them now. She'd have been nicer about it, but she discovered that they waited three days after Summer died to call her. They'd also made all the funeral arrangements without consulting her. She felt abandoned and angrier than she'd been when she left Ephraim.

She'd choked on the first sip of Chardonnay and abandoned it immediately.

While she felt the familiarity of her father as she sat on the lakeshore, throwing stones into the water as she'd done with her parents as a child, she didn't feel her mother's presence at all. That bothered her and made her angry. Fallon didn't want to cry. She wanted to rage against the proof sitting in the urn next to her. She felt like a crazy person, not a daughter grieving the loss of her mother.

Fallon heard the crunch of footsteps on the stones approaching her. She was in no mood for company, so she didn't look up. Didn't acknowledge the new arrival. She knew it wasn't one of her brothers. They both realized that she needed time before approaching her. While neither of them was overly intuitive, both valued their hides enough to let Fallon be until she was ready to walk with them.

The crunching stopped and a decidedly male presence plopped down beside her. He didn't say anything for a while. Letting Fallon get used to him, she supposed. Oddly enough she didn't care. He smelled of soap, salt, and a hint of lime. Similar to her father's aftershave but more elemental.

The next thing Fallon allowed herself to notice was his boat shoes. They were new. He wore them somewhat awkwardly, like they were foreign.

She heard him clink the bottle as it brushed against the stones. She heard the *pop* sound of the cork as he pulled it from the bottle. Then came the unmistakable sound of liquid pouring into plastic. Summer only carried plastic wineglasses outside, especially near the water, a habit Fallon picked up.

The stranger grabbed her hand where it wrapped around her upturned knees and thrust the over-sized rainbow-colored plastic wineglass into her hand. "Drink it," he demanded as if he had a right to demand anything from her. "It might not help, but odds are, it won't hurt."

Fallon took the glass, wondering why she felt comfortable taking it from a stranger. She thought she heard irony in his remark, or maybe it was commiseration. She didn't know him, so perhaps she was projecting more than she should. Maybe communing with a father she felt in the water and an urn that was supposed to be filled with her mother's ashes made one hyper-aware. Fallon hadn't known anyone with experience quite like hers to ask. She was losing it, self-aware enough to know she was on tenuous mental ground, but still losing it.

She should take the urn, the bottle, and high-tail it back to Summer's house and cry herself to sleep.

Instead of doing what she should, Fallon took a sip of her wine — which this time, tasted clean and crisp and welcoming — eyeing the man who poured it for her over the rim of her plastic glass. Eyes narrowing as he openly held her gaze.

His expression seemed more inquiring than merely affable, but perhaps that was the intelligence she thought she saw in his eyes. Eyes the color of the lake water where it hit the shore, magnifying the yellow, grey, and brown stones below — light greyish-blue with flecks of gold and brown to give them depth and interest. The dark ring around his irises only enhanced the lightness of his eyes.

The rest of him was well enough put together that she'd have approached him had he been dining alone at her restaurant. He appeared tall even though he was sitting. His shoulders were wide, but some of that was the way he held himself — straight back, chin up, chest out. He breathed from his diaphragm, which most people didn't. Fallon found that interesting and a little alarming. His face had character, like the men who frequented her restaurant in Key West. Most had stories they would never tell, not the real versions at least, but if you looked closely enough, you could see some of the joy, the fear, the will to re-invent written on the lines of their faces. Sometimes on their hands and arms as well.

Fallon took her time absorbing what she could from his appearance and demeanor.

He let her. He didn't rush or shy away from her scrutiny.

A man sure of whatever mission he was on. Fallon got the distinct impression that while she may be a part of that mission, she wasn't the center of it. He just wasn't giving off that kind of vibe.

Fallon set her wineglass down on the semi-flat rock to her left. The man was to her right. No obstacles — save the urn and the partially filled Chardonnay bottle — between her and this dark-haired creature who wanted something from her. She was a black belt. She had little to lose. She was in a kick-tail-and-take-names kind of mood.

What was the worst that could happen?

Part of her wanted to find out.

Losing it, indeed.

Fallon looked at the compelling stranger, mentally measuring the distance between the bottle and the rock. "Which are you: law enforcement, military, or ex-military?"

When he flinched, a tiny jerk he controlled quickly, Fallon knew he was one of the above. She cut the pretense of civility and said, "You are uncomfortable in your shoes."

Fallon gritted her teeth and edged closer to the bottle. "You sit up straight." When doubt or something like confusion flashed in his eyes, Fallon continued through gritted teeth, "You have a military bearing."

He gave nothing away except the tick at his jaw and the hardening of his welcoming eyes.

"You breathe through your abdomen, and you scan the horizon for every threat and every means of escape. You're good at making it appear nonchalant, but you're scanning, not mindlessly enjoying your environment."

His jaw hardened.

Fallon edged closer to the bottle. She was now equal distance between the rock and the bottle. She may have a struggle on her hands, but she'd make him bleed if she had too. Nothing in his demeanor so far hinted at aggression toward her, but she'd be a fool not to be aware of the fact that he was capable of it.

An iron grip came down on her wrist before Fallon even knew she was grabbing for the bottle.

"Don't even think about it," he said before nuzzling her neck as he whispered in her ear, "I am not your enemy." To anyone watching, they'd see an intimate moment. Two lovers enjoying the lakeshore.

He held Fallon close as she struggled.

"Don't fight me, Fallon. I'll make sure you direct all that homicidal energy in the right direction." He paused a beat, then said, "Trust me."

His voice was calm.

Decisive.

Immediately trustworthy.

His grip was strong and firm. He wasn't hurting her. He was constraining her. She hated it. The second she stopped fighting him, he let her go.

"Who are you?" Fallon asked, looking up into those compelling eyes.

He stared down at her almost sternly but not quite making it happen, begging her to believe him.

"The man who knows where your mother is."

She took one look at him and knew he was full of shit.

The second Max sat down next to Fallon, he knew he was

out of his league. She didn't startle. She didn't move away. She didn't accept his presence, but she didn't tell him to buzz off either. She sat there, eyed him up and down, and came to conclusions — most of which were spot on — before he opened his mouth.

Max's excitement at getting close to the team who stole the Flower of Scotland made his blood burn through his veins. He felt it like a tangible warmth since he carried Summer O'Hara into Julie Grace's naturopathic clinic. Dr. Grace, the naturopath with grit and sass, saved Summer's life. Max had no doubt about that. She knew what to give Summer to counteract the plant poison put into her tea.

Then Dr. Grace went five steps further. She agreed to produce a death certificate — Max's off-the-books FBI contacts helped with that. His father lent him most of the cash he needed since it couldn't be requisitioned through formal FBI channels. Max had been assured his father — a retired FBI veteran — would be reimbursed, so long as both Max and his father, Roland Scott, kept all the receipts.

Roland, aka "Rolly" Scott, had no qualms about jumping back into the fray to help his son. In fact, he seemed giddy about it. Some of that was seeing photos of Summer O'Hara in the briefing materials Max sent to him.

Summer O'Hara was a beautiful woman. The combination of red hair and blue eyes that happened rarely in nature defined her facial features. It didn't hurt that she kept herself in good shape, or that she inherited good bone structure. But that was the two-dimensional woman. Summer was far more attractive in person than photos could capture.

The intelligence in her eyes, her quick wit and easy smile, even knowing she'd been targeted by a man bent on ensuring her silenced, made her just the kind of woman his father couldn't ignore — smart, engaging, and teasingly sarcastic. Something about that combination pushed every one of Rolly Scott's buttons. Didn't hurt that she had red hair. Two of Rolly's ex-wives had red hair. Neither lasted long, but that didn't stop his father from trying to make one stick.

Max's mother, who died when Max was seventeen, had been kind, funny, sardonic—a trait Max associated with intelligence to this day. She also had red hair and blue eyes. Rolly wasn't the only Scott male who had a soft spot for women who resembled Max's mother, both inside and out. Max liked Summer instantly. He'd do anything he could to protect her. Since he knew Rolly would put Summer's safety above his own, he trusted his father to keep her safe.

The fewer people who knew Summer was alive, the better. Right now, that list was manageable: his boss's boss, Dr. Grace and her fiancé—who was also her assistant and had access to just about anything legal and quasi-legal, Summer's son Gus or Fergus—because Max needed help making funeral arrangements without a body, and now his dad.

Max had to make a choice: tell Fallon and enlist her help, or keep her and her other brother, Fingal, in the dark. Their reactions would be more authentic if he and Gus allowed them to stay in the dark.

If Max told them their mother was alive, the risk to his case escalated.

If he allowed them to continue to believe their mother was dead, he'd do damage to his soul. He'd have given anything to believe his mother was still alive, to save himself and his father the pain that still filled them both.

There was also the fact that Summer was safer if her children thought she was dead. Two of them anyway. He could mitigate the risk to Summer. He and his father knew how. What they couldn't fix was the sense of betrayal that would plague Summer and her children for the rest of their lives if they didn't come clean as soon as possible.

Max wasn't willing to tear apart a family simply to make a case—not when odds were good that he and Rolly could keep Summer O'Hara safely guarded. Odds weren't quite as good that they could keep the triplets safe without enlisting their help. Help required trust. Lying never served Max well when it came to building trust. He made a habit of keeping his lies to a minimum.

That had the added benefit of not having to remember them. Stick to the truth as far as you're able. Truth may not set you free, but it will keep you safer than the alternative. Purely a matter of playing the odds. That's what his first undercover training had taught him. It had served Max well over the years.

Until he sat down next to Fallon Murphy.

She sucked every good intention from him and left him thinking thoughts he had no business thinking. The first of which made absolutely no sense to him. *Protect her at all costs... keep her by your side...*

Max shot that line of thinking so fast his teeth hurt with the effort. How was he going to get her to trust him when he didn't trust himself?

She took one look at him and knew he was a fraud. A fake. A man uncomfortable in his shoes. How in the heck had she nailed that with a look? So much for his undercover skills. He'd blown it by wearing what every overpaid boat owner in Door County wore.

Max didn't know what to expect from Fallon. A light flirtation, a quick buzz-off, a polite "Please leave me alone." He hadn't expected Fallon to try to brain him with a half-filled Chardonnay bottle. He probably should have. Had someone like him sat down next to him while he was mourning, he'd have warned them off *impolitely*, and if they didn't high-tail it fast enough, he would have *politely* punched them in the face.

In a few days he'd had to study Fallon, her brothers, and Mr. Jack Smith, high-end boutique jeweler and master thief. He'd learned the Murphy siblings were all hard-working, life-loving, hard-headed individuals who had no issue demanding what they wanted out of life and fighting to get it. The brothers, Max understood. Fallon, he couldn't figure out.

She didn't make sense.

Graduated in the top quarter of her high school. Good, but not stellar. Did better in undergraduate school, studying history, philosophy, and comparative literature. Odd mix, but there it was. Then, she nailed her LSATs and went to law school. There she graduated in the top ten percent of her class. She spent two years at the top criminal defense firm, and then, when she was just establishing her reputation as a litigator, respected by her colleagues and the district attorneys who worked opposite her, she disappeared.

Max hadn't been able to track her movements until she surfaced in Key West. Older. More sophisticated, not less. And running a restaurant that locals and tourists frequented. Most of them with secrets. A place where deals were made and money was exchanged with the frequency of bottles of Land Shark at the bar.

She had no ties to criminality. None.

But the man who employed her walked a fine line on both sides of the good citizen aisle. Law enforcement monitored but did little more because Nick Card threw them a bad guy on a semi-regular basis — often enough to maintain his usefulness. Nick Card had his own sense of integrity. It wasn't close to Max's definition of the word, but it was honorable in its own way. What didn't make sense was Fallon's connection to any of it. Maybe, if he worked at it, he'd get a glimpse into what made her tick.

The light in her eyes made him want to try.

"Trust me," he said to Fallon as he held her close.

"Who are you?" she asked.

"I'm the man who knows where your mother is."

And he did.

"Let me show you."

Three

The orchard Gus managed with his brother, Fingal, was thriving. They'd had another hard winter which hadn't helped the cherry production, but somehow the newer trees they planted were still growing strong. The heavy, wet snowfall they had throughout the Door in late April put them behind schedule. That late, unexpected snow put every farmer in Wisconsin behind schedule, so that, in and of itself, wouldn't hinder the cherry crop.

What worried Gus about the winery, orchard, and gallery wasn't the late spring or the early dry summer; it was the lie he kept. It was eating him alive. That lie when it came out, and come out it would, would damage his relationship with his sister past the underlying strain that already existed. Letting Finn believe their mother was dead would earn him a bloody nose and, best case, a summer of barely civil mutual détente—their personal Cold War in which mutually assured destruction ruled their every interaction.

His siblings were stubborn. They held grudges. They loved deeply but forgave one another only when forgiveness was earned. Gus certainly had earned their ire. He couldn't think of one way to earn either's forgiveness.

Gus carried the case of semi-dry red Finn had asked him to get for the tasting bar from the storage house in the back. They were running low on their bestselling red. That had Finn concerned. He didn't want to lose customer base due to lack of product. There were just too many great red wine choices in their twelve to fifteen-dollar price to alienate even one consistent customer.

"We're down to twenty-four cases of the Fallon Red," Gus said. Finn had his back to him, stocking the side bar with small tasting glasses.

"We'll have to start pushing the new Rosé. Twenty-four cases won't get us through August." Finn's voice was dull. Matter-of-fact. Monotone. Like he knew he was saying the right thing but couldn't quite make himself believe it.

The Rosé was a Murphy Brother's original. Their first original was their semi-dry red with the punch of Pinot Noir mixed with the smoothness of a full Cabernet. They named that one after their sister and it was an immediate success. So much so, they couldn't keep up with demand.

They named their Rosé after their mother: *Summer Rose Rosé.*

In the blind tastings they'd had so far, Summer Rose outshined both the California Rosé they stocked and the Oregon variety. They had another winner, and neither Finn nor Fallon felt good about serving it. Finn couldn't do it without getting sullen and misty-eyed, something no barkeep could do without losing every customer who approached the counter.

Gus couldn't stand anymore what circumstance made him do. He didn't like the sense of betrayal it made him feel. He didn't even like looking in the mirror when he brushed his teeth. This necessary farce couldn't end fast enough for him. He could have just killed Jack Smith and been done with it, but that FBI agent wasn't sure Smith was the one who tried to kill Summer. He'd also planted the idea that *if* — and Special Agent Max Scott had stressed the if — Jack Smith had poisoned Summer and pushed her down her stairs, he probably hadn't acted alone.

Gus opened the case of Fallon Red with so much force, he rendered it unusable. He stopped. Stood up straight, rubbed a palm across his forehead, then through hair already mussed from the repeated act. "I'm going out," he said.

Finn turned to finally look at him. "Where are you going? There's still more stocking to do, and we haven't gone over the new labels yet."

Gus was already walking away. "Get Sully to stock. The answer on the labels can wait. If you don't think so, pick one. I don't really care anymore."

Finn's accusation followed him out the door, "You don't care about anything or anyone other than yourself anymore."

What hurt more than Finn's words echoing through Gus's brain was the certainty that when his siblings discovered their mother was alive they'd believe those words were true. Gus knew, in the dark part of his soul, that they were true.

His need to keep their mother safe obliterated his duty to his siblings because he couldn't live with himself if anything more happened to her when he could have stopped it. He should have insisted Summer stay with him after their encounter with Smith. He should have cared more about her and less about trying to bail out the gallery, keep the orchard thriving, and the shop under control.

He was feeling miserable, self-absorbed, and sick to his stomach for making this about him and not about Summer.

Gus had no idea where he would end up when he got on his Sportster and turned left onto Highway 42. But he should have known better not to stop riding until he got his self-absorbed temper under control. Anger, fear, and a sprinkling of stupid had never served him well.

Today was no exception to that rule.

Gus didn't know that today's little excursion to the dark side would put them all in more danger than he could have imagined.

Fallon looked at the man who claimed to know where her mother was with all the jaded hope she could muster. She wanted to believe him almost as much as she needed to. She sure as the day was long in Door County in the summer, never truly believed the urn next to her contained what remained of her mother. Not overtly religious in theory, Fallon was deeply spiritual in practice. Since she was a little girl, Fallon believed God lived in her. She'd grown to rely on what her inner self told her with matters of the heart and soul.

Her mother lived in her heart and her soul. She still felt her there in a way that was definitely corporal, not otherworldly.

"Tell me your name," Fallon demanded. "I'm going to scream bloody murder if you don't tell me your real name right bloody now."

He laughed, touching the side of her face gently with the back of his hand before he folded both arms over his knees. If he was trying to appear harmless, he was failing spectacularly, but with flare.

"You certainly say 'bloody' a lot."

Fallon flushed. That was true. But only when she felt off her game in a way that left the façade of control over her environment in ashes. Her eyes flashed to the ornate urn beside her. This time the ashes were literal. Summer would have hated the urn. Fallon had no idea what her brothers were thinking picking it. It was etched with white calla lilies. Flamboyantly floral. Gus and Finn would have done better with dandelions. There was a resilient bloom her mother would have approved of.

The absurdity of her thoughts brought a small smile to Fallon's face. The smile had the added benefit of grounding her. She no longer wanted to throw the word "bloody" into every sentence.

"Max," the stranger said. "My name is Max."

"Is that your real name?"

"Yes. Maxwell Scott is my full name. I work for the FBI. I'm part of the Jewelry and Gem Theft Team." He shrugged and cocked his head to one side as he scrutinized her reaction. Nothing in his demeanor nor tone suggested he was being anything but honest with her. "However, *team* might be a bit of a stretch on this one. My team thinks I've been canned. Probably would have been, too, had it not been for your mother."

"Bloody hell. You're telling the truth," Fallon said, believing him.

He smiled fully at her, meeting her eyes with real warmth. The effect was instantaneously devastating to Fallon's overwhelmed senses. She felt lighter than she'd felt since Gus's phone call — like a real weight had been lifted from her chest. She felt like invisible strings were pulling her up and nothing would weigh her down. Light as air. Buoyant even. "Take me to my mother."

Max reached into his shirt pocket and pulled out a thin, white-gold diamond eternity band. "Give me your hand."

When Fallon took too long trying to determine what she should do, Max reached out and grabbed her left hand. He slid the band over her ring finger. It fit perfectly. Since Fallon's hands were relatively small, that was almost as surprising as the ring itself.

Fallon looked at the ring on her finger.

Then she looked up into Max's eyes, guarded now, and expectant, like there was another shoe getting ready to drop right on Fallon's head. She fitted what he was saying into an unfinished puzzle in her head.

FBI. Jewelry Theft. Summer O'Hara — jewel and jewelry lover needing to appear dead. Wedding band on her finger.

Fallon swallowed past the lump in her throat. "Take me to my mother. You can explain about the ring and everything else on the way."

Max grabbed her left hand and brought it to his lips. His voice was low and gravelly when he spoke. "When we get up from the beach we will be married. I'm here to help you settle your mother's estate. We are living temporarily in Summer's house until we can get things settled. I know this is a lot to take in, but you're going to have to step up and make it happen. My case depends upon it. Your mother's safety depends on my case."

He paused, looking at her like he was willing her to get with the program. And pretty darned quick.

"My name — the name you will use for me — is Max Smart. I'm a business analyst. I help large companies stay large and up-and-coming companies grow. I travel often for business but have a few weeks downtime to help you and your family get Summer's things in order. We are recently married. We met six months ago when I came to your restaurant to meet Nick Card and help him with a new business acquisition. We had instant chemistry. We fell in love quickly and since we're both over thirty, saw no reason not to marry. You kept your maiden name. We were about to tell your family and arrange for a small ceremony here in Door County when the news arrived about the death of your mother."

Max rattled all that off with the quick efficiency Fallon associated with law enforcement. Lines of a story pieced together to make an outline of a whole while completely ignoring emotional content that made any tale real.

"Do I have your cooperation?" Max asked.

Fallon wasn't sure what Max meant by "cooperation." What he seemed determined to take from her was absolute acquiescence to everything he demanded. *That* would never happen. He'd learn that about his "wife" very quickly. Just not before Fallon saw her mother.

"You have my *help* with your case. You have my *demand* that I see my mother, right bloody now." Fallon took a deep breath and let him see the truth of what she was about to say in her eyes. "You have my *promise* that if any more harm comes to my mother as a result of your investigation, that *I* will hold you, Maxwell Scott Smart, totally responsible, and *I* will exact my pound of flesh directly from your hide."

He had the audacity to grin. "Are you threatening bodily harm to a federal agent?"

"You bet your bloody hide I am."

"We really have to do something about your choice of words."

And just like that, Fallon Murphy went from being a *me* to a *we*.

Four

Summer O'Hara had vague memories of being carried into Julie Grace's medical clinic by a disconcertingly strong and equally compelling young man who appeared to be older than her triplets but still young enough to be her son. The man had a nice voice. The problem was he used it incessantly.

She just wanted to go to sleep.

He kept moving her and shaking her and talking at her until she acknowledged him.

Then Julie and her assistant, Peter, pumped her stomach, made her drink more water than one mortal human could possibly flush through their system, and they made her drink a chalky tea that tasted like salty seaweed. If she lived through this, which Peter insisted she would while he helped her to the restroom for the eleventh time, she was never going to willingly drink that wretched tea again.

By the time she could have a coherent conversation that didn't involve asking for soda crackers or lotioned toilet paper, the FBI agent who saved her life had her ensconced on a mini-yacht with an older version of himself. Same devastating smile. Half the charm. The man was an overbearing nightmare.

And Summer was locked on a boat with him while they made their way along Lake Michigan's coast from Ephraim to his condo on the river in Milwaukee.

Rolly... his name was Rolly. What kind of name was Rolly? It sounded like some old-time baseball player with a handlebar mustache, or an eight-year-old boy who hadn't quite grown into his name. Because he insisted everyone call him Rolly, Summer refused to. It was one of the few things she could control about her life now. As an added bonus, it made him grit his teeth when

Summer needed to call him by his name: *Roland*. When she was put out with him, which was anytime he took away her iPad, cell phone, or laptop, Summer rolled the *R* in his name dramatically.

She was now a woman unconnected. That was making her want to climb the walls even more than having no one to talk to who didn't want to dictate her every move. It was bad enough she needed to hide; it was worse she had a keeper who wouldn't so much as allow her to view the online jewelry sites she loved. Summer was a reader as well as a surfer. She loved to read e-books on her iPad. Roland would not allow that.

He did cave in and let her read her morning papers from his computer. He had online subscriptions to the *New York Times, Wall Street Journal,* and *Business Journal.* He caved further and added the *Washington Post, Boston Globe,* and *Guardian.* Roland also had a nice collection of hardcovers and paperbacks, most of which she hadn't read. He had the full spectrum of James Lee Burke, Clive Cussler, and Lee Child. But he also had books by Terry Pratchett, Ursula Le Guin — including one on writing — and a trio of old historical romance novels set in Scotland by Julie Garwood. Interesting choice for a man as masculine as Rolly Scott. There was also a selection on environmental conservation, books about adventure travel, and *The Hidden Life of Trees.*

For a man of such eclectic tastes in reading material, *Roland* had one persona. All-protective-alpha-male — all the time. Summer wasn't allowed to frequent any of the sites she generally frequented online, except for her newspapers. His overabundance of caution made her want to howl at the moon and break into his stash of single malt whisky and top shelf bourbon.

Summer took off her sandals. She didn't like them anyway. They chaffed. What she needed was a good pair of walking sandals she could get wet and a good pair of boat shoes. She'd never been a fan of boat shoes, but if she was going to be held captive on a boat, she might as well look like she belonged here. She sure didn't feel like she did.

She hadn't set foot on any boat, not even a kayak, since her first husband's death. Padraig—or Patrick, or sometimes simply Murph—had been a commercial fisherman. The lake had taken her first love, the father of her children. Summer still loved the water, almost as much as she still had the irrepressible fire of first love in her heart, but she didn't love boats or ships or whitefish the way she used to. In fact, she hadn't had a Door County fish boil since the last one she'd had at the White Gull Inn with Padraig. His sister had made the trip from Galway, Ireland, and wanted the authentic Door County experience. Padraig had smiled and made sure she got the royal treatment. Then he'd snuck into the kitchen where his mate had a porterhouse waiting for him.

The thought made her smile. Padraig hated fish boils. Give the man a good steak and he was happy. Serve him the fruits of the sea—or lake—and odds were he'd be grumbling all night while waiting to eat something with hooves. The man didn't even like potatoes unless they were french-fried.

"What has you smiling so sweetly?" Rolly asked, coming to sit on the couch next to Summer. Lifting her bare feet, he sat down next to her, then placed her feet on his lap. The action wasn't threatening. Rolly acted like it was something he did all the time. Still, it felt intimate to Summer. She hadn't been touched by a man in a long time. The casual intimacy burned her to her core but didn't seem to affect him in the slightest.

Summer hoped her feet didn't stink. She didn't want to encourage Max's father. He already asked too many probing questions, but she didn't really want to repulse the man either.

"Shouldn't you be manning the deck or whatever else a captain has to do on his boat?" she asked, setting down *The Bride*. It was one of three Julie Garwood books Roland had on his shelf, secured by an ingenious yet simple system of elastic and Velcro.

Roland absently started to rub her ankles. He was good at it. Since he didn't seem to put any meaning into it at all and since it felt good, Summer let him continue. She'd been told she carried much of her tension in her feet the few times she'd gone for therapeutic massages. Summer was fairly certain being poisoned and pushed down the stairs had caused more tension to accumulate in all sorts of places.

"We're anchored for the night. We've got time before dinner. I thought we could talk or watch a movie. Maybe play some cards." Roland smiled at her. It was a light, teasing smile. The same one that took her off guard and put her at ease at the same time. It was the kind of smile a woman could learn to love, waking up to it every morning for the rest of her life.

Summer shut the book. She had no business reading romance. Apparently, it did funny things to her head. She did manage to bookmark her page with the worn jacket cover before closing it. Summer narrowed her eyes at Roland hoping he'd just go away. Or at least stop smiling at her.

As if he were reading her thoughts, his smile widened, making the lines at the corners of his eyes deepen. Roland Scott was an attractive man. No doubt about that. He also had the kind of confidence that came with age and experience. He didn't seem to care about his appearance; he was simply comfortable and confident in who he was. As dictatorial as he'd been about Summer staying out of sight and doing everything he told her to do before they left port in Ephraim, now he was more relaxed.

More open.

More compelling.

Summer felt like she was making a friend, that kind of tentative feeling of making friends before becoming a teenager and everything became about sex. It was a nice feeling. Roland was a nice man when he chose to be.

"Are you going to tell me why you were smiling when I came down? You looked lost in a memory. Judging by the far off look in your eye, it was a good one." Roland's voice was light, as if treading gently on the surface of getting to know her. Still, he seemed genuinely interested, and Summer couldn't think of one reason not to tell him. She wasn't secretive by nature or inclination which is exactly what got her into the predicament she was currently in. Had she just kept her suspicions to herself about the Zoe Tiara and the Flower of Scotland, she'd be safely ensconced in her own bed right now.

Alone.

"I was thinking about my first husband, Padraig Yeats Murphy," Summer said. Simply saying Padraig's full name aloud made Summer smile.

"Yeats?" Roland asked with genuine curiosity.

Summer snorted. She couldn't help it. Yeats was a ridiculous name to attach to someone like her first husband. Summer looked into Roland's light blue eyes, enjoying his company. He had a way of putting her at ease that she didn't fight. She needed the ease, something she hadn't felt in a very long time. "Padraig's mother loved Yeats. She'd often say, 'Watch how you walk through this world. Tread lightly, for you tread on my dreams.'"

Roland seemed to ponder that. He said nothing, simply waiting for her to continue or not. It was up to her. Summer appreciated that. Another thing in her life she had control of — her story.

"I think I fell in love with her before I fell in love with Padraig. Padraig had his mother's poetic soul but none of her culinary preferences. He was a commercial fisherman who hated the taste of fish." Summer laughed. "And a first-generation Irishman who hated potatoes." Summer's brow furrowed as her smile deepened. "What kind of Irishman doesn't like fish and potatoes?"

Roland smiled with her. "What did he like?"

"Red meat, teaching his babies rebel songs, and …"

Summer's voice trailed off as she looked away from him. Rolly wanted to see her eyes light with love and the softness of good memories again. He'd seen her fired up and full of sass. He'd seen the fear as they pulled out of port and into open water. He'd seen the loneliness when she thought he wasn't looking. He'd seen that look often enough in his own reflection not to notice it in a kindred soul. Part of him hoped he could banish that particular demon from both their souls — for at least a while.

"*And…*" Rolly urged Summer to continue.

She looked him straight in the eyes, as if she could see straight through to the heart of him with those clear blue eyes of hers, and said, "Me." She swallowed hard and those lovely eyes grew misty. "He liked me."

Me too, he wanted to say. Because it was true. Rolly liked Summer O'Hara more than he should, although he didn't try too hard not to. Summer was easy to like. He hadn't liked a woman like he liked Summer in more years than he could count. Now that he was retired, golfing, writing, and sailing simply hadn't filled him the way they used to. He wanted a friend. Not the man kind he'd have a beer with after eighteen holes, but the woman kind he could tell secrets to while rubbing her feet.

Retiring had a way of realigning priorities. It also was offering him a chance to redefine who and what he wanted to be.

Wanting to banish the mist and bring back the mellowness Summer had shown before, Rolly nodded toward the hardcover set on the table. "That belonged to my second wife."

Summer sat up a bit straighter, but she didn't pull her feet from him.

"You kept your second wife's books? How many wives have you had?"

Ah, he thought. That was better. A little give and take as far as their romantic histories went and genuine female interest as evidenced by the multiple questions — the latter of which was the more important of the two. He would have smiled at how easily he'd led her where he wanted her to go, but Summer seemed truly interested. He'd also learned she didn't have pretense in her. If she wanted something, she asked. If she was angry, she showed it. Clearly and without obfuscation. Summer didn't hide what she was thinking or how she felt. Rolly wasn't sure he could handle Summer O'Hara, but surprisingly he wanted to try.

She'd been honest with him. He found, again to his surprise, that not only did he want to answer her questions about him, he wanted her to keep asking.

"Yes," he answered nodding to the other two books in the series still on the shelf. "I kept those three. I considered them hazard pay after they were thrown at my head."

Summer was gearing up to ask more about that. He could tell by the flash of amused interest in her widened eyes. He stopped her by answering her second question. "Three. I've had three wives." His eyes narrowed of their own volition for a millisecond, and his hand involuntarily stilled its gentle exploration of Summer's ankle. "I would have had only one had Max's mother not passed."

"I'm sorry," Summer said, meaning it.

How often he'd heard those exact words over the years. Not once before now had they brought him any kind of comfort. Summer was sorry he didn't get to finish the life he'd laid out for himself on his wedding day. She hadn't been able to finish hers either. Only she'd had that particular pain not once, but twice.

"It was a long time ago. Max was already a man—or nearly so. Peggy was healthy one day, sick the next, and gone twelve weeks later."

"I'm sure she'd never have left you or Max if she'd have had a choice."

No one had said that to him before. His other two wives had left him. He hadn't given them much of a choice. Truth be told, had they not, he would have left them.

Summer surprised him by changing direction entirely. Rolly gave a self-deprecating snort at her next question.

"So, you kept your second wife's books because they made good projectile weapons?" she asked smiling sideways at him. That teasing smile hinted at the girl she had been. Only the crinkles at the edges of her eyes and bracketing her smile belied her age. A fact Rolly found vastly appealing.

"That was an added bonus."

The head cock got more pronounced as the grin dimmed to a warm smile. "Why keep the books? They don't seem like the kind of books a man like you would keep."

Rolly was curious to hear what kind of man Summer thought he was, beyond the obvious. But he was willing to wait until he showed her more of himself before he heard her assessment of him. He did raise a brow at her comment. When she kept smiling at him, he resumed his gentle stroking of her ankles. Trying to keep it light. Offhanded. Like he wasn't even aware of the heat radiating from her directly into him.

"She loved those books. I read them and a handful of others

in an attempt to get closer to her." He shrugged. None of it even hurt anymore, although he felt a stab of regret that he hadn't tried harder to make either one of his marriages work after Peggy. "I kept the books I enjoyed. Tossed the ones I didn't."

"What did you like about these books," Summer asked, truly interested. She'd never met a man who read romance on purpose. Certainly not one who's motivation was to get closer to someone he loved.

"I like the spunk, the strength, and the seemingly eternal optimism of the female characters. And the fact that after terrorizing them, they forgive their heroes."

Summer laughed. What a fabulous reason to read. And an even better reason to keep old stories. "Rolly Scott, you are a sentimental soul."

Rolly grinned at her. He was nothing of the sort. He had managed to get Summer O'Hara to use the name he preferred which pleased him almost as much as a kiss would have. *Small steps, Rolly. Small, careful steps. Tread lightly... for you tread on your dreams.*

"I'm a practical soul, dear lady. And keep what brings me joy." Let her make of that what she would. "How about a glass of Rosé while we play cribbage? I have on good authority the wine I stocked is named after you," Rolly said as he moved her legs to the side and stood. He immediately missed touching her, but he wanted more stories from her, and card and drink had a way of bringing them out in most people.

Summer sat up, letting her feet fall to the floor. She eyed his liquor cabinet. "Make that two fingers Four Roses neat and you've got yourself a deal."

"Done," Rolly said.

And just like that, a friendship that would last the rest of their natural lives began.

Five

It was a beautiful afternoon. The breeze off the lake was gentle, adding a crispness to the otherwise warm air. The sky was blue, filled with patches of translucent white clouds. The songs of robins and wrens, sparrows and finches, and soft cooing of doves filled the air away from the water and the distant sounds of motor boats.

The air smelled fresh and new, like it did every summer after the cherry blossoms fell. Tulips and daffodils bloomed. A myriad of summer annuals perfumed the air from planting boxes and baskets that filled every inch of available space not reserved for trees and manicured lawns.

Fallon found it odd how much she loved Door County in the summertime, how peaceful it was even with the constant buzz of tourists milling everywhere. She had a million and one questions reverberating through her head as she and Max made their way from the shore to Summer's home. So many in fact, she couldn't pick one.

Part of that may have been the fact that Max was holding her hand while they walked. Naturally they seemed to fall into step with one another. Like breathing. It took no effort; it just flowed. Step by step in tune. Holding Max's hand felt right. Reassuring. Like she could count on him. While none of that made logical sense, Fallon wouldn't deny the truth of it. Denial had never served her well in the past, so she'd made a concerted effort not to allow herself to indulge in its dangerous depths.

They were just approaching her mother's favorite jewelry shop when Fallon heard the familiar rumble of Gus's 2010 Harley CRD

XR 1200. Harley launched the bike only in Europe. It had cost Gus a small fortune to have it crated over from Spain. There was only one motorcycle in the Door like it and it was Gus's.

One look at Gus as he parked it in Jack Smith's small parking lot next to the jewelry store, and all Fallon saw was red. By the time Gus was taking off his Shoe full-face helmet, she was ready to take him to the ground. She may have too, if Max hadn't held her back.

He clamped down on her hand as she tried to cross the road. There was only one main route in and out of Ephraim, and it was busy throughout the tourist season. On a clear day like today, it was dangerously busy. "Calm down," Max hissed in her ear. "He's seen you. If that pale look on his face is any indication, he knows you're angry. Anger has no place here for either of you. I need you to put a lid on it and pretty damned fast."

He smiled at her through gritted teeth. "Smith is coming out of his shop. Follow my lead or risk Summer never being able to go outside again without looking over her shoulder for her would-be killer."

Max didn't wait for Fallon to answer. He started waving instead like a joyful madman at Gus. He shouted across to Fallon's perplexed brother. "Hey, Gus, thanks for meeting me, Bro. I hadn't counted on your sister being with us."

A weak smile grew on Gus's face as he slowly waved back. "Got here as quickly as I could," he said, falling into his role as follower of Max's lead.

Max crossed the road at the first clearing between slow moving, yet consistent traffic. He made his way to Gus and enveloped him in what looked to be a painful hug. "You're here *early*. I wanted this to be a surprise for your sister."

"Oh, she looks plenty surprised," Gus said, making Fallon wonder if she was the only one who noticed the sardonic and worried edge to his upbeat tone. Probably. She was sensitive to it in a way even the triplets' best friends growing up hadn't noticed.

Jack Smith made his way down the concrete steps in front of his front door. "Been kind of slow here today, gentlemen. What can I help you with," he asked amicably enough, although Fallon thought she saw a calculating shrewdness in his eyes that had little to do with how close he could come to his three-hundred percent markup.

Max turned toward Jack Smith and switched into a different person. He was warm and engaging and effusing. He didn't even look the same. Gone were the penetrating and assessing eyes. Now those eyes said everyone he met was destined to be his best friend and wasn't he just so happy to be part of that experience. The transformation was uncanny.

The smile Max sent Fallon was loving and gentle and filled with a knowing sensuality that said he wanted to hold her to him naked forever. Fallon's throat went dry as he pulled her to his side. "I was going to surprise my bride with a belated engagement ring, but this oaf came early, before I could get his sister home. He was going to help me pick out something wonderful. Now that the cat's out of the bag, I guess Gus's help is no longer needed."

Max turned to face Gus and his smile deepened. Only this time it didn't reach his eyes. Gus got the message. He smiled, too. Then he slapped Max's shoulder. As a gesture of brotherly competition couched in brotherly love, it managed to look real enough. Gus still couldn't meet Fallon's eyes, though. He hastily put on his helmet after he said to Max, "Meet you guys up at Mom's in about an hour. I'll grab Finn. He's expecting dinner and drinks on the back deck."

Gus was backing up the Sportster as Max said, "Take your time. You're in charge of the wine. Steaks are in the fridge."

Gus waved, started his bike and was gone without once looking Fallon in the eye. Fallon tamped down her anger. Max was right. With Jack Smith watching every nuance, this was neither the time nor the place to tip their hand.

Jack's gaze shifted from Max to Fallon. They'd met before. Summer managed to drag her into his shop at least once a summer when Fallon visited. They hadn't exchanged more than a dozen or so words. Her mother was the one who loved to talk jewelry. That didn't stop Jack Smith's probing words or assessing eyes. "I was sorry to hear about your mother, Fallon." He cocked his head at her and leaned down. He was a tall man, taller than her, playing at comfort by leaning in, waiting to see if she'd jerk back.

She didn't. In fact, she smiled a small sad, detached smile. Men as trained in their craft as Jack Smith had tried to play her for any number of reasons over a period of years. Her boss, and the one man she called friend, Nick Card, had taught her how to recognize their tells. She knew how to use them to her advantage, while never once giving away by word, deed, or micro-expression what she was feeling. The trick she'd learned was not to feel, to take herself out of the moment and replace herself with whomever the men assumed her to be.

"Thank you, Mr. Smith," she said, holding his gaze for a moment before looking down. Her voice was softer when she continued, "It's been a difficult time for my brothers and me. Especially for Gus. He's as angry about losing our mom as he is hurt. It makes him impulsive."

"I'm surprised you'd be shopping for an engagement ring at a time like this," Jack said neutrally, his gaze shifting between Fallon and Max.

Fallon wrapped her arm around Max's and pulled him closer into her. She looked up into his face and smiled her best *You-walk-on-water-and-I'll-love-you-forever* smile at him. She toned the smile down a bit but kept it in place as she looked toward Jack Smith. "This wasn't my idea, Mr. Smith. I'm perfectly happy with my wedding band. I'm not the jewelry lover my mother was…" Fallon let her voice trail off.

Max picked it up beautifully. He tapped her arm with his free hand. "That's why this is the perfect time to pick out a ring, love. We'll be honoring your mother's love of jewelry. You'll get to pick out something perfect from her favorite shop. Every time you look at it, you'll have a good memory of your mom and a loving memory of me."

Well, after that load of sentimental — yet convincingly

sincere—horse manure, not even someone as slick as Jack Smith could suggest it wasn't the ideal time to buy solidified carbon, compressed over millennia in the earth's crust.

"Shall we," Max asked gesturing toward the stairs that led to Jack Smith's jewelry shop.

Fallon smiled at him, enjoying herself, despite the fact that she may have just engaged pleasantries with her mother's would-be killer. Maybe she was enjoying herself because of it. Either way, she'd take pleasure in taking the man down.

"We shall," Fallon said, stepping once again in perfect time with Max and following Jack Smith, wherever that cagey criminal chose to lead.

Gus's little intervention had forced Max into Jack Smith's shop before he was ready. But now that he was there, Max was determined not to leave until he scoped out every jewel in the place. As it turned out, Jack Smith led Max and Fallon to the case farthest from the front door that held vintage diamond rings. Not a Harry Winston, Cartier, Graff, or a Van Cleef and Arpels among them. Max spotted an older Tiffany piece from about the 1940s, but the diamond was under half a carat and a higher color, maybe an "I." Not worth what old Mr. Smith was asking for it, regardless of one's affinity for the forties.

When nothing in the vintage case sparked any interest in Fallon, they made their way case by case until they hit the one filled with Jack Smith's own creations. Most of the diamond engagement rings were under a carat—nothing too obvious to draw attention. Max thought Smith had probably hidden anything that might raise a brow after Summer O'Hara called out the Flower of Scotland. He had to give it to the old fox though, his designs were lovely. Some delicate and floral. Some more bold with mixtures of 18K yellow gold, rose gold, and platinum. All had high quality diamonds.

Fallon tried on three of the engagement rings, feigning

interest in all of them. The shop was small, maybe 800 square feet. It didn't take long to exhaust the diamond selection. Then they moved to the small room housing sapphires, rubies, a few emeralds, multi-hued tourmalines, a handful of morganites, aquamarines, tanzanites, exactly three highly saturated amethyst rings, and a surprising selection of opals.

Max knew Fallon was feigning interest in the diamonds as soon as her eyes lit on the opals. They seemed to light a fire in her heart. For some reason that thrilled Max. Opals, especially ones from Australian mines that had run their course, could be every bit as expensive and far rarer than the white diamonds.

Seeing her interest, Max asked to see a strand of perfectly round opal beads.

Jack pulled them from the case, laying them out on a cushioned pad topped with black velvet. Then he grabbed the box they came in and set the box beside the stand. They were old, judging by the length, made for a small woman.

"These are from Vincent and Sons," Jack Smith said.

Max could have read that himself. It was written clearly in black script on the satin inside the cover of the hinged kidney bean shaped box.

"Vincent and Sons was a short-lived yet premier jeweler in Milwaukee at the turn of the last century. This piece dates back to the early 1900s, probably no later than 1920. The clasp is platinum, set with old mine cut diamonds." Jack held the strand up to the light filtering in from the front windows. There was plenty of incandescent light in the small space, but in the natural light, the green and blue hues of the opals appeared otherworldly. The piece was magnificent. Fit for someone who would love it as much as its creator had cared for its first recipient. Women just didn't wear things that rare and subtle today. Again, it pleased him that this piece was the one that brought a genuine smile to Fallon's face.

"Would you like to try it on?" Jack asked, obviously pleased to take out a piece of value that most people would simply ignore.

Fallon's hand went to her throat. "I…"

She caught herself quickly and started again. "It looks so delicate. I'm not sure I feel comfortable wearing it."

"I restrung these myself. I assure you, they are quite secure. You could wear this choker every day for the next decade, and as long as you took care not to swim in it, spray it full of perfume or hairspray, you'd have no issues."

Fallon tried it on. It fit perfectly.

"The total length is only fifteen and a half inches. Not everyone can wear this beauty."

Fallon looked at her reflection in the mirror. She looked like a princess. Her small smile and the look in her eyes as she stroked the beads made Max want to be the one who gave them to her. He wanted her to look at him while she touched him that reverently. He didn't dare entertain those kinds of thoughts. Not on the job. Not with Fallon. Not ever.

Before Max could direct Fallon's attention back to his real reason for being in the shop, she had the necklace off and was handing it to Jack Smith. "Thank you," she told him, meaning it, before she moved onto the next case.

Max made his way to a case that held pins made of sterling silver, replica coins taken from various ship wrecks, including some from the Atocha find. All were replicas. All were well done. None of them interested Max, because none housed any stolen gems he had on his radar.

Then Fallon, who was in the corner looking at sterling pendants, asked to see one of them. Max swung around to see what she found. She held it up for him. "Look, Max, it's a sterling impression of an old ring seal. The seal would have been used to imprint melted sealing wax to letters or other correspondence. Isn't it cool?"

Max went to her side. It was very cool indeed. Inside the seal was a tiny red diamond. No more than fifteen or sixteen points. Not the kind of thing to be placed in a pendant selling for just over a hundred bucks.

Max took the pendant and put it over Fallon's head. He turned to Jack Smith and said "Sold" as enthusiastically as he could. He didn't bother to hide his smile. "Now, my sweet girl, shall we pick out a diamond?"

Fallon grinned at him, went to the case where she'd seen the three wedding sets she liked, and pointed to the one that Max thought had the highest quality diamond. She picked a smallish diamond, over half a carat, but not quite sixty points, surrounded by a halo of small round diamonds with even smaller diamonds running down the shank. Most white diamonds under a carat didn't come with GIA—Gemological Institute of America certifications. This one didn't, but it was easy to see it was well cut and clearly in the white scale of D, E, or F color.

"We'll take the lady's choice," Max said to Jack.

Jack pulled out the ring and handed it to Max.

Max slipped it onto Fallon's left finger, on top of the thin eternity band he'd placed there less than an hour before. It fit perfectly.

His eyes captured hers. Before he changed his mind, he leaned down and brushed her lips with his. As kisses went, it wasn't more than a brief hello, still it shook him to his core. "I'll call Tiffany in Chicago and have a bigger one made for you if you want."

Jack interrupted. "I'll be happy to make the same ring in a larger size for Mrs. — "

He let the silence hang, waiting for Max to jump in with his last name.

Max said instead, "Fallon kept her maiden name. No Mrs., just Fallon Murphy."

Jack nodded. "I'll be happy to make another ring for you if you determine you'd like more substance on your finger, Ms. Murphy. Just tell me about the size and what you're looking for, and I'll get some stones in for you to look at."

Fallon smiled at him. "Thank you, Mr. Smith. I think I'll live with this ring for a while before I decide. Right now, it has all the *substance* I can handle."

Max reached into his back pocket, pulled out his wallet, and set his white card down on the counter. "We'll take the ring and the pendant; we may be back for the opals."

They wouldn't be. Max took one look at the price on the antique strand and knew he'd be skinned alive if the deputy director got wind of that kind of purchase. His white card was real — issued by invitation only with basically no limit. He even got points toward booking private jet flights. Even so, the FBI would not be amused when the bill came through.

The card served its purpose though.

It gave Jack Smith Max's assumed name. The name, when checked, would show that he earned millions of dollars a year — more specifically, that he charged and payed off more than a quarter of a million dollars in the previous twelve months. He was a mover, a shaker, a man willing to spend fortunes large and small on the finer things in life, including jewelry.

For any criminal worth his or her salt, it also told them where Max Smart lived, worked, traveled, ate, drank, and that he was willing to part with his cash freely and frequently.

Jack Smith was worth his salt.

Max had just made himself a mark.

Now all they had to do was see if he was a big enough mark to tempt a thief who made his living ensuring he never got caught.

Either way, Max was determined to catch his white whale. The only difference was Max wouldn't let the whale take him down with him.

Six

Walking into her mother's house knowing Summer wasn't there felt odd. The scents were the same. On a table near the door, lilacs and peonies sprouted from the tin-can vase Fallon had made for her mother in fourth grade. Another vase, an Irish crystal, was filled with Asian lilies and hybrid tea roses from Summer's garden in the back. Petals were falling from the lilies, but the roses still had their bloom. They seemed to scent the air even more strongly when they were in the last vestiges of life.

Fallon's stomach turned. Broken shards of Summer's tea cup, jagged and raw, the largest piece stained on the edge a sickening brown-red, lay scattered at the bottom of the stairs. Fallon had her hand to her mouth trying to control the wave of nausea when Max came up behind her and enveloped her in a hug. She turned into him and let him hold her.

One hand was at the small of her back, the other at her nape, holding her to him as he whispered, "It wasn't as bad as it looks. She had a small cut on her arm from the teacup." Actually, it was a gash that bled more than it should have. The doctor had said the compounds in the poison had thinned Summer's blood, making her bleed more profusely. The cut required about twenty stitches, but Fallon didn't need to hear that.

Max hoped that when they Skyped, Fallon wouldn't see Summer's bandages. "She bruised her arms and her left wrist. She's pretty banged up but nothing is broken. She's going to be all right."

Fallon pulled away from Max to look into his eyes. She wasn't crying exactly, but her eyes were red and glistening with unshed tears. "How do you know she's going to be all right? Someone tried to kill her."

"Because you and I, with a little help from our friends, will make it so."

"I don't have any friends here," Fallon said dejectedly.

Max smiled down at her, moving a piece of her shoulder-length hair behind her ear. "I highly doubt that. I've got a feeling you make friends wherever you go."

Fallon said nothing to that.

She wiped at her eyes with the back of her hand, taking what was left of her eye makeup and spreading it around. She had brownish sparkles around her temples and under her eyes. Nothing so mundane could take away from her earthy beauty. Fallon's features where strong, where her mothers were soft. She got her mother's spunk and apparently, her father's chiseled features. Gus had the same strong features. Max hadn't met Finn yet, but he was guessing Finn got the same chin, jaw, and cheekbones.

Fallon pushed away from him and bent to pick up the shards of the broken teacup. "Thoughtless ass," she muttered to herself. "Bloody cretin couldn't be bothered to clean this up."

Max grabbed her by the arm, lifting her as gently as he could to her feet. "Give me those," he said opening his palm.

Fallon dropped the shards into his palm.

"I'll finish this. Why don't you go upstairs? Wash your face, comb your hair, do whatever you have to do to gear up for your brothers. As I understand it, you're the peacemaker of the group. Fingal is bound to be as furious as you are at Fergus. It's none of my business how your sibling dynamic works, but for what it's worth, Gus was trying to do what was right for your mom."

He had her for a moment. He lost her with his defense of Gus Murphy. Whatever was between them, whatever happened to Summer wasn't the beginning or end of it. The coldness in her eyes said Max had overstepped. Her words confirmed it.

"You're right. My siblings are none of your business." Her tone was flat when she said it. She was up the stairs and out of sight before Max could think of anything to say to bring some happiness back into her eyes.

"Way to go, Max. Alienate the one person you need to successfully complete your investigation," he muttered to himself. Muttering seemed to be contagious. Either that, or being married, even for show, was making him crazy.

By the time Max finished cleaning up the mess at the bottom of the stairs, taking out what was now rancid trash, and throwing away the dying flowers, he was starving. There were no steaks in the refrigerator. He hadn't purchased any. He hadn't planned on having to stop Gus from doing whatever that hothead planned to do to Jack Smith. He hadn't planned how he was going to deal with the Murphy triplets at all.

Max found the keys to Summer's Mazda right where she told them they'd be. He penned a hasty note letting Fallon know where he was going, if she cared. He wrote it on a pad of paper secured by a magnet on the refrigerator that read "Things To Do" in bold block letters at the top and "Make the World Better with Your Smile" at the bottom.

He wasn't smiling when he walked out the front door.

So much for making the world a better place.

Jake Smith picked up one of his many burner phones and called the woman with the long blond hair. In reality, her hair was neither long nor blond. He knew her intimately. She did have certain attributes that made his life more lucrative, which made it far more palatable. And those side benefits suited him. For now.

She didn't answer.

Jack Smith left a message.

"I need you up here. Time for a ten-day vacation. Bring your toys."

The Fallon Murphy encounter made every hair on the back of Jack's neck stand at attention. It wasn't Fallon he needed to worry about. The man with her, the one claiming to be her husband, he was a threat. Jack thought he'd seen the man before, but he'd run his picture—taken from Jack's in-store surveillance—by every secure source he had. So far, he'd come up with nothing. The guy was smart. Knew how to avoid camera angles.

Time to get some surveillance in Summer O'Hara's house.

The funeral service tomorrow should be the perfect time to see it done. Most of the town would be at the service.

Jack Smith thought about the money still to be made from the stones he'd taken out of the stolen Zoe Tiara. He thought about all the money he had stashed around the world. He thought about his small cottage in the Cotswolds of England and the widowed teacher who lived next door. He thought about his apartment in Rome with a view of the Vatican.

Then he thought of his home in Long Grove, Illinois, and his summer home on the lake in Fish Creek, just south of his shop in Ephraim.

He was older than he ever thought he'd live to be. He was physically healthy and agile for his age. Even so, he couldn't scale walls with the same alacrity anymore. He didn't have the stamina. His reflexes had slowed, no matter how many exercises he did daily to keep them sharp. His upper body strength had waned, and sex was no longer a spontaneous thing, but a planned one, made possible with the help of pharmaceuticals.

Jack Smith really liked the widow in the Cotswolds. Liked the slow life there too. Flowers in the summer with evenings at the pub. Winters spent by the fire, reading, talking to the widow about books. Maybe even kissing her goodnight in time. It was appealing.

Jack put the thought away.

He was done running.

He liked his life here. He was going to live it as long as possible. Even if that meant cutting other lives short.

Seven

Fallon showered, changed into a pair of shorts and a T-shirt she had in her room. She kept a collection of clothing at her mother's house since she spent time here every summer. She also had clothing in the trunk of her rental that she packed in Key West. She just hadn't bothered to unpack yet.

Max was gone when she went downstairs. So were the wilted flowers. Fallon was thankful for that. She didn't like to see once beautiful living things fade into nothingness. She wasn't sure why she was feeling so morbid.

Then she looked at the ugly urn her brothers had picked for what at least Finn thought were their mother's ashes and she started to laugh. She laughed so hard it hurt. No wonder she was feeling morbid. She'd been carrying around some poor sod's ashes wishing she'd have called her mother more often.

Fallon made her way to the kitchen. She was hungry now that she didn't want to throw up. And she wanted to talk to her mother. The latter wouldn't happen until her brothers got here. A mixed blessing that. The former she could do something about.

The note on the frig stopped her in her tracks.

Hungry after our first argument. Gone out for grill food. Looking forward to make-up marital sex after we eat.

"Keep dreaming, Romeo," Fallon said smiling as she shook her head. She'd felt badly about snapping at him. It wasn't Max's fault she still felt raw about Gus's betrayal.

"Always keep the dream alive," Max said behind her.

Fallon whirled around, catching sight of him in his rumpled polo, khaki shorts, and ill-fitting boat shoes. It was the smile on his face and the devilish twinkle in his eye that made him dangerously appealing.

Fallon smiled back. "Never going to happen, slick."

He came closer to her, walking slowly, smiling so wickedly that her heart literally skipped a beat before racing in her chest. Then he leaned down, set the groceries on the counter behind her, and whispered, "Never is a long time, sweetheart. I wouldn't hold your breath."

Fallon turned toward him. Max held his breath, waiting to hear what she had to say. He'd been frustrated, mostly with himself, but somewhat with her, when he wrote that note. He didn't regret it, exactly. How could he when she looked freshly scrubbed and sweet, and she was smiling at him like he was her best friend in the world.

That made something inside him explode.

Whatever else happened, Max was going to keep the woman next to him safe.

She was gearing up to give him a royal dressing down when a voice cut in. "So, it's true. You went and got married."

Max looked toward the entrance to the kitchen. A man who looked like Gus, except for the smile, stood with open arms, looking at Fallon with love in his eyes.

Fallon ran to him.

Finn spun her around like she was five and they were on the playground. "How could you let another man hold your heart without letting me and Gus give you away. That's always been the plan, short-stuff."

Since Fallon was almost as tall as her brothers, that comment was laughable on its face. They were all tall, dark, and attractive. Suddenly Max felt like a third wheel.

Then Gus walked in and he became the fourth wheel.

He was about to catch them up on the fact that he and Fallon weren't really married. He needed to do that before they talked to their mother. Fallon had other ideas. "Put me down, you oaf. I'm not a child anymore."

Finn set her down. "Nope. All grown up and frick'n *married*. What are you going to tell us next?" he asked feigning irritation, "that there's a tribe of mini-me's running around Key West?"

Fallon hit him. "Don't say *frick'n*. It makes you sound like an eleven-year-old afraid to swear for real." Then she grinned at him, ignoring Gus completely. "Come meet Max."

Fallon walked Finn toward him. She stopped about a foot away and introduced the brother he'd only seen in photos. "Max this is my brother Fingal. Finn, meet my... *husband*, Max Smart, business consultant extraordinaire."

Max just stared at her, eyes narrowed, silently asking what was going on.

Fallon winked at him.

Finn grabbed Max in a bear hug that threatened his ribs. Then he made it worse by pounding his back like he thought Max was choking to death. Finally, he let him go. Then pulled him in for another quick hug. Mercifully, this one was quick and not nearly so tight.

"Welcome to the family, Max," Finn said, still smiling. "You must be really something to get Fallon to marry you without telling her family."

"She's still pissed at me, Finn. That's probably why she didn't tell us," Gus said. His voice sullen, flat, angry. He was leaning against the wall that opened to the kitchen. The invisible chip on his shoulder weighing down his left side.

Again, Fallon ignored Gus. Max decided to do the same.

Finn lost his smile. His shoulders dropped and his chin dipped toward Fallon. "Did Mom know?" he asked. "She'd have been so happy for you, half-pint."

Fallon reached up and touched Finn's cheek. "No," she said. "Mom didn't know." Fallon shot Max a look that he thought meant, *don't say anything about us* not *being married*. That was okay with him. He liked having an excuse to hold her hand anytime he wanted. He had no problem with that.

Gus pushed away from the wall, looked at his watch, strode into the kitchen, and said, "Isn't it time to get mom on the phone?"

Finn whirled around to face Gus, hands fisted at his sides. "That was a terrible joke."

Gus put his hands behind his back. "No joke." His gaze went

to Max. "Call her."

Finn looked from Fallon to Gus then back at Fallon.

"I just found out. Still don't quite believe it," she said.

Finn turned to Gus. "How long have you known?"

"Since the beginning. Since Max saved her," Gus said. No excuses. No empathy for what either of his siblings had been put through because he'd lied to them.

Finn punched him in the face.

For the second time in a matter of hours, Max was cleaning blood off the floor.

Eight

The journey to Milwaukee had been uneventful, which according to Rolly made it perfect. It took them two days to get there, a short time by most standards. For Summer, it was too long to be stuck on a boat. When Rolly was playing cards with her, she was fine. When he was rubbing her ankles, she was fine — better than fine, but she didn't need to tell him that.

Summer wasn't fine when she was alone while Rolly was doing what needed to done to keep them on the right course. She tried not to show it, but somehow Rolly knew. He wasn't patronizing about it; he didn't tell her how brave she was. What he did do was read to her. He played cards with her. He never let her win, which she did about forty percent of the time. The man was a cardsharp. He bluffed like a man born to it.

His condo surprised her. It overlooked the river and had a slip where Rolly docked his boat. The view was spectacular. It was in an area of the city referred to as the Third Ward — a closed art community with boutique shops and some of the city's best restaurants. The condo itself was bright and cheery, done in a shade of grey and cream and burgundy. The kitchen was outfitted for a man who loved to cook. There were two bedrooms, both en suite. One she currently lived in. The other, she hadn't seen. There was a large and open great-room that led to the balcony, which was large enough to hold a grill, a bistro set, and two full-length reclining loungers.

The art on the wall was local. Her favorites were the lithographs done by Wisconsin artist Harold Hansen. Rolly had a large loom against the wall. The man loomed in his spare time which, as far as Summer could tell, he didn't have much of. Rolly was constantly in motion. Up early. Go all day. To bed by eleven, generally after some snuggle time on the couch watching movies.

Rolly liked action movies, old Hitchcock flicks, and the remake of *Westworld*.

She liked *Midsomer Murders, NCIS,* and everything with Pierce Brosnan—including *Mama Mia* which Rolly watched with one arm around a gigantic bowl of cheese popcorn, the other around her.

As lovely as his home was, Summer was going more than a little stir-crazy. She also wanted to see another human being, even if she wasn't allowed to talk to them.

Summer was sitting in the kitchen drinking her third cup of coffee—something Rolly said wasn't good for her—when he walked in, hair still wet from his shower. He grabbed a mug from the mug tree and poured himself a cup from the pot. He leaned against the back counter, looking at her as she read the *Post* from his tablet. "Is that your third cup?"

Summer set down her cup and looked Rolly straight in the eye. He was wearing a pair of tan shorts, a white polo shirt, and grey running shoes. "This is my *second* cup of coffee, Rolly Scott. And for your information, I am a grown woman who can decide for herself how much caffeine she can ingest."

The corner of his mouth twitched, but he didn't smile. "Liar."

Summer didn't even try to fight it. "How do you always know?"

Rolly crossed the room and sat on the stool beside her. "You always look me in the eye and use my full name. Then you get defensive and say something like, 'Rolly, I am perfectly capable of making my own poor decisions.'" Rolly mimicked her voice, but he got the pitch too high and cadence too slow. Even so, he was pretty good.

"I don't make poor decisions." Summer shrugged. Letting Jack Smith know she knew he had the Flower of Scotland had been a doozie. She flushed. "Not most of the time anyway. And certainly not about coffee."

Rolly changed the subject, which Summer was beginning to learn signaled he was certain he was right and thought he'd made his point well enough to move on.

"I've got a surprise for you," he said.

"Do I get to finish my coffee?"

He grinned at her, then leaned down and kissed the top of her head. Summer couldn't tell who was more surprised, him or her, but he didn't stop grinning at her. He seemed quite pleased with himself. "Drink up, darlin'. I'll be right back."

Suddenly her coffee wasn't so necessary anymore. Summer was wide awake and having more fun than she'd had in years. What she wasn't, she realized, was lonely.

Rolly came back holding a box about a foot wide and a foot deep. It was white with a big red bow on top. Summer looked from the box to Rolly, then back at the box. "What's this?" she asked.

Rolly seemed almost giddy. He was certainly pleased with himself. "Open it. Find out."

He handed the box to Summer.

She lifted the top. She couldn't quite believe her eyes. "Are we role playing?"

Rolly spit out the coffee he'd been trying to swallow.

Summer lifted a wig out of the box. It was blond and cut short. She put it on. "Is this a gentlemen-prefer-blondes thing?"

"No. And for the record, this gentleman prefers redheads. This," he said nodding toward the wig, "is a let's-get-out of-the-condo-and-enjoy-ourselves thing. There's a pair of sunglasses in there too. I'd like you to wear a hat. I've got an extra Brewers cap that should fit."

"We can get out of here?"

"That's the plan."

Summer squealed, jumped up, threw her arms around Rolly, then ran toward her bathroom at the opposite end of the hall. When Rolly bought the condo, having the two master bedrooms on opposite ends had been a selling point. Now that he actually had a house guest, *this* house guest, he wanted her right next him. He was falling for Summer O'Hara. A woman he was supposed to be protecting. A woman who had two good marriages and by all accounts loved two good men.

He was two-time loser. He loved one great woman, he cared about two pretty good ones, and he managed to lose all three. One by a quirk of fate no one could control. Two by being a distant, self-important ass. Fate had nothing to do with that.

Now fate, or God, or the Universe had entrusted him with caring for another great woman. One who was nothing like his first love, except in her inherent kindness. One who made him laugh, kept him questioning his opinions, who couldn't lie worth a damn, and seemed to find the positive in the least positive of situations. This woman made his heart beat faster while still being so easy to be around he didn't have to try. This woman was the whole package. The thought of losing Summer scared him like he hadn't been scared since the day they got Peggy's diagnosis.

Summer came out of her room wearing her wig. It worked. She looked different enough that no one who didn't scrutinize her closely would know she was Summer O'Hara. Rolly wouldn't let anyone within scrutinizing range of Summer, so he could show her a good time in his city without worry. He was happy he could do this for her. That he'd enjoy her enjoyment was an added bonus.

She twirled for him.

Rolly loved the fact that Summer didn't act like she was older than she was. She enjoyed life and she let it show. "How do I look?"

The wig was shorter than her shoulder-length hair. She looked younger with the bangs, but that could have been the ear-to-ear grin. "Like Kelly Preston when she was blond."

Summer laughed. "Now who's lying, Rolly Scott?"

He wasn't lying, although Summer was more attractive than Kelly Preston and less flashy. "Come on, woman. Let's get out of here."

Summer was at the door, purse slung across her body, sunglasses in hand before he could fish the keys out of his pocket.

For the first time in a long time, Rolly was looking forward to simply spending the day out with a woman.

"So, tell me about your son," Summer said, popping a strawberry in her mouth. Rolly took her to breakfast at a sidewalk café that specialized in fruit crepes. She had a double order. One strawberry. One blueberry. Both were fantastic.

Rolly set down his fork. He'd finished about half his spinach omelet and red potato hash. "I thought we weren't talking about our kids."

"Five minutes."

"Okay. What do you want to know?" Rolly asked.

"What kind of man is he?"

The question threw Rolly for a second. Most people asked for the mundane facts: Where does he work? Is he married? Do you see each other often? Not Summer. But then she wasn't most people.

What kind of man was Max? Rolly said the first word that came to his mind, "Honorable."

Summer's eyebrows raised and she pulled down her sunglasses far enough to look over the rims at him. "That's it?"

Rolly narrowed his eyes. "Is there anything I could say about Max right now that would mean more to you than that?"

Summer thought about it for a second, and just when Rolly thought she'd ask him something more, she said, "No. Thank you."

Again, she surprised him. This time pleasantly. He was sinking deeper under her spell and he didn't care. "Tell me about your children," Rolly said, although the one he cared about most was Fallon. Fallon had his son's attention.

"Gus came out first. He was plucked, actually. Ever since then, he thinks it's his job to run the show, whatever the show is. He's smart, ambitious, and hard-headed. He has a good heart, and he tries to do the right thing but manages to put his foot in it about a third of the time."

Summer ate another strawberry, warming to her topic. "Fingal is kind, and funny, and determined. He makes everything work.

His focus is amazing. He has a tender heart that gets him in trouble more than it should. That hasn't made him jaded though. He still puts himself out there with more optimism than I could muster."

Rolly said nothing, but he doubted that. He'd never met another person as openly optimistic as Summer. He was betting Fingal Murphy had a sizable amount of his mother in him.

Rolly took a sip of his water, urging Summer to continue with a gesture.

She smiled, though not at him. She was staring off, lost in a memory, and judging by her expression, it was a fond one. "Fallon is a mix of both boys and," Summer paused, "she's all her own. She opens her heart, but not with regularity or blind optimism. She's strong and opinionated. That manifests as stubbornness and determination, depending on how the recipient of her strength takes it. Fallon loves hard. And when she cares deeply, she gives everything she's got to the person or project she cares about. She's loyal and seriously smart. She's got a good head for business." Summer looked right at him. "And if she feels she's been wronged, she's slow to forgive." She paused again just to make sure he understood what she was saying. "My girl holds a grudge."

Rolly got the distinct impression that Summer wasn't simply talking about her daughter.

"You're not going to scare me off, Summer. No matter how hard you try. I can out stubborn the best of them. And you, my dear, are not in the running for stubborn blonde of the year. I don't think Max is going to do anything that would give Fallon a reason to hold a grudge."

Rolly smiled at her and leaned in. "It's not like he married her, moved in, and set up house. There should be no legitimate reason for Fallon to hold a grudge."

For some reason Rolly couldn't define, Summer's slow smile bothered him. It reminded him again that women were inherently undefinable and infinitely more complex than their male counterparts. That even when they appear simple and sweet and straightforward, they almost always know more than you do.

Summer lifted her glass of iced tea in salute. "Of course, you're right," she said, solidifying his concern. "What on earth would lead any of my children to hold a grudge against Max. He did save my life after all."

Rolly groaned inwardly knowing he was going to get more than he bargained with Summer, yet grateful she was such a bad liar. One thing he knew for absolute certain, out of everything she'd just said, Summer O'Hara only believed her last sentence.

Rolly got up, slid two twenty-dollar bills into the over-sized black wallet that contained their bill, and reached for Summer. "Come on then, lovely lady. It's a beautiful day and we've got a lot to do before the sky opens up and your proverbial *grudge shoe* drops on our heads."

Summer grinned at him. "Our children's five minutes are up, sir," she said standing before executing a sloppy but endearing bow. "The rest of the day is all ours."

Now that kind of thinking, Rolly thought, was more like it.

Nine

All three of the Murphy children stared at Max's laptop screen, trying to decipher the surreal experience of speaking to a mother they were having difficulty recognizing. Each one was lost in their own internal space: Gus, biting down hard on the peanuts he kept popping into his mouth; Fingal, silently assessing, lips pursed, head cocked to one side; Fallon, openly engaged in disbelief.

For his part, Max was having a hard time reconciling his reserved, by-the-book father with the smiling, seemingly happy-go-lucky man on the screen sitting next to a now blond Summer O'Hara.

"After breakfast, Rolly took me to something called the Rainbow Race where rainbow-colored chalk is thrown on the racers as they run by. They end up being a mess, but everyone seems to enjoy it."

"It's not chalk. It's called the Color Run," Rolly interjected.

Summer waived that away, then took Rolly's hand when he tried to adjust the screen on his laptop and held it. "That's not really important, is it?" she asked.

Rolly smiled indulgently at her. "Nope."

"What's important is that we had *such* a great time today," Summer said expansively, gesturing at the screen with her free hand. Then she leaned in and said conspiratorially, "Did you know there's a place called The Witches House on the lake? Not only is it haunted by a real witch who never dies, she's an artist and her lawn is filled with exotic sculptures."

"Mom, what's that on your head?" Fallon asked.

"It's a wig, dear." Summer whispered, "I'm incognito. Isn't

it exciting?"

Max started to cough.

Finn said, "I think she's asking about the headband with the springs on it."

Summer's hand flew to her head. Then she looked at Rolly with a frown. "Why didn't you tell me I still had this thing on?"

Rolly laughed. A sound Max hadn't heard from his father in more than a year. "It's cute."

"What *is* it?" Finn asked, sounding truly curious and far less judgmental than his brother looked.

"Rolly bought this," she said seriously, peering into the screen. "It has tiny bouncing rainbows attached to it." Summer nodded as if her explanation made perfect sense.

Rolly added, "After lunch we walked to the Summerfest grounds. I took your mother to Pride Fest. That," he said nodding toward the bouncing rainbows on Summer's head, "was the least flamboyant thing she liked. It looked cute on her when she tried it on, so I bought it for her."

"Were the heart-shaped glasses your idea too?" Max asked, thinking his father had lost his mind.

"Nope. I got her a nice pair of Oakley's. She picked up the ones she's wearing from a vender on the Summerfest grounds for five bucks."

"Best deal of the day." Summer nodded, making the tiny rainbows bounce.

Fallon was shaking her head, a perplexed look on her face. It's not even seven thirty yet, Mom. Just how much wine have you had?"

Summer smiled and lifted her plastic cocktail glass. "We're sitting on the balcony watching the river. Rolly made mojitos." She took a sip from her glass. "They're delicious."

Finn smiled at his mother. "How many have you had, Mom?"

"This is my second," Summer said, holding up an almost full glass.

"Third," Rolly interjected.

Summer let go of his hand and back-handed him gently across

the chest. "Noooo," she said. "This is like that coffee thing, right? I've only had two, but you count three." Summer looked from Rolly back toward the screen. "Rolly doesn't want me to drink more than two cups of coffee." She sounded put out by that.

Gus spoke around a handful of nuts for the first time. "But apparently three mojitos *are* okay."

Everyone ignored him.

Finn grinned. He looked like he was enjoying himself. He'd only just learned that his mother was alive. After punching his brother and seeing his mother on the screen, he seemed to be over the hurt and fully embracing the joy of seeing his mother happy. Or that's how it appeared to Max. Finn was pretty easy to figure out. He was having a harder time reading what Fallon was thinking.

Finn grabbed Fallon's left hand and held it up to the screen, grinning. "Since you're in the mood to celebrate, here's some good news." He waved Fallon's hand, holding it firm as she tried to pull it away, "Fallon's married."

Max waited for the explosion he thought was imminent. If not from Summer, then from his father.

Both parents looked at the screen, taking in the sight of Fallon's left hand and the diamond rings resting there.

A slow smile began to move across Summer's face. She looked at Rolly as if their children on the screen were no longer part of the conversation. "I think, Sir Rolly, that the sky just opened. You better watch out so that *grudge shoe* doesn't fall on your head."

Rolly smiled at Summer. Then all four children watched in amazement as he took off Summer's wig, taking the bouncing headband with it. Then he kissed her. "My head will be just fine, darling. So, will yours, after tomorrow."

Rolly looked back at the screen, his gaze finding Max. "I hope you know what you're doing," he said. Then he looked back at Summer. "Say good night to your children, sweetheart. They seem to need assurance that you're okay."

Summer looked at the screen. "I'm more than okay. I'm enjoying myself immensely. Take care, loves," she said.

Then Rolly closed the computer, leaving them all to wonder how a woman who was supposed to be dead wound up enjoying life like a giddy teenager.

Seeing the look on Fallon's face, or more accurately, judging the air around her, Max asked her brothers to leave. "We all have a big day tomorrow," he said, referring to Summer's memorial service. "We should all get some sleep."

Finn kissed his sister's cheek on his way out saying, "Doesn't it feel good not to have secrets?"

Fallon pushed him out the door. "Mom should have named you, Loki. The trickster role suits you."

Gus left without a kiss or so much as a wave and a "see you tomorrow."

That was fine with Max. Tolerating Gus was beginning to feel like a full-time job.

Fallon shut the front door and surprised Max by saying, "It's still light out. Want to take a walk down by the water?"

Max wasn't sure why Fallon wanted to get out of the house. Maybe it was as simple as wanting some fresh air. It had been one heck of a day for her. Not wanting to read anymore into it than that, he said, "Sure. Let me just change my shoes." He smiled. "I've been told the ones I'm wearing don't suit me."

Max ran upstairs to the room he'd staked out as his, rummaged through his duffle, and grabbed his running shoes. He quickly put them on. Then he went to his second secure computer and pulled up the security feed from the cameras and other monitoring devises he'd had installed immediately after his covert op was authorized. By the time Summer's fake death certificate had been penned, her entire property had been rigged with monitoring devises, some of which were geared to alert Max of any intrusion through his cell phone.

None of the alarms had been triggered. No unscheduled activity around the house—although there was footage of

Fallon cutting fresh flowers from her mother's garden. Even in black and white, she was beautiful.

Max closed his computer, locked it in the high-density plastic box he kept it in, and placed the box in his duffle, right next to his backup weapon. He kicked the duffle under the bed. Not much of a hiding spot, but for now it would do.

He ran downstairs to meet his *wife*.

Ten

While Max was busy upstairs, Fallon texted her boss, Nick Card, asking what he'd discovered about stolen jewels entering the private collections via the gray and black markets. Fallon didn't know all Nick's connections, probably not even ten percent of them. The one's she knew were sufficient for her to know whatever Nick told her was the absolute truth.

He texted back: *Sending a friend to check on you.*

That wasn't good. That meant Nick was significantly worried about her safety, even knowing she had her own personal FBI agent at her side—more than anyone else had been in months.

How bad is it? Fallon texted.

Her phone rang a second later.

Nick's resonant voice sounded in her ear before she could say hello. "I've verified that several stones have made their way from Chicago to Miami and from there to London, Mumbai, Zurich, Rome, and Berlin. Three of the stones have been authenticated as coming from the Zoe Tiara. The Flower of Scotland is still unaccounted for. Given its provenance and the lore behind the theft, whoever stole it has a fluid and active market for gems—something worth killing for. Whoever purchased it has a vested interest in keeping it. That makes them dangerous too. Maybe more so."

"So, you're telling me to watch my back," Fallon said.

"I'm telling you I'm sending someone to watch your back. I need you to finish your business up there and come back. I need you back here. Having you near me dissuades the casual criminals from any number of bad acts."

Fallon snorted. "And it encourages the diehards."

"True enough." Nick paused and grew even more serious. "I've run a check on this FBI agent, quietly. He's smart. Overly ambitious when it comes to catching those involved in the spate of thefts that involved the stones your mother identified. He's honest, like his father before him, but reckless. Where his father lived by the rules, your man plays a bit fast and loose. Normally I'd cast that as an asset, but not this time. Not with you. Take care, love."

"Always," Fallon said.

"I've got a feeling things will be coming to a head there. That photo of the small stone you texted looks like one of nineteen other red diamonds from the Zoe Tiara. The one you just bought from Jack Smith for $120 is one of the smaller stones. Given its provenance, it would fetch over $100,000 on the gray market."

"Jack Smith doesn't know we know we bought a red diamond and not a garnet or a piece of polished glass."

"Don't bet on it, love. He let you walk out of his store with it because he couldn't kill you in his shop. He won't take any chances. That stone — hiding in plain sight — is proof he possessed stolen gems. No way he can explain that away easily. Even if there's not enough proof to indict him, INTERPOL and the FBI will be watching him every day for the rest of his life. He'll be audited. He'll be hounded. He'll never lead a normal life again."

"Does he know my mom's alive?"

Nick Card took a deep breath. "No. For now your mother is safe. It's you I'm worried about."

"I can take care of myself."

Nick sighed audibly into the phone. "Where's the necklace with the red diamond now?"

Fallon's hand went to the chain around her throat. She ran her fingers over the pendant, wondering how such a small stone could cause so many people to lose their minds. "I'm wearing it."

"Are you in the house?"

"Yes."

"When you click off, I want you to go outside. Walk the length of the patio that faces Jack Smith's store. Make sure you have the necklace visible. Play with it as you look at your mother's flowers. Then go in the house. Are the blinds open on the windows in your mother's kitchen?"

Fallon looked. "Yes."

"Good. Take the necklace off. Leave it in that crystal bowl your mother keeps on the kitchen table."

Nick had been to her mother's house exactly once. It was so like Nick to remember every detail—especially the layout of the rooms and every access point. Nick Card was a thief at heart, albeit a good-hearted one.

"You should add your watch to the bowl and your earrings if you're wearing them," Nick added.

"It's not like Jack Smith is watching my every move, Nick."

Fallon could hear the smile in Nick's voice. Her mentor had bone-deep affection for her. "I find your naiveté endearing most of the time. This time, dear heart, it's getting in the way. Do as I say. Leave the necklace. Leave the house. With any luck, the necklace will be gone when you return. Whatever you do, don't check the dish until the morning. When you come back home, go straight upstairs."

His next words stopped her heart. "Do not sleep alone tonight. I love you," he said, ending the call.

Fallon put the phone in her pocket and went outside to wait for Max. She did exactly as Nick instructed. She toyed with the necklace burning its way into her flesh as she imagined herself being watched. She pulled a few stray pieces of grass that found their way into her mother's planting beds. Then she went back into the house and turned on the kitchen light. Even though the late evening sun was filtering through the windows, there was little direct light. The kitchen light brightened the room, making it glow warmly. She took off her watch, setting it in the crystal bowl. Then her earrings. Finally, the necklace with its blood red stone. She was about to grab a soda from the refrigerator when Max came bounding down the stairs.

"I'm ready for our walk," he said.

"Let's go." Fallon wondered how long she would be playing the role of wife and grieving daughter. To her surprise, Fallon didn't mind the first one. The grieving part she didn't like one bit. She fervently hoped when this was over, no one in her family would have reason to grieve for decades.

It was a lovely evening. The breeze was light enough not to be bothersome but strong enough to keep away the tiny flying bugs from the lake. They left the house just after eight. The sun wasn't due to set for another half an hour or so. It was Fallon's favorite time of the day.

People raved about the evenings in Key West. Key West sunsets were said to be some of the most beautiful in the world. They were. No doubt. But the sunsets over Lake Michigan from Egg Harbor, Fish Creek, Ephraim, or Sister Bay were just as beautiful. Having grown up in the Door, Fallon thought even more so, although she'd never tell Nick Card that. Nick liked to tease that a good part of the reason he spent so much time in Key West was because of the hypnotic sunsets.

"Want to go to Wilson's and get ice cream? We could take it down by the beach. Hang in the Adirondack chairs for a while?" Max asked.

Fallon looked at him in surprise. "How do you know about Wilson's?" Wilson's burger and ice cream shop had been the cornerstone business in Ephraim for well over a hundred years. The red-and-white candy-striped exterior dotted with old Coke signs was the subject of many Door County artists over the years. To say it was iconic for Door County would be like saying the Statue of Liberty was iconic for the nation.

"Anyone who's ever been to Ephraim knows Wilson's," Max said, smiling at her. He seemed tuned up, ready for action, as if he was anticipating something but not quite ready to share what that something was. He was calm, but there was an energy about him, humming just under the surface.

"Have you been to Ephraim before?"

"Not in a long time. When I came up as a kid with my parents, we stayed in Egg Harbor. We'd camp sometimes in Peninsula State Park, but we rarely went farther north than Fish Creek." He smiled down at her, "But we made it to Wilson's once or twice."

Fallon wanted to ask more. She wanted to *know* more about Max as a child. That thought got waylaid when he asked about Gus.

"What is with two anyway?" he asked. "I get that he's a jerk, but your anger with him seems far deeper than that."

"It is."

"Do you want to talk about it?"

Fallon took Max's hand and led him to the small bench in front to the library just down from Wilson's. If they were going to talk about this, she wanted them to be alone—not surrounded by tourists eating burgers, enjoying fountain sodas, or devouring every kind of ice cream known to man.

Max sat next to Fallon on the bench, keeping her hand in his. She didn't pull away. His warmth and his presence were comforting.

Did she want to talk about it? Fallon thought about that for a moment while they sat silently watching the world go by. She really liked Max's ability to cut through to what mattered, and that he was content to sit with her while she hashed it all out inside.

Without making the conscious decision to open up to Max, she just did. It was easy.

"I think commercial fishermen are a lot like cops and professional soldiers," she said.

That didn't make immediate sense to Max, but he didn't interrupt. He'd found that the best way to get to the truth was to let it come without interruption or leading. He'd have made a terrible lawyer, he mused, silently urging Fallon to continue. After collecting her thoughts, she did. Tied it all up rather nicely too, he thought.

"They worry. They know their profession is dangerous, so they leave notes or letters for their loved ones just in case heaven finds them before they're ready to go."

Max couldn't fault the logic of that. He had just that kind of letter addressed to his father.

"When we turned twenty-one, our mom gave us our letters from our father. Those were his instructions and Mom loved him enough to follow them."

Max couldn't imagine receiving one of those letters. It would be far worse than writing them, he thought. Now that his father was fully retired, he was fairly certain he'd never be in the position of finding out. Max rubbed the inside of Fallon's wrist with his thumb. She probably didn't realize it, but she was holding onto him tighter than before. Max wished then and there that if it were possible, he'd be granted the ability to take away at least some of her pain.

"All the letters were short. Dad telling each of us how much he loved us. How we made him smile. That he carried us in his heart every moment of every day. How he was the luckiest man in the world to be blessed with a wife who loved him and three babies who proved every day that heaven was a place he lived in on earth. That's how he put it. 'Every day was heaven, so long as he drew breath.'"

Fallon blinked away tears in her eyes and gave him a watery smile. "My father had an Irish poet's soul."

Max wanted to pull Fallon to him. He wanted to hold her for the rest of his life. He was betting Fingal and Fallon had their own poet's soul. The jury was still out on whether Fergus possessed a soul at all.

"With the letters were gifts. One for each of us." Fallon paused, swallowing hard. "Things that defined who our father was and what he cared about the most. Things even as children we'd seen and known he cared about."

Now Max wanted to prompt her. What could be so hurtful about a gift? It didn't make any sense to him. He trusted it would, but so far, the story didn't match Fallon's depth of emotion.

"To truly understand, you have to know that my father loved his parents and his grandparents deeply. He loved his grandfather most of all. Whenever he was on shore, he carried his grandfather's gold pocket watch. Always. Without fail. It was the single most important thing to him. He didn't love our house as much as he loved that watch."

"What were the other gifts?" Max asked, interjecting because Fallon looked like she was going to cry. He didn't want that if it could be helped. He wasn't good with crying females as a rule. The thought of Fallon crying damn near broke his heart. He thought he knew how this story was going to play out, but he was mistaken.

"My great-grandmother's engagement ring—a small ruby surrounded by tiny diamonds. She married the man with the watch."

"And..." Max prompted.

"And my father's rose-gold signet ring. His parents gave it to him as a graduation gift when he graduated from Trinity College in Dublin. He was so proud of that ring. He used to put it over my big toe and tell me if I studied very hard, I could have a ring like his someday."

Max smiled at her. The tears that threatened earlier were gone now, replaced by a watery, but warm smile. Max wanted to take Fallon to a place where he could see that grow, so he asked a question he hoped would take her there. "What did your father study at Trinity?"

She laughed, giving him a glimpse of her heart. "English. Dad didn't just have a poet's soul. He had a poet's mind as well."

Whether she realized it or not, Fallon had fallen into a native Irish cadence. A hold over from a childhood filled with Irish rhyme and rhythm, no doubt. He didn't have to prompt her this time to continue. She looked straight at him. No more misty-eyed dew, just sadness, reflected in her clear blue eyes.

"I got the pocket watch. Fingal got our great-grandmother's engagement ring. Gus got dad's signet ring." Fallon waited for him to understand. Max knew she was waiting because her expression said *Do you get it now?*

"I don't get it," Max said.

He didn't. He didn't get it at all.

Fallon took a deep breath in. She held it. Then she let it out again. She repeated that sequence three times before she tried to explain. Someone had taught her that. No one breathed with that kind of mindfulness without guidance.

"My mom had to have a C-section. The three of us were simply too big for her body." A statement of fact. Max got that. It was the rest of the connections that he was missing.

"Our birth order was chosen by the surgeon." She paused as if this bit of information was vital.

Max said nothing.

What could he say? Since nothing came to mind, he waited.

"Gus came first," Fallon said with the gravity Max imagined God had when giving the ten commandments to Moses.

"So?" Max asked.

Fallon jerked backward as if he'd slapped her. She gave an involuntary shake of her head. Then she seemed to realize she was speaking to someone who didn't give a flying-fig about triplet dynamics. She actually smiled. "So, Gus seems to think that because the surgeon chose to pull him from our mother first," Fallon gestured with her free hand jerking it rapidly in front of her, "And, because he was born with a penis, he was entitled to the gift he believed our father cared about most."

"Okay," Max said, trying to keep up. "So, your father told all three of you what gift he cared about most? He ranked them?"

This time Fallon scrunched her face up, threw her head back, and let out a sound that was both irritated and thankful. It sounded something like a duck gurgling. What Max heard was *urrrrggghhh*. What he saw on Fallon's face was a small, thankful smile. What he felt, he didn't care to contemplate. Who met their soulmate in a day? Certainly not a man old enough to know such things didn't exist.

"No! My father didn't rank his gifts in order of importance any more than he ranked his children."

That revelation seemed to stop Fallon in her tracks. She stopped talking. She stopped everything and just sat still for more seconds than Max could count. Then she laughed. It was the kind of laugh that said she'd just figured out something she should have realized long ago.

"No," she said. "Dad didn't rank us in his head or in his heart. He simply gave each of us what he thought we'd appreciate most. I think he also cared about which of us would pass the stories and the items on to our children and grandchildren. The *passing on* is important in my family," Fallon said as if Max didn't understand the concept. He got it. He had his own bits of memorabilia and his own stories to tell.

Now that Fallon wasn't about to cry, Max had to ask, "What's the big deal? I'm not obtuse. I'm just not following. What was your gift, again?"

"Dad gave me his pocket watch." Fallon said it like she'd just put the nails in her own coffin.

"Okay…What did Gus get?"

"My father's signet ring—the ring marking his crowning scholastic achievement," Fallon said. There wasn't much to add to that, so she continued with Finn's gift.

"Fingal got our great-grandmother's engagement ring," Fallon said.

"Was Finn happy?" Max asked.

"Thrilled," Fallon answered.

"Then why the angst?" Max said.

"Because Gus thought our father cared more about his pocket watch than anything else. He also thought he was the oldest, he was entitled to it. That it should have gone to him because he was the oldest son."

"That explains why Gus would be angry with you." Max shook his head. "Although that reasoning is full of holes when looked at logically." Max lifted Fallon's chin, trying to get her to focus on him and the fact that what she was saying was ridiculous on its face. "Why would you be angry about Gus's adolescent theatrics over a pocket watch verses a signet ring?"

Max regretting his words the second they left his mouth.

He never wanted to see the absence of emotion he saw in Fallon's eyes ever again. It cut him to the quick. When she spoke this time, she sounded like a robot. All emotion was gone. There was no love in her voice or her intonation.

There was no hate. Just no emotion at all.

In that moment, Max knew what hell looked like.

Hell wasn't pain.

It was apathy.

And it was written all over Fallon's face when she said, "I was never angry over the watch, or the ring, or Gus's manufactured hurt." She paused. Her expression grew even more distant—as if hell wasn't distant enough.

"Then why the disconnect?" Max asked.

"First, Gus saw something he thought was one thing, but wasn't."

"Well, that's clear as mud," Max said.

"He saw my college boyfriend kissing me goodbye. I had told him I'd just gotten engaged to my high school sweetheart. The man I thought I'd marry was Gus's best friend. Gus told him I was cheating on him with my college boyfriend. *That*," Fallon said, "caused my engagement to come to an abrupt end. That was right after Mom gave each of us our letters from dad. The day after our twenty-first birthday."

None of that was good. Still, it was forgivable, given time.

"Then…"

"Then?" Max asked, thinking he'd heard enough to punch Gus's lights out.

"Then, Gus took one look at me and said, 'Just wait until Mom dies.' He actually said those exact words. 'Just wait until mom dies.' I couldn't believe it at the time. I still can't quite believe it as I'm telling you this."

Fallon stopped talking.

It was as if her next words had been stolen from her. Like after all these years, she still couldn't make sense of Gus's nonsensical words. She seemed stymied.

Then she looked at him quizzically, like she was questioning her ability to think clearly. "Can you imagine anyone related to you being excited about the prospect of your mother's death?"

He couldn't. Max wanted to make Fallon a twin in that moment, but Fallon wasn't done with the hurt that Gus had reigned down upon her.

"Gus couldn't wait to try to punish me with it. He's twisted in a way I don't want to understand. I'm pretty sure I'll never forgive him for taking joy in the thought of our mother's death and how it might serve him as executor of her estate." Fallon paused. "I thought I'd gotten past all that. Then I learned he knew from the start Mom was alive. He kept that from me. He kept it from Finn too. Four days I've spent thinking our mother was dead." She looked at him sideways. "Can you imagine if those four days turned into three months?"

Max couldn't think of one excuse for Gus Murphy.

Fallon wasn't done. She was angry now and Max wanted her to revel in her anger. Fallon needed to call it out and move on. If he had his way, she'd be moving on without a brother. That man was toxic. No doubt about it. Max just wished he'd get a chance to make Fergus Murphy hurt for the pain he seemed to dish out like candy. God willing, he'd get that chance.

"My brother wanted to take every bit of my mother from me. He took her rings, the only jewelry I ever cared about, from me. Then he took pleasure in making me believe she was dead."

Fallon looked at him clearly and said, "I'll do almost anything to keep my mother safe. I'll do anything you ask me too. Just don't ask me to give Gus a pass. I'm simply not capable of that kind of grace."

"Screw Gus. He's a vitriolic waste of space and he isn't worth your time right now. We've got bigger things to worry about now, like keeping your mother and you safe."

Fallon agreed.

"Help me do that."

Fallon was listening.

"I need you to be my wife until this is over. I don't want to do anything to make you uncomfortable, but I need you to act like you love me."

Fallon held firm to Max's hand. "Okay," she said, meaning it.

Eleven

ax walked Fallon upstairs. He showed her the room he set up in, including all his equipment. She didn't need to go into the kitchen to determine that the sterling necklace with the red diamond was gone. It was on the screen, clear as day.

Only it wasn't Jack Smith who broke in to retrieve it. It was a woman. A woman with long blond hair and shaded glasses. Flashy. Elegant even. The kind of woman no one would mistake and everyone would remember.

Max put a finger to his lips, gesturing to Fallon that she should watch what she said. He went to his phone and texted her, while he said, "Should we snuggle and watch a movie? Take both our minds off the memorial service tomorrow?"

He texted: *That's the woman your mother took a cell phone photo of from Jack's store. She saw the woman with The Flower of Scotland and one time before that buying what we believe is a stolen Harry Winston diamond.*

Fallon nodded toward the phone. "Sure honey. That sounds great. I'm not looking forward to tomorrow. I don't want to get up in front of all those people and say anything. I'll let Gus and Finn do that."

"You don't have to do anything you don't want to," Max said.

Fallon texted back: *Are they listening to us?*

Doubtful. Still, we should be cautious. Need to act like everything is as it appears to be. Mom dead. We're married. Nothing to see here.

Got it, Fallon typed.

And she did get it. What she didn't get was her reaction. She was comfortable around him. She didn't mind letting someone take the weight of her emotional baggage for a while. When she woke up tomorrow she intended to throw it all away. She was sick of being angry. She was sick of being sad. Neither served her well. She didn't have to hang onto ideas of family when part of that family meant harm to other members. Nothing about that was healthy.

"Do you mind moving to the room I sleep in when I'm home?" Fallon asked. "The guest room doesn't have the same warmth." Fallon found a genuine smile. "My room has a TV. Mom DVR'd every episode of *Blue Bloods* for me."

Max grinned. "Great. Nothing puts me to sleep like family drama masquerading as a police procedural."

"Okay, how about we watch *Midsomer Murder* on Netflix. It's one..." Fallon caught herself. "It was one of Mom's favorites. She liked both *Paddington* movies too."

Max came up to her, enveloped her in a hug, and said, "*Blue Bloods* it is."

The morning of Summer O'Hara's memorial service was bright and warm. The perfect summer morning with chickadees chirping and water fowl singing their greeting to the day. Most of the tourists were already greeting the day on their bikes, sitting outside drinking coffee and eating cherry crepes at cafés, or teeing off on a dewy, green course.

The street in front of Summer's church was teeming with people. Max and Fallon walked there from Summer's house after the coffee, toast, and eggs Max had whipped up for them. To Fallon's surprise, she'd been famished. Apparently, woman could not survive on ice cream alone.

Finn came up to Fallon first. Kissed her cheek. "Ready for this?" he asked, smiling.

"Not even a little bit." Fallon looked around. "Where's Gus?"

"He's at the winery. He's getting everything ready for the reception after this."

"Isn't he planning on showing up? How's it going to look if he misses his mother's service?"

Finn looked down at her, he wasn't much taller than she was, just tall enough to make her feel small. "Gus is leaving the winery and gallery. He got an offer to head the management team at one of the large estate wineries near Niagara-on-the-Lake. He's leaving at the end of week. He's just getting things in order before he goes."

"He's moving to Canada?" Fallon asked, shaken.

Finn nodded. "It's been brewing for a long time. He needs the time away." Finn looked out over the small crowd milling in front of the church. "Frankly, I could use a little distance from Gus."

"You're not sorry to see him go?"

"Running things without him will be challenging for a while, but it's time. Gus has to find his own way. He needs to forgive himself for the way he treated you. For the way he used Mom to hurt you. I don't think he ever really got over dad's death or Geoff's. Seeing you again solidified his decision. It's time for him to grow up. He can't, or won't, do that here."

Fallon linked her arm with Finn's. "You've got a good heart, brother-mine. Definitely the best of us. Shall we go tell everyone how wonderful our quirky, gem-obsessed, wig-wearing, rum-drinking mother once was?"

"That woman you described is the one we'll be saying hello to when this is over. Let's go say goodbye to the woman who spent too much time alone, whose life was on standby, waiting to hear about her grown children's day. I'm happy to say goodbye to that woman if we get to welcome the woman Rolly brought out. I want Mom to be happy. She's way too young to act so old."

And that's what they did. They said goodbye to the woman who defined herself by the men she'd loved and lost, and said hello to the one she'd let play since dying. Fallon shook her head, she fervently hoped that almost dying had jolted her mother back into living life well.

Fallon stopped and looked around at the town she'd been raised in, taking in the community, the landscape, the sights and sounds and scents of home. Not everything she needed was here, but the most important things were.

They were hiding in plain sight.

Twelve

*L*ife is a grand adventure, Jack. Always has been, always will be," said the woman in the long blond wig as she walked into Jack Smith's shop. She had expertly picked the lock and now locked it again behind her. She pulled the shade on the front door, making the interior a little dimmer than before. The store was still filled with light from all the west and southern facing windows, none of which had shades to pull. But the woman knew that. She was making a point. Giving Jack fair warning.

"Sign on the door says closed for a funeral," Jack said, looking up over his reading glasses from his accounts.

"Didn't think that applied to me," she said, coming closer to the case Jack was standing behind. "Don't worry, Jack. You'll make it to your funeral."

Jack reached for the Walther he kept under the case. He pulled it out, aiming it straight at her. "Didn't have to be this way," he said.

The woman smiled slowly. "We had a good run, Jack. Better than most ever get. But you and I both know it was always going to be this way."

Jack aimed at her head and pulled the trigger.

It landed making a clicking sound. The gun was empty.

The woman made a *tsk* sound. Her smile deepened. This time it reached her eyes. "When your gun don't shoot, it's time to leave the game, Jack. Your gun hasn't shot for quite some time."

Before Jack could reach for the shotgun he kept in a secret compartment in the wall behind him, he felt the cut. She was fast. Precise. The blade so sharp he barely felt it.

Jack touched the side of his neck. Pulling his fingers away, he saw his own blood staining them. It wasn't much. Just a small tear in the skin.

The woman reached into her beach bag and tossed a handful of tiny periwinkle cut flowers. They were lovely — star-shaped with five petals each. He recognized them immediately. They were freshly cut from the small flower garden in front of his shop.

It wasn't the cut that would kill him. Jack realized it the second the flowers hit the glass top of his case. The blade she cut him with was laced with the same poison he'd given Summer O'Hara before pushing her down her stairs. The woman had introduced it directly into his bloodstream.

He'd be seeing Summer O'Hara sooner than he thought, in less than thirty minutes if he didn't get to a hospital. He reached for his cell phone.

The women held up a boxlike devise. "Don't bother. I've jammed the signal."

"Why?" Jack asked.

The woman didn't even try to misunderstand. "Nick Card is younger than you. He'll be around a long time. He pays better. Did you know about Fallon Murphy's connection to Nick when you poisoned her mother?"

He'd known. Jack made a judgement call. A fatal one. It never occurred to him that Nick Card would place one woman above what was good for business.

That misjudgment cost him his life.

The woman stuffed the wig in her bag. She went in the back and cleared out what stones she thought she could use, leaving enough — per Nick Card's instructions — for that FBI agent to find. Case closed. He wouldn't get all the stones, not even the best ones, but he'd get his man.

Hopefully, that would be enough.

Nick asked her to do one more thing on her way out of town.

She did what he asked and disappeared. St. Moritz was lovely this time of year.

Thirteen

allon walked into the reception with Finn and Max at her side. Tables were laid out with place settings. Warm and cold dishes were spread throughout the shop. The wine bar was stocked with tea and coffee and open, half-corked bottles of Murphy Brother's wine.

Gus was nowhere in sight.

A woman Fallon had never seen before with short black hair and deep green eyes bumped into Max. He steadied her, smiling. His gaze lingered a bit too long. "Do I know you?" he asked.

The flash of jealousy that surged through Fallon irritated her. It was irrational and unwanted. It wasn't like she and Max were really married or that last night meant anything more than two lonely people sharing the night together, staving off the hurt and aloneness that defined both their lives, up until the moment Max approached her at the shore.

A time that could be measured in hours as much as in days.

She had no business feeling jealous.

That didn't stop Fallon from grabbing Max's hand.

The woman, who would have stood apart from the crowd no matter where the crowd was, raised a brow at her, then turned back to Max, ignoring her completely. "No, I don't think we've met. Perhaps we'll meet again." She stumbled on her high heels, catching herself on Max's arm. As soon as she did, she was gone, leaving Max staring after her.

"She isn't that beautiful," Fallon said, regretting the words the second they were out her mouth.

Max looked at Fallon briefly then back toward the space

where the woman disappeared. He was searching the crowd when he said, "Yes, she is."

Fallon jerked her hand away.

Max didn't seem to care. He kept scanning the crowd. "That's not it. The way she moved. It...it's familiar..." Max took off at a run. He made it through the side door and into the parking lot before Fallon could call after him.

He scanned the parking lot, seeing the long blond wig in the middle of it. The woman was nowhere in sight. The phone in his suit jacket pocket began to vibrate. Max fished it out. It wasn't his phone. His thumb slid across the surface. He held it to his ear.

"Summer O'Hara can come home now."

"What are you talking about?"

"Don't be obtuse, Max. You're no good at it. The threat's over. No one will come after her or her family. If I were you, I'd stick close to the daughter. If that flash of jealousy is any indication, she's fallen for you already. Don't go chasing stones when you could be catching hearts."

Max said nothing. He continued to scan the immediate area, trying to ignore the regret he heard in the woman's smoky voice.

"I'll find you," Max said, knowing that wasn't going to happen anytime soon.

"No," she said. "You won't. Check your jacket, Max. Let the rest go." The phone went dead.

Max reached into his opposite jacket pocket. He pulled out the pendant with the red diamond he purchased from Jack Smith's store. He felt the coldness of loose stones as well. He pulled them out and looked at them, a blue diamond about a carat in size, two small red diamonds, and a yellow cushion cut about 10 carats that he thought was from the Graff theft.

The Flower of Scotland wasn't among the stones.

He was fairly certain it was halfway around the world by now. Max could keep chasing it.

Or he could close this case, a feat made easier by the stones that literally fell into his pocket. Then he could take the woman's advice and start chasing the only heart he cared about.

Fallon came out the side door walking slowly toward him.

"What's wrong?" she asked, stopping at his side.

Max pulled her too him and kissed her. Deeply. Fully. Like she was the only woman in the world and now was the only moment that mattered.

Fallon kissed him back with every ounce of feeling she had in her. There was something urgent in Max's kiss as if he'd made up his mind about something important.

"Tell me what's wrong, Max."

He smiled. Then he threw his head back and laughed. "Not a thing, darling. Not one thing." He kissed her again. "Everything about you makes me smile."

Epilogue

ack Smith's jewelry shop reopened after his death to wide speculation and acclaim. People came from all over the world to purchase synthetic stones based on the great collector gems they represented. Summer O'Hara-Scott, the woman responsible and the owner of the shop, could be seen there from Memorial Day through Labor Day most summers, telling anyone who would listen all about gems and jewelry. She earned more than enough from her shop to purchase her own fancy colored diamond which she wore on her right hand—a 2 carat yellow diamond in the shape of a heart. She wore that ring until her granddaughter's twenty-first birthday when she gave it and the shop to her.

Fallon's daughter inherited her grandmother's love of jewels and her mother's love of opals. And her grandfather Rolly's love of sailing—a love he had in common with her biological grandfather, Padraig Murphy. In time, she'd name her first son, Roland Patrick, honoring them both.

One day, long after her children were grown, she would inherit her mother's journal.

In that journal, Fallon Murphy Scott, wrote of her joys and her sorrows, her triumphs, her travels, and her walks on the wild side—a life made possible by balancing her work with Nick Card while loving and living with Max Scott, a stickler for the law.

That journal began with the line:

> *On what I thought was the worst day of my life,*
> *the day I thought my mother died, I looked around me*
> *and chose to see what was in plain sight.*
> *Life is simple.*

It's defined by hope and light and holding on to those who make our hearts smile.

It is possible to fall in love in a day — all it takes is a moment of real connection — and to keep that love alive every day for the rest of your life.

I did.

So can you.

The End

About the Author

A native mid-westerner, Leigh lives in Southeastern Wisconsin and dreams of owning a cottage in Scotland.

Leigh is currently working on two series of stand-alone contemporary novels: The Warrior Chronicles, with a tie to the martial arts, and the Shute Pond novels, featuring the quirkiness of small town life. Adventure, romance, and themes such as 'what constitutes a family' and 'living by a personal code' all wrapped up in a tail-kicking package that will make you laugh, cry, and feel good about the world and your place in it.

To become a Leigh Morgan Minion, visit:
https://www.facebook.com/groups/533531666752263
Follow Leigh's blog on Authors of Main Street at: https://authorsofmainstreet.wordpress.com/
You may visit Leigh at:
www.leighmorganauthor.com

E.Ayers

To George, who believed in me

One

Kimmie tried to scrub the worst of the dirt from her fingernails and prayed the rest would come out when she washed her hair. She jumped into the shower. Being late was not an option.

Twenty-three minutes later, she was ready. "Gran, Patricia, are you ready?"

"Coming, Mommy." Eight-year-old Patricia darted down the front staircase of the old 1950's Cape Cod home. "Gran-Gran is in the backyard. She's afraid you're going to forget the flowers."

Seriously? "Gran, come on, or we'll be late," she hollered out the kitchen door. "I have everything!"

Gran hurried across the patio. "I was concerned that you'd forget."

Kimmie passed a box to the older woman. "Here's your corsage, Gran."

"Do I get one?" Patricia asked.

"No, honey. Go jump in the car, and don't mess with anything."

Gran grabbed her black lace shawl from the mirrored table in the foyer. "Just in case I get chilly. Did you pick up the lilies for the grave?"

"Yes. Everything is handled. Just get in the car, please." She didn't want to fuss at her grandmother. The woman wasn't as quick on her feet anymore and Kate Silverlake's passing had been a tough blow.

As soon as Kimmie had everyone settled in her car, her grandmother began to fuss. "I've heard that Kate's son isn't coming. Maybe he thinks he's too important to come. Can you imagine not going to your mother's funeral? What has happened to children these days? No respect for anything. Simply shameful."

Kimmie didn't feel like explaining that not everyone can drop everything and travel. "I heard that Dr. Silverlake is in South America with a medical missionary team. It took days to locate him."

The scuttlebutt said that the grandson was returning in his father's place. Too many years had passed since she'd seen the grandson of her grandmother's best friend. The last time she'd laid eyes on her childhood friend, she was probably twelve, and he'd ignored her. Kimmie drove a little further and spotted the funeral home with the cemetery behind it. She offered up the town's newest rumor to her grandmother. "Flint is coming in his father's place."

After pulling into the parking lot of the funeral home, she grabbed the pot of pink calla lilies. Funerals kept her floral department thriving, but to her they were horrendously depressing. Attending funerals was twice as hard on her since her husband had died. She handed the pot of lilies to the director's wife, signed the guest book, and followed her grandmother into the Celebration Room.

The room had been painted to look like a bright day, with pretty white clouds in a vibrantly blue sky. The carpet was dark grass green. Several tropical trees were placed around the room, and if someone didn't water the fig tree, she feared it might just shutter and drop every leaf.

The expression on Gran's face softened. "Oh, look. Isn't it lovely? Kate would be so thrilled."

Kimmie wanted to roll her eyes. Miz Kate's ashes were in a pearl-white urn shaped like a calla lily with two cherubs that doubled as handles. Her grandmother burst into tears as she stepped to the table that held her best friend's remains. Patricia wrapped her arms around her great-grandmother. "Don't cry, Gran-Gran. Now she's in heaven with Daddy."

Kimmie blinked hard and fought her own sadness. *I don't need all these tears. You're going to make me cry.*

She tucked Patricia into a seat in the second row. "Try not to fidget, sweetheart. It's not polite."

"I won't. I promise,"

Oh please, let this be quick.

Miz Kate and her grandmother had been best friends since they were in their teens. Quick math said that was about sixty years of friendship, and most of that time they had been neighbors.

Kimmie spent her childhood summers with her grandmother while growing up. That meant Kimmie couldn't remember a time that she didn't know Kate Silverlake. It was as though she were another relative. Kimmie had been as at home in Kate's house as she'd been in her grandmother's. The only difference between the two houses was Flint's presence, and it wasn't unusual to discover him at her grandmother's kitchen table scooping up oatmeal cookies and drinking a vanilla cream soda on a hot day.

Patricia fell sleep before the second reading from the Old Testament and now leaned against her great-grandmother. Kimmie had a difficult time keeping the smirk off her face during the funeral. Miz Kate was religious but not exactly a churchgoer. Nature and the cycles of life were much more meaningful to her, and hearing a minister spouting Bible verses would've had Kate grumbling. Kimmie would have preferred to have placed Miz Kate's crystals around the urn. That would probably have upset some of the town's folk, so she made a mental note to place a few on the tiny grave. It was one of Miz Kate's legacies to Kimmie, a gift of knowledge of an ancient practice. Miz Kate swore it never hurt to respect old practices.

A man walked to the mic near the urn. "Thank you all..."

Kimmie snapped to attention. *Flint Silverlake? Whatever happened to the Flint I knew?* Before her stood a man dressed in a black suit, gray shirt, and black and gray striped tie. Gone was the scrawny young kid that had once climbed trees and dared Kimmie to wade through the Felding's duck pond while dressed in her Sunday clothes. The dark linen suit didn't camouflage the form that hid beneath it. Flint filled his attire with the body of a mature man. He had broad shoulders, slender hips, and powerful legs. There was no wedding band on his left hand, but not every married man wore one. There didn't appear to be anyone with him except for a mixed breed Doberman wearing a service vest.

She tried to count the years since she last saw him. *Hmm,*

sixteen or... It was an enigma. *Long time.* Then she stared at the dog and wondered what Flint's problem was. He'd always been a healthy kid. *Why do you need a service dog? What happened to you?*

Flint looked around the room. There were faces he hadn't seen in years, plenty with names that had escaped him, a few faces that seemed to be missing, and there were several more faces he didn't recognize. *Probably newcomers.*

Flint finished regaling the praises of his grandmother and her many wonderful deeds for the community and her fellow man. He tossed in a few anecdotes, which lightened the mood and produced some giggles before he walked to the side of the room to await the close of the celebration of the woman's long life.

His grandmother's death had hit him hard. She had been more of a mother figure to him than his own mother. His mom had worked full time, so he'd spent most of his after-school time with his grandmother. She was the one who had attended school conferences for him, taken him to baseball practice, taught him to drive a car, and doted over him when he was ill. He'd spoken with his grandmother only a few days before she died. She had been thrilled at the news of his impending return. No one was prepared for his grandmother's quick demise from a massive stroke. She'd rarely been sick and had just undergone her annual checkup that she claimed she'd passed with flying colors. *Maybe that's the way to go, fast and effortlessly.*

Grady stood as he'd been trained, never leaving Flint's side. Flint lightly scratched behind the dog's ear with a single digit as if to tell the animal he wasn't forgotten. Poor creature had thought he was going to get a new owner, but after two weeks, he was returned to Flint. Now the dog awaited another chance to become a service animal for someone in need of sight assistance. If the animal had been kept a few days longer, Flint would have been forced to retire the young dog from service work. It always saddened him if a dog didn't make it through the orientation period. Often it wasn't the dog's fault but rather the human who really wasn't prepared to share life with a four-legged creature.

Lost in his own thoughts, Flint wasn't paying close attention to anything around him. He found himself shaking hands. "It was so kind of you to come, Mrs. Peabody."

"Everyone loved your grandmother." The gray-haired woman gazed tenderly at him.

"Yes, I believe you're right." He gave her his sweetest smile and turned to the next person in line. He pressed hands with those who stopped, and was introduced to several of his classmates' spouses and children. A child ran up to him with a large bottle of icy-cold water.

"Mr. Flint, my mommy said you must have this before your tongue gets glued to the roof of your mouth and your lips get stuck to your teeth."

"Well, thank you." He uncapped the bottle and swigged half of it. Ice cold, it cooled his parched throat.

The child before him fisted her hands on her hips. "You should never eat glue. Some glues will kill you and then you will have to live with my daddy in heaven."

It took everything that Flint had to keep from laughing at the brazen little girl in front of him. "And so that I know who to thank for this cold bottle, who is your mommy?"

The child turned and pointed. "Kimmie."

Kimmie? Where? The name seemed to strike him like a punch in the solar plexus. But he didn't see Kimmie. He remembered her as blonde-haired with the prettiest pale brown eyes and dark eyelashes. He used to tease that her eyelashes were caterpillars. With two school grades between them and almost three years, she had been his little playmate every summer. They played, explored, and got into plenty of trouble together.

"May I pet your dog?" Patricia asked.

"Yes, but would you mind waiting until we are outside?" The child's question brought him back to the moment. Yet, his gaze searched in vain for someone resembling that little girl who had come every summer and most holidays to visit her grandmother.

Mr. Boyd stopped to ask a dozen gardening questions as Kimmie scanned the lawn for her family. Her search ended when she spotted Flint. As the sun rose to its apex, she watched him slip out of his dark jacket. The man's gray shirt clung to his moist skin. She closed her eyes against the rawness of the masculine form and the feelings the man elicited in her. It had been almost four years since her husband's death. Illness had ravaged his body, and he had slowly wasted away. He had once been so strong and muscular, invincible…or so they had thought. Both of them had believed that he'd beat the cancer. Instead, it had defeated him and taken a little piece of her. Sensing her inability to cope and get back on her feet, her parents had suggested that she move to the country and stay with her grandmother for a while. The woman was getting older and could use someone close to help with simple chores around the house and at the garden center. Kimmie had been there less than two weeks when Gran and Miz Kate convinced Kimmie to utilize her horticulture degree and take over Posy's. She'd be the fifth owner in the family, having only skipped her mom who couldn't stand to get her hands dirty. But Kimmie was the first to ever do it with her college degree.

Like many small towns, the tiny hamlet of Clear Creek didn't offer many opportunities to meet eligible men. She resigned herself to accepting the few wonderful years she and Steve had shared together. Considering she was raising a daughter, operating a garden center, and helping her grandmother, there honestly was no time to date even if she did meet someone.

Her grandmother didn't charge her rent, but her grandmother also immediately retired. Now it was Kimmie's turn to provide for the three-person, all female household. The first year, she almost put Posy's in the red, but the little garden center had grown and was now thriving more than ever. The place had changed with the times since opening its doors in 1903. During World

War II, it had been divided into Victory gardens, allowing the community to eat healthily and abundantly, when so many foods were rationed. Gran firmly believed that the center's ability to adapt and change with the times had accounted for its success. *Maybe I have what so many women want, a beautiful daughter, a job I love, my own company so I'm the boss, a house, and enough money to live. And I'm not dependent on anyone.*

She stood a little straighter and then gently broke into Gran's chitchat with Miz Ellen, a friend of her grandmother's. "Excuse me, ladies, I do need to get back to the center. It was so nice seeing you again, Miz Ellen. I know how much Gran enjoys talking with you. And I do hope you can stop by soon and look at my newest hanging baskets. I've got some gorgeous new pink geranium varieties that I know you will love. And they will look lovely with the dahlias that bloom beside your porch."

It was enough to send Gran to the car.

"I want a puppy, Mommy." Patricia climbed into her seat and began to buckle up. "I met Grady, and he even shook my hand. And when I kissed him on his nose, he gave me a big kiss. Mr. Flint says dogs are very important."

Kimmie let out a deep sigh. "I know how much you want a dog, but now is not the time to get one for you. End of discussion."

The only thing that occupied Kimmie's mind was Flint, and she figured that was one fine specimen of masculinity to contemplate. It was not what she needed to take up head room, though. She had more pressing things to consider.

"You are being quiet. Is something wrong?" Gran asked.

"No. I-I was thinking about Miz Kate...and then about Posy's... and what I need to do this afternoon."

"Did you get a chance to talk to Flint? You two were inseparable when you were children."

Kimmie pulled into the long, shell-covered driveway that led to her grandmother's house. "No. I'm sure he has no desire to rekindle that friendship. I'm not about to be put in the position of making some wife jealous. He's merely come home for his grandmother's funeral or whatever they want to call it these days. A funeral is simply a society event forced upon people. The person is dead and those who cared have had their hearts ripped out. No amount of flowers or pretty words can repair that ache."

"Darling, I had no idea this funeral would be that hard on you. It's been four years. Maybe it's time to move on with your life."

"I have." She put the car in park. "Please, stop playing matchmaker. Having my heart ripped out once was enough for me. I have no desire to marry again."

Flint returned to his grandmother's house and spent what remained of the day clearing and cleaning things from the three story Federal-style home. Already he had plans for this place. The structure was sturdy and had been kept well, but it needed updating and normal maintenance. Maybe he needed the old place more than it needed him. The desire to put down roots, to find a place to call home, was strong. This place had always felt like home, it just wasn't his until now.

Grady asked to go out. Flint flipped on the back floodlights and took the dog for the last walk of the evening. The air had cooled to a reasonable temperature. Across the way was the Overton house where Kimmie spent her summers with her grandmother, Iris Overton. He never did spot Kimmie during the funeral, but when little Patty scampered to a parked car, he saw someone with shoulder-length hair. But she was too far away to recognize. Uncertain, he was left with the impression that it was Kimmie. His heart had skipped a beat.

Grady stopped under the low-hanging branch of a tree. It was at that moment that Flint decided he was determined to catch up to his childhood friend. Too many times, he wished he had known how to reach her. There were so many things he wanted to talk to her about, as if they were still little kids sharing secrets. The times he wanted to ask what was going wrong and how he could he fix it. He was certain she would listen, she always had. But back then they were just kids. She had probably married and moved on with her life. Patty was a bit of a shock, but in a way, she wasn't. The child was merely the confirmation of what he had supposed. But still he wondered about Kimmie. Was she happy? Maybe they could share yearly Christmas cards. Or maybe her husband might be a great guy and they could hit a few golf balls.

His thoughts turned bitter as he reflected on Haley. She swore her undying love to him. Yet, every time they set a wedding date, she would change her mind. He wanted children. She didn't. Then one day he realized that she was not being faithful to him. Those feelings of betrayal still lingered.

He discovered she had been pregnant... It took forever before he came to grips with that. Eventually, he realized it might not have been his child, but to dispose... It would eternally haunt him. Women had choices and he could understand that, but he didn't agree with it. To him, it was wrong. *Maybe if... But not mine. No. Never. Life is precious.* He wondered what he had done wrong. *Why?*

Kimmie climbed into her bed. She had plenty of important things to contemplate before she drifted to sleep, except Flint crept to the forefront. He was handsome. His black hair reached over his collar but not in an unkempt way. It looked as though it had been cut that length. He hadn't changed; he'd only matured.

Her mind drifted to a place that she'd tried hard to forget. She realized she was smiling at the fantasy of Flint. The fire that she thought had been extinguished years ago burned bright and heated her body until she was certain she might self-combust. *Oh, what a fantasy. I wonder if he's really that good.*

Two

efore dawn had broken, Flint found himself wide awake. He'd barely slept. His dreams seemed semiconscious as they had tossed through the memories of Haley, the child who might have been, his grandmother's cooking, his time in her garden weeding, picking beans, shelling peas... And Kimmie with her infectious smile, their adventures through the woods behind his grandmother's house, and swimming in the lake.

He lay there rehashing the memories, but he kept coming back to the ones of Kimmie. As the sky became light, he got up and found a can of coffee. In the pantry, his grandmother had left a brand new container of powdered creamer, and he was grateful. He'd spent time yesterday tossing out her milk and dozens of other items from her refrigerator. This morning he made a pot of coffee. As the water dripped over the grounds, he decided he'd visit the market in a few hours. *And I'll look for Kimmie.*

The coffee finished brewing. He poured a cup and stepped onto the front porch of the house. Barely able to see the Overton's driveway, it didn't take much to determine that the car he'd seen yesterday at the funeral wasn't there. *She's left town...only came for the funeral.*

Grady finished and returned to Flint's side. A moment later, he took off as though he was about to chase a squirrel, but instead of stopping by the tree line, he bolted into the Overton yard. *If he did this with his...*

Flint took off across the yard without shoes or his shirt, only wearing a pair of ragged shorts. When he reached the trees, he spotted Grady being petted by Patty, and returning her attention by licking her face. *Oh, are you in trouble, boy!*

"I'm so sorry. Grady knows not to bolt. He's been trained as a service dog. There's no reason for him to act this way." Flint called to Iris Overton.

Mrs. Overton smiled at him. "No harm. They seem to adore each other. Patricia has been bugging us for a dog for the last three months. Kimmie says she doesn't have time to train a dog." The older woman held out her arms to Flint. "Come here and give me a big hug. It's been too long."

Flint found himself wrapped in her comforting arms. "It has been a long time. How are you doing?"

"Ha! Me? I'm a tough old bird, but I've already decided that I miss Kate. You get to my age and… Well… We don't live forever. How are you handling it?"

He steered them to the chairs under a tree that flanked the house and moved one chair so that he could chat with the older woman. "I'm doing, okay. She knew I was coming home. I had called her last week and asked if she minded my staying with her for a few days. I've been thinking about moving and calling this place home."

"What about your job?"

"With the Internet, I can keep up. Occasionally I'll have to visit my various coffeehouses. Cup of Joe is simply a coffee café. But I try to hire good people at each one." He pressed his fingertips together. "Maybe I'll start one here."

Squeals of laughter filled the air as Grady and Patty romped across the yard. Flint didn't miss the bond that was forming between them. Grady had been promised to a little girl about Patty's age. But it was her parents who claimed that Grady took too much of their time. Walking him each morning and evening became an issue as was food and water. Flint worried about their daughter - maybe she cramped their life, too. What did they expect?

He and Grady had met with them several times but never in their home. An agency had put them together. Had Grady bonded with the little girl and missed her? Did Patty remind him of that child? Or do dogs form their own friendships? He suspected it was a little of both.

"Where are you going to stay? Are you selling your grandmother's house?"

Mrs. Overton's questions made him turn his attention to her. "I'm not certain. I'd like to stay at the house. I was asked to meet Roger Britter at his office Monday morning. He wants to go over the Will with me. I found a copy of it last night as I was clearing some things from the house, and unless there's some sort of a change that I'm unaware of, the house and properties are mine. She left my parents a chunk of insurance money, but the largest portion went to Dad's mission work with him overseeing the money. She also left some money towards a scholarship fund. But what physical property she owned is mine."

Mrs. Overton laughed. "Complete with warts?"

He chuckled. "I was looking at the roof of the house. It might need to be replaced."

"She did own property in town, quite a few pieces, including that old gas station next to Posy's. I offered to buy it a few times, but she never wanted to sell anything. Thought it would make a nice produce stand."

"That was a gas station?"

She nodded. "I was still a kid when that place sold gasoline. You could buy an entire tank full for what a gallon costs today."

"And a man didn't make much back then either."

"It's all relative." She waved her hand as though dismissing the subject. "My father would buy me a bottle of Coca-Cola from the machine in there. That was a real treat. I'd save the cap."

Grady came to Flint with his tongue hanging out. "Guess that's my cue to take him home and give him some water."

Kimmie walked out of the house. "Was that Flint I heard?"

"Yes. He's such a nice man and he's turned into a very handsome one."

"I don't need a matchmaker. I need to get to work. Are you going to church this morning?"

"Of course. Did you want Patricia to wear anything special?"

"No. She can wear her sundress. That's fine. Or I can take her to work with me. I don't mind. I don't open until noon. I'll be spending most of this morning deadheading petunias."

"She can stay with me. Who will be there with you?"

"Jimmy and Kelly. They both are hard workers." Kimmie leaned down and kissed her grandmother. "Let's go out for dinner tonight. My treat." Kimmie rolled down the window on her vehicle and let the warm air blow through the car. She loved this time of year. Everything was so fresh and the balmy weather suited her.

At Posy's, she parked and pulled her favorite pair of tiny snippers from her pocket and started deadheading the plants that faced the road.

As she finished each row, she turned on the drip irrigation for that section. Quick and efficient, it didn't take her long to complete the task. Then she moved to the store. *Oh, I forgot to sweep last night.* With broom and dustpan, it was a chore that she wished didn't need to be done. The only good thing was the sweet, earthy scent that filled the interior of the shop. Her floral designer had cleaned that area Saturday before leaving and placed the closed sign on the counter. It would stay closed until Tuesday.

She was about to walk into the courtyard in the back when her front door opened. She was expecting her two workers but instead it was a man's form. With bright sun backlighting him, panic took hold and she almost screamed, but managed to squeak, "I'm sorry, we don't open until noon."

A slight chuckle could be heard. "I know that. I was hoping to catch you before you got busy."

She let out a breath. "Flint?"

"Were you expecting someone else?"

She flicked on the store's overhead lights. "Don't scare me like that! Do you want to give me a heart attack before I reach my thirtieth birthday?"

"Kimmie, it's only me. I'm not... Oh dear. I wanted to talk to you...just say hello. I wanted to... but I didn't... I'm not..."

She went to her old friend and touched his arm. "What wrong? Take your time." She pulled him to a bench seat and forced him down. "Sit. You know you can always talk to me. I will always be your friend."

"Well, that's nice to know, but you're acting strange." He looked around. "I came because... A lot of years have passed, and I don't want to make a boyfriend or husband jealous."

"Nothing to worry about there. I'm widowed and there's no boyfriend."

He smelled of soap and shampoo. It was clean and fresh with a woodsy scent that was doing wonderful things to her.

"How about you? Are you hiding your wife or lover in another town? Didn't see anyone with you." She sucked in a quick breath. "Did something happen, I mean you have a service dog. Do you want to talk about it?"

"Wait a minute." A single chuckle was heard. "Back up! No partner hiding." He got to his feet and rubbed his temples. "Grady is a service dog. He's with me because I train these dogs for the blind. It's my hobby, but I take it very seriously."

"How did you get into that?"

"Two days after I graduated from college I read an article about how much these dogs were needed, and how expensive they are to train. I kept reading everything I could on service dogs and decided I'd try it. Grady is my twelfth dog. Two never got placed and Grady has been rejected so he's waiting for another opportunity."

"Oh. I thought something had happened to you."

"No. I'm fine. I've had my own hell over the years and maybe training these dogs has helped me get through some rough spots. What about you? What happened to Patty's father?"

"Cancer. Who would have figured that at twenty-four he'd get cancer?"

"That's a hard blow."

"Patricia was a baby. Three years later, I was a widow." She walked to the front windows and looked over the parking lot, hoping Flint wouldn't see the tears welling in her eyes. "My parents were supporting us, and I fell into a very deep depression that I tried to hide from my family and child."

She felt Flint's arms encircle her. She leaned into him and let her tears fall. *Typical Flint.* He merely held her. That gentle support that he'd delivered as a kid still came through, letting her know that he'd be there for her and that everything would be better.

She turned and faced him. It was the same Flint that she had always known. Only now he was grown up. She sniffled and fished a tissue from her pocket. "I'm sorry. I didn't mean to do that to you."

"Aw, Kimmie. Anytime, you know that. Can you escape for the day?"

"Not really. I own Posy's now. Gran gave it to me."

"That's a no?"

"I'm only open until four today. But I'm closed on Monday."

"Then I shall steal you at four this afternoon and again tomorrow. I think coming home was the best thing I could have done. I've missed you, Kimmie."

His face was so sincere.

"I missed you. I miss our friendship."

"We were kids and a lot has happened. We're going to have to start over as adults if you're interested in being more than just casual old friends."

She shook her head. "I loved my husband. I can't see myself having any sort of relationship right now. Don't expect too much from me."

He dropped a kiss on the top of her head and vanished out the door with Grady keeping step beside him.

She walked into her office and let another round of tears flow. This time she wasn't certain why she was crying.

Flint looked at the old gas station and realized he could tell what it once was. He didn't feel like stopping or giving it much consideration. Holding Kimmie in his arms made him feel truly alive, as though nothing else mattered.

He turned onto his grandmother's driveway and parked his car in the usual spot. But instead of going into the house, he took the old path through the woods to the lake. *She isn't the only one with emotional battles to fight.*

At the lake, not a single human sound could be heard. He stood and looked around. It was as he remembered it. He stripped off his clothing and plunged into the cold water. It took his breath away. The summer sun had not yet warmed the water. He shook the wet hair from his eyes and made his way to the pebbled beach.

Grady stared at him as if begging to have the same fun. Flint stepped out of the water and shivered for a moment. He took Grady's service vest off and picked up a stick. "Fetch!"

Using his hands, he slipped the water droplets from his skin and pulled his shorts on before Grady returned with the stick. Their game of fetch lasted for quite awhile. When it ended, Flint stretched out on the beach and closed his eyes against the sun. He wanted Kimmie back in his arms. It was the same feeling he had when he'd last seen her. Except he was still too young to realize what the feelings were that she stirred within him. That last summer so many years ago, his father had forbidden him to see Kimmie and sent him to a summer boys' camp in the mountains.

As an adult he understood why, but he never understood why his father had not been more forthcoming about the budding feelings of a young teen. Flint vowed that he'd be more open with a son if he ever had one.

Grady whined and Flint opened his eyes to a darkening sky. He wasted no time gathering his things and heading back to the house. He didn't quite make it. As he stepped from the woods, lightning cracked overhead. By the time he reached the house, he was drenched.

He fixed a pot of coffee and changed into dry clothes. Whatever plans he may have had prior to his grandmother's death, he could feel them sliding away much like the water that poured off the roof. Coming home to his grandmother's had become a new beginning. He could feel it deep inside. The sensation was strong. Every fiber in his body was alive, and for once, he felt as though he'd been freed from his past—freed from the domination of a father who treated his son with less respect than was warranted.

He walked into the sunroom of his grandmother's house. There in the center of the room was a small mosaic table that his grandmother had created from bits of semiprecious gemstones. Scattered across the table were pieces of the whitest quartz. He'd almost swept a few out of his way but realized he'd better not. He was certain they were placed there for a reason.

It took a few moments to find her little book that she kept filled with what she called her nature notes. The last entry told part of the story. Nothing made sense to him. But when he put the book back where he found it, he discovered an envelope with his name on it.

Using her letter opener, he slit the envelope and began to read.

My dearest and only grandson,

If you are reading this, then I have died or I'm totally incapacitated. I pray it's the first and not the second as that's not the way I want to leave this life. I need to tell you a few things. Maybe you've discovered them on your own and maybe not.

I'll start with heritage. There's more Indian blood in you than your father wants to admit. And this is where I will spill the family secrets. Your grandfather was Native American. I have a small amount in me because my father married a woman with French and Indian blood. That made your father more than half. It was something that he preferred not to recognize in spite of my trying to instill some pride in him. He rebelled.

I thought our problems with our often-wayward son were over until he came home one spring from medical school and informed us that in spite of his marriage to Jennifer, he'd had an affair. That affair caused a pregnancy.

Alicia came to stay with me that summer and when she neared full term, your father took her to Jackson Medical Center and registered her under the name Jennifer Silverlake. He then forced his wife, Jennifer, to accept you as her own.

The rift between your dad and his wife probably affected you in ways you'll never know. That is part of the reason that you seemed to be at my house so much. Years have helped soften the chasm between your parents, but that's their problem.

Alicia walked away and never made any contact after you were born. There is no doubt in my mind that she also was of American Indian heritage. During her stay, She taught me things that I didn't know, often recounting great deeds of the forefathers and of the Great Spirits.

I can tell you that she was adorable and I enjoyed having her. She loved your dad and also felt very betrayed when she discovered he was married. All of this information is best if no one knows that I've told you the truth of your birth.

He read the next page and the following one.

I've left a puzzle for you on the table. I started it after Haley left you. I wanted to know if you would find happiness or would your father's sins follow you. I've prayed that your life will be filled with joy and laughter. I've allowed the quartz to move without my help. Rain and wind have moved the stones - along with the help of a bird or squirrel on occasion.

I don't think life is predetermined. But I do believe how we live it will determine our happiness. The placement of the stones doesn't matter. The magic is inside of us. We establish how we face our life and what we do with it.

Happiness has nothing to do with what we accumulate or buy. It is how we look at what we do have, and how we treat those around us. Stay true to yourself.

The love you seek has always been there. Embrace it.

Grandma

PS: Forgive your father for his mistakes. His infidelity gave you to me, and you've always brought joy into my life.

Flint stared at the quartz and grinned when he realized where each piece rested on the ancient pattern. His grandmother had taught him well. He picked up the one piece of quartz and held it tightly in his hand. *I hope you are right.* A slight breeze stirred the air. He placed the stone back where he'd found it. Then he read the letter a second time before returning it to the envelope. His feelings were raw. He was glad he'd not read it as a teen or even as a college student. But he doubted she wrote it back then.

The knowledge of his birth answered many questions, yet left him with a few new ones. At least now, he had an inkling into the dynamics of his strained relationship with his mom and dad. But he still couldn't understand why he was punished for his father's mistake. He was the innocent child.

He looked at the time and called Posy's.

Three

immie was certain that Flint hadn't planned to go out to dinner with Gran and Patricia, but he wasn't complaining. He drove to what they jokingly referred to as the "city." It was another small town but large enough to have plenty of dining options along with shopping and lots of other amenities that a tiny country town with only two signal lights didn't.

He took them to a family-style steakhouse swearing it was very casual dining. Kimmie was glad she'd taken a quick shower and changed to something more suitable for a friendly get-together. And as always, Grady came along.

Patricia held Grady's leash as Flint had instructed. Patricia looked at the dog with total adoration, and the dog acted as though he was in charge of the child.

Kimmie expected the restaurant to say something about the dog, but the employees accepted the dog with his blue service vest. A few of the patrons mumbled under their breath and quite a few stared.

The meal was delicious. They all laughed and caught up on old times. Gran swore she didn't have room for dessert but managed to eat the Baklava anyway.

When the waitress brought the bill, Flint grabbed it and insisted he was paying. He stuck his credit card inside the leather binder. "I'm not allowing my favorite women to pay for their meals. I said it was my treat, and I meant it."

"But what about women being independent?" Kimmie asked. She waited to hear his answer.

"I'm totally in agreement with women having the right to

independence." He smiled as he spoke. "The days of women being dependent on a man are long gone. A woman is entitled to equal pay for equal jobs and all the rest." His facial expression turned very serious. "Women should never be made to feel dependent. But that doesn't mean that men should get away with being jerks and expect women to pick up the meal tab." He looked directly at Gran. "Call it my Southern roots and training, but I was raised to be a gentleman at all times and especially around women. I would never stand back and allow a woman to change a flat tire. That is wrong. A man needs to be a man."

Kimmie scrunched up her nose and teased, "Chauvinist. I can change my own tire."

He raised his eyebrows. "Am not! But I would never allow you to do that if I am with you. And if you are stranded on a back road, I will find comfort knowing you can change a tire without help."

As soon as he was able to sign the receipt, they left the restaurant.

"Patty, it's best if we give Grady the option of visiting the grassy area over there. Would you like to try walking him, if your mother says it's all right?"

Kimmie nodded and walked with them. "What if Grady needs scooping?"

Patricia turned to Flint.

"That's the polite thing to do. If Grady were going to someone in certain cities, he'd be trained to use the curb. If he were being trained as a different type of service dog, he'd expect his human to clean up behind him. But since he's been trained for a blind person... Where would someone blind know to scoop?" Flint grinned. "I've taught Grady to use non-traffic areas. He knows not to go near the restaurant."

"I never thought about all the things a service dog must do." Mrs. Overton said. "I never considered all the ramifications of training a service dog. I assumed they only had to learn to watch for cars. I find it very interesting."

"Service dogs cover a very wide range. Even police dogs

are service dogs. They undergo some of the exact same training as Grady, but police dogs are highly specialized. They learn to do their job, just as Grady knows to lead a blind person. It's not interchangeable. You wouldn't expect your dentist to know how much fertilizer to give a rose bush or how to perform heart surgery. But we expect everyone to know how to wash their hands."

"Just fascinating." Gran watched as Grady obediently walked to the far end of the parking lot and then brought Patricia back to the proper car. "Amazing. What a smart animal."

Flint grinned. "Thank you. Most animals are intelligent. Training allows them to develop the skills that they need as companions. And just as humans like to take pride in what they do, so do dogs."

The sun was hanging low in the sky, signaling the end of day as they all piled into Flint's SUV. Kimmie appreciated the outing but she wanted some time alone with Flint. She knew that if Flint had been a stranger, she would never have considered being so forward. "When we get back, would you mind giving me a chance to settle Patricia into bed? I'd like very much to spend what is left of the evening with you."

"Mommy! I don't want to go to bed."

"It's a school night, and eight-thirty is your bedtime. By the time we get back to the house and you get cleaned up, it will be bedtime."

"It's not fair!"

Flint jumped into the conversation. "Hey, squirt, no one said anything in this world is fair. But I doubt that Mommy is making you go to bed early. Judging by the time right now… You're going to need every possible minute to get ready for bed. And I'll warn you, if you were at my house and you had to help Grady brush his teeth, you'd need extra time."

"Grady doesn't brush his teeth." Patricia said defiantly.

"You are right, he doesn't. I have to do that for him. He has peanut-flavored toothpaste, and he thinks it's great."

Kimmie groaned. "Don't tell her things like that. Now she'll want to brush his teeth."

Flint shrugged his shoulders. "Well, if she does as she's told tonight, I'll allow her to brush Grady's teeth tomorrow night. She may come over after dinner and I'll show her what Grady does before his bedtime."

"What's he use, a doggie toothbrush?" Kimmie almost snarled. She didn't mean to sound so negative, but she hated someone filling the child's head with nonsense.

"Yes. Oral health is just as important for dogs as it is for humans."

Kimmie decided that continuing such a conversation was only going to lead to a dozen questions from Patricia and delay bedtime even more. The child resisted going to bed every evening and had from the time she was a baby.

And as she predicted, Patricia asked a gazillion questions about Grady, and then asked if she could spend the night with the dog.

It was almost nine o'clock when Kimmie dared to creep downstairs and join Gran and Flint. Gran fixed Kimmie a cup of coffee before excusing herself and vanishing to her bedroom.

Kimmie motioned to Flint to follow her to the front porch. "I'm sorry it took me so long."

"It's fine. I didn't mind waiting."

"You are happier tonight than you were this morning."

He smiled at her and a little piece of her heart melted. "This morning I didn't know if you were married or had a boyfriend."

"What would you have done if I had?"

"If you had a husband, I would have asked you both to dinner tonight. But I wouldn't have been as generous if you had a boyfriend. I probably would have prepared for battle."

"Ah, a pistol duel or a joust?"

He laughed. "I'm a law abiding citizen, and since pistol duels are illegal, I'd have to settle for a jousting match which I'm certain I'd probably win."

"Cocky, are you?"

"Maybe. My desire is in my favor. I'm willing to do anything if it meant I could win your heart."

She fell into giggles. "You really can lay it on thick. Are you forgetting who you are talking to?"

"No. I wouldn't say that to someone else. I'd put on my smooth persona and charm her. Then I'd take her for dinner, have an enjoyable meal, and go home alone." He slipped Grady's vest off of him and patted him on his head. "Be good."

Grady wandered off and chased a few fireflies.

Flint took her hand and pulled her from the porch chair. "Walk with me."

Kimmie stood and wrapped her arm around Flint's waist. He snuggled her to his side as they took off towards his grandmother's. She found comfort in his closeness and with it came the sizzle of sexual attraction. She was certain that he felt it, but he didn't attempt any moves that suggested more.

With Grady in tow, they walked to the lake and around to the small dock. "Seems odd not seeing the canoe. Still have it?"

"I came to the lake today and at first I thought nothing had changed, then I noticed something had changed. I couldn't put my finger on it. You're right. The canoe is missing."

He stopped in front of the old wooden structure that protruded into lake. "Stay here. I'll make certain the boards are safe." He walked the length of the dock and then returned. "It's fine, but I've solved a mystery."

As they walked across the old boards, Flint pointed next to the dock. The little canoe was sitting on the bottom of the lake with its ropes still attached.

"Oh, dear. Now what?" Kimmie asked, remembering all the summer hours they had spent in the not so little aluminum boat.

"I guess I'm going swimming. Probably filled with rainwater over the years, I'll try raising it and seeing if it's still usable. I'm certain Patty will enjoy canoeing."

"Her name is not Patty. I named her Patricia for the grandmother who started Posy's in 1903. That's her name, not Patty."

They stood staring at the small sunken boat. Then Flint broke the hush. "I didn't realize you were so sensitive about the name. She seemed to like my calling her that."

"It's not her name."

Flint wrapped both his arms around her waist. "We're going to discover all sorts of things about each other, aren't we?"

"I'm sorry. I didn't mean to snap at you over Patricia's name. I just don't want someone trying to undo what I have done."

They took a few more steps and reached the end of the pier. Flint dropped to the edge.

"Have a seat."

She sat beside him. "Been a long time."

"It has, and yet it doesn't seem like it tonight. My feelings for you were changing back then and my father forbid me to see you. He did what he could to keep us apart."

"Why? I didn't do anything wrong."

"Neither one of us did. I think he thought that I would hurt you in some way. Just the fact that I was older and maybe more ready to have a girlfriend and not a little friend."

"That was mean."

"I thought so too, but now... Maybe he did us both a favor. Maybe we had to experience a certain amount of life before we found each other."

"Some of what... I've had so much pain. When I met my husband, I thought the world was this wonderful place. Love was the great driving force, and life was going to bring us all the things that we wanted." She looked across the lake to the dark outline of the trees creating a ragged edge against the silver sky. "We had a small but lovely wedding. I had a maid of honor, one bridesmaid, the long white dress and a nice reception with a pretty cake. It was a real wedding. Steven wore a tux and we both thought it would last forever. Shortly afterwards, I discovered I was pregnant – a little sooner than we had planned. Then three days after Patricia was born, Steve's test results came in and we discovered he had cancer. I still had another year of college. Everything was wrong, we just didn't know it."

"Did you graduate?"

"Yes. I never took that first real job. I had a toddler and a very sick husband. We refused to believe..." Tears began forming and then one slipped down her cheek. The pain flooded her.

"You're not the only one to have lost someone special."

She wiped at her cheeks and stared at Flint through her

blurred vision. A tear poised above his cheek for a moment before rolling downward.

"We both lost a precious life, Kimmie. How will we ever reach beyond the pain?"

Flint awakened when Grady yelped and put his paw on Flint's chest. He eyed the dog and realized the sun was shining. Stretching his arms over his head, the reality of the previous evening began to populate his mind. The sun shone through the blinds creating stripes on everything. Grady whimpered. "Okay, give me a second, and I'll let you out."

He managed to make it downstairs to the kitchen and open the back door. Grady took off and didn't go very far before stopping to relieve himself. Grady began to bark as a truck pulled into the driveway and parked not far from the house. A man stepped out and walked towards the back door, sending Grady to Flint for further instructions.

Flint gave the command for Grady to stay yet remain alert.

The man, dressed in a camel colored pair of work pants with a matching shirt came close but stopped, leaving a fair distance between him and the dog.

"I'm here to cut the grass if that's what you want. Been doing it for years."

"Who are you?"

"John Hotchkins. I own JH Lawn Service. I cut this yard and the one over there." He raised his thumb in the direction of the Overton's.

"Go right ahead. How often do you come?"

"Once a week and then the first Monday of the month I do more than cut. You want a copy of the contract I had with Mrs. Silverlake?"

"Yes, that would be nice."

"I can mail it or bring it."

"What's easier?"

"Don't much matter. I'll bring you a copy tomorrow. I'll need a new contract being she died. She's already paid for this month."

Flint eyed the man with the beer belly and slightly curled, graying hair under his wide brimmed hat. "You related to the John who played football in high school?"

"That's me. Played all four years, JV and then varsity. Had a scholarship to Clemson, but I hurt my knee the first year, so I had to come back home. Started this here company. Been working ever since."

Flint nodded. He remembered the guy, but obviously, the man didn't remember him. *Years have a way of changing people.*

It didn't take Flint long to start a pot of coffee and take care of his morning ablutions. His hair was still damp from his shower when he came downstairs. Grady sat by the door and kept vigil over John as he worked on the landscaping.

The rumble of a lawn mower was a distinctive noise. No matter where Flint took his morning coffee, the sound of the mower followed. Flint decided it meant he didn't have to take the time to mow the yard with the smaller ride-on that he saw in the barn. He was grateful for John's services as the mower zipped across the acres of his grandmother's place.

It dawned on Flint that John's shattered dreams of fame were turned into a hometown business. The man was a small town resident with a story. There were plenty of them in every little community across America. Maybe that was all Flint really had. Maybe he and John weren't that different.

Flint called Grady and they headed into town. He had an appointment with Roger Britter. *Let's see what there is or isn't.*

Four

Kimmie stood on the porch while Patricia caught the school bus. Watching the child as she left gave Kimmie a feeling of satisfaction that she was certain only a parent could understand. Patricia was an excellent student and seemed to have lots of friends. Like any child, she had her strong points and some not so wonderful ones. But Kimmie knew from experience that Gran's influence was a good thing and a major help. Gran was there when Patricia got off the bus, and Gran oversaw the homework each afternoon.

The child didn't spend most of her free time playing video games. She spent it playing outside and helping Gran with chores. *Maybe a dog wouldn't be a terrible thing. Grady is well behaved, and certainly there are other dogs like him.* Kimmie pondered the situation a little more and then decided once again that dogs were work. She really didn't have time for one. *It's like adding another child to the household.*

Flint promised to pick Kimmie up before noon, but it was never decided what they would do. Not knowing his plans meant she didn't know what to wear. Did he intend to take her someplace special? She pulled on four different outfits before settling on a simple, tea-green, cotton dress with a white cotton, crocheted, short-sleeved jacket and paired it with some flat, strappy sandals. She added a touch of makeup, button earrings, and spent a few minutes on her hair. Then she stood in front of the full-length mirror and silently declared that she was as good as she'd ever get.

"You look fabulous." Gran smiled over the rim of her coffee mug.

"Thanks. He's got an appointment in town this morning and said he'd pick me up afterwards."

"Britter's office, I suspect. Kate used him for her Will and everything else."

"I wonder what will become of Miz Kate's house."

"One day it will be sold off and they'll put one of those big housing communities there, waterfront property and all that. Kate owned that lake but she couldn't interfere with the water. The government controls that."

"I thought she stocked it?"

Gran nodded. "She could add certain fish. I know she added some a few years back. It keeps the mosquitoes down. Kate's husband was the one who was the fisherman. He loved going out on the water. I don't think there's a fishing hole within fifty miles that Jack didn't fish. Kate wasn't as fond of cleaning fish as Jack was of catching and eating them."

Kimmie opened her laptop as Gran continued to talk. The garden center was closed on Mondays, but Kimmie never was able to escape from it. Putting the center online took serious thought and forced her to learn about web design. She hired someone she knew from high school to help handle the more complicated aspects of her site. He designed it so that she could easily add, subtract, or tag an item as sold out. Her Internet orders had started out slow, real slow as in almost non-existent. But this year, she'd spent serious money advertising. Online orders had picked up and outsold her little center in town. She had already begun adding to her small greenhouse operations to be certain she'd have enough stock for next spring.

Posy's was a family, always female-owned business that had been around since the start of the twentieth century. Its small-town operation appealed to people. The other drawing cards were her wide variety of cooking and medicinal herbs, and the fact that she kept everything organic. Miz Kate often worked at Posy's and she had been responsible for the introduction of the lesser known and used herbs. When Kimmie went to put Posy's online, she had spent several long days with Miz Kate going over the use and popularity of the various herbs. Now it was one of her strongest lines and she was thrilled.

But being responsible for Posy's was very different from working there every summer as a teen. Gran had run the place for over forty years and there wasn't much that she didn't know about plants, retail, or accounting. She was still there to help when Kimmie needed it. With luck, Patricia would probably follow in the family tradition, but Kimmie also wanted her daughter to be free to choose her career.

Posy's income for the month was on the computer's screen, but Kimmie failed to concentrate on the numbers. Instead, she found herself thinking about last night with Flint. How easily she had talked about her husband and how openly she had been able to grieve. It was something she'd not done. Always attempting to hide her feelings and carry on, putting her sorrows into some sort of makeshift box that she believed she should never open. She had dragged out the proverbial box, and together they had sorted out some of its contents. Maybe now she could begin to find hope for a brighter future.

Her phone rang and it was Flint. "Hi."

"Hi, I'm done. May I come get you and steal you for the day?"

"Yes. I was sitting here working on the books, except my ability to focus kept taking a walk to last night's chat on the dock."

"I hope you aren't rehashing the negative things."

"No, quite the contrary. I was thinking about how much better I feel. Except I will admit that lack of sleep isn't helping. I had to get up with Patricia and get her ready for school."

His warm laugh came through the phone and rolled across her like a gentle breeze.

"I'll be there in about three minutes. I just finished walking around that lot next to Posy's. I'll tell you about it when I get there."

For the last nine years, Flint had worked hard at opening coffee shops where people could relax, meet with friends, study, or just grab a cup of delicious coffee. His constant attention to detail meant that people relied on knowing that they could have a consistently good cup of coffee at Joe's. His dedication to the farmers growing and roasting the beans gave him a reputation that was gaining international recognition.

Today, with Grady at his side, he was hit with an idea that he knew would not be easy for some people to accept but would please others. Now he couldn't wait to share it with Kimmie. They were more than just childhood friends; they were both independent entrepreneurs. They understood retail and what it took to make an idea become a reality.

He drove up the Overton's driveway and sprinted from the car, leaving Grady on his own.

Kimmie immediately appeared. "Do I need to bring anything?"

"Oh, no. And you look pretty enough to devour right here. I can tell that I'm going to have to work extra hard to remain a gentleman."

She scoffed. "Don't sling me compost ingredients. I know all about you, Flint, and I know that you were taught to be good, very good."

He raised his eyebrows. "I am good. And I believe that you'd love to discover how good."

She giggled. "I'll settle for a little kiss."

He promptly obliged and broke it off when Kimmie's grandmother walked into the kitchen.

"Well, it's about time. I've been waiting for you two to discover each other as more than apple tree raiding bandits." Mrs. Overton laughed.

Flint prayed that the flush of warmth on his cheeks didn't show. "I'd rather not remember that stomachache."

Gran waved her hand. "Speaking of stomachaches, how long will it take you two to decide on giving me a grandson who's as cute as his daddy?"

"Gr-r-ran!" Kimmie protested.

"Well, you're not getting any younger,"

Kimmie's anger flashed. "How dare--"

Flint broke into laughter. "I'd be more than willing to accomplish that mission, but I think we'd both better wait for your granddaughter to approve. We've only managed to make it to the kissing stage."

He took Kimmie by her elbow and quickly escorted her to his car. "Oh, darn. Grady! Car!"

The dog bounded from across the yard and jumped into the backseat of his master's auto. Flint promptly snapped the dog's seatbelt, checked on Kimmie, and then opened the driver's door.

"I can't believe she said that!" Kimmie was still upset.

Flint took Kimmie's hand, leaned over, and kissed her one more time. "I think our grandmothers have planned our wedding for us."

"We need to give ourselves time and not jump into anything too hastily."

He turned the car around in the driveway and headed to town. "Hasty, no. It's not hasty. I know how I feel and I'm waiting for you to admit to your feelings. But! We both have responsibilities and although we need to make snap decisions on some things… implementing those or others often takes time."

He pulled the car into the lot that had once been a gas station. "It's a great location because it's on Main Street but not crammed against other buildings. That makes it even better. It's located next to a thriving garden center, and the structure is quite sound."

Kimmie looked at him as though he'd lost his mind. Maybe he had.

"What are you getting at?" she asked.

"Hear me out because with or without you, it will affect you."

"Huh?" She tilted her head slightly to the side.

"Imagine a place where you can come and get great coffee"

"Okay. You're going to open a Cup of Joe."

You're catching on. "Now imagine where you can come and sit with Grady and your daughter."

"Grady is a service dog. He has to be allowed to come into your coffee shops. I understand that."

"Right, but let's say Grady isn't a service dog and merely the family pet."

"Where are you going with this line of thought?"

"A coffee shop where all dogs are welcome. It would take some extra doing because of health laws, but wouldn't it be nice if Grady or Fido, Spot or Fifi could come, too? Maybe even have a few special healthy treats for the dog to enjoy while his or her human sipped coffee? A set of outside tables as well as indoor ones. Maybe a little grassy area in case the dog needs--"

"I get it!" Her face brightened. "Is it possible?"

"Anything is possible." He took a key from his pocket. "Not totally certain what we'll find here, but from the outside, it looks solid."

The door squealed as Flint forced it open. Cautiously they stepped into the deserted building. The musty odor that faintly reminded him of motor oil accosted him. It didn't look much like a gas station. It looked more like a general store. But, as he made his way to the back, he could see the addition. Faded oil stains on the concrete floor marked where the cars had been. A tiny hole somewhere overhead had allowed rain inside and streaked a wooden support post. "I think it'll work. The basic place is here. Modernize it, update it with heat and air conditioning. It's bigger than it looks from the outside. Plenty of room for refrigerators and storage...lots more for seating. What do you think?"

"Miz Kate owned this?"

"I do now. Would you like a coffee shop for customers?"

"On a hot summer day, they will want something other than hot coffee."

"I was thinking about that, too. I do have tea at my coffee shops. The iced tea is always a big seller during the summer months."

"So Joe's is coming to my town?"

"I was thinking Joe Wags. Slight name change along with an addition to my logo that will include a dog and voila! Joe Wags."

"Now try to get it through the health department. You know they are sticklers."

"I'm fairly certain I can."

Kimmie found herself tagging along with Flint and his pursuit of this new adventure. It was fun and exciting. Watching Flint was even better.

He had a way about him. He could wheel and deal with a smile. His confidence never wavered even when opposition was tossed at him. They stopped long enough to order a sandwich at the bakery in town. Then he bought two loaves of artisan bread, one for each household.

But as the afternoon drew to a close, they left the small town and drove several miles. She wondered where he was taking her, but she didn't question him. She'd never been so willing to let someone take her wherever they wanted. It had something to do with the basic trust that always seemed to be there.

He took an exit off the highway and pulled into a restaurant. She wondered if they were dressed for such a place, but apparently, he had reservations because they were quickly seated. The private patio had a view of the river below. Candles graced the table covered in a dark blue cloth with lighter blue napkins shaped into fans. The *maître d'* brought a bottle of wine and poured it. Soon the meal was served. Flint must have ordered everything ahead of time. Never had she experienced anything like it. Nor had she ever tasted such food.

Their little date became the most exciting one she'd ever had. She snapped photos with her phone's camera and managed to convince Flint to join in a few selfies with her. She couldn't wait to share the pictures with Gran and a few online friends.

The wine was going to her head and she knew she shouldn't drink another drop, but when the frosted dessert wine arrived, she didn't say no.

When morning came, she awakened with a terrible headache. She drank several glasses of water before she even took her shower. Somehow, she managed to dress and get to Posy's. She hid in her office. When an employee knocked on the door, she thought she might die from the sound cleaving her brain into pieces. "What is it?"

"The plant supply truck arrived. They want to know where you want the pots."

"Take them to the third greenhouse from the right and let

them unload in there." *Oh, my head. What happened last night?*

She dropped her head to her desk and wondered if it would ever stop throbbing. When she opened her eyes, Flint was sitting across the desk from her.

"What...?"

He handed her a large travel mug of coffee. "Drink up. You obviously need it."

She took the cup and stared at him. "What did you do to me?"

He laughed so softly that it sounded like breathy huffs. "Nothing, darling. I fed you a fabulous meal. Do you remember any of it?"

She fought with her clouded memory. "I think I ate frog legs and snails."

He nodded. "Anything else?"

She tried to nod without rattling her brain. "Yes, I remember having the most amazing night, but this has to be the worst headache I've ever had. I think it was the dessert wine."

"Oh, I do believe you enjoyed that sweet wine." Whiskey brown eyes twinkled as he spoke. "But I don't think you remember much beyond the raspberry wine. Do you even remember coming home?"

She closed her eyes and drew a blank. "What did you do to me?"

"Nothing. You giggled your way to my car and promptly fell asleep. When I arrived at your house, you seemed to revive at least enough for me to get you inside without waking your grandmother or Patricia." His grin widened. "Do you remember giving me this and telling me to throw it away?"

He held up her tiny wedding band that she'd switched to her right hand after her husband died. That caused her to look down at her hands as a slight gasp broke the silence.

"I don't think you should toss it. It was your wedding band. It's very much a part of your life. Don't allow your sorrow over losing Steve to erase all that time from your life. You loved him and he's Patty—Patricia's—father. Embrace what you had."

She stared at the ring, and then took it from him. No longer did she want to wear it. But Flint was right; Steve had occupied a very large and important part of her life.

"I wanted to discuss something last night, but you obviously don't drink. I'll remember that the next time when there's important items on the agenda."

"Ugh! Don't remind me. Nothing against it, but I've only had a few drinks in my entire life."

"Feeling better?"

"Yes."

"Ready for more coffee?"

She nodded.

He produced a small bottle of water and a thermos filled with coffee. "Drink the water and then the coffee. You're dehydrated."

She followed his instructions.

"I am going to have to go away for a few days. I've got to go to South America and visit one of the families who grow coffee for me." He pressed his lips together for a moment. "I have a favor to ask. May Grady stay with Patricia? They seem so happy together and she knows most of the basic commands for him."

"Oh, I... That's a lot to ask. My time is so limited." Panic rushed through her.

"I've already checked with your grandmother, and she's willing to keep him so it's up to you."

"I don't know. When are you leaving?"

"Tomorrow, if you'll keep him. I've got almost a direct flight, otherwise I'll have to take him to a friend who also works with the dog agency. That will delay me by several days, and extend the time that I'll be gone. Besides, I promised that I'd show Patricia all of Grady's routines."

She sighed. "I guess, if it's only for a few days. That's probably enough for her to realize how much work a dog can be. Maybe she'll stop begging for one when she realizes what's involved."

"Thank you." He brushed the subject of Grady away as if he'd known her answer the entire time. "The second thing is this." He handed her a small box. "Before you open it, I want you to know that I love you as my childhood friend, but also as the young girl that I believed you'd become, so I used you to measure everyone else. But a few short days have shown me that the girl you once were has matured into a woman who is more than I ever could have dreamed... I want you, Kimmie, not for a torrid fling or to prove anything, but for a lifetime. I know we still have much to overcome, and that we need time to work out the kinks in our relationship. There are all sorts of aspects when it comes to building a life together. We have busy schedules, companies to run, and we're going to need to be completely certain. But I want you to have this as a reminder to consider the concept of us. I think you feel it, too"

"I'm not ready for a ring or even to consider committing to a long-term relationship."

"I know that and it's why I chose this." He walked around her desk. In the small space of her crowded office, he pulled her to her feet. "Now open it."

She lifted the lid and gasped. Inside was a gold necklace with a pendent. Small diamonds formed a heart that encircled a heart-cut diamond that was larger than any diamond that she'd ever seen. "Is it real?"

"As real as my love. It's not a proposal. It's a token of the way I feel towards you. Wear it, Kimmie. And when you are ready to say yes to marriage, I'll propose properly and give you a ring. I love you."

She looked at him and leaned into his chest. His lips found hers. Her arms wrapped around him as though he was about to be torn from her.

"Come back to me. I don't think I can bear losing you too."

"We can say our goodbye's tonight after Patricia is asleep. I'll be gone by the time you wake up tomorrow morning." He took the necklace from the box and hooked it around her neck. "I'll be back, Kimmie. I don't want to lose you. It's taken us all these years to find each other again. I'm not giving you up."

Five

Kimmie heard sound emanating from Miz Kate's property. She walked beyond her front porch and looked towards the sound. Several trucks were unloading temporary storage units. *What is he doing?*

Two days later, it was apparent. Several women had packed boxes of things and placed the boxes in the big storage bins. Later that same day, her grandmother called Posy's and said the furniture was being removed. Kimmie was certain that meant Flint was moving out and the land was going to be sold.

Sadness washed over her as she thought of the old place being turned into a housing development. She knew then she wanted to go see the lake one more time. When Saturday morning dawned, she packed up Patricia and Grady and took them to the lake. Next to the dock floated the canoe sporting new ropes and two new life vests sitting inside. One was child sized. On the dock beside the long thin boat was a brand new set of paddles. *When did he do that?*

Kimmie reached into the canoe and lifted the life jackets. She placed the one on Patricia and then put on her adult-sized one. Uncertain about taking Grady with them in the boat, she left him on the dock. Listening to the squeals of delight coming from Patricia was worth it. They spent an hour in the boat. It eased through the water as though it was made of Teflon. Not being used to handling a paddle also meant she'd probably feel it the next day, so she made her way back to the dock and they disembarked. Patricia didn't want to leave and made Kimmie promise that they could return.

Grady looked exhausted. He had followed them along the coastline, never allowing them out of his sight the entire time. As much as she didn't want to admit it, she enjoyed Grady's quiet company. Plus he was a constant reminder of Flint.

A few more days and he should be home. She was certain he was returning. She fingered the pendent that he'd given her. Part of her still feared ever being close to another man again, but she couldn't stop her feelings for Flint. His smiling face popped into her brain all the time. His gentle manners, the things he did for her, and the way he treated her meant so much more to her. He didn't hide his physical attraction, but he never forced the issue. They were adults and capable of making decisions when it came to sex. He knew where she stood on the subject, and she was well aware of his feelings. Death had hurt both of them. His unborn child would have been about the same age as Patricia. From everything he said, she didn't think it was his child. Too many games were played to trap a man into marriage, especially one who wanted children. This pregnancy wasn't the same. It was hidden. The timeframe of Haley's affair with another man, a man that Flint knew… *It wasn't his.*

"Mommy, may I go swimming now?'

Kimmie looked out at the lake. "It's very cold water. I don't want you beyond where the water is no longer waist high. Stay close to the shore." She scowled at her daughter. "You don't know how to swim, at least not enough to swim into the deep water. Okay?"

The child nodded. "I'll be good, Mommy. I promise."

Grady followed the child who scampered into the water. Patricia didn't make it past her thighs before she ran to shore. "It's cold!"

She grabbed for her towel while Grady shook the water from his fur. Looking at the dog, she attempted to shake, but discovered that she wasn't as skilled at shaking water off her body. Kimmie giggled until Grady decided he needed to remove more water from his fur and sent a shower of water pellets onto Kimmie. "AHHH! No, Grady!"

Now it was Patricia's turn to laugh at her mom. She plunked down beside her mother. "Can I keep Grady forever?"

"No, sweetie. We're only dog sitting him until Flint gets back home."

"When is he coming back?"

"Any day now. Any day…" Her phone rang and she answered it. "Hello."

Posy's employee had questions and that's why Kimmie kept her cell phone close at all times. "That's fine. Tell her those new purple Echinacea will be beautiful behind the gray of her Artemisia. The butterflies will love the coneflowers blooms and the finches love the seed heads. Oh, and did she get her hummingbird vine?" She listened. "Great. No problem. I'd rather you call if you don't know the answer." She listened to her newest employee. "If you see Mr. Martin, make sure he gets his roses." She smiled. "Good. And he left the photos… That's awesome. I'll be in this afternoon."

It was her little store and she loved it. Flexing her hours with her employees allowed her to spend extra time with Patricia. It wasn't easy raising a child. Even with her grandmother's help, Patricia still needed some mommy time, and Kimmie needed time with her daughter. This was the busiest season at the garden center yet she managed to take a few hours off.

Patricia stood, shed her towel, picked up her little plastic bucket, and began to explore the area around them. Grady as always followed. The child was turning into a rock hound.

"Don't expect to take every stone around here home with you. You need to leave some so we still have a beach."

"Mommy, you're so silly."

She grinned at her daughter, but knew the child would bring home a plastic pail full of rocks. That little pail's handle would be straining with the weight. Patricia's great-grandmother encouraged the interest in rocks. The rock pile on the back patio was becoming unwieldy. But Patricia's grandmother promised to make stepping-stones that were decorated with Patricia's "important finds." They were waiting until school was out.

Kimmie's phone alerted of an incoming text message. Her

new birdbaths had arrived. She quickly responded that she'd handle them when she came in this afternoon. The alert sounded again but it wasn't Posy's. A strange number appeared and then was followed by a text. It was from Flint.

"Come, Patricia. We've got to go home."

It took a few minutes to convince Patricia to leave. The trek back always seemed sad. It always signaled the end of something fun. It meant the conclusion a fishing trip, a day in the sun, and now had taken on a different meaning, the end of an evening with Flint. She missed him. Maybe she'd been missing him since that summer after she had turned twelve.

Her thoughts returned to when she was twelve and staying with her grandmother during her winter break. Every year she'd arrive on the day after Christmas and stay until it was time to return to school. That particular visit Flint kissed her. She wasn't certain that she liked being kissed like that. He'd run his tongue around her lips and then pushed his tongue into her mouth as if searching for a piece of gum. He swore that's how grownups did it.

She'd spent the next few months watching every movie kiss, her parents, and even people on the streets kiss. The best she could figure was they didn't slobber as much, but that part inside the mouth remained an enigma. She kissed everything she dared, trying to get the hang of this adult act. It wasn't until Tommy Halloway kissed her that she discovered some of what she had done wrong. But he didn't complain about her inexperience, instead he had proclaimed that she was 'the best kisser.' She never realized she'd have to wait seventeen years to try kissing Flint again. This time *he* knew what he was doing. His lips were gentle and soft, yet insistent. His tongue knew how to tango. But she would have willingly accepted the most wet, slobbery kiss from him, because when he kissed her, she could feel it to her toes. And she wanted to feel it again. She wanted to feel his body pressed--

"Grady come back!" Patricia called.

The dog had bolted ahead of them and begun barking.

Pulled from her thoughts, she nodded to her daughter. "Let's go; something is wrong."

Her lungs burned and her side was beginning to hurt. Twice she almost lost her balance, as her cheap flip-flops provided no support or traction on the uneven ground.

Patricia was out of view. The dog's barking was more of a bray than a bark. Discerning what would change Grady's bark was impossible, but it sounded like a cry. *If anything has happened to him...*

As she broke free of the trees, she slowed for a moment and gasped for a few deep breaths. She spotted a flash of neon pink from Patricia's bathing suit as she dashed to her own backyard.

"Mommy, hurry up. It's Gran-Gran." Her words were faint and clouded by the distance between them. "Hurry, Mommy, hurry!"

Kimmie sucked in a deep breath and called, "I'm coming."

Adrenalin was probably the only thing keeping her feet in motion and she still had quite a distance to run. Aware that the dog had stopped barking, Kimmie called again. "Are you and Grady..."

"Mommy, it's Gran-Gran. She's fallen. She says she's all right, but she can't get up."

Kimmie slowed, unsure if it was from relief or if her legs could no longer run at that speed. Her breath kept catching in her throat and she mentally cursed herself for being in such lousy physical shape. Shoveling dirt and hauling heavy pots of dirt was not the same as running.

Now she could see her grandmother's form on the ground. Grady sat at attention and Patricia was sitting beside her great-grandmother.

"What happened? Does anything hurt?" Kimmie blurted out as she drew near.

"I'm fine. I could have lain here watching the clouds until you returned. I promise, I'm glad you are here because I don't know what I would have done. I can't feel my left leg. I think I twisted it."

Heavy breaths rammed their way through Kimmie's chest, and she wasn't certain if her breathing would return to normal anytime soon. "Don't move. I'm calling an ambulance. That leg is definitely twisted." She pulled her phone from her pocket and dialed 9-1-1.

"Carroll County Emergency Dispatch. Officer Lock speaking, what is your emergency?"

"Lorie, it's Kimmie. It's my grandmother. We're in the backyard. I think she's broken something. Her leg is lying at a strange angle, and she says she can't feel it."

"I'm sending the ambulance. May I speak to her?"

"Yes." She handed Gran the phone. "It's Lorie, she wants to talk to you."

Gran took the phone. And Kimmie decided she liked it better when she was talking to dispatch. "Patricia, go watch for the ambulance so you can show them where Gran-Gran is."

The dog started to follow and Kimmie commanded, "Grady, stay."

She held her grandmother's hand while the woman chatted about her fall to Kimmie's friend at emergency services. Her grandmother looked a little pale but was in good spirits.

Strains of sirens filtered through the air and Kimmie could feel herself relaxing. She wasn't certain when her breathing had returned to normal. Looking at her grandmother, she began to make plans. She needed to change, get Patricia dressed, and do something with Grady. *Do I just leave him at the house? Inside or out? Oh, I don't know. How do I know what to do with a dog?*

The siren was louder and then turned off. As another round of panic shot through Kimmie, Patricia shouted, "They're coming down the driveway!"

Four hours later, it was determined that Gran would be spending a few days in the hospital. The doctor explained what happened and what they would be doing. But they wanted to be certain that she really would be fine and they were scheduling a variety of tests. At least nothing was broken, but her grandmother's overall health and good physical condition had been a true blessing. There was nothing Kimmie could do but allow the hospital to settle her grandmother in for the night.

Kimmie returned home to find Grady waiting patiently by the back door. He immediately ran out to handle his business. She had a child and dog to put to bed.

Patricia put the proper amount of food into Grady's bowl. She let him out one more time before making him come upstairs. Then she brushed his teeth and brushed his hair. She checked his paws and looked in his ears. When she finished with Grady, she proceeded to put on her pajamas and do her own teeth. "Okay, Mommy, we're done!"

Kimmie went upstairs. The child extended her hands as she opened her mouth for inspection. "Yes, my darling. And what about Grady?"

Kimmie had no desire to check his mouth or paws. Her concern was with her grandmother who was miles away. But it was then that she realized Grady was a hero. She knew they claimed that dogs can hear things that people cannot. She had no idea if he heard her grandmother or had sensed the situation. Kimmie pointed to the bed that had once been hers when she'd come for visits. "Let's say our prayers."

Patricia got on her knees by the old canopy bed. Grady wiggled next to her and put his front paws on the edge of the child's bed. Together they said their prayers and added. "Please watch over Gran-Gran and make her all better. And bring Flint home soon because we miss him. Amen."

"Amen. That was sweet—"

Grady gave a small bark and sat upright for a moment before settling on his bed at the foot of the child's.

"I think Grady prays too. We just don't know what he's saying." Patricia said as she slipped under the cool sheet. "I'm sure he misses Flint."

"I'm certain he does. And thank you for remembering Flint in your prayer." She kissed her daughter and walked downstairs. No more fighting over bedtime. The child had taken care of Grady and brushed her own teeth without a single complaint since Flint was gone. She'd been left in charge of the dog and she took her responsibility very seriously.

Grady had become quite an asset to their little family, and Kimmie didn't doubt that he'd be very good with Gran when she came home. As much as Kimmie wanted to talk to Flint, she didn't want to call when she didn't know where he was. She fixed a cup of coffee and then took her cup to the patio. Patricia's window was directly above Kimmie and the window was open. Everything was quiet, except for the chirping of the crickets and the distant sound of a barn owl. She was alone.

She knew she'd have to leave Posy's in the hands of a few employees while she took her grandmother to therapy and with summer on her doorstep, the garden center tended to be extremely busy. Now she was glad that she'd hired the new gal. The woman was new to the community but she wasn't new to gardening. Kimmie attempted to shake the tension from her shoulders. *I've got to learn to relax and put some faith in my employees.*

She wondered how Flint could open a coffee shop and virtually walk away. She wondered how Flint was doing, and what had delayed him. Her desire to feel his lips… That was far from accurate. It was him she wanted.

That night on the dock had stayed with her. Her friends dated and broke up with guys. Most of them had married, divorced, and were now remarried or in a committed relationship. She wasn't the type to hook up with a guy just because she needed her hormonal needs satisfied. She truly didn't need a man to make her life better.

Fingering the pendent that Flint had given her sent her back in time. They'd both grown up, but those wonderful basics that had been instilled in them as children remained. Flint encouraged, but never demanded. His personality had never changed. He was her friend. She basked in that sensation for several minutes and then went back to considering some of the things she knew about him.

He'd grown up to be efficient and organized. It was a quality she liked. But it was the way that he treated her that meant so much. Maybe because they had known each other for so long… maybe not, yet when she was with him, the air zinged with his presence. Even the scent of him sent her heart racing. The slightest touch heated her. It was a feeling unlike any other.

She looked at her empty coffee cup. The grandfather clock near the front door began to chime. It was time for her to lock up and go to bed for the night.

She had too much to do at Posy's in the morning. Patricia would have to come. Then they'd make their way to see Gran. With plans firmly in her head, Kimmie made her way up the stairs. She stopped by Patricia's room and Grady lifted his head for just a moment. "Goodnight, boy."

The dog responded with a tail wag.

As she slipped between the covers of her bed, her phone rang. Her heart stopped.

Six

id I wake you?" Flint asked.

Kimmie's voice was breathy. "No, just not used to phone calls this late. You scared me."

"Why would a late call worry you? Wouldn't you have known it was me?"

"No. I-I thought it might have been the hospital. I thought something…I panicked. I figured it was about Gran."

"What? What's going on?"

"Oh, I'm sorry. Gran fell today. She's at the hospital. I was scared she'd broken her hip, but the doctor said her hip was fine. She injured something in her back. And overextended a ligament or something."

"Kimmie, will she be okay? How did she fall? Does she need surgery? Is she going to be--"

"Stop! I can't answer that fast. She fell in the backyard. We were at the lake at the time. Grady must have heard her. He took off running. Patricia ran after him. I ran all the way from the lake."

He assumed he was hearing Kimmie sitting up and turning on the bedside lamp.

"Anyway, she fell in the yard and I called 9-1-1. They took her to Kingston Hospital. They checked her out and nothing is broken. But she can't feel her leg. Something about her back, and they're giving her an injection tomorrow for it. But she's going to be out of commission for a little while."

"If she can't feel her leg… I'll get the next flight out of here. I don't want you to be overburdened." He stood and opened his suitcase.

"No, there's no reason for you to do that. I'll be fine. We'll all be fine."

"Kimmie, I'll come home. Certainly they have late night flights."

"No! You don't need to do that. We'll be fine. Really. I promise."

He looked around his hotel room. "If I get home and find out that's not true…"

"It is. And everything is under control. I'm capable of handling the situation."

"I know you are, but if you want me, I'll come." He started to place a few things in his suitcase.

"Really, Flint, I can handle this." Her voice sounded tinged with frustration.

"Okay, I'll believe you. But I've got your back. You know you can lean on me."

"Thank you, but I can do it. There's no need for you to come home early."

"I won't argue with you. But, I am worried about you."

"Flint, I'm fine. I have lots to do, and I need my sleep." She emphasized each word.

"Okay, I'm sorry. I don't mean to make you angry, or even sound as though I'm being overbearing. Please allow me to be concerned for you." He took a quick but deep breath. "I'll let you go. I only wish you were sleeping in my arms." He sensed her silence was not over her tiredness. "I miss you."

"I miss you. I'd love to have your arms around me. Call me tomorrow night?"

"Yes, my darling. I will call."

They said their goodnights and hung up the phone. But Flint couldn't let go of the feeling that he was needed. When morning broke, he made several calls and managed to cut his trip short.

He spent another day filled with meetings. The last one ended late. He found a taxi and went to the local airport. The flight home was long with several layovers. It had been days since that initial phone call. He'd texted her several times during that period, and each time she swore everything was okay. As much as he wanted to believe her, he still worried.

He hated flying. Twenty-two hours of airports and airtime left him exhausted. When the last flight landed, he found his vehicle and headed home. But as he drove, he could feel the pull that Kimmie had on him. He took out his phone and called her. "I'm on my way home. May I see you?"

"Now?"

"Yes."

Another long silence followed.

"Kimmie, are you still there?" He drove through the darkness with nary another vehicle on the road.

"Yes."

"Is something wrong?" He waited for her answer.

Kimmie rushed to Flint's vehicle and tossed her arms around him as he stepped out. "Seeing you at the moment doesn't seem very real. But I'm so glad you are here. I've missed you so much."

He cupped her face in his hands and kissed her. She wasn't certain how her legs managed to keep her upright because her body truly relaxed against his for the first time since her grandmother's fall.

As she neared the kitchen door, she spotted Grady waiting for Flint. She opened the door and the dog jumped onto Flint and licked his face.

"Off."

The dog did as told but looked so sad even when Flint petted him.

"He was so happy to see you. Why did you fuss at him?"

"He knows better."

Since Flint's house was being torn apart, Kimmie offered the guest room.

Flint raised his eyebrows. "The guest room? Is that really where you want to put me?"

She bit her lower lip. "Not really, but I do have Patricia, and I've not…since Steve…I'm not certain…"

"Kimmie I've been flying since this time last night. As much as I'd enjoy a romantic night with you, I need my sleep. But I'd love to have you in my arms."

In less than an hour, they were both in bed. There was an awkwardness to the simplest things. Even when he turned out the light, she was uncertain. Did he really expect her to sleep or was it just a ploy? She wasn't very sure of anything. She asked herself if she really did want to be in his arms. *Maybe I should have taken the right side of the bed.*

"Kimmie?" Flint's voice was so soft that she barely heard it.

"Yes," She whispered.

Flint's movement beside her made her freeze.

He wrapped his arm around her and tucked her to his body as though she was a feather slipping across the sheets.

"I love y…"

Kimmie awakened when the sky had changed from navy to a shade of pale purple. It was then she realized that Flint was missing. Her bathroom was filled with humidity from his shower and contained the scent of a man. It had been too many years since she had been around a man's morning rituals. It was familiar yet different. These were Flint's.

She dressed for Posy's. She couldn't take off or afford to lose even an hour from work. Patricia had to come first, her grandmother second, and Posy's was third. There was no time even for her to contemplate her own needs. Morning coffee was her only luxury. She poured her cup and then sat with her laptop showing Posy's bookkeeping.

Flint seemed to be missing, but his vehicle was still in the driveway and his laptop was charging on the kitchen counter.

Kimmie lifted a blank three by five card from a kitchen drawer and began to make notes to herself. She liked this old-fashioned way of tracking what she needed to do. Several generations of Posy's women had kept cards and she'd even found a few very old ones tucked in the oddest of places.

Her phone pinged the morning alarm, reminding her to awaken Patricia. The morning rush had begun.

"You can go to Posy's. I'll put her on the bus," Flint offered.

"I don't need anyone to *put* me on the bus. I'm not a baby!" Patricia scooped a large spoonful of cereal into her mouth. "Uu khan oo et mmiseelpf"

Flint laughed. "No talking with your mouth full. I know you're not a baby."

"I'll just make certain I'm nearby with Grady. But I do have a question. Am I allowed to acknowledge that I even know you and I see you on the bus?"

"You mean like wave at me?" She made a horrible face as though she'd been fed lemons for breakfast.

"Well, does that mean I have to pretend I've never seen you in my life?"

The child nodded.

Kimmie giggled. "That's the way it is. I've heard it gets worse in middle school." Kimmie kissed Flint on the cheek. "Sure you don't mind?"

As soon as the school bus drove off, Flint started his day. At nine o'clock, he went to the house to check on the progression. It had been totally gutted.

He could see what would become the new kitchen and the larger living room. The formal dining room would remain and the jumble of small rooms that had been added over the years would be his office. He corrected himself, our office. *I need to check with the architect. Kimmie will need her own space and work area.*

He ran up the steps to the two front rooms that would become a play area. Several more rooms were being combined, making them larger with private baths. He loved what would be the master bedroom. The third floor would probably be Patricia's. The plan would give her plenty of space yet still provide storage areas. He loved what was happening to his grandmother's house to transform it into his home.

Then he drove to the old gas station. The whole back end that had once been a car service area had been demolished and rebuilt.

The new metal roof was in place. The electricians were pulling wires and the HVAC people were fitting the place in ductwork. The place might have been minus the gasoline pumps but it still looked like an old service station.

"Hey, Flint. Saw you standing there and decided to stop. This is going to be another Joe's?" A school buddy asked.

"Yes, but this will be a Joe Wags. Got a dog?"

"Yeah, I got a Pointer last year to go with my Golden."

Duck hunting? "When Joe Wags is ready for its grand opening, stop by with your dogs. I think you're going to love it." A few minutes later, he said goodbye to his friend.

Flint checked his phone for the time and went to the bakery. He emerged with a half dozen sandwiches. Surprising employees was always good for morale, but his real reason was to visit with Kimmie.

She was with a customer when he walked in, so he took her sandwich and his to her office. It was locked. The other sandwiches, he lifted from the bag and placed in the break room. After alerting one employee of lunch and asking her to spread the word, he went back to wait on Kimmie.

"Sorry." She opened her office.

"No reason to be sorry." He passed her the sandwich that he knew she liked. "Where might I find your grandmother in Kingston?"

"Room 414. I'm to bring her home tonight. Fortunately, her bedroom is on the first floor. If it wasn't, she'd be going into a rehab center or I'd be turning the living room into a bedroom."

"That's a problem today for many people."

"We have a bigger one."

He stopped mid-bite and stared at Kimmie.

"Having you last night in my room... I thought about it this morning. It's wrong. It's giving the wrong impression to Patricia, and I can't have you in my room with Gran there. She'll have my hide."

"Let me deal with both problems. Okay? By the time you get home with your grandmother, it'll be solved."

"How?"

As soon as Posy's closed, Kimmie was on the phone with Flint.

"I promise, Patricia's homework is done and I made homemade pizza."

"What? How'd you do that - ketchup on toaster muffins?"

"No. I made real pizza and enough for you and your grandmother. And before you totally freak out, I worked in a pizza joint while in college." He dried the last of what once was a sink full of bowls, measuring, cups, etc. "I learned all the stuff that school didn't teach me. Nothing like a hands-on education in the food industry."

"What's your degree?"

Flint laughed. "Business administration. I think a few of those professors could have used a part time job in retail."

Kimmie laughed. "Okay, see you later. Not certain how long it will be before I can bring Gran home. I'm going there first."

"I'm certain she's packed and ready to leave."

By the time Kimmie reached her grandmother, she discovered Flint was correct. Gran had a large rolling suitcase filled and was sitting on the edge of the bed waiting to be released.

"Where did you get that?" Kimmie pointed to the suitcase.

"Flint gave it to me. He said there are more pieces and he's sending me on a cruise as soon as I'm well enough."

"Cruise?" *I'm going to kill him for filling her head. Gran doesn't have that kind of money.*

"Kate and I always talked about going on one. She wanted to do it this coming winter. She always wanted to go to the Bahamas and to do the Caribbean islands." She gathered the papers together that she had signed and placed them in a small carrying bag that matched her suitcase. "Did you know there's coffee grown on several islands? He told me he buys coffee from a coffee plantation on St. Something. I forget which one. There are several islands that start with Saint."

"I didn't know he used coffee from there. Cup of Joe is well known for its coffee. And knowing Flint, he's very picky. He's changed your coffee at the house and bought a new coffeepot. He says you need to drink the good stuff."

Gran smiled. "He told me. And he told me you two are sleeping together."

Kimmie thought she might faint when her grandmother dropped that bomb. "Um, he spent the night... I didn't have the guest roo--"

"Kimberly Anne Croff, it's about time you two set a wedding date. That boy is head over heels in love with you, and you've done nothing but float on air since he returned. Everyone around knows it except you."

Kimmie could barely hear her grandmother for the blood rushing in her ears.

"Kate and I knew you two would tie the knot one day. She almost had a stroke when you married Steve."

"Leave him out of this."

"No way. You think he'd be happy seeing you mope around for years? He's probably sitting on a cloud cheering right now. Flint is no dog. He's a darn good catch, and he loves you and Patricia. You can't beat that."

Kimmie's gaze landed on a magazine by Gran's bed. She wasn't familiar with the name, but there on the front cover was Flint with a line about giving real coffee lovers a serious cup of coffee at an affordable price.

"Gran, where did you get that?"

"On the cart that comes each morning. They have several newspapers along with a variety of magazines. I spotted Flint's picture and had to buy it. I've shown his picture to all my nurses today. I think they are quite jealous that you are going to marry him."

Kimmie knew her jaw had dropped. "He hasn't even asked me to marry him."

Gran shook her head. "Kimmie, a man doesn't put a diamond like that around a woman's neck unless he's marrying her. Wake up and smell the rose— Oh, hi, Doctor Spiro."

Kimmie was glad to bring her Gran home, but as she stepped inside the house, she began to panic. The place was quiet, no television blaring, simply silent. "Anyone here?"

Flint came around the corner. "Need some help?"

Mrs. Overton made her way to the kitchen table using only her cane. "I'm doing quite well. I do hope that you saved me a piece of that pizza that I was told you made." She made a terrible face. "I'm tired of hospital meals. It was terrible. The only thing I ate for dinner tonight was the salad. Other than the soggy squash, I couldn't even identify the other foods."

Flint produced two slices of pizza from the oven and put them on a plate. "I saved some for both of you." He looked at Kimmie. "Ready for yours?"

"Starved."

He opened the refrigerator. "Salad, too?"

She nodded. "Where's Patricia?"

Flint laughed. "Reading. Totally absorbed. I tossed down the gauntlet and she picked it up."

"What? Patricia? What have you done to my child? She abhors reading?"

"Not anymore. She's in the living room."

Kimmie turned and went to find her daughter. Patricia was exactly where Flint said she was, except she was reading on a tablet.

When Kimmie returned to the kitchen, she went to Flint. "What did you do?"

"I made the text extra large. I think she needs reading glasses. I noticed that at times she was struggling with her homework."

"I feel like a horrible mother. My daughter needs glasses and I never realized it. How could that have happened?"

Flint shrugged. "Minor. Just call your eye doctor. We can't be sure of anything except she's reading with larger text. That doesn't make you a bad mother."

Kimmie went upstairs with her daughter at bedtime. Patricia was quick with her nighttime routine, which included Grady's.

Patricia kneeled by her bed with Grady and said her prayers. "And please help Mommy to tell Flint yes, because I really want a baby sister. And Flint said that I can't have one until Mommy marries him. Amen."

Grady said his amen and Kimmie managed to say hers as she remembered that Flint said he'd talk to Patricia. *Oh no! Oh, please, Dear God, what did he tell her?*

Seven

Flint was in Mexico when his phone rang.

"What did you do?" Kimmie's voice was breathy.

There was no question in his mind what Kimmie had found. His full color postal ad cards were due out this week. An adorable rendering of Joe Wags with Posy's in the background was on the front, and the back of the card said 'The town of Clear Creek, best known for America's favorite small town garden center, Posy's, has become home to Cup of Joe's newest coffee shop, Joe Wags, where you can enjoy great coffee and your dog can enjoy staying with you.'

He chuckled. "Why, are you busy?"

"Swamped. And the Internet orders are pouring in this morning."

"When I have the grand opening, be certain to keep extra help on hand that day, just in case you get busy."

"Did you mean to advertise Posy's?"

He chuckled. "Why? Don't you want the business?"

"It's my business."

"We'll talk when I get home, but if you'd like to write Joe Wags a check for a dollar, I'll gladly accept the co-op advertising money."

"Next time, tell me."

"But I did tell you I was going to do this, and you even liked the image with Posy's in the background."

"I thought you were joking."

"When it comes to money, I don't joke."

"I love you and miss you, Flint." Her voice was whispery.

"I love you, too. But being married to me, means I'm going to be chasing coffee beans all the time. Can you handle it?"

"I know. Since that day you returned home, you've been gone more days than you've been here. But being married to me, means dirt under my fingernails. I'm not giving up what I have."

The overhead sign lit with his flight back to the States. "We're going to be just fine. They just posted my flight. I think it's going to be another long day."

"Without you it's always a long day." She was shuffling papers. "My friend wanted to know how I could stand having you gone all the time."

"Kimmie, we're never going to be like other married couples. You have Posy's and I have Joe's. But the most important factor is we have each other. The fact that we are independent makes us click. We need that."

The overhead sign flashed a delay to his flight and he groaned. "I swear I'm going to buy my own jet. My flight just got delayed."

Kimmie laughed. "If you buy your own jet, I might never see you."

"No such luck. You know I could never stay away that long."

"Are you certain you don't mind a very little wedding?"

"That is perfect for me. Did you pick out a dress?"

"Yes. It's white but with a pink cast, and it's accented in a deeper pink. Perfect for a garden wedding."

"As long as you love it. Do I get to see it?"

"I'll take a picture of it in the catalog. It doesn't look as pretty on the hanger."

"What goes under it?"

"You mean you want to know about my lacy pink panties that match?"

He stifled a groan. "Maybe we need to change the subject. I am in an airport."

"Too bad. I was going to ask if you wanted natural or should I trying waxing."

"Don't do that to me when I'm almost two thousand miles away."

She laughed. "Got to run."

"Natural." But he wasn't certain she'd heard him as she disconnected the call.

Joe Wags opened with a bang. Friday, Saturday, and Sunday people could purchase coffee for a quarter. It was part of a fundraiser. Every penny went to the local dog rescue. The group had come with a tent and dogs that were looking for a forever home. People came because they wanted to see how Flint managed to have a place that also served dogs.

The interior was split into sections so that guests who didn't want to be near animals could remain isolated from them and know that the air was being filtered with state of the art equipment. But in the other section, dogs were welcome and there were several large booths that people could use as private areas or for when an animal needed some alone time with its owner. The coffee brew stations went non-stop and the dog treats were a big hit. From simple bone-based treats to the frozen types, the dogs could enjoy a little extra indulgence, and water was always available and free. The big draw was a patio that overlooked the fenced play park for dogs. And of course, there was an area for dogs that needed to make a nature call. Plenty of cleanup stations dotted the property. The whole place was functional, complete with WiFi for human visitors. Flint managed to keep its adorably quaint look on the outside. And as predicted, visitors stopped by Posy's.

Friday had been so busy that Flint and Kimmie had skipped dinner. Saturday was the same. But both places closed early on Sunday, and they left to enjoy a nice dinner in a nearby town.

Kimmie's grandmother and Patricia had already eaten. Grady stayed at the house. He walked into the living room and instantly plopped in the middle of the pretty area rug and closed his eyes. It had been a long weekend for him at Joe Wags. And after using his likeness on the logo, everyone recognized him and wanted to make friends.

Fame had taken its toll on the four-legged family member. Grady would never work as a service dog. He bonded with the people in the house and this was his home. Always there for

Gran, he'd fetch something that might have dropped or he'd retrieve something for her. But when Patricia would open the door, Grady was ready to run and play.

"Ready for the wedding?" Flint asked as he and Kimmie ate dinner at the steak house.

"Yes. All of your family and my parents... Forty-three people will be there. It's a little larger than I expected." She took a sip of her glass of cold tea. "The bakery is catering everything. Everything is ready."

"Except us."

She tilted her head at Flint. "Don't tell me you have to make another trip to South America or something."

He quietly chuckled. "No. I'm here. But we've never seriously talked about children. I'd like to have a few. Would you consider it?"

She dragged her fork through her mashed potatoes. "When will we have time for children?"

"We don't. We make time for them."

She drew crosshatches on the potatoes with the tines. "I'm glad you want a child. I'm in love with the idea of another baby, but with Posy's, it's scary."

Flint smiled brightly. "I'll create a cabbage patch corner complete with a stork built in the showroom. Crib, playpen, the whole works – we'll put the baby online. Everyone loves babies. They'll come online to your store just to keep up with this garden child. While they are there, they will buy things."

"Do you ever stop?"

"They tried to say I was hyperactive in school. I was bored. I wanted more. I don't think I've changed. If I'm hungry, I want to totally enjoy my meal. If I'm playing, I'm going to play and enjoy every second. Sleep? I want to be comfortable and to sleep well. As for a child, I'll do anything. What's wrong with that?"

"You also never stop looking for a money angle."

"Kimmie, if you spotted the newest, most wonderful, lightweight pots, you'd show them off and do everything you could to get people to try them, right."

She hesitated. "Yes."

"No difference. Guess I tend to look larger and take more chances. There's a thrill out of making something from nothing."

"From the looks of it, Joe Wags is going to be a huge success."

"I'm tossing enough money at it. Time is the true test. I'm counting on marrying my childhood sweetheart and sitting on the front porch of the house when we're old and gray." He chuckled. "Actually, I'm not. I'm planning to take my wonderful woman on every adventure we can conceive. Because as much as I enjoy spending some quiet time watching the fireflies, I want to experience everything I can."

"You scare me."

"I shouldn't, because I've no intention on doing anything from a ledge. I want to keep my feet on firm terra."

She reached across the table and took his hand. "I never thought I'd ever say this. I've grown too independent, maybe as a form of self-preservation. Posy's is mine. My family is in that land. I have a history with it. I can't imagine ever doing anything else. With luck, Patricia will want it."

Flint nodded, but concern rolled down his throat and settled in his stomach. "Of course. I'm not trying to take you away from Posy's."

"I never planned for another man to enter my life. And I promise I'll balk and stand my ground on occasion."

Flint put up his hand to say stop. "I'll never take that independence from you. It's why we're so good together. I've learned not to worry too much about you when I'm gone. I'm aware you are very capable of handling most anything. I couldn't marry someone who needed me home every night. That doesn't work with my career, nor would a strangling hold on me."

Kimmie nodded. "I promise that's a two-way street."

"But I'd love to know that it's my child…"

Kimmie laced her fingers with his. "It is your child."

"What? Did I just hear what I think... Did you say...

"I tested this morning. There was something very special about the other night when we slipped down to the dock. I've never been so certain about us as I was that night in your arms."

"That calls for champagne...ah, no that, ah... a hot fudge sundae?"

"You want me to get fat?"

"Would anyone even notice a sundae?"

The following weekend, Flint put on his summer suit and stood in front of the mirror checking one more time to be certain that nothing was amiss.

Patricia knocked on his door. "Gran-Gran wants you to eat something. And she said no milk on a hot day when your tummy is nervous."

He'd heard the same nonsense from his grandmother. He walked down the stairs and into his newly renovated kitchen. Sunlight filled the room with a soft morning glow. He dropped an English muffin in the toaster and poured a cup of coffee while he waited.

Patricia flounced into the kitchen wearing her special dress that Kimmie had bought her daughter for the wedding. The polished cotton material was printed in flowers, and the back of the dress had crisscrossed-straps that buttoned at the sides. Her skirt was full but not stiff. It flowed around her with every move, and Patricia seemed to constantly move. It was cute on her.

Patricia tried very hard to be very grownup in spite of her excitement. "Mommy said the caterers are due any second."

He stood over the sink to eat his crunchy toaster muffin. The clock said he had a long wait ahead of him. "Where's Grady?"

"Gran-Gran is making him stay in her room."

"Oh." He nodded at Patricia. "You look very pretty today."

"Thank you. I got to pick out my own dress."

"Really?" He grabbed a paper towel and wiped his mouth.

"Gran-Gran wanted to put my hair in pigtails, but I wanted

to wear it down."

"Well, I think it looks very nice the way you have it." He motioned for Patricia to follow him. "I have something very special—just for you."

He opened a drawer in the living room, took out a fancy box, and handed it to her. "I had it made for you. I figured since I was putting a ring on your mother's finger then I should give you a forever item so that you will know how much you've become part of my life."

She opened the box and gasped. "For me?"

"Yes, for you. Read it."

"Let me get my glasses." She put the box on the table and scampered off. When she returned, she picked up the necklace, and began to read. Flint smiled as he watched her.

"Who is S L C?"

"Your father, Steven Lawrence Croff. He will always love you and you will always be his little girl."

"And P M C is me for Patricia Madeline Croff."

He nodded.

"And Mommy is K A W C S, Kimberly Anne Wilkins Croff but what's the S stand for?"

"Silverlake. That will be her new last name after we marry. And in case you wanted to know, she is taking my name."

"Why wouldn't she take your name?"

"Sometimes today women prefer to keep their name for a variety of reasons."

"Oh."

He was relieved she accepted that explanation so easily.

"And who is M F S?"

He chuckled. "That's me. Mathew Flint Silverlake."

She scrunched up her nose and looked just like her mother when she made that face. "I didn't know you were Mathew. Why does everyone call you Flint?"

He took the necklace from her, leaned over, and managed to latch the gold strand around her neck. "My grandmother liked Flint better, and eventually, everyone used it." Satisfied he'd secured the necklace around her neck, he checked the way it draped. "We are all very much a part of your life. I love you, too."

Patricia grabbed him around his neck and hugged him so tight she almost knocked him off balance. "Do I get to call you Daddy, because you are marrying Mommy?"

Flint returned her hug and lifted her off the ground. "If you want to call me Daddy, I'd be honored."

"Does that mean yes?"

"Yes. Patricia, I'll be your daddy. But I don't ever want you to forget that your father loved you very much."

She shrugged. "I don't remember much about him."

"That's because you were little, and he was very sick. But I know he loved you, and he didn't want to leave you and Mommy." He put Patricia back on her feet. "I don't want to wrinkle that pretty dress."

She smoothed it out. "It's got lots of flowers like the ones at Posy's."

She pointed to the various ones and called them by their botanical name. He couldn't help but smile at the child who was prepared for the biggest party of her life.

An hour later, he mingled amongst the guests who had come. Most were family, old friends, and faithful employees of Posy's. When he spotted his parents joining the guests who had collected on the large deck behind the newly renovated house, he went to them. His father greeted him as always. His mother was her usual self, pleasant but slightly cool. It was as if they resented returning to the little town – hated to admit their roots were there along with memories. They were so different from Kimmie's parents who bubbled with enthusiasm and seemed happy to see him again after so many years.

Mrs. Iris Overton appeared with her cane hanging on her wrist. She wore purple dress pants and a white blouse printed in large purple irises. Her silver-white hair had been pulled into its normal, braided style, and a large floppy white hat was decorated in purple flowers. Her back was getting stronger and with the new lawn, her footing was sure. She smiled at everyone, pleased that she and her dear, departed, lifelong friend had grandchildren who were tying the knot. She told anyone willing to listen that she and Kate had predicted this marriage.

Flint caught up to Patricia. "Go to your Gran-Gran's house and let Grady out. There's no reason to keep him inside. He'll be fine."

The backyard and deck were beautifully decorated in flowering plants. Posy's had closed for the day. Flint decided that was because Kimmie had probably used half of her merchandise to decorate for the wedding. But he loved what she had done.

The caterers had three very large grills by the side of the house. The day's food really was more of a picnic than a wedding reception. He liked that. He reached into the large fancy cooler and grabbed a bottled, vanilla cream soda. It was an icy cold treat that brought back childhood memories.

There were plans for later in the season when Kimmie wasn't as busy at Posy's. That's when he'd arranged to take her on a honeymoon where he could show her the more romantic side of life.

Overhead, he heard the soft cooing of a raven. He looked at his rooftop and there sat the black bird with the distinctive tail. It dropped something from its mouth and they both watched it roll down the roof. Taking a few quick steps, he caught the small round object in his hand, and then laughed. It was a lake pebble of the whitest quartz. Barely audible, he looked up as he spoke. "Thanks, Grandma, for bringing Kimmie and me together."

A second raven joined the first, showing off some flying skills and eventually snuggled close to the first. There was no doubt in his mind what he was seeing. "Grandma and Grandpa, stick around and watch what you've created."

They answered with their comforting song that ravens used around their nests.

Everyone found seats and was anxiously waiting when Kimmie made her entrance. In her hands was a bouquet of pale pink calla lilies, a tribute to his grandmother. The crowd hushed. Flint smiled as he walked to his bride. She had never looked more beautiful and her smile could be seen in her eyes.

He took her hand and lifted it to his lips, depositing a soft kiss on her fingers. Then he held out his other hand to Patricia. When she grasped his right hand, he led both females to the local minister. Grady followed and took his place beside Patricia. Flint leaned to Kimmie and whispered, "This time, we'll grow old together. I love you, Kimmie, with all my heart."

She smiled at him and mouthed the word forever.

Kimmie was the love of his life. She always had been. There was no question in his mind that they needed the time apart as teens and young adults. They needed to know something about life in order to appreciate what they now had with each other. Together, they sparked with an electric current. It glued them together. *My beautiful bride. You are everything I've always wanted.*

In the backyard without a lot of fanfare, they quietly married. With family, friends, a dog, and a pair of ravens to share the event, it became a day of fun. But a little further away, under the shade of an old live oak, a squirrel sat in the center of Flint's grandmother's table munching on a nut and leaving the shell behind. Her white quartz stones once again were scattered across the mosaic table, foretelling a future to whoever was willing to take the time to read it.

The End

About the Author

E. Ayers is a true believer in love at first sight because it happened to her, she thinks everyone should find that special someone. When it happens, it's magical. Writing about that love is what she enjoys doing and when she's not spending time with her two dogs and waiting on his royal highness (the cat), she's busy writing. The official matchmaker for all the characters who wander through her brain, she likes finding just the right ones to create a story.

She writes a slice-of-life novel, the romantic slice in two characters lives. In today's world, most people have careers and responsibilities. Figuring out how to blend two separate lives into one can be a huge dilemma. No one is perfect. She brings that into what she writes.

The fantasy of a handsome hunk who will sweep the damsel off her feet and carry her off to a castle in the clouds is still there, but that castle is probably a condo. And that damsel isn't going to be persuaded by a few smooth lines.

More Books by E. Ayers

A note from the Publisher:

Indie Artist Press and the Authors of Main Street hope that you enjoyed reading *SUMMER ROMANCE ON MAIN STREET!* If you did, please drop by the review venue of your choice and spread the word.

Coming Soon to Paperback

Christmas on Main Street - Volume 1
Christmas on Main Street - Volume 2
Christmas at the Inn on Main Street
Christmas Babies on Main Street
Christmas Wishes on Main Street
Love Blooms on Main Street
Weddings on Main Street

Indie Artist Press | Brackettville, Texas

www.ingramcontent.com/pod-product-compliance
Lightning Source LLC
Chambersburg PA
CBHW050056120726
47904CB00004B/1112